COLD BLOOD
&
COLD SHOULDER

LYNDA LA PLANTE

COLD BLOOD
&
COLD
SHOULDER

PAN BOOKS

Cold Blood first published 1996 by Macmillan
Cold Shoulder first published 1994 by Macmillan

This omnibus edition published 2002 by Pan Books
an imprint of Pan Macmillan Ltd
Pan Macmillan, 20 New Wharf Road, London N1 9RR
Basingstoke and Oxford
Associated companies throughout the world
www.panmacmillan.com

ISBN 0 330 41513 1

1 3 5 7 9 8 6 4 2

A CIP catalogue record for this book is available from
the British Library.

Printed and bound in Great Britain by
Mackays of Chatham plc, Chatham, Kent

COLD BLOOD

To Liz Thorburn

ACKNOWLEDGEMENTS

I sincerely thank Suzanne Baboneau, Arabella Stein, Philippa McEwan, the real Lorraine Page whose name I borrowed, Susanna Porter and Harold Evans of Random House, Gill Coleridge, Esther Newberg, Peter Benedek, Hazel Orme. With special thanks to Alice Asquith, researcher at La Plante Productions, and Vaughan Kinghan, editor at La Plante Productions. To everyone at the Pasadena Police Station and Sheriff's Office, thank you for your time and expertise.

With thanks for their contribution to: Eliot Hoffman, Arthur Q. Davis, Clara Earthly, Geoffrey Smith, Paul Lovell, Priestess Miriam Chawani, Brandi Kelly, The Voodoo Museum, Yosha Goldstein, Centre for New American Media, Sergeant Barry Fletcher and Lt. Sam Fredella of the New Orleans Police Department, John Gagliano, New Orleans Coroner's office, Dr Munroe Samuels, Tyler Bridges, Arthur Hardy, Mardi Gras Guide, Luke Delpip, Zulu Social Aid and Pleasure Club, Warren Green, NOMTOC krewe, Ed Renwick, Institute of Politics, New Orleans, John Maloney, Lakefront Airport, Dr Ragas, University of New Orleans, Kim Brown, Housing Authority of New Orleans, Kara Kebodeaux, New Orleans Chamber of Commerce, Wayne Everard, New Orleans Public Library, Jerry Romig, University City Hospital, Rodney and Frances Smith, Soniat House Hotel, Norman and Sandra King, Betty Baggert, Longue

Vue House, Wade Henderson, 6 WDSU Television, Courtney Marsiglia, WVUE TV Channel 8, Alcoholics Anonymous, L.A. County Coroner's office and the *Times-Picayune*.

But above all my thanks to a very admirable lady who brought me the story of her life.

PROLOGUE

Mojo is an African word denoting a fetish or sacred object, which can be used either for good or for evil. Gris-gris, meaning 'grey grey' in French, is the name given in New Orleans to the combination of 'black' and 'white' mojos made by a voodoo practitioner to achieve his or her ends – to safeguard the life of a person to whom the charm is given, protect against disease, and ward off the evil wishes of enemies to avoid bad luck in love and life. A personal gris-gris must be kept secret, and will lose its power if seen or touched by anyone other than the owner. For that reason, gris-gris are usually worn close to the body, on the right side by men, on the left by women.

CHAPTER 1

ANNA LOUISE Caley remained beneath the shower for a full half-hour, scrubbing herself clean, making sure every inch of her perfect body was cleansed. She could blank what she had done from her mind – that was easy – but it was the abuse she inflicted on her body that worried her, and she examined herself with care, pleased to see that there was no bruise or other mark to show what she had done the night before.

With just a soft white towel swathed around her, she re-examined herself, checking and patting her flesh until she was satisfied, then oiled and powdered her body and got dressed. White tennis socks, white cotton panties, white tennis dress and, lastly, pristine white tennis shoes. She laced them up, then chose one of a row of professional-standard racquets and unzipped the cover, tapping the taut strings with the flat of her hand before she slipped the cover back on. She checked her hair, putting on a white stretch head-band to keep her long blonde hair back from her face.

Anna Louise left nothing out of place in her room, placing the towel she had used in the laundry basket along with the previous night's soiled clothes. She liked the fact that she was not like a normal teenager, prided herself on being meticulously neat, and she slowly appraised her immaculate room before she headed for

1

the tennis court. She passed through the kitchen, still empty at 6.30 in the morning, before any of the domestic staff had begun to prepare breakfast, and went outside, where a gardener was already turning on the sprinklers and sweeping up any dead leaf that might have fallen during the night. He did not look up, however, as Anna Louise headed for the changing room where the tennis balls were kept, picked up a large basket of them, then made her way to the court. First she examined the net, making sure it was precisely the correct height, then fed the balls into an automatic delivery machine and set the dial for speed and direction. She carefully removed her racquet from its cover and switched on the ball machine, ready to begin to play against it – against herself. She stood on the service line, her weight thrown on to the balls of her feet, poised and ready for the first ball to shoot out, then began to practise her double-handed backhand. She was a precise player, fast, meticulous and very powerful, and she slammed ball after ball up the court until she was sweating with exertion, each stroke accompanied by a low grunt of satisfaction.

Her concentration lapsed for a moment and she missed the next ball, which struck her hard in the chest. Someone was laughing, and she recognized both the laugh and the accompanying soft, low giggle.

The balls continued to pop out of the machine, but Anna Louise ignored them now and walked off the court towards the summer-house, through the shrubbery, where she knew her approach could be neither seen nor heard.

Some time later, the machine fired out its last few balls, but now Anna Louise was slashing furiously at them, sending them crashing around the court as Tilda Brown,

2

her closest friend, opened the court gate. Tilda was as blonde and as pretty as Anna Louise and dressed in a similar white tennis dress, but Anna Louise didn't stop playing even for a moment to acknowledge her.

'Hi, Anna!' Tilda called. 'Sorry I'm late, I've got a terrible headache. Maybe I won't play this morning, I feel real bad,' she continued, pulling a face.

Anna Louise made no reply, but switched off the machine and picked up the basket to begin collecting the stray balls. Tilda, still complaining of a headache, balanced some balls on her racquet and carried them across to the basket to tip them inside.

'Did you hear what I said? I don't feel like playing.'

Anna Louise smiled.

'Ahh, but I've been waiting for you. I want to show you my backhand, it's really progressed.'

'It was always good,' Tilda replied.

'Yes, but now it's better,' Anna Louise said nonchalantly.

'Maybe later!' Tilda carried the basket over and tipped the balls into the machine. 'I'll refill it for you.'

Anna Louise stood on the service line, bouncing a ball up and down on her racquet, then suddenly took aim. The ball slammed into Tilda's back, making her turn round, gasping. The blow had hurt so much she could hardly speak, and the next ball hit her so hard in the stomach that she staggered backwards, winded.

'Stop it, Anna, STOP IT, THAT HURT ... YOU HURT ME.'

Anna Louise moved closer. 'Get Polar to kiss it better ...'

Tilda was scared and tearful; her belly ached, while her back felt as if it was burning, and Anna Louise was bouncing another ball, ready to aim at her again. Tilda ducked for cover as the third ball came towards her.

3

'What are you doing? STOP IT!' she screamed.

Anna Louise grinned as she picked up a fourth ball.

'You can't get away from me, Tilda Brown.' She was now throwing the ball up in the air as if to serve. Tilda moved further back and bumped into the ball machine, hitting the switch with her arm. The machine began to pump the balls more rapidly towards Anna Louise, who laughed as she swung her racquet, forehand and backhand in perfect unison, every ball viciously directed at the cowering Tilda, who screamed, running this way and that to avoid the swift hail of tennis balls, until she squatted sobbing behind the net.

Even behind the safety of the net, balls slammed into her arms and legs through the mesh, Anna Louise first taking aim at Tilda's body, but then at her face.

'Stop it, please stop it,' sobbed Tilda, looking up to see Anna Louise standing over her.

'You stay away from him, Tilda, he's mine. I see you with him again and I'll make you sorry, I'll hurt you more than any tennis ball, I'll hurt you so bad, Tilda Brown, you're gonna wish you were dead . . .'

Tilda was crying like a baby, terrified as much by Anna Louise's verbal threats as by her violence, and she sobbed with relief when she recognized the figure coming towards them. Anna Louise saw him too, and gave Tilda a final quick, hard blow on the side of the head, then lowered the racquet, smiling sweetly, her whole manner altered.

'Hi, honey,' Robert Caley smiled to his daughter, then looked towards the weeping Tilda. 'What's happened, Tilda?'

Anna Louise linked her arm through her father's. 'It was my fault, you know that serve o' mine, Papa, poor little Tilda here got right in the way of it . . . and you got to take some of the blame for coachin' me to serve so hard, but I didn't mean to hit her, I guess she just isn't up to my standard.'

Robert Caley had one arm around his daughter as he reached out to Tilda with concern. 'You all right, sweetheart?'

Tilda wouldn't look into his eyes, but held her hand to her head feeling the lump where Anna Louise had hit her. 'I want to go home, Mr Caley, today,' she said in a low, but firm voice.

'She is just bein' silly 'cos she lost the game,' Anna Louise said petulantly. She tried to keep hold of her father's arm to stop him following Tilda, but he pulled free of her, and she was infuriated to see him help Tilda to the gates and walk her back to the house. She smashed the racquet against the tarmacked court, then examined it, afraid she had damaged one of her favourites. Long strands of Tilda's hair were caught between the strings.

Tilda had packed, and refused to say anything else to Anna Louise through her locked bedroom door other than that she was going home at once. Anna Louise tried to cajole her, saying she was sorry, that she hadn't meant to be nasty, but Tilda refused to unlock the door. Now Anna Louise was worried about what Tilda might say to her mother, and was beginning to think that perhaps the sooner she left the better.

'Fine, you leave, Tilda Brown, I don't care,' she said angrily, but she was worried enough to decide to go and sit with her mother. Tilda would certainly want to say goodbye to her, and more than likely would tell tales. Anna Louise tapped on the door of her mother's suite and waited; it was often locked in the mornings as Elizabeth Caley hated being seen without her warpaint, even by her own daughter. Anna Louise knocked again, then walked in: all the curtains were drawn and the room was in darkness. She called out to her mother, but receiving no reply wondered if Elizabeth was still sleeping or, worse, had gone downstairs and would see Tilda. She hurried through her mother's sitting room towards her bedroom.

'Mama,' she whispered, then pressed her ear to the door, listening. 'Are you awake Mama? It's me, it's Anna Louise.'

She eased the bedroom door open and peeked inside, adjusting her eyes to the darkness of the room, then called out softly again, but saw that the bed covers had been drawn back. Her mother was known to fly into an even worse rage if she was woken from sleep than if she was surprised without makeup. She suffered from severe insomnia and her sleep was precious, if rarely natural.

Anna Louise looked across to the bathroom door and heard the soft sounds of bath-water running. She was about to leave when she noticed the low, flickering light of a candle on her mother's bedside table. The candle was sputtering, and she crossed the room to check it out, not expecting to find anything else.

The gris-gris had been consecrated, because it was positioned on top of a worn black Bible, a small white cotton sack of salt to the left and a tiny green bottle of water to the right. Above the Bible a blue candle, representing the element of fire, guttered in its candlestick; below the book was a square of sweet-smelling incense, the symbol for air. Anna Louise felt the hairs on the back of her neck prickle when she opened the gris-gris bag and looked at the contents, unaware of their meaning and of what it meant to have seen and touched a consecrated gris-gris. Fascinated, she picked up the old Bible and opened the fly-leaf: in old-fashioned scrolled handwriting whose ink had faded from black to brown there was an inscription to Elizabeth Seal – her mother's maiden name. Anna Louise carefully replaced the book, flicking through the tissue-thin pages to try to make sure it was in the same position she had discovered it.

Back in her own room, she sniffed her fingers and decided they smelt musty, so she filled her wash-hand basin with hot water and soaped her hands clean. She was just drying them when she heard her mother calling for her and returned to the suite.

'Tilda wants to go home today,' Elizabeth said, toying with a silver spoon on her breakfast tray. 'But that's silly as we're all leaving tomorrow.'

Anna Louise sat on the edge of her mother's bed, noticing that the bedside table had been cleared. 'Oh, we had an argument, we'll make it up.' She was anxious to change the subject, so asked with concern, 'How you feeling today?'

'I'm just fine, honey. Now you go and talk to your friend, it's stupid for her to go if we're all going to New Orleans tomorrow.'

'Okay, I'll make up with her. Do you want me to take your tray?'

'Mmmm, I'll sleep a while maybe, I had a bad night. Kiss kiss?'

Anna Louise leaned over to plant a kiss on her mother's cheek and then carried the breakfast tray out of the room and closed the door behind her.

Tilda had already left by the time Anna Louise returned her mother's tray to the kitchen. Anna Louise was unconcerned: she'd make it up to her, buy her something expensive. She wandered into the kitchen where Berenice, the housekeeper, had just baked a tray of fresh blueberry muffins, and began picking at one with her fingers, remembering the strange, musty smell from the Bible she had seen upstairs.

'Tilda told me somethin' weird, something she'd seen . . .' she began casually, still picking at the muffin's crispy top.

Berenice was emptying the dishwasher, not paying too much attention to her employers' daughter, only half-listening as she went back and forth stacking the clean dishes in the cupboards. She poured a glass of milk for Anna Louise and set it beside her.

'Miss Tilda sure was upset about somethin', crying her eyes out. We thought maybe she'd had bad news.' She continued putting the clean crockery away.

'What does it mean if you got a Bible, a blue candle and funny little bags of salt and incense, you know, like those gris-gris bags they sell back home?'

The cupboard door banged shut.

'You don't wanna know, Miss Anna Louise, an' you stop pickin' at each muffin. You want one, then you take one.'

'What does it mean?'

The housekeeper was replacing the cutlery in its drawer now, buffing each knife and fork quickly with a clean cloth before she put it away.

'Well, it depends on which way the cross is placed on the Bible.'

'Ah, so you do know what it means?'

'All I know is, if you and Miss Tilda are playing around, then you stop and don't be foolish. That's voodoo, and nobody ought to play games with things they don't understand because evil has a way of getting inside you, like a big black snake. It sits in your belly and you never know when it's gonna uncoil and spit . . . and if you touch another person's gris-gris, then you got bad trouble.'

Anna Louise broke off a large piece of muffin and

8

stuffed it into her mouth. 'You don't believe in all that mumbo-jumbo, do you?'

She took a gulp of milk, swallowing it the wrong way, and started coughing and spluttering as the muffin lodged in the back of her throat. She gasped, her eyes watering and her cheeks turning bright red. She couldn't breathe – it felt as if she was being choked, and Berenice had to hit her hard in the middle of her back as she retched and clung on to the edge of the table before at last she coughed the mouthful of food up, heaving for breath.

The housekeeper fetched some paper kitchen towel to wipe up the mess.

'You see, what did I say about that snake? It just come and hissed an' spat right now, almost chokin' you, so you hear me right and don't go meddlin'.' But when she turned back Anna Louise was gone, so she went out into the hall, catching sight of the girl as she ran helter-skelter up the stairs.

'Are you all right, Miss Anna Louise?'

Anna Louise looked down and then leaned over the bannister rail, whispering, 'It was in my mama's room. It wasn't Tilda that saw it but me!'

She laughed suddenly and continued running up the stairs, not seeing the fear on Berenice's face as she slipped her hand inside her uniform dress to feel for her own gris-gris. It was safely tucked into her underslip, on her left-hand side, beneath her heart.

Berenice returned to the kitchen: that silly spoilt child had no notion of what went on in the house, and she hoped to God she never would. She cleaned up the mess from the table, and finished putting the dishes away, then tipped all the freshly made blueberry muffins into the trash. She would make a fresh batch, just in case a drop

9

of the snake's venom that had hissed from Anna Louise Caley had touched them: there were some chances that just weren't worth taking.

The following afternoon, accompanied by her parents, Anna Louise flew from Los Angeles to New Orleans. It was 15 February, and on 16 February, Anna Louise was officially reported as missing. Police in both Los Angeles and New Orleans attempted to trace her, and when they failed to do so, her parents brought in private investigators.

The weeks became months – no body and no ransom note were ever discovered, and even with top investigation agencies on the case, no clue as to the whereabouts of the missing girl, or her body, ever came to light. After nine months the disappearance of Anna Louise Caley was no longer news, and she had to all intents and purposes become just another statistic, another photograph on the missing persons files.

Eleven months passed, and with no new information, Anna Louise's distraught parents faced the possibility that she might have been murdered. By this time, more than fifteen investigation agencies had been involved with the case, the Mississippi had been dragged and helicopters had searched the swamplands of Louisiana. Agnews Investigations, along with three other less well-known agencies, were still retained on the enquiry: the Caleys had paid out millions of dollars but the expenditure had yielded no motive, no suspect, no result. All the grieving parents were left with was an aching period of waiting, while they longed for a sign that their beautiful Anna Louise was still alive.

All the PI agencies involved had made a lot of money, and some had even traded information with one another, but the Anna Louise Caley bonanza was coming to an end. Pickings were getting slim for private investigators – it was a tough business in which contacts and recommendations by word of mouth were a necessity, as Page Investigations, a small PI company, had found out the hard way. Even getting a foothold on the lowest rung of such a competitive ladder had proved impossible, and the attempt had been financially crippling for Lorraine Page: now, her agency was virtually bankrupt.

Even though she was a former police lieutenant, her own case history as an alcoholic and an officer who had shot dead an unarmed boy while drunk on duty meant that instead of being welcomed into the PI fraternity, she was being frozen out – just as she had been kicked out of the LAPD. The hardest part was explaining to Rosie, the assistant whom Lorraine jokingly called her partner, and who was also a recovering alcoholic, that they were going under. Dear Rosie, who still hoped, Rosie who still maintained that business would pick up – but there had never been any business. There was nothing to pick up from: it had all been a gamble, a dream even, but now it was over.

Lorraine had the phone cupped in her hand, half-listening to the call, half-wondering whether tonight would be the night she would tell Rosie – she knew she would have to do it soon. She listened, interjecting twice how sorry she was as the man's deep rumbling voice made incoherent references to his wife's passing.

Rosie, a plump woman with a kind, open face, was reading her star signs, a cup of coffee and two orange chocolate cup cakes beside her. She had flicked a glance at Lorraine when the phone had jangled through the silent office and sighed when she had heard Lorraine's over-cheerful 'Hi, Bill, how ya doing?'

Rosie had been trying a new diet: proteins one meal,

11

carbohydrates the next, with fruit forty minutes either before or after each meal, and no fats or fried food. She had stuck to it for a month and felt better for losing a few pounds, but today she was indulging in a binge of chocolate cup cakes, hating herself with each bite. Still, it was just one of those days – she couldn't face another chicken breast without crisp golden skin or French fries, or another salad without dressing, and a whole month with no fresh crusty bread spread thickly with peanut butter had been excruciating.

At last Lorraine was able to replace the receiver. 'That was Bill Rooney,' she murmured, lighting a cigarette. 'His wife died.'

'I didn't know he had a wife,' Rosie said, lowering her magazine.

'I don't think he did,' Lorraine said as she counted the butt-ends in her ashtray. She sighed and leaned back in her chair. By turning her head a fraction she could just make out the cheap sign printed in fake gold leaf on the outer office door – 'Page Investigations Agency'. There was a stack of calling cards on her desk with the same inscription. It was a farce.

'Well, the end of yet another over-active sleuthing day.' Rosie chomped on her cup cake, staring at the free digital alarm clock she got from ordering some non-stick pans. It was almost six. Unaware of the smear of chocolate over her right cheek, she looked over at Lorraine, watching her as she inhaled deeply on her thirtieth or so cigarette of the day. Her eyes were staring vacantly across the small white painted office. Rosie hated it when she did those vacant stares. Sometimes her silences could last over an hour and Rosie could never tell what her partner was thinking. She hoped this was not going to turn into one of Lorraine's moods. 'You should cut down,' she said with her mouth full.

'So should you,' Lorraine retorted, looking at the trash can filled with empty silver foil cup cake moulds.

'I don't smoke, so it's expected to crave sugar. That's half of what alcoholism is about too, you know, sugar craving.'

Lorraine pushed her second-hand typist's chair back from her empty desk. 'Is it? Well, well, isn't that interesting. And just what are hamburgers and fries, are they a craving too?'

'For chrissakes, don't start having a go at me! You and your brown rice and your vitamins make me wanna throw up.'

'Might do you some good!'

Rosie now pushed her large ass back in her catalogue sale of the month office chair. 'Right, that is it.'

'Yep, I guess it is, Rosie.'

It was hard to explain how each day Lorraine felt more isolated, because in physical terms she wasn't: Rosie and big Bill Rooney were always there. It wasn't that she didn't have anyone to talk to, interact with – it just felt that way. Her mind seemed to be atrophying and she felt drained, lethargic; sometimes she wanted to weep, out of a deepening feeling of utter loneliness, or was it loveless-ness? Whatever it was, it was having a more and more destructive effect on her, and she felt its undertow sucking her down.

Lorraine flicked the old venetian blind that didn't quite fit the windows. She gave a sly look at her plump room-mate as she stubbed out her cigarette. She didn't even live in a place of her own, but was sharing Rosie's small apartment in a run-down district off Orange Grove. She was thirty-seven years old; almost six of those years had been lost in a sea of drugs and alcohol addiction, and sometimes, especially at times like this afternoon, she felt it was all a waste of time; in reality she was never going to get back into the only business she knew or had known when she had been a cop.

The two women had met when Lorraine had been recuperating from a near-fatal hit-and-run accident. It wasn't the vehicle that had almost killed her, but her drinking and self-abuse. Now she had been sober and attempting to get her life organized for nearly two years. As an ex-lieutenant attached to the Pasadena Homicide Squad, she had experience not only in the field but as a detective, and she had been a very good one. 'Had' being the operative word: after drinking took over her life it had cost her the husband she had loved and the two daughters she had adored.

'What you thinking about?' Rosie asked, pretending to be immersed in her magazine.

'Nothing,' Lorraine answered, but she quite obviously was. She wondered if she should attempt another reconciliation with her kids. Yet as always whenever she thought about them, she decided they were better off without her intruding on their new life, a life she had not been a part of for too many years. Added to that, her ex-husband had remarried and her daughters called his new wife 'Mother'. They didn't even want to see her.

Rosie pored over her magazine again. Lorraine's long sighs made her aware that something was coming, but she said nothing, flicking over the pages to a new diet that guaranteed you could lose weight with ease if you sent off for their special-priced 'slimming drinks'. But as she'd attempted most diets, including slimming drinks, and none had worked, she flicked over to a knitting pattern.

'This is a farce, you know it and I know it. I mean, I

dunno what else we can do. How many more adverts can we afford to run, if we don't drum up any customers by the end of the week?'

Here it comes, thought Rosie, scowling. 'You've said that every week.' She hated it when Lorraine started on this tactic, partly because she knew everything she said was true but also because it made her afraid. Afraid Lorraine would leave, afraid that without Lorraine she would go back on the booze, afraid Lorraine would too.

'Got to face reality.' Lorraine prodded her empty cigarette carton, hoping she'd overlooked a stray one. But it wasn't to be, so she looked over the stubs in her ashtray again.

'Yes, I know, I know, and I hear what you are sayin', but at the same time we got to stick at it. Everyone knows any new business takes time to lift off, even Bill Rooney told us that.'

Lorraine appeared not to be listening as she rummaged in her purse and started to check her loose change.

'I mean, we could get a case in tomorrow that'd make everything you just said obsolete,' Rosie said a little too cheerfully.

'What?' Lorraine asked challengingly.

'Obsolete,' Rosie repeated flatly.

'Really? Well, you've been saying that for the past month and we've not had so much as a telephone call. And if you want to check the diary out, we are hardly likely to get some case off the street that'd pay for your cup cakes and my cigarettes, never mind the rent on this place and your apartment, so straighten out, Rosie. Shit, I need a cigarette.'

Lorraine crossed to the hooks by the toilet closet. She yanked down her raincoat.

15

'Maybe the rain'll stop soon.'

Lorraine pulled on her raincoat. 'Oh yeah, so it's all gonna be okay if the sun shines, is it?'

'Maybe.'

'You're a dumb optimist.'

'What?'

'Optimist, Rosie. Even if the sun cracked the paving stones that's not gonna help us. Two stray dogs, a missing senile grandfather, a two-week stint in a department store to cover for their in-house detective's vacation, five car traces, four warrants and a woman suspecting her husband of having an affair with his secretary, and as the wife was your size and his secretary looked like Julia Roberts, it didn't take us long to investigate, and that . . . that is it, Rosie, that's been all there's been for the past nine months.'

'You always gotta get personal. If you look on the good side, you've been sober nine months more, so have I come to think about it, so my guess is we'll make it. This is just a bad patch.'

Lorraine clenched her teeth. 'No, it isn't, Rosie, it's just a fact. We are flat broke and searching my ashtray for dog-ends is not exactly what I had planned for the future. We might as well admit it, face it, before we get any deeper in debt.'

'But we are facing it,' Rosie said stubbornly.

Lorraine closed her eyes as if talking to a child, her voice sounding annoyingly over-patient. 'No, we are not. Fact is this whole idea was shit, and to be honest I am not feeling like patting myself on the back 'cos I remained sober. Truth is, right now I feel like tying one hell of a load on and the only thing stoppin' me is that I have no money.'

'Never stopped you before,' snapped back Rosie.

Lorraine's eyes were like cold chips of ice. 'What's

that supposed to mean? What are you suggesting, Rosie? Come on, spit it out, are you saying I go out and screw a few guys to keep this place open? That what you think I should do?'

Rosie blushed and turned away. She loathed Lorraine when she was like this, she could get so cold, so unapproachable, so downright nasty. But unlike the times they'd bickered about the agency before, there wasn't another sarcastic retort forthcoming, just an ominous silence.

Lorraine was staring at herself in the small mirror glued to the back of the door. Her hair needed a cut and new highlights. She leaned closer, frowning, as she checked the scar running from her left eye down to midway of her cheekbone; that needed to be fixed but plastic surgery cost. She stepped back, giving herself a critical appraisal. Considering the punishment her body and insides had taken from all the abuse, her skin looked remarkably clear, but there were fine lines at the sides of her eyes and they were getting deeper. Either way, she didn't like what she saw, and kicked the door closed.

Lorraine picked up her gym bag and flicked off the main overhead light switch. Her shadow etched across the main office wall as she reached for her purse. Caught in the half-light from the lit-up screen on Rosie's word processor, Lorraine's chiselled features never ceased to make Rosie's heart lurch. She obviously didn't see herself as Rosie did, because she was still a very attractive woman. Perhaps not as ethereal as Rosie thought, but for her age, and considering what she had been through, Lorraine Page was still a looker. The stronger she had become physically over the past twenty-one months, the more her natural beauty shone through. Lorraine's strict diet, her almost obsessive work-outs at the gymnasium, had proved that a woman who lost six years drinking

17

herself into oblivion, who had become a hopeless, scrawny, sickly alcoholic when she and the overweight Rosie had first met, could now pass for an athlete. The only thing ex-Lieutenant Lorraine Page could not recapture was her career, and her husband and two daughters. She never spoke of them, either to Rosie or at AA meetings, whereas Rosie spilled many tears about wanting to be reunited with her son.

Rosie now took a long deep sigh; maybe, as she herself had half-suggested, the failure of their business would send Lorraine back to the bottle, back to a life in the gutters. Rosie was therefore totally unprepared for what Lorraine had to say as she hovered by the main office door, about to leave.

Lorraine swung the door slightly with her foot. 'I meant to tell you, the department store have offered me a full-time job as their store detective. Remember the job I took over for two weeks? Well, apparently she had one hell of a holiday and came back pregnant.'

'What?'

'So, we close up at the end of the week and at least I'll have enough for the rent on the apartment.'

'What about Page Investigations?' Rosie asked as the tears started.

'Like I said, it's over, end of the week we close up shop.'

'What about me?'

Lorraine wouldn't look at her friend, still tap-tapping the door with the toe of her shoe. 'Well, I guess you got to go out into the big world, Rosie, and get a job. Shouldn't be too tough, you can use a word processor and . . .'

Rosie turned away, her eyes brimming, and Lorraine felt awful. She went over and slipped her arm around her friend's shoulders.

'I'm sorry, sometimes I say things and they come out all the wrong way. What I am trying to say is – you got a life, Rosie, and maybe I have too, not just doing what we're doing, okay?'

Rosie nodded and felt in her pocket for a paper tissue. Lorraine hesitated, knowing that to stay with Rosie would only involve going over old ground, but was saved by the ring of the phone. Rosie snatched up the receiver, hoping against all hope that the call would mean a job, but didn't even get out 'Page Investigations'. It didn't matter anyway – it was only her sponsor, Jake, wondering if she'd be at AA that evening. By the time Rosie had replied that she would, Lorraine had gone.

'You okay, Rosie?' Jake's friendly rasping voice enquired.

'Nope, we're shutting up shop. Can I see you tonight before the meeting?'

Jake agreed and Rosie replaced the phone, feeling the tears welling up again. Was it ever going to end? Did she have a life of her own, as Lorraine had said? Did she hell, as without Lorraine, Rosie knew she was hopeless – sure, she could use a word processor, but she didn't have enough confidence to go out alone into the big wide world. That was the difference between them – Rosie needed Lorraine, and without her, the world scared the shit out of her. Or maybe it wasn't the world, just her own weakness and low self-esteem. Just seeing the empty cup cake carton made her want to weep – she couldn't even stick to a diet! How could she cope without Lorraine? By having a drink, that would be how, and that realization made her want to weep even more. She badly needed to go to that meeting.

*

Lorraine went to her weightlifting class. She pushed herself to breaking-point, wanting to exhaust herself so she'd crash out and sleep when she got home. She blanked out Rosie's doleful face. In truth, she was just as sad at the failure of the business, but unlike Rosie she knew she could not let it swamp her. If she had to move on, then she would do what had to be done. She knew she could not take responsibility for Rosie, it was tough enough taking it for herself, and if she was to survive then she had to put herself first, otherwise she'd go down. She had not been kidding when she had said she wanted a drink. She did. But she was not going to take one, well, not tonight. She knew by now that it never ended, the 'thirst' was never over. It was, and would continue to be, a constant battle for the rest of her life. Part of her wanted to fight it but sometimes, just sometimes, it seemed so pointless.

Rosie was in floods of tears, sitting beside her dear friend Jake Valsack, who was patting her hand.

'Well, maybe she's right, Rosie. If it's not working out on any front, more specifically financially, why flog a dead horse?'

Rosie blew her nose. 'She just came out with it, like she must have known a while back about this offer of a job. You see, she's pregnant.'

'What, Lorraine?'

'NO! The goddamned store detective, the bitch!'

Jake raised his thick, matted eyebrows. He was having a tough time following what Rosie was going on about, but surmised that Lorraine had a job and Rosie didn't, and their so-called investigation business was kaput.

'I mean, how could she do it, Jake? I decorated and painted the place, we got all that office furniture ... I

20

know it's not much, but we got phone extensions put in, I got a word processor to pay off, a fax machine and a . . . It was me that got the desks, you know, and the furniture. It took us months to set up, how could she do this to me?'

'She did it, Rosie, because you got no work offered, right? Am I right?'

'That is not the point,' she said stubbornly.

Jake sneaked a look at his watch; the meeting was about to start. Rosie could carry on like this for a long time, he knew it of old, and no matter what he said she paid no attention, she just went round and round in circles.

'What about that ex-captain, Rooney? I though you said he was gonna drum up work?'

Rosie blew her nose. 'Oh, him! He's boozed out, his wife's just died.'

'Oh, I'm sorry. I don't know him, but how is he coping?' Jake asked, trying to change the subject.

Rosie continued as if there had been no interruption. 'I mean, if you don't stay with something, you know, really see it through . . . we got the office furniture and I schlepped all over yard sales for that . . .'

Jake gripped her hand tighter. 'Rosie, sweetheart, maybe Lorraine did just that, saw it through and came to the conclusion it wasn't gonna work. It hasn't worked.'

'She never gave it a chance,' Rosie snapped back.

Jake sighed in frustration. He was in the chair this evening and he could see that the crowd of people arriving for the meeting was thinning out as they entered the hall. 'Rosie, I got to go in now. Maybe talk this through after?'

'I need to talk it through now, Jake.'

He was trying to hold on to his temper. 'Rosie, I have

been talking it through with you for over an hour but you won't face facts.'

'Facts are, Jake, she just dumped me. We might have got overflow work from the other agencies.'

'No, honey, facts are Lorraine's talking sense. I mean, you think about this, you know her history, she was a drunk cop on duty, she got kicked out of her station, she shot a young kid, for chrissakes. You ever think that maybe, just maybe, none of the other agencies can take the risk of an ex-junkie, ex-alcoholic orderin' their toilet paper, never mind taking on any overflow of cases? They know about her, so even if it's tracin' stolen vehicles—'

'But we did a trace, we got three.'

Jake rumpled his thinning hair; she was refusing to listen to him. 'I got to go in, Rosie, like now, so come on, wipe your nose and let's go in. You need a bit of stabilizing.'

'I need a drink, Jake.'

He closed his eyes. It was going to be a long, long night.

They were just about to go back to square one when there was a tap on the window of his beat-up Pontiac. 'Jake, it's me, only I've welcomed everyone as I don't think we're going to get any more here tonight. Coffee is served and everyone's waiting for you to take the chair.'

The thin-faced woman in a rather expensive tailored suit stepped back from the car. Phyllis Collins didn't even glance at Rosie, who was blowing her nose loudly.

'Okay, Phyllis, I'm comin' now.' Jake stepped from the car, bent down to Rosie. 'Let's go, Rosie.'

'No, I'm not coming in.'

Jake gestured to Phyllis. 'Do me a favour, Phyllis, she needs a bit of encouragement tonight. You've met, haven't you?'

22

Phyllis nodded and peered towards the passenger seat. 'Good evening.'

Rosie didn't even acknowledge her as she delved into her bulging purse for a clean tissue. Jake raised his eyes to heaven and Phyllis gave him a reassuring smile.

'You go in, I'll stay with her. Go on, you can't keep everyone waiting.' Phyllis bent down to the car. 'We've met a few times, I'm Phyllis Collins.'

Rosie glared. She had no recollection of ever meeting the woman before and she had no intention of getting out of the car.

'Jake can't not go in, he's chairing tonight. You mind if I sit with you?'

Rosie shrugged, looking away, but she didn't stop Phyllis from getting into the car. If nothing else, she was someone she could repeat the entire scenario to; she'd have spilled it all out to anyone, she was feeling so wretched.

'My partner just dumped me.'

'Oh, I am sorry, were you married long?'

'My business partner. I've worked my butt off and tonight she just told me she had another job, just like that.'

Phyllis nodded, her thin, plain face concerned. 'Oh dear, no wonder you're not feeling good.'

Lorraine eased the wet iced cloth further over her sweating face. The heat in the sauna was so intense she could take only another few minutes. She was lying naked on the highest bench, two other women were flat out on the benches beneath her. No one spoke.

Lorraine was wondering if Rosie was okay but she figured if Jake was with her she wouldn't do anything stupid. She decided to clear out the change in her purse and get a bottle of alcohol-free cider to cheer her up. It looked like champagne and tasted like gnat's piss, but Rosie loved it.

'Excuse me,' Lorraine murmured as she swung her legs down to the lower bench and then eased her body past one of the prone women who leaned up on her elbow to allow Lorraine to pass. She remained half-upright, staring at the tall woman as she left the sauna. She envied the beautiful, straight, muscular body and then became curious when she saw the patched scars across Lorraine's arms, the small jagged razor lines and round burn marks.

The same woman caught sight of Lorraine again in the changing room. Using a brush, she was blow-drying her fine silky blonde hair rather expertly.

'I wish I could do that.'

Lorraine turned, slightly puzzled, wondering if the woman was talking to her.

'Save a fortune at the hairdresser's. I can never do the back of my head.'

Lorraine switched off the hair-dryer. 'Oh, it just takes practice,' she said politely, and concentrated on finishing her hair. When she walked out from the changing cubicle the nosy woman was talking confidentially to someone else, both their overweight bodies cushioned together in their white fitness club-issue towels.

'She used to be a police lieutenant, drunk on duty, that was what I was told. She knows the gym instructor and he told me that . . .'

Lorraine let her cubicle door bang hard and they whipped round like startled hamsters. She would have liked to tell them where she would like to ram the hair-dryer but she didn't. She said nothing. And all the tension her exercise and sauna had relaxed from her body

24

was back. By the time she passed through reception she was wired and angry.

Arthur, the gym instructor, gave her a friendly grin and called out, 'Goodnight.'

Lorraine kept on walking.

Some friend he'd turned out to be. She decided she would not come back. She just knew she had better head directly for home instead of getting Rosie's cider because that feeling of wanting a real drink was growing out of her control.

Three bottles of Evian water downed between them, Phyllis and Rosie were sitting in a small café. Only it wasn't Rosie spilling out her tales of woe, it was Phyllis, and she had Rosie's rapt attention.

'I suppose in some ways I stayed on because it was all so dreadful and I keep on saying to myself, "When it's all over, I'll leave." But it's not over, maybe it never will be. Sometimes it gets so bad with her I just don't think I can take any more of it. She is so demanding, expecting me to be ready to drop whatever I am doing any time of day or night. If she wakes up at four in the morning, she can't be bothered to use the intercom, she just screams my name. Sometimes I wake up in a cold sweat because I think I've heard her shrieking for me, and other times, when she's very sick because she's taken so many pills to sleep, I just get rigid with fear and all I do is feel her pulse to see if she's still breathing. It's a wretched, terrible time for all concerned, a tragedy really . . .'

Rosie took a big breath. 'I used to see all her movies.'

Phyllis poured the rest of the Evian into her glass. '"Used to" being the operative words. She hasn't made a movie for maybe fifteen years.'

Rosie leaned closer to Phyllis. 'Why, why do you take it? Is it the salary? Oh, I'm sorry, that was rude, you don't have to answer that, I'm sorry.'

Phyllis pursed her lips, becoming defensive. 'No, no, it's not the salary, believe me, and lately we've not travelled the way we used to, she's hardly left the house.'

Rosie nodded. 'Yeah, I guess it must be awful.'

'It is, every time the phone rings. Not that she answers, just screams for me to do it, and so I get all tensed up, over and over again, hoping for news and afraid it will be bad, the worst . . . She was such a pretty girl.' Phyllis started to sniffle, opening her purse to take out a small lace handkerchief. Rosie noticed it was a very expensive suede-lined purse, with a gold chain threaded with leather for a strap. 'I'm so sorry to get like this, but I don't have many friends, no one to really talk to. That's why since I joined AA, it's meant so much to me, you know. And Jake, he's such a dear man, he's been wonderful.'

'Oh yeah, I know, he's a godsend to me too. Would you like another glass of water, Phyllis? Or we could go on to something stronger, like apple juice?'

Lorraine was waiting to apologize to Rosie when she heard heavy footsteps on the stairs leading up to the apartment.

'Rosie?'

Jake opened the screen door and then peered in. 'Nope, it's me. She's not here then?'

'Nope.'

'I'll drive around, see if I can find her. She took it hard about the business folding.'

Lorraine lit a cigarette. 'Yeah, well, I'm not out

26

celebratin' myself, Jake, but one of us has got to earn the rent.'

'You're right, you're right. So stay put, I'll drive around.'

'Was she at the meeting?' Lorraine asked with just a tinge of concern.

'Outside it, I left her with Phyllis whatever her name is. I just hope the two of them aren't out some place tying on a load. See ya.'

Her heart sank when not long after Jake had left she heard a bellow from the street and then Rosie's footfalls. The small apartment, which only had one bedroom, a tiny bathroom and a lounge with a kitchen crammed into a corner annexe, was on the second floor of an old house on Marengo Avenue. The apartment below was occupied by an ever-growing family of Hispanics. Luckily, they created much more noise themselves, their radio and TV sometimes turned up so loud you could hardly hear yourself speak; anyone else having to live beneath the thunder of Rosie's footsteps would have had a nervous breakdown.

'Hey! You won't believe what I got to tell you.' Rosie's cheeks were flushed pink with the exertion of hurrying home. She gasped for breath.

'Rosie, how much have you had?'

'I've got more bottled water swilling around inside me than the main water tank.' Rosie kicked off her shoes and chucked her coat aside, hurling her purse on to the sofa, and then, with her hands on her wide hips, she beamed from ear to ear. 'I think we just got lucky.'

'You want some coffee?'

'No, sit down and listen, right now. Go on, siddown.

Okay, now, you ever heard of a very famous movie star called Elizabeth Seal?'

'Nope.'

Rosie threw her hands up in the air. 'Of course you have, *The Maple Tree*, you remember that one. And you gotta remember *The Swamp* and *Mask of Vanessa*, yes?'

'Nope.'

'For chrissakes, we saw it on cable. The movie star Elizabeth Seal is famous, you gotta know who I'm talking about, late seventies, eighties, she was . . . *huge*!'

'Have you been drinking with her?'

Rosie flopped down on the sofa bed, which creaked ominously. 'Don't be dumb, as if Elizabeth Seal would be out drinkin' water with me in Joe's Diner. She's a *big movie star*! Maybe you heard of the name Caley? Elizabeth Caley? That's her married name.'

'Nope.'

'Holy shit, I don't believe you. Elizabeth and Robert Caley have been headlines, well, almost a year ago they were. Every paper ran their story, even the TV, it was headlines because of her bein' so famous. Their daughter went missing, you listening? Their eighteen-year-old daughter, Anna Louise Caley, disappeared.'

Lorraine was trying to recall their names but she still had a blank. Nothing new in that, there were big gaps of months, even years, when she hadn't even recalled her own name, never mind anyone else's.

Rosie sipped the coffee. She was so excited she was sweating, her eyes bright like a child's. 'She disappeared without trace. They had the police involved, they had mystics, psychics, 'cos they had a big reward on offer. But they got no ransom note, no phone calls, no notes, nothin'. Like she just disappeared into thin air. Cops reckoned she might have been kidnapped and it went wrong and they killed her . . . They think she's been bumped off and . . .'

Half an hour later, Lorraine was sitting with her head in her hands, still unsure what Rosie was so excited about. 'I mean, Rosie, if according to this Phyllis woman the Caleys have hired the top private investigation agencies, why come to us?'

'Because nobody has found her yet and they're still spending thousands. They're mega rich, Lorraine, and they keep on shellin' dough out.'

Lorraine held up her hand. 'Wait, wait, Rosie, please, just you hear me out now. If the . . . Caleys, yes? have already over the past . . . how long did you say?'

'Eleven months or so, happened during Mardi Gras in New Orleans,' Rosie said eagerly.

'What? In New Orleans? Are you serious?'

'Yeah, what you think, I'm makin' all this up?'

Lorraine sighed. 'Rosie, if it went down in New Orleans they're not likely to hire private dicks located in LA, are they?'

'Yes, they already have, Phyllis told me. Cops were working on it here as well, they live here, right?'

Lorraine raised her eyes to the ceiling. 'If they have paid out all this money and still got no result, what makes you think they would be willing to shell out some more, say, to us, which I presume is what all this hysteria is about?'

'I'm not hysterical, for chrissakes.'

'Okay, but facts are facts, Rosie. Why do you think they'd be interested in taking on Page Investigations Agency, i.e. you and me? Just because you're in AA with the family's secretary is not what I would call a great introduction.'

Rosie yelled, 'I never fuckin' mentioned *you* were a

29

soak, I built you up, said you were one of the best. I even gave a good line about havin' Rooney as part of our team, you know, him bein' ex-Captain, that kind of thing. She was impressed, she was real impressed.'

'She was?'

The sarcasm was lost on Rosie. 'Yeah, she was. I gave her our card and she said she was gonna talk to Mrs Caley.'

'Oh, and when she's talked, then what?'

'Look, she's trusted by them, worked for them for years, right? And she knows that Elizabeth Caley is desperate, like going nuts, because she just wants to know what happened to her daughter, and she'll pay anythin' to find out.'

'And you gave them our card?'

'*Yes!* An' I'm not stupid, you know, 'cos first I was all upset, right? Like tellin' her about my partner quitting, but soon as I smelled a big fish on the line I sort of made out the new job you got offered was some big murder investigation, not just actin' as a store detective. I'm not dumb, I know how to spin a good yarn when I need to. I said you was in demand.'

'So how long do we wait for her to get back?'

The phone rang. Lorraine stubbed out her cigarette, nodding to it. 'That'll be Jake, you got him all wired up. He's been looking for you so you answer it.'

Rosie snatched up the phone. But it wasn't Jake, it was Phyllis, and she wanted details of Page Investigations' company background sent round as soon as possible for Mrs Caley. She replaced the receiver with a smirk.

'See? She did talk to her, just like I said.'

*

The following morning, after a hurried session on the word processor, they had what they felt looked like a reasonable folder, Lorraine giving full details of all her recommendations as a police lieutenant, listing the cases she had been involved with. They also included as part of Page Investigations' team the experienced and dedicated ex-Captain William Rooney, recently retired from the Pasadena precinct.

Rosie went off to deliver the freshly printed folder to the Caleys' home in Beverly Hills. Lorraine sat in the empty office brooding over the new events. She had a couple of days before she had to give the store job a yes or a no so she didn't see any reason why she shouldn't hang in there. Rosie *may* be right, they might be able to earn a few bucks, but she somehow doubted it.

The buzzer on the office front door sounded as Bill Rooney wove in with an over-bright 'Hi, you called, didn't you? So as I was just passin' . . .'

'Oh yeah? Via which bar, Bill?'

Rooney gave her the finger as he squashed himself into Rosie's swivel chair. He looked unshaven and well hungover, his big, florid face and bulbous nose a shade of mulberry. One side of his shirt collar stuck up at an angle, and his tie was food-stained and pulled to one side; the seat of his pants was shiny, and the whole suit had a crumpled, worn-too-often look.

'You look in good shape,' Lorraine said, smiling.

'I feel it, I feel real good. Lost half my pension on the PI agency I never got off the ground – in fact, I think the paint's still wet on the door. Never was a business-man, never any good with figures, an' the bastard that sold me the place must have seen me coming – he fuckin' saw "sucker" written right across my forehead. I got a computer compatible with no one, least of all myself, a cock-eyed telephone system, and I had my mobile no more than half an hour before I lost it. I hadn't gotten the insurance arranged, so I got no cover, an' now I can't sell the equipment for what I paid for it. So, I don't know about passing any overflow cases to you, I'm looking around for myself, business pretty thin on the ground. You got much going?'

He looked over the office and smiled. 'I see business is flourishing, can hardly hear myself talk for the sound of telephones ringing!'

'Very witty, considering your own fiasco.' Lorraine fetched some clean mugs and prepared coffee. Rooney had glossed over the fact that he had been in no shape to run an agency – with Ellen dying, and making arrangements for her funeral, he had been in a deep depression for weeks. Lorraine felt sorry for him, as for all his bluff manner he was probably lonely, and she watched out of the corner of her eye as he leaned on Rosie's desk and looked at the new Page Investigations Agency folder.

'Makes interesting reading. I like the way you skim over the missing years, sweetheart. Readin' this it's as if you left the Force with glowing recommendations instead of out the back door on your ass.'

'Yeah, your section reads pretty good too.' She banged down the mugs.

Rooney laughed as he read about himself and then he let the folder drop. 'I tell you Ellen passed on?'

'Yes, I'm sorry.'

'Yep, went to collect her urn. I said to the guy, how can I be sure these are my wife's ashes? I mean, I know it's the urn I ordered but you could've filled it with any crap.' Rooney shook his head as he continued. '"It's your wife, Mr Rooney sir, you see her name is on it!" Fucking crazy, whole life and it's packed into one tiny brass jar this size.' He indicated with his hands and then

32

rubbed his face. 'She was in the kitchen, cooking. Her radio was on, always had her radio playing, used to drive me nuts. And she fell, I heard her sort of thump to the floor.'

Lorraine poured water into the percolator. He didn't seem to be talking to her or to care particularly if she was listening.

'She was lying on the floor, still with a wooden spoon in her hand, and she had this sort of look of surprise on her face. She was dead.'

'I'm sorry, Bill.' Lorraine leaned on the cloakroom door.

'Yeah, I guess I am. I mean, I know I've not been easy to live with. I've not even cleared her clothes out yet, hadda move into the spare bedroom. It's like any minute she's gonna call me, tell me food's on the table. I dunno what to do with myself, Lorraine, I'm goin' nuts. The house is quiet, I even miss her goddamned radio.'

'Don't you still see all the guys down the station?'

'No. I did for a while but you know the way it is, once you're outside it, you're an outsider. Old drinking bars don't feel right any more, they all talkin' about this or that case and I gotta be honest, it's all high-tech nowadays, you know, everything's computerized, breeds a different kind of cop.'

Lorraine went to his side and patted his big, wide shoulder. He gripped her hand for a moment.

'I'm not in the way, am I?'

She felt sorry for him so she punched him lightly. 'Like you said, we're not exactly rushed off our feet. I'm sorry it hasn't worked out for all of us.'

Rosie stormed in.

'What a place, it's like a palace, I've never seen nothin' like it . . . gardeners and servants, and the grounds are

33

like some showpiece, ferns and flowers and swimming pools, two pools, and pool houses, and tennis courts and . . . Hi, Bill, how ya doin'? I was real sorry to hear about your wife.'

Rooney rose to his feet. 'Thank you.'

'You ever heard of a movie star called Elizabeth Seal?'

Rooney nodded. 'Sure, used to have the hots for her.'

Rosie turned, pointing to Lorraine. 'See? I told you she was famous. Well, that's where I just come from, Elizabeth Seal's home, like some kinda palace.'

Lorraine passed coffee to Rooney and indicated a mug to Rosie.

'I'll have one,' Rosie said as she took off her light coat. 'They even got an English butler, I'm not kiddin' and a maid. They left me in the hallway a while until Phyllis came down. It's enormous, the hall, like you could roller-blade around it. They got some cash, reeks of it, got paintings worth millions, I'd say. These old movie stars sure know how to live in style.'

Lorraine poured Rosie a coffee. 'Did Phyllis say anything about us working for them?'

'Nah, she just took the envelope, thanked me for coming round and said she'd see me at the meeting day after tomorrow. Never even offered me so much as a glass of water. To be honest she seemed edgy, know what I mean? Kept looking over her shoulder . . . Maybe we should have sent it by courier.'

'Elizabeth Seal, I remember her,' Rooney said, closing his eyes. 'She's originally from New Orleans, starred in a movie called *Swamp* somethin' or other, while back. She was real sexy . . .'

Rosie nodded and began to list Elizabeth Seal's later films. Lorraine sat at her own desk with her coffee. Rooney frowned as he listened to Rosie, then nodded his head.

'Yeah, yeah, I remember now, she was all over the papers a while back, somethin' about a girl – kidnapped, wasn't she?' Rooney was pinching his nose, trying to recall what he'd read about the case.

'I said it made all the press, didn't I?' Rosie was nodding and beaming.

'Her daughter, her body was never found?' Rooney pondered.

'Right, and they are still trying to find her. But it wasn't here in Hollywood, it was in New Orleans. She went missing there, didn't she?'

Rosie pointed. 'Yes, disappeared into thin air. She went there with her parents during Mardi Gras. She goes out and is never seen again.'

Rooney chewed his lip and then looked at Lorraine. 'I think a friend of mine, Jim Sharkey, handled the case here . . . all comin' back to me.'

'Lorraine didn't even know who Elizabeth Seal is,' Rosie interjected.

The phone rang, making Rooney jump as he was sitting on the edge of the desk closest to it. Rosie answered, feeling very superior by now.

'Page Investigations.' She then commenced a waving pantomime to Lorraine, gesturing towards her desk and her phone. 'Would you hold one moment and I will see if Mrs Page is free to take your call.' Rosie covered the phone with her hand and took a deep breath. 'Elizabeth Caley, line one!'

CHAPTER 2

LORRAINE CHECKED her appearance. Her tan shoes looked scuffed so she kicked them off and Rosie was ready with polish and a brush. Rooney would drive her to the Caley house, not only saving money on a cab but, as an ex-captain of the Pasadena Homicide Squad, his presence might add extra weight to Page Investigations Agency.

Rooney had jumped at the opportunity of filling up his empty days and had tracked down a few back issues of the papers that had run the story about the missing Caley girl. He had also used his police contacts to try to get further details from the officers that had been overseeing the case. Jim Sharkey, the officer heading the LA side of the investigation, had not been very helpful; Rooney reckoned he'd have to take him out and give him a night on the town to gain any decent information. But Rooney did have something regarding the private investigators that had already been hired – and it was an impressive list. Lorraine adamantly refused to allow him to begin digging up anything from the agencies as she felt it might all be a waste of time. They didn't have finances to fritter away; they didn't have finances, period.

She gave herself one final check-over. Rosie finished polishing her shoes and then they heard the blast of a car horn from the street as Rooney arrived to collect Lorraine.

He had made an effort: his shirt looked as if it had come straight out of the wrapping paper, with two large creases adorning the front, and his tie had flakes of cigarette ash, but not the usual breakfast stains, Lorraine was relieved to note.

'Rosie not coming with us?' he asked as he pushed open the passenger door of his Hyundai.

'Nope, no need to overplay it. Just you and me.'

'Fine. I drove by their place last night, impressive. It's a mile past the Bel Air Hotel. In fact, it's so impressive I almost hadda double-check it wasn't a hotel.'

'Yep,' Lorraine said. 'So, how you reckon we play it?'

Rooney drove carefully, wearing his shades as the mid-January sun was so strong it already felt like summer. 'Let 'em do most of the talking, we sit and listen. We don't have to do a hard sell, well, not to begin with. Don't look good. We don't want to look desperate.'

Lorraine nodded, staring out of the window.

'What you make of it?' he asked nonchalantly.

Lorraine leaned back against the seat, eyes closed. 'Well, from what I've read in those newspapers you got it sounds to me as if it was maybe a kidnap case that went wrong – no note, no ransom . . . she's probably dead a long while. What do you make of it?'

Rooney headed off the San Diego Freeway, the 405, then on to the Sunset Boulevard turn-off heading towards Beverly Hills.

'Well, as far as I can make out, the kid didn't seem the type to go off with any kind of rough trade. She knew the area, been there many times, parents have homes there. Maybe she went freely, but it was Mardi Gras so who knows . . . If we get the case we'll get to know more details from New Orleans. Can't do much this end, guys in LA just covered statements, you know, from family and associates, to see if there was a possible link to the case back here.'

'Was there?'

'Not as far as I know, they got fuck-all here.'

'No ransom note,' Lorraine repeated to herself. She remained deep in thought for another ten minutes or so as they drove on, then she opened her eyes. 'Remember that case, 1986, young girl disappeared, turned up eighteen months later in Las Vegas as a show girl? The family really thought she'd be found dead, instead she was found wearing a G-string and her new silicone tits decorated with a few sequins.'

Rooney shook his head. 'Nope, don't remember it.' He stopped at traffic lights, then turned into Beverly Hills. Lorraine lit a cigarette, puffing it alight from the car's dashboard lighter.

'Reason I remember it is because of the time it took tracing her, eighteen months. If they want us on this, we gotta think about how long it takes tracing anyone, alive or dead,' Lorraine said thoughtfully.

Rooney reached out to the glove compartment and, flicking it open, handed Lorraine an envelope. 'They're a sort of guideline of expenses. Pal gimme them a while back, you know, when I first thought about bein' a dick for hire, useful information. If we get the job we got to know how much to ask for. Check 'em out.'

Lorraine skimmed over the notes and tucked the sheets back into the envelope; she'd already had a good idea how much to ask for, but nowhere near what some of the agencies were charging for their high-tech equipment, from bugging and tracking devices to computerized files and camcorders.

'We'll undercut those other agencies but give the same crap about our high-tech gear. We don't wanna come on cheap.' She replaced the envelope and snapped the glove compartment closed on seeing the stashed bottle of bourbon.

'Right,' Rooney grunted as they drove past the high hedgerows and the ornate houses patrolled by security guards with dogs at electronically barred gates. 'Some of these places remind you of a prison?' he asked, and Lorraine laughed softly.

'No way, man. If you'd been banged up, no way you'd describe these millionaires' mansions as prisons.'

They reached a small roundabout with an arrow sign pointing to the Bel Air Hotel. They turned left, passing the Bel Air, and continued up the quiet road.

Rooney slowed down. 'Next house on the left.' He noticed she straightened up in her seat, pulling her jacket down. She looked great, and, compared to his bulky, unhealthy body, she looked fit. Amazing, considering the punishment she'd heaped on herself. Her resilience constantly amazed him, and he admired her for it. Not long ago she had been arrested for drunkenness and vagrancy, but she'd come a long way since then.

He swung the car in front of the gates, opening his window to a blast of hot air. 'Shit, it's hot. Weather's crazy, one second it's pissing down, the next they're saying it's going to be way up in the seventies today.' He reached out to press the intercom and announced their arrival.

The gates remained closed for a couple of minutes, then eased smoothly open. From the entrance the house could not be seen but the plush gardens were even more exotic than Rosie had described. They were like a hot-house jungle of ferns and carefully planted screens of evergreens, with palms of every shape and size covering each side of the pale gravel drive. They drove slowly past tennis courts, manicured lawns and flower-beds blazing with colour where water-sprinklers ensured they flourished in all the seasons. The water-spraying jets spinning in a wide arc gave the garden a hazy, surreal quality. Not until they turned a wide bend in the drive did the house itself come into view. The white pillars of the three-storey Southern-style house were reminiscent of something out of *Gone with the Wind* – any moment one expected Scarlett O'Hara to come running down the white stone steps saying, 'Why, I do declare.' But there was no Scarlett. Instead, a butler in a black suit and white waistcoat stood poised at the ornately carved front doors.

'Rosie said it was some place.' Lorraine was in awe.

'Money,' muttered Rooney.

A manservant appeared as if from nowhere to open the passenger door for Lorraine. She hesitated a moment before she stepped out and noticed that Rooney had broken out in a sweat by the time they began walking up the steps.

'Good morning, would you please follow me, Mrs Page, Mr Rooney?' said the butler stiffly. He was English, his frozen face devoid of any expression as he gestured for them to go ahead of him into the hall. The white marble floor was so polished it glittered, light sparkling on the surface as they followed the butler towards closed, ceiling-high white and gold-embossed double doors leading off to the right of the hall.

'Mrs Caley will join you directly,' the butler said as he gestured for them to head into the room. White sofas with white frilled scatter cushions in satin and silks were everywhere, and everything was white on white with a gold embroidery finish. The white silk Japanese wallpaper had faint outlines of shimmering birds, and hanging between the impressive gilt mirrors on every wall were large oil paintings of Elizabeth Caley in all her many movie roles.

'Ah, I remember her in that one,' murmured Rooney as he stared at a painting. '*The Swamp*, it was called, and she danced with a big snake.'

'May I offer you any refreshments?' the butler asked as if he'd just smelt something bad.

Lorraine asked for a glass of water. Rooney would have liked a beer but he shrugged. 'Fine for me too, just water.'

The austere butler departed and they were able to have a good look around the white palace, almost afraid to sit and disturb the carefully arrayed cushions. Rooney chose a white Louis XV chair, not that he had any notion it was the real McCoy. Only after he'd eased himself down into it did he worry that he might be too heavy for its spindly legs.

Lorraine looked around the room, noting the many beautifully framed photographs of a young girl. She gestured to one. 'This must be the daughter.' She looked towards the doorway and then moved closer to inspect a photograph. The girl was exceptionally pretty, with waist-length natural blonde hair, a small, up-tilted nose and wide pale eyes.

Lorraine sat down in the centre of the vast white sofa, sinking so low into it that she felt self-conscious: her weight had disturbed the carefully arranged scatter-cushions, which tumbled inwards.

'I don't suppose I could light a cigarette,' she said almost to herself, looking over the white marble-top coffee table with its carefully placed objects, all either bronze or gold. None resembled an ashtray. She stared down at her shoes, almost hidden by the dense white pile of the carpet, and worried that Rosie's quick brush might have left a smear of brown boot polish. She looked up as the clink of ice cubes could be heard.

A maid in a black dress with a white pinafore entered

41

with a tray of iced waters, fizzy, still, with lemon, all in tall crystal glasses in silver and gold containers. Lorraine could barely hide a smile as Rooney murmured his thanks and his chair creaked ominously. The maid passed each of them the water of their choice and then put the tray down. As she returned to the door, Phyllis appeared.

'Don't get up, please. I'm Phyllis Collins, Rosie's friend. You must be Lorraine? If I may call you, er . . . Lorraine?' She scurried across the room and shook Lorraine's hand, and then acknowledged Rooney. 'And you are William Rooney, Rosie told me all about you. Please don't get up, Mrs Caley knows you are here and will be with you shortly.'

Lorraine nodded her thanks. Rooney felt even more awkward in his chair but at least no longer felt the heat. On the contrary, the room was icy cold.

'This has been a very distressing time,' Phyllis said, hovering by the matching Louis XV chair opposite Rooney's.

'Will you be staying for—' Lorraine couldn't think how to describe the meeting.

'No, no, Mrs Caley has asked me not to. I am really just her companion. She should be down any moment.'

The moment stretched to three-quarters of an hour. They discussed Elizabeth Caley's films and paintings, and Phyllis's English background, but whenever Lorraine tried to steer the conversation towards the reason why they were there, Phyllis changed the subject. Lorraine had drunk two tall glasses of water and refused any further as she knew she would need the bathroom. Rooney had gulped his down and wished he hadn't asked for carbonated water as he could feel the gas roaming around his belly. A clock chimed and all three looked at the large gold-embossed and glass-domed ormolu clock on the white mantel.

'I presume these are photographs of Miss Caley?' Lorraine asked, quietly indicating one of the ornate silver frames.

Phyllis nodded, and was about to say something when they heard footsteps in the marble hall, the click-click of high heels, and then the doors were opened by the butler.

'Mrs Elizabeth Caley.'

Phyllis made the introductions and Lorraine rose to her feet, the cushions scattering around her. Rooney creaked out of his chair but Mrs Caley only fluttered her hand in his direction and he eased himself back down.

Elizabeth Caley gently brushed Lorraine's outstretched hand, just giving it a light feather touch, then smiled warmly at Rooney who blushed bright pink. She was, as one would picture a movie star of the late fifties or early sixties, perfectly made-up – her black hair was glossy and worn swept up from her beautiful, strong face, neatly clasped in a tortoiseshell comb. At a distance she could still be taken for a woman in her thirties, yet she was very much the wrong side of fifty, her many face-lifts giving her skin a tight, fragile falseness. Her creamy, low-cut blouse showed just enough cleavage of probably equally fake bosoms. She wore a straight, tight black skirt and pale stockings, which showed that her wondrous legs were still like a young woman's, and high-heeled sandals which accentuated her slender ankles.

Rooney was almost overcome. He could feel his heart thudding as her perfume seemed to wrap itself around him, a heavy magnolia that made one even more aware of her soft white skin. Elizabeth Caley was still a very stunning and sexy woman. She had full red lips, matching long red fingernails, and on her wedding finger a diamond and emerald ring the size of a small bird's egg. She was also charming in her manner, almost deferential

43

as she sat poised as if for flight on the edge of a small, hard-backed gilt chair. She gave only the slightest incline of her head to indicate that Phyllis should leave them alone. Phyllis silently closed the doors behind her.

'My daughter.' Mrs Caley gestured slowly towards a large colour photograph on a glass-topped corner table. Rooney and Lorraine both turned in the direction of the fluttering hand.

Anna Louise Caley was as fair as her mother was dark. Similar wide eyes stared from the photograph but Elizabeth's were a dark tawny brown while her daughter's, judging from the photo, were light blue, and she had a faint smile on her sweet, childish lips, a secretive, shy smile.

'She is very beautiful,' Lorraine said softly.

'Yes, she is.' But Rooney couldn't take his eyes off Mrs Caley, recalling all her films, one after another, and almost had to pinch himself to realize that he was sitting within a few feet of her.

'I know you have already hired a number of private investigation agents,' Lorraine began, as Mrs Caley stared vacantly ahead. 'If we are to reopen the case—'

'It is not closed,' Mrs Caley said quietly.

'I'm sorry, of course it isn't, but if Page Investigations are also to begin making enquiries into your daughter's whereabouts, then we will have to ask you a lot of questions. It may be very upsetting for you, but perhaps we will be able to uncover—'

Mrs Caley bowed her head. 'A clue?'

'Yes. Often an individual or a company like my own, coming on to a case fresh, can uncover something that might have appeared inconsequential to others.'

Mrs Caley nodded, her eyes studying the sparkling ring on her finger. 'The reason I was interested in meeting you is that Phyllis explained to me that you had been involved in other similar cases.'

Rooney frowned, giving Lorraine a questioning look. She ignored it, wondering just what Rosie had embroidered, and covered fast, keeping her voice low and encouraging.

'Tracing missing persons can be a lengthy and costly process and we cannot give any guarantee of success. But that said, I am very confident that with my previous experience as a lieutenant with the Pasadena Police, and with the assistance of my partner, Mr Rooney, ex-captain, we will promise you . . .'

'No stone will be left unturned?' Elizabeth Caley's wide eyes looked from Lorraine to Rooney and then returned to her ring. She laughed softly. 'They have all promised me that, dear, and quite honestly I am not interested in the cost or how long it will take. I want my daughter found because every day is like a nightmare, every phone call a hope, and every night . . .' She caught her breath and swallowed, taking a moment to gather her composure. If this was any indication of her acting prowess, her films must have been good. 'I have never given up hope, even though it has been implied that after so long . . .' Another intake of breath and her delicate hand stroked her milky-white neck. 'Do you have any children, Mrs Page?'

'Yes, I have, two daughters,' Lorraine said softly.

'Well then, you must be able to understand what it means to a mother. Every night I mark in my diary, another day passed, another night ahead without my darling, and I pray, I have prayed so much. And I have wept so much that I don't think I have any more tears to shed.'

Again came another slow, flowing hand gesture in the

45

direction of her daughter's photograph. 'I stare at her face, saying over and over, where are you? Oh, my darling, dearest child, where are you?'

Rooney was almost in tears. Lorraine looked suitably moved but was still of the mind that Mrs Caley was talking, or acting, as if she was in one of her movies. She thought this all the more when Elizabeth Caley sprang to her feet and began pacing up and down, her emotion spilling out as she moved soundlessly back and forth on the whiter-than-white carpet, her voice lifting slightly.

'It was February fifteenth. We went to New Orleans, we always go for Mardi Gras. She didn't come down for dinner, but we had only arrived a few hours earlier and we just thought she wasn't hungry.'

Elizabeth Caley began to move towards one of the gilt and glass-topped tables displaying one photograph after another of her pretty daughter – as a debutante at one of the Mardi Gras balls, at a special surprise birthday, at a film premiere. Elizabeth seemed almost to be dancing in front of them, then she traced one small gilt frame with her finger, tears brimming and then spilling down her perfectly made-up cheeks.

'I will not give up, I cannot give up.'

Rooney could have fallen to his knees, a fan for life. Lorraine simply wished that Mrs Caley would stop the dramatics and talk straight so that they could discuss how long they would be given to work on the case. Throughout Mrs Caley's monologue, she had been calculating how much she could charge to keep three of them on the case, including travel expenses and meals, and as they would obviously have to go to New Orleans, they would have hotel expenses, car hire, etc.

Lorraine coughed to draw Mrs Caley's attention. 'Mrs Caley, if you wish Page Investigations to begin work, can we discuss finances for a moment . . .?'

Mrs Caley spun round on her high heels to face Lorraine. 'Of course I want you to begin, why do you think I've asked you to my home? I want to hire you, I want you to find my daughter, haven't I made that abundantly clear?'

Lorraine licked her lips. 'Good, but we must discuss what contracts you have with other private investigation agencies, as they are a little territorial and—'

'They've done nothing! It's been eleven months, *eleven months, and I don't care who we've hired*. Not one of them has found a single clue as to where she is.' She was giving an Oscar-winning performance, her voice rising as she became more and more emotional. She picked up one of her daughter's photographs and clasped it to her chest. 'She is a sweet, innocent girl, she could not just disappear, she must be somewhere. Someone is doing this to me, it's breaking my heart.'

Lorraine looked at the bedazzled Rooney, wishing he'd help her. She could tell that Mrs Caley was building to a climax and could well collapse on them. Then they'd have to return, maybe even go through this a number of times before they had an agreement on paper. Then, to her consternation, the doors banged open.

'Elizabeth, *Elizabeth*!'

Mrs Caley turned towards the door, holding out the photograph of her daughter in a theatrically helpless gesture.

'She is alive, Robert, I know it, she is alive. I won't give up, *I won't give up*.'

Robert Caley didn't even glance at Lorraine as he gestured to Phyllis, hovering behind him in the doorway. 'Phyllis, help Elizabeth to her room, please, straight away.'

'No, Robert, I won't go. I need to talk to these people, they will trace Anna Louise.'

47

Robert Caley was like a movie star himself. His face was etched with deep lines, made more prominent by his suntan, and his thick black hair, with two wings of grey at the temples, gave him an austere quality that matched the steel of his controlled voice and piercing dark blue eyes.

'Please, Elizabeth, go to your room. It is pointless to upset yourself like this, to put yourself through this over and over again.'

Elizabeth placed the photograph back in its position like a naughty schoolgirl. She pouted petulantly. 'They are highly qualified, darling. At least give them a chance . . . give Anna Louise a chance.'

Robert Caley studied the carpet for a moment, and Lorraine detected that he seemed to be desperately trying to control his anger. Then he looked up and stared coldly at her.

'My wife, as you can see, Mrs Page, is distraught. I think it is better if you leave. At the moment we have more than enough investigation agencies, along with the police, attempting to trace my daughter without needing to hire anyone else. This is a waste of your time.'

Elizabeth Caley confronted her husband, her hands clenched tightly. 'I want them to begin as of this afternoon, Robert, I insist. Mrs Page has daughters of her own, she knows what it is like for a mother, and she has come very highly recommended . . .'

'Really? I think all Mrs Page is interested in is ripping you off, Elizabeth. This has got to stop. I will not have you bringing these people into the house.'

Lorraine stepped forward. 'Excuse me, Mr Caley.'

He turned that cold, arrogant stare on Lorraine again. 'No, you excuse me, Mrs Page, because I don't know what cock-and-bull story you have fed my wife but I do not think you are in any way qualified to assist us in tracing my daughter. We have had enough of journalists, enough of blood-sucking people calling themselves private investigators, people who care only for what they can milk out of us, people who are no better equipped to find Anna Louise than . . .'

'Excuse me,' Lorraine blurted out again.

'I will not allow my wife to be subjected to yet another—'

Lorraine interrupted him. 'Yet another what, Mr Caley?'

He took a deep breath, looked away for a moment and then turned back to Lorraine. 'Sham, Mrs Page, and I think you are perhaps the lowest we have sunk to date. You see, I know all about your agency, if you can call it that, just as I am aware of your record for drunkenness. You were thrown out of the police for shooting a young and, I believe, innocent boy. You are an alcoholic with no experience whatsoever in private investigation work. And as for being a mother! You have had no contact with your daughters since you were divorced. Perhaps the agencies hired to trace my daughter have been incapable of gaining results but they were very swift and very informative regarding you. I would therefore be grateful if you would leave my house and not come back.'

Lorraine felt the thick-pile carpet rising up and choking her. She turned and picked up her purse. Rooney, who had sat like a silent Buddha, now stepped forward, his face flushed red.

'Mr Caley, I am Bill Rooney, and before you start in on me, if you have also done some background work on me, then you'll know I recently retired from the police. I have started working with Mrs Page . . .'

'Just leave, please.'

'Oh, I'll leave, Mr Caley, but not before I set a few

49

things straight. Mrs Page may have been an alcoholic but she isn't now. And whatever she did, she's paid hard for it. But what she's doing now is what she was good at, and I should know because I worked alongside her for long enough. She's got more street knowledge, more intuition than any of the officers I've ever worked with, and she's better than any hired dick you could find in or outside LA. If your daughter's alive, she'll find her, and without ripping you or your wife off, because first and foremost Lorraine Page is a professional. Thanks for the iced water.'

Rooney's face was even redder as he turned with his hand out for Lorraine. She had never needed it so badly since she'd quit drinking. They would have both walked out there and then had not Elizabeth Caley caught hold of Lorraine's arm.

'No, please don't leave, please . . .' She was not acting now, she was for real, and up close her youth had flown, leaving her face etched with pain. 'Find my baby for me, please. Dear God, I beg you to help me, please.'

Rooney tried to ease Lorraine out of the room, as Mrs Caley turned pleadingly to her husband.

'Don't send them away, you can't send them away. Don't let me give up hope, don't do this to me, please.'

Robert Caley deflated, refusing to look at any one of them. He had lost all his anger and now he sounded simply tired out. 'You're hired for two weeks, all expenses paid, whatever you need, whatever your charges. If you wish to talk with me, I can be contacted at my office during office hours. Phyllis, please take Elizabeth for a rest and then draw up whatever contract is required.' He walked away.

Elizabeth Caley sighed, leaning against the door. 'I'm too tired to talk now, you'll have to come back. Tomorrow maybe, Phyllis will organize everything.'

'Thank you, Mrs Caley,' Lorraine said.

Elizabeth beckoned to her. She was not in any way out of control now, but almost steely. 'I want a private word with you. Will you assist me to my room?'

Rooney watched them leave before he smiled at Phyllis. She closed the doors with an abruptness that made it obvious she was angry that Rosie had misled her. She turned her small, frosty eyes to Rooney.

'Well, what payments do you require, Mr Rooney?'

'There are three of us who will be working on this. Thousand a week.'

Phyllis nodded, moving further into the room. 'Three thousand a week and expenses, which I presume will be at the same rate the other agencies have requested?'

Rooney's jaw dropped a fraction; he'd sort of calculated the thousand dollars was for the three of them.

'I will need receipts of all your expenses,' Phyllis said curtly as she flipped open a small note-book.

Rooney beamed. 'You'll have them, Miss Collins.'

He couldn't believe their luck.

Lorraine did not get in to see Elizabeth Caley's bedroom. As they reached the door to her suite, she drew Lorraine closer.

'Can you find her?'

'I will most certainly try, Mrs Caley.'

She nodded, chewing her lip, and then leaned closer still. 'I will give you an incentive. If you find her, you will get a one-million-dollar bonus.'

Lorraine blinked. 'One million.'

'Yes. I want my daughter traced, Mrs Page.'

Lorraine turned to look down the wide staircase and then after a moment, keeping her voice as steady as she could, she repeated, 'One million?'

Mrs Caley nodded.

Lorraine eased her weight from one foot to the other. Her voice was soft, as low as Mrs Caley's, but she didn't hesitate. 'Dead or alive, Mrs Caley?'

'If you trace her, dead or alive, Mrs Page, you will receive one million dollars.'

'Can I have that in writing?'

The soft white hand with the blood-red nails gripped hold of Lorraine's in a firm, fast handshake, and she once again got the impression that Elizabeth Caley was like two people; publicly, she was the showcase movie star, the consummate actress, but beneath the show there was something else, something she had not picked up on earlier – and it wasn't the underlying steely quality she'd expected. Elizabeth Caley was very, very frightened. Up close, the pupils of her slanting brown eyes were over-large, and Lorraine knew she was using drugs of some kind.

Not until they had driven out of the electronic gates did Rooney let out a whistle. 'One grand each for two weeks, all expenses on top. Plane tickets, hotels, we got total carte blanche, no expenses spared. Rosie was fucking right, this is a big cash deal all right.'

Lorraine gave him a sidelong look and then stared ahead. 'There's a bonus,' she said quietly. He looked puzzled. 'If we find Anna Louise we get one million dollars.'

He braked, and she had to press her hands on the dashboard to stop herself from sliding down the seat.

'What? Are you kiddin'?'

'No, not kidding. She's going to put it in writing.' She slipped on the safety belt.

'Fuck me, one million. Holy shit.'

52

Lorraine gave a tiny smile. 'Dead or alive.'

'Fucking hell.' He shook his head in disbelief.

'Just one thing, Bill, two actually. Thanks for backing me up in there with that bastard Caley.'

Rooney accelerated again. 'Think nothin' of it, only said what I meant, he got to me. So what's the other thing you wanna talk about, the split?'

Lorraine smiled. 'No, that goes three ways. It's just I run this investigation, Bill, not you, me. I give the orders, understood?'

He nodded. 'Yeah, I hear you, it's your show.'

'Yes, it is,' she said softly and then let out a yell, thumping his big wide shoulder. 'One million!'

CHAPTER 3

THAT SAME afternoon, Lorraine, Rooney and Rosie discussed how they would begin the investigation into the disappearance of Anna Louise Caley. First they would invoice the Caleys for an advance of salary. Rooney would approach the officers he knew had been or were still involved on the case in LA. This would cut down a lot of questions they would have to ask Mr and Mrs Caley, and before Lorraine talked to either of them she wanted as much background information as possible. All back issues of newspapers that had featured the girl's disappearance had to be checked over at the library and xeroxed copies filed at the office.

They felt they were on a roll. One million dollars was one hell of an incentive.

That evening, Rooney met with the Dean Martin look-alike Detective Jim Sharkey for a liquid dinner. To begin with, Sharkey was non-committal; as far as he was concerned, the police had done about all they could do their end.

'Consensus is, or was, she was kidnapped by persons unknown, though no ransom note was delivered. Other cases with similar characteristics would not have been kept open as long as this one.'

Rooney sniffed. 'You sayin' you had a lot of girls just disappearing?'

'Yeah, a lot, Bill, and you gotta know it. We got a file

54

as long as my arm on missing kids, and we try checkin' out most of them. Believe me, we spent more time on this one because of the high profile of the Caleys. She disappeared in New Orleans anyway, so there was not a lot we could do this end. We even sent a few guys there to dig around but they came up with nothing, and they're not the friendliest bunch of bastards, kinda suggested we back off.'

'So you did?'

'Yeah, we got nothin' from LA, and we interviewed every kid she knew.'

'Was the Caley girl into drugs?'

'Nope, squeaky clean. You know, with no body discovered after eleven months, some of the guys reckoned the girl maybe just took off.'

Bill sighed, leaning back in his chair. 'Anythin' come up against the parents?'

Sharkey looked askance. 'What? Give me that again? They've fuckin' hired the best in the business, if they'd had anythin', anythin' to do with their own kid's disappearance, believe me, we'd have sniffed it. And the broad, she was weepin' her heart out.'

'Mrs Caley?'

Sharkey nodded. 'She must have been one hell of a woman, still is. Geez, what a figure, and I'm tellin' you, Bill, I never been one for older women, know what I mean? But fuck me, well, I'd like to give her a roll in the hay, no kiddin'.'

Rooney nodded. The fact that the pair of them hadn't pulled a woman in twenty years unless they'd paid for it did not prevent their classic male ego from believing they could. They sank a few more beers, then switched to vodka. The dinner had been a long one. At midnight they called a cab, and made their way back to Sharkey's precinct in uptown LA. Sharkey held his liquor well and

55

even though he was off duty, he refused to let Rooney come into the station with him. To have ex-Captain Bill Rooney in tow breathing beer fumes over everyone could cause problems, even more so considering what he had agreed to do.

Rooney waited in the cab. It was almost an hour before Sharkey rejoined him and slipped him a thick xeroxed file of information. It had been an expensive afternoon, Rooney thought as Sharkey accepted the folded bills with a wink. He'd asked for five hundred dollars and a guarantee that if any questions were ever asked the files never came from him. Rooney never even mentioned the thirty-five-buck cab fare, he was too eager to get the statements back to Lorraine.

Lorraine worked on Sharkey's information well into the night. As far as she could make out, Anna Louise Caley was a well-liked, friendly and very pampered young lady. The students in her year who had been questioned didn't have a bad word to say about her. All the students and teachers alike made references to her being very pretty or even beautiful; none referred to her academic prowess but she was said to have been an excellent tennis player, swimmer, horse rider and all-round athlete. She had no steady boyfriend but Lorraine ringed the names of the boys that had admitted to dating her up until the time of her disappearance. She decided she would target them first. She had the names of numerous female students who all claimed to have been Anna Louise's best friend, so they were lined up second. Then came the coaches and the college teachers. It was going to be a race against time: with only two weeks on the case, she had set aside only two days to complete the LA research.

Next morning, Page Investigations Agency was busy for the first time since they had opened. The phone in

56

the office rang constantly, and Rosie was flushed bright pink and sweating as the calls came in.

Lorraine pointed to a large cork board on which she had pinned lists of names for interview, and those for her to cross reference and delete when necessary.

'Okay, Rosie, you list every name, all the students I got to see in alphabetical order. We cross them out as we go along.' Rosie nodded. There was a buzz in the office and it felt good.

Rooney had been assigned to make very discreet enquiries into the private investigation agencies hired by the Caleys, to see if there was an ex-colleague working anywhere he could palm money to, like Sharkey, and if they had any information worth digging into. He listed the companies on Lorraine's big board.

'My God, are they all on the same case?' Rosie asked.

'Yep. Caley's sure been shelling out a lot of cash.' Lorraine chewed her pencil and then stuck it in her hair.

'Okay, this is how we work it, I do the college kids, you, Bill, start seeing what you can come up with about Caley, tap your old associates, whatever you need to do. Rosie, you'll be the anchor-woman, you hold the fort here, we call in if we get anything, most important is that we get moving and come up with what we can as fast as possible . . . agreed?'

Rooney nodded as Rosie made a note of Lorraine's mobile phone number and passed it to him. 'We can all keep in constant touch,' she beamed.

Lorraine flicked a look at Rooney and winked. 'That's what it's all about, Rosie!'

Lorraine began the tedious and laborious interview sessions and hired a car, an '88 Buick which had seen better days, with a portable telephone to keep in touch with the office while driving herself from one meeting to another. Armed with two photographs of Anna Louise, she talked to fifteen students at UCLA. To be confronted with fresh young girls, eager to talk and full of youthful exuberance, made her feel tired and jaded beyond belief, but the mental picture she was gradually forming was basically the same one which had already emerged from the old police files. Making the kids feel relaxed with her was painstaking work and her fixed smile was wearing thin, but she persisted. By twelve in the afternoon she only had two names left on her list and went to the tennis courts to meet Angie Wellbeck, listed on Sharkey's statements as a 'best friend'. After Angie, she was meeting one of the kids listed as dating Anna Louise, Tom Heller.

Angie was wearing tennis shorts, a white T-shirt, Reeboks and little white socks with bobbles at the heel. She carried her tennis racquets in a very professional-looking white sling sports bag. She constantly plucked at it as she answered the routine questions Lorraine had asked all the students very politely – did she get on with Anna Louise? Did she know of anyone who did not like her? Anyone who might have a grudge against her? Who did she socialize with? Did she take drugs, drink too much? In essence, what was the missing girl like?

Angie sat on a bench, staring at her tennis shoes, and Lorraine could see faint freckles on her lightly tanned pale skin.

'Well, she was real pretty, and always wore the most up-to-date clothes, you know, if something was in, AL always was the first to have it.'

'AL?' asked Lorraine, knowing full well that it was a nickname because it had been repeated to her so many times.

'Yeah, we all called her AL. You know, Anna Louise is boring. I don't mean she was boring, just her name.'

Angie said nothing untoward, or even gave the slightest hint that her friend wasn't anything other than perfect. She just reiterated that although she was not academically inclined, she was great at sports and very competitive.

'Like how competitive?' Lorraine enquired.

'Well, she liked to win, tennis anyway. We played a lot together, sometimes we played doubles. Her dad is a great player, he used to play with her I think, that's why she was so good. Great backhand, very strong, although her serve wasn't so hot, but she was a good player. Got enough practice in, I guess.'

'Did she get angry if she lost?'

'Sure.'

'Aggressive?'

'Sometimes.'

'Did she argue or get angry with anyone specific?'

'No, she was kind of more angry at herself.'

'How do you mean?'

'Well, if she missed a volley she'd shout and yell at herself, you know.'

'Ah! So you never saw her fighting or shouting with anyone?'

'No, but maybe you should ask some of the others. I mean, I played a lot with her but I wasn't the only person she played with. Tilda Brown played with her mostly. She was closest to AL, but she hasn't come back to school, not after AL disappeared, but I guess you know that.'

Lorraine nodded, underlining Tilda's name in her note-book.

'Did you all have the same coach?'

'Geez, no way, AL was rich, you know, and her coach was ex-Olympic standard, a real professional. We'd all have liked to be coached by him,' she giggled.

'Did this create jealousy?' Lorraine was even boring herself.

'Yeah, but nothin' to do with tennis.'

Lorraine looked at Angie who had removed her headband and was plucking at it with her fingers, picking off strands of fluff. 'How do you mean?'

'Jeff Nathan, the coach, is like a movie star, I think he coaches a lot of famous people. Sometimes when I went over to their place he'd play with us, you know, make up a four with her dad. That was the only time I got to meet him.'

'The coach?'

'Yeah, and her dad, he was real nice.'

Angie's tennis partners were hovering, so she asked if she could go. Lorraine could think of nothing else to ask. Like everyone else she'd spoken to, Angie hadn't given any real insight into Anna Louise but, like three other girls, she had mentioned the handsome tennis coach.

'Were you her best friend?' Lorraine asked as Angie sprang to her feet, eager to leave.

She turned and smiled. 'I dunno about her best, I think Tilda was, but everyone liked her – she was a real nice girl.' Angie's face puckered for a moment and she hesitated, chewing her lips. 'You think something terrible has happened to her?' Lorraine looked away, as Angie moved closer. 'Some of them say she's maybe been murdered, is it true?'

'I really don't know, but thanks for your time.'

'That's okay. Bye now.'

Lorraine watched Angie join three other girls, all in similar white tennis gear. They looked over and smiled. She sat for a few moments, watching the girls warming up, slicing the ball over the net. Judging by the hard thudding crack of the ball she could tell, even though she was no tennis player, that the girls could play well.

So if AL, as she was known, was better, she must have been very good.

'I'd say she could have turned professional, if she'd had the inclination.'

Lorraine was outside the squash courts, talking to a gangly boy with a white sweat-shirt slung round his shoulders. Tom Heller was at least six feet two and good-looking in an ordinary, neat-featured way.

When Lorraine asked if he had played regularly with Anna Louise, he shrugged.

'Yeah, sometimes on weekends at her house. Her dad is a great player.'

Lorraine nodded. 'What about the coach, er . . .'

'Jeff Nathan? Yeah, I played with him at her place. He gives private lessons.'

'Did you like him?'

He frowned. 'I didn't really know him.'

'Did Anna Louise like him?'

'I don't know.'

'You used to date her, didn't you?'

'Few times, nothing serious, beach parties, we were just buddies really.'

'Did you have sex with her?'

He blushed. 'No.'

'Do you know if she was sexually permissive in any way?'

'No, well, no more than anyone else.'

'How many boys do you know had a sexual relationship with Anna Louise?'

He blushed again. 'I don't know, like I said, we dated a few times but no more than that.'

'What about the coach? This guy Nathan, did he have a scene going with her?'

He looked with distaste at Lorraine. 'I have no idea.'

She was suddenly pissed off by his supercilious attitude.

'Look, it's Tom, isn't it? Well, I am trying to trace Anna Louise, she's been missing for eleven months and she could be lying in a shallow grave or she could be dancing in Las Vegas. I am just trying to do my job, okay? So if she was screwing this tennis coach, and you maybe knew about it as her buddy, then I'd be grateful if you'd tell me . . .'

'I have no idea.'

'Do you know where I can find the tennis coach, Nathan?'

'Maybe in the Bel Air. He plays there.'

'Thank you, Mr Heller. Sorry to interrupt your game!'

It was almost lunch-time when Lorraine called the office on her mobile.

'How's it going?'

'Fine, waiting for Bill to call in with any developments,' Rosie said.

'I'm on my way to see the tennis coach – what are you doing?'

Rosie pursed her lips. 'A lot, I've got to arrange hotels, flights and . . .' The second phone rang on Rosie's desk. 'Hang on, Lorraine, it might be Bill on line two.'

Bill it was, to say that he wasn't getting much of a result from any of the other investigation agencies attached to the Caley case, but he was still plugging away. Rosie passed this on to Lorraine, who suggested that perhaps he should interview the psychic whom the Caleys had hired in LA. Rosie repeated this to Rooney and listened to his reply with both receivers pressed to her ear before coming back to Lorraine. 'He says they're all a fucking waste of time.'

Lorraine snapped back to Rosie, 'You tell him that so are a bunch of racquet-swinging rich kids, but before we hit New Orleans we gotta cover ourselves here, *you tell him that.*'

Rooney could hear her and laughed, and, still laughing, told Rosie to tell Lorraine she was the boss, but when she tried to do so the line was dead. Rosie put both phones down and began to check out the telephone manual for a way to connect calls on two lines.

Jeff Nathan had the kind of muscular body that most women fantasize about. His tight white T-shirt and his brief white tennis shorts showed strong tanned limbs which were very desirable, but within minutes Lorraine had sussed that all his masculine muscles would more than likely be wrapped around another equally tanned male's body.

'You gay, Mr Nathan?'

'My, my, you are very aggressive.'

'No, I don't think I'd say that was an aggressive question but one I need to ask and know the answer to. You see, Mr Nathan, I am trying to find a young girl who's been missing for eleven months, and if you had sexual relations with her then . . .'

He smiled, and relaxed his macho tennis pro image. 'Yes, Mrs Page, I am,' he said, looking at the card she had passed him.

'Thank you. So, tell me what you know about Anna Louise Caley.'

'Well, I was her personal coach, so I've lost a nice income. Anna Louise could have played professional

63

standard, she was very coordinated, strong, but she had a major fault; if she made a mistake she couldn't forget it. She became very angry at herself and it usually fouled up the rest of her game. The more anger she felt, the worse her game progressed.' He cocked his handsome head to one side. 'You see, I really did only know her as her coach, I can tell you about her game but nothing about her personal life.'

'What about her father?' Lorraine asked.

Nathan shrugged. 'Good player, hard hitter, but no speed. He'd wait for the ball to come to him, never used the court. She was never interested in being a serious player, all she ever wanted was to beat her father, but whenever they played she lost it. And she could have beaten him.'

'Did she come on to you?' Lorraine asked as they walked towards the court. She found his fake capped-toothed smile unattractive but realized that for a young kid it could be devastating.

'Come on to me? My dear, that is, sadly, the main part of why people, well, women, girls or whatever, keep hiring me. I have to look and act the stud.'

'Were you?' she tried one more time.

'Was I what? A stud? Oh, please . . .' Nathan's tanned neck stretched, his perfect features wreathed in smiles.

'So she was, say, infatuated?'

He smiled, showing his perfect white teeth. 'Maybe, but I assure you it was not in my interest to encourage her in any way. Like I said, the Caleys paid me well to coach their daughter and I would have been foolish to foul up a good weekly income.'

'Weekly?'

'Yep, although sometimes I'd get to their place and she didn't feel like playing, but I was always paid.' Nathan turned as a petite blonde woman with a frilled white tennis skirt waved across to him from a court. 'I gotta go, but if you need to speak to me again, any time. Do you play?'

Lorraine looked at the blonde attempting to knock a ball over the net. 'About as good a game as maybe she has!' He laughed, she quite liked him. 'Thanks for your time, I appreciate you seeing me.'

She hadn't got much from Nathan, again nothing that had not already been recorded by the police files. She watched him in action with his 'student' and realized on closer inspection she was well into her late forties. Poor woman, she thought, she must have the same infatuation with Jeff as his students, staring at his rippling muscles as he began to drag his ball basket to the centre of the court opposite the blonde.

'Let's just warm up with a few easy ones, shall we, Mrs Fairley? See how you've progressed.'

Lorraine made her way back to the car park and she heard Mrs Fairley squeal a lot of 'Oooppps' and 'Oh, I'm so sorry . . .' as the balls she attempted to swipe expertly dribbled into the tennis net.

Lorraine felt totally drained by the time she drove out of the university complex, and she was also irritated. Maybe it was the students' youth, their nonchalance, but no one had given her any real insight into the missing girl. Just as nobody seemed to have a bad word to say about her except that she got a bit itchy when she missed a fucking volley.

Lorraine called Rosie at the office from her car phone. 'Any developments?'

'No, not as yet,' Rosie replied.

'Rooney gone to see that psychic?' asked Lorraine.

'I think so, but he sort of thought it was a waste of time.'

'Yeah, okay, I'm on my way to the Caleys'. I haven't come up with anything positive yet so I'll interview them and then call in when I'm through.'

'Oh, I think Rooney wanted to be in on your meeting with the Caleys, didn't he?'

'Rosie, I am running this case, not Bill Rooney.'

No sooner had Rosie replaced the phone than Rooney barged into the office.

Rosie smiled. 'Lorraine just called in, she's on her way to the Caleys'.'

'Shit, I wanted in on that meet.'

'I know, I told her, and she said she was running the case, so . . .'

Rooney tossed his hat at the stand and missed, then took off his jacket, showing his sweat-stained shirt. 'Well, I got a contact. Old buddy of mine used to be on the Force 'bout ten years ago, now works with the top investigation agency hired by the Caleys, Agnews. To be honest I didn't think he'd still be working, got a good pension when he was invalided out. Poor bastard got a leg full of lead . . . I've arranged to see him tonight.'

'What's his name?'

'Nick Bartello.' Rooney frowned.

'Italian, is he?'

'At one time. She won't like him. Dunno if they met, they were attached to different departments, he was drugs, she was with me on homicide.'

'Why won't she like him?'

'He's a dead ringer for her old partner Lubrinski, same kind of guy. Nick and he were partners, short-lived 'cos Lubrinski moved over to my team.'

'Who's he?'

Rooney frowned. 'She never mention him to you?'

66

'No.' Rosie crossed to the coffee percolator and began to brew up a pot.

'They were partners at the old station.'

'So why won't she like him? If he's a pal of yours maybe he can give us some inside information.'

'Maybe. So she's never mentioned Lubrinski to you?' Rosie returned to her cluttered desk. 'No . . .'

'He's dead.'

'Well, maybe that's why.' She sat down.

'He was one hell of a guy, Lubrinski, great cop. In fact, I gotta tell you, Rosie, during my time I saw a lot go down, not all died, some just folded, you know, mentally, but Lubrinski, when I was told he'd bought it, he was the only officer for whom I cried. Not because he was one hell of an officer, he was that, but he was also a main guy, could drink any man under the table. Loner, crazy son of a bitch. When I partnered him with Lorraine I reckoned on fireworks . . .'

'And?' Rosie asked only half-listening. But because Rooney remained silent she looked up. He was staring into space.

'They were one fucking good team, best I ever had. He was injured in crossfire, took three bullets. He bled to death in the ambulance. She'd made a sort of tourniquet to try and stem the blood, used her pantihose . . . but it didn't work. He was dead on arrival at the hospital, and she wouldn't let go of his hand. Orderly told me they'd had to force her to let go, that she kept on saying he was gonna be okay.'

Rosie raised her eyebrows. 'Well, she's never mentioned any of this to me. What happened after?'

Rooney sighed, shifting his bulk. 'She requested to be returned to duty immediately. About six weeks later she killed that kid . . .'

Rosie knew about the boy Lorraine had shot by mistake, a young kid caught up in a drugs bust. 'Maybe this Bartello isn't such a good idea. Maybe she won't want to be reminded of the past.'

'It was a long time ago,' Rooney said, trying to change the subject. 'And the guy's good.' Then the phone rang, so Rosie's attention was diverted. As she answered she didn't hear Rooney say softly, 'I think she was in love with Lubrinski.'

Rosie held one hand over the phone, waving the other to Rooney. 'It's Nick Bartello.'

'Hey, Nick, how you doing? You got my message then? So can we meet, have a few drinks? Sure, where are you?' Rooney jotted a note down on Lorraine's notepad. 'Okay, I'll be there, gimme half an hour . . .' He slowly replaced the receiver. 'Okay, I'm out of here. If she calls in, tell her I've gone to Joe's Diner, lemme suss the guy out.' He picked up his jacket. 'Rosie, maybe you don't say anything about Lubrinski. Like you said, it was a long time ago and I don't want her to think we've been gossiping, okay?'

Rosie nodded, distracted yet again by the telephone. By the time she had answered, Rooney had departed. The call was from Robert Caley, asking to speak to Lorraine to say his wife was indisposed and he would be at home rather than the office as arranged. His manner was abrupt, cold. A man, Rosie determined, very used to handing out orders.

Rosie called Lorraine on her mobile and passed on the message. She got a blast of foul language as Lorraine had actually been on her way to Caley's plush office complex, the Water Garden, in Santa Monica. She did not mention Nick Bartello or Lubrinski as Lorraine cut off her call as abruptly as Robert Caley had, but she wondered about what Rooney had said about Lubrinski. The dawning realization of just how little she knew of Lorraine's past life made her feel uneasy, perhaps because it also meant, if she were truthful, that she didn't really know ex-Lieutenant Lorraine Page, the woman she shared her home with.

The same austere butler ushered Lorraine into the Caleys' lounge and asked her to wait. She did not sit down, choosing instead to study the other photographs of Anna Louise in their ornate frames. One particular picture caught her eye: Anna Louise was standing between Nathan, her tennis coach, and her father, Robert Caley's arm around her shoulders, as if he was showing her off to the camera, a look of paternal pride on his face.

Ten minutes ticked by. Lorraine now studied the large oil paintings of Elizabeth Caley's film roles. She really was an astonishingly beautiful woman. She crossed over to one that Rooney had pointed out, which depicted one of Elizabeth's earliest starring roles in which she looked no more than twenty years old. She was wearing heavy golden hooped earrings and a pale blue silk turban like the headcloths black women sometimes wore, arranged in an odd way Lorraine had never seen before, with the material knotted into points to give the impression of a crown over the young woman's head. Her shoulders were bare, the skin of her whole body tinted a tawny brown, and she was covered only by the brief draperies of a brightly coloured scarf. A small plaque was set into the embossed gold frame, inscribed with the words 'Marie Laveau, Queen of New Orleans'. Looking from paintings of Elizabeth Caley to the photographs of Anna Louise and her father, Lorraine could see little family resemblance.

Twenty minutes passed and Lorraine checked her

watch, then the ormolu mantel clock. It was almost 5 p.m. She was about to walk out of the room when the butler returned, and, remaining at the open door, gestured for Lorraine to follow him, giving no apology for the fact that she had been kept waiting.

Lorraine followed the silent, black-uniformed figure past the wide sweeping staircase and into a corridor, turning left into a wonderfully light, glass sun room. The vast conservatory was, she thought, some kind of extension to the main house. Tropical plants were in such profusion that it resembled a florist's, with the heady perfume of magnolia and jasmine lingering in the air and condensation misting the lower glass panes. They continued through the jungle, out into a courtyard shaded with plants growing from white painted tubs. Crazy-paved paths and a gazebo with white trailing curtains dominated the end of the courtyard, and primrose-yellow cushions adorned the white garden furniture. A table with chilled orange juice, an ice bucket with two bottles of Chablis and an array of glasses stood in the centre of the gazebo.

'Mr Caley will join you shortly.' The butler wafted his hand for Lorraine to sit, and hovered over the table. 'May I offer you wine, juice, or . . .'

'Still water,' Lorraine said curtly, irritated that Caley was still keeping her waiting. She sat on a white wicker chair, shifting the yellow cushion to one side, glad of the shade given by the trailing muslin curtains. The butler poured her some still water into an ice-filled glass, and with a pair of silver tongs expertly picked up a ready-cut slice of lemon to rest on the edge of her glass.

'Thank you.' She accepted the glass, watching as he uncorked the wine, first feeling the bottle with his hand, then wrapping a napkin around the neck, before placing it in the ice bucket.

'Excuse me, Mrs Page.' He actually backed up two steps before he turned and walked back into the house. Lorraine looked at her watch; she had been there well over an hour, and with only two weeks on the case, it was an hour lost. She sipped the iced water, and seeing a large glass ashtray leaned forward to draw it closer. She hesitated for a moment, then lit up a cigarette. She looked around the yard, and turning in her chair, she could just see the edge of the tennis courts. She got up and walked to the narrow pathway. To her right she could see the entire double tennis courts, to her left was a vast swimming pool with rows of sunbeds laid out next to each other, each with pale lemon towels, with small tables between, like a hotel patio. Beyond the pool was a large pagoda-style building which she assumed held the changing rooms and showers. Water fountains at either side flanked a path which led into a Japanese garden or what she supposed was one because of the bonsai shrubs and trees. There was no one visible, not one gardener, swimmer or tennis player. Apart from the chirping of the birds, it was all strangely silent: so silent it was unnerving. Again she checked her watch and physically jumped when Caley appeared as if from nowhere.

'I'm sorry for keeping you waiting. Did your secretary explain that my wife is indisposed, which is the reason I am here and not at my office?'

He did not seem to require a reply to his apology. He was standing by the table, pouring himself a glass of wine. There was a moment of hesitation and she saw him flick a glance at her glass of iced water. He did not offer her wine but filled his glass and sat on one of the yellow-cushioned wicker chairs. Half-turning, he picked up the cushion and tossed it on to the chair nearest him. He was dressed casually in light brown slacks and loafers. His arms were bare, his pale blue silk shirt-sleeves rolled back

71

casually. Robert Caley lifted his glass to her and sipped the wine, but she could not see the expression in his eyes behind his gold-rimmed shades. Everything about Robert Caley had that LA gloss, that mark of high fashion, from the thin gold wrist-watch on his left wrist to the single fine loose gold band on his right. He wore no wedding ring.

'You have a very beautiful garden.'

'Mm, too manicured for my taste, and this flimsy thing reminds me of something off a movie set, but it has a purpose.'

Lorraine sat down and drew her glass closer, feeling very self-conscious.

'My wife never sits in the sun, she is too pale-skinned.' He obviously did; he was one of those men Lorraine presumed had a year-round suntan. Caley was also a very confident man and apparently in no hurry to ask why she wished to see him.

Lorraine stubbed out her cigarette and felt his eyes giving her a swift appraisal from behind the shades. She coughed lightly and crossed her legs, reaching down by the side of the chair to retrieve her purse.

'Do you play tennis, Mrs Page?'

'No, I don't.'

He smiled, and sipped his wine. 'I didn't think you did, but you work out, correct?'

She hated the fact she was blushing, and busied herself with opening her purse to take out a note-book. 'Yes, but as you checked up on me I am sure you must be aware I was not, until recently, in what one could describe as being in the best of health.'

He lifted his glass to her. 'Well, you certainly look well today. Is your hair naturally blonde?'

'Yes, but I have streaks.' She suddenly laughed, finding their conversation ridiculous. No man had ever asked her whether or not she was naturally blonde.

'My daughter's hair is as blonde, ash-blonde, but then you must know, you have photographs.'

'Yes, I have, thank you. And thank you for sending the retainer fee so promptly.'

'Ah, that will be Phyllis's doing.' Caley reached for the bottle again and refilled his glass. 'Would you like more water?'

Lorraine shook her head. 'I don't think I can deal with your butler, he reminds me of a character from one of those British television series on PBS.'

Caley laughed, a lovely deep warm laugh, and he crossed one leg over the other, leaning back in his chair. 'Close to the truth, actually. He used to be an actor, a lot of Brits come out here for the pilot season hoping for work. When they don't get it, I suppose they take what work they can, but Peters has been with us for many years. I think he's refined his role rather well. The other servants are from home, or Elizabeth's old home in New Orleans – Berenice is our housekeeper, and we have two maids, Sylvana and Maria, plus Mario the chauffeur. I think we also have about four gardeners who maintain the grounds and the pool.'

Lorraine made a note of the servants. 'Can I ask you some questions?'

'Of course, that is the reason you are here, go ahead.'

'I gathered from talking to her friends that your daughter was very well liked. In fact, it's a rare occurrence when—'

'She is very well liked,' he corrected, as if resenting the use of the past tense.

'I met her coach, Jeff Nathan.'

He nodded. 'Yes, he's a good coach and Anna Louise

is an excellent player. I'd hoped she would think about turning professional, she is a natural athlete.'

'Are you?'

He leaned forward. 'Sorry?'

'Are you a natural athlete?'

'Good God, no, but you're not here to talk about me. Did anyone you have spoken to come up with anything new?'

'No, they did not, so it will obviously be necessary for myself and my team to go to New Orleans when I've completed my interviews here.'

He nodded, sipping his wine.

'I know you have gone over and over this, Mr Caley, but would you tell me in your own words exactly what occurred the day your daughter went missing?'

He drained his glass and stood up. 'We had breakfast. My wife was checking her packing so she did not join us, it was just Anna and myself. She was in good spirits, looking forward to the trip. We usually go for the last weeks of Carnival, have done for many years. The date of Mardi Gras itself is worked out backwards from Easter, so it can fall on any Tuesday from early February onwards, from February third through to March ninth.'

Lorraine smiled and consulted her notes. 'Thank you. So last year you left on February fifteenth?'

'Yes. At about nine-thirty I spoke to my wife and said she and Anna should be ready to leave at noon. I had some business to take care of at the office and when I returned a little before twelve, the cases were already in the limousine. I showered and changed and we left for the airport just after twelve-thirty.' His voice was expressionless, having repeated this many times before. He stuffed his hands into his pockets and walked to the side of the gazebo, leaning against one of the pillars. 'I have a private jet. I did not fly it myself as I had some

74

papers to sort through on the flight, so we used my pilot, Edward Hardy. Anna sat with her mother, looking through the magazines on the central table, and asked Elizabeth if she could arrange for Phyllis to collect one of the evening gowns she liked on the fashion pages. Elizabeth called Phyllis and arranged it there and then, shortly before we landed. My car was waiting at the tarmac and we went directly to the hotel. Anna Louise was as excited as she always was. She was planning to see a friend.'

Lorraine flicked through her notes. 'Friend would be Tilda Brown, yes?'

He nodded so Lorraine continued, 'And you all went straight to the hotel?'

'Yes, we always have two adjoining suites booked for the entire Mardi Gras month.'

'That is the Hotel Cavagnal?'

'Yes, Rue Chartres. It's an old hotel in the heart of the French Quarter, the balconies overlook the courtyard on one side and the streets on the other.'

'Why do you choose to stay at a hotel when you have houses in the city?'

'Well, during Carnival it's good to be central to all the action.'

Lorraine looked at Caley, unconvinced, and he continued evenly, still meeting her eyes, 'And sometimes I prefer to conduct my business away from a domestic setting.'

Lorraine looked back to her note-pad. 'So you arrived at the Cavagnal . . .'

'Yes. The maid, she's called Alphonsine, unpacked my wife's clothes first, then mine, and then she went to Anna Louise's suite. We have various functions and parties we always go to, so she checks that everything is pressed or that nothing requires laundering.'

Lorraine nodded, and waited. 'Alphonsine lives in New Orleans?'

'Yes, we have staff at one of our homes there. They help us at the hotel, see if we want anything taken to the house and get everything ready there, as we generally go to one or other residence when Carnival ends.'

Lorraine flipped through her notes. She had the addresses of the Caley households and lists of their staff. 'So what time—'

He interrupted her. 'As soon as we arrived, Elizabeth arranged for a massage; I remained in the suite making some business calls. Anna Louise joined us for tea and we decided we would dine at the Cavagnal, early, as we had a number of invitations and er . . . She has a wicked sense of humour, and began to mimic some of the more elderly ladies who had asked us for cocktails. At one point Elizabeth ticked her off, said that after that evening she would be free to see her friends, but for now she had to behave. Elizabeth is quite a celebrity and enjoys being the centre of attraction on these occasions, probably reminds her of the old days when she really was a star.'

'Did Anna Louise argue with your wife?'

'No, in fact they began to discuss what they would wear, girls' talk. I went for a swim, came back around seven. I showered and changed, Elizabeth was already dressing, her hair had been done. She always used the same hairdresser, again someone she has known for many years.'

'Oscar Cloutier?'

'Yes. He left at about seven-fifteen. We both went down to the dining room for seven-thirty. We had some champagne ordered. At seven forty-five Elizabeth asked me to call Anna Louise's room, so I did. There was no reply, so I returned to the table, presuming she was on her way down.'

Lorraine looked over her notes. Robert Caley had repeated his original statement almost word for word, even down to the dates of the Mardi Gras. He went on to say that he and his wife began to order, and he even ordered barbecued shrimp, her favourite New Orleans dish, for Anna Louise.

'When it got to about eight and Anna Louise had still not come down, I asked the waiter to call her room again. He said there was no reply, so I went up to her room and as it was locked I used the connecting door between our suite and Anna Louise's. Nothing that I could see was out of place and the gown she was going to wear was laid out for her on the bed. I went into the bathroom and the sitting room, and saw her purse, or at least the one she had been carrying on the flight, so I simply thought she had gone out to visit someone and had been delayed. I returned to the dining room.'

'But you had asked her to join you for dinner. Did she usually disobey?'

'Well, sometimes she would say she would do something, but like any teenager she could not always be relied on.'

'But your wife had specifically asked her to join you both on this particular evening.'

'Yes, yes.'

'Did she seem not to want to? You said your wife reprimanded her for mimicking some of the people who had invited you for cocktails later in the evening, correct?'

He sighed, irritated. 'I wouldn't call it reprimanding, in fact I said "ticked her off", so it was not a very serious exchange.'

'At any other time when you were in New Orleans had Anna Louise agreed to dine with you and not turned up?'

'I suppose so, but I can't recall any single time it was

77

of importance. She knew the city and was very aware of the obvious dangers about being out alone in certain neighbourhoods. We had both been very firm about her not wandering out alone at night. And she never did, or not to my knowledge.'

'She knows the city well, knows the old French Quarter?'

'Yes, of course. Elizabeth is from New Orleans so Anna Louise had been there off and on since she was a child. She even made her debut at one of the Carnival balls.'

'So Anna Louise also has many friends there?'

'Yes, well, not that many because she was educated here, but one, Tilda Brown, is a close, if not her closest, friend. She was also studying at UCLA but came from New Orleans, so they have much in common.'

'So you presumed that she might have gone to see Tilda?'

'Yes, I did.'

'Did Mrs Caley also think she had gone to see Tilda Brown? Only I believe Tilda had been staying here in LA with you shortly before you left.'

He nodded, then shrugged. 'They'd had some tiff and Tilda left the day before we did. Stupid really, as we were going to give her a ride with us, but . . .'

'Did you know what the girls argued about?'

'No, I did not.' He seemed irritated, his foot tapping. These were obviously questions he had been asked before.

'According to previous statements you did not call Miss Brown's home until very much later that evening.'

'Yes, that is correct.'

'Why did you not call Tilda Brown immediately?'

'Because we finished dinner and, as I said, we had engagements, commitments, if you like.'

78

'So even though you saw your daughter's purse left in her room . . .'

Caley turned to face Lorraine. 'I did not call Miss Brown's family or anyone else because I did not think anything untoward had happened and nor did my wife.'

'How did your wife react to your daughter not coming down to join you for dinner?'

He sighed. 'Elizabeth is a little more volatile than myself. She was very angry with Anna. We left the hotel at about ten to go to our first engagement. When we returned to the hotel at about fifteen minutes after midnight, we became concerned. We called Miss Brown's family. Tilda was in bed so we spoke to her parents and they told us that Anna had not been by or phoned. They had not seen her.'

'May I ask if you are wearing prescription lenses?'

'What?'

Lorraine stared at him and he slowly removed his sunglasses. 'Thank you.'

He moved closer so she could see his eyes. He leaned on the table. 'You think I'm hiding something?'

'No, but I like to see—'

'What, the whites of my eyes? Or do you and your type get a kick out of the pain? Because, Mrs Page, every time I have gone through this, every statement I give, you don't think I feel somehow to blame? That if I had acted faster my daughter might have been traced? Well, I do blame myself, every minute of every day. My daughter has been missing for eleven months, Mrs Page, and every phone call, every letter is a hope, and every hope makes my heart thud in my chest. What did you expect from me, tears?'

'I'm sorry, but I have to ask.'

'You ask whatever you want and I will try to answer, just as I have done with every single agency we have hired. I know the police here have given up, but I also know the case is still open in New Orleans. How do you expect me to behave? I want my daughter back, I pray she is alive, whether she has run off with some unsavoury character or whatever she has done, I will forgive her because this is hell. All I want is to see her again, I love her, I was proud of her, and I miss her.'

He was bitterly angry and yet his eyes brimmed with tears. It was unexpected and it threw Lorraine. His open emotion and obvious declaration of love for his daughter were distressing. This sophisticated, handsome man was suddenly more vulnerable than any man she had ever met because he was unable to control himself. Half-turning from her, he started to cry, awful low sobs.

'I miss my lovely daughter, Mrs Page. If I pass the tennis courts I hear her laughing, shouting out to me. Just sitting here in this stupid fucking gazebo hurts because I hear her laughing about it, sending it up, like the ridiculous Japanese garden we both hated. And then I have to listen to my wife crying every night, watch her face when the telephone rings. This house is dead without our little girl.'

'I'm so sorry.'

'I don't need your sympathy, Mrs Page, I need my daughter found. Or worse, I need to know she is never coming home, then I can get on with my life.' The tears spilled down his face and he wiped them away with the back of his hand, replacing his glasses. 'Excuse me, if you need to ask any more questions go ahead.'

Lorraine closed her note-book. Everything he had told her was on record, he had given no further insight into what had actually happened to Anna Louise. She picked up her purse and replaced her note-book, then hesitated.

'There is just one more thing, Mr Caley. You said you made calls from the hotel, to business associates, I presume, and I have no record of who you actually called.'

'You'll have a list delivered by morning.'

'Your business is real estate. Could I ask you to give me a more precise account of your business transactions in New Orleans and here in Los Angeles?'

He turned away. 'What in God's name has my business got to do with my daughter's disappearance?'

'Maybe nothing, but then again it might, so I really would like to have as much background on you . . .'

'You'll have it. Now if you would excuse me.'

'Yes, of course. Er, just one more thing, I know your wife is indisposed, but would I be able to speak for a moment with Phyllis?'

He nodded and walked to an intercom phone she had not noticed at the side of the gazebo. He picked it up. 'Phyllis, would you come into the yard, please? Mrs Page would like to speak to you.'

Robert Caley collected the open bottle of wine and walked out towards the tennis courts as Lorraine remained seated, looking after him.

Rosie was trying to decipher Bill Rooney's appalling handwritten scrawl.

'I can't make this out, what is this?' she asked.

Rooney yawned. 'The psychic the Caleys used. She wasn't at home and I been back twice. I left two messages.'

'Juda?' Rosie enquired.

'Yeah, that's her name. I reckon she's a waste of time, all flakes if you ask me. I'm gonna go for a few more

81

drinks with Nick Bartello, he's on to something, so if her ladyship calls in, tell her she can catch me at home later. A lot later, if I know Nick.'

Rosie nodded and jotted down Juda's name, phone number and address. 'I gotta go to a meeting tonight but I'll leave a message for her here and at home.'

'Good, you do that. See ya!' Rooney thudded out as the phone began to ring.

'Mr Rooney there?' said a thick, drawling voice with a real down-home Louisiana accent.

'No, I am so sorry, he's not available. Who's calling? Can I take a message?'

'I'm just returnin' the man's calls. It's Juda Salina. You know what it's about?'

Rosie perked up, becoming the partner in the investigation agency. 'Yes, we are investigating the case of Anna Louise Caley and . . .'

The phone went dead. Rosie looked at the receiver, wondering if it was something she had done her end. She wrote a memo for Rooney and Lorraine, saying the psychic made contact. Rosie also noted the time and date the call had come in. She was being very professional.

Phyllis toyed with her glass of mineral water. 'She needs pills to make her sleep and sometimes she can't get up. Today is one of them, we had the doctor out but he prescribed a different sedative. It's all very sad, poor woman, but I'll make sure she can see you tomorrow.'

'Thank you.'

Lorraine sipped the melting ice, the deftly placed slice of lemon now floating on top of the residue of tepid water. 'So you didn't see or hear anything untoward the day the family departed for New Orleans?'

'No, I did not.'

'And Anna Louise was happy and carefree, excited by the forthcoming trip?'

'Yes, they were often more like friends than mother and daughter. I mean, they had the odd little argument, only natural, she was quite wilful but she never sulked.'

'The day they left, February fifteenth, you received a call from the Caleys' private jet?'

'Yes, I did. Anna Louise had seen something in *Vogue* she wanted me to purchase for her.'

'Did you?'

'Yes.'

'Did she often just call you to get what she wanted? According to the files a three thousand, five hundred dollar black chiffon Valentino dress. I would say that stinks of a spoilt kid.'

Phyllis pursed her lips. 'The Caleys happen to be extremely wealthy, Mrs Page, and I assure you that was not unusual. You may say she was spoilt, but at the same time she was also one of the sweetest, most natural young girls I've ever known.'

'But she was spoilt.'

'No more than any other child of rich parents.'

Lorraine hesitated, and then said quietly, 'Or parent . . .'

'I'm sorry, I don't quite follow?'

'Yes, you do. Surely it is obvious that the main money in the Caley family is Elizabeth Caley's.'

Phyllis pursed her lips. 'Mr Caley is also a very successful businessman.'

'But he was not that successful when they first married. An old press cutting hinted that he was not a wealthy man and they met when he was showing Mrs Caley a property.'

Phyllis froze. 'I am afraid this is not something I can answer. I have only worked for the Caleys for ten years

83

so whatever happened previously I have no knowledge of. All I do know is Mr Caley works exceptionally hard.'

'What work is he involved in specifically in New Orleans?'

'Mrs Page, I am not privy to Mr Caley's business. I am Elizabeth Caley's companion and secretary.'

'But you settle the bills. You did, I believe, pay my fees and will continue to pay them, is that correct?'

'Yes, Mrs Caley instructed me to pay your retainer.'

'You didn't discuss it with Mr Caley?'

'I made a note for him to be aware of exactly what I had done, as I always do.'

Lorraine made no mention of the one million bonus Mrs Caley had promised to pay. She was beginning to feel tired; it had been a long day and she had to drive back to Pasadena.

'Thank you. Oh, just one more thing – Tilda Brown, Anna Louise's girlfriend, was staying here and she was supposed to return to New Orleans with the Caleys but instead left the day before. Do you know why?'

Phyllis rose to her feet. 'No, but probably over a tennis match, they were always playing tennis. I think Tilda used to make up her own rules and it infuriated Anna Louise.'

'Did you hear them arguing at all?'

'No. Tilda just asked me to arrange a ticket for her and she was driven to the airport by Mario.'

'Thank you, Miss Collins. I'll walk out via the gardens.'

Phyllis nodded and said she would warn the security guard to open the gate.

'Is there a full-time guard on duty?'

'Yes, since Anna Louise's disappearance we've had a lot of press hanging around outside, and Mr Caley didn't want his wife disturbed, so we now have full-time security guards patrolling the estate. To begin with it was feared that perhaps Anna Louise had been kidnapped, so the guards were employed for everyone's peace of mind.'

Lorraine prepared to leave. Just as she walking away from Phyllis she stopped. 'Is this house Mrs Caley's?'

'Yes, I believe so.'

'And the property in New Orleans?'

'Yes, I think a lot of it belonged to her family.'

Lorraine hesitated, wondering whether or not she should ask Phyllis the next question, or leave it until she spoke to Elizabeth Caley personally.

'Was there something else?'

'Er, yes, it may be nothing, but who is the main beneficiary of Elizabeth Caley's will?'

Phyllis glared, and Lorraine knew she had made a mistake.

'It's probably inconsequential to the investigation but at the same time you must understand that I—'

She was interrupted. 'I really can't help you, I'm sorry.'

'That's okay. What time shall I call in the morning?'

'About eleven.'

'Thank you, I'll see you tomorrow no doubt.'

'Yes, you will.' Her sharp features were even more pinched as she stared at Lorraine. 'You certainly do a lot of research.' She did not say it as a compliment but Lorraine smiled as if it had been one.

'I believe that is the point, is it not? And you must understand, Phyllis – I hope I can call you Phyllis – that everything you say to me is in total confidence. If there is anything that you feel would help my investigation, anything at all, I hope you will feel free to call me at any time.'

She caught it, just a flicker of hesitancy, but then Phyllis covered with a tight, brittle smile. 'You keep to the left walkway and it will lead you round to the front of the house. Good afternoon, Mrs Page.'

Lorraine walked from the courtyard along the immaculate paved path. She passed the tennis courts and stopped. Robert Caley was sitting on a white painted bench, the bottle of wine held loosely in his hand, seemingly staring at the empty tennis court. She continued on past the vast swimming pool with its carefully laid out sunbeds, and could see a maid folding up the unused towels.

Lorraine would have gone on but Robert Caley called her and she turned to face him. He still wore the dark glasses but removed them slowly as he looked at her.

'I'll be going to New Orleans. If you need to go there within the week, please call me. You can . . .' He gave a boyish smile. 'I'm offering you a ride.'

She returned his smile. 'Thank you, I'll call you.'

He nodded and stood watching her as she walked round to the front of the house.

Lorraine had found Robert Caley very attractive, she'd known it when he had leaned towards her across the table in the gazebo, but any sexual desires had to be dismissed because if she discovered that he could benefit from his daughter's disappearance or death, he would be under suspicion. And by now Lorraine intuitively felt that Anna Louise Caley was dead.

CHAPTER 4

'ROONEY SAID he reminded him of someone called Lubrinski.'

Lorraine reacted, giving Rosie that funny half-squint look, her hair covering part of the scar on her cheek. 'Did he now?'

'Yeah, said he was injured in some shoot-out. He's got a nickname, Nick the Limp.'

'Really?' Lorraine said non-committally.

'So who was this Lubrinski guy? And what was that about you using a pair of pantihose as a tourniquet, is that true?'

'You should know Rooney by now, Rosie, he's full of crap. He should have been doing what I told him to do, like contact the psychic. We got two weeks, Rosie, just two weeks.'

'But you told Bill to check out all the agencies, and I'm not exactly sittin' on my butt doin' nothing all day, thank you very much!'

'Oh, shut up. And if you don't wanna use the shower I will. Maybe see if I can see her tonight.'

Under the water-jets of the shower, face uptilted, eyes closed, the memories came back. The way Jack Lubrinski had looked up at her in such agony and gripped her hand.

'You're gonna be okay,' she had lied. 'Ambulance's gonna be here any second, you old bastard, but in the meantime . . .'

'Hell, if it takes being shot to see you whip off your panties I'd have done it before.'

'Shut up, you perverted shit.'

He'd died in her arms fifteen minutes later as the ambulance, siren screaming, cut its way through the traffic to the hospital. He was still holding on to her hand like a child when she saw the light go out of his eyes. They'd had to prise his hand away from hers. She hadn't wanted to let go, sure that maybe there was hope, but there had been none. The black-haired, dark-eyed Lubrinski had left a deep empty place inside her. Was that why she wanted Robert Caley? Was that gonna be the game plan for the rest of her life, the look-alike Lubrinskis? Was that why she was attracted to Robert Caley, because he was dark-haired, with fierce, scared eyes? That was what she had seen when he'd taken the shades off, fear and pain. Lubrinski had always hidden behind the smart remarks, the tough exterior, until he was dying; then she had seen something in his eyes that squeezed her heart. What was it? Why did it attract her? What she felt was in no way a mothering feeling. She didn't want to mother Robert Caley: she wanted him to screw her, just like she had wanted Lubrinski. But at that time she had been married with two kids. She wished she had just once told him before he died that she loved him. She shut her eyes tightly, clenched her teeth together; she wasn't going to cry now, it was all too long ago. But she couldn't stop the tears, because for the first time she was admitting to herself that she had been in love with Jack Lubrinski. She had fought and denied it, even after his death, but now all these years later she wept for him and whispered to herself, 'I loved you, Jack, and I still miss you.'

Rosie opened the shower curtain. 'I called the psychic. She says she won't see nobody.'

Lorraine reached for a towel. 'Wanna bet?'

'You going there now?'

'Yep. We've got two weeks Rosie, just two weeks.'

'Oh, can I come with you?'

Lorraine was about to refuse, but Rosie's child-like eagerness changed her mind.

'Sure, why not?'

The address was good but the apartment was in the lower ground floor and at the end of a corridor. The apartment block was an expensive one with intercom buzzers, top-level security and an underground car park for residents. Lorraine had been lucky; she had simply followed a car into the parking area, waving at the woman in front who had smiled back, unaware that Lorraine had no right to be there.

'Bingo, we're in. We can surprise Mrs Salina unless she saw us coming in her crystal ball,' said Lorraine as she followed the woman into the car park.

'Learn something every day,' Rosie said, impressed, but Lorraine was already hurrying out of the car.

'Afternoon,' Lorraine smiled as the woman parked her Saab convertible.

'Afternoon,' she replied, switching on her blinking alarm and heading towards a private entrance door.

Lorraine moved quickly to join the woman as she punched in the security code to access the elevator into the building. 'Weather's strange, nearly seventy already today.' She glanced behind her, irritated to see that Rosie was still getting out of the car. The woman nodded, more intent on getting her house keys out from her purse than concentrating on Lorraine. The elevator door was still open, and Lorraine rammed her foot against it in case it closed.

'Are you having problems with your air conditioning?' Lorraine asked, keeping up the conversation and giving Rosie a glare.

'No, but I noticed it was a lot warmer today.'

'Yep, could be heading up in the eighties according to the weather report.' Rosie stepped in and the elevator door shut.

The elevator from the garage opened on to the main corridor by the apartment elevators. The woman turned towards them as Lorraine carried on down the corridor with Rosie tagging behind, neither of them realizing that they were in actual fact heading in the right direction for Mrs Salina's place.

'Yes, who is it?'

Lorraine leaned close to the door. 'My name is Lorraine Page.'

'What do you want?'

'Mrs Salina, I really need to talk to you. I am a private investigator looking into the . . .'

'I don't know how you got into the building but you'd better leave immediately or I'll call security.'

'You go right ahead and do that, Mrs Salina, but I'm sure Mrs Caley won't like it.'

There were a few moments of silence. Rosie stood to one side, still more impressed by Lorraine. Then came the sound of a chain being removed, a bolt pulled back, and a higher lock opened before the door inched open.

'I'm goin' out in five minutes.'

'Fine, this won't take long. Can I come in?'

'You with the police?'

'No, this is my card, my name is Lorraine Page of Page Investigations, and this is my assistant, Rosie.'

Mrs Salina snatched the card and then the door inched further open. 'Five minutes.'

Rosie pursed her lips – she didn't like the assistant line, since she was a partner in the agency, but she said nothing as they were led along a dark, narrow hall. The main room of the apartment was at the end of a narrow corridor, the walls lined with framed photographs of well-known and not so well-known stars, alongside certificates for psychic readings, palm readings, crystals, tarot cards and more. It seemed Mrs Salina dabbled in every form of psychic phenomenon and had a certificate to prove it. Rosie glanced at everything, wishing she had brought a note-pad. This was really interesting, she thought – no wonder Lorraine liked her job, you got to meet all kinds.

It was not until they followed Juda into the small sitting room that they got a good look at her. She was exotic-looking, olive-skinned, with thick, black crinkly hair tied in a knot at the nape of her neck. She weighed at least 280 pounds, yet like a lot of very heavy women, she moved lightly and had tiny, delicate hands. Lorraine estimated her age to be about fifty, and her shawls, bangles and thick beaded necklaces were reminiscent of the 'Flower Power' days. In contrast, her perfectly made-up face was very much a nineties work of art, with well-placed false eyelashes, lipstick similar in colour to the one Mrs Caley had worn, and even the lips outlined in the same way.

'Sit down,' she said as she eased her bulk into a hard-backed armchair. 'Like I said, I got five minutes. Why do you want to see me?' She had a New Orleans accent, not heavy but easy to detect by the way her voice drawled and lifted in a musical manner.

She stared hard at Rosie, who tried to blend into the wallpaper, uncomfortably balanced on a stool. She had let Lorraine take the better chair, or rather, Lorraine had taken it automatically: she behaved as though Rosie wasn't there.

'Tell me about Elizabeth Caley.'

'I'm sorry, but unless I have Mrs Caley's permission I cannot discuss her. My business is just like a priest's or a doctor's, my clients' private consultations with me are exactly that, private.'

'But, like me, you have been hired to help trace their daughter.'

'Yes, that is correct.'

'How much contact have you therefore had with Mrs Caley?'

'I am afraid I cannot divulge that.'

'Did you travel to New Orleans?'

'I did.' She levered herself up from the chair and crossed to the dresser. She opened a drawer and took out a photograph. 'She is a very strong presence.'

'Anna Louise?'

'Why, yes. This was given to me by Mrs Caley.' She thrust it in front of Lorraine, and there was the sweet face, the long blonde tresses.

'She is very beautiful.'

Juda nodded, then passed the photograph to Rosie, who leaned forward to look at it.

'Yes, she is very pretty,' Rosie nodded. Juda returned the photograph to the drawer.

'She most surely is, and I would say she is still in New Orleans.'

'Alive?' Lorraine asked sharply.

Juda shut the drawer and remained with her back to Lorraine. Then she turned slowly and, with her eyes closed, pressed herself against the dresser. Rosie studied the big woman: if she had been worried about her own weight, Juda had even more of a problem.

'I sincerely believe Anna Louise is alive.'

'Why?'

The false eye-lashes fluttered. 'Why? Like I said, she has a presence. The little girl is alive, I am sure of it.'

'Why?' Lorraine persisted.

The eyes opened. 'I have just told you, I feel her presence.'

'Well, that may be so but I am not quite as fortunate as you, Mrs Salina. My job is to find her, I can't feel any presence, I am not in touch with the . . . forces, so to speak.'

'They are forces, Mrs Page, strong ones, and I am telling you that little girl is alive. I take my work very seriously and when I feel her, become her, she is not saying to me she is cold.' She turned her dark eyes to Rosie again, and Rosie felt a frisson of fear. She looked away, biting her lip: there was something unpleasant about the woman, about the whole apartment.

'So, what is she saying to you?'

Juda pointedly looked at her watch, and then at Lorraine. 'Mrs Page, you ain't paying, Mrs Caley is, and I have told her all that I have been able to receive, that is, Anna Louise is alive.'

'Well, I'll pay you, is that what you want?'

Juda stared hard at Lorraine. 'I have to go out now. If Mrs Caley personally tells me that I can give you what I have received, then you may call again. But right now all I can tell you is that I feel her presence, an aura of light, every time I look at her sweet angel face.'

'Well, if this presence should indicate where Anna Louise is, then I'll talk to Mrs Caley and I'll come back and make you tell me where she is. You see, I deal in facts, not fantasy, and she has been missing nearly a year. Now, that is a very long time to have no word, no letter, no contact. I'm hired to find her.'

'But I presume you are being paid.'

'Yeah, but then so are you.'

'No. The husband has refused to allow me to see my poor dear Elizabeth.'

'Did you tell him his daughter was alive?'

Juda crossed to the door and stood there. 'I have had no dealings with Mr Caley but I have known Elizabeth for many years.'

'She's a drug addict, isn't she?'

Juda gave Lorraine a surly look. 'I said five minutes, now I ask you to leave. I only agreed to see you because you implied Elizabeth had asked you to see me, but I think you are lying, just like all the others who have tried to talk to me. My clients have my total loyalty.'

'What other people have talked to you?'

Juda again gave that direct, rather eerie stare. 'Private investigators, and the police. They treat me with no respect, Mrs Page, I can feel it, see it in their faces. They don't have to say a word, I know what they think of people like me.' She moved back to the dresser and opened a drawer. 'Here, take this, but now you gotta go.'

She handed Lorraine a cheap computer-printed document, clipped together. Juda didn't wait for her even to glance at it before moving impatiently into the hallway. Lorraine handed it to Rosie and indicated by a nod that Rosie should follow her to where Juda stood by the open front door, waiting.

'Good afternoon, Mrs Page. Er, just one thing, will you come real close to me for a moment?'

Lorraine stepped closer and Juda stared up into her face. She lifted her delicate hand and touched the scar running down Lorraine's cheek. 'Honey, you should get that fixed, you'd be real lovely. What was your first name?'

'Lorraine.'

'Nice to talk with you, Lorraine.'

Rosie was squeezing past her when the woman leaned forward again.

'Rosie. Your name is Rosie, and your spirit is kind. You take care now, honey.'

The chain was replaced, the bolts banged across. For someone who was about to go out, it was weird to lock themselves in. Was she expecting someone or simply lying? Lorraine suspected the latter; Juda Salina was not about to go out.

Lorraine and Rosie had to wait fifteen minutes in the car park before a resident came down and used the special code to open the security gates. They sat discussing Juda and, as Bill Rooney had done before them, came to the conclusion she was one big fake, able to make a lot of money from people as desperate as Elizabeth Caley. Her computer-printed advertisement was crude, unprofessional, stating how many people had been saved by Juda Salina predictions, and how many times. She also listed a number of police cases she had assisted in. It was all rubbish; saying she felt a presence and that Anna Louise Caley was alive only meant she could keep asking for more money from Mrs Caley.

Rosie read the print-out, and frowned as she turned the pages.

'I hope she's right.'

'About what? Your sweet soul?'

'No, that the little girl is alive. I hope she is.'

Lorraine was now more convinced the girl was dead but she decided that Rooney should at least check out the so-called police investigations listed in the print-out and Salina's part in them. She had gained only one thing of interest: Robert Caley did not like Juda Salina. She respected him for that.

Juda sat wondering whether or not she should call Mrs Caley. She didn't like the fact that yet another private investigator was questioning her, and supposedly with Mrs Caley's permission. In fact, it annoyed her that she had been told by some faceless employee of Robert Caley's that she was no longer allowed to visit his wife and that there would be no further payments. She had made a lot of money out of their misery, even a trip back home. But this time she was worried.

She went over in her mind everything Lorraine had said. The woman hadn't asked anything new, so what was it? The scar? She had a feeling that it had been inflicted by a man, but the message had been very hazy. She sighed, feeling tired, unsure whether or not to put herself through it, and without being paid. But even as she fought against doing it, she got up, drew the dark crimson curtains and turned off the overhead lights so the small room was in virtual darkness. She sat down again. An onlooker would have thought she was nodding off to sleep, her eyes drooping like those of someone heavy with exhaustion, unable to keep awake. She moaned softly, as though with sexual gratification, and sank deeper into the chair. Her big bosom rose and fell as she took slow, deep breaths.

'Yes, oh yes, yes,' she whispered, and her tiny, delicate hands clung on to the carved arm of her uncomfortable chair. She continued to take deep laboured breaths, her bosom heaving, her head beginning to feel light as she began to go slowly into a trance. The darkness seeped into Juda's consciousness. Nothing for a while, then it started to happen, just as it had when she had been with Elizabeth Caley. First came the distorted sounds of music, then of a street. She couldn't grasp the area, it was happening too quickly and she couldn't control it, but she felt the place was familiar. Exactly as it had played out before, something began to terrify her, and this time she felt it even more strongly. She began to gasp, her hands clawing at the chair; there was a pain in the centre of her chest, as if a weight was pressing down, squeezing the air from her lungs. She began to flap her hands; someone or something was astride her, a man, it was a man and he was taking out a knife. She couldn't see his face, just knew he was going to slice her throat.

Her own scream cut through the dark void of panic, and she lurched forward, coming to fast, fazed for only a few moments before she realized she was safe in her own apartment. The sweat trickled down her cheeks and she involuntarily patted her neck and chest, frightened by the still awful feeling of choking, of someone squeezing the life out of her. But it wasn't her, she knew that, it wasn't Juda Salina being murdered, it was someone with a name beginning with the letter L.

The initial L: did it stand for Lorraine Page? She was tensing up, remembering what she had just put herself through, and for a second time. Juda'd had a similarly jumbled message when she'd gone into the trance at Mrs Caley's, someone's name beginning with the letter L. She knew she had frightened Elizabeth Caley but she didn't know what it had meant. Often she didn't, the messages for one client could get confused with another's, but this one had been particularly strong. She'd presumed then that the letter L was for Louise, Anna Louise, because she had had an overpowering feeling of imminent danger, and death. She had lied to Mrs Caley, said the powers had been strong and that her daughter was alive, but she had felt death very close.

Juda tried to recall the exact day she visited Mrs Caley. She found the entry in her diary and turned over the page to the next day. She read the scrawled message from Robert Caley's secretary that she was not to see his wife again. They were the only notes in the diary for that day. Juda drummed the blank pages with her painted fingernails, made a decision and dialled the Caley residence. Phyllis answered.

'Phyllis, this is Juda . . .'

'You must not call here again, I thought Mr Caley had made that clear to you. He will not allow you to speak to Elizabeth again.'

'I know. It was you I wanted to talk to . . .'

Phyllis was almost whispering. 'If it's about any further payments I have been instructed by Mr Caley that—'

'It isn't, I just need to know something. I've had a visit from a woman working for a private investigation agency.'

'You mean Mrs Page.'

'Yeah, Lorraine Page, isn't it?'

'Yes, she's been brought in.'

'What day did you hire her?'

'Last Tuesday, the same day you last came to see Mrs Caley. You know she was very distressed after you left and . . . hello?'

Juda was silent.

Phyllis sounded worried. 'Hello? Are you still there? Is something wrong, has Mrs Page said something?'

'No, no, I just needed to clear up my diary entries. Thank you, Phyllis, and please tell Elizabeth I am thinking of her and keeping Anna Louise's presence in my mind, and I'll wait for her to contact me. Bye now.'

Juda replaced the phone before Phyllis could ask anything else. She could tell herself it was coincidence but she knew it wasn't. She sensed much more strongly than she would ever admit that Anna Louise Caley had been dead a long time – she knew that. What she hadn't been able to make sense of until now was that on Tuesday night the message she'd received was so strong it had made her physically sick. A connection to the letter L had come up and burned in her brain, surrounded by fire and imminent danger. Now she was sure the L was for Lorraine Page, and there was a lot more than imminent danger . . . she was sure the woman was going to die, and in the same way as she had seen so clearly in her second trance state – Lorraine was going to get her throat cut.

Lorraine had borrowed Rosie's heated Carmen rollers to style her hair. She wore a cream silk blouse, a tight, straight skirt with a slit down one side, and high-heeled shoes. She eased a dark blue linen jacket round her shoulders and stepped back to admire the effect.

Rosie stood in the kitchen, spooning up a vast bowl of cereal. 'I dunno how you manage to get bargain of the month at every yard sale, nothin' ever fits me. Very smart.'

'Thank you, I need to feel good to take on Elizabeth Caley.'

'Mm,' Rosie muttered, milk dribbling down her chin. 'You gonna take up his offer? Be nice to travel in style, private jet.'

Lorraine checked her purse and slim briefcase. 'I'm not ready to leave LA yet, so we'll see. In the meantime, there's a list of things for you to be doing: arrange tickets, hotels and start packing. Call me if you need me on the mobile, maybe early afternoon, and see what Rooney and this hop-along guy come up with.'

'Okay.' Rosie looked down the neatly written list.

Shortly after Lorraine drove off down the road, Rooney screeched to a halt outside the apartment. He tooted the car horn; he'd started giving Rosie a ride into the office if he was passing. She thudded down the wooden steps and crossed over to his car as he opened the passenger door.

'You just missed Veronica Lake, she's gone to the Caleys'. But we have a list of orders and she wanted to know how you got on with Nick Bartello.'

Rooney pushed his shades up his shiny nose. 'I got one bitch of a hangover, but any money he's got an even worse one.'

Rosie looked at him more closely. 'Jesus, where in hell did you get those shades?'

'Found 'em in a drawer, I think they were my wife's, why?'

Rosie grinned. 'Well, I just didn't reckon you'd be the kind of guy to wear pink-framed shades but they suit you, match your colouring, sorta flushed.'

Rooney drove on, his gut pressed against the steering-wheel. 'Well, when I'm through with 'em you can have them. They'll match whatever colour you describe your hair.'

'Aw, shut up, you, it's the perm. I'm a natural redhead and if you want I can prove it.'

'God forbid, I couldn't take that even without a hangover!'

Lorraine and the butler had another formal bowing session before he led her towards the drawing room.

'I won't be kept waiting again, will I?' she asked.

He actually half-smiled. 'Mrs Caley is expecting you, Mrs Page.'

At that moment Phyllis appeared and gestured for Lorraine to follow her up the wide staircase.

'Please bring Mrs Caley's breakfast, and for you, Mrs Page?'

'Oh, I'd like a coffee, black with honey if you have it, thank you.'

He gave a curt nod and departed towards the kitchen corridor, as Lorraine continued up the stairs.

'What's his name again?'

'Peters, Reginald Peters.' Phyllis tapped on the double doors on the first landing.

'Come in.'

Phyllis stepped back and ushered Lorraine into Elizabeth Caley's drawing room, almost bumping into her as she stopped dead in her tracks. The drawing room was a profusion of perfumed flowers in vast displays on almost every available surface, and even though the shutters were drawn over the open windows, the pale lemon walls, drapes and carpet seemed to blend into each other as if the room was ablaze with sunlight. White muslin curtains billowed from brass curtain rods in contrast to the stillness of the designer-draped silk curtains with their golden fringes and tiebacks.

Elizabeth Caley was reclining on a white shot-silk chaise-longue, wearing a flowing kimono of dark green and yellow printed flowers. Her thick, pitch-black hair was braided in a long plait down her back and a tight white bandanna was wrapped round her head. She was creaming her delicate hands and smiled warmly at Lorraine.

'Come in, darling. Please excuse me for not shaking hands but I have just had a manicure and the girl never uses enough moisturizer. Sit down.'

Lorraine looked around. There were scatter-cushions in profusion on every lemon shot-silk-covered chair and before she could decide which one to sit on Phyllis made the choice for her, drawing forward a spindle-legged armchair.

'Thank you, Phyllis dear. Is Peters bringing refreshments?'

'Yes.'

'Good, then you may leave us.'

Phyllis crept out, and Lorraine sat down, unzipping her briefcase and taking out her note-book.

'Have you done something different to your hair?'

Lorraine smiled. 'No, just washed it.'

'You do it yourself?'

'Yes. Thank you for seeing me.'

Peters entered, wheeling in a gilt trolley which held coffee, croissants, tea and iced water. He eased the trolley to beside Mrs Caley, passed her a white, stiffly laundered napkin and poured a greenish-looking tea. The china was fine porcelain. He poured black coffee and indicated a silver dish with honey for Lorraine.

Mrs Caley eased herself to a sitting position and wafted her hand. 'Thank you, thank you, I'll ring if we need anything else.'

'Very good, Mrs Caley.' He performed his backward half-bow out of the room and closed the doors silently behind him.

'Would you care for a croissant?'

'No, thank you.'

Lorraine spooned in the honey, careful not to let any drops fall on the white tray cloth. Elizabeth Caley picked up silver tongs and placed a warmed croissant on a plate, then some jam from a silver pot. Lorraine noticed that her smooth hands with their long, talon-like red nails were shaking, and she had to use both hands to sip from her delicate tea cup.

'I'm sorry I couldn't see you yesterday but I am sure Phyllis made my apologies.'

'She did.'

'I don't know what I would do without Phyllis. That is a very pretty blouse.'

'Thank you.' Lorraine balanced her cup and saucer on

the arm of her chair, as she eased her note-book on to her lap. 'I am sorry if I ask you questions that must have been put to you many times, but it is important. I will try not to take up too much of your time, as it must be distressing to . . .'

Elizabeth Caley nodded. She resembled Merle Oberon, with the same high forehead, enhanced now by the bandanna, and flawless skin. Her make-up, like everything else about her, was immaculate, her lips lightly outlined in a dark fuchsia. Whether or not her beauty had by now been assisted by surgery was immaterial, even at this close proximity her face appeared unlined. In comparison, Lorraine felt jaded, as any woman would. Elizabeth Caley had a fragility and femininity that in this day and age was ridiculed by feminists because, perfect creature as she was, she belonged to a different era. She would not dream of opening a door for herself – this was a woman used to having men break their necks to get to the door first.

'Could you just tell me about February fifteenth, the day you left for New Orleans?'

'How do you mean?'

'Well, I know you and Anna Louise were together before your husband returned from his office and—'

'Oh, I see, yes, well, I had to oversee all the packing, we had some engagements, cocktail parties, dinners . . . Peters usually packs for Robert but I am very particular, I always have special tissue paper; it avoids creases, you know, if you lay tissue sheets between each garment.'

'Did you pack for your daughter?'

'Good heavens, no. Anna Louise is dreadful, and you know how young girls dress these days, jeans and T-shirts, and more jeans and T-shirts, sneakers. I think whoever invented those awful things should be shot. She just hurls things into cases, in fact, we had a little tiff about it because I asked Phyllis to make sure she had some of her nice things because we had a few formal engagements. Anyway, Phyllis oversaw her packing, I think, and then we had brunch on the terrace and waited for Robert. We then went to the airport and . . .' She frowned. 'Oh, yes, on the plane she saw something in *Vogue* or *Elle* magazine, a little black cocktail dress, and I was surprised because she really liked it. So we called home to ask Phyllis to collect it and arrange to have it delivered for when she returned.'

She frowned again, one long fingernail tapping the centre of her forehead. 'Anna Louise was in high spirits, really looking forward to the trip and seeing her friends, especially Tilda Brown, an adorable girl. She often stayed here, we are all very fond of Tilda.'

'Tilda Brown was scheduled to travel with you to New Orleans but—'

'Oh, yes, yes, yes. She said she wanted to go earlier so Phyllis arranged it. I've no idea why, but you know young girls, silly waste of money, I suppose. Anyway, we left, drove to the airport and . . .'

Lorraine listened as Elizabeth Caley repeated, as her husband had done, almost word for word her original statement given to the police, from the moment that they arrived at the hotel until the dinner.

'Can you think of anything, no matter how trivial it may seem, that you have not mentioned to anyone else?'

'My dear, I have gone over and over those hours, as if seeing them on a screen, trying to find some clue, but there is nothing, nothing at all that I can recall. And that is what makes it so horrible, because I cannot think of a single thing that would be of help. She was happy, cheerful and looking forward to Carnival . . .'

'Had she ever gone off alone before?'

'Of course, but never without letting us know where

she was going to, or who she was seeing. She is an intelligent girl, aware of the dangers of being out alone in the evenings, especially in the old French Quarter. I had even discussed with her the importance of always making sure we knew where she was. Obviously any young girl from Los Angeles is made very aware of the dangers of going off with strange men or accepting a ride, or drugs . . .'

'Did she ever use drugs?'

'I'm sorry?'

'Did Anna Louise to your knowledge ever use drugs, smoke cannabis, for example?'

'No, most definitely not, she doesn't even smoke cigarettes. And very rarely drinks, perhaps a glass of champagne, nothing more. She is, you see, very health-conscious, very athletic really. She loves sports and obviously any over-indulgence in drugs or alcohol would be adverse to her. I am not making her to be a goody-two-shoes, she is not perfect. She can throw tantrums and get angry, just like any other girl of her age.'

'Tantrums?'

'Well, I don't know if that is the correct description. She is very spoilt, I know, more by Robert than myself, and she can twist him round her little finger, always has done since she was a baby. He dotes on her but he can also be very firm.'

'Is your daughter the main beneficiary of your will?'

'Why do you ask?'

Lorraine chose her words carefully. 'Well, there is no evidence that your daughter has been kidnapped, no ransom note, no contact. I am simply trying to find if there is a motive . . .'

For a fleeting moment Lorraine saw Mrs Caley hesitate.

'Yes, she does benefit from my will.'

'Your daughter is the main beneficiary?'

'Yes, but she is also the main beneficiary of my husband's will. Did you ask him the same question?'

Lorraine kept her eyes down as if concentrating on her notes. 'Yes.'

'Ah, I see. Yes, well, if anything happened Anna Louise would automatically be the sole beneficiary. And if, God forbid, anything did happen to Anna, then Robert is obviously the next of kin, and vice versa.'

Lorraine looked up, concerned, because Elizabeth Caley was shaking and now it was not just her hands, her whole body visibly trembled.

'Are you all right?'

'What has happened to my daughter?'

'I don't know, Mrs Caley, but I will do everything I can to find out.'

'Do you think she is dead?'

'Until I have more details I really can't answer that question.'

Elizabeth slowly rose to her feet, holding on to the edge of the chaise-longue. Lorraine watched as she used the furniture to cross the room, grasping the back of a chair for a moment, then the edge of a cabinet. 'Excuse me, just a . . . Please help yourself to more coffee.'

Lorraine stood up, ready to assist her, but Elizabeth supported herself against the door leading into her bedroom and before Lorraine could help her had walked out, the door banging shut behind her.

Lorraine poured herself a cup of fresh coffee and then noticed a dark wet stain on the chaise-longue where Elizabeth Caley had been reclining. Was she incontinent? She tried to recall the moment when she had noticed Mrs Caley shaking or trembling – was it when she asked about who was to be the main beneficiary?

106

Phyllis entered, nodded curtly at Lorraine and uttered a quiet 'Excuse me' before she slipped into the bedroom.

Lorraine waited about ten minutes. Phyllis came out of the bedroom and gave a brittle smile. 'I'll just get some fresh tea. Would you care for more coffee?'

'No, thank you, I'm fine. Is Mrs Caley all right?'

'Yes, she just gets tired very easily so I hope you won't keep her much longer.'

Phyllis quickly slipped one of the scatter-cushions over the stained chaise-longue and then began wheeling out the trolley. As she got to the doors, a shrill, high-pitched voice from the bedroom called out her name. '*Phyllis . . . Phyllis!*'

Lorraine watched as the woman scuttled back to the bedroom and disappeared from view. She could hear her whispered voice but was unable to make out what she was saying. Then Peters walked in and before Lorraine could say a word he had wheeled the trolley out. She saw the intercom on the telephone flashing and again heard Phyllis's low voice. This time she crept closer to the bedroom door.

'I think you should. I can ask her to leave. Fine, yes, I'll tell her.'

Lorraine only just made it back to her chair when Phyllis walked in from the bedroom. 'Peters took out the trolley.'

'I think, Mrs Page, you had better leave because—'

'Get out, Phyllis.' Elizabeth Caley now wore a different kimono and was tying the silk sash tightly around her waist. 'I'll tell Mrs Page when she can go, not you. Go on, get out. And I want some fresh tea and she wants whatever she was having.'

'No, I'm fine, thank you. And if it is inconvenient for me to stay—'

107

'It isn't. Go on, Phyllis, go away.'

Phyllis sighed and walked out.

'She can be so bloody interfering.' Elizabeth crossed to a glass-topped table crammed with photographs and ornaments. She opened a cigarette box and took out a long, thin cigarette. She flicked an onyx lighter, shaking it.

Lorraine took out her own and was just about to light Mrs Caley's cigarette when the onyx lighter caught. She sucked in the smoke and tossed the lighter down on to a chair.

The beauty had gone, her perfectly made-up face like some kind of mask. '*I don't want you interfering!*' Her voice was shrill, and her hands, with the claw-like nails, tightened the kimono sash. Like a cheap whore, she let the cigarette dangle from her fuchsia-coloured lips. 'Mrs Page, you do what I paid you for. And I will withdraw my offer of a bonus if you see Mrs Juda Salina again. She knows nothing about my daughter.' Elizabeth held up a sheet of her private notepaper. Scrawled in her own handwriting was her agreement to pay the bonus. 'As I said, one million if you find my daughter. But if you talk with Juda Salina, I will not pay you a cent. Do you understand what I am saying? You won't get one more payment.'

Elizabeth Caley's voice had changed. The elongated vowels were creeping in, as if she was reverting to her Louisiana accent. It fascinated Lorraine, and she knew that whatever Elizabeth Caley had taken in her bedroom was either cocaine, speed or some kind of stimulant because she was hyper – smoking, pacing, clutching continually at the belt of her kimono. 'I need to trust you.'

Lorraine folded the note. 'You can, Mrs Caley, you can trust me.'

'Okay, okay, that's fine, that's good. Yes, that's good, I need to trust, I need to, understand me? You understand me?'

'Yes, I understand.' She didn't, she still didn't know what was going on, but just as she might have found out, the doors opened and Robert Caley walked in. He ignored Lorraine and went straight to his wife, seeming to wrap her in his arms.

'Come on, come and lie down now, sweetheart. Say goodbye to Mrs Page.' He kept his arms around her, steering her towards the bedroom. 'I think you had better leave, Mrs Page.'

Lorraine was getting into her car when Robert Caley hurried out of the house. 'Mrs Page.' He had a vivid scratch mark down his right cheek.

'Yes,' she said innocently.

'A moment please, er, perhaps I was not as, er ... honest as I should have been when we spoke yesterday.'

'I'm sorry?'

'I told you my wife could not speak to you, that she was indisposed, as a good PR agent would say. Well, you just saw what my wife's indisposition is . . .'

Lorraine didn't let him off the hook but looked at him with as much innocence as she could muster. 'I'm sorry?'

He turned away, rubbing his head. 'My daughter's disappearance has obviously affected my wife deeply. I don't know what she has said to you but I think you should be aware that she can be very irrational and ... Elizabeth has had, over the past few years, a drug-related problem mainly due to an old injury ... During the filming of *Santa Maria* a gallery collapsed on her and she suffered extensive injuries. The studio doctors made

109

sure she would be on the set the following day by prescribing heavy pain-killers and . . . er . . . well, she still suffers a great deal of pain, and over the years . . .'

Lorraine waited, watching him trying in every way to explain or excuse his wife's behaviour.

'She is, I suppose, a sick woman, and with Anna Louise's disappearance . . . what I am trying to explain to you is that my wife has a dependency on these so-called pain-killers. It is controlled, obviously, but now she is not using these drugs for any physical pain, just mental . . .'

'I understand.'

'Good, because I would hate you to misconstrue anything or, God forbid, report this to the press.'

'I wouldn't do that.'

'Good, thank you. It's just that I have been able to control her dependency with the help of her doctors but sometimes if I am not here she . . .'

If he was lying he was good, because he seemed genuinely disturbed and caring.

'I do understand, Mr Caley. This must be a very distressing time, not just for your wife, and obviously anything that is said to me, or anything I see, will remain strictly between us.'

He turned away. 'Just try and find out, Mrs Page, if my daughter is dead or alive, because not knowing is destroying me, and killing my wife.'

CHAPTER 5

ROONEY LOLLED in Lorraine's chair behind her desk. The door buzzer went off and both he and Rosie looked towards the door. Nick Bartello lounged in the doorway, gazing down at the doormat. He wore his thick, black and unruly curly hair almost to his collar and he needed a shave.

He limped into the office. His crumpled denim shirt and torn jeans didn't detract from his immediate attraction. He was one of those guys you knew just by looking at him had a big case history. His limp wasn't bad, it sort of made his walk just that bit lopsided.

'Hey, Nick, how you doin'?' bellowed Rooney.

'I'm fucked, I feel it an' look it. You got some coffee brewing?'

'Sure. Nick, this is Rosie, by the way.'

'Hi, Rosie.' Bartello slumped into her vacated chair. 'Hey, man, did we tie a load on last night or didn't we?'

'We did, Nick, we did.'

Rosie started to brew some coffee as Nick pulled a crumpled note-pad and bits of paper out of his pocket. 'Okay, this is how the land lies. I know I only got handed the case when our top dicks gave it the thumbs down, maybe because they'd like to stick one up my ass. Like I said last night, I get fired if I don't get a result an' to date I got fuck-all. And today, like ten minutes ago,

111

Robert Caley is threatening the agency to get screwed unless we get some results.'

Rosie returned to her desk. 'Coffee is on.' She hovered, and he gave her a marvellous smile.

'Thanks, sweetheart, make it strong and black.' He turned back to Rooney, who grinned.

'Nick's being paid a grand a week plus expenses, Agnews is getting about five grand. They probably put out to Caley they got three of you workin', right, Nick?'

'Yeah, but in reality the main guys are on a new gig finding some bitch's ex-husband. They'll drag it out as long as possible so basically I got the Caley case solo. Company don't wanna lose their five gee's per week, I don't wanna lose my job.'

Rooney cocked his head at Nick. 'You tell 'em about us?'

Nick shrugged. 'I didn't say nothin'. They know you're on the Caley payroll and, hey, Rosie, what about that coffee? This is a desperate man you're looking at.'

Rooney snorted as Rosie checked the percolator; it was just bubbling. She liked Nick Bartello, crude maybe but there was a lovable quality to him. That smile he had was a killer.

'Bill, I am prepared to split my fee, you gimme what you got and vice versa.'

'But you got fuck-all.'

'Correct.' Nick laughed. It was as good as his smile, a lovely chortling sound.

'So why should we pool with you? We're on a good slice ourselves.'

'Yeah, well, maybe I got a bit extra that bein' drunk didn't loosen out of me. You think I didn't know what you were up to?'

Again Rooney snorted; for all his easygoing manner

Nick was nobody's fool. 'It'd have to be somethin' if you want in with us.'

Nick Bartello rubbed the stubble on his chin. 'Well, maybe I just got somethin' that'd be worth wantin' to split that one million pay-off Mrs Caley promised as a bonus.'

Rosie looked at Rooney; he'd obviously been drunk enough to tell Bartello, and for a moment he had the temerity to look abashed.

She banged down the mug of coffee. 'Don't you think we should discuss this with Lorraine?'

Bartello laughed. 'Look, I know her type, if Jack Lubrinski rated her, she's cool, she'd go for this. She's a drinker, right?'

'Not any more,' said Rosie angrily.

'Okay, maybe she isn't, but all I am suggesting is we pool info and you cut me in on the one million pay-off. I dump my job and everyone is happy and able to pay the mortgage with a few extras on the side.'

Rooney gave Rosie a frown and then turned to Bartello. 'Okay, I agree, Lorraine will, what you got?'

'We should wait for her to be in on this,' Rosie interjected as she poured more coffee.

'Come on, you only got two weeks,' Nick said.

Rosie glared at Rooney, knowing he must have told Nick everything about their case.

'You're already almost one day down and I been on this for a few weeks, so I got information that'll save valuable time.'

'You got nothing,' Rooney said flatly.

'Okay, I'll come clean, I got something I didn't tell you last night, but no way am I gonna spill the beans unless we shake hands.'

Rooney looked at Rosie and she shrugged. 'Okay, we got a deal.'

The two men shook hands. Then Bartello sipped his coffee. 'Right, try this for starters, I got from a very reliable source that Elizabeth Caley is into drugs in a big way. So maybe, just maybe, the disappearance of her precious daughter is connected.'

'Fuckin' hell, is that true?' Rooney asked.

Nick sipped his coffee. 'Yep, it's true, like she's got a habit of over three thousand dollars a week. I'm checkin' into dealers, I mean, she might owe some shit that got nasty with her daughter. I got the name of her doctor as well. He's like top drawer for the stars, but he's also known on the street for passing on dodgy prescriptions.'

'Is it cocaine?'

'Apparently the lady will take whatever she can lay her pretty hands on. She's been in two drug rehab centres, the type with a lot of glamour.' Nick passed over some crumpled xeroxed medical sheets, stuck together with a safety pin. 'Got those from a sweet-faced nurse for a hundred bucks. By the look of the docco I'd say this angel could make a few thousand bucks on the side passin' this kind of stuff to the tabloids.'

Rooney looked over Elizabeth Caley's medical sheet. 'Says the woman is called Maureen Sweeney.'

'Yeah, well, she's not likely to put her real name on their register, is she? But it's substance-abuse routine . . .'

Rooney finished reading and then passed it to Rosie. 'That it?'

Nick rocked back in his chair. 'Well, for starters. What you got?'

'Lorraine went to see this psychic,' Rosie said, and got a kick from Rooney.

Nick stared at Rosie. 'Juda Salina?'

Rosie frowned. 'Er, I'm not sure.'

Rooney turned back to Nick. 'She give you anythin'?'

Nick shook his head. 'Nah, she's a fake.'

114

Rooney nodded. 'Yeah, I agree, that's why I never bothered seein' her. Dunno why Lorraine's so interested.'

'So, what else you got?' Nick waited, saw Rooney glance at Rosie, and then threw his arms up into the air. 'Holy shit, you lyin' bastard, you got fuck-all.'

'Rooney did *what*?' Lorraine yelled into the receiver of her mobile phone.

'Now calm down,' Rosie said, quivering.

'*Calm down?* Are you crazy? You tell me that stupid fat bastard has brought on some half-assed guy, not only *told* him everything we got, but even offered him a share of the one million bonus and you tell me to calm down?!'

'They were trading information,' Rosie stammered.

'I don't give a shit what they were trading.'

'But Nick's information was good—' She was interrupted.

'It stinks. You think I didn't already know Elizabeth Caley was stoned out of her mind? Jesus Christ, Rosie, I knew it the first time we met her.'

'Well, I didn't.'

'You've never met her,' Lorraine snapped.

'Well, maybe we can sort it out,' Rosie said nervously.

'Oh, yeah, the bastard works for Agnews, doesn't he? Yes? *Yes? And don't you think he's gonna go straight back there and tell them?*'

'I don't think he will,' Rosie said nervously.

'You don't think, full stop, and nor does that stupid son-of-a-bitch Rooney. How could he do this?' Lorraine thumped the dashboard in frustration. 'Where are they now, Rooney and this Bartello character?'

'At home.'

'I'll see you there.'

It took Rosie about twenty minutes to walk from the office to the main Orange Grove junction, then she headed down Marengo Drive. She saw the rental parked at a bad angle, right under the no parking zone plaque. She also saw Rooney's car across the road from the apartment.

Rosie could hear them arguing from the street.

'I told you, Bill, that *I* was running this case, not you. *Me*.'

'Okay, okay, I'm sorry, but no way is Nick gonna report back to his agency.'

'Oh yeah? You know that for sure, do you?' Lorraine was shouting.

'I fucking know Nick Bartello, an' I'm telling you he's on the level.'

'Oh, you're telling me, are you?'

'*Yes!* An' if you'd just get off your box for a second and calm down—'

'Don't tell me to calm down, Bill, because I am steaming!'

Rosie banged in but neither Rooney nor Lorraine even glanced at her. Rooney was red-faced and looked guilty.

'Nick'll be here any minute and we can talk this through.'

'No way am I splitting this four ways!'

'Shouldn't we put this to the vote?' Rosie interjected, and then wished she hadn't.

Lorraine glared at her as she unbuttoned her blouse, heading for the bedroom. 'When are you two gonna get this together? This is my case, *mine*, no fucking votes, I make the decisions!'

*

116

Rosie was on a carb meal of pasta and salad and had actually lost four pounds since they started on the Caley case. She had surprised herself, and she decided that she really would cut out cup cakes and pastries between meals. The no-fat regime was making her feel a lot better – physically and mentally.

'What is this?' Lorraine asked, jabbing a spiral piece of pasta with her fork.

'It's just fusilli with garlic and tomato sauce. You don't like it, there's more for me and Bill.'

Lorraine took a mouthful and grimaced. 'My God, you went heavy on the garlic.'

'You wanna cook, then the kitchen is all yours,' Rosie said.

'So what time is this Nick guy arriving?'

'Any time now,' Rooney said.

Lorraine got up and fetched her note-book. 'Okay, Juda Salina told me nothin' apart from the fact she was hired not by Robert Caley but by his wife. She wouldn't say much because of her so-called client confidentiality shit, and Mrs Caley is prepared to withdraw the bonus if we make contact with her again. I'm gonna have to have another talk to Mrs Movie Star who is hooked on so-called pain-killers. Robert Caley admitted his wife is hooked on drugs, and to my mind she seemed scared of her husband, or if not of him, maybe of me finding out she's a druggy. Anyway, he was pretty straight, but as a possible suspect his motive could be that if his daughter is out of the way, he stands to inherit the fortune as he's the main beneficiary. That's just supposition because Mrs Caley said that they *both* named their daughter in their wills, so whoever should go first, bingo, the other's a hell of a sight richer.' She looked up as Rosie lifted her plate, about to fork her leftovers on to her own. 'Shit, Rosie, I haven't finished.'

'Sorry, but I thought maybe the garlic—'

'No, it's great.' Lorraine drew her plate closer and took a mouthful.

'He a suspect then?' Rosie asked.

'Right now maybe, I need to know the financial—'

They turned as Nick Bartello opened the screen door and peered in, having overheard the last few lines of their conversation.

'I'd say it's a motive, the will. Elizabeth ex-movie star Caley is worth about fifty-five million dollars.'

Rooney pulled his napkin out of his shirt collar and rose to his feet. 'Hi, Nick, lemme introduce you, this is—'

'Lorraine Page of Page Investigations,' Nick said, smiling, his hand outstretched. Lorraine did not take it, but lifted her glass of water.

'So you're Nick Bartello?'

'Yep, that's me.'

'Have we met before?' Lorraine continued to eat.

'Nope, but you got one hell of a reputation.'

'Have I?' Lorraine said.

Nick looked at Rooney, puzzled by her coldness. He drew up a chair and Rosie poured him a glass of water.

'What's your reputation, Nick?' Lorraine said sarcastically. 'Or is "the Limp" sufficient?'

'I'm a real lovable motherfucker, how's that for starters?' The smile that had smitten Rosie cut no ice with Lorraine. She'd come across a lot of Nick Bartellos, invalided out of the Force or not, and he didn't even have that much of a limp.

'What division were you in?'

'Mine, well, at one time, when I was with the drug squad,' Rooney said flatly.

'Really? So you an' Bill are old friends?'

'Yep, in so much as I got a leg full of lead courtesy of

118

this fat fucker sending me out on a domestic, but not informing me that the coke-head had a personal armoury that'd make the US artillery think twice before they sent in tanks.'

Lorraine nodded. 'So you reckon Bill here owes you?'

Suddenly Nick Bartello quit the jokes. 'I got nobody but myself to blame, Mrs Page, nobody owes me nothin'. What I did was my business and I got a pension to prove it. Bill and me are just old buddies.'

Rooney, feeling very uneasy, thought he'd better get it in before Nick blurted it out. 'Nick partnered Jack Lubrinski for a few weeks. When I moved I took Jack with me.'

'Yeah, thank Christ, he was a mad fucker.'

'My, my, you must have been some double act.'

Nick hesitated. 'Yeah, we were, Mrs Page, for ten minutes.'

She turned away. 'And now you work for Agnews Investigation Agency? Lubrinski would be real proud of your progress.'

'Yes, ma'am, I most sincerely do work for them and maybe I know what Jack would think a whole lot better than you. Way I heard it, you were quite a lush.' He lifted the glass to his lips, trying to fathom her out. She was cool, he'd give her that, because she didn't rise to the cutting remark.

'So, have you informed Agnews about us?'

'No.'

'You haven't? Really? Not even tipped them off we been offered a big bonus?'

'No, I'll tell them fuck-all, especially not if I get a cut.'

'Does that mean you will tell them or you won't, Mr Bartello?'

'Nick.'

'Okay, Nick, why should I believe a word you say?'

He put his glass down carefully. 'Because I'm just a hired hand and a cut of the bonus would mean the finger to Agnews and all who sail in her. What is it with you? You want a fucking résumé? Hasn't Bill told you we worked together?'

'Yes, but limping around is not what I'd call a really good recommendation, Mr Bartello.'

'Fuck you! Hey, Billy, what is this? What's with this broad?' He was angry, and his eyes glinted at Rooney as he tried to control his temper.

'She's the boss, Nick.'

He turned and stared at Lorraine. 'My, my, my, haven't you cleaned up your act. Lady Boss now, huh?'

'My, my, my, Mr Bartello, haven't I just, so why don't we cut the bullshit and you tell me why we should cut you in if we find Anna Louise Caley? Because what Bill here got from you about Mrs Caley I already knew, and it's not worth enough to give you a slice of our possible bonus.'

He leaned closer to her. 'Maybe, bright eyes, I got something else.'

'I'm all ears, Mr Bartello. Can you match what we got?'

He smiled that killer smile again. 'Oh yeah, what you want me to do, give you a round of applause? So far you got shit . . .'

'You've not come up with much better,' she said, and she was warming to that smile. As Rooney and Rosie watched their interaction they could almost see the sparks between them.

Nick rocked back in his chair and took out a crumpled pack of Kool cigarettes. He flicked one out and flipped open his lighter, then gave Lorraine a hooded look. 'You got Robert Caley ear-marked as a suspect? Well, you

120

might be close. Way I see it is, with his daughter dead, he's the main beneficiary, isn't he?'

'Yep, but he'd have to kill the old movie star to get his hands on her cash.'

'Maybe he is planning it.'

'Maybe he is.'

'You think a guy who has bumped off his own daughter wouldn't go to those lengths? The top agencies were hired not by Mrs Caley but her husband, so the same reasoning could apply to her. She might want his dough.' Nick waited for the comeback.

'Has he got any? Old newspaper articles say he was just selling real estate when they married.'

'That was more'n twenty years ago. Now he's got a lot of real estate, I checked up on that too, so he's not short of cash. Anythin' else?'

Rosie and Rooney were out of it, watching Lorraine and Nick as they concentrated on each other across the table like chess players.

'If you only have Robert Caley as a possible suspect then you are in a very small canoe, *Mrs* Page, and you got no paddle.'

'Why?'

'Because if I had done my own daughter in, I wouldn't hire half of LA's top private dicks, myself included . . . But your problem is, if Caley is our guy, he *would* hire the world an' its mother but only if he was goddamned sure there was not a shred of evidence to prove his guilt. With me?'

'Not really.'

He smiled. 'Oh, I think you are, Mrs Page, I think you have sussed me out by now.'

He was knocked sideways by her husky laugh. He was beginning to like everything he saw about Lorraine Page. At the same time he would not give her any indication that he did. He reckoned this lady ate Nick Bartellos for lunch.

Rooney lit a cigarette. 'So, we together on this or not?'

Nick looked at Lorraine and cocked his head to one side. 'Up to the lady.'

'What you got, Nick?' Lorraine asked bluntly.

He dug into his pocket and brought out a quarter. 'Toss you for who goes first.'

She took the coin. 'Okay, heads or tails.'

'Your call.'

'Heads.' She tossed it on to the table and prodded it. 'I guess it's me first.'

Nick watched her get up. He was aware of every line of her body as she seemed to uncoil from the chair. She lit a cigarette and inhaled deeply. He liked the way her mouth pursed up, how it hung half open as she let the smoke trail out.

'I think the girl is dead, trail is too quiet, no sightings, et cetera. There again, people have been found after a much longer time on a few cases, but my gut feeling is Anna Louise is long dead.'

Nick nodded. 'But Bill said the million dollars still stands, dead or alive, right?'

Lorraine hesitated. 'That mean you agree with me?'

'Yeah, I do, and Bill's of the same opinion.'

Rooney looked at Lorraine. 'Yeah, I think she's a goner.'

Nick lifted his hand. 'Chick's dead, we all agreed?'

'No,' said Rosie. 'I'm not sure she is dead, well, not until we've got more information. She could have just taken off. Kids of her age do. I mean, I know kids that have taken off and years later resurfaced, maybe Anna Louise is one of them.'

Lorraine met Nick Bartello's bright blue eyes and

122

there was mutual understanding; they both believed Anna Louise was dead.

'Yeah, I guess you may be right, Rosie.' Lorraine kept looking at Nick. 'You talk to this Juda woman?'

Nick nodded. 'There're a lot like her, all she needs is a fuckin' crystal ball and a tent. She's full of bullshit and the money rolls in 'cos we got a town full of desperate people. I'd say she's been cleaning up with Elizabeth Caley, you know how these movie stars get into this kind of psycho stuff. Her rap about client confidentiality sucks, and it's bullshit about her being used by the cops for their enquiries, I checked it out. She more'n likely read it in the *National Enquirer*. From police records she never came up with anything they could use, she just got in the way and got publicity for herself.'

Rooney felt he should put his ten cents in. 'You want to see her again? Mrs Caley doesn't want you to see her.' He looked at Nick. 'She told Lorraine she would withdraw the bonus . . .'

Lorraine interrupted. 'We've gotta get to New Orleans. Robert Caley offered me a trip in his private jet. I'll accept, it'll give me more time to talk to him.'

Nick smiled. 'Oh yeah, gonna join the mile-high club, are you?'

'What's that supposed to mean?'

Nick ran his hands through his unruly mop of hair. 'No offence, but he's a looker and . . . Come on, just a joke. Is this all you got so far?'

'If you and Bill here have talked it over, you know we got fuck-all.'

'Yeah, I hear that, but what are *you* holding out on?'

Lorraine laughed at him. 'Who says I'm holding out, Nick?'

'Call it intuition, sweetheart. You got a gut feeling the girl is dead, what else is your gut saying?'

Lorraine sat down, drawing her chair close to him. 'There is something going on in that palace the Caleys call home. Elizabeth Caley is scared, maybe of Robert Caley, I dunno.'

'But you intend flying out on his private jet?'

'I intend to try.'

Nick smiled at her again; it was too intimate and she turned away. He rested his hand on her arm. 'Don't get uptight, he's a great-lookin' guy. If I was in your shoes, I'd try and get in his pants.'

'For chrissakes, back off me.'

'No, you do what you have to.'

'What's that supposed to mean?' she snapped.

'If you can get information, fuck him. Like I said, if I was in your position, and a woman, I'd maybe do the same thing because the three of you haven't got much, and not a lot of time either. An' screwing the guy is just a way of cuttin' corners. However, that said, maybe I have . . .'

'Have what?' Rooney asked, leaning forward towards him.

Nick lit a cigarette from the butt of his last and rocked back in his chair. 'Okay, is that it? All you got to date? So I guess it's my turn, right?'

'Right,' said Lorraine, annoyed and yet slightly embarrassed by his innuendoes, because it was as if Nick Bartello had read her mind. Robert Caley *was* attractive to her. But he'd also hit the nail on the head on another matter – she or Page Investigations had little to go on so far. Maybe a few hunches but she never mentioned those. 'Well, we're waiting, Mr Bartello,' she said, cocking her head to one side mockingly. 'I'm sure you must have so much more. You've been on the case a while, so stop fucking around.'

He took a drag on his cigarette and then slowly

removed a crumpled mess of paper from the back pocket of his jeans. He carefully straightened out a couple of pages, taking his time. They looked like pages torn from a small note-book, the edges ragged.

'I'll check my files, see if there's anything I can cross-reference,' Nick grinned, indicating his scruffy bits of paper.

'Why not start with the drugs?' Rooney prompted. He felt tired and in need of a drink.

'Okay. I picked up a guy called Gerry Fisher 'bout ten years back. Anyway, he turned out to be married to one of the officers on the drug squad, not my team, but I kind of got a hint to go easy, you know the game. I let Fisher off the hook, so he owed me, right? And then I pick the bastard up again eighteen months later, still running drugs, and I say, "I'm gonna bust you an' I don't care if you're married to the President." Fisher was a kind of middle man. He scored from his main dealer and then did back-door deals with a society-type doctor called Hayleden with a lotta high-profile patients who didn't want straight prescribed drugs. He didn't know who he was dealing for, he'd just take the orders then deliver to the surgery. In fact, he said he rarely even saw Hayleden. I was gonna do somethin' about it but then I got a leg full of lead an' was invalided out. So Fisher—' He was interrupted.

'What's this got to do with the case? Get to the point, Nick!' Rooney banged the table.

'Okay, okay, right. Now, before I was even working on this Caley thing, I was doin' a search for another movie star's kid. His family reckoned he was dealin' because he was loaded all the time and they hired the company to tail him and sort him out, you know, before the law did, put a bit of a squeeze on him. And bingo, I meet up with Fisher who still owes me, right? So he tips me off that this kid is scoring from him an' dealin' to college kids.'

'Anna Louise Caley?' Lorraine asked, suddenly interested.

'No, wait a second. I do the business, put the hand on the kid's collar, et cetera and we cop a nice fee for the agency. Next thing Fisher's scared shitless, thinks it's gonna be an arrest, but the family don't want that, just a rap over their asshole kid's knuckles. So Fisher bargains with me, telling me that he'll give more info on a lotta high-profile people if I don't hand him over to the law. I tell Fisher to fuck off and, to cut a long story short . . .'

They all moaned but Nick held up his hand. 'Hey, hey, wait, I'm getting there. I get pulled on the Caley investigation, so I use Fisher, ask him if the kid was dealin' to Anna Louise. He said he'd never heard of her and didn't recognize the photo, so I say she is Elizabeth Caley's daughter, used to be Elizabeth Seal, the movie star.'

Nick squinted at his bits of paper. 'Now it starts gettin' good. Fisher ain't dealin' to Anna Louise Caley but her mama! Goes like this, one night Fisher gets an emergency call from Doc Hayleden who's skiing in Aspen or some place, and he asks Fisher to deliver some quality goods to his surgery ASAP, says a nurse will pay him.' He listed on his fingers. 'Items required, cocaine, amphetamines, some crack and a load of downers – sleeping tabs, temazepam – like it's obvious somebody is havin' a party. So he takes the goods to the surgery, gets paid the usual way, then he goes back to his car. He thinks to himself, why not cut out the middle man? Fisher waits, and about half an hour later, a thin woman drives up. He sees her go into the surgery then come out and fast, and get back into her car. He follows, 'cos he knows the surgery is closed, so this chick hadda be the buyer, right? And she leads him straight to the Caley residence. She parks by the security gates and he takes his chance. He goes up to the car and she freaks and says she doesn't know what he's talking about, she was simply collecting a prescription, and if he doesn't get away from her car she'll call the police. She drives in . . . he reckons maybe he got it wrong but he gets a few more emergency calls and sees the same woman collecting, so he susses he was right to start with. He stops her again, and this time she is more than freaked but he calms her down and tells her he's not the law, just—'

'You talking about Phyllis Collins?' asked Rosie.

'Yep, only now she is scared that he's gonna turn her and her movie star in, so she agrees from then on they will deal direct. Phyllis would call him, place the order, meet up in cafés or wherever. So the Doc loses his cut, Fisher is raking it in because he starts doin' the same thing to a few more of the Doc's customers. Then Phyllis tells him no more deals, Mrs Caley's gone into rehab, nice earner down the drain. But somebody in that house still has a real bad habit, according to Fisher several thousand dollars a week habit.'

'My God, Elizabeth Caley?' Rooney murmured.

Nick shrugged. 'Next, an' this may or may not be connected, my friend Fisher—'

'Can I see him?' Lorraine asked.

'Be tough. He was found dead three weeks ago, he's still on the slab, they've got a backlog. Probably back on heroin, had a needle in his hand.'

'Shit,' Lorraine said as she poured herself more coffee.

Nick turned to the next crumpled page. 'So, we know the secretary scored for her ladyship. I'd say that's a good area we can work on, or work on Phyllis because she must know a lot more than she's admitting to. You said you reckoned Mrs Caley's still using, so maybe she got another dealer or is dealing with the Doc again. At the same time, we don't want to rock the boat as Mrs Caley is the one offering the one million bonus.'

'Did this guy Fisher ever mention meeting or dealing with Robert Caley?' Rooney asked.

'Nope.' Nick stubbed out his cigarette.

'Is that it?' Lorraine asked.

Nick shrugged. 'Phyllis should be pushed a bit . . . we could have a possible drug connection. Maybe Fisher's dealers got pissed, or the Doc, so that's all got to be checked out. Next, and this *is* good . . .'

Nick studied his notes, chewing his lower lip as he flicked a glance at Lorraine. 'Right, Robert Caley. He may be cute-looking, sweetheart, but to me he's our suspect number one, and if not him, his associates.'

'Because of the will?' Rooney asked.

'That's a good opener. We don't know if he's intending to bump off his drug-addled wife in a few months' time, but with no daughter, and *if* Elizabeth Caley dies, he gets the lot. And believe you me, it's a fucking fortune. We're talkin' in the region of fifty million. That mansion they live in is worth twelve million alone and they've got big property in New Orleans.'

'But this is just supposition, right?' said Lorraine.

'Yeah, but so is everything until we get results, and when I said earlier that our Mr Caley is not short of cash, it's not exactly true. You know what business Robert Caley is into?'

'Real estate,' said Rooney impatiently.

'Yeah, right, businesses both here and in Louisiana, and he's making a lotta dough.' Nick paused for effect. 'Well, he was.'

Rooney and Lorraine glanced at each other. This area they had not as yet checked into, so they waited as Nick prodded his crumpled notes.

'Robert Caley and his partners are trying to open a casino in New Orleans, right? Gambling is big business, it coins in the dough, and they've also sold it to the city on the basis that it will jack up the economy and give everybody out of work a job. But somehow, they're being fucked over – suddenly, there's zoning objections, architecture objections, bad for family life objections, and Robert Caley still hasn't got a casino licence, while another local consortium has had time to crawl out from under a rock and say it ought to go to them. The reason I put my money on Mr Caley as numero uno suspect is that he's losing credibility and every delay makes it more likely that his partners will pull out. If he doesn't get the green light for this casino soon, he's gonna go down millions, because he bought the proposed site.'

Nick beamed at them; he knew he'd opened up one hell of a can of worms. He continued, 'So we got quite a few possible motives, one is the missing daughter could have been kidnapped and connected to a drug dealer, two, she was snatched as a threat to Caley to pull out of the casino deal, maybe just removed as a warning. Caley is mixing with very heavy hitters and as far as I can make out, it's the wife bringing in all the private dicks, not Caley . . .'

'He didn't want us hired but he sort of implied it was because he reckoned we were no-hopers,' said Rooney, draining his coffee cup.

'Lemme wind down, Bill. My number three theory is Caley needs money for the casino, and bad. You know what the politics is like down there – if Caley had a big enough sweetener to slip into the right civic-minded vest pocket, his problems would all just melt out of his way. So he knocks off his daughter, next comes the wife, and we got one very rich and happy guy with a licence to print money for the rest of his life.' Nick folded his scruffy notes and stuck them back into his pocket. 'Well, that's what I got. May I make a suggestion? I think Lorraine or even Rosie should see what we can pump out of Phyllis Collins, I'll do the Doc's drugs scene and, Bill, you see if you can dig up more on the Caley casino property deal.'

'Sounds okay to me,' Rooney said, easing his sweaty tie up to the equally sweaty collar of his shirt.

Nick lit another cigarette and crossed to the front door. 'Thanks for the coffee, Rosie, and so, partners, I'll be seeing you . . .' He hesitated and looked at Lorraine. 'Seeing that Mr Smoothy has offered you a ride in his private jet, take it, because I don't know about you but I reckon he's our prime target.'

Rooney pushed back his chair. 'Yeah, I'm outta here too. I'll see what I can get from my old department. We all call in, right?'

'I'm looking forward to it,' Rosie said, smiling.

'To what?' Lorraine asked, irritably.

'New Orleans, I've never been there. And with expenses we can book into a real nice hotel. And I can interview Phyllis Collins, she'll be at the meeting tomorrow.'

'See you,' Rooney said, already at the door.

'Bye, y'all,' Nick called.

Lorraine looked up. 'Just one thing, Mr Bartello. This is my case, I run the show, so after today you don't tell me what to do.'

'Hey, that's cool.'

Lorraine caught the glance between Nick and Rooney as they left. It really infuriated her and she was angry at herself for coming out with such a crass statement. She should have played her hand better by far. She carried the dirty dishes across to the sink.

'Maybe I'll talk to Phyllis, Rosie.' Rosie ran water into

the sink and couldn't hide her disappointment. Lorraine put her arm around her shoulders.

'You can see her as well at the meeting, two heads are better than one Rosie, okay?'

CHAPTER 6

LORRAINE GOT on the freeway: Rosie had already contacted Phyllis Collins and she had agreed to see Lorraine, but not at the house. Phyllis eventually suggested they have coffee in the Plaza on Rodeo Drive as she had to be there to collect something for Mrs Caley from the Georgette Klinger shop.

'What's that?' Lorraine asked.

'I dunno, maybe a boutique, I didn't ask.'

'Okay, if you need me, I'll have the mobile with me.'

'Right, over and out.'

Lorraine checked her watch, parking the rental on a meter on Rodeo Drive. She had over an hour to kill so she decided she'd have her hair trimmed and chose a salon at random, asking if they could do her hair straight away.

'Okay, Lorraine, gonna make you a new woman.'

Lorraine watched as Noël, the flamboyant Afro-American hairdresser, cut and snipped, looked at her with critical eyes, cut and snipped some more. She noticed on the shelf below the mirror some white tubes, the name Georgette Klinger printed down the side.

'What is that stuff?'

He looked up. 'Oh, those are the real expensive treatments, they've a shop further up the Drive. Some of our customers,' he made a sweeping gesture with his scissors, 'swear by it.'

At 2.45, armed with Noël's card, she walked out. She still had fifteen minutes before she was to meet Phyllis so she walked down Rodeo until she got to the Georgette Klinger shop, peeked in, and then stepped back to admire herself in the window. The cut was good, tapered to the nape of her neck and long at the front. He'd made one side much longer, the scar side, and she liked the way it hid half her face when she leaned forward. In fact, she liked her new image. She was so busy admiring herself that she didn't see Phyllis parking on the opposite side of the road, didn't see her continue on to another parked car, a metallic green stretch Lincoln with black tinted windows, and get into the back seat.

'Hi, I'm supposed to meet a friend, collecting something for Mrs Elizabeth Caley.'

Lorraine's confidence in her new look faltered slightly as the elegant French woman behind the counter swished back her waist-length blonde hair.

'I am zo zorry, who?'

'Mrs Elizabeth Caley.'

'No, I am zo zorry but I am not expecteeng anyone, unless . . . one moment, pleeze.' She checked a leather-bound book. Lorraine busied herself looking over the various Georgette Klinger serums and lotions. 'No, Mrs Caley is waiting for some of our sun protection creams but they have not arrived yet, not until next week. I am zo zorry.'

Lorraine asked for shampoo and conditioner and had a near heart attack when the bill was rung up. A second assistant walked in from the back of the shop, eager to help sell more products.

'Theeze lady is a friend of Mrs Caley's, she said she was expecting a delivery . . .'

The second woman smiled at Lorraine. 'I called two days ago to apologize for the delay. The sun creams won't be here until the end of the month.'

Lorraine collected her goods in their neat white plastic bag and left the shop. She checked her watch, worried she was going to be late for Phyllis.

Juda's heavy breathing and sweet perfume made Phyllis feel sick; she disliked the woman intensely. 'I am afraid Mrs Caley's husband has put his foot down, there is nothing I can do. Please do not call the house again. Mrs Caley said she would contact you at a later date.'

'I see, well, it's up to her. But you know she can't make appointments and just keep cancelling like this. I make the time for her and I have a lot of clients.'

Phyllis handed Juda an envelope. 'I think this will suffice . . .'

Juda took the envelope. 'Please tell my dear Elizabeth not to give up hope. I still feel a strong presence of Anna Louise, tell her not to give up hope.'

'I will.'

Juda nodded, passing Phyllis a small square package, wrapped in brown paper. As Phyllis reached for the door, she said, 'Perhaps Mr Caley is going away and Elizabeth can see me?'

'I am sure Mrs Caley will call you. I must go . . .'

Phyllis got out of the car. The driver half-turned towards the back seat; he was only about twenty, with deep olive skin, and he wore a white shirt open at the neck. He watched as Juda opened the envelope and began to count 100-dollar notes, a lot of them.

'Where to now, Aunt Juda?'

Juda glanced up, quickly stuffing the money into a soft leather purse. 'Get me back home, Raoul, then go do a grocery shop. And keep your eyes to the front or you'll be on the next bus.'

He chuckled. 'Nobody messes with you, huh?'

She leaned back, staring out of the dark window. 'You said it, sugar, an' when they do, they get real sorry. Wait, stop a second, I just seen someone.'

Lorraine hurried along Rodeo towards the Plaza. She saw Phyllis get out of the Lincoln, saw her waiting at the roadside, but by the time she had actually crossed the road, she was already ahead of Lorraine.

Lorraine presumed the Lincoln was Mrs Caley's, the chauffeur dropping Phyllis off for their meeting, so she didn't give it a second glance. But Juda leaned forward in her seat as the nose of the Lincoln eased out from the parking bay. She was sure the blonde was the woman who had called on her, and by the look of it she was tailing Phyllis.

'Lorraine,' Juda said softly.

'What? We stopping or moving on?'

'Drive,' Juda snapped.

'A client?' Raoul asked.

'No, she's no client that one, she's a private investigator.' She repeated the name Lorraine to herself and then clasped her fat sweating ringed hands together. Her chest heaved as her breath caught in her throat in loud rasps.

'You got trouble?' Raoul asked.

'No, I not got trouble, but that lady is gonna have it, bad trouble.'

He didn't joke any more. When she said stuff like that, when her big, false-eyelashed eyes stared sightlessly as if she was seeing through and beyond him, his aunt scared him like his mama could . . . but then they were sisters. His hands clenched the wheel as he took another furtive look at Juda, then at the wing mirror, wondering if he would catch a glimpse of the woman his aunt had referred to. But Lorraine had disappeared.

Lorraine caught her breath, joining Phyllis just as she sat down at one of the small white tables outside the coffee shop.

'Sorry I'm a bit late but I wasn't sure exactly which shop.'

Lorraine smiled. 'Would you like coffee?'

'Yes, please, a cappuccino. No need to go to the counter, a waiter'll bring it, it's not self-service.'

Phyllis spoke fast, nervously. Her eyes couldn't fail to see Lorraine's plastic bags from Georgette Klinger.

'I don't think you've been very truthful, Phyllis.'

Two pink spots appeared on Phyllis's cheeks and her mouth tightened. 'I'm sorry, but I can't imagine why you think that. You've had your hair cut.'

'Yes, I had time to spare, and I also went to this store.' She held up the bag of cosmetics and smiled.

'Ah, yes, I was going to collect something for Mrs Caley.'

'But it's not in until the end of the month, I know.'

'Yes, very irritating, waste of a journey. Still, I am free to see you, and you did want to see me, Rosie said, rather urgently.'

A waiter hovered and Lorraine ordered the cappuccinos. Phyllis's right foot tapped nervously against the chair.

'But you knew they wouldn't have Mrs Caley's sun protection, they called you. Well, so the assistant told me.'

'Good heavens, did you ask them? Well, really, I think that is all rather unnecessary.'

'Maybe, but as I was there . . .'

'If that is what you term being dishonest, then I am sorry. I was going to call in just to make sure it hadn't arrived. I also have other things to collect, so I wasn't lying, and I rather resent your implying that I have been. Mrs Caley suffers so much from the sun, she cannot sit out in it at all . . .'

Tap tap went her foot, the table rocking a fraction, but she seemed unaware of it, constantly looking around, fiddling with her blouse collar. Lorraine let her stew for a while. The two pink spots on Phyllis's cheeks faded before she spoke again.

'Your hair is very nice, good cut, it's all in the cut really, isn't it?'

'Yes, I just got lucky, I went to the salon further up the drive.'

'St Julian's?' Phyllis asked. Her face reminded Lorraine of a bird's, pecking, her thin nose sharp as she twisted her head and kept up the nervous kicking of the table. 'My, you are taking your work to rather silly lengths.'

'I'm sorry?'

'That's Mrs Caley's salon. Well, it was, they come to her now. But Anna Louise used it, she was always very particular about her hair.'

'Really? Then it was just a coincidence, I walked in off the street. As I said, I got here early.'

The coffee arrived, with tiny flaky pastries. Lorraine smiled her thanks to the waiter.

'How long has Mrs Caley been a drug addict?'

Phyllis's pink spots returned with a vengeance. She stirred her coffee, her foot still tapping, and now her head twitched. 'I have no idea what you are talking about.'

'Yes, you do, and that's why I wanted to see you.'

'I really do not see that whatever medication Mrs Caley requires is any business of yours or Rosie's.'

'Medication? Come on, Phyllis, I know she's on uppers, downers, cocaine, speed, you name it. Even her husband admitted—'

'Mr Caley told you?' Phyllis said, astonished.

'Yes, but he implied they were simply pain-killers for an old injury and that Mrs Caley had, well, become dependent on them. But speed, cocaine, et cetera, are not what I would call pain-killers, and when I last saw her she seemed very hyper. She was also very disturbed.'

Phyllis's jaw was working overtime now. 'I think in the terrible circumstances, Mrs Page, anyone would be disturbed. Her daughter is missing, she could obviously be dead . . .'

'Yes, I know, Phyllis. That's why I have to investigate every possible motive.'

'You mean you suspect Mrs Caley?'

'No, but I need to know who she was getting her drugs from because there may be a connection.'

'There isn't, I assure you.'

'You assuring me, Phyllis, is not good enough, I'm afraid. And if you care about finding out the truth, then you'll stop this silly game. You could be arrested for procuring drugs, you know that, don't you? You see, I know how it used to work, Phyllis. The friendly, sympathetic doctor – he could be arrested for dealing. I know you collected from his surgery, just as I know you later dealt direct with a man called Gerry Fisher.'

'Oh, God,' Phyllis was shaking now. 'Does Mr Caley know you are talking to me?'

'No, this is a private discussion between you and me,

it won't go any further. But I need to know if anyone got nasty or made threats to Mrs Caley. A three thousand dollar a week habit is big money for some, it gets to be competitive, understand me? And I know you cut out the doctor at one point so he lost his share.'

'It's not three . . .'

'Come on, Phyllis, we're not here to worry about a few hundred dollars this way or that.'

'It's five . . .'

'What?'

'Sometimes a bit less, and obviously I would say a lot of that is for . . . confidentiality. I mean, if it was ever to get out, she is very famous, sits on a lot of charitable boards, and then of course there is Mr Caley to consider. If it was ever to be made public, it would be dreadful for him.'

'He doesn't use drugs of any kind?'

'No, no, not at all, he's very much against them. He has tried every means possible to persuade Elizabeth to stop. She's been in so many clinics but no sooner is she released . . . it starts again, and with this tragedy it's made things a lot worse. She's in a stupor for most of the day, and then when Mr Caley comes home she starts taking anything that'll wake her up, so then of course she can't sleep and the spiral begins. It's a wonder she hasn't killed herself yet. She must have the constitution of a horse, the abuse her poor body takes, but she still manages to put on a good show when it is needed. Nobody would know, and that's part of the problem. She's very sly, very devious, and will swear on a Bible that she was clean if you asked . . .'

Lorraine drained her cappuccino, Phyllis had hardly touched hers. She was not so agitated now, her hands folded in her lap.

'How we've managed to keep it secret for so long I

don't know, I really don't, but at least I haven't got to meet that dreadful man.'

'So who do you deal from now, Phyllis?'

'Please, I don't deal, Mrs Page. When Mrs Caley went to a rehabilitation centre, I told Mr Fisher his services were no longer required. Then it started again, I picked up her prescriptions from the surgery again, just something to help her sleep and relieve the anxiety. She's not using the other things, that is the truth. He should be struck off but if he didn't get what she wanted she would go elsewhere.'

Lorraine nodded, really needing a cigarette. 'So you never contacted any other street dealer, just the doctor?'

'Yes.'

'So no one else knows, nobody is putting any pressure on her to use their goods?'

'If they are, I don't know about it.'

'Mr Caley knows you are getting the stuff for her, does he?'

Phyllis chewed her lips. 'He knows about the painkillers.'

'Do they sleep together?'

Phyllis looked shocked. 'I cannot discuss that, really.'

'Do they share the same bedroom?'

'They have different suites. What they do in their own time I really have no notion of. He is, to my mind, very caring and patient with her, and she can be extremely difficult, you know.'

'What about Anna Louise?'

'I'm sorry?'

Lorraine sighed. 'Phyllis, did Anna Louise know about her mother's addiction to drugs?'

Phyllis looked away. 'Perhaps, well, it is hard not to if you live in the same house. Mrs Caley has extreme mood swings and sometimes she is quite irrational.'

'Did they argue a lot?'

Phyllis nodded.

'Did Anna Louise use drugs?'

'No, no, she hated them, she wouldn't even smoke a cigarette, hardly ever drank. In fact, sometimes she seemed more like the mother than the child, which is why this is so awful for Mrs Caley.'

Lorraine picked at her tiny pastry. 'The day they left for New Orleans, what state was Mrs Caley in?'

'She . . . she had taken something. She was very tense, always made the excuse she hated flying, that she needed something to calm down her nerves, but she was . . . I think the expression is "wired". She kept on changing her mind about whether or not to go, but we got her packed and ready, and by the time Mr Caley returned, she was quite calm.'

'How was Anna Louise?'

'Well, she hated it when Mrs Caley got anxious, and I think at one point she said she didn't want to go. But when Mr Caley came home they talked for a while, and then they all left.'

'So the last time you spoke to Anna Louise was from the plane?'

'Yes, that was the last time. She asked me to collect a dress, but you know this.'

'And she sounded okay, not stressed out?'

'She sounded relaxed and happy, as did Mrs Caley.'

'So you also spoke to Mrs Caley?'

'Yes, she was making sure I'd get the dress sent to the house and then I was to give it to the pilot who would return for it and take it on to New Orleans.' Phyllis suddenly bowed her head. 'It was a lovely dress, and . . . she never got to wear it. You think she's dead, don't you?'

Lorraine signalled to the waiter. 'I am not in any position to say that, not until I know more. Do you?'

'Pardon?'

'Do you think she's dead, Phyllis?'

She nodded, twisting her hands. 'Yes, she would not do this to her mother, and especially not to her father, she was a very thoughtful girl. You know, if she was going to be late she'd call home, and when she went away she would call her father two or three times a day.'

Lorraine settled the bill for the cappuccinos; she could have bought a full meal in an Orange Grove coffee shop for what they charged. She collected her purchases and was rising to her feet, preparing to leave, when Phyllis spoke again.

'It was very hard when she had friends to stay.' She had sipped her cold cappuccino now and had a froth stain on her upper lip. 'She was protective about Mrs Caley, afraid anyone would find out. You know, in this day and age it's so difficult to trust people not to sell out to the tabloids. Poor Anna Louise was worried about how it would affect her mother, it seems so incongruous that she should be the one to make such headlines, in every paper too. And you know something extraordinary, sick really . . . after fifteen years, during which she could not get a phone call returned, well, not for serious work, maybe television but she would never do television parts, she's suddenly been offered numerous scripts from some of the big studios. And one, it's hard to believe, even hinted that they may make a film about Anna's disappearance and they wanted to discuss Elizabeth playing herself. Disgusting, just disgusting. So it is understandable why she is so dependent, isn't it? Even if it is very hard on me.'

'Thank you for agreeing to see me and for being so honest, Phyllis. Obviously everything we have said was in confidence. And if there is anything, anything at all that you think may help me, will you call me? Or Rosie.'

'Yes, yes, I will and . . . well, thank you for coffee.'

Lorraine hurried out of the Plaza on to Rodeo, leaving Phyllis still sipping her cappuccino. She was relieved that Lorraine had only wanted to discuss the drug situation. She had been scared she knew more, and she could not, would not have talked about Juda Salina, she daren't. She dabbed her lips with her napkin and looked around. Not until she saw Lorraine actually disappear from view did she get up and go into the café to use the public telephone. She gave a quick, furtive look around as she punched in the number, and waited.

'The Caley residence.'

'Peters, will you check on Mrs Caley? And will you say to her that everything was all right and she has no need to worry. I will be home in half an hour or so.'

Lorraine sat in her car. It was sweltering, the seat burning her backside, so she opened her windows all round. The portable buzzed and hissed.

'Rosie, can you call Robert Caley? He'll probably be at his office, so try there and ask if he'll see me.'

'Sorry, hang on a second.' Rosie was munching a carrot, her cheeks bulging. She swallowed quickly. 'Sorry, let me put Bill on, he wants a word. While you're on to him I'll call Caley, okay?'

Rooney picked up the phone. 'I've been trying to check out this casino deal.'

'Yeah, what you got?'

'Not a lot but I got what I could. Caley heads a consortium made up of him, a couple of local moneymen

143

and a casino outfit from out of state. They're ready to back the deal to the tune of around two hundred and fifty million.'

'What?'

'Yep, lot of dough, but Caley will take the major slice of ownership as he laid out the initial payment for the land, massive site near the riverfront. The complex will have a hotel and a lot of high-class shops as well as the casino.'

'So what's Caley's problem?' Lorraine interjected.

'Well, there's a number of little hitches. One, he's been wanting to set this deal up for five years, but unfortunately the state of Louisiana hasn't been too quick about getting legalized gambling on the statute book, while their good neighbours next door have been straight off the blocks – a lot of the gambling revenue for the whole of the south-east already has a happy home up the coast in Mississippi, and maybe it ain't gonna move. Second, there's some old money elements in the city that are dragging out some case about re-zoning the area, saying it's prohibited by federal law: load of fucking horseshit, but they could hold things up quite a while. And third, get this, there's some very fucking weird provisions in this gambling statute – the city gets to choose the guy who develops the site, but the state gets to say who runs the casino. Everybody has been thinking it would be Caley and his friends, as soon as they could get this legal mess straightened out about the site, but lately people are getting to wondering what's holding things up. Some other rich guys down here seem to have got the message that maybe somebody else might just get the licence to run the show, so now Caley's got a rival consortium on his back, call themselves Doubloons. One of his backers has dropped out until he has the operating licence in his pocket, and the other may walk too.'

'You got the backers' names?'

'Yep, two guys named Bodenhamer and Dulay. They're big-time owners of major corporations, Bodenhamer construction, Dulay liquor. They both stand to make a packet out of the casino, not only out of the gambling, but by selling the stuff they got to sell, and as yet they don't stand to lose a cent. Caley's in a lot deeper though.'

'What do you mean?' Lorraine asked, trying to assimilate all the information.

'Caley paid for the land leases on the site. If he doesn't get the licence he's stuck with them. This is all common knowledge in New Orleans, but I'd get a lot more from being there.'

'It might be common knowledge, Bill, but how come this isn't detailed in any of the reports your pal Sharkey xeroxed for us?'

'Maybe he was looking out for his own ass, I dunno, or maybe they didn't think it important.'

'No? Well, I think it is. You're sayin', in so many words, Robert Caley's got to get the casino deal?'

'Sure. He's been cash-poor for years – he liquidated a lot of his assets, sold off properties in LA and Louisiana. If the deal is greenlighted he stands to make mega-bucks. So maybe Nick was right about Caley. He's up against very tough opposition, mainly from this other consortium, but the door's wide open now for anyone else to walk in.'

'We got to get as much as we can and fast. I'll see if Caley will give me further details. Rosie contacted him yet?'

Rosie took the phone. 'Yes, be there about four-thirty. He's warned security to expect you.'

Lorraine tucked the phone under her chin and started up the engine. 'Okay, I'm on my way.'

Rosie replaced the receiver and bent down to start removing tin-foil dishes from a carrier bag of takeaway, spreading a newspaper as tablecloth on Lorraine's desk.

'It's Japanese, Bill, nothing fattening – that's prawn, that's salmon and that's fish, raw fish. It doesn't taste so good first time, but give it a good chew and a dip in the sauce. Then we got grated lettuce and broccoli.'

'No thanks, I'll get a hamburger.'

'This is better for you – at least just try it.'

'No thanks, I'll wait.'

Rosie laid out all the dishes, then speared a piece of fish on a fork and carried it to Rooney.

'Just have a taste, it's good, healthy, and if you don't mind me saying so, that suit'd fit better if you lost a few pounds.'

Rooney made a face, but opened his mouth and chewed, while Rosie leaned over him, waiting. He swallowed, nodding his head.

'Not bad, bit like Chinese, isn't it?' Rosie prepared two platefuls as Bill hovered over the dishes, picking up a prawn and nibbling it.

'No rice? Didn't you get any rice?'

'No, you can't eat rice with protein because it's a carbohydrate and you can't mix them. Next meal we can have a huge plate of pasta, as much pasta as you can eat, but no protein.'

'That's interesting. Where you getting all this from?'

'Lorraine, she put me on to it.'

Bill sat down in front of his plate, tucking a paper napkin in his collar. 'She knows a thing or two, does Lorraine.'

Rosie nodded, pouring some spring water into two cups. 'She always impresses me, sort of takes me by surprise. She's a funny woman, though, and I don't mean to bitch about her behind her back, but sometimes she can have a sharp tongue, and then other times she's as soft as a baby.'

Rooney had his mouth full, or he would have contradicted her vehemently, because in all the years he had known Lorraine Page he had never seen a side of her character that could be described as soft as a baby, but he said nothing, chewing in unison with Rosie. Even if what he was eating did taste like rubber and he would have preferred a huge hamburger special with sausage and bacon on the side, he liked the fact that he was not sitting at home alone. French fries he could get on his way home, sweet company he could not.

A young man with slicked-back hair, wearing a grey designer suit and floral tie, led Lorraine into Robert Caley's office. He tapped at an immense floor-to-ceiling door, a green light blinked on an intercom by the side, and the floral tie opened the door. He peered in, Lorraine just behind him.

'It's Mrs Page, Mr Caley.'

He turned with a whiter than white, capped-tooth smile. 'Please . . .'

The office was a vast windowed room, with blinds cutting out the afternoon sunlight. An enormous black desk with black glass top dominated the room. The carpet was grey thick-pile, and soft leather bucket chairs formed a semicircle in front of the black monster. Expensive prints lined the walls but there were no filing cabinets, no stray tables. Only a bronze sculpture of what looked like an elongated man on a plinth pointing to heaven was placed discreetly in a corner.

Robert Caley was speaking on one of the eight

telephones lining his desk. The high back of his chair was facing Lorraine so she couldn't see him, but his assistant indicated one of the bucket seats.

'Fine, Bel Air, see you there.' Caley eased round to face Lorraine as he replaced the phone. 'Excuse me one moment, Mrs Page.'

He looked at his assistant. 'Call my five o'clock appointment and move him to six – I have to go out to the Bel Air for a while. And grovel some more to Dulay's office, Mark, he's really pissed off.'

'Yes, sir. Do you want any refreshments?'

'No, unless . . .' Caley turned his attention to Lorraine.

'Nothing for me, thank you.'

Caley gave a curt nod and the doors were closed silently. 'You wanted to see me, Mrs Page?'

He swivelled from side to side, and, not waiting for her to answer, tapped the phone he had used with his forefinger. 'That was trouble.'

'I'm sorry, if it is inconvenient . . .'

Caley smiled glumly and leaned on his elbows, cupping his chin in his hands. 'It is, but maybe I need something to take my mind off the fact I might go belly up. You want to see something?' He sprang out of his chair and pressed a button at the side of the desk. Lorraine turned as part of the grey wall to her right slid back to display a large architect's drawing. 'This is what might do me in. Come here, let me show you.' He showed her the proposed casino site, hotels, shopping precinct, and talked her through his plans, much as Rooney had outlined. 'Looks good, huh? As I owned the entire site, I would of course be the main shareholder. But I didn't count on the state fannying around for fucking years while they commission fifty reports on how gambling corrupts widows and orphans and makes you

148

go blind, before they get around to deciding that actually it's an emerging area of the leisure industry, worthy new area of economic development, provision of employment, economic stimulation, just what the city needs. They realized all of that first time around up the coast. Five years of my life go into this plan, and my partners, who unlike myself have not laid out so much as a dollar, are getting cold feet, while a gang of other guys around town decide they might like a piece of the pie and get themselves into a little huddle too. So . . .'

Lorraine looked over the model. 'So if your partners pull out, what are you left with?'

'A lot of land, and no money. So you see, I need those partners, without them I couldn't build myself a shed. That's how deep in this mess I am.' He clicked off the screen, pulled back the wall panel across the model and returned to his desk.

Lorraine sat back in her chair. 'Are your partners dumping you?'

'Yep, one gone and one just about ready to. He called in the last hour – asked me what I propose to do to ensure this goes through when he's the one pushing the Governor's fucking golf cart for him every weekend. There's only so long you can string people like Lloyd Dulay – the brewery magnate, if you don't know who he is. When you have his kind of money there are a lot of people like me dangling deals and you know these mega-rich bastards are always intent on anything that's gonna make them even richer, they just don't want to wait.'

'You mind if I smoke?' she asked.

'No, go ahead.'

He opened a drawer and placed an exquisite onyx and gold box on the table. She took a cigarette, and he clicked open the gold Cartier lighter from inside the box for her. As she inhaled, she looked up and met his eyes.

They stared at one another for a brief moment, then he let the cigarette box lid close with a snap. He passed across a black glass ashtray. 'I need a drink.'

She watched him cross the thick-pile carpet to yet another hidden section in the pale grey walls. Another panel slid aside to reveal a large drinks cabinet. She could hear the clink of ice against the glass and her heart began to beat rapidly. Was he going to offer her a drink? More importantly, would she be able to refuse it?

Lorraine was there for a specific reason – to discover if Caley was financially in as much trouble over the casino deal as Rooney had surmised. Yet he had, without any prompting, told her. Either he was a consummate actor and had pre-empted her reason for being there, or he was being honest. He had confused her and she was at a loss as to how she should continue the meeting.

'This office is a bit crass, isn't it?' he chuckled. 'When I first took it over, I used to go down the corridor and down a back flight of stairs to the john. I didn't know which button to press for my own en suite bathroom. Fucking nightmare of grey on grey, but it's only rented.' He placed a long crystal glass of sparkling water with ice and lemon on the desk. He had a small, square, cut-crystal glass with brandy.

'Thank you,' she said softly.

Again he met her eyes, and this time he smiled. 'You didn't think I'd offer you alcohol, did you?'

'For a moment I did.' He was throwing her sideways.

'I wouldn't do that to you, I know you have a problem. I should do, I live with a woman who has not one, but a number. But then I think we have already discussed my wife's situation.'

She nodded, wondering if one of the grey walls also slid back to reveal a bed. If it had done and he did reveal

150

it, she wouldn't know how she would react. She found him even more attractive today, liking everything about him; his hands were strong and tanned, his suit more casual than the floral-tied assistant's, and he wore a collarless shirt with two buttons open at the neck, and simple loafers. Everything about him was casual, apart from his blue eyes: they were as dangerous as his smile.

'I have to go to New Orleans, tomorrow maybe. You want to come with me?'

'Yes.' She sipped the iced water.

'I guess you want to see what you can dig up there.' He laughed. 'Dig being the operative word. I might be digging for the rest of my life if I don't pull this deal off.'

'But surely your wife has a considerable amount—'

He interrupted her. 'Let me make this very clear, Mrs Page. My wife's money is hers, I make my own. We have separate bank accounts, always have done, and in case you haven't unearthed it yet, I signed a pre-nuptial agreement. What is my wife's is hers, what is mine is mine, for what it's worth.'

'If she dies . . .' Lorraine said quietly.

He glared. 'What?'

'You are her main beneficiary, aren't you.'

'No, Mrs Page, my daughter is . . .'

'But if Anna Louise is dead?' she said, keeping her voice soft.

'I hadn't thought of that. Dear God, is that the reason you are here? What the fuck do you think I am, huh? We are talking about my daughter, what do you think I have done, killed her so that I can get my wife's money? Do you think I'm making plans to kill my wife, is that it? What do you think I am?' He shook his head. 'Jesus Christ, that is so sick.'

151

'I'm not here for that.'

'Well, I'm glad to hear it, because if you were I'd throw you out of here myself.'

'I'm looking for motives for Anna Louise's disappearance, Mr Caley. Maybe you've given me one.'

He glared again. 'You seriously think I would be capable of murdering my own daughter?'

'I don't know you, Mr Caley, but as an investigator I have to look at all possibilities. You are, as far as I can see and in so much as you have just told me, the only person that, like it or not, would benefit from Anna Louise's death.'

'And I'd benefit a whole lot more if my wife also died, yes?'

'Yes.'

'So you think I am arranging to kill her? Is that what you came here to discuss? To find out by what means I intend to murder my wife? Well, in your capacity as a so-called investigator, maybe you could give me some tips.'

'I am not, Mr Caley, a so-called investigator.'

'You weren't much of a cop.'

She stood up and leaned towards him across the desk. 'You have no idea what I was and I am not prepared to sit here and be insulted.'

'But you can insult me? Anna Louise is my daughter, now you get out of this office and do the job my wife hired you to do, because I did not kill my daughter and I have no intention of murdering my wife.'

Lorraine coughed, trying as best as she could to appear nonchalant. 'Perhaps one of your business associates may have a connection.'

He sat back in his chair and stared at her, then swivelled round so she could not see his face. His voice became deeper, quieter. 'Go on, Mrs Page . . .'

'Well, you've just made it perfectly clear; there's a lot

of money to be made, there's you and a rival consortium, and things would be a lot easier for them if you were just suddenly to lose interest in this project. Plus there's the riverboats – presumably a casino like yours would take a lot of their business, right? So there is a possibility that your daughter may have been part of some kind of plot.'

'Like what?' he snapped.

'Well, someone may have kidnapped her to persuade you not to go ahead with your project. You own the land, and your partners haven't put in a cent so far . . .'

He remained silent for a moment and then slowly swivelled round in his chair to face her. 'Go on.'

'It's just a theory, but someone may have been considering using her to make you back off. Has anyone approached you directly, warned you off personally?'

He stared, then shrugged. 'No, no, they have not. You mean hold her to ransom?'

She nodded. 'Has anyone offered just to buy out your land?'

He began to toy with his empty glass, moving it slowly along the desk top. 'No, but tell me this, why, if what you are saying were true, was there no ransom note, no request for a meeting, no contact whatsoever? The Doubloons consortium has so much muscle that I do not believe for one moment they would resort to kidnapping Anna Louise as a means of threatening me.'

'But they may have used some unsavoury goons to pick her up, maybe hold her, and it went wrong.'

'You mean they killed her?'

There was that awful pain in his eyes, and she had to look away. 'Possibly, which would explain why there was no note or no contact with you. All the publicity surrounding your daughter's disappearance must have had an adverse effect on the deal.'

Caley pushed his chair back and stood up. 'But they

are successful enough at blocking any advancement of my development without my daughter, they didn't need her. And if I continue to lose my partners, then . . .'

'You've considered this, haven't you?'

He nodded, sighing. 'Yes, briefly, but then I dismissed it because I truthfully do not think they would sink so low.'

'When millions are at stake you would be surprised how low people are prepared to sink, Mr Caley. So, if you had even considered the possibility, then you must understand why I must also look into it and why I will need to know who all the other parties are, specifically your competitors. Then by a process of elimination—'

'You won't get anywhere with this so-called elimination.'

'Try me,' Lorraine challenged.

'Okay, you want to talk to the opposition, yes?'

'Obviously.'

'Well, Mrs Page, I think you will come up against the same brick wall that every other agent has met with, but far be it from me to dissuade you. In fact, I will do everything I can to assist you, as I have done throughout the enquiries. Now if you'll excuse me . . .'

'Did the other agents and the LA police question you about these people?'

He strode towards the huge doors. 'Of course, and they also at one time suspected me.'

'I see.'

'No, Mrs Page, I don't think you do. I had expected, after we had talked, that you would have believed I could not have harmed a hair on my daughter's head, let alone be the type of man who would put his wife through such torment. You have suggested nothing new, nothing that I have not been subjected to before. Now excuse me, Mark will give you all the details you require.'

154

He walked out, closing the door behind him. A few moments later, the floral-tied assistant appeared with a thick file and crossed the office to Lorraine.

'Mr Caley has asked me to give you these files, but please understand this is private and confidential information. You may make notes but not remove the file from the office. Mr Caley's secretary will give you every assistance if you need anything clarified—' He was interrupted.

'So I remain in here?' Lorraine took the files.

'Yes, Mr Caley suggests you use his office so that if you require any assistance, or anything xeroxed that we agree to be released, his secretary or I will be on hand to help you. The file contains plans for the proposed casino development and—' Again he was interrupted as Lorraine moved round Robert Caley's desk.

'Fine, thank you. I'm sorry, I didn't actually catch your name.'

'Mark Riley, I am Mr Caley's personal assistant.'

She sat at Caley's desk, opening the file. 'Thanks, Mark. If you could just show me what button I press to talk to you or . . .'

'Margaret is on line five, I am on line two.'

She smiled. 'Thank you very much, Mark.'

He hesitated at the half-open door. 'I'll leave you to it.'

'Did you know Anna Louise, Mark?'

He looked surprised. 'Yes, of course.'

'Did she come here a lot?'

'No, just occasionally for lunch with Mr Caley.'

'Did you ever see her socially?'

'No. I only met her when she came to see Mr Caley.'

Lorraine was left alone in the vast, cool office, sitting in Robert Caley's soft leather chair. She opened the file and then reached for her purse to get her note-book. She found it, but no pen, so she looked down the side of the desk to rows of black steel-fronted drawers discreetly built into each side, to try to find one. There were no handles. She tried pushing at them, trying to fathom out how they opened, but they all seemed to be locked. She frowned and looked over the vast desk top and saw that it had a built-in square directly in front of the chair. She pushed at it but nothing happened. Then she noticed a small black raised button so she pressed it and the inlaid section eased back. The opening housed a blotter, a row of pens and pencils, note-books, memo pads, paper clips, all in neat compartments, and two photograph frames face down. She turned one over and it was of Anna Louise; the other was of Elizabeth Caley.

Sitting at his desk in his office, Mark Riley watched Lorraine on a small monitor. He turned to a dark-haired woman who was typing on her word processor.

'Mrs Page is having a good snoop round the office.'

Margaret looked at him. 'Yes, I noticed, but I've secured all the drawers so she can't poke her nose any further.'

Mark looked over the diary. There was no record of the new appointment. 'Who's he meeting right now?'

'Who do you think?' Margaret said, half-raising an eyebrow.

Saffron Dulay was late, she always was, and Robert Caley checked his watch again, missing her entrance. But no one else did – she was hard to miss. Saffron moved gracefully between the tables, led by a maître d' who bowed and gestured towards Caley's discreet table in one of the alcoves of the Bel Air garden restaurant. Pausing just a fraction to smile and acknowledge a number of

156

people she knew, Saffron gave only a slight incline of her beautiful head, behaving as if she was royalty, and the maître d' was treating her as such.

Caley immediately rose to his feet as Saffron joined him, bending her head towards him for a kiss on the cheek.

'Robert,' she said huskily, 'I'm sorry, I know I am late, please don't get up.'

He did, pulling her chair out for her as she sat down with the passing swans at her back. He knew she liked to get a good view of the place and invariably knew anyone that was anyone. Saffron was rich, the only daughter of a brewing king, sole heiress to billions. She wore her wealth in that covert, simple way that only the truly rich can. Almost six feet tall, the sheer simplicity of her white negligée-type dress enhanced her height, while her glowing golden tan was set off by slim gold sandals and a million dollars' worth of solitaire diamonds in her ears. As she eased her slender body on to the cushioned seat, she removed her only accessory – her gold-rimmed shades.

'Hi, how you doing?'

Saffron was the wrong side of forty but one would be hard-pushed to estimate her age; her confidence in herself, boosted by her millions and her obvious physical perfection, gave the appearance of youth. Four marriages and endless lovers had not managed to dent her innocent girlish act, one she had perfected better than any hopeful starlet half her age.

'You got any news about that little girl o' yours?' she asked in her Southern drawl.

'No.'

She reached over and touched Caley's hand lightly. 'It must be s'ah hard.'

'Yeah, it is.'

Her eyes flicked round the tables, then back to Caley. 'You always choose this place.'

'Yep, I can smoke, outdoors.' He signalled to a waiter. 'I've already ordered you your usual – I take it your tastes haven't changed.'

She laughed, her eyes still darting around the restaurant, and all he could think about was Lorraine Page. She was as blonde, almost as tall, but so flawed, so real a woman in comparison with Saffron. He no longer wanted to fuck Saffron, that had been over a long time ago. He had never disliked her before, now he did. Perhaps Lorraine attracted him because she was so direct. He would like to screw Lorraine, and just thinking about it made him smile.

'You got one hell of a smile, Robert Caley,' Saffron said softly.

'Why, thank you . . .'

She cupped her chin in her hands. 'What you want, darlin'? You runnin' short of funds again?'

The waiter brought her an elaborately decorated cocktail and another whiskey sour for him. It irritated him that she knew instinctively why he had asked to see her, that he had to play out the game. She sipped a tiny drop from the glass and then placed it on the table; she wouldn't touch it again, she never did.

'Ah'll never understand why you don't get that movie star wife of yours to finance you.'

'I don't want money from my wife.'

'No, but you sure as hell need it, an' you'll take it from elsewhere.' She leaned back, only now giving him her undivided attention. Being rich, she knew how to handle anyone about to put the touch on her, she was an old hand at it.

'I don't want a cent from you, darlin', but I do need

158

you to easy-talk your daddy. No need to go into details, you know we're into this development deal together, but he's hinted he might pull out and I know you can talk him round, so—'

'Ah already talked to him, darlin', soon as Ah put down the phone from you he called me. In fact, we must have been playin' telephone games – he calls you, you call me, then he calls me ... He may be more than seventy years old, but, man, he is a wily old bastard. Said he wants me to go to some function back home, you know, always keepin' tabs on me and it drives me crazy. Since Mama died, he is trying to get me to go live back home, find a nice steady man and produce a grandchild.'

'It's understandable, you're his only daughter. So did he mention my project at all?'

'Why don't we drive around a while to discuss this?' She smiled sweetly, not waiting for him to reply, then tossed her napkin aside. Caley half-rose from his seat, watched her get up, then finished his drink, knowing she would be table-hopping for a good fifteen minutes. He paid the check, and knew he was now about to pay even more. As he threaded his way through the tables, he checked his watch; he had only forty-five minutes before his next meeting.

The driver could not see or be seen through the dark-tinted glass partition. Saffron's limo had a wide couch section, a television and drinks cabinet, plus a fax machine, telephone and a computer deck. Caley sat opposite her; she was lying across a deep cushioned seat, unwrapping a peppermint.

'You want a sweetie?'

'Nope.'

'No calories.'

He opened the drinks cabinet, filled a crystal tumbler with ice cubes and topped it up with water. He looked at Saffron, holding up the glass, but she shook her head.

'I have to be back at my office by six.'

'Fine, we'll drive nice and slow . . . just the way Ah like it.'

She eased one shoulder strap down, then the next, and wriggled out of her white dress. She wore no underwear and was totally unselfconscious as she carefully folded her dress and spread her long tanned legs wide. She wore only her thin-strapped gold sandals. Caley watched her as he sipped the water and then drained the glass, leaving just the ice cubes. He jangled the glass for a moment, and she giggled.

'Well, well, it's been a while since Ah was cubed up, and you know how Ah like it . . .'

He didn't even loosen his tie or remove his jacket; he didn't need to. Saffron didn't want to be held in his arms and wouldn't want to have her discreet make-up disturbed by frantic kisses. She knew exactly what she wanted, and so did he. She began to massage herself, cupping her neat breasts in her tapering fingers until the nipples hardened. He knelt between her legs. With his right hand he stroked her nipples with an ice cube, making her moan softly, as his left hand began slowly to caress her thighs, inching up gradually between her legs until his thumb rubbed her, knowing the exact spot to arouse her, and she spread her legs wider and wider, eyes closed.

'Oh, yes, yes, Ah like that, Ah like that.'

Slowly he let the ice cube slither down from her breasts, making her shiver, and her body arched as he adeptly inserted the melting ice cube high up into her vagina. He quickly reached for the rest of the cubes still in his glass and pressed in one after another until he could feel the cold ice with his thumb.

'Oh, God, yesss, yess . . .' She bent forwards, drawing his head down as he began to suck and lick her clitoris. She came quickly, letting out a scream, but still held his face between her legs with her hands. 'Ah wanna come three times, make me scream three times, baby, do it, do it.'

Nick breezed into the office eating a hamburger, and Rosie wrinkled her nose.

'That's full of cholesterol, not good for you, Nick.'

'I know, but I like it.'

He sat in Lorraine's chair and swivelled round, stuffing the remains of the burger into his mouth as Rooney walked in.

'Caught you, you've had a hamburger, I can smell it,' Rooney said accusingly to Rosie.

'I have not,' Rosie replied self-righteously, 'but he has.' She pointed to Nick, who was wiping his mouth on his shirt cuff.

'What the hell is this place? A health clinic?'

Rooney sat on the edge of the desk, grinning at Rosie.

'Just a private joke. What you got – anything or nothing?'

Nick dug in his pockets, bringing out his scraps of notes.

'I got a line into Elizabeth Caley's doctor, pal of mine is sniffing around for me, and . . .' They waited as he thumbed his way through his crumpled papers.

'Fisher's girlfriend is rapping to a pal of mine on the drug squad, and . . .' Nick continued.

'And?' prompted Rooney. Nick ruffled his already untidy curls.

'We got to move fast, word is they're going to arrest Doc Hayleden for dealin', so I'd kind of like to get to him before the bust, may be nice if her ladyship came with me, you know, see how a real pro works!'

Rosie said she'd call Lorraine on the mobile, and was about to dial when Nick held up his hand.

'What is it with her? She got a problem with me?'

Rooney shrugged, looking across at Rosie.

'No, why do you ask?'

Nick cocked his head to one side. 'Well, I'm working my butt off, but I don't want to get screwed.'

'By Lorraine?' Rosie asked.

'Yeah, I know she's edgy about me being on this gig, so . . . I'm asking you straight: I'm in, aren't I?'

'Of course you are,' Rosie replied, and Rooney jabbed a finger into Nick's chest.

'Listen, we cut this four ways and that's it.'

Nick grinned. 'Okay, just needed it confirmed . . . is she screwing anyone? Not metaphorically. Just wondered.'

Rooney laughed. 'You don't stand a chance, Nick. Does he, Rosie?'

She hunched her shoulders. 'I dunno, but do you want me to contact her or not? She's over at Caley's office.'

Nick grinned again. 'You call her, but don't you say nothin' – about anything personal.'

Lorraine remained at Caley's office desk, making notes, monitored by Mark and Margaret, but she called for no assistance from either of them. She sat at the big desk, ploughing methodically through the thick file, knowing it had been checked over by all the other investigators, but she could not afford to skim just in case she missed

162

something. By six o'clock she had half-filled her note-book, and she sat back in the big leather chair.

Robert Caley's finances were stretched to the limit. It appeared that all his money was tied up in properties, which still made him a rich man but one with no ready cash-flow. As he had told her, he had banked everything on the casino deal, and if it did not come off, he would still have to pay off the outstanding monies due on the land. If his partners pulled out, he would lose millions and would be forced to sell properties fast and thus at a loss in order to pay his debts. Lorraine had no access to information about Elizabeth Caley's fortune and as far as she could ascertain, the Caleys did not have any form of joint finances or joint accounts.

Mark looked at the monitor and saw Lorraine stand up and stretch her arms above her head, yawning. He watched her close the file and begin to pack away her things.

'I think she's through,' he said to Margaret. She was talking to Robert Caley's chauffeur, who had just got back to the office.

Margaret pursed her lips. 'I hope he's not going to be late, Mario left him at the Bel Air. That bitch Saffron Dulay, dunno why he even sees her.'

Mark shrugged as he pointed to the video screen. 'It's called being fucking rich, Margaret! Mrs Page is leaving. Can you blast the air conditioning on in there? She's been smoking . . .'

Mark hovered as Lorraine walked out of the office carrying the file. 'You all finished?'

'Yes, thank you. Is Mr Caley here?'

'No, I'm sorry, he's at a meeting and then he has another one at six o'clock. Do you need to speak to him?'

'Er, well, not really, just thank him for me, would you?' She passed him the file. 'And, oh, just one thing. Mrs Caley, she has nothing to do with the business here, am I correct?'

'Yes.'

'I see, and she has not financed any of the real estate companies?'

'Not to my knowledge,' he said tartly.

'They have no joint interests?'

'None that I am aware of.' He carried the file to a cabinet. Lorraine followed, standing just behind him.

'She is very wealthy then, in her own right?'

'Yes, I believe so, but I work for Mr Caley. I have never been privy to Mrs Caley's private finances.'

'But you must have some idea of what she's worth. I mean, is it a few million, one million or a sort of clutch of millions?' she smiled jokingly but he would not give an inch.

'I really have no idea, perhaps you should discuss it with Mrs Caley herself.' He turned as Margaret approached with Mario. 'Mario, will you walk Mrs Page to the elevator? I'll inform security she's leaving. This is Mr Caley's chauffeur, Mario, Mrs Page.'

Mario nodded and headed for the door, holding it open for her. They went down in the elevator together.

'I thought Mr Caley was still out.'

'He is, ma'am.'

'Are you employed by both Mr and Mrs Caley?'

'Yes, ma'am, eight years now.'

He gestured for her to go to the security desk and she unpinned her badge, handing it over. He then opened the main doors of the building for her.

She hesitated. 'Did you know Anna Louise?'

'Yes, ma'am, I sometimes drove her and Mrs Caley.'

'Did you drive her to any specific place? Particularly just before her disappearance, anywhere unusual?'

'No, ma'am, I only used to drive them on shopping trips, sometimes to a social event, but Miss Caley had her own car. She was a really cute girl, always polite, always treated me with respect.'

'And Mrs Caley?'

'I'm sorry?' He looked away.

'Did Mrs Caley treat you with respect?'

'Yes, ma'am.' He still held the door open but she got the feeling he wanted to get rid of her.

'Did you drive Mrs Caley to and from her doctor's at all?'

'No, ma'am.'

'Really? So you only drove Mrs Caley infrequently? Just shopping trips, a few social events?'

'Yes, ma'am, that is correct.'

'Did you ever take Mrs Caley to a Mrs Juda Salina's apartment over on Doheny?'

'I did sometimes take them.'

'Them?'

'Ah, well, yes, Miss Anna Louise went to see Mrs Salina a few times. Mrs Salina used to come by the house but Mr Caley didn't like it, so then they used to go to her place.'

'Did Anna Louise ever go by herself to Juda Salina?'

'Er, maybe, once or twice.'

'Immediately before she disappeared?'

'I don't want any trouble, please. Mr Caley doesn't know I took them, he didn't like her, and I don't believe in all that stuff.'

'So Anna Louise went to Mrs Salina's just before they left for New Orleans, yes?'

He nodded his head.

165

'You're from New Orleans, aren't you, Mario?'

He seemed to be very uneasy and the sweat stood out on his forehead. 'Yes, ma'am, a number of the Caleys' employees used to work for her family, and sometimes we go back there with them, when they're gonna stay a while.'

'If I need to talk with you, Mario . . .'

'You can call me at the house or here, Mrs Page. I live in, I got an apartment over the garages.'

Mario looked at the security section, then back at Lorraine. He took out his card and wrote on the back. 'That's my portable, you can always get me on my portable, but you got to know I got nothing to say about Mrs Caley, or Mr Caley. They're fine people and I am real cut up about Miss Anna Louise, as is everyone that knows them.'

Lorraine slipped the card into her pocket and smiled. 'I'm sure it must be a very distressing time for everyone. Thank you, Mario.'

She walked out of the building and headed towards the car park. She saw the white stretch limo parked by the security gate. Robert Caley was bending into the passenger side, with his back to her. Lorraine hurried along the neat pathway and took a short cut across the grass, ducking under the white barrier. She was within feet of Robert Caley, who seemed angry.

'All I'm asking is for you to see if he'll give me time. Jesus, you play games, you know that?'

'Me? *You* play the games, Caley, you get what you deserve. What you want me to do? Tell my daddy that you'll go down on him?'

'I'll tell your daddy what his fucking bitch of a daughter gets up to . . .'

'Hi, I was just leaving,' Lorraine said from directly behind him. He whipped round, the door of the limo

166

ajar, and she could see the still naked Saffron lying on the back seat. He slammed the door shut, the car backed away from the barrier and did a U-turn.

'That was some meeting,' Lorraine said, smiling.

He covered fast, shrugging his shoulders. 'Yeah, but sometimes old partners can push their luck.'

She could see a small muscle at the side of his jaw twitching and she continued to smile. 'Thank you for letting me use your office.'

'Any time.' His hands were clenched at his sides and although she knew he was trying hard to be civil, his eyes gave him away. 'If you'll excuse me, I have an appointment.'

'Sure, if I need to speak to you again . . .'

He was walking away. 'You know where I am, Mrs Page.'

As Lorraine turned around towards her car, the security guard tipped his hand to his hat and headed towards her.

'Evening, Mrs Page.' He walked with her to her car. He even took her keys to unlock the car for her, holding the door wide. Everyone in the place seemed over-polite.

'Must have been up in the seventies today,' he remarked, making conversation, waiting for his tip. She passed him five bucks.

'That was a nice limo.'

'The big white one?'

'Yeah, with the Louisiana plates. Whose is it?'

'Used to come by a lot but not lately, business associate of Mr Caley's.' He shut the car door, tapping the roof with his hand. She wondered if she gave him another five bucks whether he would recall whose limo it was, and she lowered the window, keeping a fixed smile in place.

He lifted the security pole for her to drive through. As she came alongside him, she let the smile drop.

'Who owns the limo, pal? Save me time checking it out at the station. Yeah, that's right, I'm a cop, we come in all shapes and sizes now.'

He hesitated. 'Miss Saffron Dulay, she's Lloyd Dulay's daughter, he uses her limo when he's here in LA.'

'Thank you,' Lorraine said crisply, driving out through the barrier. So that was the business meeting. Well, maybe it was; Lloyd Dulay, Robert Caley had told her, was one of the casino partners, the brewery magnate.

Lorraine was heading back towards Hollywood when Nick called her on the mobile.

'Hi, honey. If we wanna talk to Caley's doc, we got to make it quick. I got a tip-off he's gonna get busted, so meet me there as soon as you can make it.'

'Okay, I'll head straight over there, I've just got to make one call on the way.' She punched out the office number.

'Hi, Bill, anythin'?'

'Nope,' he answered. 'How you doin'?'

'I had a couple of hours at Caley's office, I got some names to check out. He gave me access to the casino deal file, which makes interesting reading. Will you dig up what you can about Lloyd Dulay's daughter? She's in Hollywood, name's Saffron Dulay. I think Robert Caley's got a scene going with her, so can you check her out?'

'Sure, but Lorraine—'

She knew he was about to hassle her about wasting time in LA. 'I got to go now, I'm on my way to meet Nick.'

The line went dead. Rosie leaned over Rooney's

shoulder, reading his notes. 'Who's Saffron . . . what's the name?'

'Dulay, daughter of one of the guys on the casino deal, rich, rich family. Lorraine seems to think Robert Caley's screwing her, so I'll check her out, start ringing round the social columns and society diaries.'

Rosie nodded. 'I'll do that, if you like.'

'Okay, thanks. You smell nice, you wearin' perfume?'

Rosie beamed. 'It's gardenia.'

'Smells nice, fresh.'

'Thank you.'

'S'okay.'

Nick watched Lorraine drive into the car park adjacent to the doctor's surgery on Santa Monica and Bedford, get out and head towards the building. He liked the way she walked, with long, easy strides. A raunchy woman, he thought to himself, *all* woman. Even with her blonde hair all ruffled and her suit crumpled, she looked good to him. He'd always liked leggy, tough blondes and Lorraine was a natural, kind of coordinated. He couldn't help but smile, intuitively guessing she was also raunchy in bed.

'What's so funny?' she snapped.

'Nothin', but you look like you want to sock somebody. You in a raw mood, are you?'

'Yeah,' but she was smiling when she answered. Nick Bartello had that ability to put you at your ease immediately.

He gave her that great smile of his. 'Okay, this is what's going down. You wanna sit in my jeep? I'm in the Doc's parking bay. He's inside by the way, but he's also gonna be *inside* inside sooner than he knows.'

They crossed to a beat-up Cherokee jeep; even the seats were torn and shredded.

'Holy shit, Nick, where'd you get this?'

'Engine's good an' it was cheap. My dog screwed up the seats.' He whistled, and a weird, long-haired head shot up from the back seat.

'This is Tiger. Tiger, meet Lorraine Page, of Page Investigations.'

The dog, part German Shepherd and part sheepdog or maybe wolfhound, was as unkempt-looking as its owner, its freaky pale blue eyes like Nick's.

'Found him in a trash can two years ago, he's a great guard dog but he craps everywhere, so he kinda lives in the jeep.'

'Yeah, I can see that.' Lorraine looked over the disgusting jeep's seats; a food bowl, a water bowl, and an old blanket, along with Tiger, occupied the entire back seat. As Lorraine sat inside and shut the door, Tiger gave a low, rumbling growl.

'Hey, back off, this is my partner.'

Tiger settled down, his head resting on Nick's shoulder as he tapped out a cigarette from a squashed pack of Kools.

'Remember the Fisher guy I told you about? My now deceased informant?'

Lorraine nodded.

'Well, I made some more enquiries, autopsy report revealed it wasn't a heroin OD but a blood clot, caused by injecting temazepam, that caused death. Kind of makes sense because he'd said the last time I met him he wasn't using, but I just presumed he'd got back on the smack. His type usually do. This doctor is sellin' prescriptions like it's going out of fashion and he is still supplying temazepam to Elizabeth Caley. But if we want to go in there, let me do the talking. We won't have long because

Fisher's girlfriend has been rapping to the cops, they picked her up a couple of nights ago. Don't ever accuse me of not movin' my ass, I been at this since early morning. Anyway, my tip-off is they're gonna bust him any second, so if we need a bit of a lever to make him talk we can use Fisher.'

'Okay, let's go talk to the guy.'

The surgery was like a luxurious lounge, deep sofas, drapes and coffee tables, while Dr Hayleden, with his rimless glasses, pristine suit, coiffured hair and facework, resembled something from a waxworks.

'I cannot discuss any patient. Unless, of course, he or she is privy to the discussion or you have a legal, written consent form.'

Lorraine said nothing. Nick remained silent.

'So I think that concludes our interview.'

'Not quite,' Nick said softly.

'Oh, I think so. You walk in off the street, you say you are a private investigation company, you ask questions about one of my patients, and obviously one that the media know only too well, and expect me—'

'To cut the bullshit,' said Nick quietly, 'I know you have been prescribing Elizabeth Caley not just pain-killing drugs, but sleeping tablets, mild tranquillizers, right? And over a long period of time . . . only she's got enough to tranquillize a fucking elephant.'

'I don't like your insinuations, Mr Bartello.'

'Quite honestly, Doc, I don't give a fuck. I know nobody, no matter how much of an insomniac they may be, who requires per week the bulk load of temazepam you have been prescribing for Elizabeth Caley. Enough to melt down the tabs and inject six or seven times daily. Now, we're not talking the usual prescription-sized

171

orders here, I mean two hundred a time. The reason I know this is a friend of mine was also dealing for you, a Mr Fisher. He and his pals were breaking into warehouses at chemical plants and delivering to your door. I know and you know, Doc, anybody doing that amount of gear is heading for thrombosis, like our pal Mr Fisher. He is dead, you know that?'

Dr Hayleden stared hard at Nick, trying not to show that he knew exactly what he was talking about. But they'd got to him, they could feel it. The sweat was breaking out on his forehead and his eyes widened in panic. Lorraine kicked Nick's ankle lightly – no way did they want to frighten him too much.

Lorraine leaned forward. 'We're not from the drug squad, this is a private investigation. All we need to know is if Robert Caley is aware of what his wife is hooked on.'

'I don't know of any patient on my books called Fisher.' Dr Hayleden was sweating profusely, his perfect hair-weave now damp round the edges, his lips dried out as he constantly flicked his tongue from corner to corner of his mouth. 'You must understand, if a patient insists on misusing prescribed drugs there is little I can do about it.'

Nick got up. 'If a doc continues to prescribe drugs knowing the dangers, I'd say he was in shit up to his armpits. Why don't you answer the question? Better still, tell us if Robert Caley has ever picked up one of your little sweetie bags for his wife in person.'

Fifteen minutes later Nick and Lorraine knew that Elizabeth Caley was sometimes ordering over a thousand tabs a week and that Hayleden, never having met Robert

172

Caley, had no reason to believe he was in any way aware of his wife's drug abuse. Mrs Caley's personal assistant had on occasion collected the tablets. Anna Louise Caley had never at any time been to his surgery.

By the time Nick and Lorraine had driven back to Pasadena, the LA drug squad had arrested Hayleden. He was to be charged with the selling of prescriptions and illegal drugs, would probably get off with just a fine, and be struck off the medical board. But his type just moved on and started up again in another state. Elizabeth Caley, using an assumed name, was only one of his many clients. Her real name would probably never even be linked to the case.

Over dinner back at the apartment, Nick remained adamant that Robert Caley was still their main suspect. Rooney listened as Nick and Lorraine filled him and Rosie in on their session with the doctor. The consensus was that they should now begin work in New Orleans. Only Lorraine held back, not satisfied that Robert Caley was their number one suspect. The others felt she was becoming obsessive with the Juda Salina scenario, and she insisted she still needed to talk with Phyllis again and have yet another session with both Elizabeth and Robert Caley.

Nick threw his hands up in agitation. 'Why the fuck are you wasting time, sweetheart? It's Caley, he's got the motive.'

Rooney nodded in agreement. 'Yeah, we got to prove it though, Nick.'

Nick wound some spaghetti round his fork and looked at Lorraine. 'You give us reasons why we don't go for him, push him hard.'

'I honestly don't have one, just a gut feeling.'

'You mean you want to get into his pants,' Nick said, laughing.

Lorraine sprang up. 'Fuck you, that isn't true. All I'm saying is, if he was involved in his own daughter's disappearance, why give me access to his private files, why give me reasons or a fucking big motive? He's not hiding anything, on the contrary.'

Nick poured a beer which he had brought himself because he knew neither Lorraine nor Rosie drank. 'Hey! Let's just hold it there. A guilty man is bound to want you to know before you find out, rules of the game, Lorraine, you know that. And you caught him out with Saffron what's her name. We have got to move fast so that Elizabeth Caley doesn't kill herself before we get him or we'll lose out on that one million pay-off.'

Lorraine felt tired out. 'You got anything on Saffron Dulay, Rosie?'

Rosie, more official then ever, opened her note-book. 'For starters, she's had more husbands than I've had hot dinners. She's the only daughter and heir to a fortune and she puts it about, a lot. I contacted Melissa Dewhurst from the Hollywood grub mag and she filled me in without much preamble because Saffron sued her magazine for a lotta bucks 'cos Melissa wrote some article implying she was a nympho. By the way, she sued another mag because it hinted that she'd had breast implants. Judging from the pics I got sent over, I'd say she's had a lot more than her tits lifted, she looks fantastic. And take a look at the apartment she lives in.' Rosie spread out the magazine pictures.

Nick leaned forward and whistled. 'Now, she's a motive. What a body, and rich with it, nice one. Lorraine, have a look at her with clothes on. You saw her in the back of a limo at Robert Caley's place bareass naked, right?'

Rooney stared. 'You're kiddin' me!'

Lorraine sat back, pushing her half-finished plate away. She opened her briefcase and passed out her notes from Caley's office files, putting them on to the table. 'Don't get food over them, but you two, and you, Rosie, should get clued up.' She got up from the table.

'What about Robert Caley?' Nick asked, uptight.

'That is about him, Nick, just read it, all of it.'

Nick yawned, winking at Rooney. 'How about a drink? We can go through these in a bar.'

Rooney snapped the book shut. 'Okay by me. See you tomorrow, Rosie, thanks for the spaghetti.' He leaned over and kissed her cheek. It took her by surprise, and she blushed.

Nick gave her a wink as he held open the door for Rooney to pass. 'Goodnight, see ya tomorrow.'

Rosie started clearing the table. It was nice having men around the place, it was a good feeling, and as she passed a mirror carrying the dirty plates to the sink, she gave herself a quick glance. Maybe tomorrow she should have her hair trimmed, start wearing a bit of make-up. Rooney's peck on the cheek had meant a lot; she hadn't been kissed by a man for a very long time. Not that Rooney had kissed her properly, but it was a show of affection and she hadn't had much of that either.

Lorraine remained sitting at the table as Rosie began clearing up. She could hear Rooney and Nick laughing in the street below. She got up and stood by the window, looking out, then turned to Rosie.

'Goodnight, Rosie, go to bed now, it's late, and I'm tired out.'

'Goodnight. Turn off the air conditioner or you won't sleep.'

Lorraine turned off the air conditioning, then the lights, and stood in the semi-darkness by the window, arms folded, deep in thought. Nick Bartello had virtually taken over the case, she knew it, and she knew she would have to top him, to prove not only to Rosie but to Rooney that she was still running the show. He was ahead of her and he was good, she knew that. He might be laid back but he had come up with motives, and good ones. Was she losing her touch? Had her physical attraction to Caley made her fail to see through him? She sighed as she lay down on her sofa bed.

Was Robert Caley capable of covering up why his own daughter had been abducted, possibly murdered? Or was it Elizabeth Caley covering up not only her drug addiction but something more sinister? If so, why the hiring of private investigators? Unless it was a role she was acting out from one of her old movies?

Lorraine yawned, feeling her eyes droop with tiredness. Either way, she was convinced that the key to the disappearance of Anna Louise Caley was connected to her parents. The question was, which one? They had only two weeks to get that million, and two days were already gone.

The faces became blurred; one moment Nick Bartello was calling out to her, then Lubrinski. She was trying to drag the body to safety from a hail of bullets . . . She was screaming, the body was heavy, bleeding and moaning. Lubrinski's face became Nick Bartello's, then Lubrinski's again, and she was weeping, unaware she was crying out loud. It was her own cry that woke her: just before she came to, the man cradled in her arms had become Robert Caley. She sat up shaking, panting for breath, her body drenched in sweat, and it took her a moment to realize where she was. Then she flopped back on to her pillows, closing her eyes, but she couldn't go back to sleep. She didn't want the nightmare to return, didn't want to go back to the memory of Jack Lubrinski dying in her arms. She felt cold, very cold.

Nick Bartello was so like Lubrinski. He too always kept his notes in his back pocket, ripping pages out of her book to write in his thin, scrawled, unorthodox shorthand.

Rosie had heard the screams. She had sat bolt upright in her bed listening then crept to her door. She eased it open and peeked into the living room. She saw Lorraine curled up like a little girl, hands clenched under her chin.

'You all right, partner?' she whispered.

'Yep, just had a bad dream. Did I wake you?'

'Nope, see you in the morning.'

'Rosie, you always go for the same kind of guy?'

Rosie leaned over the sofa and gently stroked Lorraine's hair. 'Listen, I been without one for so long, I'd go with anything offered, short or tall, fat or skinny, bald, blond or dark. Maybe not a red-head, never fancied red-haired guys.'

Lorraine turned over and smiled up at Rosie. She had such a lovely, sweet smile, it was sad she so rarely used it. 'I always liked dark-haired guys. You know, maybe that is what I need.'

'What?' Rosie looked worried.

'A man.'

Rosie laughed. 'Thank Christ for that, I thought you were gonna say a drink. Mind you, in my experience they're both as bad for you.'

'Yeah, I guess so.'

Rosie's gentle hand stroking her head was calming and Lorraine was asleep before she knew it. She didn't even feel Rosie carefully lay her duvet cover over her, didn't know Rosie waited until she was asleep, watching in part-fascination as Lorraine's long slender hands slowly

177

uncurled from fists. It was moments like these that made
it all right between them; only to Rosie did Lorraine show
her frightening vulnerability. Whatever bad dreams made
her scream in such a terrible way were never referred to.
But they were now less frequent, like her sweet smiles.

CHAPTER 7

LORRAINE ARRIVED at the Caley home at two minutes to eleven, exactly two minutes before the appointment time which had been agreed through Rosie and Phyllis, but Mrs Caley was with her beautician and asked if Lorraine would be kind enough to wait. Lorraine was furious, and told Peters, the dour butler, that it was impossible for her to wait as she had other pressing business, and eventually Elizabeth agreed to see her despite the inconvenience, and she was led into the sun room.

Elizabeth had a thick face-mask on, a soft towelling robe belted at the waist and a towel wrapped around her head. Two young women in white uniforms were hovering around her, one giving her a pedicure, the other a manicure. They were in the small massage room off the gymnasium built on to the rear of the house, with a polished pine sprung floor, weights, bicycles and a punchbag, and leather reclining chairs. Classical music drifted from hidden speakers and all the blinds were drawn on the arched windows, excluding the morning sunlight.

'Mrs Page, this is Angela at my feet, and Barbara.'

The two pretty, immaculately groomed girls smiled and continued working.

'Pull up a chair, darling.'

Lorraine drew a wicker basket chair forwards and sat down. 'Thanks for seeing me, Mrs Caley.'

Elizabeth was sipping her usual mint tea from a china cup placed on a small side table. 'My dear, I am paying you, if you need to ask me about anything it would be rather stupid not to see you, would it not?' She eased up into a sitting position and sipped her tea again. 'You have any news for me?'

'No, not yet, I'm sorry.'

Barbara finished the last coat of blood-red varnish on Mrs Caley's left hand and stood up. 'I'm all through, Mrs Caley.'

'Thank you, Barbara.'

'I won't be a moment, Mrs Caley, then I'll take your mask off,' said Angela, as she carefully massaged oil into the delicate feet.

Lorraine did not want to ask any questions until the face-pack had been peeled, the skin cleaned with tonic lotion, then massaged and moisturized. It took a long time. Elizabeth kept her eyes closed throughout.

Angela gave a series of small discreet smiles to Lorraine and then whispered, 'She's asleep.'

Lorraine smiled understandingly back when she would really have liked to get up and shake Elizabeth Caley awake. But she sat there like a fool as Angela crept around, packing up her vanity case. When she finished, she gave a silly little wave and crept out, closing the door silently.

Elizabeth remained motionless, head tilted back on the head rest, seemingly deeply asleep. Lorraine stared at her first with irritation, then with a strange fascination: there wasn't a line on the woman's face or neck and, completely devoid of make-up, her skin was still flawless. Her beautiful hands rested on the white towel robe, and she was absolutely still.

Lorraine suddenly felt panic-stricken – was she dead? She eased out of her chair and crept closer, sighing with

180

relief when she could see her breathing, deep, slow, rhythmic breaths. Elizabeth Caley had a perfect face: cheekbones, nose, chin, lips – whether they were man-made or not was immaterial. Lorraine looked over the sleeping woman – could she really be ramming that amount of junk into herself? She could see no needle tracks, none on her slender marble-white arms, and none between her toes. Then she saw a small bruise and needle puncture on the right side of her neck, but only one. If Elizabeth Caley was injecting herself, then she must be very adept, possibly using her groin. But to move aside the towelling robe could wake her and God knows what the implications of that would be. Lorraine checked her watch and walked out, leaving the sleeping Mrs Caley to her Beethoven concerto.

Peters was unsure, but Lorraine made it clear that as she had been hired by Mr and Mrs Caley to trace their daughter, it would be necessary to see Anna Louise's room.

'Perhaps you should ask Mr Caley for his permission,' she said impatiently.

'I'm afraid Mr Caley is dining out this evening.'

'Well, it's up to you, Peters, you are capable of making a decision, aren't you?'

It was no simple room but a vast suite consisting of a bedroom, lounge area and a bathroom bigger than Rosie's entire apartment. It was like a showcase: unreal, unlived in, nothing out of place. The furnishings were soft shell-pinks and whites, and the king-sized bed had a row of white stuffed bears so pristine they were obviously for show rather than ever having been used as toys.

Lorraine slowly looked around; no normal, full-blooded young girl could occupy this room and leave no trace of herself. She sat on the bed and let her eyes take in every corner, as if hoping the room itself would talk to

181

her. She asked herself where she would put something if she wanted to hide it. Was there some kind of hidden safe?

She moved through the suite, her feet buried in the soft thick oyster-pink pile of the carpet. She looked beneath the bed and found nothing, she searched behind the curtains, underneath the scatter-cushions and the bears: nothing. She went into the bathroom, looked inside the huge cabinet, the toilet cistern: nothing. She went back into the vast walk-in wardrobe and looked through the shelves: nothing, not even a faint smell of old perfume on any of the clothes. They seemed, like everything else, unused and unworn. She was just about to return to Mrs Caley when something caught her eye. All the shoe boxes had the contents stamped on cards – sandals, mules, loafers, brown, black, cream, etc. – apart from one; it had the same neat card, but without any description at all; it was blank.

Lorraine eased the box out and discovered it was a designer-made shoe box, the cardboard covered in white silk. She took the lid off and smiled to herself. Inside she found little bundles of letters, birthday cards, mementos, a Valentine card. At last she was finding something interesting, something she could get a fix on. She opened the Valentine card.

My one and only Valentine. Love, Polar.

Most of the other birthday and little gift cards were from Anna Louise's various aunts and uncles, her mother and father, but five cards in all, accompanying floral deliveries, were from the same Polar guy. Lorraine sifted through the box, reading the letters. There were poems and a couple of invitations to college functions.

She found nothing of interest until she had almost emptied the box – then she saw the condoms, held together with an elastic band. Anna Louise sure as hell had a neater-than-neat complex. Next came out several matchbooks, also tied together, not from any elegant restaurants but from the Viper Room, On the Rox, and the Snake Pit – all notorious nightclubs. But not until she drew out the pornographic magazines did she sit back, because they were not cheap material bought over the counter, but heavy hardcore porn.

She flicked through them and found a folded note sellotaped to one of the centre-folds. Written on the note in tiny neat capital letters were the words,

I LOVE YOU, I WANT TO FUCK YOU, I WANT YOU TO WANT ME, I WANT TO TAKE IT UP THE ASS, I WANT YOU TO LICK MY PUSSY UNTIL I COME AND I WANT YOUR DICK IN MY MOUTH. SMACK ME HARD, PLEASE, PLEASE HURT ME AND KISS ME BETTER.

Lorraine slipped it into her pocket; it was the only thing she took out of the room. She had checked that the childish print was Anna Louise's against one of her poems before slotting the 'shoe box' back into place.

Peters was standing at the bottom of the stairs as she slowly made her way down.

'It is a very beautiful room.'

'Yes, it is. Mrs Caley is still sleeping and I really do not think I should wake her.'

'I'll come back tomorrow morning, say about nine.'

'Mrs Caley does not rise until ten-thirty.'

She hesitated. 'I'll be here at eleven. Goodnight.'

Lorraine called Nick from the car.

'Hi, how ya doing?'

'You fancy going clubbing?'

'What?'

'You know the club the Viper Room?'

Nick laughed. 'You're a bit old, sweetheart, and far be

183

it from me to say, not famous enough. You won't get past the door.'

'Wanna bet? Pick me up from Rosie's about eleven-thirty.'

Nick hesitated. 'Shit, Lorraine, I ain't no dancer, I got one and a half fuckin' legs. What's this about? You come across another chick screwing Robert Caley?'

'Nope, I just got an insight into our sweet angel Anna Louise, some guy called Polar was givin' it to her up the ass. See you later. And, Nick, have a bath, maybe a shave, huh?'

Lorraine replaced the portable, well pleased. She figured she had now come up with something that no one else had even hinted at knowing. She was buzzing, and fully intended driving straight back to her apartment, and then on to an AA meeting before meeting Nick at the Viper Room. She had no intention of going to see Juda Salina again, but she pulled over as she drove along Doheny Drive, checked the time, and sat thinking for a moment. She couldn't understand why she felt so drawn to follow up Juda Salina, but she was – maybe because Anna Louise had visited her, maybe because she knew intuitively that the woman knew a lot more about the missing girl than she was admitting. If she had the mystic connection she claimed with Anna Louise, maybe she might have some insight into who the character calling himself Polar was . . . And as Lorraine was virtually on her doorstep, why not?

Lorraine pressed the intercom from the main apartment entrance. This time she was not about to play games trying to get in or out without permission. A bored voice asked who was calling.

'My name is Lorraine Page, I need to speak with Mrs Salina.'

'She's sleepin' right now.'

'Then wake her up, this is important.'

'What you say your name was?'

The main door to the apartments opened and she stepped inside, heading directly down to the apartment along the narrow corridor.

Juda slapped Raoul across the face, hard, and he pressed himself against the wall.

'I dunno who she was, and you gotta a lot of freaks comin' in, all jumpy and sayin' it's important. I thought she was a client.'

She pushed at him again. 'I said you check out my appointment book, you don't let nobody in here unless *I* say so. Now you've gone and let this bitch in, well, I'm not seeing her.'

'I said you was sleepin' and she said to wake you.'

'Fine, now you tell her I'm sick and not getting up for her or nobody else, you got it?'

The door-bell rang and Juda swayed down to her bedroom, slamming the door shut. Raoul inched open the door, leaving it on the chain.

'Hi, it's Lorraine Page.'

'She can't see you, she's sick.'

'Who are you?'

'Raoul, Ah'm her . . . Ah is her driver.'

'Okay, Raoul, go tell Mrs Salina that unless she gives me ten minutes, I'm gonna go to the guy who runs these apartments and I'm gonna tell him that your aunt is runnin' a business out of this exclusive apartment block. Now you go and make sure she understands that I am not moving away from this door.'

Banished to the kitchen, the door firmly closed, Raoul put the kettle on. He was already wishing he hadn't come to LA, but he couldn't go back home, not for a

185

while, and he had no other place to go. Living with his aunt was hideous; only if he sat in the box-like kitchen could he escape her bulk, but it was dark and claustrophobic, and Raoul didn't like the dark, didn't like what happened in the darkness.

Juda lit an incense stick and wafted it for a moment. Lorraine sat in the same chair she had before.

'I didn't mean to be so pushy, Mrs Salina, but I really needed to ask you some questions.'

'I'm sick, I got a migraine.' She was wearing big dark glasses, another tent-like creation folded around her massive body, and a green turban. The long red talons wafted the heady incense perfume across the room, making Lorraine's eyes water.

'You never told me that Anna Louise Caley came to see you.'

'I don't recall you askin'.'

'Did she come to you the day before she left for New Orleans?'

Juda sighed. 'I'll check my book, but you know, I already told you I have to respect my clients' confidence.' She eased herself up and swayed slowly to the door, opening it. The apartment was so small she didn't need to shout but she did. 'Raoul, get me mah appointment book.'

Raoul appeared at the door and passed a red leather book to his aunt. 'Go get the car, Raoul, I need to be some place in fifteen minutes. Park outside, go on now, get your butt moving.' She shut the door and flipped open the book.

'Mrs Salina, I don't want to see your appointment book, I want you to tell me if Anna Louise—'

Juda shoved the book under Lorraine's nose. 'You see, Miss Page, you threaten me and tell me you're gonna report me. Now, there it is in black and white, whole

186

weeks before February fifteenth, and there is no Anna Louise listed, okay?'

Lorraine stood up, flicking through the book, and saw that Juda did actually have an appointment that afternoon with a client called Eunice Bourdreaux. She closed the book. 'Thank you. Why did Mrs Caley bring Anna Louise, were you reading her cards too?'

'Sometimes she needed assistance, she used not to feel so good.'

'I know why she didn't feel so good, she was out of her head on drugs, so Anna Louise used to . . . what? Help her down the corridor?'

Juda shrugged. Like her nephew, she seemed to enjoy slipping in and out of her Southern accent, sometimes accentuating it, other times not. Now she drawled, elongating her vowels.

'Ah do not know about any drugs, Ah don't know what you are trying to imply or why you are so interested. The little girl came, sat awhile and when Ahhh finished the session with her mother they left.'

'Did you talk to Anna Louise, I mean, read her palm or tarot cards, for example?'

'I may have, I don't recall . . . mah client was Mrs Elizabeth Caley.'

Lorraine sucked in her breath; the woman really annoyed her, with her sing-song voice and her huge dark glasses. She crossed her legs, one foot swinging with irritation.

'You read tarot cards, you read palms, you feel people's auras, and according to all those credentials you got pinned up on your walls, you also call yourself a medium . . . and you're saying you cannot remember? Now, I personally don't believe in all this, but that is just my opinion.'

'You are entitled to your opinion, honey.'

'I also know that you hand out a leaflet, where you state you assist with police enquiries. But the police told me you never helped solve any case. You just got a lot of publicity from it, and judging from the red appointment book, I'd say you need a whole lot more. It's not exactly bulging with clients now, is it?'

Juda smiled, her hands resting over her belly. 'Right now I'm not doin' so much business, in fact I might just well retire.'

'Unless you don't always note down your clients. So let me ask you again, did Anna Louise Caley ever come to see you alone?'

Juda remained smiling, then shrugged her fat shoulders. 'No, she did not. Like I said, she just came a few times with Mrs Caley.'

'Who is the young man that let me in?'

'Raoul? He's my nephew, I am taking care of him, Miss Page, that's all. Nothing illegal about that now, is there?'

Lorraine leaned forward. 'What did Anna Louise ask you about? Was she worried about something? Was she scared of something?'

Juda sighed but did not answer. Lorraine was becoming angry at her inability to get Juda to talk. She tried a different tactic, almost pleading.

'I am trying to find her, Mrs Salina, so if there is anything she said to you that would give me an insight into a problem she may have had, even a relationship . . .?'

Juda turned away.

'Was she seeing someone? Mrs Salina, don't give me any more clients' confidentiality, et cetera. Please, Anna Louise has been missing without trace for eleven months.'

'I have been interviewed over and over again and if

188

there was anything, don't you think I would have already told the police, told the other private dicks? But there is nothing, and what I saw for Mrs Caley has nothing to do with anything.'

'Okay. What did you see *for* Mrs Caley? Please.'

Juda licked her lips. 'I saw nothing good, I saw she needed to go to a rehab clinic, I saw she would have marriage problems, I saw that she might have a resurrection of her career, a lot of publicity, but not good . . .'

Lorraine wanted to snatch the dark shades off her fat face, but instead she gave up. 'You know, people like you make me sick.'

'I think you made that clear the last time, honey, but to be honest I am not struck by you all that much. You think you can push your way into my home, make threats, only because you're being paid a lot of cash to do so. You ain't offerin' any to me, and even if you did I'd throw it back in your smug face. I suggest you start taking lessons in politeness because you are a rude bitch. Like I said before, I got nothing to say or add to what I already told the police and what I told you the last time you came burstin' into my home.'

Lorraine walked to the door, opened it. 'You still see a big bright aura round Anna Louise Caley? You still telling that poor woman to keep up hope? Well, I may be pushy, I may be getting paid for my job but it's sure as hell a lot better than being paid for spouting bullshit to poor desperate people who could probably do with a good shrink. Thanks for nothing.'

Lorraine didn't wait for Juda to show her out but she slammed the front door hard to let the whale of a woman know she had left.

Juda remained sitting in her chair, her hands clasping the arms. She sure as hell could feel Lorraine Page's presence; one part was obvious, the bitch was a pushy ex-cop. But the other part confused Juda. To begin with she had been positive she'd felt something bad, really bad: was it because she was different from all the other PIs? After all, she was digging that much deeper. Or was it because she knew that someone with the initial L was going to be in bad trouble, like a clock whose tick-tick-ticking was about to stop, for good?

Juda had felt it the moment she had met Lorraine, that something inside that lady was about to escape from control. What it was she couldn't put her finger on, but it unsettled her and she began to be afraid, as she knew she would have to go deeper and she feared that the consequences would suck her into the darkness herself.

Lorraine stepped out on to the pavement, which was shimmering in the blistering sun. As she headed for her rented Buick parked at a meter, a limo drove out of the parking lot. She could not see the driver because of the dark tinted windows, but she recognized the car. When she had seen Phyllis get out of it earlier that morning, she'd assumed it was Elizabeth Caley's. Now as the driver's window glided down, she knew she had been wrong: Raoul, in his mirrored shades, looked towards her, smiling.

'You were on Rodeo Drive this morning with Phyllis Collins.'

He looked nonplussed.

'Mrs Caley's companion,' Lorraine said, as she walked towards him.

Raoul gave an even wider smile. 'Maybe I was, but to tell you the honest truth, ma'am, I am new around town so I don't know where I am or who's in the back . . .'

Lorraine moved closer until she could see her own face in his mirrored shades.

'How long have you been staying with your aunt?'

'Oh, a while, maybe a few weeks.'

'You came here from New Orleans?'

'Yes, ma'am, I did, no work back home.'

'Did you know Anna Louise Caley?'

He turned off the engine and removed the keys. 'Who?'

'Anna Louise Caley, you know who I'm talking about.'

He sucked at the small monkey-like mascot dangling on the end of his key ring. 'I know, well, I read about her but I never met her. I seen her photographs, ma aunty show-n them to me, and I know she was real pretty.'

'Didn't you meet her in New Orleans?'

'No, ma'am.'

Lorraine stepped back, sure he was lying. 'Thanks for letting me into the apartment.'

'That's okay, you have a nice day now.' As she walked off he shouted out to her, 'Hey! Miss! Hey!'

She turned back to him; he was leaning out of the window, his elbows resting along the rim, still sucking the key ring.

'You shouldn't be so mean to my aunt.'

'What?'

'She is not the kind of person you want to get on the bad side of. Trust me, you be nice to her.'

'Why?'

'Maybe she's seen bad things for you, she's got the . . .' He tapped the centre of his forehead. 'You cause any trouble for her and she'll make bad things happen, she's got the sight, know what I mean? Bye now, ma'am, and lemme tell you, you got real nice legs.'

He eased back inside the car and she heard loud music begin to thud out, some kind of screaming reggae, then

191

the window slowly closed. She felt uneasy, because, although it was the middle of the day and hot, she suddenly felt icy cold.

She unlocked her car and got inside. She could still see the car parked up ahead of her; Mrs Juda Salina was obviously not that short of money. She started the engine, pulling her safety belt on. She stayed there for another five minutes and physically jumped when the phone rang.

'Hi, it's me, just checking in.' It was Rosie. Lorraine kept her eyes on Juda's limo up ahead.

'Rooney's here and wants a word,' Rosie said, sounding loud and perky. Rooney came on the line.

'We got to get over to New Orleans real soon, I don't wanna talk to my contacts there over the phone, better face to face. You got anything?'

'I want anything you can get, from anyone you can get it from, on this Juda Salina bitch, the so-called psychic.'

'I think we got as much as we could. She's a joke, isn't she?'

Lorraine saw Juda exit from the apartments and get into the waiting car. 'She's got a young nephew staying, Raoul, from New Orleans, comes on like a young Lothario, à la Robert de Niro. Get him checked out, try the same surname for starters. If you get nowhere, use the licence number; fat woman can't drive and the car's got Louisiana plates.'

Rooney jotted down the registration. 'Okay, but you know we got to get over there. Time's moving fast, we only got two weeks – three days down already.'

'Yeah, yeah, I know. Ask Rosie if she's gonna go to a meeting this evening and if it's one Phyllis attends . . . shit, hold on.'

Lorraine saw Raoul drive off, honking his car horn as he inched into the traffic. She swerved out, narrowly missing an oncoming car that hooted at her. She waved her hand in apology, the phone tucked under her chin.

'Hi, it's me. It's Rosie,' came her bellow.

'You meeting tonight?' asked Lorraine, heading up Doheny about four cars behind Raoul.

'Yep, you want to come?'

'I will if Phyllis will be there.'

'She will be – she usually is.'

'Okay, see you later, bye now.'

Rosie replaced the phone. 'She's got a thing about this Juda Salina. Dunno why, waste of time, I think. I mean, I was there, I met her, and Nick checked her out.'

'You think she's a flake too?' Rooney asked.

'Well, I have to be honest – I couldn't tell you. She was sort of strange, gave me a weird feeling like when she looked at me she was seeing through me. She's got strange eyes, very deep and dark, or maybe it was just the false eyelashes.' She chuckled.

'I've lost four pounds,' Rooney said.

Rosie clapped her hands. 'That's wonderful. I have lost, well, not as much as I'd like. Do you think I'm looking thinner?'

Rooney gave her a long, studied appraisal, and then nodded. 'There is just one thing, Rosie – when we get to New Orleans can we forget the diet? I mean, they have the best food in the world, and I'm not going there to eat raw fish. It might mean a few extra pounds going on, but . . .'

She held out her hand. 'It's a deal – we diet now, but we come off it when we get to New Orleans.' They shook hands, and Rooney felt suddenly embarrassed. He'd never had this kind of intimate conversation with a woman before, even with his poor wife, who had been stick-thin when he married her and stick-thin the day she died.

'Can I tell you something?' he asked hesitantly, and she looked over at him.

'Sure, tell me what?'

'Don't tell Lorraine,' he said, like a kid. Rosie waited while Rooney rubbed his head and pulled at his big nose.

'Maybe it's age.'

'What is?'

He coughed, now pulling at his tie. 'Well, don't take this the wrong way, I mean, hell, I'm not backing out of anything, no way, but . . .' He sighed, unsure of what he was saying and how to say it.

'I just can't get the energy up the way I used to, you know, that adrenalin that pumps through you on a case. I used to feel it down to the soles of my feet, itching all the time to get to the bottom of something. I wouldn't sleep, couldn't even eat sometimes, and I know I was hell to live with. I must have put poor Ellen through it, and I keep thinking about her, thinking what a bad husband I was. She never had much of a life.'

He seemed so vulnerable, trying to express something that he couldn't release, and Rosie went over and put her arms round him, which embarrassed him even more.

'I just feel so bad about her, Rosie, because she was looking forward to us going on this camper trip right round the US, and . . .'

Rosie said nothing, but just held him and rubbed his back. Rooney rested his head against her.

'I'm sorry about this, you must think me a big old fool, but she was a nice woman, Rosie, never would hurt a fly.'

'It's always good to let it out, Bill, you'll feel better,

and don't you worry about that itch – I think you're a very special person. Too many people hide their real feelings – I know I hid mine in a bottle, but I'm getting better, much better.'

There was a moment of embarrassment as Rosie drew away and Bill blew his nose hard.

'Lorraine should be here any minute,' Rosie said to cover her own confusion.

'I'd be grateful if you didn't mention this to her, I don't want her to feel that I'm not giving one hundred per cent.'

'Nothing happened here, you old buzzard,' Rosie smiled warmly, but they both knew something had happened. Perhaps they were afraid to admit it at once, but there was now a bond between them and it felt good.

Lorraine tailed the lunatic Raoul as far as she could, but he then cut across traffic and she lost him. Maybe Raoul knew she'd been on their tail, but judging by the way the kid drove, he was more than likely to cop a speeding ticket and Lorraine with him.

They were parked across the road from the AA meeting. It was almost eight.

Lorraine looked in the driving mirror. 'Here she comes now. Okay, I'm out of here, you wait in the car.'

'But I want to go into the meeting.'

'Fine, can you just give me a few seconds with Phyllis?'

Lorraine crossed to Phyllis, smiled and shook her hand. Then they walked to a bench seat outside the church hall.

Phyllis clenched her hands together. 'I really do not

see that it is any concern of yours, I was simply passing the car and Mrs Salina called out to me, so I went over and—'

'Is she still seeing Mrs Caley?'

'Er, no, well, Mr Caley has objected to her coming to the house and so, no, she doesn't see her anymore.'

'Does Robert Caley know Elizabeth is pumping herself full of temazepam . . . that's what she's injecting, right?'

Phyllis had those two red dots in her cheeks again. 'You don't understand.'

'I am trying to, Phyllis, I really am. Do you have any idea how dangerous it is? That she could induce a thrombosis and kill herself?'

Phyllis seemed ready to burst into tears.

Lorraine continued. 'The stuff is lethal, Phyllis, and you would be partly responsible if she killed herself. You're procuring the stuff for her, you have admitted to picking it up, so why don't you stop lying to me? Does Robert Caley know what his wife is taking?'

Phyllis shook her head. 'No, he has no idea. You see, when she last came out of the rehab clinic, she was no longer taking cocaine, not even alcohol, but then with all this terrible thing about Anna Louise . . . She couldn't sleep and she became very anxious and . . .'

'The doc prescribed the temazepam, right?'

Phyllis nodded. 'Just a small amount to begin with and then she needed more, and . . .' The tears came and she fumbled in her sleeve to take out a tiny lace handkerchief. 'Oh dear, dear me, I can't stop her. And she's threatened to sack me if I mention it to Mr Caley, she'll also sack me if I don't collect them . . . it places me in such a terrible position.'

'Well, she won't be able to get any more, Dr Hayleden's been arrested.'

'Oh God.' Phyllis pressed the handkerchief to her watery eyes.

'Yeah, oh God, but you should thank God, Phyllis, because without her supply she's not likely to kill herself, is she?'

Phyllis closed her eyes and sniffed, her mouth turned down. 'Oh, she'll find someone else, or something else. I don't know if I can take much more. That's why I started drinking, you know, she wore me out. She just never sleeps, she can't sleep without something, and now she has an excuse. All she thinks about is Anna Louise.'

'She took her to see Juda.'

'Yes, I think so, but I wasn't with them, she would never let me go with her.'

'And Mr and Mrs Caley took Mrs Salina to New Orleans, yes? To try and help trace Anna Louise?'

Phyllis nodded, chewing at her thin lips. 'Yes, Elizabeth insisted. You see, Mrs Salina was sure that if she was close to where she had been, in the hotel or wherever, she would pick up her aura.'

'And?'

Phyllis shrugged. 'Well, she was sure the poor child was very much alive and I think she stayed on for a few days after Elizabeth returned because as I recall Mr Caley sent his private plane to bring her back to LA.'

Lorraine nodded. 'Why did he forbid her to see Elizabeth?'

Phyllis sighed. 'Mr Caley suspected that the woman was a charlatan, building up Elizabeth's hopes; he never approved of her, and he was deeply angry when he discovered that Elizabeth had taken Anna Louise to Mrs Salina's apartment.'

'Was that when he banned Juda from visiting the house?'

'No, that was after they returned from New Orleans.'

197

'But she was a calming influence!'

'*Yes*, she was, but not after the disappearance. Elizabeth would become very distraught and called Mrs Salina in hysterics. She gave her hope, you see . . . Mr Caley was only doing it for the best.'

Lorraine nodded, checking the time. 'Why did Anna Louise go to Mrs Salina's?'

'I don't think she got involved in any of that mumbojumbo thing, it was just that sometimes Mrs Caley was not very steady. I think Mr Caley had words with Anna Louise, and she promised never to go there again . . .'

'And did she?'

'No, no, she wouldn't go against her father's wishes. She was a very obedient girl. And she had Tilda Brown staying at the time, so she had other things on her mind. The girl used to stay a lot, well, with her family being so far away, most weekends actually. In fact, Anna Louise was looking forward to going to New Orleans because . . .'

Phyllis suddenly hesitated, turning away from Lorraine. It was as if she had thought of something and was deciding whether or not to mention it. She covered by tucking her little handkerchief back up her sleeve.

'Because?' Lorraine said softly.

'Er, nothing really, it's just that the girls had a bit of a falling out, nothing serious, and Tilda went home the next morning. She was meant to stay on another day and travel with Mr and Mrs Caley but you know young girls, probably argued about a game of tennis.'

'Must have been quite an argument to leave so abruptly, and also as they were all to travel together the following day.'

'I suppose so, but you know young girls.'

'Have you ever met Saffron Dulay? I think she's a close friend of Mr Caley's.'

Phyllis looked at her watch and stood up, smoothing down her skirt. 'No, I have not had the pleasure. Is there anything else you wish to ask me? If there isn't, I really should go in.'

'No, I don't think so. Thank you very much for your time.'

Phyllis patted her hair. 'I am sorry if, well, I know you think I am not always honest, but you see, Mrs Page, part of me has to be so very careful. I signed a confidentiality agreement with Mrs Caley, all her staff have to . . .'

'I understand, Phyllis.'

'It's just I am so scared of losing my job. I have a very elderly mother and aunt I take care of back in England. They are dependent on my income and the Caleys have been so very kind over my own little problem.'

'Yes, I am sure Elizabeth Caley would be, considering her own.'

Phyllis gave an eerie, high-pitched titter. She put out her hand to shake Lorraine's, rather like a little fragile claw which clasped for a moment and then released.

'Was Juda Salina paid a lot of money?'

'Money, Mrs Page, is not something that Elizabeth Caley has any worries over.'

'Just one more thing, Phyllis. How close to the time of Anna Louise's disappearance did Mr Caley forbid her to see Juda Salina?'

'Oh, weeks before. Then after Anna Louise disappeared, Mr Caley agreed to allow Mrs Salina to visit but stopped her coming after about three or four months. Now please, I really should go in. Good evening.' And with that, Phyllis hurried into the church hall.

Lorraine frowned; why did Elizabeth Caley have such a prissy woman caring for her?

Rosie banged the car door shut, shouting, 'I got to go in, Lorraine! *Lorraine!*'

Lorraine was still frowning as she joined Rosie. 'You know, I don't think Phyllis even likes Elizabeth Caley.'

'You going into the meeting?'

Lorraine shook her head. 'No, you go ahead.'

Rosie sighed with irritation as she watched Lorraine walk towards the car. 'Maybe you should.'

Lorraine whipped round. 'We got two weeks, Rosie.'

'I know that, but how am I going to get home?'

Lorraine sighed. 'Ask Phyllis to give you a ride.'

Rosie was tight-lipped: sometimes she really didn't like the way Lorraine treated her, and she was just about to say so when Lorraine turned back and gave her a hug.

'Sorry, didn't mean to sound so pushy . . . but we are pushed for time, Rosie, and I think I'm on to something. Not sure what it is yet, but if you can't get a ride, take a cab, okay?'

Rosie patted her friend's shoulder. 'Don't you worry, I'll get home. You know Nick will look after you, don't you?'

'What?'

Rosie winked. 'I never said nothing, but he's kind of got the hots for you, so you treat him nice.'

Lorraine laughed. Sometimes Rosie could be so dumb. 'No, Rosie, he just wants a cut of the one million, that's what he's got the hots for, and we may just be getting closer to it. See you later.'

CHAPTER 8

IT WAS 11.30 p.m., already the third night of the investigation, and Lorraine was not as confident as she had led Rosie to believe. She gave herself the critical eye; she was wearing a short black dress, second-hand naturally, but with its Donna Karan label, she knew it had once been expensive. She had also acquired, from the daughter of the Hispanics living in the apartment below, a pair of red platform high-heeled shoes. The black stockings were her own. She had washed her hair, still unsure about the new cut, and was just wondering if she should put even more make-up on when there was a knock on the door.

Rosie had got a ride home from her meeting and was sitting in front of the television with a bowl of grapes.

'Come in, it's open.'

'Hi, is she ready?' Nick said loudly.

Rosie nodded, and used the remote control to switch the TV off. 'What's this Viper Club like then?'

Nick sauntered in. 'Viper *Room*, you don't call it a club, Rosie. Is she for real then?'

Rosie shrugged. Lorraine walked in and Nick tried not to over-react, because she looked so different. 'My, my, we are pulling out the stops.'

Lorraine looked at him. 'Wish I could say the same for you, you rolled out of bed to get here?'

'I most surely did. So this is on, is it?'

'You think I got dressed up like this for fun?'

'Turns me on, I think it's the shoes. Man, you gotta be six foot in them.'

Lorraine put on a pair of shades and waved at Rosie. 'See you. Come on, Nick, let's go.' She peered at his denim jacket. 'Holy shit, you got dog hairs all over you.'

'Well, I would, I got a dog. G'night, Rosie.'

Nick glanced over the note found in Anna Louise Caley's bedroom. He said nothing as he passed it back to Lorraine. He was still taken aback by her appearance, and when she leaned close to him, he got an erection. It annoyed him that she could make him react to her so physically.

'I want to find out who this guy Polar is. She had matches from the Viper Room so we'll start there. And there were other matchbooks from On the Rox and . . .'

'Look, no need to explain, we'll suss it out, okay?' He seemed irritated and she didn't have the slightest inkling that it was because he found her so attractive. They turned on to Sunset and drove past the flash parade of yuppie wannabe Hell's Angels on their shiny chrome bikes, past the neon-lit zone, the hookers and the pimps, past the open-fronted bars and cafés, until he pulled over into a vacant parking bay outside a sleazy joint called Alfredo's Live Striptease.

'We're here?' Lorraine asked.

'Nope, but I need to see a friend. Just hang in there, I'll be a couple of seconds.'

Nick hopped out of the jeep and went into the strip joint. Lorraine waited with Tiger's hot, panting breath wafting past her face.

'Sit back a bit, you stink.'

He looked duly miffed and squatted back, then the sides of his huge mouth lifted and he gave a low growl.

'Hey, sit on my knee if it makes you happy, just don't bite me.'

She heard the thud-thud of his tail as it whacked against his food bowl. There was no growl, but his lip curled up to reveal his teeth and it looked like he was smiling, which made Lorraine laugh.

'Good boy. I could get to like you, you know that?'

And she really believed she could when two drunk, leather-clad bikers stumbled against the jeep and one looked in, sneering, to ask, 'How much?'

Tiger went for the jugular, fast, and the biker reeled off, scared shitless.

Lorraine reached out and patted his big head. 'Nice one.'

'Winning you over, is he?' Nick said as he opened the driver's door. He started up the engine. 'Okay, I got our calling card so maybe we can get in . . . But if you don't mind me sayin' so, you're the wrong side of thirty and there are not a lot of chicks in there over twenty. Guys can get in any age so long as they're famous an' their wallets're heavy. Still, we'll have a go.'

They drove out into the night traffic and Lorraine asked if Nick had some movie star contact. He laughed, shaking his head. 'Nah! Feel in my pocket, I've gone one better.'

She slipped her hand into his denim jacket and pulled out a plastic bag. 'Nick, what you playin' at?'

'Cocaine, well, some of it, rest is scouring powder. You ain't somebody unless you have something that the somebodies want, right?'

'You mean you just scored this?'

'Nope, well, in a way. Remember me tellin' you about Fisher?'

'Yes, but . . .'

'Tony T. Loredo owns that dive. I busted him in eighty-five but I did him a favour. Since then he's come up in the world, and he supplies young meat, chicks, dope, you name it, to the movie stars. I'm gonna use him as an intro. All right with you?'

They pulled up outside the Viper Room's dark, nondescript entrance; the only indications that it was a club were the heavy-duty bouncers on the door and the stretch limos pulling up and moving off as their clients staggered into the venue.

Nick leaned out of the jeep and called out to one of the bouncers. 'Hey, man, gimme an ear, will ya?' He turned back to Lorraine. 'Bend your head forwards, look like you're out of it, cover your face with your hair. Do it!' The bouncer came up closer. 'Keep your distance, I got a mad dog in the back and a real one beside me . . . I also got some merchandise Tony said he wants me to deliver.'

The bouncer stared at Lorraine, then at Nick, who eased out his bag a fraction. The bouncer stepped back, nodding, and pointed for Nick to park up a way down the road.

'Right, we're in . . .'

'In' blew Lorraine's mind. The main club room was so dark she could hardly see and the music was so loud it was deafening. She tried as best she could to see through the darkness. She focused on a young girl wearing black bra and panties, and fish-net stockings. 'You think she maybe had a dress on when she arrived?' she said to Nick, but he was looking around. He then turned back and leaned in close.

'Over to your right, clutch of supermodels.' Nick

pointed up above them. 'That's a room with a two-way mirror on to the dance floor. Some of 'em get a kick out of screwing up there on top of all these assholes. Still, takes all kinds . . .'

'Yeah, and maybe Anna Louise Caley was one of them. How do we go about it?'

Nick shrugged. 'I think we're wasting our time. Come on, that note you found in the girl's bedroom is juvenile dementia, a kid writing dirty, so what?'

'It might mean something if we track down this guy Polar.'

Nick signalled to a waiter. She could feel he was edgy, his eyes darting around all the time. He searched in his pockets and took out a picture of Anna Louise.

'You got any cash on you? Like fifties, ten bucks no good, I need a few big notes.' Lorraine opened her purse and he suddenly leaned in close and whispered to her, 'Head down and stoned, sweetheart.'

She looked up as a waiter closed in on Nick. 'Hi, man, gimme a Mexican and a Diet Coke. Hey, a second.'

The waiter leaned forward.

'I need to get shot of this.' Nick jerked his thumb at Lorraine, and then winked at the waiter. 'My friend Tony, Loredo T., wants to know if this chick's been in. Reason is she owes him, understand? Lot of dough. And if you can tip him off, there's something in it for you . . .' Nick drew out the plastic bag. 'Worth fifteen big ones . . . all yours. Act real cool about it, man, but I need to know if she used to hang out down here.'

'Sure, a Mexican beer and one Coke.' The waiter took the photo without looking at it and two fifty dollar notes with a nice swift move so they were hidden under his tray.

Lorraine hissed. 'A hundred bucks, Nick, are you crazy?'

205

He kept looking around the dark dance floor where a girl was stripping; nobody seemed all that interested. 'That's shit, some of these kids drop ten, fifteen thousand bucks a night down here. I'm gonna take a leak, you okay to hang out on your own?'

She turned away. 'I been in places a lot worse than this.'

He leaned close. 'This is class, sweetheart. Won't be long.'

He was away at least twenty minutes. Lorraine watched the stoned kids, some openly snorting coke. One girl was so high she sat with her legs apart in a stupor. As guys walked past her, they groped her and all she could do was just about hold her head straight.

Lorraine got up and headed for the restroom. She was pushed and jostled, and saw more lines of coke laid out and young teenage girls huddled together, wearing as little as possible. Lorraine felt old; not that anyone bothered even to look in her direction, they were too intent on getting noticed by one or other of the 'stars'.

Nick had still not shown when she made her way back to where she had been sitting, but the seats were now occupied by a couple on the verge of copulating, so she picked up her glass and turned away. She took a gulp, then freaked because it wasn't straight Coke, it had rum in it, and a lot of it, mixed with God knows what else.

The alcohol hit her throat like a fireball. She swallowed. It took a lot of will-power to put the glass down but she did. She edged away and was pushed against the wall by a group of guys dancing with each other. She pressed her back hard against the suedette wall, could feel the panic starting and wished Nick would show. Her dress clung to her as she broke out in sweat, the heat stifling, the thudding music overpowering – but not as hard to ignore as her need to finish the drink.

'Where's your friend?' the waiter hissed, and she turned to be blinded by spinning spotlights. 'He in the john? Or upstairs? Don't look at me, act like I'm taking your order.'

She closed her eyes, sweat trickling down her body. She swallowed, her mouth felt rancid.

Nick appeared right behind the waiter. 'Hey, man, you got a guy fuckin' a chick in the john.'

'So? Listen, I can be out the back door in ten, my break's due, okay?'

Nick nodded, and as the waiter took off he grinned at Lorraine. 'Quite a show in there.'

'Get me out of here, Nick.'

He laughed. 'What? Can't take it? But you said you . . .' He suddenly knew she was in trouble and gripped her elbow, easing her forward and out into the cool night air.

Lorraine leaned against the side of the jeep. 'Somebody spiked my drink or I picked up somebody else's and . . . sorry, sorry, I got all hyper in there.'

She was so vulnerable, her whole body shaking, and he put his arm around her, walking her to the jeep door.

'Come on, sit inside, you're okay . . . You want some water?'

She stumbled and he held on tightly as he helped her. He reached over to the back seat. Tiger's head appeared and he gave him a quick pat as he unscrewed a bottle of Evian.

'It's Tiger's but I guess he won't mind.'

She gulped at the water; it was lukewarm but it was liquid. She was scared to feel so dependent. 'Sorry about this, sorry.'

He gently stroked her cheek. 'Sweetheart, you don't have to be sorry, I shouldn't have stayed in the john but the floor show was somethin' else and . . .'

She turned away, her hand clutching the dented old plastic. 'Oh, shit, Nick, does it never stop? That was the first drink I've had in months, months . . .'

He opened the glove compartment and took out some peppermints. He unwrapped one and touched her lips. 'Open your mouth.' He popped in the mint and cuffed her chin lightly. 'You stay put, I don't want to miss out on this guy. Besides, he's got a hundred bucks of our dough and,' he tapped his pocket, 'he's gonna do some nasal damage in there with this gear. You okay if I leave you?'

She nodded, her mouth bulging with the mint. 'Yep, and I got Tiger. Go on, I'm fine.'

Lorraine wasn't. She couldn't stop the tears as they welled up and spilled down, and she sucked hard on the big peppermint, angry with herself.

'I lost it in there, Tiger,' she whispered. It frightened her how quickly her confidence could be swiped from her, the realization that everything she was or thought she was could be so easily ripped apart. All it took was one drink and the craving was back.

Nick was leaning against a wall where he could see the cordoned-off back yard. He waited for almost ten minutes. They had bouncers even out back with the trash cans as kids tried to get in that way. He was beginning to think they'd lost a hundred bucks when out came the waiter. He had a leather studded jacket slung over his shoulder and was wearing dark shades.

'Gonna check out my wheels, be back in five,' he called out to the bouncers.

Nick remained half-hidden against the wall until the waiter was clear. He was very edgy as he joined Nick.

'My bike's parked upaways, you wanna walk with me?'

208

'Sure, you got a name?'

'Frankie. You got to be real careful, any one of us caught passin' on anythin' so much as a cigarette pack and we're fucked. This is a big earner, man, I don't wanna lose my job.'

'I never seen you, it's cool.'

The waiter's Harley had more bolts and alarms than a security firm. It was a highly polished, chrome on chrome custom shovel-head.

'Nice bike.'

'Yeah, the fuckin' bastards use trucks now to lift them. I've only had it a few months.'

'Like you said, you got yourself a nice earner and maybe you gonna earn even more. You got something for me?'

'This is the chick that's missin' right? An' I'm not gonna get involved with any cops, that's got nothin' to do with the action . . .'

'I'm not a cop, for fuck's sake. I'm gonna hit on her family for Tony, she owed him. I don't give a shit about anythin' else.'

'I don't think anyone's sussed who she is, they got a lotta this kind of material, know what I mean?'

'I'm trying to, I just want to do the deal an' get out of here.'

Nick eased out the bag as a taster and Frankie flicked a furtive glance in both directions. He drew his jacket forward and exposed a newspaper with a brown manila envelope tucked inside.

Nick gave Lorraine a wink as he got back into the jeep, starting it up straight away.

'Let's put some distance between me and my new pal Frankie.'

He swerved into the traffic with a screech of his balding tyres and they headed down the strip. He eased the manila envelope out of his denim jacket.

'Oh, my God,' Lorraine said, as she took out the photograph.

'You said it, blew me away, part of a private collection they got up in the office. You were right, I was wrong.'

Nick lived in a house similar to Rosie's, but even more dilapidated. His apartment was a shambolic mess, the bed unmade and dirty dishes stacked in the sink. 'Guess the place needs a woman's touch. Problem is, although I get a lot of chicks up here, none of them stay long enough to hoover.'

He wasn't apologizing, he obviously didn't care. Out of the corner of her eye Lorraine saw him open the fridge and take out a bottle of iced vodka. He took a small thick glass, filled it once, knocked it back and refilled it twice, each time downing the contents in one go and letting out a satisfied 'Ahhhh'.

Everything in her wanted to join him in the neat ice-cold vodka. Her body was shaking.

'Nick . . .' she said softly.

'Yep? Coffee's on, won't be long.' He came and stood above her and gently patted her head. It was a sweet, affectionate gesture, and she had to swallow hard because she felt herself wanting to weep. 'How you doing?'

'Okay.'

It was hardly audible and he squatted down in front of her, resting on his old beat-up cowboy boots. 'You want to talk?'

Her voice was husky. 'I want a drink, it's all I can think about.'

'S'okay, I can go over to the fridge and pour you one right now, but that would be dumb.'

She bent her head. 'Just gimme a drink, Nick.'

He stood up, hands on his hips. 'You want one, *you* get it! You get up off your ass and the bottle is there in the freezer compartment, go on.'

She got up slowly, licking her lips, and crossed to the fridge. Her hand reached out and she turned to look at him.

'I'm not stopping you, you know the road you're gonna take better than me.'

She rested her head against the cold front of the big old-fashioned fridge, and he remained watching her, hands resting above his snake hips, the old Mexican silver-buckled belt askew. He waited. The way she pressed her body against the fridge turned him on, she was virtually kissing it like a lost lover. She pushed herself away and turned to the coffee percolator, her hands clenched at her side.

'How well did you know Jack Lubrinski?' Her voice was strained. She turned to him, her face tilted to one side, the scar hidden by a fold of her soft blonde hair.

'Good cop, great guy.'

She nodded, and as she pushed the hair away from her face he could see the jagged scar down her cheek. She had the bluest eyes he'd ever seen, but she didn't seem to be looking at him, more like through him.

'I miss him.'

'Yeah, I know.'

Suddenly she focused on him, studying his face. He blushed under her scrutiny. 'You sometimes remind me of him.'

He lit two cigarettes and passed one to her. As he

211

held it out, she touched his hand lightly with one finger, then took the cigarette and inhaled deeply.

'You see, what happens, Nick, is like corners of my mind open. It comes on unexpectedly, kind of throws me sideways, and I feel this terrible panic. Just when I think I have it all under control, just when I think I've got myself together . . .' She sucked on the cigarette. 'One spiked drink, one goddamned mouthful, and . . . nothing else matters.'

'Yes it does, you didn't open the fridge.'

'No, I didn't, but I would have done if I was on my own. That's what scares me, Nick, that and . . .'

'And what?'

She shrugged and sipped her coffee.

'Go on, tell me, and what?'

'Oh, my kids, I think of them and Michael.'

'Who's Michael?'

'He was my husband.'

'Ah, well, we've all got ghosts, we've all got corners, Lorraine. Maybe you shouldn't hide them away but talk more.'

'I can't.'

She suddenly bent her head forward so he couldn't see her face, and let out a soft moan. He wanted to hold her in his arms, cradle her, kiss her, but he got up and moved further away. He couldn't deal with the emotions she was wrenching out of him, it had been a long time since he had wanted to love a woman, and that's what he knew was happening: he was falling in love with her. He changed the subject fast.

'Right, we should talk over what went down tonight, sugar, because it's late an' we got to get moving on this case and out to New Orleans.'

She sniffed. 'Yes, you're right, and I'm okay now.'

212

She sprang to her feet, pulling her skirt down, kicking off the red high-heeled shoes. 'Gimme the picture, let's have another look. And this Frankie didn't know of anyone called Polar?'

'Nope.' Nick picked up his jacket off the floor, fished inside the pocket and brought out the envelope. She took it from him and slapped it against her thigh, no shakes now, no vulnerable lady. She was back in shape.

Lorraine leaned on the edge of the Formica-topped kitchen table, studying the photo. He stood next to her, quite close, but couldn't touch her, not like before; her need for him and a drink he knew had gone.

'Well, she's out of her head, that's for sure, look at her eyes.'

'Nice body,' he said softly.

Anna Louise Caley was naked, lying on a table. There were bottles around one shoulder, one glass fallen on its side. The three boys were all around twenty and they looked drunk, their clothes half off, their trousers down, and all their faces in shot. One boy was fucking her, one was kissing her tits and one was jerking off over her, semen glistening over her flat, tanned belly. Anna Louise Caley was smiling, one hand holding a bottle of tequila.

'Miss Goody-Two-Shoes,' she said softly.

She was peering at the picture closely. 'I think one of the little shits was the freckle-faced kid I interviewed at UCLA, I'm sure of it.'

Nick lit another cigarette and inhaled deeply. 'According to Frankie, and he only started working at the club about the time this was taken, he only saw her once or twice, with a blonde girl about the same age. They came together, got smashed and royally screwed. He didn't know any of the kids porking her but remembered her from the photo we passed him.'

213

'He also know who she was? Newspapers had her picture on the front page so how come he didn't contact the cops?'

'Hey, kid's scared to lose his job, and you don't think he was the only guy that must have recognized her and kept their mouths shut.'

She frowned. 'But if this kind of thing is a regular scene, why would he remember somebody who only used the place once or twice? I mean, you said they were screwing in the john.'

'Well, firstly, a so-called bag of coke worth fifteen thousand dollars is a pretty good incentive, and this action we got here wasn't done in the john but in a private room, this happened like real late. You know, just the main guys there, the so-called stars that gang-bang, and only a couple of waiters on duty, Frankie being one of them. He said he remembered her because he reckoned he'd get his dick wet, but she passed out . . .'

'But this bunch of shits aren't movie stars, one is a college kid.'

'Maybe rich enough, who the fuck knows?'

Lorraine frowned. 'Frankie have a picture of her girlfriend?'

'No, he said she was taken up to the top room and he wouldn't get up there, they had their own waiter.'

'Who took this photograph?'

Nick cocked his head to one side. 'Seems they got hidden cameras in the wall of mirrors in the private room. They take a lot of snaps, so many he wasn't even worried they'd miss one.'

Lorraine stuffed the photograph back into the envelope. 'Well, I got something to discuss with Mr and Mrs Caley, but I don't think they're gonna like it.' She started to put on her red shoes and then pulled a face. 'I'll go barefoot, you wanna give me a ride home?'

'Sure.'

In the jeep she stroked Tiger's head while the dog tried to lick her face. 'I think we really gelled, Nick, he's a real character.'

'Yep, he is.' Nick slammed his door shut.

'You know, this new direction kind of excludes Robert Caley. You think the photo might have been used for blackmail?'

Nick rammed the car into gear. 'Like Frankie said, they got a load of snaps and all they're used for, I'd say, are sick kicks. But maybe we don't exclude blackmail.'

As they drew up outside Rosie's place, Lorraine laughed. 'Hey! We got one big breakthrough tonight, Nick. I'll talk to the Caleys in the morning, maybe see if I can get that Tom Heller to spill something, and then . . .' She punched his arm. 'New Orleans, here we come . . .' She clapped her hands. 'Oh, Nick, one million dollars! I am sure we'll crack this, we'll find her, and like Mrs Caley said, dead or alive we still get the pay-off.' Lorraine rubbed Tiger's head. 'G'night, talk tomorrow. Oh, Nick, you won't give this information to Agnews, will you?'

His smile wiped fast. 'No, but is it okay if I collect my pay cheque?'

She laughed, and he stayed watching her running barefoot up the stairs, two steps at a time to the first floor. She seemed full of energy, her confidence seemingly restored. She also, Nick noticed, made sure she had the photograph. Lorraine Page was back on the case. He rubbed Tiger's head.

'Dangerous lady, that one. Gets to the core, understand?' Tiger licked his face. 'No, I guess you don't.'

Nick finished the bottle of vodka and lay spread-eagled on his crumpled bed. He picked up his guitar, strummed a few bars and began to tune it. He had liked her when she was vulnerable, liked it when he could take charge, sort of care for her. He hadn't felt that way about anyone in a very long time and he knew he was caring too much, she was touching him deep down.

'Oh, Lorraine, Lorraine, filled up with pain . . . Oh, Lorraine, let me . . .'

He was a much better guitarist than he ever admitted, but his lyrics stank and he knew it so he just lazily plucked at the strings that kept on saying her name . . . Lorraine.

Lorraine was curled up on her sofa bed, planning exactly how she would deal the ace she held in the brown manila envelope to the Caleys. Nick was far from her mind, so was the craving. The vulnerable Lorraine had crept back into her secret corner, along with Jack Lubrinski, her daughters and ex-husband. In fact, the person she was thinking about when she drifted asleep was Robert Caley, wondering how he would react to the photograph. In a way she was relieved that in her mind he was no longer their main suspect. She was still wondering about his possible involvement in his daughter's disappearance and, lastly, what it would be like to lie naked next to him, when she fell asleep.

CHAPTER 9

LORRAINE STOOD in front of the case chart pinned up on the wall in the office, 'Day 4' underlined. It was only 7.15 in the morning and she'd been there since six. She hadn't had more than a few hours' sleep but she wasn't feeling tired; on the contrary, she was buzzing.

Marked up under her name were the names Robert Caley, Elizabeth Caley, Tom Heller, the freckle-faced student from UCLA, Noël, the Rasta hairdresser; four people she wanted to interview again.

Listed under New Orleans were Caley's business partners in the casino development, Tilda Brown, Anna Louise's girlfriend, and all the Caley staff. Uppermost on Nick and Rooney's list was to make contact with the New Orleans officers involved in the investigation to get an update and any background on Juda Salina.

Lorraine watched as Noël blow-dried her hair.

'You want the same style, right?'

'Yeah, just like before. By the way, did you ever do Anna Louise Caley's hair?'

He cocked his head to one side, holding the dryer aside a moment. 'Yep.'

'You ever go to the Viper Room?'

217

He continued working, his attention on her hair. 'Nah, I got better things to do with my time.'

'Anna Louise Caley used to go.'

He looked at her reflection in the mirror, seemingly intent on her hair.

'Really? Didn't think she was the type.'

'Why do you say that?'

'Well, she was always kind of cute, bit shy. Obsessed with her hair though.'

'Was she always on her own?'

He turned off the dryer and leaned against the mirror shelf. 'What's this? Why all the questions?'

Lorraine leaned forward, looking at her reflection. 'Because I have been hired to trace her and all I get told is that she was a real cute, nice little rich girl. But I don't think she was, in fact, I know there was another side to Miss Caley.'

'You think I know about it?'

'Maybe. I'm a private investigator, Noël, not a cop, so there's no need to get edgy. I want to show you something.' Lorraine drew out the photograph. 'Take a look at this.'

Noël glanced at the photograph, then whistled between his teeth, holding it closer. He muttered something to himself and then passed it back to Lorraine. She slipped it back into the envelope.

Noël continued to blow-dry her hair. Twice his eyes met hers but he said nothing.

'You know any of the guys in the photo?'

He nodded. 'You see the cat at the end, right at the end of the salon, finishing a tint? He's the one giving it to her. His name is Cal, Cal Thompson, real little prick, if you'll excuse the pun.'

Lorraine looked along the row of salon chairs. Cal had

his back to her so she couldn't get a good look at his face.

She walked down the salon to the end chair. She stood behind the young man who was washing out his tint bowl and brushes.

'Excuse me, it's Cal, isn't it?'

Cal Thompson turned. He was good-looking, tanned like everyone in LA, one of those young men full of confidence in his own looks.

'Hi, could I talk to you for a moment?'

He frowned, looked towards the main reception, back to Lorraine.

'In private.'

He hesitated. 'I'm busy right now, if you want to make an appointment . . .'

Lorraine took out the photograph. 'You want this plastered over the *National Enquirer*? I'd find a few minutes if I were you, Cal.'

Cal drew a curtain across the doorway. Lorraine sat down and took out her cigarettes.

'You a reporter?'

'Nope. Sit down a second, Cal.'

He sat down, still holding on to his cool, pushing the ashtray towards Lorraine. 'What do you want?'

'Information. I'm a private investigator. Look at the picture, Cal. Gang-rape is an offence, right? She was just a kid, so just answer a few questions, then I'm out of here.'

'Listen, man, she's no fucking minor. Look at her face, she was loving it.'

'I'd say she was stoned out of her mind. You do know who she is, don't you?'

He sighed, turning away. 'Yeah, yeah, I know who she is.'

Lorraine waited; he was losing his cool now. 'So you know she's been missing?'

He nodded. 'Yeah, but it's got nothing to do with me. I mean, *that* was just a one-off, know what I mean? We were high and . . . that's all there is to it.'

'All? There's three guys here fucking a young kid stoned out of her mind and you say that's all? Can you name the others?'

'No.'

'So what happened after this?'

Cal shrugged. 'I put my dick away, had a few more drinks and went home. She'd already left with her friend.'

'Who was the friend?'

'I dunno. She was here once at the salon.'

'Tilda Brown?'

'I dunno, I get a lot of clients, some walk in off the street so it might not be in the appointment book. Look, I obviously know Anna Louise, but then so did everybody else. She had the reputation of being open to offers, she'd been there a few times before, turning the same tricks. She liked it.'

'Was she always stoned?'

'I dunno, I think it was booze rather than drugs but everybody's taking stuff down there, it's on offer, know what I mean?'

'I'm trying to, Cal. Did you ever see her with anyone specific? Heard the name Polar mentioned at all?'

'No, like I only saw her that time at the club and a few times in the salon. She's not even my client.'

'You saw her leave the Viper Room on the night this photo was taken?'

'Yeah, and her friend. We hung out for a while longer.'

'We?'

'Couple of friends. It was real late anyway, the place

was getting quiet so it hadda be around four or five in the morning.'

Lorraine slipped the photograph into the envelope. 'Do you recall when this was taken?'

'Yeah, because it was my girlfriend's birthday. We had a bust-up in the Viper, I hung on in there. February thirteenth last year. Look, I'm being dead straight with you, I'm married now and I don't get into that kind of stuff anymore.'

Lorraine stubbed out her cigarette. 'You recall how she got home? You said you saw her leaving, did she drive or was she driven, or did she get a taxi?'

'Man, she was too out of it to drive. I think maybe somebody collected her, but I dunno, I honestly don't remember. I did nothin' wrong, I mean, she was loving it.'

Lorraine walked to the curtained doorway. 'Thanks. And Cal, I hope you have been straight with me because I don't want to have to come back.'

'Hi, you remember me?'

Tom Heller was drenched in sweat after a tennis game, tying a white cotton sweater round his shoulders. He stared at Lorraine a moment, then took out a pristine white towel from his kit-bag and wiped the sweat from his face, rubbing his hair. 'No, I'm sorry, I don't.'

She opened her purse as he stowed his racquets into their cases. 'Lorraine Page, Page Investigations.'

He zipped up the bag. 'Oh, right, yeah.'

'Anna Louise Caley, you said you had dated her.'

He slung his bag's shoulder strap on to his shoulder. 'Right. Look, I should go get a shower.'

'You also said it was a platonic relationship, just

221

picnics, beach parties . . .' He started to move away. 'Wait one second.' Her voice made him pull up fast. 'You lied, you knew her very well, didn't you?'

'No more than anyone else.'

She slapped the photo into his chest. 'No more than anyone else? You mean everybody fucked her like this? Take a good look, because that is no beach party or teenage barbecue, now is it? It's a gang-bang and you, sunshine, are jerking off over her belly. It is you, isn't it?'

He stared at the photograph and then let out a long sigh. 'Oh, shit.'

'Let's sit on a bench and talk. This time you'd better be honest with me or a copy of that is sent to your parents, to the principal of this place . . . you understand me?'

Mario was polishing the Caleys' limo. He turned as Lorraine walked up to him.

She smiled. 'Doing a nice job, Mario, remember me? Lorraine Page.'

Mario nodded and continued polishing.

'Tell me, on the night of February thirteenth last year, did you collect Anna Louise from the Viper Room?'

'What?'

Lorraine leaned on the side of the car. 'The family left for New Orleans two days later, on the fifteenth, same day Anna Louise went missing, so I'd say you've got a pretty good memory of events close to that date 'cos you were questioned by the cops, right?'

He nodded again, still polishing.

'So, February thirteenth last year, did you—'

'Yes, ma'am, I picked up Miss Caley and her friend, drove them back here.'

'Stoned out of their heads?'

'I dunno, ma'am, I just collected them. They was waitin' on the pavement.'

'Did her parents know?'

'No, ma'am. Anna Louise called me on my portable, I had to get up an' dressed. It was comin' up to around five o'clock.'

'How come you've never mentioned this to anyone before?'

He walked round to a bucket and dunked his leather into the soapy water. 'I didn't want no trouble, they were just foolin' around, the way kids do. I brought them home, no more to it.'

'You ever picked Anna Louise up from a club before?'

'No, ma'am. She'd call me from a few parties, never wanted to drive when she was not sober. We hadda kind of arrangement, safer that way.'

'Who was she with?'

'Most times with her friend Tilda. She didn't go out much, only when Miss Brown was stayin'. Everyone said that Miss Brown was a nice girl, but me, well, I didn't. I think she was a bad influence on Miss Anna Louise but I never said nothin' to nobody, not my business.'

'You know anyone called Polar?'

'No, ma'am, I do not, an' if you'll excuse me, I need to wash over the wheels now.'

Lorraine stepped aside. 'Did you take Tilda Brown to the airport?'

'I did.'

'She say anything?'

'No, she knew I didn't like her, she never spoke to me. Miss Tilda Brown is a high and mighty little minx.'

Lorraine turned as she heard her name called. Phyllis was standing on the front steps of the house. She looked confused. 'Why, Mrs Page, I've only just sent off your money. I didn't expect to see you, is there a problem?'

223

'No, I just need to speak to Mrs Caley before we leave. She is in, isn't she? Only I arranged to see her at eleven but I've been held up.' Lorraine joined Phyllis on the steps.

'I doubt if she will agree to see you, she never mentioned to me that you would be coming over and she is meeting her agent, so . . .'

Phyllis walked into the hallway, as if to close the front door, but Lorraine was right behind her.

'I need to talk to her, it's very important.'

'I really can't interrupt her, she is dressing.'

'Yes, you can, Phyllis, because I am not leaving this house until I see her.'

'I am sorry, but Mrs Caley cannot see anyone.'

'Don't you think you should ask me, Phyllis?' Elizabeth Caley stood at the top of the stairs, looking poised and immaculate. 'I'll come down, Mrs Page, but I only have about half an hour.' Elizabeth stepped brightly and steadily down the stairs, her perfume reaching Lorraine long before the delicate white outstretched hand tapped her shoulder.

Lorraine followed Elizabeth into the sun room. All the blinds were drawn and the overpowering smell of lilies mixed with Elizabeth's flowery perfume made her want to gasp for fresh air. They sat at a small white table on two delicate cushioned chairs among the profusion of plants.

'I'll get straight to the point.'

'I hope you will, darling. My agent will be here shortly, it seems I am being offered work. Since Anna Louise disappeared I've had so much press, disgusting really, I think a lot of people in the industry thought I was dead. Of course, I won't do it but he is most insistent that I at least discuss the offers. There is nothing sadder than resurrecting old has-beens like myself.' She laughed.

'You look wonderful,' Lorraine said, and meant it. Not a hair of the coal-black braided bun at the nape of Mrs Caley's neck was out of place, her make-up was perfect, and her simple pale lemon suit with tight-fitting pencil skirt showed off her slim legs and feet in their white high-heeled sandals. She was wearing a tiny gold ankle chain with a diamond drop, diamond earrings and the large diamond and emerald ring on her wedding finger. Beside her, Lorraine felt and looked cheap; this make-over job on Elizabeth Caley had cost a lot of money and it showed.

At that moment, tea and coffee were brought in by the mute butler.

'Thank you, Peters,' Mrs Caley said as she poured her pale greenish tea. She looked at Lorraine. 'You've found out something, haven't you?' Her voice was soft, almost frightened.

'Yes, I have.'

She closed her eyes. 'It's not good, is it?'

'No.'

'Well, get straight to the point, Mrs Page, don't keep me in suspense.'

Lorraine reached for her briefcase. 'I am sorry, but what I'm going to show you will be very upsetting.' She passed over the photograph and waited, watching Mrs Caley like a hawk. She saw her eyes widen, saw her swallow once, twice, then breathe in deeply as she stared at the photograph of her daughter. She then passed it back to Lorraine.

'Why? Why would she do something like that? Why?' Her lips quivered, then her brow puckered. She seemed to be trying not to weep in order not to spoil her make-up. 'Who are those people with her?'

'I know two. One is a hairdresser and the other a fellow-student.'

225

She shook her head. 'Dear God, they should be arrested. Where was it taken?'

'In a club. It's called the Viper Room.'

'Don't show it to Robert, please don't let him see that disgusting display or he'll ... he'll kill them. He wouldn't believe it, he has no idea.'

'Did you have any idea?'

'What? Did I know my daughter was making a public spectacle of herself? Did I know my daughter was being fucked by a group of men like a whore? *No! I did not know!* But I wish to God I had.' She clenched her hands. 'What kind of a woman do you think I am?'

'You have a drug problem, I know that.'

'I beg your pardon?'

'Let's not play games, Mrs Caley, I know about your doctor. Do you know, really know, what chances you are taking?'

'Who told you this?'

'I found it out, Mrs Caley, that is my job. But are you fully aware of the enormous risks you are taking with your own life? You are using temazepam sleeping tablets.'

'Wouldn't you, under the circumstances?' she snapped.

'What you are doing is lethal and you must take medical advice and as soon as possible. I believe you are injecting temazepam—'

Mrs Caley pushed at the table. 'Phyllis, has Phyllis been talking to you?'

'Your doctor has been arrested . . .'

'Oh, my God. Did he tell you? What has he said to you?'

Lorraine opened her cigarette pack and proffered one to Elizabeth Caley, who swiped the pack out of her hand.

'You are supposed to be investigating the disappearance of my *daughter*, not delving into my private life.

226

You had no right to make any enquiries about my personal—'

Lorraine interrupted, her voice controlled and very firm. 'I am trying to ascertain the whereabouts of your daughter. And I would say your drug problems might have some connection. So I am asking you again, did your daughter also use drugs, Mrs Caley?'

'No, she did not.'

'Did she know of your drug addiction?'

Elizabeth Caley sighed impatiently. 'Yes, but she would not even contemplate using drugs herself. She saw too much anguish and pain, regret and dependency in her own mother.'

'Were you aware that Tilda Brown also frequented these clubs with your daughter?'

'Tilda was with Anna Louise?'

'I believe so. Did you know the two girls had some kind of argument the day before you left for New Orleans?'

'I don't know what they were arguing about, just that Tilda decided to leave, silly really. I just let them get on with it.'

Lorraine wasn't going to let Mrs Caley off the hook. She tried again.

'Do you have drug dealers in New Orleans?' She knew she had hit a red zone; Elizabeth Caley's face was glistening with sweat and she was becoming more agitated by the second.

'Oh God, Robert will be so angry, this is terrible. You see, he is in the middle of this big business deal and—'

'I only need a name, Mrs Caley, someone you usually contact there.'

'No, no, please, if this was ever to get out, if anyone there was to know . . .' She seemed to fall apart in front

227

of Lorraine's eyes, slumping into a chair and crying. The make-up smeared, and she held her head in her hands as though it ached, pulling loose her tightly coiled hair. She continued to sweat profusely.

Lorraine leaned forward to touch her. 'Please, I will be discreet, I promise you, but I do need to question everyone possible. You want me to find your daughter, don't you?'

'Yes, yes, I do,' she murmured, and then her body began to shake uncontrollably and she screamed, 'Phyllis, *Phyllis, Phyllis!*'

Phyllis came running as Elizabeth Caley lost control of herself. Urine trickled down her legs, her limbs jerking and her head twitching.

'It's all right, I'm here, *I'm here, Mrs Caley*, just hold on to me, you're going to be all right, just hold on to me. Oh, my God, help me, for God's sake, help me, she's going into a spasm . . .'

Peters came running and between them they helped her from the sun room. Lorraine followed them out into the hall and watched as Peters carried Elizabeth up the stairs.

'Please stay down here,' he said angrily to Lorraine.

'Yes, just leave her alone,' Phyllis interjected.

Lorraine sighed with irritation but there was nothing she could do. She knew she would get little sense out of Mrs Caley now, so there seemed no point in remaining at the house. She returned to the sun room to collect her purse and cigarettes. A maid was already clearing up the tea trays.

Lorraine suddenly picked up the tea pot, took off the lid and sniffed; it smelt of mint and something else, a herbal smell. She sniffed again.

'Excuse me, Mrs Page, may I take that from you?' It was the dour Peters.

'What the hell is in it?'

'Just a herbal remedy, Mrs Caley has it delivered.'

'Where from?'

Peters picked up the tray. 'The Natural Health Store, I believe it's called. Excuse me, I hope you won't take offence but why don't you leave her alone? She is very sick and it's tragic to see her this way, just as she was recovering and—'

'Yes, very reminiscent of Sunset Boulevard, but I wonder who will end up in the swimming pool?'

He stared hard at Lorraine and did not hide his disdain. 'You should perhaps take great care or it could be you.'

He walked out. Lorraine was about to follow him when the maid gave a small nervous cough. Lorraine turned towards her. She gave a furtive look at Peters's disappearing ramrod back before she whispered to Lorraine.

'She gets it from home, ma'am. It's no remedy.'

'I'm sorry, what did you say?'

The girl chewed her lip and then made to pass Lorraine, frightened.

'Wait, don't go. Are you talking about the tea?'

Phyllis hurried in. 'Get back into the house, Sylvana, go along, quickly now.'

Sylvana shot a frightened look at Lorraine before scurrying away.

Lorraine turned to Phyllis with concern. 'Is Mrs Caley going to be all right?'

Phyllis shook her head and shrugged. 'She'll sleep it off.'

Lorraine took Phyllis's arm as they walked back to the house. 'Phyllis, you had better get Mrs Caley some treatment and fast, otherwise she's going to kill herself.'

'Yes, I know,' Phyllis whispered, and then stopped

in her tracks. 'What did you say that made her get so upset?'

'Who's her drug dealer in New Orleans?'

Phyllis closed her eyes. 'Oh God, this is dreadful, if Mr Caley was to know. Please, is it really necessary to—'

'For chrissakes, Phyllis, I am trying to find her daughter! Now if you know and persist in withholding information from me, in giving me half-truths . . .'

Just as it seemed that Phyllis was about to confide in Lorraine, Robert Caley strode in. 'What has been going on out here? Phyllis, you should be with Elizabeth. I want you to sit with her until a doctor comes to see her.'

'I'm sorry, Mr Caley, I'll go straight to her now.'

'And stay with her, if she vomits she could . . .' Robert Caley sighed, waited for Phyllis to go and then looked at Lorraine. 'What did you say to her? She's hysterical.'

'I'm just trying to do my job, Mr Caley, but it seems everyone who works around here is so busy protecting your wife—'

'You saw her, don't you think she needs protecting?' he snapped.

'Yes, I do, but I don't think you know how serious her condition is, Mr Caley.'

'How dare you! I get her into a rehab centre and she's cleaned up only to get back on whatever drugs she can get her hands on. Well, she's going away this time whether she likes it or not . . .'

'So you know what she's taking?'

'You name it and she'll shove it up her nose, down her throat or inject it. Unless I put her under twenty-four-hour watch I can't stop her. But believe me, I've tried.'

'Right now, Mr Caley, your wife is using drugs that could very easily kill her. They are very dangerous used

230

in the quantity she is injecting and she could easily induce a thrombosis.'

He closed his eyes. 'Oh, my God, what is it – heroin?'

'No, they are prescribed sleeping tablets.'

He sighed, giving a helpless gesture with his hands. 'The last thing I need right now is some asshole to get hold of her condition and the story to be plastered over every shit-filled tabloid there is. My competitors'd love it, with Anna Louise missing you can bet any money they'd link her drug abuse to—'

'What if it is?' Lorraine interrupted. He frowned and looked at her. She was sure he was unaware of the exact drugs used by Elizabeth Caley. 'Do you know who she used to procure drugs for her in New Orleans? Your wife has a very expensive habit, Mr Caley, and she'll either take stuff with her or score it there, so maybe there is a link.'

He sat down, head in his hands as he rested his elbows on the table. 'I doubt it, she has a pretty well-organized network of people who I think procure whatever she needs. And she pays highly for it, I have no doubt.'

'You know any of them?'

'I know her main contact is her own doctor. It's madness, like a Catch-22 situation – if I report him he will obviously use my wife's name, even more so now.' He got up and stuffed his hands into his trouser pockets. He seemed tired out. 'I banned Juda Salina from the house but it didn't do any good, she just went to her place . . .'

'Juda Salina procured drugs for your wife? Are you sure?'

He cocked his head to one side. 'Sure as I can be, but what can I do? Put the cops on her and then she informs the press who her client is?'

231

Lorraine leaned forward. 'I don't think her doctor will be able to practise for some considerable time – he was arrested two days ago, and as I believe your wife did not use her own name I doubt if there will be any adverse publicity. Well, I hope not for her sake as much as yours.'

'Thank you,' he said softly, and smiled, then gestured for her to walk beside him. 'I need some air, let's go into the garden.'

They walked side by side in silence along the narrow pathway past the manicured lawns and flower-beds. She felt him begin to relax and he gave her that gentle smile again.

'You mind if I ask you something personal, Mr Caley?'

'No, Mrs Page, you go right ahead. And if you don't mind me being personal, I like this new haircut, it suits you.'

Lorraine ignored the compliment. 'Do you love your wife?'

He wasn't expecting the question and took a moment before he answered, shaking his head, 'Of course I do, but maybe "care" would be a better description. If it wasn't for her I'd still be bumming around selling real estate. That's all I did, you know, when I met her, I was a real estate agent. In fact, I was trying to sell her a property.'

'You got lucky,' Lorraine said softly, and his pleasant manner changed. He lost that vulnerable quality, his eyes hardened and his voice was cold.

'No, Mrs Page, I fell in love with a very beautiful, sweet lady. Now unless you want to ask any further personal questions, I had better see to my wife . . . Oh, I offered you a ride, I'm flying to New Orleans tonight. If you wish to join me, call Phyllis, I'll send my car round.'

'I accept the ride but I'll make my own way to the airport.'

'Fine, Phyllis will give you details of which hangar my plane's parked in. About six-thirty?'

'Thank you, I'll be there.'

'I bet you will be, Mrs Page.'

He returned to the house, not looking back, and Lorraine remained standing alone, angry at herself. There was no need for her to have asked Caley if he loved his wife; she knew he didn't but she believed he really did care about her.

She was getting into her car when she saw the private ambulance pull up in the drive. She took a long time unlocking the door, as she watched the two attendants hurry into the house. A third car was parked in the drive, a dark, four-door Mercedes Benz saloon. After a few moments the two attendants appeared on the steps, holding Elizabeth Caley between them. She was wearing a pair of dark glasses and a head-scarf swathed round her head and she was sobbing, needing the support of both men, but she made no attempt to resist as they helped her inside the ambulance.

Phyllis and Robert Caley came out behind Mrs Caley, accompanied by a tall man in a grey suit carrying a doctor's bag. Lorraine could not delay leaving any longer, as all three turned towards her.

'Goodbye, see you later,' she called out, and then at once regretted her failure to say something more appropriate – even more so when she drove past the ambulance and caught a glimpse of Elizabeth Caley just before they closed the doors. She was weeping inconsolably, repeating her daughter's name again and again – 'Anna Louise, Anna Louise . . .'

CHAPTER 10

LORRAINE HAD expected a small twin-engined plane but Robert Caley owned a 1993 Citation Jet which made her Russian cab-driver whistle with open admiration. As she picked up her suitcase a tanned blond man jumped down the steps of the plane.

'Mrs Page?' His wide smile seemed over-bright. 'I'm Edward Hardy, Mr Caley's pilot. Let me take your case. Mr Caley has been delayed but he called in to say he would be here shortly. As it turns out it's not a problem as we haven't yet got clearance for take-off.'

Lorraine stepped inside and Edward moved ahead of her to indicate a plush leather easy-chair. He stowed her case away in a compartment at the rear of the plane, keeping up a friendly conversation.

'If you need the bathroom it's right here, and the bedroom is just beyond.'

She flicked him a glance but the remark was innocent.

'If you need to wash, or do whatever ladies do. In the meantime, can I offer you a drink? We have champagne, chilled Chardonnay or a nice Merlot, if you prefer. There's gin, whisky, Martini, or I can make up a cocktail . . . anything you want.'

Lorraine felt so self-conscious as she sat stiffly in the leather easy-chair. 'Just iced water, please.'

A diminutive Chinese man appeared, carrying a deep basket and a large silver foil-covered tray.

'Hi there, how you doing? Yung Sin, this is Mrs Page.'

She smiled as the little man began to lay out his many different covered dishes.

'You like lobster, Mrs Page?' he enquired.

'Yes.'

'Flown in from Maine.' He opened a table, deftly placing on it white linen cloth and napkins, flower bowls, cutlery and cut-crystal glasses.

Lorraine drew a *Vogue* magazine towards her and flicked through the glossy pages. Had Anna Louise Caley sat in the same chair and read a similar magazine?'

'Did you know Anna Louise?' she asked as Edward refilled her glass.

'Yes, of course.'

'You were flying the plane on February fifteenth last year?'

'Yes, I was.'

Lorraine smiled, sipping her water. 'Anna Louise called home?'

'She did. We have a phone, do you need to make a call?'

'No, thanks. How was she on the flight?'

'I was in the cockpit.'

'But you must have welcomed her aboard.'

'Yeah, she was like usual, you know, cute kid, always real friendly.'

'You've worked a long time for the Caleys?'

'About eight years.'

'So you knew Anna Louise quite well?'

Edward hesitated and then put his hands on his hips. 'She was my employer's daughter, ma'am, she was a nice kid but I never knew her, I never saw her outside business if that is what you mean.'

'You are a nice-looking young man, Edward.'

'I'm also married, Mrs Page, with a two-year-old boy.

No way would I start up anything that'd jeopardize my job, my marriage, or show disrespect to Mr Caley.'

'How did you get on with Mrs Caley?'

Edward was beginning to show his irritation at her questions. 'Mrs Caley is one of the nicest women I know, always friendly. I know she has a few problems but that isn't my business. When she's aboard she's real quiet, she's nervous about flying. You nervous at all, Mrs Page?'

'No.'

'No, I didn't think you would be.'

He was about to walk away when she slapped the magazine down.

'Edward, a second. Don't get lippy with me. I'm hired by the Caleys to find their daughter so I have to ask you a few questions, be they personal or not. I don't mean to insult you but I've had a lot of people tell me what a cute, sweet kid Anna Louise was, when I know she was not quite so cute, not quite so innocent, and liked to be fucked.'

'Excuse me, ma'am.' Edward walked to the exit door.

Lorraine sighed, surprised by her own brusqueness. She looked out from the window as Caley's limo drew up close to the plane. Edward was waiting to take Caley's suitcase. The two men smiled warmly at one another.

Caley appeared, waved at Lorraine, and slipped his arm around Edward's shoulders. 'Sorry about the delay. Will we have problems with take-off?'

'Nope, just got clearance, we can go any time.'

'Right, let's get going.'

Caley started for the cockpit, then turned. 'Will you put your belt on, Mrs Page, just a precaution. I'll be right out.'

Take-off was smooth, hardly disturbing the cutlery neatly laid out on the dining table. It was a few moments more before the plane began to climb, and Caley returned. He fixed himself a whisky, checking his watch.

'Flight's just over three hours. We'll eat in about an hour, is that all right for you?'

'Fine, thank you.'

'I hope you like lobster?'

'I do.'

'Good.' He smiled and picked up his briefcase. He sat opposite her and selected some papers from his case. Lorraine continued to flick through the magazines, aware of his presence, aware of him seemingly paying her no attention. It unnerved her.

'You can smoke if you want,' he said quietly.

'No, I'm fine, thank you.'

'If you'll excuse me, I just need to read through these, sorry.'

'Don't apologize, I'm grateful for the ride. Thank you.'

He didn't answer, becoming intent on his papers. As he worked, he eased off his jacket, tossing it aside. He then unbuttoned his collarless shirt, one, two, three buttons, still intent on reading, and undid first one cuff, then the other, rolling the sleeves midway up his forearm.

Caley fixed himself two more drinks, checked in with Edward, then sat in another area of the plane and used the telephone for almost three-quarters of an hour, his back to Lorraine. She listened, even though he kept his voice low. The calls were to business partners, Phyllis, the hospital to discuss Elizabeth's condition, his staff in New Orleans, and a lengthy conversation with Mark, his assistant, and Margaret. He listened, swore under his breath, sighed a lot, and then got up to refill his glass. He paused at her side.

'Do you want a refill?'

'Nope, I'm fine.'

He smiled, but she could see his mind was elsewhere so she continued to look at another magazine. By now they all seemed to have the same model wearing similar dresses. She didn't look up when he sat opposite her again.

'I like your suit.'

She looked up and blushed. 'It's new.'

'Are you hungry?'

'Only if you are. If you have to continue working, please, go ahead.'

He didn't. Instead he offered her his hand and led her to the table, drew out a thick padded leather seat for her and lit the candles.

During the meal, they hardly spoke. When they finished, he prepared coffee as she returned to her seat. She didn't know if it was the air in the cabin or the churning of her stomach, but she was finding it hard to breathe because she wanted him to touch her. It was driving her crazy, it was all she could think about, and it physically hurt, the wanting.

'I need to use the bathroom.'

He pointed to the end of the cabin, a cigar clenched in his teeth as he poured their coffee and then opened a bottle of brandy for himself. Lorraine pressed the door closed and gasped. Not until she had run some water and patted her face did she feel calmer. Her hands were shaking and she felt like a sixteen-year-old, scared to walk out and see him, scared he'd know what she was feeling.

She knew the bedroom was next door, even had a moment of fantasy that she would walk out and he would be waiting for her. What would she do if he was? It was madness. She flushed the toilet, telling herself to get it together. She caught her reflection in the vanity mirror above the small washbasin – her cheeks were flushed from the cold water, and her mascara had smudged. She spat on a tissue and wiped beneath her eyes. 'Suit might look good but you look a mess,' she told her reflection, forcing herself to open the door and walk out.

Her coffee was on the table, but there was no Robert Caley. She looked towards the closed bedroom door: had he gone in there? Was he, as she had just fantasized, waiting for her?

Edward opened the cockpit door. 'Will you put your belt on, Mrs Page, we'll be landing in ten minutes.'

She nodded, pulling up the seat-belt strap as Edward popped his head round the door again. 'Just so you won't panic, Mr Caley is not landing the plane, says he's had too much to drink. He's finishing up some work, be out when we land.'

Lorraine noticed the briefcase had gone and she shut her eyes with relief; just not having him close made her calmer.

Caley was lying on the bed, the cigar in his hand. He'd had too much to drink, he knew it, but he couldn't handle the fact that he wanted Lorraine; it was making him feel like an inadequate teenager. He imagined her walking in and, without needing to say a word, lying down beside him. He could feel the slow downward spiral of the plane matching the churning in the pit of his stomach. He had to force himself to straighten out. He checked his watch, got up and shaved, then put on a clean shirt.

Caley rejoined Lorraine as the undercarriage lowered. He snapped on his safety belt, placing the briefcase he hadn't opened at his side. Lorraine stared out of the dark window.

'I put the candles out.'

239

'Oh, thank you.'

He straightened a magazine on the table between them as the plane made a good smooth landing. 'Good pilot,' he said.

'Yes,' she said, but neither of them looked at the other.

The stretch limo was waiting outside the private Lake-front airport, and beyond the tarmac the dark waters of the huge salt lake stretched as far as Lorraine could see. As Caley helped her into the car, he asked her where she was staying. She sat as far away from him as possible, opening her purse to check Rosie's notes. The St Marie Guest House. The chauffeur waited until Caley gave him instructions to drive directly to his hotel.

'It is the hotel we stayed at the night Anna Louise went missing. I've booked both suites again as I thought perhaps you would want to question the staff.'

Lorraine nodded, and Caley turned towards the window, seemingly staring at the bulk of an old, garishly painted paddle-steamer, now refitted as a floating gaming palace, brilliantly lit and emblazoned with a huge casino sign. The competition? Lorraine wondered.

'If you want you can use Anna's suite . . .'

Lorraine told herself she was being insane, one minute afraid to be close to him, the next wanting to accept a suite in the same hotel. He stared out of the window, asking himself what the fuck he thought he was playing at, one moment avoiding her, the next asking her to sleep in the adjoining suite. If Elizabeth knew she would scream blue murder, always wary about any scandal that might smudge her fame in her home town.

'Maybe not,' he said softly. 'Sorry, I don't want you to get the wrong impression, it's just . . .'

240

'Just what, Mr Caley?'

He turned and faced her as the chauffeur swung on to the Interstate to cross town; the houses, all with their Southern shutters and verandas and many already sporting Carnival decorations, seemed small and huddled together in the darkness, and the city cramped, spaceless after the sprawl of LA.

'It's a connecting suite,' he said with embarrassment.

'Yes, you said.' Her heart was thudding and she knew she should refuse the offer. Instead she gave a tiny laugh, trying to make a joke of it. 'You afraid I'll sneak up on you in the middle of the night?'

There was a long, strained pause and he never took his eyes off her. 'I am not afraid of what you would do, Mrs Page, it's what I would do, or might not be able to stop myself doing.'

There was another strained pause. She inched her hand across the seat towards him. She couldn't speak, and when she felt the touch of his hand on hers she felt as if she would explode. They had left the highway now and were approaching the old French Quarter, and Lorraine was glad of the excuse to look away, pretending to be absorbed in observing the historic streets. Only a few blocks away were the high, modern towers of a business district like any in America, but here was an atmosphere unlike anything Lorraine had encountered before, half village, half cosmopolitan, Babylonian city.

The buildings at first seemed low and unimpressive, flat-roofed, two-storey town houses for the most part, their plaster fronts painted within a narrow range of muted shades that had once been bright – ochre, putty, ashes-of-roses, mustard. All had long, elegant shuttered windows and door frames, often picked out in a contrasting deep green, but most distinctive was the iron-work, as fantastically wrought as spun sugar, with which

241

balconies, galleries, walks and window-boxes were all lavishly decorated. In its heyday the place must have been something to see, Lorraine thought, but now the fading paint, peeling woodwork and untended hanging baskets and jardinières were noticeable even at night.

Caley grimaced slightly as the crowds became thicker and the buildings more and more festooned with the purple, gold and green of Carnival flags, masks and streamers, and they slowed almost to walking pace to avoid the pedestrians of every age and nationality who thronged the streets. 'Sorry. There's only a couple of blocks of this – it's tourist gulch down here, I'm afraid.'

Lorraine knew he too was making small-talk to try to conceal the tension between them, and glanced up at the street sign as they took a left: Bourbon. Farther down the block she could see the neon naked girls and triple X signs of the strip clubs, and every store front they passed seemed to be a jazz bar, a restaurant, or a gift emporium full of tacky T-shirts, mugs, figurines, Carnival masks and Cajun cowboy hats by the score. Music and the smell of spiced food were everywhere, spilling from doorways and sometimes from broad galleries above; everywhere people were eating, drinking, singing, begging, the young guys staring and calling after the girls, tourist ladies in their seventies holding tight to their purses and their companions' arms. But all were out in the night and the Quarter: the raw life of the place hit Lorraine like a shot of liquor, and suddenly it didn't seem quite so fading and unimpressive. On the sidewalk a young black kid of ten or twelve tap-danced effortlessly, expertly in a pair of trainers with metalled heels and toes. He had a wide, ingratiating smile pasted to the lower half of his face, but Lorraine caught the age and the knowing in his eyes, and suddenly she felt the power of the past. This place had seen a lot of human foibles, she reckoned: there was nothing that couldn't happen here.

They picked up speed again as they drove on and the streets became quieter and the goods for sale changed to jewellery, art and antiques, displayed in smarter shops closed at this hour of the evening.

'We're almost at the hotel, Mr Caley,' the chauffeur said as they turned into a block as perfectly preserved as a museum, and Lorraine moved her hand away. They pulled up outside an exquisite three-storey town house with broad galleries and iron-work as delicate and elaborate as the lace of a ball-gown: there was nothing to indicate that this was a hotel, but when the chauffeur rang at a pair of high double doors, a smartly suited young man appeared and greeted Caley warmly by name.

He led them through an arched *porte cochère* into a lantern-lit, paved courtyard, and Lorraine knew she was entering a world apart from the tacky burlesque of the tourist traps, one where every aspect of her surroundings had been carefully designed to leave no sense unsoothed, unrefreshed. The trees exhaled an intense, herb-sweet scent, strange at first, then delicious, revivifying, while in the background the sound of two fountains was just audible, and an array of ferns, palms, citrus trees and vines grew lushly and seemingly at will around the courtyard's borders and balconies. Lorraine knew at a glance, however, that this sweet neglect was an effect achieved at considerable cost in terms of both time and money: the balance of wildness and cultivation was as perfect as a note in music.

The young man ushered them into a small, graciously appointed office and an interminable time seemed to pass while Caley exchanged pleasantries first with him, then with the still more courteous and urbane general manager before their bags were taken by the bell-boy. Lorraine noted wryly that the South, though perhaps in slightly reduced circumstances, still moved at her own grand old lady's pace.

'Lieutenant Page will want to ask your staff a few questions,' Caley said as the manager at last motioned them towards the elevator.

'Anything myself and my staff can do to assist in any way, you only have to ask.'

The bell-boy was waiting at the elevator, a dainty cage of mirrors and gilding. Despite the confined space, Lorraine and Robert Caley remained well apart and said nothing to one another. When they reached the third floor, Caley took his keys from the boy, walking ahead.

'Show Lieutenant Page to her suite, if you would,' he said without a backward glance.

'Yes, sir. You follow me, ma'am?' Lorraine was shown to a plain white door: the hotel was clearly too exclusive for room numbers, or even names. Further along the corridor Caley's suite door closed.

'Enjoy your stay, ma'am.'

'Thank you.'

Alone, Lorraine glanced around the suite: the sitting room was large and airy, lit by a heavy crystal chandelier, and again Lorraine knew that the day-bed, the magnificent fireplace and mirrors, and the figured rugs, as soft and fine to the touch as a cat's ear, were genuine antiques, not the ostentatious reproductions favoured by anything approaching an expensive hotel she had encountered in the past.

Beyond was the bedroom; an embroidered half-canopy hung from a corona above the double bed, and a separate bathing and dressing area was screened from the balcony by muslin-draped French doors. Lorraine opened them and stepped out, noting a narrow spiral staircase, presumably the fire-escape, trailing vines and plumbago, which gave access to the balcony below and then the ground. She wondered half-heartedly if Anna Louise Caley had left that way. If she had, no one would have seen her leave unless they'd been in the courtyard.

She unpacked, hung up her new clothes, wondering if she should contact Rosie and the others now, but then knew that if she did she might have some explaining to do. She went into the bathroom, set her few cosmetics out on the imposing marble washstand and ran herself a hot, deep bath.

Nick Bartello knocked on Rosie's door as Rooney appeared at the end of the corridor. 'I got five beds in my room, how many you got, Nick?'

'Oh, just a double, a single and a cot!'

Rooney shrugged. 'Well, we ain't payin' for it.'

Rosie opened her door and beamed. 'Hi, come on in. I got a huge room and my own bathroom, it's so cute.'

'Any word from Lorraine?' Nick asked as he sat down on a boxy foam-filled sofa, upholstered in the same Dralon and fringes as the drapes. An old TV was perched high on a repro tall-boy; the oversized nylon lampshades were full of dust and the room smelt of cigarettes and air-freshener.

'Not yet, no, but I called home and the office and got no reply, so maybe she's on her way.'

'I'm hungry,' Rooney said flatly, and Rosie beamed again.

'Why don't we go eat, see a few sights, maybe wander round the French Quarter? I mean, as it's our first night we can kind of relax, right?'

'Let's go,' Rooney said, gasping for a beer.

Nick hesitated, then shrugged. 'Okay by me, but you

245

got to get on to the cop shop here, Bill, find someone we can get some inside information from.'

'Way I hear it, any one of the cops'll do anythin' for a few extra bucks.'

'Hey, we can pick up the streetcar, take a ride, have a look at the riverboat casinos.'

Nick looked at Rooney as Rosie headed out. 'Dumb broad thinks we're on holiday.'

Rooney shrugged. 'For tonight we can be . . . why the hell not?'

'Okay, man, why the hell not?' Nick strolled after Rooney as Rosie locked her room, clutching tourist guides and leaflets in her hand. 'But we're already five days down. That leaves us nine to break this case.'

'I've been looking forward to this,' Rosie said as they trooped down the stairs, passing four old ladies with crimped perms protruding from their straw sun hats with 'Laissez les Bons Temps Rouler' printed on them.

'Hell, Rosie, this is zimmer-frame location,' Nick said.

'Now don't start, Nick Bartello. Like I said, we're lucky to get into some place as central as this, it's coming up to Carnival.'

'Sure is,' Nick said as a group of yet more chattering women met their tour guide in the reception area.

'Ladies, are we all set? Tonight we are going to the historic Voodoo Museum, please all have your special party tickets ready,' their slick black-haired guide bellowed.

Rosie slipped her hand into Rooney's arm. 'I want to go there, to the Voodoo Museum.'

'Let's eat first, huh?' Rooney said, that beer calling him.

*

Lorraine wrapped the hotel courtesy robe around herself as she dried her hair, conscious of the door to the adjoining room that had remained closed. In his suite, Caley, a towel around his waist, made some calls, the first to Saffron Dulay's father to arrange a meeting.

It was almost 10.30 but he still continued to call each one of his partners to say he was in town and needed a meeting. Normally, he would have waited until first thing in the morning but he needed to occupy his mind. The door that connected the two suites drew him like a magnet.

Had he said it? she asked herself, or had she misheard? Hadn't he said he was afraid of what he might do?

'Shit,' she muttered, knowing it was ridiculous. 'Go repack your things and get out before you do something you'll regret.' But she did nothing, telling herself that she should go down to the front desk and start asking a few questions. This was the room Anna Louise Caley disappeared from; the dress she was going to wear had been laid out in readiness, and Caley had said he saw her purse in the sitting room. By which door had he entered the suite – the connecting door? Had he said it was unlocked? She couldn't remember. She finished drying her hair and decided she would go to bed and ask questions the following morning.

Lorraine had closed the doors to the balcony and was pulling back the bedspread when there was a tap on the main door. Her heart lurched as she heard the key turning.

The maid peeked round. 'Oh, sorry, do you want your bed turned down, ma'am?'

'No, thank you, er . . . one second. Come in.'

The maid hovered at the door. She had two foil-wrapped mints in her hand, and she curtsied to Lorraine as she scuttled to the bed.

247

'Do you mind if I ask you something?' Lorraine smiled sweetly.

'No, ma'am.'

'Do you recall Anna Louise Caley at all?'

'Yes, ma'am, she often stayed here.'

Lorraine came closer. 'Were you on duty the night she disappeared? It was February fifteenth last year.'

'Oh yes, I was, ma'am.'

Lorraine looked at her watch. It was 10.45. 'Did you turn back her bed?'

'I did not, I knocked but received no reply.'

'But you just unlocked my door so you obviously have keys, and as I didn't reply, you walked in.'

'But you didn't have a Do Not Disturb sign on the door, ma'am.'

'Did Anna Louise Caley?'

'Yes, ma'am, but I came by earlier than tonight. We had a lot of new guests check in this evenin' so I am late on my round.'

'So what time did you try to turn down Miss Caley's bed on the fifteenth?'

The maid looked to the ceiling. 'Be about eight to half past.'

'Did you come back to try again?'

'No, ma'am, I did not, because when I finished my round there was still the sign on the door. That was about ten-thirty.'

'Thank you. Er, what's your name?'

'Ellie, ma'am, Ellie Paton.'

Lorraine slipped her a couple of dollars and sat on the bed. If Anna Louise Caley had stayed here often then she would know the routine of the night staff, so she obviously intended not to be disturbed or found out.

'Goodnight, ma'am, enjoy your stay.'

Ellie closed the door silently and Lorraine listened,

wondering if she would also turn down Robert Caley's bed. She could hear nothing so she inched open the door and stepped into the corridor. She could see the Do Not Disturb sign on Caley's suite door.

Lorraine eased off the robe and slipped between the cool sheets. The two mints had been left by the telephone at her bedside. It was now almost eleven and she used the dimmer switch to lower her bedside lamp. Distant voices echoed from the streets outside the courtyard: music, someone singing. She lay there waiting, wondering what he was doing. No way could she sleep.

Nick was tired out. He'd had too much to drink and the hot spicy food had given him one hell of a thirst. He was also feeling the buzz between Rosie and Rooney. Hard to believe, but they were acting like a pair of teenagers, tasting each other's food, ordering more and more ridiculous dishes. The Cajun restaurant had been as big as a barn, but hot and crammed to capacity, full of tourists being 'sold' the atmosphere by over-expansive waiters, all out-of-towners eager to eat their blackened shrimp and jambalaya off greasy check oilcloth and add their business cards to the thousands stuck on the posts that supported the roof. A band played rapid, lurching Zydeco while the singer yelped about his Cajun queen, and middle-aged couples shuffled round the dance floor as though it was the first time they had touched one another in years. The place irritated the hell out of him.

'You two mind if I split? I'm kind of tired out.'

'Ah, no, don't you want a streetcar ride to the riverboats?' Rosie asked.

'Another time. I'll just get some shut eye.' Nick delved into his tight jeans but Rosie put her hand out. 'It's okay, Nick, all on the agency, remember?'

Nick grinned and eased out of his chair. 'See y'all in the morning for grits Creole-style. G'night.' He sauntered out, ready to hit some of the strip joints in the real city; the tourist section was all show, all done to hit the wallet, and judging by the packed restaurant a lot would end up well and truly creamed, unaware maybe they'd seen nothing of what really went on just a few streets deeper down.

Lorraine tossed her sheet aside and, stark naked, reached for her robe. She knew if she stopped moving she'd back out but just as she got to the adjoining suite door, it opened. They didn't say a word. He slipped his hands beneath her open robe and drew her close. She rested her head against the nape of his neck, inhaling his clean smell, like fresh scented soap, and she could feel his heart thudding alongside her own as she curled her legs around him. He lifted her higher and closer, carrying her towards his bed, then eased her down so her back lay flat against the sheets, her legs still entwined round his waist. He slowly stroked her legs as he knelt down until they opened wide for him to kiss her thighs, her belly. She felt herself opening to him totally as he licked her, kissed her cunt until she was moaning, feeling the rush of heat flood through her as she tilted her hips upwards. Not until she came with another soft purring moan did he begin to strip off his towel. Then he gently moved her so her head lay on the pillow and he lay beside her, stroking her, kissing her body, gentle, sweet kisses. He eased his body over hers and nuzzled her neck until his lips searched out her mouth and his tongue traced hers. Not until she drew his head closer, not until he felt her hungry passion, did he move her hand down to his erect penis as if

250

wanting her permission to fuck her and she murmured, 'Yes . . . yes . . .'

Caley was the most experienced lover she had ever known. He never at any time seemed to be just screwing her; he was caring and in turn rough, but she began to feel that he was only wanting to give her pleasure, wanting her to orgasm, asking softly what she liked, what she wanted him to do. Without embarrassment she told him; it made her feel as if she was in control and yet she knew she wasn't. And not until she began to make love to him, caressing him in turn, did she feel him withdraw slightly, and she pulled away from him.

'Let me love you now . . .'

He closed his eyes as she eased on top of him, looking down into his face. She bent her head close. 'Look at me, open your eyes . . . I want you to see me, know me.'

Slowly he opened his eyes. Gone was the experienced lover, instead she saw a raw innocence, almost a fear, and she stroked his face. 'What are you scared of?'

'You,' he said softly, because the countless women he had fucked, women like Saffron Dulay, had never touched him so deeply as Lorraine. He was not used to accepting sexual pleasure, only to giving it, and there wasn't a trick he didn't know. But tonight there were no games, just two people with the same physical passion for each other, and the more she aroused him the more at ease he became with allowing himself to be desired, until they were equal. His first orgasm left him gasping for breath. Their bodies glistening with sweat, they remained clinging to each other as they drifted into an exhausted sleep. They woke alternately, arousing and waking the other. The night felt long and the dawn was still to come, and they could not get enough of each other.

'I am loving you, Lorraine Page,' Caley whispered.

'And I you, Mr Robert Caley,' she smiled, leaning up

251

on her elbow, looking down into his handsome face. 'It's been a long time for me.'

He laughed softly. 'Much longer for me, my love, I never believed I could feel this way again.'

'Again?' she mocked.

Caley drew her close. 'It's as if this is the first time I have ever been with a woman who doesn't play games because . . .' He kissed her lips. 'We don't need to, more importantly I don't want to. That said, what was the last position?'

She laughed, tracing his face in the dim light, feeling his rough chin, liking the fact that it had been so smooth when they had first kissed. 'Remind me.'

Rooney looked at the big riverboat casino, gaudy as a Christmas tree with its rows of gold lanterns and golden illuminated crown encircling the funnel, the lights dancing on the wide Mississippi.

'Maybe whilst we're here we'll treat ourselves to a few chips one night,' Rosie suggested.

'That'd be nice, I've never been inside a casino.'

They walked on, Rosie now totally at ease about them linking arms. 'You know, according to the papers two of these riverboat casinos have gone bankrupt. In fact—'

Rooney stopped and looked around. 'We can't be far from Caley's site for his proposed casino.'

Rosie was about to get out her street maps when he took her hand and tucked it under his arm. 'We'll start work tomorrow. Maybe we should think about getting back to the hotel.'

'Okay, fine by me.'

He grinned. 'You're good company, Rosie, I've enjoyed tonight, good choice of restaurant, real authentic atmosphere. I dunno why Nick dived off the way he did, anti-social bastard.'

'I'm glad he did,' Rosie said as they continued walking.

'Me too,' Rooney said gruffly, and his big arm tightened on hers. 'So you were married, right?'

'Yes, and I got a son, but that part of my life is best forgotten. Not my boy, but you know, Bill, I was a lousy mother. I had this drink problem, and now they've moved to Florida, my husband remarried, like Lorraine and her ex, he remarried and her daughters are settled, so is my boy. But one day, well, I hope one day he'll come to me so I have a chance to explain that no matter what I did I never stopped loving him.'

'I'd have liked a son,' Rooney said gloomily.

'Maybe walk back towards the big hotels, people bound to be getting cabs there,' Rosie said as if reading his mind.

They turned back and continued walking at a slow, unhurried pace.

'You ever think about it?' Rooney asked.

'Think about what?' Rosie said.

'Starting up another family?'

Rosie stopped, looking up into his big round face. 'I think about it all the time, Bill, but I'm forty-two now . . .'

An empty cab passed and Rooney interrupted her as he stepped out on to the cobbled road to flag it down.

'What's the name of our hotel, Rosie?' Rooney bellowed.

'The St Marie,' she said as Rooney opened the passenger door.

The cab driver nodded, about to do a U-turn when Rooney leaned forward. 'We far from the old Convention Centre?'

'No, sah, two-minute ride.'

Rooney looked at Rosie. 'Might as well just drive past, huh?'

'Sure, Bill.'

'You know anything about a new casino complex near here?' Rooney asked the cabbie.

'I heard they bin thinkin' about it. These rich guys keep on sayin' they are creatin' work for the locals but it's a load of hogwash. They bring in outsiders, don't hire locals, not classy enough, so they say, not intelligent enough to deal a pack o' cards. Good enough to spend their money there though. They is corrupt, this whole city is corrupt, an' I know it, my cousin is a cop.'

'You don't say,' said Rooney, leaning forward.

Nick had walked a little further than he meant: he'd followed Dauphine quite a way, glad to get away from the bright lights, and then taken a left somewhere. He was bored now with the cheap bar; it must once have been a strip joint, and still had the pink light to make grey-fleshed and jaded girls look younger, and the stage surrounded by sheets of DIY mirror tiles. Old electric cable and piping now hung off the walls, which were covered in tacky seventies posters, and even the red light couldn't conceal the dirt and neglect. Some young guys played the video poker machines, while an elderly jazz four-piece played with surprising verve and expression under the old glitter ball.

The guys were good, but Nick had had enough, so he signalled the waitress to get his check and she sauntered over. Two kids started screaming at an old black dude who had been sitting on a bar stool for almost as long as Nick had been in the bar. The old guy had played a set and he was a real good horn player. When he had been on, the place had been jumping. One of the kids pushed at the old man who rocked dangerously on his stool. Nick kept one eye on them as he flicked out his wallet, paying the lazy waitress who seemed more interested in her tip than in the fracas.

The two boys, both black, were really yelling now.

'We paid you, man, we want the goods, man, you owe us.'

The barman was easing down to the bar phone, his eyes out on stalks. The kids got louder.

Nick was almost at the door when the gun came out. There was a hushed silence. No one seemed to want to make a move.

'Gonna blow your fuckin' head off.' The muzzle of the gun was rammed into the old boy's face.

Everything in Nick was telling him to walk away. But there was something about the old dude and his beat-up trombone.

'Hey, take it easy, kid.'

The boy turned, waving his Magnum, and close up Nick could see he was well spaced out.

'Who you tellin' to take it easy, motherfucker? Stay out of this, none o' your concern.'

Nick came even closer. 'You threatening me?'

'You want your head blown off, man?'

Nick eased into position just behind the old man, who was shaking badly.

'Sonny, I suggest you put that big Mama away and cool down because you are kind of making this whole place jumpy.'

'You a cop?'

'Nope, just a guy enjoyin' an evening out.' Nick smiled, then made his move. He was fast, jabbing the kid hard in the groin and at the same time twisting his arm hard up behind his back. 'Drop it . . .' The gun clattered to the floor. Nick kicked it away but not one person reached for it. 'Get the fucking gun, man,' Nick said to the old boy, who eased off his stool, placed the trombone on the bar and picked up the gun.

'Okay, now everything's cool. You two walk out and chill out.'

Nick pushed the stoned kid off him. He fell on to his backside and as his friend hauled him up on to his feet his mouth was frothing with fury. 'I'll get you, motherfucker.'

They ran out, still shouting abuse as Nick helped the old man back on to his stool.

'You okay?'

'Sure, brother. You wanna beer?'

Nick didn't, but he nodded his head. The barman removed the weapon and placed a chilled beer on the counter.

The old boy turned to the band. 'You guys lost your wind?'

The band started up and the bar buzzed as the old boy gave the barman orders to serve drinks on the house. He then turned his lined face to Nick, and when he smiled he displayed four gold teeth, two top, two bottom.

'This is my place, my bar, who the fuck are you?'

'Nick, Nick Bartello.'

The gnarled hand gripped Nick's. 'Name's Fryer Jones. That was a real nice move you just peeeformed, you a cop?'

'Was, long time ago.'

'Ah,' Fryer said as he slurped his beer.

'What was that about?'

The old man fingered his trombone. 'Nothin' much. Happens most nights, they get high. I got to pay a pot of protection and you can see the place ain't a gold mine. We call the cops an' they ask for even more dough.

Sometimes we just let 'em shoot up the place a bit, don't bother me, why should it, I had my day.'

Nick drank his beer and another bottle was placed down in readiness.

'So you deal on the side, huh?'

The old guy chuckled. 'For somebody that ain't no cop y'all sure ask a lot of questions. What the fuck you doin' in this area anyway?'

'I've been hired to trace Anna Louise Caley.'

Fryer kissed his teeth. 'Ah, little Caley gal, been a lot 'bout her in print.'

'So you know who I'm talking about.' Nick hadn't really anticipated such a direct reply.

'Know her mama, everyone knows Eeelizabeth Caley, man. And if you want some advice—'

'Take any you've got,' Nick said, liking the old man.

'Git your ass outta here or you'll get burned real bad, man.'

'Why?'

'Just like I said, lotta people been here before you.'

'What, to this bar?'

Fryer chuckled, shaking his head. 'Nah, man, the city is jumpin' right now, afloat with millions of bucks, and just a handful gettin' the pickin's . . . it creates a deep murky pond. Dig up some of the slime and like I said, you'll git yo'self in bad trouble, might have even got yourself into some tonight. Those two kids . . .' Fryer fingered his trombone. 'They got heavy connections.'

'Didn't look too heavy to me.' Nick drained his beer.

'Nothin' is how it looks, man, some got connections to gangsters, some got deep roots, and I'm just givin' you some friendly advice. Now if you'll excuse me, I got my second set comin' up, I like to keep my wheels oiled.'

Nick got off his stool as Fryer unwound from his neck what looked like small animal bones bound with a leather

257

strip. 'Here, brother, wear this, and go easy now. Help ward off evil, they're the real thing. Go easy now.'

Fryer watched Nick walk out, then turned to his barman with a half-raised eyebrow. 'Crazy fucker.' He signalled to a young guy drinking solo at the far end of the dark bar and he took off after Nick.

The barman stashed Nick's empty beer bottles in a crate beneath the bar. Right by the side of the crate was a double-barrelled shotgun: if Nick Bartello hadn't stepped in to help Fryer, the kids were within inches of getting their heads blown off. But he was not to know, Fryer Jones was old and he hadn't survived this long without taking good precautions. There were a number of dudes quietly drinking that were ready to step in, but Fryer usually took care of things his own way and unless they got a nod from him they left him to it.

'Lookin' for that little Caley girl,' Fryer said as he sucked at his trombone piece, wiping it down on his dirty shirt front. The barman washed out some glasses, gave a dead-eyed stare around as the place was filling up. Nothing really kicked off until after midnight when a lot of the regulars would come in from their work at other clubs and restaurants. Some of the musicians, having trotted golden oldies all night, needed to jam, and played at Fryer Jones's bar. These sessions were almost a nightly ritual, and a lot of hookers would drift in at dawn to have a few beers and a dance before crashing out to sleep the day away.

Fryer made his way to the small raised platform with the old beat-up plastic chairs, a microphone and sound-box circa 1956. He patted a few shoulders, then stopped by a young black girl with her hair plaited and decorated with metal beads. She was fanning herself with a folded-up newspaper, eyes closed, her cheap synthetic version of a satin slip dress clinging to her young pubescent body, showing off rather than hiding her small tits with their large brown nipples.

'Hi, Sugar May, your mama know you're out this late?'

'Yeah, she knows. I wanna be a singer, Fryer, she knows I hang out here, she don't care either way.'

'Mmm, you said you were gonna stay with your aunty in LA, said you needed two hundred bucks, so how come you're not singing at one of them Hollywood clubs?'

Sugar May shrugged her pretty little shoulders. 'Mah brother took mah money, Fryer, Raoul'd take mah cherry if I didn't keep my legs crossed. He's been gone a few weeks now. So you gonna let me sing?'

Fryer looked around, then bent really close to Sugar May, gripping her braids so he drew her head back. 'You tell that mama of yours if she send any mo' your relatives squeezin' me for protection I'll shove my trombone right up her ass. That was dumb, hear me, girl?'

'I didn't know my brothers was comin', Fryer, they're just stoned.'

'They shoot their mouths off, threaten me with an old pistol in front of my cli-hon-telle, Sugar May, an' one of 'em was an outsider.'

'I'll tell her, Fryer, I will truly, and I wasn't lyin' about going to stay with Aunt Juda, honest I wasn't.'

Fryer released his hold on her braids. 'You also tell her the guy was looking into Anna Louise Caley and this one don't look like he'll be bought off. He was here, right? So maybe he knows somethin'. And now get your tight little ass home.'

Sugar May eased away from him, scared, her big brown eyes wide as the old man creaked up on to the platform. She didn't dare push for singing tonight but she'd push those two dumb bastards that made a show of themselves. She'd most certainly tell on them.

*

Nick Bartello crashed out on one of the many beds in his hotel room, without even undressing or removing Fryer's leather thong with the animal bones from around his neck. He liked it, it reminded him of his hippie days. He hadn't noticed he'd had a tail on him from the moment he left Fryer's bar.

Edith Corbello, Juda Salina's sister and weighing two hundred pounds, was asleep in front of the TV set. The house was one of a run-down, one-storey row, with a sagging felt roof and maybe ten feet of battered frontage facing the street. There was a veranda all right, tiny, the front railing missing half its posts, but even on fine evenings Edith rarely sat out – there wasn't much enjoyment in looking across a vacant lot full of weeds at the raised section of the I10's concrete underparts, or the trash stuck on the barbed wire round a disused warehouse, or the slack utility cables slung right in front of the house: she just stayed put and dreamed. Edith woke with a start when Sugar May nudged her.

'Fryer is blazin', Mama. Willy and Jesse went into the bar tonight threatenin' him and waving a gun around. He also said there was some guy asking questions about Anna Louise Caley an' he said this one didn't look like he'd go away easy.'

Edith Corbello eased herself on to her big flat feet, her swollen ankles spilling over on to her heels. She was wearing dirty old slippers, about the only thing her bloated feet could get into.

'I swear, I'm gonna teach them both a lesson. I'm gonna scare the fuck out of them both.'

'They were stoned, Mama,' Sugar May added, almost gleefully, and received a swipe to her head from Edith.

'An' you should be in bed, go on, git out. *Out!*'

Edith shuffled to the door and into the dark hallway. She passed the closed door to her 'company' parlour, making her way down to the back of the stifling hot kitchen. She looked in. The place was filthy, grease on the walls and floors, littered with old takeaway cartons and empty beer bottles and stinking of decaying food and cigarettes. She pulled the cord of a rickety ceiling fan and pushed open the screen door to the yard. Willy and Jesse were flat out, one on a hammock and the other on the back seat of an old wrecked car. For her size she moved fast, picking up a broom, and with one swing she brought it down first on Jesse's head and then side-swiped Willy so that he fell out of the hammock with a scream.

'I'm gonna fix you both good, I warned you. What's this about you going down Fryer's place, shooting more'n your yapping mouths off?'

The broom swished again, catching Jesse in the eye. He howled as Willy tried to dodge it, but she clipped him hard on the top of his head, and he sank to his knees, holding on to his head with the flat of his hands. Her breath heaved in her chest, her eyes bulged and the sweat streamed off her body.

'Pair o' you git in that kitchen and make it presentable, then you come see me in the front parlour. You're gonna have to make good with Fryer or so help me God I'll put a snake in your guts, an' you know I don't make empty threats. *Move!*'

She sank on to the old car seat, tossing the broom aside. Since Raoul had left she'd had her hands full with those two and sometimes she just got so angry with Juda. All that money she was making and she still living in a pile of ramshackle rooms with four kids. She wished she had never set eyes on that rich bitch Elizabeth Caley.

CHAPTER 11

LORRAINE WAS woken by a shaft of sunlight, diffused and softened by the gathered muslin curtains, coming through the doorway to the bathroom and the balcony beyond. For a moment she was unsure where she was until she saw Robert Caley already showered and shaved.

'What time is it?' she murmured.

'Seven.' He walked to the closets, just a small towel round his waist, and selected a shirt, suit and tie, tossing them on to an elegant spoonback chair. Lorraine sat up and blinked. He turned and smiled.

'When you sleep you look like a ten-year-old, but for that scar. How in God's name did you get it?'

Lorraine drew the sheet around herself. 'Oh, some bar someplace. I'd better get back to my room.'

'No hurry. You want me to order some breakfast?'

Lorraine squinted up at him. 'You think that's wise?'

He laughed, dropping the towel to pull on his briefs; he was completely relaxed about his nudity.

'Maybe not, but you can call from your room then we can eat together.' She sat up, watching him pull on his trousers. 'I have a meeting, eight o'clock.'

Lorraine swung her legs from the bed and he came towards her, bending down to kiss the top of her head. He leaned over and traced the scars on her back, then on her arms. 'How did they all happen?'

Lorraine drew away from him. 'Well, at some point I didn't care too much about living. They're the self-inflicted ones, the others . . .'

He cupped her face in his hands. 'Wherever you've been, my darlin', is past. You're with me now.'

She looked up into his face, trying to fathom him out. 'I was there though, Robert, like it or not I was a drunkard.'

He kissed her, holding her tightly. 'But you're not now. You're my lovely Lorraine, and last night is one I will remember for a long time.'

'Me too,' she said softly, wishing he would get back in the wide boat bed again, wanting to hold him naked, wanting him to make love to her again. For a moment she felt that he wanted it too but his phone rang and he eased away from her to answer it.

'Hi, Phyllis. No, no, I'm already dressed. How is she?'

Lorraine picked up her robe from the floor and slipped it round her shoulders. He had his back to her.

'She is? That's good. Well, tell her I'll call later.' He turned to face Lorraine as he pressed line 2 to pick up a waiting call. 'It's Phyllis, says Elizabeth is fine, maybe another week.'

He returned to his call, his manner changed. 'When? It was set for eight this morning . . . what? Shit, okay, no, I can make it. Call him back and tell him I'll be there, and thanks, Mark.'

He replaced the receiver and sighed. 'Lloyd Dulay wants me to meet him at his place so I'm going to have to move fast. Will you leave me the number of your hotel so I can call you?'

She nodded. He finished dressing and put on his shades.

'Talk to you later.' He kissed her cheek and closed the door behind him.

Back in her own suite, Lorraine sat on the balcony. What the hell did she think she was doing? She must have been out of her mind; no matter what the night had been, or meant, she couldn't help but feel depressed and listless. She called down for a pot of hot, strong black coffee, and drained three cups and smoked two cigarettes before getting ready to leave.

Lorraine walked back into Robert Caley's suite. To her surprise it had already been cleaned and the bed made up. There was no indication of their night together: it was as if it had never happened. She crossed to the escritoire to leave her hotel and phone number, pulled the lid down to write, and then saw a stack of documents left neatly in order and a file with 'CASINO DEVEL- OPMENT' printed on it. She wondered if Caley had forgotten it in his hurry to make the meeting; she opened the cover and saw the site for the proposed casino underlined three times: the Rivergate Convention Centre.

Lorraine picked up the file and returned to her own suite. She began jotting down notes. Some of the information blew her mind. Two hundred thousand square feet of gaming area, two hundred tables, six thousand slot machines, and a projected five and a half million annual customers. Lorraine was filling up the pages, salaries estimated at a hundred and seven million. The sources of funding listed were as mind-blowing: a hundred and seventy million equity, almost five hundred million in bonds, a further hundred and forty million bank credit, and on it went to mount up, the grand total well in excess of eight hundred million. The document listed the hard costs, including the parking structures, gaming equipment, state taxes, city taxes, interest, cash load pre-opening, finishing fees and expenses. She noted that the expenditures totalled as much, if not more, than the sources. Finally listed was the projection of revenue, ending up with a profit margin target of around a hundred and twenty million.

Detailed on the following pages were the proposals of what seemed to be the rival consortium, Doubloons, consisting of nine Louisiana residents, nine wealthy men clearly eager to make themselves even wealthier: no wonder Caley was so strung out about whether he or they would be awarded the concession. Lorraine noticed that the costs in excess of forty million dollars had been incurred in securing leases on the site where the casino was to be completed, and wondered if Caley had borne all of these himself. If he had, then not only must he be very wealthy but, as he himself had implied, was stretching himself to the very limit too.

Lorraine returned the file to his room and could not resist opening up every drawer in the desk. She found his real estate licence, his New Orleans office address, details of new hotel developments, mostly in the riverfront area, and one of the hotels which was part-owned by both Robert and Elizabeth Caley. Contrary to what he had said about his wife having nothing to do with his business, her name appeared on numerous deeds. But most shocking to Lorraine was a folded document in the name of Anna Louise Caley. It was secured with a seal and a red ribbon, and contained details of Anna Louise's trust fund. Using the paper knife, warming it over her lighter, Lorraine worked on easing the seal up without breaking it until it came away from the paper. The thick, yellow-papered deed was deeply creased and brittle and she opened it with care. She gasped: there had never been a mention at any time, verbally or in any statement she had seen, of a trust fund for Anna Louise Caley, and the amount was a staggering hundred million. The trust fund was to be managed by her mother until Anna

Louise became twenty-one, and should she fail to live to that age, then the fund would automatically revert to Elizabeth Caley.

Rooney had put on a suit he hadn't worn in a while, and had been surprised that it fitted him, but those few pounds he had lost had made him look and feel better.

'My, you look snazzy,' Rosie remarked as he walked into the restaurant across the street from the St Marie, and he flushed.

'Remember our deal? No diets while we're here.'

'Sure, and I'm game – while we're here, we can eat anything we like.'

Rooney clapped his hands and grinned. 'Right, let's go, they got pancakes here that are delicious, and Nick and Lorraine will be down in a second.'

Hungover, dressed in the clothes he slept in, dark shades on, Nick listened as Lorraine recounted her findings. Watching Rosie and Rooney eating pancakes with syrup, Lorraine realized she was hungry. She hadn't eaten anything since dinner on Caley's private plane. She ordered scrambled eggs and smoked salmon, which made Nick feel even more ill.

'How did you get your hands on all this?' Rooney asked with his mouth full.

'I stayed at the same hotel, in the same room Anna Louise disappeared from. When I went in to thank Mr Caley, he had already left.'

'Went in?' Nick enquired.

'Yeah, there was a connecting door, I had the key. Caley had a breakfast meeting with Lloyd Dulay.'

Nick poured himself more coffee. 'So you stayed in the room next to Caley's?'

Lorraine nodded. 'Yep. I questioned the staff, which

266

was the reason I accepted his offer, so quit with the snide remarks, Bartello. What is that shit you got round your neck?'

'It's a gris-gris.' He leaned close to Lorraine. 'What's that on your neck, sweetheart? Get bitten in that fancy hotel, did you?'

Before Lorraine could answer, Nick took off, and she inched up her collar. 'Mosquito bite. I must have given one little bastard a real night out.'

'I'll give you something for it,' Rosie said at once. She had brought a first aid kit with every conceivable thing they could require.

'It's nothing, just forget it.'

Rooney was scratching his ankle, now sure he had been bitten by something too.

'I think the same little bastard just got me. Heat's like a blanket an' still only January. What this place must be like in the peak of summer, God only knows.'

'Well, hopefully we won't be here more'n a few days,' Lorraine said, a little sharp as she was not getting much response from anyone to her findings. In fact, they seemed to accept it all, as if they knew it already – Robert Caley was still their number one suspect!

'I'm out of here, see you later – we'll meet up in my room. It makes me feel like Snow White or something, by the way, Rosie – it's got about five beds.'

Rosie was getting rattled by all the complaints about their hotel rooms.

'Listen, if you think you can do better, go ahead, but it's Mardi Gras, there wasn't much on offer.'

'Don't get pissed, I was just mentioning it.'

Rooney sniffed.

'If we get short of cash, we can all bunk in together or maybe make a few bucks rentin' them out. You want some more coffee?'

Lorraine drained her cup and nodded. 'I'll be right back.' She set off towards the restroom and Rooney signalled to the waitress to order a fresh pot of coffee.

'Where's Nick?'

'Getting cleaned up, I don't know,' said Rosie, still irritated.

'What's the matter with everyone this morning?' Rooney asked, puzzled.

'I was in a perfectly good mood when I came down for breakfast,' Rosie snapped back.

'Now, don't get all steamed up about Lorraine, we've all mentioned that we got enough beds for a basketball team.'

Rosie banged the table.

'Well, we can check out, one of you can try to find accommodation that can take all four of us at the same time. I spent enough time trying to get the best deal I could, but not so much as a thank you, it makes me sick.'

Rooney reached over and patted her hand.

'Come on now, no one minds, and you never know, one of us might get lucky.'

'What's that supposed to mean?' she glowered.

'Have a few friends call in! Just a joke, sweetheart.'

'Well, I don't find it funny, it undermines my confidence. You might all have been doing this investigation work a long time, but I haven't, and you make me feel inadequate.'

'Then I'm sorry, Rosie, but you know, you could take it as a compliment – cops always get at each other, joke around, it's the way we interact. Treat you any different and you should worry.'

She flushed and suddenly smiled. 'That right?'

'Sure. Now, did you want another coffee?'

Rosie nodded.

She felt a lot better – in fact, she always did when she

was with Rooney. He was restoring her confidence, especially as a woman, in more ways than she had ever hoped possible.

At the turn of the century the Dulay home, an amalgam of Victorian gothic turrets and towers and an incongruously Mediterranean-looking front portico, might have been thought a vulgar, ostentatious hybrid, but it had cost a king's ransom to build, and Lloyd liked to let people know that there was nothing shabby genteel about his family: they had had money then, and they had money now.

Robert Caley drove along the allée of specially trained oaks through Lloyd's extensive grounds – the formal garden, the wilderness garden, the kitchen garden, the cut-flower garden, the water garden – which the Dulays had laid out on several acres of prime site near the agreeable cool of parks and country clubs between river and lake shores, and which glowed like green velvet even when every other yard of ground in the state was a bleached grey-brown. He rang the door, and a uniformed maid ushered him through several waist-high bronzes of the Dulays' favourite dogs and horses into the breakfast room. Caley never ceased to marvel both at the crassness of Lloyd's taste and the boldness of its execution: the modelling of plaster- and woodwork throughout the house was overall heavy, and Lloyd had decided to offset the darkness of the breakfast room's panelled ceilings by commissioning modern murals around the walls, in which neo-classical nymphs and satyrs peeped through more thick foliage. There was something lascivious in the painting, and Caley wondered whether the young Creole goddess, attired in French maid's costume and presently pouring coffee at the mahogany table, might perhaps have been the inspiration for one of the voluptuous nudes to which she bore a striking resemblance.

There was only one place-setting at the table, where Georgian silver-covered dishes faced a large, abstract sculpture in coloured perspex which served as épergne: Lloyd fancied himself as a collector of modern art, but his reforming zeal had not yet encompassed the 200 feet of glazed chintz fussily swagged, draped and festooned across the room's huge picture windows by his grandmother, nor the half-hundredweight of early Anglo-Irish glass hanging from the ceiling, the chandelier's enormous pendants almost touching the plastic structure beneath. The effect was grotesque.

'Just coffee,' Caley said, and the maid acknowledged him with only the smallest of nods of her beautiful head with its wide cheekbones, pale coffee-coloured skin, delicate nose and large, slanting, almond eyes.

The heavy door burst open and Lloyd Dulay strode in. He stood at six feet three and, despite being in his seventies, ramrod-straight, his shock of white hair combed back from his high forehead. He was a formidable man and beside him Caley felt small in comparison.

'Sit down, boy, sorry to change the meeting place but I had a round of golf this morning that hadda continue. I made five birdies, *five*. Thank you, Imelda, honey.'

Dulay touched the maid lightly with his big wide hand and she smiled, eyes downcast, almost too demure, too beautiful. Caley knew she was probably Dulay's mistress, he was famous for keeping them 'in house', and perhaps in this case, on display to his guests.

'How's Elizabeth?' Dulay enquired as he removed the cover from one of the dishes and forked a large portion of Charentais melon and berries on to his plate.

'She's fine, Lloyd, be out soon.'

'I sincerely hope so. Carnival wouldn't be the same without her and we got some fine entertainment this year.'

Lloyd went on to discuss the floats, the big parties and masked balls that different krewes – the local name for Carnival organizations – planned to hold, the new King of Carnival and the young society girl who would be presented as his Queen. Then, seated in his throne-like carver chair and gesturing expansively, he eulogized about the time his own daughter was presented as a maid of Rex, his voice booming round the vast cavernous room.

'Saffron looked more beautiful than ever that day. I tell you, Robert, that girl could have had her pick of any man falling at her pretty little feet, begging her for a dance. You know, I even offered her, *offered*, ten million dollars if she got herself married for long enough to give me an heir. That is one of the blights of my life.'

Caley chewed his lip. He couldn't recall how many times he'd sat opposite this bully of a man, forced to listen to his loud adulation of his whore of a daughter. He even wondered at times if he wasn't in some round-about way hinting that Caley should fuck his daughter – which Robert and almost everyone else had – but if he knew her reputation, Dulay never gave so much as a hint. He just seemed to enjoy the sound of his own rasping voice, and not until he had finished his fruit, sausage patties with a variety of savoury confits and old-fashioned Southern biscuits did he fall silent.

As though summoned by telepathy, Imelda re-appeared and cleared the table, and again Caley saw that big hand stroke his little 'in house' woman. He was sure that if he didn't have a legitimate heir, he most certainly had a number of illegitimate kids. Rumour had it to be around ten or eleven.

Dulay looked over the cigar box held out for him by Imelda. He chose one, sniffing at it with his big hawk nose, then she clipped the end, brought to the table an antique silver perfume bottle remodelled into a lighter, and slipped out. Not until the cigar smoke rested like a halo above Dulay's head did he focus his beady, ice-blue eyes on Caley.

'The Mayor's meeting with the Governor and some of the legislative leaders in Baton Rouge sometime this week. Way I see it, he ought to save himself the trip – what we got to worry about is right here in New Orleans. Some people just seem to want to stand in the way of change until it rolls right over them, though it seems like there might be something in all this federal law stuff. Or so my attorney is bleatin'.'

'That's bullshit, Lloyd, and you know it. They're just trying it on.'

'Robert, you're not hearing me. It's the delay. Don't you see, the more they delay granting you the go-ahead, the longer it drags out . . . and no matter how much you kick against it and say it's not you they're turning up their noses at, nobody's gonna believe it.'

Casey sat back. Even in the chill of the air-conditioned room he could feel the sweat break out on his body: he knew that Dulay had brought up the zoning objections purely as a pretext to cover some move of his own.

'So are you pulling out?' he said nervously.

'Hell, no, I am right behind you. But you are gonna have to give me some proof that it's not just me in deep in this.'

'Right now, Lloyd, the only person in deep is me. It's my own money that's bought those leases. So far you haven't put in so much as a cent.'

Dulay stared hard at him and his eyes seemed to shrink. 'No, Robert, you got my name attached and here

272

that means something, understand me? My name carries a lot of weight in these parts.'

'I know, I know . . . sorry, but right now, Lloyd, I'm being squeezed, you got to know that.'

'Sure I do, nobody likes their balls held in a vice, but at the same time you're gonna be the man who makes the most, so unless you want to carve up your interest . . .'

'I don't.'

'Maybe not now, not today, but perhaps you should give it some thought. If you're gonna go belly up then nobody's gonna back your development, even if the land you got is worth something.'

'More than something, Lloyd.'

'Right, right, but can you keep afloat?'

'Depends on how long. What's friend Siphers doing in Baton Rouge?'

Lloyd shrugged. 'They have to go through some sort of little pantomime of discussing the Doubloons proposal – crease the pages before they toss it out.'

'You're sure the Governor is going to toss it out?'

Lloyd pushed back his chair. 'Sure. This is your show, Robert. You're the one who made the commitment and got ground broken people said couldn't be broke. A bunch of guys trying to jump on your bandwagon will just find they fall off on their ass.'

'So when do you think we might get a yea or nay?'

'Oh, any day now, Robert, and you'll be the first to know. As you know, the Governor is a personal friend,' Dulay said silkily.

There was something in his manner just a shade too smooth to trust, but Caley was too tired to press the old man further and stood up, forcing himself to smile.

'I'll look forward to it, Lloyd.'

'You count on it,' Dulay said, and gestured towards

the door. The meeting was over. He paused as they walked out into the huge entrance hall with its bronze menagerie. 'They found your little girl yet?'

Caley shook his head. 'No, but Elizabeth has hired a new agency, they'll maybe get some results, they seem very capable.'

Lloyd glared. 'Capable? Holy Jesus, Robert, she's your daughter! You just hired *capable* . . . I'd leave no stone unturned if it was my little girl, I'd hire the best this country has.'

'We did,' Caley said flatly.

Dulay held out his arm and it felt like a dead weight on Caley's shoulders. 'You sure you can keep going? Money-wise?'

Caley nodded, and the big man hugged him close. 'I feel for you and my lovely Elizabeth, she must be going through hell.'

'She is.' Now all Caley wanted was to get out, but the big man's arm held him like a vice.

'You call on me, Robert, I mean it. You're like family to me and that sweet child keeps me awake at night. What do these agencies think might have happened?'

Caley stepped aside. 'That she could have been abducted, you know, kidnapped by the opposition, maybe to stop me from opening up.'

'Bullshit, they're too big to play that kind of game. Jesus, I know every man on the Doubloons board, lot of old friends, some I was in knickerbockers with, and I can tell you every man is a gentleman.'

'Why didn't you kick in with them?' Caley asked quietly.

Dulay shrugged and walked into the marbled hallway. 'I wasn't asked . . . and I like to be asked. I'm not a man that barges in on anybody's deal, they gotta come to me. With my kind of capital I don't get into anything without being shown a little respect.' He towered above Caley. 'You've always shown me respect, Robert, and for that reason alone I'm with you on this deal. You're a man that's climbed up from nothing and I admire you. I also care about that wife of yours, we go back long ways, and I look forward to seeing her soon as she arrives. My house is yours, you know that, Robert.'

Caley looked back at the huge house, riding like an ocean liner above the smooth lawns, and Dulay's empty words rang in his ears. 'My house is yours, you know that, Robert.' What a joke! Dulay was squeezing for a much bigger chunk, it was obvious, squeezing and waiting like a shark to step in and offer to bail him out for a percentage that Caley could see – sixty:forty: and the sixty wouldn't be his but Dulay's.

The chauffeur headed back to the hotel. Caley closed his eyes, thinking of Lorraine and the previous night. No wonder he felt worn out. But he wanted to see her again, needed to see her, because at the moment he knew Dulay was shifting the ground under him, and it felt like he was going to go down.

Nick rejoined the black iron courtyard table washed, shaved and wearing clean clothes. Rooney was making notes on the back of an envelope. 'I'm going to have a chat to this cab driver's brother.'

'Really? Can you fill me in, I mean, what cab driver and who's his brother?'

Rosie leaned forward. 'We used him last night, Nick, drove past Caley's proposed site for his casino, and this guy was full of it. He said his cousin, not his brother, was a cop, said they're all corrupt.'

Lorraine was sitting with her eyes closed, face tilted to the sun.

'Okay, I think I'm gonna go back to the bar I wound up in last night. This old trombone player sort of warned me off.'

'Off what exactly?' Lorraine asked without moving.

'Anna Louise Caley.'

Lorraine turned to face him. 'Go on.'

Nick shrugged. 'That's it, he just said to get the hell out, and thinking it over he's got to have a good reason and a better one than . . .' He leaned forward, frowning. '. . . "Murky waters" – he said something like that, roots go deep . . . I dunno, just got a feeling he knows something. And you, what you gonna do?'

Lorraine yawned. 'Well, maybe start interviewing Caley's business associates and, er . . . what's her name? Anna Louise's friend. I think that'll more than take up my day.' She checked her watch. 'So what say we all meet back here about six tonight?'

Rosie looked at Bill who was still scrutinizing his notes. 'Anybody want me to do anything? If you don't, I'm gonna go to the Voodoo Museum.'

Rooney tucked the envelope into his pocket and got up. 'I'll hire a car, drop you off there if you like, Rosie.'

'Oh, thanks. See you all later.'

Lorraine held up her hand. 'Just a second, before you scoot off, Rosie, will you get me appointments to meet all Caley's business partners and Tilda Brown?'

Rosie nodded. 'Sure, I'll do it straight away. You arrange the car, Bill, and I'll meet you in the lobby.'

Lorraine watched them go off, easing between the tables.

'They're getting very friendly, aren't they?'

Nick rocked in his chair. 'Yeah, hadda terrible meal

276

out with them. Rooney gettin' all coy and a bashful Rosie are hard to take.'

'You serious?' Lorraine said, laughing.

'Yeah.' Nick watched her, wanting her. He instinctively knew she'd had a lot more than just a dinner on the plane with Caley.

'What did you get from the staff at Caley's hotel?' he asked.

'Not much. Only one thing that's not on any report was that the maid did not turn down Anna's bed at around eight to half past because there was a Do Not Disturb sign on the door. Which could mean she'd already left, or . . .'

'Nice suite, was it?'

'Yes, it was.' She wanted to take off his shades, see his eyes, because he had that irritating smile.

'You fuck him?'

Lorraine picked up her purse and her note-pad. 'What you think I am, Nick?'

'I'd sure take a chance like that, but then chance'd be a fine thing, right?'

'You said it.'

She edged past his chair and he caught her hand. 'No offence.'

'None taken, Nick, but back off about me and Caley, it's starting to get on my nerves.'

Nick got up and walked with her. 'Just being cautious, sweetheart, he is our main suspect, right? Even more so now with that little legacy you found.' He took off his shades. 'You know, maybe Caley had been dipping into the trust fund. It must be like a red-hot carrot, one hundred million bucks is fucking hot.'

Lorraine felt dizzy. 'Yeah, I thought of that, and I was wondering if there was any way we could find out.'

Nick slipped his arm around her shoulder as they went into the lobby. 'You could ask him.'

Lorraine sighed. 'Yeah, but then he'd know I went through his papers. I don't want to frighten him off if we're right . . .'

'That is some mosquito bite you got, you should get calamine lotion on it.' She turned angrily towards him and he pulled her close. 'Don't bullshit me, I know what it is. I don't care if you fucked him or not, just so long as you don't start to . . .'

'Start what?'

'To care. Because I don't want you to get hurt, you mind if I say that?'

She rested against him, it took him totally off guard and he held her a moment. 'Also, I have to admit that it makes me jealous as all hell. Not that there's any hope for me but . . .'

She smiled up at him. 'You never know, Nick, when you're all washed up and smellin' cute you're not a bad-looking guy. Just not . . .'

'Your type?'

She laughed softly. 'You would have been once, like Lubrinski was, but, Nick, you'd be hell on any woman who cared about you. I know your kind, you love the chase but when it's over you're bored and on to the next.'

'Ah, you got me sussed, huh? But you know, me and Tiger, we're looking to set up a place, one with a back yard so he won't piss on the carpets, and with the right woman—'

'I'm not the right one, Nick, and we're wasting time.'

She saw the hurt look pass quickly over his face and then he gave her that smile of his. He kissed her lips before he sauntered off with his lopsided walk in his beat-up cowboy boots.

As she unlocked her room at the St Marie, Lorraine wished she hadn't been so dismissive because Nick, like Jack, didn't come out with those kinds of words easily. In many ways she was attracted to Nick, it was hard not to be, but it wasn't anything she would allow to happen because what she had said about him was the truth – Nick would never settle down, even with his 'back yard' routine. He was and always would be a loner, like Jack.

She sat on the coloured synthetic bedspread and looked up at the bubbled wallpaper and air vent clogged thick with dust; after last night it all seemed ugly and depressing, and although it was still only eleven o'clock, she felt tired out. That awful feeling in the pit of her stomach that Caley was involved in his daughter's disappearance wouldn't go away, and even after a night with him, a wonderful, special night, she couldn't help but be logical. She was able to subjugate her emotions towards Caley, and allow the professional judgement to take over.

There was a sudden tap on the door and Rosie peeked in, carrying a sheet of paper.

'I've listed those I could get hold of and those you'll have to maybe see tomorrow. I got a car booked for you with a driver at a real low cost as some of these are quite a way apart, and Tilda Brown's place is twenty-odd miles out of town.'

Lorraine glanced over the handwritten notes. 'So it's Tilda Brown first, then Lloyd Dulay? Okay, I'll get cracking.'

The phone rang. It was Robert Caley.

'Hi, you free for lunch?'

'Ah, ten minutes ago I was but I'm just on my way out.'

He sounded disappointed. 'How about dinner?'

'Can I take a rain-check on it?'

'Sure. I'll be back at the hotel early evening, maybe go out to the house, so just give me a call.'

'Will do.'

There was a moment of silence, both wanting to say some kind of endearment, but neither did. Rosie hovered nearby, listening as she pretended to check her notes. She wondered who the call was from, as Lorraine was suddenly acting coy, and she was blushing.

'Talk to you later.'

'Yes, about six-ish,' she said, and the phone went dead. She replaced the receiver and looked at Rosie.

'Who was that then?'

'Robert Caley,' Lorraine said dismissively.

'Oh, you seem to be getting along very well.'

'That's the idea, Rosie – you get along with somebody, you get more information from them, they talk more freely.'

'Mmmm, I'm sure they do. So, you going out with him this evening or are we having a case update? Only I got to let Nick and Bill know.'

Lorraine brushed her hair. 'I just said I would call him, Rosie.'

'Okay, I'll make a note of that, shall I? We'll meet down in the lobby.'

'Fine, see you later.'

'Okey dokey.' Rosie started for the door.

'You and Bill seem to be getting along pretty well too,' Lorraine said nonchalantly.

Rosie had her hand on the door handle, her back to Lorraine, and her whole posture suddenly became defensive. 'Yes, well, I make it my business to get along with him. We're partners after all, and like you said, you get a lot more out of people if you get along with them.'

'But Bill's not a suspect,' Lorraine said, amused.

'Maybe he's not, but as someone learning the business, I need some guidance to keep up with someone as experienced as you.'

'Ohh, that was a bit near the knuckle, Rosie.' Lorraine laughed.

'It wasn't intended that way, but you can get real nasty if I make the smallest mistake, so all I am doing is making sure I don't make any more.'

Lorraine was suddenly concerned. 'Hell, Rosie, you know me well enough that if I snap at you, you know you can have a go right back.'

Rosie smiled. 'Yeah, well, sometimes I just get the feeling you don't rate me, but I won't forget what you just said.'

Lorraine crossed the room and put her arms round her friend. 'You just always be honest with me, Rosie. Jesus, we all make mistakes.'

'No!' Rosie smiled again, assuming a look of mock surprise which made Lorraine laugh again as she crossed back over to the dressing table.

'I'm glad you and old Rooney get along, he's a good man. He was a good cop too – bit rusty now, or maybe it's just he's not as hungry as he used to be.'

Rosie's cheeks went pink. 'You undermine his confidence, Lorraine, like you do mine. He and Nick are working hard, we all are. We're all after the same thing, and there's nobody not pulling their weight.'

Lorraine accepted the put-down gracefully, to some degree impressed by her friend – Rosie was more centred than she had ever known her.

'Yes, I'm sorry, you're right. See you later.'

Rosie opened the door. 'Take care, and check in with us, because we are all backing you to the hilt.'

The door closed, and Lorraine frowned. Rosie was

different these days: maybe it was working alongside Bill, maybe it was her diet boosting her confidence. Lorraine stared at her own reflection.

'Maybe,' she murmured to herself, 'you should start straightening out as well.'

She touched the bruise of the love bite on her neck, and could not prevent the warm feeling that began in her groin flooding right through her body until she hugged herself. She was happier than she had been for a long, long time.

Tilda Brown's family home had been built on the lake in the 1970s, a low white ensemble of rectangles and cubes with a nod to tradition in the form of modern reworkings of traditional architectural features, square columns and vestigial balconies barely six feet off the ground which reminded Lorraine of the wingstumps of some flightless bird. Still, it clearly hadn't been lack of money which was responsible for its boxy blandness, and money was still much in evidence: a European convertible and a fancy off-road funmobile were parked outside, and a gardener was working outside. The large, well-tended yard adjoined the levée, and Lorraine told her driver, a sullen black boy of twenty, to pull up a couple of hundred yards away so she could walk round the back.

'Wait for me, okay?'

'Yes, ma'am, you got me booked for the day.'

From the levée she could see a tennis court and pool, each with floodlighting and a flanking cubist pavilion: by the pool a young blonde teenager lay stretched on a sun-lounger, and Lorraine went round to the front of the house before the girl – Miss Tilda, she presumed – looked up and saw her. She rang the door-bell, and a maid in a pink house-dress opened the door.

'Come along in, Miss Page. Miss Brown is pool-side and she says to ask if you'd like a cool drink.'

'Thank you.'

Tilda Brown had a perfect, all-over golden tan, her waist length blonde hair silky and well cut, and she wore only the smallest of bikini briefs and top.

Feeling the heat, Lorraine was relieved when Tilda got up from her sunbed and suggested they go to the small air-conditioned pool house, further shaded by large palms. She sat in a chair made of stainless-steel 'wicker', its cushions covered in what seemed to be hot pink Spandex, and motioned Lorraine to its twin.

'It's real hot already,' Tilda said, smiling, 'but I got all goose-pimples, coming in from the sun. You mind if I just fetch a wrap?'

Lorraine returned the smile. The maid appeared to serve home-made lemonade, and Lorraine had drunk half her glass before Tilda returned, draped in a long silk kimono, wearing large dark sunglasses with thick white frames and smelling of fresh flowers. She was very nervous, her little hands shaking as she poured herself a lemonade.

'Can you tell me about your relationship with Anna Louise?'

'Sure, she's my best friend. We both come from here, I mean, not that she lives here full-time like my family, but we first met when we were real young, you know, six or seven years old. Then we didn't see each other for quite a while, maybe five years, but I got to go to UCLA and we met up again and it was like no time had passed at all. It was nice to be made so welcome at her home because I sometimes got so lonely.'

'So you knew each other really well?'

'We did, and I miss her.'

Lorraine asked if she could smoke, and Tilda shrugged, fetching a small chrome ashtray. 'You had an argument the day before she left LA,' Lorraine said as she lit her cigarette.

'We used to argue a lot, Mrs Page, we didn't always agree on everything even though we were best friends.'

The girl flicked her silky hair over her shoulder with an immaculately manicured hand, the nails lacquered oyster-pink to match those on her toes. Lorraine envied the Tilda Browns of this world, their ability never to perspire. This was money in front of her, and young as Tilda was, one could tell she had never wanted for anything in her life.

'Can you tell me what the argument was about? It'd be the morning of February fourteenth last year.'

Tilda's eyebrows furrowed. 'Well, you know Anna Louise was a good tennis player and she used to get impatient with me because I was not in her league. Even when we were just warming up she'd do these smashes and I just used to get so angry because it wasn't a competition. But with Anna Louise . . .' She hesitated.

'Yes, go on, Tilda.'

'Well, Anna Louise was competitive in everything and I just got tired of it. I said to her that I wasn't going to play with her anymore and she threw a tantrum, and believe you me, Mrs Page, she could get so angry sometimes, say such horrible things. I had just had enough so I said to her that unless she apologized to me I was not going to travel home with her, no way. I would prefer to travel alone than with somebody as bad-tempered and mean as she was being towards me. Well, she just refused to apologize and so I went in to tell Phyllis that I wanted to leave straight away.'

'Just like that?'

'Yes. Phyllis arranged for Mario to take me to the airport and she also got me my ticket. I called my mama and papa and they collected me here. I said I didn't want to discuss it, but that I was not going to stay with Anna Louise ever again.'

Lorraine drained her glass and Tilda immediately refilled it. At last she removed her big white-framed sunglasses. Lorraine wanted to see her eyes, to try to ascertain just how good a liar Tilda Brown was going to be.

'I never saw her again. And I have felt so guilty. The last time we were together we were fightin', had those cross words with each other, and if . . . if she won't ever be coming back, then . . . It just gets worse, and sometimes I cry about it because we would have made up, no doubt about it, we always did.'

'So she didn't call you when she arrived here with her parents?'

'No, she didn't, but I wish very dearly that she had.'

Lorraine sipped the ice-cool lemonade, wondering how to play it. Tilda seemed to be the genuine forlorn best friend and even at one point had tears in her grey-blue eyes, but she never looked directly at Lorraine and she was exceedingly nervous.

'On the night Anna Louise arrived in New Orleans, where were you?'

'At home. I had a dress fitting, and I ate supper with Mama and Papa before going to bed, 'bout ten o'clock.'

'And she never came round to see you, to make up to you?'

'No, but like I said, I wish that she had. All I do now is pray that she is still alive, because I will make up to her for that silly tiff we had . . . and it was *so* silly.'

'Do you know somebody called Polar?'

Tilda frowned. 'You mean like polar bears? No, I never heard of anyone with that name.'

'How about Tom Heller?'

'Oh, I know him, he was at college with me.'

Lorraine was becoming irritated by her sing-song voice. She decided she had waited long enough. 'You ever go to the Viper Room with Tom?'

Bingo, the cheeks flushed bright pink. 'I beg your pardon?'

'The Viper Room . . .'

The baby eyes blinked and the blush deepened as Lorraine drew out the picture of Anna Louise being fucked by the guys at the Viper Room.

'Oh, my goodness . . .'

'Mmm, oh, my goodness me. That was taken the night before your little tiff, wasn't it? You were upstairs, weren't you, in the private section of the Viper Room?'

Tilda crumbled fast. She bent her head and started sobbing, begging Lorraine not to tell her parents. If her family were ever to know she would be in such trouble.

Lorraine passed Tilda a tissue from a box, covered in the same pink synthetic fabric as the cushions, and she blew her nose. 'I am so ashamed.'

She continued to sob for a while, then quietened down. 'Anna Louise used to take pills from her mother. The first time we took them we just acted silly but then she started to take them real regular, you know, and she'd make me drink vodka, she liked vodka. Then we'd go clubbing and . . . I cannot tell you how ashamed I am . . .'

'No need to be in front of me,' Lorraine said, encouraging her to talk.

'I don't remember what we used to do or what I did, I just used to blank out.'

'But you both used to get screwed, right?'

She nodded, and down came the tears again. 'I guess so.'

'The morning you had the little tiff was after you had been out clubbing with Anna Louise so you were probably a bit hungover, weren't you? So was the "tiff" really about tennis or was it something more important?'

Tilda sighed. 'Oh, it was just awful, she could be such a bitch about things. She wanted to make sure we had our stories straight so her parents wouldn't find out. We were down by the tennis courts and you're right, we weren't playing. I had such a headache, I was feeling sick, and Mr Caley came by on his way to work. When he stopped and asked if I was feeling unwell, I just started to cry. I know what we did was bad, but she could be very insistent, you know? She'd make threats that if I didn't do what she wanted then she'd tell my parents.'

Lorraine waited as she dried her tears and then sat back.

'He was so kind, Mr Caley, sat me down and asked if I was sick, if there was something wrong. He even gave me his handkerchief . . . and I just cried and cried because I couldn't tell him what I was crying about. He sat with me until I stopped crying and said that if there was something worrying me it was always best to share, that if ever I wanted to talk to him then all I had to do was call. He was so worried, so kind and thoughtful, more like a friend . . .'

'Was Anna Louise sitting with you and Mr Caley?'

'Er, no, she had gone into the pool house, said she was going to have a swim and . . .'

'And?' Lorraine asked impatiently.

'Oh, Mr Caley left. He gave me a real nice kiss on the cheek and said he had to go into the office. Then she just flew at me.'

'Who did?'

'Anna Louise of course. She began hitting and kicking me, real crazy. She used her tennis racquet and hit me real hard, and then she got me down on the ground and was clawing and scratching at my face and pulling out my hair. She was on top of me, pushing my head into the ground.'

'Did she think you had told her father about what had happened at the Viper Room, was that why she attacked you?'

'Yes, she said she had seen me with her father. She wouldn't listen to me – she said she was gonna make me sorry. I hit her back and then she spat at me, right in my face, saying she would tell my parents, tell everybody that I was trying it on with her father. I was so shocked . . . I was speechless.'

'But he was just being kind and fatherly, right?'

'Why, yes, of course, but she was crazy about him.'

'Wait, wait, what do you mean, crazy about him?'

Tilda had her hands clenched at her sides. 'She was obsessed by her daddy, she talked and talked about him, that no man ever lived up to him and that . . .' Tilda turned away and up came the flush, her cheeks burning bright red.

'Go on, Tilda, and what else?'

'She said they were lovers, that they were in love.'

Lorraine lost it for a moment, so taken aback by what Tilda had said. 'She actually told you that she was having a sexual relationship with her father, Tilda?'

'Yes, yes, that is what she said.'

'Did you believe it?'

Tilda twisted her fingers, pulling at a ring. 'I just had to leave, Mrs Page. I ran into the house and asked Phyllis to get me a ticket, I never wanted to see her again.'

288

Lorraine's heart was thudding. 'You didn't answer the question, Tilda, this is very serious. Were Robert Caley and his daughter lovers?'

Tilda licked her lips and turned away, her voice strained, hardly audible. 'I don't know, but he was just friendly to me, really and truly, he never made any advances.'

'What about her other friends?'

'She only had me, I was her only true friend. She couldn't tell anyone else about things, everybody thought she was so wonderful, they didn't really know her. And no one liked to stay at the house because of Mrs Caley acting weird, you know, all boozed up and sometimes so out of it it was just plain embarrassing.'

Lorraine stayed for another half-hour, carefully taking Tilda back over her entire statement to the police and the reasons why she had never before admitted the truth about her argument with Anna Louise that morning. It boiled down simply to her being afraid it would get out that she, like Anna Louise, used to go clubbing, stoned and drunk. Tilda did not seem to realize the importance of the question of whether Robert Caley's relationship with his daughter had sexual overtones or not. When pressed by Lorraine for proof, she became agitated and tearful.

'Was Anna Louise just infatuated or do you believe there was more than a father–daughter relationship, Tilda? Did you ever see them together?'

Tilda refused to look at Lorraine, chewing at her lip. Lorraine patiently told her that if what she had said was true it could be the reason behind Anna Louise's disappearance, the reason she might have just run away and might still be alive but afraid to return. What Tilda finally came out with made Lorraine feel wretched.

'She told me they slept together, that he had put her on birth-control pills because he was afraid she would get pregnant.'

By the time Lorraine got back to her driver, she had left Tilda Brown looking like a rag doll: her face was puffy from weeping, her nose red from wiping it, and even her little rosebud lips looked chapped and ugly. Lorraine instinctively believed Tilda's reasons for not admitting what she and Anna Louise had argued about. She had also been given yet another reason why Robert Caley, even more than before, was their main suspect. Lorraine needed a drink, a real one, and she was scared she'd stop and get one so she ordered the driver to take her on to Lloyd Dulay's mansion. Her initial shock on being told about Robert Caley and Anna Louise made her whirl through a spiral of emotions. Having slept with Caley the night before made her want not to believe it, but why would Tilda Brown lie? And gradually her feeling of betrayal and foolishness turned to burning anger. Robert Caley most certainly had a motive to get rid of his daughter and she was going to prove it.

Nick swore. He knew he'd got off the streetcar a couple of stops too early, and he studied his own route map, ignoring the neat bundle of street maps and locations Rosie had given him with telephone numbers of restaurants, taxi ranks, etc. He didn't like carrying around anything more than he needed, or anything that he couldn't stuff into his back pocket. He was near the new Convention Centre, on Lafayette, looking out for Francis X. Roper's Investigation Agency. He had an old buddy who used to work for them; it was a long shot and he'd not seen or spoken to Leroy Able for over ten years, but worth a try.

Nick got the brush-off from Roper's agency, a surprisingly smooth-looking place, when he eventually located it. The receptionist, a red-haired spitfire with green-rimmed glasses, gave him an appraising look that'd have stopped a streetcar dead in its tracks, never mind Nick, and she snapped that she did not know of any Leroy Able – she made even the name sound distasteful. This was a high-class agency dealing with fraud cases and working closely with the police. She seemed to give a lot of weight to the word police.

'You maybe got a forwarding address?'

'Check the telephone directory.'

'You got one?'

She pursed her lips and pushed a big yellow directory across her pristine desk. Nick thumbed through it, taking covert glances around him at all the posters and advertisements the company displayed – missing persons, domestic undercover security work, installation of video cameras, surveillance work. Every case, a poster proclaimed, was the firm's top priority.

'You busy?' he enquired, as he checked down the As.

She was about to reply when the telephone rang, and she snapped the name of the agency into the phone, listening with one eye on Nick and suddenly assuming a sweet voice for the potential client on the other end of the line.

'Yes, sir, we have a full-time staff of six investigators, all licensed and highly trained, and we have our own camera equipment, which includes a variety of long-range lenses and high-powered binoculars. Our teams also carry hand-held radio communications and mobile telephones. I can make an appointment for you, just one moment please.' She reached for a large desk diary as Nick jotted down Leroy Able's address. Whether he was still in business was something he'd find out.

He thanked the woman in green glasses who appeared not to even notice his departure, and headed for Magazine Street in the warehouse district. When he found Able's address, he double checked he was at the right place as the ground floor seemed to be a boxing gymnasium.

Nick went up the stairs into the gym, peering through the double door. 'Anyone know a Leroy Able?'

'Top floor,' came a bellow from a stout boxer well into his fifties, slamming the hell out of a punch-bag.

Leroy was thumbing in leisurely fashion through the *Times-Picayune*, a cup of coffee from which rose the unmistakable smell of New Orleans chicory in front of him, his feet up on his desk.

'Hi, Leroy Able around?' Nick asked.

The paper was slowly lowered. 'Who wants him?'

'Old buddy, shit, it's you, isn't it? Leroy?' Leroy slowly took his cowboy boots off the desk and stared hard at Nick. 'Nick Bartello, LA Drug Squad, last saw you 'bout ten years ago, maybe more.'

'Oh, yeah? Well, I've not got a good memory for faces, what you say your name was?'

'Shit, man, Nick, Nick Bartello.'

'Oh, yeah, yeah, recall the name now. Siddown, want a coffee?'

Nick was a little fazed by Leroy, he didn't show any recognition at all. 'I went to Francis X. Roper's place, I reecalled you mentioned working for his agency.'

Leroy handed Nick a paper cup of black coffee and perched on the end of his desk. 'You know what I hate? People who start talking with a Southern accent ten minutes after they get to New Orleans. What's this reecall crap, Bartello, you wop?' Leroy cuffed Nick's head and gave him a wide grin. 'You had me wondering there for a second, man, it's the gris-gris round your fucking neck.'

Nick fingered the leather thong and the bones. 'I dunno what the shit it is, was given to me last night down some cruddy bar.'

Leroy fingered the bones, raised his eyebrows. 'Well, you must have got well and truly loaded, this isn't tourist shit, this is the real McCoy.'

Nick shrugged. 'So, how's life?'

Leroy eased back into his swivel-chair. 'Ah, not bad, making some dough, of late mostly for the dental board, you know, carrying out medicative investigations.'

Nick laughed as Leroy leaned back and let out a big loud bellow, showing his splendid white and gold-capped teeth.

'Yeah, man, long way from the LA Drug Squad, but at least I don't have a leg full of lead. And I'm my own boss.'

'So you *do* know who I am,' Nick said, reaching for his coffee.

'Yep, just was worried for a second I owed you dough. I don't, do I?'

Nick shook his head, and looked round the office. Leroy's joke about the dentist wasn't right on the level. His office was in good repair and looked like the business was coming in.

'You want a job?' Leroy asked, seeing Nick's curious looks.

'Nope, I'm on one, that's why I'm in New Orleans.'

'Oh yeah, and what's that?'

'The Anna Louise Caley girl, she disappeared eleven months ago.'

Leroy nodded. 'Yeah, I know the one, lot of private Is brought in on it, but me? I stayed clear: I stick mainly to salvage myself.'

'But you must have heard about it?'

'Sure, like I said, it was pistol-hot at one time, but as

293

far as I know they all came up with zilch. Word was the girl must just have flown the coop – they do down here, you know, especially around Mardi Gras. Kids flock here, get laid, get stoned and move on with some drifter. City draws them like a magnet.'

'This one's different, she's rich as hell.'

Leroy leaned on his elbows. 'Rich kids, Nick, are just like everybody else. They like to get stoned and laid, preferably with a little dash of danger thrown in, and then it's back to Mama and Papa who welcome them home with open arms.'

'But she's been gone eleven months.'

'Then I'd say she's dead.'

Nick got up and paced around the office. 'Yeah, I think so too. Question is who killed her, and if I find out I get a nice bonus.'

'Well, I'd like to help, man, but like I said I got this dental case.'

Nick smiled. 'So what's putting you off, huh?'

Leroy hesitated, and suddenly became serious. 'You want it on the level?'

'Sure I do, I want whatever you've got that'd help.'

Leroy ran his hands through his iron-grey curls.

'Okay, the Caleys and the types you're dealing with are high-powered money people. Elizabeth Caley is a big star round these parts, so you'd get a lot of people coming forward with bullshit just for the rewards they offered. I think it was twenty-five thousand bucks. I know that to date something like twenty people have said they seen her, and you chase it up and find it's nothin' and then . . .' Leroy rocked in his chair. 'Money runs out and you find you spent half your fee gettin' fuck-all results. So for the time being I'm sticking to salvage and dental.'

Nick drained his coffee. 'What d'you know about an

old black jazz player goes by the name of Fryer Jones?' Leroy stared as Nick flicked the bones at his neck. 'He gave me these.'

'Fryer Jones did?'

'Yep, last night.'

'He's famous where he hangs out, round the French Quarter and Ward 9. All the young kids wanna hang out at his bar, play a few sets with him and the old guys – he used to be one mean trombone player. They drift there, score some dope, maybe play a few numbers. He uses kids like most use toilet paper but the cops leave him well alone. If he's not openly dealing on the main drag, he's out of their hair, out of the main tourist routes, an' that's all this city cares about.' Leroy rubbed his thumb and finger together to indicate money, then he leaned back. 'I'd say Fryer must be worth quite an amount by now. No kiddin', he's been running that bar for decades, got a string of little girls whoring for him, all in the name of jazz, brother! But if you want my honest opinion, he's a piece of shit, because it's not all singing the blues that holds them to that stinking bar ... it's what you got round your neck too.'

Nick touched his bones. 'What?'

Leroy shook his head. 'You don't know, do you? Gris-gris is supposed to ward off evil voodoo spells, and old Fryer used to have a few connections in that field. In fact, I think he may even be related to one of the Salina sisters.'

Nick tensed up. 'Hold it, Salina?'

Leroy nodded. 'Yeah. One was called Juda, the other ... er, shit, can't recall right now, but she married. They were real high priestesses. Word is that ... shit, I wish I could remember her name, but Juda's sister has a daughter, Ruby, Ruby Corbello, 'bout eighteen, she works in a hair salon. She does some modelling on the side and some new black krewe that's getting together for the Carnival has put her up as their queen.'

Nick hitched up his jeans. 'Wait, wait, you're going too fast for me, man. There's a Juda Salina in LA, reads tarot cards, that kind of stuff?'

'They do a lot more than tarot readin', Nick. If it's the Juda that's related to the Corbello family, she's almost like royalty in some areas . . . and I don't mean for the tourists. These are supposed to be the real thing, related to the big voodoo queens they had last century, and they can put the fear of God into people. Like I said, it's more than booze and drugs gets the kids hanging round those people, and if you got your head screwed on right, you'll stay well clear of Jones an' anyone who has anything to do with the Salina sisters. I tell you, you wouldn't even get me through the door of their place and I wouldn't go to Fryer's unless I had a good reason.'

Nick felt uneasy, and his leg was beginning to hurt from all the walking. He rubbed it hard with the flat of his hand. 'I saved the fucker's life so maybe he owes me.'

Leroy lit a cigarette, the smoke drifting from his aquiline nose as he looked hard at Nick.

'Pack up and go home, Bartello, don't you go getting involved in all this shit. Like I said, you'll come out with nothin'.'

Nick moved painfully down the stairs, past the gymnasium now full of heavy grunts from kids sparring and thwacking the punch-bag. It was strange, and it always had worked that way, but the more he was warned off something the more it fed his adrenalin. And he didn't believe in all that voodoo shit anyway.

CHAPTER 12

LORRAINE SAT on a wide and slippery banquette sofa, richly upholstered in vermilion silk damask printed with gold fleurs de lys, while Lloyd Dulay lowered himself into a matching chair opposite. Lloyd had decided to receive Lorraine in the drawing room to impress her with the full splendour of his house: his improvements to this room were limited to covering one wall with floor-to-ceiling mirrors, in which two Hepplewhite chairs were reflected as though standing in an airport lounge. Golden scrolls and swags were everywhere visible – the drapes, of course, were a mass of corn-coloured fabric tied back with chocolate-box bows, and ornate gilded plasterwork adorned the fireplace, the huge overmantel mirror and the firescreen which stood in front of two artificial logs on a stand. The central ceiling medallion extended for six feet of plaster wheat-ears, garlands and rosettes, and another splendid chandelier hung like a huge gilded lily beneath. A number of modern abstract paintings were suspended by taffeta ribbon bows from the picture rail and every surface in the room was cluttered with lamps, knick-knacks, bibelots, and bulky arrangements of both dried and fresh flowers. Lorraine hated the place and she was uncomfortable, her mouth dry and the thought of a drink coming persistently to her mind, but she forced it out of her thoughts.

'You wanted to see me, Mrs Page, on a personal matter?'

'Yes, Mr Dulay, I did.'

He nodded his mane of white hair and pointedly looked at his watch. 'Then get to the point, I have people for lunch.'

'I am investigating the disappearance of Anna Louise Caley.'

'Are you now? Well, I wish I had a million dollars for every one of the so-called agents I have spoken to. Quite truthfully, I don't think there is anything I can add that would be of any use at all. I have business dealings with Robert Caley and I have known his lovely wife for more than thirty years, so I have known little Anna since she was knee-high to a grass-hopper.'

She loathed him, his loud voice, his condescending, imperious manner. His vast house made her cringe because it was the very reflection of the man – big, loud and heavy. She felt there should be a family crest over the doorway that read: 'I have billions of dollars, so fuck you.'

She pushed on. 'Everyone I have spoken to about Anna Louise says the same thing, that she was naive, shy, beautiful. Tell me what you thought of her.'

He closed his eyes. 'She was all those things, and affectionate, sweet, with a smile that would break any man's heart. I loved that little girl, Mrs Page, I loved her.'

'Did Robert Caley love his daughter?'

For a fraction of a second he was thrown. 'Why, yes, he was her father.'

Lorraine met the tiny, cold blue eyes. 'What do you think of Robert Caley?'

Dulay laughed, but she knew he was confused. 'Why do you ask?'

She held his nasty stare and he was the one to look away. 'Maybe if he was fucking his own daughter she had reason to disappear!'

The huge man rose out of his seat. 'If you were a man I'd knock you right through that wall.'

'But I am not, I am just investigating the disappearance of a young girl, sir.'

He towered above her. 'Lemme tell you this, Mrs Page. If I thought for one moment that what you have just said could be true, I'd get a gun and shoot the bastard myself.'

'If you also discovered that Anna Louise was not as sweet or naive as everyone makes out, how would that make you feel?'

'I don't follow you, Mrs Page.'

She took out the photograph, slowly, and his eyes narrowed with suspicion.

He scooped it up in one massive hand and held it up to the light, his eyesight, unlike his presence, not so strong. 'What the hell is this disgusting thing?'

'A photograph,' she said sweetly.

'I know that, woman, but where in God's name did you get it? Because this isn't the little girl I knew, this is . . . Dear God, it breaks my heart.'

'Maybe Robert Caley isn't the man you know either, so what can you tell me about him?'

He was really shaken. 'Does Elizabeth know this exists?'

'Yes.'

'And Robert?'

'No.'

He shook his big head, slumping back into his chair. 'She was as precious to me as my own beloved daughter. Dear God, why did she subject herself to this disgusting show?'

'Maybe because she was abused, angry, I don't know. All I am hired to do is find her, dead or alive.'

'Is she dead?'

Lorraine looked away. 'I hope not.'

She could hear the clock ticking on the mantel as he continued to stare at the photograph. At one point he withdrew a printed silk handkerchief and wiped his eyes.

'I know that Anna Louise has a large trust fund.'

His head jerked up, the photograph forgotten.

'Mr Dulay, I am looking for motives for Anna Louise's disappearance. And that is why I am asking you about Robert Caley. The trust's assets amount to one hundred million dollars.'

'Do they?' he said softly.

'I am also aware that right now, with this casino development, Mr Caley is stretched to his financial limits and—'

'Mrs Page, I said before that if Robert Caley harmed a hair on that little girl's head I'd get a gun and shoot him, not just for myself but for Elizabeth. That said, I do not believe for one moment that the man I have known for twenty-odd years would have any such inclination towards his own daughter. The thought is sickening, degrading and unjust. He's not a great man, but he's a hard worker and has earned his money the hard way. I am one of a number of advisers who take care of Elizabeth's money and investments, and a trusted family friend, so much so I feel that I must make sure you leave this house with no aspersions cast on Robert Caley's name.'

Lorraine retrieved the photograph, slipping it back into the envelope. 'Do you know that Elizabeth Caley has a very serious drug habit?'

'No, I won't believe it.' Lloyd got up and stared arrogantly into the mirrors behind Lorraine's head, as though finding confirmation of his beliefs in his own image. The purpose of the mirrored wall was more than clear – it allowed Lloyd to enjoy the sight of his reflection as well as the sound of his own voice.

'I can give you the address of the clinic she is in right now.' She waited as he sat down, his face concerned and confused. 'I am sorry if what we have discussed disturbs you, and obviously I must ask for your total—'

'I would never divulge what you have told me, Mrs Page, not to anyone, so help me God. I am stunned, stunned . . . shocked, because if what you say is true it means that those nearest and dearest to me are nothing but liars.'

'Not necessarily.' She smiled.

'What?'

Lorraine snapped her briefcase closed. 'Perhaps they chose for you not to know. As an investigator, it is my job to find out what lies beneath the surface.'

'Isn't your job, Mrs Page, to find Anna Louise?'

She nodded, walking to the door. 'Yes, Mr Dulay, it is, but if during my attempts to trace her I uncover certain discrepancies or illogical statements, then I have to follow them through. If you have nothing to add or nothing that can help me, then I thank you for your time.'

'Robert Caley is a good man,' he said lamely.

She turned at the door. 'Yes, I think he is, but I have to make certain that he is in no way connected to his daughter's disappearance so I can eliminate him as a suspect.'

He rose slowly from his chair, moving towards her. 'Is he suspected by your agency?'

'Everyone I meet is a suspect until I get to the truth, Mr Dulay. If there is any way you could find out for me if Mr Caley has been using his daughter's trust fund, I'd be very grateful if you could let me know. May I call you again?'

Dulay agreed. He didn't say goodbye as Lorraine closed the door behind her and found her own way out. The big man sat in a dazed, uncomprehending state, feeling outraged and betrayed. He decided there and then that he would withdraw from the Caley development. He wanted to confront Robert Caley to his face, but first he wanted to know if the bastard had touched a cent of Anna Louise's trust fund. He more than anyone could check it out – the hundred million dollars had been his.

Lorraine felt used up and disgusted with herself at the same time. She knew what she had just done was wrong and unprofessional. Part of her didn't know why she wanted to put so much pressure on Dulay but perhaps in reality it was a roundabout way of putting it on Robert Caley because of what Tilda Brown had said. She hated him to be under suspicion, wanted him to be innocent. At the same time she was sure he was guilty, but of what? She refused to believe that it was now more than likely that he had murdered his own daughter.

Rosie at last found the sign for the Voodoo Museum on Dumaine and entered the building nervously to find a group of eight other people, mostly women, standing in a small reception area buying a variety of charm powders, novelties, dolls and candles offered for sale, while they waited for the tour to begin. Behind the young woman at the desk was the portrait of an imposing woman dressed in the costume of the last century; she wore a kerchief on her head and gold hooped earrings, while her skin was a rich yellow-brown with just a hint of copper, her eyes a fathomless black. Even in painted form her gaze seemed to penetrate the years, and her presence dominated the room. When the tour guide appeared, it was to this painting he first drew their attention.

'This, ladies and gentlemen, is a portrait of Marie Laveau, the most powerful queen of voodoo this city has ever seen, called the Popess of Voodoo by the time she was forty years old because she was consulted by the gentlefolk of that time, as well as by her own people, and even by royalty, so that her reputation was known all over the world. Her powers were legendary, and when she walked in the streets the crowds would stand silent and hold up their children to catch sight of her: it was as if they knew people would still be talking about her for a hundred years after she died. She held her rituals near the Bayou St John, and people said they saw her walk on the water; she could make the sun go dark and call down the spirit of the storm, and she could call up the spirits of love, and, of course . . .' he stopped and smiled, 'of destruction too.'

Rosie looked into the ageless eyes of the great sorceress: she felt certain she had seen the face before, but she racked her brains to remember where.

A hush had now fallen on the gaggle of tourists as the guide led them down a narrow passageway in which hung the portraits of a number of voodoo queens, none, however, of Marie Laveau's pre-eminence, some she had been taught by, and then vanquished or eclipsed. The guide stopped in front of a portrait of another light-skinned young black woman in a formal, old-fashioned dress, with black ringlets knotted at the back of her head and arranged in front of her ears: these eyes were cruel.

'This, people say, is Marie's daughter, Marie II, if you want to call her that, said to be more drawn to the darker side of her powers than her mother. People said they saw Marie Laveau up to 1918, 1919, and it was more likely Marie number two they saw, though there are people say Marie her mother never died: you go rap on her tomb and she'll hear you.'

'Did Marie Laveau have any other family – like, are there any of her relatives living today?' asked one of the group with interest.

The guide laughed. 'There's a lot of voodoo practitioners say they can trace a connection to the bloodline of Marie Laveau, but the strongest claim is that of the Salina family – there are two sisters who were both practitioners at one time, and those of you who are staying for Carnival will have the opportunity to see a daughter of the family, Ruby Corbello, who will be queen of a new black krewe that has been formed this year.'

The guide ushered them further down the passage to a room from which issued a rhythmic and strangely tranquillizing drum-beat; the group stepped hesitantly inside to find themselves surrounded by an eerie collection of carved masks and statues, some decorated with beads and jewellery, and with dishes containing offerings of various kinds and lighted candles arranged in front of them. One corner of the room was separated from the rest by old iron cemetery railings: inside were tombstones and animal and human bones that made Rosie shudder despite the guide's explanation that, for a religion believing in communion with the departed ancestors, signs of death were not to be feared, but cherished for protection. He pointed out one glass case of drums and other shamanic instruments to facilitate the journey to the spirit world, and another containing a wide variety of bones, dried animal claws and skins, roots, powders, beans and barks: each one of these, he told them, was a mojo, and their combination by a skilled practitioner yielded a gris-gris, a powerful protective amulet often worn in a sealed bag around the neck. In the final corner of the room was a large number of small statues and dolls, for the most part crudely made of a handful of straw or dried grass tied around two crossed sticks and covered with a few scraps of material, with tiny, oddly fierce skulls and faces then painted on. Some of these, the guide said, were to enhance fertility: he said nothing about any other use.

The sweet smell of incense greeted them at the door of the next room: here the masks and statues were brightly painted and seemed joyful and celebratory after the shadows next door. Richly worked hangings and religious paintings showed many signs of Christian influence and images of Catholic saints were pinned up over a cloth-covered table on which stood more candles, statues and a bottle of rum. In front of them a picture of the crucifixion faced a small prie-dieu, and the guide proceeded to explain how voodoo was not a set of evil spells, but a religion which had been the only link with their own culture black people had been allowed to retain in the days of slavery, and which had sustained the people through those harsh times. It saw God latent in the whole of creation and later had blended easily with Christianity, the loas, or individual spirits, becoming identified with the angels and saints.

Marie Laveau herself, he went on, had attended mass regularly at St Louis Cathedral, had friends among the clergy and had done much charitable work among condemned prisoners and during the fever epidemics. None the less there was a frisson of unease when the guide indicated that the small wooden structure in the corner housed a python named after Marie Laveau's famous snake, Zombi, symbol of the bridge between spirit and material planes, and a few members of the group craned their necks to peep nervously through the glass panes.

The tour was officially over, and Rosie stepped closer to the altar while other members of the group looked at the snake or examined the old tree-stump into which Marie Laveau's followers had dropped prayers and petitions, and saw four more of the disturbing dolls arranged on a rack above the candle flames. The presence of a world she did not understand, but which still lived in the city around her, filled her with awe and a touch of fascination, and she bought some souvenirs and a booklet describing the career of Marie Laveau before she left. The beautiful and commanding face seemed to haunt her, provoking a persistent feeling of *déjà vu*, but perhaps Marie Laveau had made everyone who had ever seen her feel that they had always known her, that in her the mysterious and the familiar met.

Rooney sat sweltering in his rental. He'd been parked outside the designated meeting point for over half an hour, and felt a little uneasy to be sitting in the tough downtown waterfront area with a rental firm's sticker in the back window, someone obviously off his home turf. He was about to give up the wait when he saw the patrol car cruising slowly behind him. He adjusted the driving mirror to watch his contact approach. He shook his head. Men, and cops in particular, come in all shapes and sizes, but he had never seen one that resembled Harris J. Harper.

'You Rooney?' Harper said at the car window. Close to, his face was as weird as his fat, wobbling body. He must have been one of those beautiful bonny babies with an upturned nose, rosebud mouth and bright blue eyes, because whereas the rest of his body had grown, his face had remained the same size, his cheeks puffed out, and his layered chins gave him the unfortunate appearance of having no neck whatsoever.

Rooney nodded, and Harper waddled his way round to the passenger door. When he sat inside the car it felt like the springs would give way.

'You been waitin' long?'

Rooney nodded. 'Yep, since ten, but that's okay.'

'Could do with a beer, huh?'

'You said it.'

'Okay, Captain Rooney, you follow me, I know a bar a block away, just stick on my tail.'

'Thanks.'

Harper eased his blubbery body out and then leaned in. 'Er . . . five hundred bucks okay with you?'

Rooney hesitated. 'Hope it's worth it, that's a lot of dough.'

Harper shut the door and patted the top of the rental. 'Be worth it, Captain, be worth it.'

Rosie continued. 'Voodoo is a religion as serious as any other. There's a lot of occult, kinda dark stuff that's got associated, but that's not the point. It is a way of connecting with positive, spiritual parts of experience, and is very natural, an important part of a lot of people's lives . . .'

'It's all bullshit,' Nick said, yawning.

Rosie leaned forward. 'I don't think so. Everyone thinks it's a lot of evil stuff about killing people and turning them into zombies, you listening, Nick?'

'Yeah, it's rivetin' Rosie.'

'What making someone a zombie actually is is a form of sanction against people who committed some very serious crime, like murder maybe—'

Nick rolled his eyes. 'Give me the good ol' electric chair any time, baby.'

Rosie looked at him in irritation. 'I won't tell you if you mess around. The priest could give them a kind of nerve poison that would produce a state a Western doctor would think was death, and the person would be what they called "passed by the ground" – buried and then dug up again. That's why white people call zombies the walking dead.'

Nick looked up and saw Lorraine heading towards their table. 'Here comes one now.'

Rosie looked up. 'What?'

'A zombie. It's Mrs Page.' Lorraine slumped into a seat beside Nick and Rosie in the shaded garden of the hotel.

'Listen, we maybe need to rethink a few things. I paid a call to an old pal, used to be in the drug squad with me, Leroy Able. In fact, I've not been in contact with him for more'n ten years but we used to get on . . .' Nick drained his beer before continuing. 'Okay, you know there are high priestesses in the voodoo church, they are pretty powerful women, and the top of the heap in the voodoo pile is always, you will be pleased to know, a woman. It's a big deal, Lorraine, they are like royalty down here and very powerful.'

'I've been to the Voodoo Museum,' Rosie began, but Lorraine cut her short. Neither of them had given her a moment even to say hello.

'Christ, Nick, what has this got to do with our case?'

He snapped, 'I'm gettin' there, all right? There are two sisters who are real big-time, very dominant with the potions, whatever the hell they do. Rosie's got some stuff from the museum you can read for yourself. According to Leroy, Juda Salina and her sister are the top dogs.'

Lorraine was stunned. She reached for a Coke can and shook it – empty. She looked over the table for something else to drink. The thirst had started.

'Why didn't you tell me that?' Rosie asked.

'I was getting to it, Rosie.'

'Juda Salina's sister, Edith Corbello, still lives here in a real low-grade area, though she's not so active now. Remember you wanted Raoul checked out? Well he is Edith Corbello's son, Juda Salina's nephew. There are another two boys, called Willy and Jesse, and two daughters, the youngest called Sugar May and last but not least, Ruby Corbello, hairdresser, wannabe model, who is going to be a queen in the Carnival this year.'

Lorraine now really did need that drink – her mouth was dry, and her head throbbed. 'Okay, now let's piece all this together because my hair's standing on end, Nick – oh, and can you pour me some water?'

Rosie poured a glass of water for Lorraine, her attention on Nick.

'Just forget all this voodoo crap and look at Juda Salina. She had a hold on Elizabeth Caley, knew her from here, they even brought her back here to try and help trace Anna Louise.' Nick lit a cigarette and passed it to Lorraine, then lit one for himself. He had seen the way she had gulped at the water Rosie had passed to her, noticed that her hand was shaking visibly as she drained the glass.

'All along we've been looking for a motive, a reason, what if it was blackmail? I mean, you found those pictures of Anna Louise, you dug up stuff on Elizabeth Caley . . .'

'Wait, wait, Nick, not so fast. You suggesting the motive all along was blackmail and it went wrong?' Lorraine frowned, rubbing her temples as she tried to assimilate everything that was being said to her.

'Yeah, led by that fat bitch Juda Salina. She's got enough family down here to move a body, she may have even gone to them . . .'

Lorraine dragged on her cigarette. 'I better see this, what was her name, Corbello? Any more water, Rosie?'

Nick took her hand. 'A second, I don't believe in all this shit, right? An' my pal Leroy said he doesn't, but what he does believe is that these people are dangerous, not with the spells and that crap but they'd kill you soon as spit in your eye. And he warned me to go very carefully because they got a whole army. They beat them drums and you're never seen again.'

'Like Anna Louise Caley?' Lorraine said softly, her hand already reaching for the glass of water Rosie was pouring for her.

'Exactly, but this moves Robert Caley into second position now because we got something outside, something that maybe makes more sense, nothing to do with his casino or his money . . .'

'Drugs?' she asked, gulping at the liquid.

'Could be. We know Anna Louise boozed and got stoned with her little friend Tilda Brown. Maybe on that night she disappeared she went to the Corbello woman's house to score and saw something? Say that Juda Salina, whom we know she went to see, was drug-pushing, not just here but in LA.'

Lorraine ran her hands through her hair. It was wringing wet – she was soaked in sweat. 'Shit, Nick, I think you're right, we've been on the wrong fucking track all along.'

Nick nodded. 'And I don't think Elizabeth Caley's involved either. Maybe she's just one hell of a good customer and we know she needed to score drugs, so the link is Juda Salina and her family.'

Rosie left the table and made her way out of the

courtyard: Lorraine hardly seemed to notice that she had got up.

'Where are you going?' Nick called after her.

'Going to get some more refreshments if it's all right with you,' she replied, without even turning round. Nick stubbed out his cigarette, looking sidelong at Lorraine.

'What's up, sugar?'

'Nothing's up, Nick, maybe I'm just tired.' She hunted for another cigarette in her purse: Nick tapped another out of his own crumpled pack, lit it and passed it to her as before.

'I hate this brand, like smoking something from out of the refrigerator,' she said, none the less dragging hard on the cigarette, her foot tapping nervously against the table leg.

Nick acted as though nothing were out of the ordinary. 'Been a tough day, huh?'

'Nothing I can't deal with.' She reached for a can of Coke that Rosie had left, but knocked it on to its side and the dregs spilled over the table.

'Shit,' she snapped, dabbing at the tablecloth, and now Nick gripped her hand.

'You're all stressed out, just take it easy.'

Lorraine bowed her head, holding on to Nick's hand.

'I want a drink so bad sometimes, Nick, it drives me nuts. It comes over me and I just can't think straight, or maybe I'm thinking too much . . .'

He moved a strand of her hair gently away from her cheek and leaned close to her.

'Just hang on in there, Rosie's bringing some more Coke an' I'll get you some more of your cigarettes.'

'Thanks.' She liked the strength of his hand, didn't want to let it go, but she glanced up and saw Rosie on her way back with another bag of Cokes and potato chips. She banged it down and yelled, 'Ah, look what you've done to my book, I was reading that and you've got beer and Coke all over it! Honestly!'

Lorraine leaned across the table and picked up the blue paper booklet, shaking Coke off it. As she did so, she noticed the picture of Marie Laveau on the front.

'What's this?' she asked Rosie.

'She's Marie Laveau, the most famous voodoo queen ever.'

'Why is this so familiar?' Lorraine said, almost to herself.

Rosie took the booklet. 'Well, I felt the same thing, like I'd seen it before, her face.'

'The turban, the robes . . . gimme it back, Rosie.' Lorraine was up on her feet, walking up and down. 'Shit! I don't believe this, it's staring us right in the face, Rosie.'

'What you talking about?'

Lorraine slapped the photograph down. 'This is Elizabeth Caley, she's got this painting in her drawing room, it's from a film.'

'No, it isn't. That's from a painting of Marie Laveau, I got it from the Voodoo Museum, but you're right, she's the spittin' image of her.'

'*Swamp*,' Lorraine said, clapping her hands, congratulating herself. 'The film was called *The Swamp*, it was the first movie Elizabeth Seal made, wasn't it, Rosie?'

'Maybe it's on video,' Rosie suggested.

'Good idea, let's see if we can get it. She's a big number round here, so you never know. Attagirl, Rosie, this is really good.'

'Thanks.' Rosie smiled.

'I mean it, you're doing good – make an investigator of you yet!' Lorraine stood up and gave Rosie a hug, beginning to feel better herself.

'If it's okay with you, I'm going to take myself off for a zizz, I'm exhausted, maybe take a shower.' Rosie put the paper pamphlet away in her purse as Lorraine touched Nick lightly on the shoulder.

'I'm okay, Nick,' she murmured. 'Don't keep looking at me. I just need a couple hours' rest.'

Nick shrugged his shoulders as she walked away.

'What was that about?' Rosie asked.

'Nothing,' Nick replied.

'Oh yeah? She looked pretty strung out to me, you think I should go up and sit with her?'

'Nope, maybe get on to tracking that video. I'll hang around here, wait for Bill.'

Rosie gathered her things together and looked at him sidelong. 'Maybe you'd like to babysit her ladyship? She looked like she needed a friendly shoulder.'

'Well, I'll be right here. And leave the Cokes, huh?'

Left alone, Nick sat toying with the chilled can of Coke, wishing he could go up to Lorraine's room and lie next to her – and not just as a comforting friend.

The Crawfish Bar sat on a dingy corner of the wharf district, a peeling clapboard building with windows covered in rusting wire mesh. It had been an old grocery store and you had to buzz the door to get inside: it was clear they didn't want any casual trade. The place was almost deserted and Rooney and Harper sat on two stools at a counter against the back wall under the television, the commentary of the basketball game masking the sounds of their conversation.

'I'm not sure if I'm gonna like these,' Rooney said, looking at his plate of boiled crawfish and the ugly black plastic dish, virtually the size of a trash-can lid, which had been slapped down to take the heads and shells.

'Sure you will, these little critters are known as "mud bugs" because they live in the freshwater streams, and this place, lemme tell you, pal, serves the freshest in the whole of New Orleans,' Harper said as he tucked a napkin under his chin. Rooney stared disbelievingly at what looked like toy lobsters to him.

'Right, now, you follow me. First you grasp the head between thumb and forefinger of one hand like so . . .' Harper demonstrated, dangling it in the air, and Rooney dutifully followed suit. Harper was more interested in his lunch than talking, saying they should eat and down their beers before they got to business. So it was at least half an hour before he volunteered any information, and not before his 500 bucks were stuffed inside his wallet.

'So what you need to know, Bill?'

'What you came up with on the disappearance of Anna Louise Caley.'

Harper shrugged his fat shoulders. 'Sweet fuck-all!'

'That all I get for five hundred fucking bucks?' Rooney snapped.

Harper gave a furtive look around. 'Depends on what else you want to know . . .'

'Any dirt on Robert Caley?'

'No, sir. Well-respected man, got his real estate licence, hadda wait a while even though he is married to Elizabeth Seal, but he didn't give any bribes, just applied as a resident of New Orleans through the right channels.'

'But he's not exactly a resident, is he?'

'You kiddin' me? They got palatial residences, three, maybe even four. Rich as Croesus. Mind you, rumour was while back now, more'n twenty-five years, that she, Elizabeth Seal, and a big tycoon by the name of Lloyd Dulay were an item, and he kind of added to the lady's fortune.'

'He's one of the partners in Caley's casino development, isn't he?' Rooney asked.

314

'Yep, a couple of heavy hitters on his side. I'd say it'll go through eventually. Just a question of time.'

'You ever hear any rumour 'bout Elizabeth Caley having a drug problem?'

'What, you kiddin' me? No fucking way.'

Rooney sighed. 'So, can you give me more details on how your investigation was set up? There was a big reward out and quite a few claimants, right?'

'True, but by the time we sifted through their so-called eye-witness reports it was all bullshit, and a number of 'em had been set up by a few officers trying to get their hands on the reward . . .'

'What do you think happened to her?'

Harper wiped the sweat from his face. 'The girl picked up some drifter, they got into an argument and he killed her. There was only one arrest, old jazz player by the name of Fryer Jones, somebody said they'd seen him talking to her out in the Quarter.'

Rooney frowned. 'You had an arrest? But that's not in any report back in LA.'

'Well, it wouldn't be, would it? LA is LA, this is New Orleans, and things happen a little bit different down here. You might not even find a report on Fryer Jones in our department either.'

'Why?'

'Because nobody likes to get on the wrong side of that old buzzard. He's very influential and we got people here with heavy superstitious minds. Fryer's real clever at twisting minds to suit himself.'

'I don't follow, how strong was the case against him?'

Harper shrugged. 'Just someone thought they had seen Anna Louise Caley talkin' to him. Like he's not far from the hotel, not in the same kind of district, mind, but his place is no more than a ten-, fifteen-minute walk away. We got nobody else to verify the eye witness's report and he was found floatin' in the river 'bout five months back, so like I said—'

'You think he was murdered because of his report against this Fryer?'

'Quite possibly, but there again he was a junkie so he could'a easily tripped and fallen into the river.'

'So no charges were brought?'

'Nope. Fryer denied seeing Anna Louise Caley and he had 'bout twenty witnesses that said he never left his bar that night, so we let him go.' Harper checked his wrist-watch. 'I'm on duty.'

'You think he'd talk to me?'

Harper hitched his pants over his belly. 'Up to you, but I wouldn't go near his bar alone or at night, it's kinda off limits. We don't bother him and he don't bother us, and like I said, he's a man I keep my distance from because believe it or not, that voodoo crap really fucks with your head, know what I mean?'

Lorraine felt better after she had taken a shower and two aspirin, and not until she was wrapped in her bathrobe did she check the messages that had come in for her. There were four messages to contact Robert Caley and one to call Lloyd Dulay. She stared at Caley's name, wanting to call him but afraid even to hear his voice, so she called Lloyd Dulay, who was not at home. She was just about to lie down on the bed when there was a rap at her door.

'It's me and Bill,' Nick called.

She sighed, not wanting to see them.

'I was just going to take a shower,' she lied as she opened the door.

'Go ahead, I'll join you,' Nick grinned.

316

Rooney was not amused. He was hot and sweaty, his feet felt like swollen balloons, and he sat on a straight-backed chair as Nick slumped down on the single bed.

'Well, you can both hang on until we've talked a few things through,' Rooney said with a touch of irritation. 'Right, this cop had some very interesting information.'

'I hope so, you coughed up five hundred dollars for it,' Nick yawned, his face twisting as he rubbed at his leg. 'Christ, I hate this city, my leg is driving me nuts, it's the damp.'

Rooney flicked out his notes. 'Can we get down to business?'

The phone rang. Lorraine looked at Nick. 'Can you get it? If it's Robert Caley, say I'm not here, and if it's reception, will you tell them to hold all calls?'

'Sure.' Nick reached over and picked up the bedside phone, pleased by the fact that she didn't want to see Caley. 'Mrs Page's room.'

'I interviewed this cop, right?' Rooney went on, 'And he told me that the bastards down here had made an arrest.'

Nick gestured to Lorraine. 'She's right here.' He covered the phone.

'Who is it?' she whispered.

'Something to do with Tilda Brown, it's the cops.'

She pulled a face and took the phone, inching on to the bed beside Nick.

'Lorraine Page speaking.' She listened, then her body straightened. 'Yes, I did, today, yes. I'm sorry?'

Rooney and Nick were all ears; just by her body language they knew something was up.

'Yes, of course, I'll come straight away. Oh, then I'll wait outside the hotel.'

Lorraine replaced the receiver. 'Tilda Brown hanged

317

herself sometime this afternoon. They want to interview me, they found my card in the pocket of her robe, they know I was there this morning . . .'

'Shit,' Nick said softly.

Lorraine was really shaken, pressing her hand to her forehead. 'They're sending a squad car . . . Oh, shit, goddamn it! The stupid, stupid girl.'

Nick reached for her hand. 'Come now, get yourself together. If you want I'll come with you.'

She eased away from him. 'No, no, stay here, talk over everything we've come up with. Oh, God! Why did she go and fucking do this, why?'

'Come on, you can't blame yourself, Lorraine,' Rooney interjected.

Lorraine headed for the bathroom and then turned. 'No? I really grilled her, I even showed her that fucking picture of Anna Louise and . . . I didn't have anything to do with it? Who you kidding?' She slammed the bathroom's inadequate louvred door.

Nick looked at Rooney. 'Maybe go to my room, leave her alone for a while.'

Rooney sighed. 'Okay, but I need a beer or something, this heat is wearing me to shreds.'

'I'll be right with you.' Nick waited for the door to close before he got up and walked to the bathroom; he didn't knock, but walked straight in. Lorraine was standing shaking, gripping the wash-hand basin with both hands, tears streaming down her face. She didn't even have the energy to tell him to leave, and he prised her hands loose, then drew her close, holding her tightly as she rested her head on his shoulder.

'Sshhh, don't fight me, you just let it all out. It'll make you feel a whole lot better, believe me, I know.'

She clung to him, and he scooped her up in his arms

318

and carried her into the bedroom. He laid her down on the bed, and as he had so wanted earlier, lay beside her, holding her in his arms, and even kissing her gently as she wept. She needed him, though she didn't want him as badly as he wanted her, but even being close to her gave him hope, still more when she leaned on her elbow and looked into his face.

'You're one of a kind, you know that, Bartello?'

'Yeah, it's been said before.'

She smiled, and he wiped her cheek with his finger. 'That's my girl. Now, do you want me with you?'

'No, I've got to straighten myself out, I've made enough mistakes already, Nick.'

She took him by surprise when she cupped his face in her hands and kissed him on the lips, sweetly and platonically, but he was thrown into turmoil none the less. He was wise enough – and had enough self-control – not to push things any further, but the kiss had given him more hope than ever before.

'You got me, Mrs Page, you know that, don't you?'

She drew away from him, already disciplining herself to get moving and face the police.

'Did you hear what I just said?'

She turned and looked at him in the way he adored, her head on one side and her hair falling across to hide her scar. 'Maybe, Nick, I ain't worth having!'

He laughed as he sauntered to the door, and walked out without looking back. 'I'll be the judge of that!'

By the time Lorraine was dressed, two little white message envelopes had been posted beneath her door: Lloyd Dulay returning her call, and Robert Caley, saying that he needed to see her urgently and that Elizabeth

Caley was arriving in New Orleans that evening. She picked them up as she left for the waiting patrol car.

'I was here this morning with a group,' Rosie said to the young man who had taken over the later shift at the Voodoo Museum: he seemed graceless in comparison to the smiling young woman who had been at the desk earlier.

'If it's lost property we ain't found nothing today,' he said, without even looking up from his newspaper.

'It isn't. I want to make enquiries about a video,' Rosie persisted, passing over the Page Investigations Agency card.

'This isn't a video store, ma'am.' He didn't even glance at the card.

'I know that, but it's a particular video, an old film called *The Swamp*, starring Elizabeth Seal as Marie Laveau, and none of the video stores have it. I know the film was made, I've seen the portrait of Miss Seal as—'

The paper snapped shut. 'I think you must be mistaken, Elizabeth Seal is white, Marie Laveau was coloured. If you want another guided tour . . .'

His eyes bore into Rosie, frightening her, but she didn't back off. 'They use make-up, you know, and . . .'

'And you didn't hear me right, ma'am, you got the wrong information. And if you don't want a tour then you should leave.'

'Thank you, I'll have another tour.'

He sullenly took her money for another tour ticket and ignored her as she moved past him and said she would wait for a guide inside. She stood in the dim, scented room for some minutes, but no one joined her. She waited on, her heart beating. Then came the soft drum-beat, and she wondered if the young man had turned on a tape.

Rosie stepped into the hallway and looked at the portraits of the queens, but it was Marie Laveau's image she saw constantly in her mind's eye, the glowing face, the eerie, pitch-dark eyes. She physically jumped when she heard someone behind her, not the young guide but a tall, austere-looking black man with iron-grey hair. He wore a smart grey suit and a white shirt with a stiff collar and tie. He held Lorraine's card in one large, finely made hand.

'Are you Mrs Lorraine Page?' His voice was quiet and deep.

'No, I am her assistant, well, partner, my name is—'

'Please come through,' he said, gesturing to the room at the back.

Rosie was so scared she was hyperventilating. She was sure it was much darker than it had been, and the drum-beat was becoming unnerving.

'What precisely are you investigating?'

Rosie shifted her weight from foot to foot. 'Well, that is really a private matter, but we have been hired by Mr and Mrs Robert Caley.'

'What for, precisely?' the man enquired, keeping his eyes fixed on her face.

'Er, they had a daughter, her name was Anna Louise Caley and she disappeared eleven months ago from here. Well, not exactly here here, but from her hotel in New Orleans.'

'Mmm, yes, I recall reading about it,' his deep voice rumbled. 'So what has this film to do with ... Caley, you said?'

'Yes, it's just that Mrs Caley used to be Elizabeth Seal.'

'Ah, yes, so she was, the film star, a very beautiful woman.'

Rosie felt more confident and stepped closer. 'Her first film was called *The Swamp* and there is a painting in her home, almost identical to the portrait of—'

'Queen Marie Laveau.'

'Yes. And we, that is Mrs Page and I, and Captain Rooney who is also part of the agency, well, we would like to see the film.'

'Why?'

Rosie licked her lips. 'Er, I don't know, to be honest, it's just that we are trying to piece together backgrounds, that sort of thing, and it was such a coincidence, me being here and seeing the painting, that's all really.'

'Mmm, that's all. But you see, it isn't quite as simple as that.'

'I'm sorry?'

He leaned forward, the candlelight illuminating his handsome features. 'Let me try to explain something to you. Queen Marie is a very special part of our heritage. We are proud of her, we worship her, she brought hope and faith when there was none. We took great exception to this film you referred to. It was a betrayal of our faith, a typical Hollywood commercial vehicle that was a distortion of the facts. This film is dismissed, disowned, and no one in New Orleans, in the state of Louisiana, will acknowledge its existence.'

'So it was about voodoo, this film?'

He stared at her and then shook his head, smiling. 'Let us say it was an attempt to portray our great queen and it was an insult to her memory. To begin with, they cast a white woman in the role: Elizabeth Seal may have black blood in her veins but she is ashamed to admit it, even though she has for many years been a generous benefactor to our cause.' He gave a formal bow. 'So if you will excuse me.'

'Are you saying that Elizabeth Caley—'

'Is a believer and a very generous and caring woman. Please pass on my condolences to her regarding her daughter. Good evening.'

'Thank you very much,' Rosie stuttered, still unsure if she had heard correctly. But she didn't wait around. The drum-beats were in time with her own heart and it scared the hell out of her.

Lorraine sat in the stifling, overheated office in the New Orleans police department. A female officer was taking down her statement. A wiry detective sergeant sat behind a cluttered desk, his chair creaking at every twist of his body.

'So you do not know of any reason why Miss Tilda Brown would have taken this tragic course of action?'

'No. As I have already said, I was there for no more than three quarters of an hour, going over, in fact, your previous enquiries, whether or not Anna Louise Caley visited her on the night she disappeared, routine questions . . .'

'Did she seem perplexed or upset?'

'Yes, she was Anna Louise's best friend so she obviously got upset.' Her brain was ticking over at ninety miles an hour, deciding not to mention the photograph, or the insinuations regarding Anna Louise and her father being lovers.

'Well, it's a tragedy, but who knows what goes on in a youngster's mind?' said the sergeant, his chair creaking ominously.

'Yes, who knows?' she repeated, and then hesitated. 'Are you sure it was suicide? Did she leave a note?'

He frowned. 'We have no indication any other party was involved.'

'So there was a note?'

He nodded. 'I am unable to disclose its contents as it was personal to her parents. She was their only child.'

'But it was suicide?'

'Yes, it was. She was wearing only a silk kimono and she had taken the belt, tied it to a curtain rail, stepped up on a small dressing-table stool and kicked it away. There were no visible signs of violence on her body other than the marks left by the belt. Her mother found her, and is under sedation. As I said, she was an only child.'

Lorraine stopped at the hotel reception, said that although she was in she wanted no calls and did not want to be disturbed by anyone, that included her associates also staying at the hotel.

There were more white envelopes with telephone messages posted beneath her door, but she stepped over them. She hadn't even opened the ones she had taken with her. She felt drained and didn't want to face anyone, talk to anyone, even Robert Caley, because she blamed herself for Tilda Brown's death. She wanted to go over everything that she had said, everything Tilda Brown had said, because somewhere there would be a clue as to why a beautiful eighteen-year-old girl with everything to live for had gone to such tragic lengths. Maybe there was even a clue to Anna Louise Caley's disappearance.

CHAPTER 13

NICK HAD sunk more than a few beers with Bill Rooney. They had traded notes, discussed the new findings, and Rosie joined them with her notes about the meeting at the museum. They'd continued to discuss their developments over supper together in a nearby bistro. All three felt that Robert Caley was no longer their main suspect and they should concentrate on the Juda Salina, drugs and voodoo connection, especially after hearing that Fryer Jones had actually been questioned by the police regarding Anna Louise Caley's disappearance.

It was after ten when they got back to the hotel. Rooney and Rosie were tired out but Nick was fully alert; he had always been a night owl. When they were told that Lorraine was in her room but had requested not to be disturbed, it irritated the hell out of Nick but the other two were thankful.

Nick went up to his room, paced around, and drank a quarter of a bottle of vodka he had bought before he decided to go and see Lorraine. He tapped on her door and waited, then looked quickly up and down the empty corridor and took out his own room key. He'd been in more hotels than enough, and he wondered if, as was often the case, the security aspect of the keys left a lot to be desired. He was right – his key fitted, and he opened Lorraine's door.

He stood looking at her, slowly unscrewing the cap from the bottle and taking a long slug. She lay on her belly, one arm hanging over the side of the bed, the other tucked under her pillow, and the sheet thrown back to the base of her back. He padded closer, sitting on the bed opposite to drink her in, wanting to lie naked beside her more than anything he had ever known. Lorraine slept soundlessly, her lips slightly parted, and even in the dim light he could see the scars on her arm and back. With the alcohol, his inhibitions relaxed more and more, until he tucked the bottle down beside the bed and ran his palm gently along the curve of her spine: she stirred, and slowly turned to face him as she woke.

'Nick?' she murmured, still half-asleep.

'Yeah,' he said softly. She turned over, reaching unhurriedly for the sheet to cover her naked breasts.

'How the hell did you get in?'

He smiled. 'Oh, I huffed and I puffed an' I blew the door down.'

'You're drunk,' she said, yawning.

'Not yet, but I couldn't stay away from you.'

She sat up, drawing the sheet closer. 'You'd better go, this is crazy, Nick.'

'I know, but like I said – I couldn't keep away.'

Lorraine sighed: she didn't need this, and it was beginning to irritate her. 'I need to sleep, Nick.'

He stood up, suddenly almost boyish. 'I know, I'm sorry, I always was a dumb bastard, but . . .'

She flopped back, looking up at him. 'But what?'

He hitched up his jeans, avoiding her eye.

'But what, Nick?'

He laughed softly. 'Do you think I could have just one kiss, just one, and then I'm gone.'

'You're nuts, you know that, don't you?'

'Yep, but that's all I want – well, it isn't, I'd like a

whole lot more, but maybe this isn't the time for you and me to dive between the sheets.'

'You'd better go,' she said again, but she was smiling. She couldn't help it, he was getting to her, she knew it, and maybe so did he.

'Come here, Bartello, an' the deal is . . .'

'One kiss,' he said, almost jumping across the bed to sit close to her and wrap her in his arms. She reached up and kissed him on the lips, and as the sheet fell away from her breasts he bent his head to kiss her nipple.

'Nick, that's enough.'

He moaned, tracing her breast with his tongue, and then drew the sheet gently back over her.

'Goodnight, princess. I love you.'

She watched him limp to the door, half-turning for a last look at her, and then he was gone. Sometimes he was so like Jack Lubrinksi it made her want to weep, but he wasn't Jack, he was Nick Bartello, and as she snuggled down she felt the warmth of his love, and although she didn't want to admit it, it felt good.

Back in his own room, Nick found it impossible now to sleep. He was still restless by eleven, so decided he would go back to Fryer's bar, see what else he could pick up. It was almost twelve when he passed through the silent lobby, where only the night porter was on duty. Like Rosie and Rooney, the other, mostly elderly guests had all flaked out, it seemed.

Robert Caley sat with a bottle of Scotch. He had been drinking since around seven and had now almost drunk himself sober. The only woman he had cared about for so long he couldn't remember not only didn't return his calls but had betrayed him to such an extent he didn't know whether he wanted to kill her or himself. Lloyd

Dulay had been round like a man possessed, accusing him of fucking his daughter and telling him with pleasure that the Governor had told him privately that there was no question of Caley being awarded the licence to operate the casino. An official public announcement would be made shortly, but the Governor had indicated that he considered a broader distribution of ownership to be appropriate, and he, Lloyd, had had no hesitation in accepting the invitation to join their number which had been extended to him by Doubloons. Finally, Dulay said grimly, he figured that Caley had walked himself into one hell of a mess, and if he used one cent more of his daughter's trust fund to bail himself out of it, he would find himself in court.

'Who did you get all this crap from?' Caley had snapped angrily.

Dulay had hesitated, and then looked Caley straight in the face. 'The investigator, Lorraine Page.'

Caley was stunned. The accusations had been like blows to his heart. Why, he kept on asking himself, why was she doing it? How could she lie in his arms one night and the next day systematically try to destroy him, unless that had been her intention all along? He just couldn't believe it. The booze helped numb the pain and the more drunk he became the more he convinced himself she wouldn't have done this to him. But when call after call to her remained unanswered, he began to get angry at himself for being a sucker, angry that maybe all his adult life he had been just that, a sucker.

The anger built when he received a cable saying that Elizabeth had discharged herself from the clinic and had ordered Edward to stand by to fly her to New Orleans. Caley called Phyllis in LA to be told that Lloyd Dulay had called to speak to Elizabeth. Phyllis had given him the clinic's phone number.

328

By twelve Caley was drunk, hurt and bewildered – and also facing bankruptcy. But he kept on calling Lorraine, needing to speak to her, to give her the chance of explaining to him, because he still could not believe that she would betray him. Nothing else mattered to him, not the money, not even Anna Louise, just that Lorraine, the woman he had fallen totally and stupidly in love with, had used him. Even when he received a call from Elizabeth, he felt numb. She sounded calm and distant, and angry. She refused to tell him why she had discharged herself, merely stated that she would not be coming to the hotel but going straight to their home in the Garden District.

Caley knew that Dulay must have said something to her but he didn't have the energy to argue on the phone, preferring to see her face to face. He did, however, ask if Lorraine Page had also contacted her at the clinic. Elizabeth seemed surprised. Then he heard the fear creep into her voice.

'Has she found out something?'

Caley sighed, dragging on a cigarette. 'Maybe, but I don't think it has anything to do with Anna Louise . . .'

'What, then?' Elizabeth asked, her voice wavering.

'You're the one with the secrets, Elizabeth. I'm just the dumb bastard that went along with everything.'

There was a lengthy pause. 'You think we should stop payments?'

'We? *We*? You're the one who instigated this investigation, Elizabeth, not me. You hired her, you fire her. She's only on it for two weeks, isn't she? Just stop the payments.'

Again there was a long pause and he could hear her rapid breathing, knew she was suffering a panic attack, but this time he didn't care, this time he wasn't on hand to sort it all out, carry her to bed.

329

'There was a bonus,' she said softly.

'What?' he asked, lighting another cigarette from the stub of his last. 'What are you talking about?'

Again there was a pause and then he heard a deep intake of breath. 'Don't be angry at me, but I offered to pay a one million bonus if they found Anna Louise.'

He closed his eyes. She was crying and he felt like weeping himself. 'Well, that's your business. I'll see you at the house.' He replaced the receiver before she could reply, then pressed for the desk and gave instructions he was not to be disturbed.

Caley lay on the bed, inhaled deeply and let the smoke drift slowly from his lungs. One million bonus! No wonder she made love to him. A man who felt foolish and betrayed, a man who felt as inadequate as he now felt was dangerous, because if Lorraine Page had walked in at that moment he would have taken her by her throat and squeezed the life out of her.

Lorraine was in a deep, dreamless, exhausted sleep. She had pushed away the sheet and lay curled up naked, her body glistening with perspiration. But nothing woke her, not the red blinking dot on her telephone as the calls came in, one at midnight, one at a quarter past, and the last at one-fifteen.

Juda Salina woke, her massive body soaked in sweat. She could feel the horrific restriction on her throat and knew that what she had seen a few days before was now happening.

'Raoul,' she croaked, and then screamed out, '*Raoul get in here.*'

330

He stood bleary-eyed at her bedroom door. 'Yes? What you want?'

'Water, get me some water.'

It was going down, it was happening, and there was nothing she could do to stop it. What she had seen, what she had felt, she would have to go through, and it made her angry that she was an open avenue for such pain. But that was her God-given power, and as much as she hated it, she had to give way and let it happen. It was the will of the spirits, she had been chosen, and there was nothing she could do to stop it.

Raoul passed her a glass of tepid water and she gulped it down, her fat hand shaking as she drained the glass. He hovered, waiting. 'You sick?'

She shook her head and lay back on her mound of pillows with a sigh. 'No, I'm not sick, we'll still be going.'

'You want some more water?'

'No, maybe just sit with me a while, talk to me.'

He sat on the edge of her bed, his short cotton wrap tied tightly round his waist.

'All be buzzin' back home, starts any day now, and Ruby is all jumpy with nerves.'

Juda sighed again. 'You talk to your mama?'

He nodded. 'Sure, said she'd whacked Jesse and Willy with a broom, they been getting drugged up at Fryer's bar, and Sugar May's a handful, wants to be a singer so she hangs out there as well. It's making Mama go crazy with worry.'

Juda nodded her head. 'Ruby's got a beautiful face and a lovely tight body, but I don't think she has the knowledge, that's why I think she's gonna be okay. But when we get home you sit your brothers down and you tell them they should keep well away from Fryer Jones.

If they don't, they're gonna get hurt bad, and the same goes for Sugar May.'

She closed her eyes and he chewed his fingernails, his foot tapping against one of the bed legs.

'You don't do those drugs anymore, do you, Raoul?'

'No, Aunty Juda, not now I'm working for you.'

'That's a good boy, they no good for you. Stop that tapping on the bed, Raoul, gettin' on my nerves. You're a real jumpy boy lately so if you can't sleep, make yourself some of that tea I get for Mrs Caley.'

'That'd take an elephant out,' he said, still chewing his nails.

'Well, I've had to increase the strength over the years . . .'

He uncrossed his legs and then promptly recrossed them, his foot tapping into the dark night. He couldn't stop it, his whole body was twitching, and he needed to get back to his pipe, had just been smoking up when she'd called out to him. If she'd looked close into his eyes she would have seen for herself: Raoul had advanced; he was no longer rolling the ganja, he was using crack cocaine now, and most nights. As soon as he saw she was asleep he would slip out to the clubs, and be back before she woke, back before she knew he'd been out to score.

Nick headed towards Fryer Jones's bar, hands stuffed into his jeans pockets, cigarette dangling from his mouth. He heard the car backfire, like a gunshot, and he automatically ducked, turned and side-stepped to the wall. Crack, it backfired again, and then he heard the loud, screeching music as an old broken-down Camaro careered towards him.

Willy was high, his brother Jesse hanging out of the

332

window, yelling, 'I said it was him, *it's him, Willy!* Pull on over now.'

Nick sighed with irritation, not in any way scared of the two stoned kids, but his hands were out of his pockets and he was looking up and down the road, making up his mind which way to go, to see if there was anyone who'd witness what he knew was going to go down.

'Eh! *You mother fucker, you!*'

The old Camaro lurched to a standstill just a few yards ahead of Nick. He moved closer to the wall, fists clenched, ready to thrash them both, knowing that if it came to it he'd go for the .22 stashed in his boot.

Willy crashed the gears into reverse and the Camaro screamed backwards. He hadn't intended to mount the pavement, he just misjudged the kerb. Jesse was still hanging out of the passenger window, swearing and cursing at the guy who had beaten the hell out of them the previous night. Only tonight he was on his own, no old bastard Fryer Jones around. As Nick moved to one side to avoid being crunched by the car, his leg gave way. He stumbled and had just straightened up when Jesse came at him, screeching, doing a farcical kung fu side-kick. Nick grabbed his foot and twisted it, throwing Jesse off balance and making him fall on his hands and knees.

'Get the shit, Willy, get him!'

Willy ran at Nick, carrying a baseball bat, and swung wildly, striking him on his forearm as Nick protected his face. His leg buckled again, giving Jesse a few moments to get back on his feet. He grabbed the baseball bat from his brother and as the two of them closed in on him, Nick ducked and dived and took off, heading towards a lit-up bar. He ran as fast as he could, hampered by his bad leg, needing a moment to get his pistol out of his boot. But the kids were on his heels, Jesse swinging the baseball bat in a frenzy. He clipped Nick on the shoulder but he kept on running. Just before the safety of the bar he stumbled again. Willy moved in front of him and Nick saw the knife come out. He held up his hands, gasping for breath.

'Hey! Come on, just take it easy, huh . . .?'

Nick saw the alley right across the road and dived between them both, but not before Jesse took another swing with the baseball bat. This time it hit Nick just on the left side of the head above his ear, making him reel. He could see the neon sign of a liquor store and was trying to make it there, hoping there would be someone around to help. His breath rasped in his chest, the shooting pains in his leg were crippling him and his head thudded, but he made it right up to the doorway. The door was locked. He jammed his finger on a security buzzer and hurled his body against the door.

'Open the door, open the fucking door.'

The two boys were grinning, one swinging the bat, the other opening the flick-knife. They had him cornered; the alley was a dead-end and there was nowhere to run to. Nick was trapped.

Raoul still sat by his aunt's bed, his whole body twitching now, and he was desperate to get back to his pipe.

'You still need me to stay with you?'

She didn't answer. He stood up and leaned closer, sure she was sleeping, when she scared the hell out of him. She sat bolt upright, her hands clutching at her throat, and started retching. He backed away, not that he hadn't seen this before, his mama often went into spasms and he hated it, just like he hated the way all his life people had come to their run-down house and started screaming and shouting in that dark front room, the kids banished to the back yard.

She twisted and turned on the bed, making it creak and groan from her weight. At one point part of the bed actually lifted as she rolled to one side. He saw it then, the old wooden box, and became even more agitated, frightened by her grunting and moaning. Saliva trickled down her fat chin, frothed at the corners of her mouth, but all he could think about was the box, because he knew what was inside it.

Nick Bartello couldn't run anywhere. He'd tried to reach his hidden .22 but the baseball bat had swung down on his arm and he'd felt the bone crack. He was defenceless but he remembered their faces, so young, the two arrogant black kids he'd given a whipping at Fryer's bar. When they hemmed him in he still put up a good fight, but he knew it was the end, and with the pain in his leg he didn't have a chance to defend himself. He curled up as they kicked at him, putting his hands up to protect himself. Then one of the boys leaned over him and he saw the blade close up, saw his whole life as it ran before him. Lorraine's face was the last image he saw as they cut his throat, giving him one last kick to turn his body over.

Fryer Jones was in his usual seat at the bar. Willy and Jesse Corbello walked in and drew up stools next to him. Fryer held on to his trombone as Willy threw the gris-gris necklace on to the bar.

'This yours, Fryer?'

He picked it up, felt the blood still sticky on the white

bones, and he sighed. 'Boys, you just done somethin' bad, these were mine, given in good faith.'

'You not given us what you promised, you old bastard, and besides, you gonna do the same for us as we done for you, right? We been here all night, man, never left your bar,' Jesse said, and leaned over to get himself a beer.

Willy opened Nick Bartello's wallet. 'Who gives a fuck? Nobody saw us anyway, we was cool. Hey! Drinks on the house, we just scored a few bucks.'

Fryer eyed the boys and kissed his teeth. They were running out of control, getting into bad trouble, just like their crazy brother Raoul. He looked at the gris-gris he had given to that poor bastard. He picked it up, tipped his beer over it, washing the blood away with his gnarled thumb, then hung it round his neck.

'Think I'll play a set,' he said to no one. He eased off the bar stool and wended his way back to the mirrored stage. As he passed two thickset black men playing bid whist, he murmured, 'Thrash 'em hard, they gotta be taught a lesson from somebody, and they're getting outta hand, way out.'

The two young boys were sitting on the bar stools, laughing and joking, guzzling their free beer, confident they were running the show, confident no one would touch them. They were the Salina sisters' boys.

'Where's Nick?' Lorraine asked as she joined Rosie and Rooney at the breakfast table for waffles and cream.

'I dunno, but we all had an early night,' said Rooney, squinting over the menu. 'I called his room, no answer.'

Lorraine sat down and brought out all the small white envelopes with her messages.

'How did it go last night?' Rosie asked as she signalled for the waitress.

Lorraine began slitting the envelopes open. 'They haven't got the exact time Tilda Brown hanged herself but they think about two or three hours after I left.' There were fifteen messages from Robert Caley, one saying his wife was arriving in New Orleans. Dulay had called four times, and Nick twice. She noted the time of the last call. 'I would say Nick is sleeping one off, seems he didn't take such an early night.' She tossed the message over to Rooney.

Rosie had been studying the menu and turned to Rooney.

'Maybe we should cut down on all this sugar. I know we had a deal, but I don't know about you, I felt a lot better before we made pigs of ourselves here.'

He nodded. 'You order for me, then.'

'Okay, maybe just some fresh fruit.'

'Fine,' he said, and then flushed as he caught Lorraine looking at him and smiling.

'What you looking at me like that for?' he said defensively.

'Because it's nice to see you two getting along so well.'

'I noticed you and Nick were real friendly too,' Rosie put in, afraid that Lorraine disapproved of her friendship with Rooney, or thought it unprofessional.

'Hell, don't be so defensive, Rosie, and you're right, I'm getting on really well with Nick, he's okay, but that doesn't mean we're up for a double wedding or—'

Rooney gasped. 'Who's talking about weddings? Me and Rosie are just on the same diet.'

Rosie brought her menu up quickly to cover her face, not wanting Rooney to see that his remark had upset her.

337

'So,' she said expressionlessly, 'it's fruit all round, is it?'

Juda Salina eased her bulk into the shower, calling out for Raoul to put the coffee on and bring round the car to take them to the airport. It had been a bad night but it was over, the dark cloud had lifted. It came down like a blanket fifteen minutes later when she kicked open the kitchen door and there was no coffee on the stove, just Raoul's sleeping bag left in the middle of the floor. And it got darker when she went back into her bedroom, because just sticking out from under her bed was her precious box. Fat as she was, she got down on her knees fast and dragged it out. It was never this close to the edge, she was no fool. In fact, she slept feeling it through the mattress and the bed springs on purpose so nobody would ever steal it from under her at night.

She screamed out loud when she realized all her savings were gone, every single dollar, more than 150 thousand dollars. Money to put towards Ruby's float, her Mardi Gras gowns, money for her sister, her kids. Her savings, all gone.

At first Edith Corbello thought it was one of her clients screeching down the phone; it was a while before she realized it was her own sister.

'Hush now, Juda, hush now, I can't understand a word you're saying.'

Juda eventually gasped out that Raoul had stolen everything she possessed, all her life's savings; everything she'd worked so hard for in order to come back to New Orleans and live in style was gone.

'No, no, honey, you got to be mistaken.'

338

'I am not mistaken, he's even taken my car, *my car*, Edith, that little shit's got my fucking car.' Juda gripped tightly on to the bed, gasping for breath, her massive bosoms heaving. 'I never done evil work, Edith, you know that, but so help me God, I will on Raoul. I'll fill that boy full of stuff to eat his guts alive, he's gonna wish he never saw the light of day!'

Juda slammed the phone back on the hook. She slumped into a chair, put her head in her hands and wept. How many times had she been told by Mrs Caley to put her money in the bank and she had always refused? Through her tears she ranted and raged against Raoul. She didn't even have enough money to go home for Carnival, wouldn't see Ruby crowned.

Eventually the tears and rage subsided into a deep depression and she sat as if wedged into the chair. 'How could he do that to me?' she said to herself over and over, and then looked at the ceiling. 'How come the spirits talk with me and I don't know when my own blood is stealing from me?'

She wiped her face with a tissue and sniffed, and picked up the phone again. Maybe *she*'d help her out, like she'd helped *her* for all these years.

Phyllis answered, stunned to hear the plaintive voice at the other end. 'Juda? Mrs Salina, is this you?'

'Yes, Phyllis. Something terrible has happened and I need to speak to Mrs Caley.'

Phyllis pursed her lips; she was going to enjoy this. 'I'm sorry, Mrs Salina, but Mrs Caley is not at home.'

'Can you get her to contact me?'

'Well, if she calls home I will tell her you rang.'

Phyllis was sure the horrible creature was crying, and when she thought of all the years she had been treated

339

like a piece of worn carpet by the big fat woman, she enjoyed her moment of power.

'You know, Phyllis, I've been a good friend to Mrs Caley, we go back a long time, so please, I'm asking you, if she calls home, tell her to contact me. This time it's me that needs her and I need her bad.'

'As I said, Mrs Salina, I will relay the message to Mrs Caley. Goodbye.'

She replaced the phone as Peters walked into the hallway.

'Who was that?'

Phyllis followed him into the breakfast lounge. 'That wretched fat woman, Juda, wanted to speak to Mrs Caley. I said I would relay the message, but somehow I think it might just slip my mind. I've always hated her, she's a blood-sucking leech and Mr Caley loathes her as well.'

Phyllis sat opposite Peters as they ate breakfast together, and Peters stared from the window.

'Nice to have the place to ourselves, isn't it?'

'Are you all right, Mrs Caley?' Edward asked, and Elizabeth dropped the magazine.

'Shouldn't you be at the controls?'

He smiled. 'It's on automatic pilot, Mrs Caley.'

She turned away. '*You* are paid to fly this plane, Mr Hardy, not the automatic pilot. Please stay in the cockpit, you know how nervous I am about flying.'

Mario looked up from his book, seated at the far end of the plane. Edward flicked him a glance and returned to the cockpit.

'Can I get you anything at all, Mrs Caley?' Mario asked.

'No, nothing, thank you.'

She picked up the magazine again, the glossy pages blurring before her eyes. The models in their glamorous poses and gowns only reminded her of the last trip with Anna Louise, and she could hear her voice: 'I like this one, Mama, what do you think?'

She had replied that she simply adored it, not even really looking at it. Just watching her daughter had pained her; she was so young, so very pretty, with her whole life ahead of her. She was envious of Anna Louise's youth, her athletic talent. She took after her father so much it sometimes unnerved Elizabeth just to look at that fair hair and bright blue eyes.

Elizabeth sighed. The secret of Anna Louise's parentage didn't matter in this day and age, nobody would care, but when she had been Anna Louise's age, and coming from where she did, it had mattered a great deal. She closed her eyes and thought back over her life, knowing without doubt that if she had it to live over again she would not have become involved with the movies – or that movie. It had destroyed her, made her dependent on Juda Salina and her kind, and somewhere deep inside she yearned to be free of it all. Perhaps that was why she took so many drugs, dicing with her own life. She longed for freedom, for air, for sunshine, the sun she was afraid to let touch her milky-white skin – not because it burned, but because it turned a rich, dark shade of brown.

Elizabeth's beautiful slanting eyes brimmed and tears spilled as if in slow motion down her cheeks. She'd used the ability to cry on cue often in her film career and had been proud of it, but now there was no 'action', no cameras. The tears were for her own empty, silly, frightened life.

*

All the diners had left the breakfast room, leaving Rooney, Rosie and Lorraine the only people still sitting round their table.

'Okay, let's get the day started,' Rooney said, pushing his chair back.

Lorraine stubbed out her cigarette. 'Try Nick's room again, Rosie. If he's not back, shove a message under his door, tell him where we'll all be so he can make contact.'

'Will do, and you take care.'

Lorraine smiled. 'Yes, ma'am . . .'

'Listen, about this video—'

Lorraine walked towards the exit, her arm loosely round Rosie's shoulders.

'What about asking Lloyd Dulay? He's known Elizabeth all these years, and as you're going to see him, I just thought . . .'

'Good idea, I'll ask him, Rosie.'

Rooney was standing by the lobby desk. He turned as the women approached. 'That bastard's not in his room, he's been out all night.'

'Well, he's probably with some hooker someplace,' Lorraine said, slightly irritated, as she headed for the elevator. Her reaction surprised her: she was jealous, but concealed it immediately. She smiled and told Rooney to let Nick sleep it off, but not for long. They had only one week left.

Edith Corbello found Jesse out back on the old car seat. He had been severely beaten, his nose and right arm broken. He was bruised and crying in agony, but when she asked who had done this to him, he just whimpered that he had fallen down the stairs.

She had just started to clean her son up when she

342

heard the front door closing and footsteps shuffling down the corridor.

'That you, Willy? *Willy get your ass in here!*'

She believed that Willy had beaten up his brother and when he came into the kitchen she was sure of it. Both his eyes were black, his nose was bleeding and he had a lump on his forehead the size of a mango. She would have slapped him hard but he could only just about walk.

'I had enough of you boys fightin' each other, I'm gonna get Fryer here to sort out the pair of you. I can't handle you no more, and it's time he took some responsibility.'

'It was Fryer that done it,' Willy said, and Jesse kicked him so hard that he howled in agony. He had so many bruises to his body it was hard to miss one.

'You tellin' me that bastard did this to you both? *Yes?*'

Jesse shook his head. 'No, Mama, we done it to each other, honest, we just started foolin' around and . . .'

Edith glowered. 'You git your brother to a hospital right now, you both lookin' all beat and your sister about to be crowned. I'm wiping my hands of you both. I am ashamed, you hear me? *Ashamed!*'

Edith banged out. She wanted to weep; what with Raoul gone and Juda screaming at her it had been a bad day and it wasn't even nine o'clock. But she knew it would get worse, a whole lot worse, when she had to tell Ruby that there was no money for her gown, already half stitched up and near finished.

Ruby was lying on her bed, in the best bedroom of the tiny rundown house, with a treatment pack on her face. She was being photographed tomorrow for one of the hair trade papers, just a promo for the salon where she worked, but it was a start. When she heard what her mama had to say, she got off the bed in a rage. 'You tellin' me Raoul stole all Aunty Juda's money, he *stole* it?'

'That's what she said, and she don't even have the money for the plane ride for the parade.'

Ruby screamed with rage; she was damned if her crazy, crackhead brother was going to stand in her way out of this house and away from everyone in it. She sobbed and clawed at the walls with her nails, her tears making trickles on her white mask until at last she hunched up in a corner like a little girl, the fight gone out of her.

'Ah, Mama, what are we gonna do, what are we gonna do?'

Below, Sugar May listened up and grinned from ear to ear. Served that mean stuck-up bitch right. Ruby Corbello always got everything she wanted, never had to wear anyone's cast-off clothes like she did. She skipped out of the house in delight as an old yellow cab drew up to take Jesse and Willy to the hospital.

Edith sat on her daughter's bed, near to tears herself. She felt worn out by it all.

'Maybe ask Father Leroy, Ruby?'

Ruby shook her head. 'With a wife and two kids he needs his money, Mama. There ain't no fortunes to be made in the kind of investigation work that's on his level. You know who the only one with money is, you know.'

Edith shook her head. 'I'm not asking Fryer, I wouldn't ask him to spit in a jam jar.'

'I didn't mean Fryer,' snapped Ruby. 'Why don't we ask her lady friend, one who's been paying out all that money for years? We ask her direct, she's rich, isn't she?'

Edith shook her head. 'No, we don't cross Juda's territory, Ruby. That Mrs Caley is her wages and it's her

344

money been keeping us all. I wouldn't go behind Juda's back.'

Ruby stood in front of her mother. 'I know you done things for money, things you've always been against, I know that, Mama.'

'You shut up now,' Edith said with a warning slap.

Ruby dodged aside. 'I saw you making it, Mama, I saw Juda coming here for her so-called tea. I know.'

Edith hit out again. 'You saw nobody come in here, girl, *you hear me*? You say one word about that business to anyone and I am warning you—'

Ruby stood her ground. 'No, Mama, I am warning you because my day is gonna be the best day in my life and nobody will mess it up for me.'

Ruby ran out of the room and Edith covered her face. She heard the front door slam hard and crossed to the window. There was Ruby striding down the street, arms swinging, still with treatment cream all over her face. It was a terrible morning, like some kind of train running out of control. And there was more to come.

As she made her way heavily down the narrow staircase, Sugar May passed her with a rolled-up newspaper. She swatted a fly with it.

'If that is today's paper, Sugar May, don't you go screwing it up like that before I've even cast my eye over it.'

The young girl chucked the paper at her mother. 'I'm gonna run away, I'm gonna find Raoul and share in all his millions.' She stuck out her tongue and her mother used the same paper to hit her across the side of the head. Sugar May just laughed and ran out.

Halfway down the front page was an article headed 'Former Debutante Commits Suicide'. Edith sank on to the stairs, her eyes popping out on stalks as she read the detailed article about the suicide of Tilda Brown. She felt

345

as if there was a noose round her throat, getting tighter and tighter, taking the breath out of her body.

Ruby knelt in front of the high white tomb in the First St Louis Cemetery. On the ground, in front of it she had drawn the ve-ve of Marie Laveau, the swirling hieroglyph that would invoke the spirit of the voodoo queen, and now she drew another cross to add to the hundreds already on the monument, pressed her hand flat against it, and knocked on the tomb. She was so intent in prayer to the dead priestess's spirit, straining every fibre of her being, that she did not hear Leroy Able's soft-footed approach. Her face was still streaked with white cream and for a moment Able thought he was seeing a woman risen from the tomb, and he froze.

'Ruby?'

She turned round.

'I thought you didn't believe in all that.' It had been one of Edith's great griefs that her elder daughter seemed to have no time for her heritage, sneering at it as a lot of superstitious African rubbish that would keep her in the ghetto when she was going to go to New York and be the new Veronica Webb.

'Well,' said Ruby gruffly, embarrassed to have been seen. 'Can't do no harm, I don't reckon. Something terrible has happened. Raoul run off with the money for my gown and it's half-stitched, I only got two more fittings.'

'Come out of sight here, quickly now, the place is full of tourists coming round looking at the graves. Hurry up, get out of sight.'

Ruby let Leroy draw her away from Marie Laveau's tomb to a less frequented part of the cemetery where the brick-oven tombs of people too poor to afford a private

346

sepulchre lined the perimeter walls. She took the handkerchief he offered her and sank down to sit on the ground, cleaning her face and stretching her long slender legs out in front of her. She had changed since last time he saw her, and her beautiful, oval face, deep, slanting black eyes and waist-length, wavy hair had begun to look more and more like those of the great queen; she could have been her daughter, or Marie Laveau herself come back to life and youth a second time.

'We'll find the money, Ruby, everyone will give towards the gown, you don't have to worry about that. The krewe won't let you go without. You're just being a silly girl.'

She sighed. 'Maybe, but things are bad at home, Leroy, really bad, and my brothers are all messed up. Even my sister is going to get herself in trouble, she hangs out at that shit bar, they all do.'

He bent down and stroked her soft hair. 'But you don't?'

'No,' she said softly.

'Because you're different?'

'You know I'm different. I have more in front of me than that neighbourhood or this whole damn city, least I had till Raoul fucked things up, but there's nothing I won't do to get that money and have my day, I even told Mama to call up . . .'

She bit her lip and turned away. He frowned. 'Call who?'

Ruby shook her head. 'I said too much.'

'No, Ruby, you haven't said anything at all. Who did you tell your mama to contact?'

Ruby kept her head down. 'Mrs Caley.'

Leroy stood up, towering above her. 'No, you don't do that, you hear me? Since her daughter disappeared there've been police enquiries, private investigator enquiries, and they're still going on, you hear me? You stay away from all that. I mean it, Ruby, you don't ever get involved.'

She looked up rebelliously. 'But what about my gown, Leroy? If we don't pay Alma Dicks she won't finish it.'

He drew her to her feet. She seemed so light, so fragile. 'Your gown will be ready, Ruby, and you will be the most beautiful queen Mardi Gras has ever seen.'

She smiled. 'Wanna see something Leroy?' She began to move her body sinuously. 'I can do the snake dance, Leroy, like Mama used to do.' She twisted her hips and rolled her head. She was as lithe, as hypnotic as a serpent, and he wanted to reach out and draw her into his arms, but she danced towards the high tombs and suddenly she had passed between two of them and was gone. It was as if she had never been there. Leroy sighed. He had changed in so many ways since he had come back from LA. It was not just the responsibility of having a wife and two children; he had come back and found his roots, rediscovered himself and his beliefs, but sometimes it was hard to lose that other Leroy that would fuck anything that swayed in front of him in a skirt. And being confronted by beauty such as Ruby Corbello's was a real test of his faith.

Nick Bartello's naked body was in the morgue, his clothes folded into paper bags. They found no identification on him, and as his pockets had been stripped, it was surmised that it had been a mugging, even though he didn't look like a tourist from the main routes, more like a drifter coming in for the Carnival. There were a lot of Nick Bartellos found and never identified, and they would have left it that way but for a tattoo on his left forearm: a shield, the LAPD badge.

Leroy Able was back in his office and back in his public persona when he got the call. When the sergeant asked if he'd been contacted by any old buddies, he frowned and leaned his elbows on his desk. 'Nope, why do you ask?'

'We got a stiff found early this morning, an' you was in the LAPD, weren't you?'

'Yeah, why?'

'Well, this guy's got a tattoo of a shield, no other ID found on him. He's also got a couple of bullet scars in his right leg.'

Leroy hesitated. 'You want me to take a look?'

'Found him up in an alley two blocks from Fryer's bar, wouldn't you know!' The fat officer waddled ahead of Leroy, who came up to his elbow. 'Throat slit and he'd taken a beating, no witness, no nothing.'

The sheet was drawn away from Nick's face and Leroy stared down. He breathed in. 'Nope, sorry, never set eyes on him. You know these old hippies get tatted up, don't mean anything too much.'

Lorraine had time to study every bonbonnière, trinket tray, hand-painted lampshade and china parakeet in Lloyd Dulay's cavernous drawing room: he had kept her waiting for over an hour, and she was furious when he eventually strode towards her, hand outstretched.

'My apologies, but I was kept waiting at the airport, I was there to meet Elizabeth Caley. Then I had to drive with her to the house and it was hard to get away.'

'That's all right,' she said coldly.

He sat on the scarlet and gold sofa, stretching out his

long legs. 'Even harder when we talked about Anna Louise's trust fund . . .'

She stared. 'Really?'

'Yes, down by near forty-two million.'

She coughed. 'Robert Caley?'

He made an expansive gesture with his huge hands. 'Couldn't be anyone else. He knows I know, and I also pulled out of the casino deal, man is nothing but a thief. He didn't deny it and I wanted to beat the hell out of him. He wanted to do the same to me when I told him I knew about him and Anna. He denied it, swore to me he had never touched her. I don't know if he was telling me the truth or not.'

She licked her lips. 'You think he might àlso have killed her?'

'What?'

'If what you say is true, and Robert Caley has used Anna Louise's trust fund, do you think he might have anything to do with her disappearance?'

'You didn't say that at all, Mrs Page.'

'No, well, I'm asking it now.'

He got up and rubbed at his shock of white hair. 'He wouldn't need to kill his daughter to cover it up, she probably wouldn't find out.'

'If the casino deal went through.'

'Yes.'

'But if it didn't?'

He shrugged. 'I can't give you an answer because I truthfully don't know.'

'Could you tell me just how much money Elizabeth Caley is probably worth?'

He crossed the priceless Bessarabian rug to stand by the windows. 'She's always used the best financial advisers to invest her money, I know because I am one of them . . .' He remained with his back to her. 'Elizabeth had a very substantial inheritance, so I would estimate her fortune to be somewhere in the region of two hundred million, perhaps more.'

Lorraine blinked: she had not been in any way prepared to hear a figure like that.

Dulay turned towards her. 'You know, Robert also had access to a lot of that, from what I can gather, but he's a stiff-necked bastard. Wanted to make it on his own. 'Course, she was always bailing him out.' He gestured dismissively. 'I guess Elizabeth will bail him out of this fuck-up he's got himself into right now.'

'Is that possible?'

'Is what possible?'

'For him to be bailed out, as you say?'

He looked at her as if she was a stupid child. 'Well, yes and no. The way the wind's blowing, he's not going to get any casino licence, but I guess whoever does will have to negotiate with him for the land. If Elizabeth gives him something just to tide him over, maybe he won't have to sell at an undervalue because he needs the cash.'

She was taken aback again and looked away, not wanting him to see her confusion, but he was not looking at her. He was fiddling with a gold chain tucked into his waistcoat. 'I'm going to tell you something that is highly confidential, Mrs Page, and as such I want you to swear it will not go further than this room.'

She folded her arms. 'Well, I can't really do that, if it has any criminal connection . . .'

'It doesn't.'

'Then you have my word, Mr Dulay.'

He sat down heavily again.

'If there was anything going on, it would not exactly be incest.'

'I'm sorry?'

351

'I said, Mrs Page, it would not be incest. I am referring to what you suggested yesterday, that Caley was having a sexual relationship with Anna Louise.'

'I don't understand.'

'Anna Louise is not Robert Caley's daughter. She's mine, Mrs Page, which is why I was able to find out about the trust fund, because the funds in it were mine too. Anna Louise is my daughter, not Robert Caley's.'

'Does he know?'

'Of course.'

'Did Anna Louise know?'

'No.'

She took a deep intake of breath. 'You confronted Robert about the trust fund, and he admitted it, but you said you were not sure if he was having a sexual relationship with Anna Louise?'

'If you want it word for word, I said that if he was abusing my daughter, I would shoot his head off his shoulders, and he said, and I quote, Mrs Page, that if I was ever to make such a disgusting accusation again, then the head would come off my shoulders!'

'But did you or did you not believe him?' she asked quietly.

'Yes, I suppose I did, because he was very shocked. In fact, he went through a range of emotions I didn't honestly think he was capable of, but in the end he was just violently angry.' He leaned forward in his chair, his small, hard eyes bored into her flushed face. 'Maybe check out all the facts before you throw dirt, Mrs Page.'

She stood up and snapped back at him. 'If I had been given them maybe I would not have needed to. I am just trying to do my job, Mr Dulay.'

He stuffed his hands into his pockets and as she was already walking to the door he followed. Suddenly she stopped.

'Do you have a video of Mrs Caley's film *The Swamp* I could see?'

'Good God, whatever do you want that for?'

'Just part of my job, to know everything I possibly can know about my clients.'

He went to an antique fruitwood cabinet in the corner of the room and slid the doors apart: this was where he kept his video library.

'She won't be happy about this, it's a terrible film, cheap, shoddy, but she is wonderful.' He handed her the video.

Lorraine put it in her briefcase. She was shaking and angry with herself. She had jumped so quickly to such disgusting conclusions she was ashamed of herself. If she had been unable even to return Robert Caley's phone calls the previous evening, the thought of facing him now made her cheeks flush with shame, so she pushed it to one side, refusing to dwell on what she would have to do to repair the damage.

She ordered her driver, the same one as the day before, to take her back to Tilda Brown's house.

'You know, Bill, I'm getting worried,' Rosie said as they sat at a sidewalk café near the French market.

'Me too, it stinks. They pick up this bastard, an anonymous tip off says they saw him talking to Anna Louise Caley and—'

'I'm not talking about Fryer Jones,' Rosie said.

Rooney looked at his watch. 'He always was a horny son of a bitch.' But it sounded hollow even to him.

'Why hasn't he called in?'

'I don't know, do I?' Rooney snapped and then patted her hand. 'Sorry, sorry. Look, tell you what, say we give it to one o'clock when Lorraine's due back at the hotel. If Nick's not shown, then we'll start looking for him.'

'Like where? This is a big city.'

Rooney downed his third café au lait. 'Start with the cop shop, if they haven't got him banged up or on a slab . . .'

'What?'

He wiped the froth from his mouth. 'Morgue, Rosie, start at the lowest point and work upwards. I know one thing for sure, until that two-bit shit shows up I'm not going near that bar of Fryer Jones, and I hope to God Lorraine doesn't take off without coming to us first. If you look at the list of so-called eye witnesses that give that trombone player one hell of a tight alibi, half are made up of Juda Salina's relatives, including Raoul Corbello.'

'I tried to get in touch with Juda, it was engaged for almost an hour then no reply.'

'What about Edith Corbello?'

Rosie's cheeks went pink. 'She's not in the phone book, I was going to try other ways when you came back.'

Rooney stood up. 'Well, let's go back to the hotel and have another try. Right now, until Lorraine gets back, we got nothing else to do.'

Mrs Brown's sister, Helen Dubois, came into the drawing room, a modern interior of metal and glass and bare boards polished to shine as though lacquered, the walls covered in severely tasteful beiges and oatmeals the better to display a collection of fashionable yarn paintings and Primitive art. In this stark setting, the plump, distressed woman looked all too human and out of place. 'I am afraid neither Mr or Mrs Brown can see you, Mrs Page.

354

They are still very shocked and my sister is under sedation.'

'Yes, I'm so very sorry, please pass on my sincere condolences.' Lorraine took her time gathering up her purse and her briefcase. 'The police called me in to give a statement, I was here earlier in the day, I interviewed Tilda.'

'Yes, I know.'

'I can't help but think that maybe it was something I said that may have sparked off . . .'

'We won't ever know, will we?' Mrs Dubois said sadly.

'But the police said Tilda left a note.'

'Yes, but it didn't give any reasons.'

'May I ask what it said?'

Helen Dubois took out a handkerchief and pressed it to her eyes. 'Just, "May God forgive . . . Tilda".'

They walked towards the front door, Lorraine really taking her time as they passed more Mexican-looking textiles and a jardinière of desert flora in the hallway. 'Mrs Dubois, do you know why I was here, why I came to see Tilda?'

'Yes, I believe you wanted to question her about Anna Louise Caley.'

'Could I see Tilda's bedroom?'

'Why?'

Lorraine hesitated, trying to think of the best way around it. 'Well, for one, Anna Louise may still be alive, it is a possibility, and she and Tilda were very close friends. After yesterday's tragedy, I would pray to God that I did not leave any stone unturned in my search for her. At the same time, even though I cannot think of anything, maybe I did inadvertently say something . . . I have a terrible feeling of guilt, Mrs Dubois, and I just think if I could perhaps sit a moment in Tilda's room, rethink everything we discussed, perhaps I will have more of a clue as to why she did it, and it would give some comfort to her poor parents.'

Mrs Dubois hesitated, looked up the open-tread wooden staircase. 'I don't know.'

'Is the police cordon still in place?'

'No, no, they took it down about two hours ago.'

Tilda's bedroom had a similar feel to Anna Louise Caley's – large enough to accommodate a turquoise sofa on back-tilted metal legs, a dresser, cheval mirror surrounded by more Mexican-looking embossed metal, and a king-size bed. All but the sofa was white, and the room seemed strangely bare, characterless, but the exigencies of decorator taste had been relaxed to permit a fitted white carpet and a wall of built-in closets on each side of a door which led to a spacious bathroom. The room showed few signs that the occupant had only been in her teens.

The carpet was marked near the window by a number of dust footprints, more than likely from the police and the medics that had removed the body, and some faint, washed-out brown stains, already dry, which could have been coffee or perhaps, as is usual in suicides by hanging, Tilda's bowels might have opened and the mess been cleaned up. There was no other sign that anything untoward had occurred in the room; even the curtain rail Tilda had hanged herself from remained in position, and the dressing-table stool, covered in white fabric with silver upholstery buttons like out-size sequins, was back in place in front of the triptych mirrors.

Mrs Dubois stood in the open doorway, pressing a handkerchief to her eyes to try to stop herself from weeping.

'You don't have to stay with me,' Lorraine said softly.

'Thank you.' Mrs Dubois turned away, just as Lorraine saw the white bear resting on the pillows of the bed. 'Oh, just one thing, Mrs Dubois.' Lorraine picked it up, sure it was similar to the white fluffy bears she had seen lined up on Anna Louise's bed. 'Do you know where Tilda got this bear from?'

Mrs Dubois swallowed, her brow puckering.

'It's just that Anna Louise had the same bears, and I wondered who gave it to Tilda.'

Mrs Dubois shook her head. 'I really don't know, it's been there quite a while, I think. I recall seeing it before . . . it's a Polar bear, is it?'

'Polar,' Lorraine said softly.

'Yes, that's what she called it, Polar.'

Mrs Dubois began to weep again and excused herself as Lorraine replaced the bear on the pillow. As soon as she was alone she drew back the covers and felt beneath the pillows, the sheets and the mattress, getting to her knees to look beneath the heavy woven cotton bedspread, but there was nothing hidden in the bed or underneath it.

Lorraine made a slow tour of the neat bedroom, sitting at the dressing table and opening each drawer. Some contained underwear, lingerie, all very expensive items folded with tissue paper placed between the garments. Even the rolled-up tennis socks were lined up like balls. In the closets, Tilda had as extensive a wardrobe as Anna Louise's and rows of shoe boxes. Lorraine bent down, wondering if she would get lucky twice, that any personal mementoes might have been hidden in the same way Anna Louise kept hers, but she found nothing other than shoes. She recalled the room she herself had had as a teenager, full of junk, books and magazines, cards stuck and pasted to the shabby wallpaper, and all the pictures of the rock stars and movie stars she'd had the hots for.

But it was clear that in Anna Louise's and Tilda's rooms their parents' decorators' taste predominated, and they had hardly a knick-knack of their own, apart from the somehow pitiful soft toys. Even the display of cosmetics and perfumes was more fitting for a much older woman; Tilda's creams in the immaculate bathroom were for dry skin and wrinkles, intensive moisturizers, serums and chemical peels. Nothing was used – everything down to the toothbrush looked brand new.

Lorraine sighed. A girl had hanged herself inside this whiter than white, innocent room, but there was no sign of the tragedy, no sense of who Tilda Brown was. She closed her eyes, trying to remember their conversation. According to Tilda, Anna Louise was jealous of anyone being shown any affection by her father: had Robert Caley given the girls the white polar bears? Was that the reason she used the name Polar on her secret messages? Was that who the Valentine cards and birthday gifts were from? Did Robert Caley use the name Polar?

Lorraine picked up one of the tennis racquets stacked neatly in a row in the closet Tilda had set aside for her sport and ski equipment. Even if Robert Caley did sign himself Polar, what did that matter now? Even if he had been sexually abusing Anna Louise or having willing intercourse with her, she was not his own flesh and blood.

Lorraine leaned forward and replaced the racquet alongside the row of others. She glanced at one racquet, whose cover bulged slightly on one side – perhaps a pair of socks? Lorraine drew back the zipper and felt inside. Her fingers touched a package of some kind and she took it out. The newspaper-wrapped package was about eight inches long, string wrapped tightly around it. Lorraine sat on the dressing-table stool, carefully untying the knot, then unwinding the string. She put it to one side and placed the package on to the mirrored dressing table, moving aside mother of pearl-backed combs and brushes.

The paper, she noted, was dated February 15, the year missing where the newspaper had been torn across. It was also dirty, stained with what looked like mud, some of the print smudged. She eased the paper away from the contents and almost dropped it, springing up from the stool with shock because of the horrible smell. Urine and human faeces were caked around a doll, whose trunk, arms and legs were made of crudely stuffed and tied sacking wound round with wool. It had a white dress, equally crudely hand-stitched, made from what looked like an old piece of T-shirt. The head was cheap plastic, like the head of a Barbie doll, and glued on to the face was a picture of Tilda. An ordinary dressmaker's pin was stuck through the left eye of the doll, protruding right through the back of the head. When Lorraine turned it over there were two or three long blonde hairs and what appeared to be dried specks of blood attached to a tiny, pinkish-brown fragment of skin tied to the torso with cross-bands of wool.

'Mrs Page,' called out Helen Dubois, and Lorraine quickly rewrapped the doll and put it in her briefcase just before the door opened.

'I think perhaps you should go. Mrs and Mrs Brown have the chaplain coming to arrange the funeral, and . . .'

'It's all right, I was just leaving.'

The driver started the engine as soon as he saw Lorraine emerge from the house. She sat back in the hot, stuffy car, slowly rolling down one of the windows. She could smell the doll in her briefcase, so she pushed it away from her. She didn't want to take it out, didn't want to handle it again unless there was soap and water handy. She washed her hands as soon as she got back to her hotel room, over and over again. Then she dried them, sniffing at them, and stared at the wrapped parcel.

'Lorraine? Are you in there?' It was Rosie.

Lorraine let her in, turning straight back towards the bed. 'You will not believe what I found at Tilda Brown's place, it's already stinking out the room, and . . .'

Rosie was red-eyed from weeping, clutching a big white handkerchief. 'Lorraine . . . I've got something to tell you.'

She knew something was wrong when the big, bulky figure of Rooney walked in behind Rosie and quietly closed the door.

'What is it? What's happened?' She could feel her legs shaking.

Rooney didn't mean it to come out so bluntly but there was no other way. 'It's Nick, he's dead, Lorraine.'

Her face drained of colour. She looked at Rosie, back to Rooney, hoping it was some kind of a joke, but she knew it wasn't by the expression on their faces. She felt for the end of the bed and sat down, trying to keep calm and steady.

'How did it happen?'

Rooney helped Rosie to sit down. 'He was murdered, throat cut. The cops found him in an alley early this morning, no wallet, no ID on him, and he was taken to the city morgue. They haven't done an autopsy yet.'

Rooney gestured helplessly. 'The only identifying mark was a tattoo of the LAPD badge on his arm, lot of them had it done when they were rookies.'

'Yes, I know,' she said softly. 'Jack Lubrinski had one, wasn't on his arm though, it was on his butt.'

Lorraine's lips trembled and she clenched her teeth,

needing to be alone. 'You mind giving me a few minutes by myself, just want to be on my own for a while.'

Rooney nodded and took Rosie's arm. 'Sure, you give us a call when you want us.' He knew intuitively that it was better to leave, but Rosie hung back.

'Just go, Rosie. Come on, sweetheart.' He pushed her towards the door and closed it behind them, leaving Lorraine still standing motionless, her hands clenched by her sides.

Rosie turned on him in the hall. 'God, she's a cold-hearted bitch, imagine even talking about that guy Lubrinski, I mean, Nick, Nick's . . .' Rosie began to sob and Rooney put his arm around her and supported her down the corridor.

'She didn't show any feelings about him at all,' Rosie wept, but Rooney knew different: he'd been a cop too long not to recognize that look on someone's face, often followed by a joke or some casual comment, anything to conceal the blow to the heart. Lorraine would weep for Nick, he knew that, but not in front of anyone else. She would try to come to terms with Nick's death in her own way, the way he knew too, privately – you never wanted to show anyone the pain.

Lorraine splashed cold water on her face, still dry-eyed and shocked, still not really registering the fact that she wouldn't see Nick again. She whispered his name, over and over again, half-questioningly, as she patted her face dry, and then walked into the bedroom and looked first at the bed where she had been sleeping when he woke her, then at the bed opposite where he had sat. She lay down on her own bed, curled up facing the empty one, wanting to reach out to him as though he were still there.

'Nick?' she whispered again. 'Oh, Nick . . .' she repeated, and then the tears came, her face crumpling like a child's as she wept for Nick Bartello, lovely and crazy as he had been. She wept until she was exhausted, cried out, and then sat with her head in her hands.

It was then she caught sight of the bottle of vodka he had left. It had fallen on its side and rolled just beneath the bed. She stared at it, unable to look away, and it drew her like a magnet until she got down on her knees to retrieve it. She held it in her hands, examining the bottle, almost caressing it, and then slowly unscrewed the cap. Just one drink: she just needed the one to get herself back together and be able to work. Just the one and she'd be able to put the bottle away. She was sure of it.

CHAPTER 14

ROONEY ARRANGED for Nick's body to be sent home when the autopsy was finished. He had called Nick's sister to tell her the news and she had been silent and uncommunicative, but had said she would bury him and gave Rooney the address in downtown LA. Not until the end of the call did she ask how he had been killed. Her voice broke just a fraction when Rooney told her.

'Lenny was always getting himself into trouble.'

'Lenny?' repeated Rooney, confused.

'Yes, he called himself Nick, but we, the family, always use his middle name, Lenny, well, Leonardo. Er, just one thing, Mr Rooney – we can't take his dog.'

'That's okay, I'll see to the dog.' They had nothing more to say to each other, so he paid his condolences and replaced the phone.

'I'll take care of Tiger,' Lorraine had said quietly. Rooney had nodded and then excused himself. She knew he needed to cry, and he did, leaning up against the elevator, returning later to force them all to get on with the job.

Lorraine drank from a can of Coke, seemingly more preoccupied with getting the day's work started than discussing Nick, and her apparent lack of emotion confused and worried Rosie. Rooney had warned her to leave Lorraine alone, and not to ask her questions, but

Rosie couldn't stop looking at her: Lorraine's face was chalk-white and her eyes red-rimmed, but that apart, she seemed almost over-bright.

'Rosie, will you quit gawping at me all the time,' she snapped.

'I'm just wondering if you are all right.'

'I'm fine, Rosie – now how about we get back to the reason we're all here?'

They discussed the hideous, rotting doll, and then Rosie wrapped it in two newspapers and stuffed it into a drawer. Lorraine did not have any energy to interview anyone, but she knew she would have to speak to Elizabeth and Robert Caley. They also discussed the importance of Fryer Jones's arrest and release, and his implication in some way with the disappearance of Anna Louise, but Rosie and Rooney would not allow Lorraine to go alone to his bar. Nick had been murdered a few blocks from there, and if there was a connection they would have to find out. Nick's stupidity in going off alone made them angry, as now they had no idea where he had been or who he had spoken to. But their anger did nothing to ease their grief.

Rosie pulled a face at the smell coming from Lorraine's briefcase as she withdrew the video of *The Swamp* and knelt down to slot it into the video recorder she had persuaded the receptionist to lend them from the lounge downstairs.

Lorraine drew the curtains and perched on one bed as Rooney and Rosie sat on the other. She saw him give her a gentle pat and lean in close. 'You all right, darlin'?'

Rosie nodded, returning his pat of comfort, making Lorraine feel excluded, but she ignored it as the film began. It was faded like some old sixties Technicolor film. Even the old Columbia Studios logo was fuzzy and the music was sliding badly. The pre-film script made them all lean forward.

'This film has carefully researched the life and times of the voodoo queen Marie Laveau, who arrived in New Orleans in the early nineteenth century.'

The film was tedious, it took a long time for the actual plot to unfold. Despite the faint picture and blurred lines across the print, Elizabeth Seal was certainly a great beauty, and her dance with a live snake was the high point of the first twenty minutes.

'They really did a good job of her make-up, she really does look black,' Rosie murmured. The film rolled on, the plot at times very confused. Even though the film spanned more than one generation and everyone else became grey and wizened, the star remained looking about twenty throughout. Even when they laid her body in her coffin she looked young and beautiful, whereas the real Marie Laveau had lived into her eighties. It really was a Hollywood-style distortion of the true facts.

The end titles began to roll and Rosie picked up the controls to switch it off when Lorraine shouted, 'Wait, wait! Roll it back, Rosie, STOP!'

They looked at the last section of the artists' credits, and under the group heading of 'SNAKE CHARM DANCERS' were two very familiar names, Juda and Edith Salina, and under the group of 'VOODOO PRIESTS' they found the name of Fryer Jones.

Rosie turned off the TV and opened the curtains, while Lorraine picked up a fresh can of Coke and opened it on her way to the bathroom. There, she poured part of its contents down the toilet, and then topped it up with Nick Bartello's vodka before returning to the bedroom. She sat down, drinking from the can, her foot tapping.

'Well, I've got my energy back. I want to talk to Elizabeth Caley this afternoon . . .'

Rooney puffed out his breath. 'You want me with you?'

'No. We need to get to Juda Salina's sister, you got an address, Rosie?'

'No, not yet, I was about to when . . .' She was about to say Nick's name but covered fast. 'She's not listed in the phone directory but I got a directory of clairvoyants, voodoo advisers and experts from the museum. She may be in that, I haven't checked.'

'Do it, but you don't go near her until I'm back. From now on we stick together, report in frequently, and if we move on, we give time and location.'

Rooney looked pissed, and Lorraine turned to face him. 'Bill, I handled the Caley situation badly. In an interview with Lloyd Dulay, I said things I shouldn't have done without checking the facts first. So I have to see him alone and apologize.'

'Okay, you know what you're doing.'

'Not always, Bill, and I was out of line with Caley.'

'Well, you got results.'

'Yes, I did.' She hesitated. 'Nick gets murdered, Tilda Brown commits suicide. I got those results all right because I was angry and tired out, tired because I had been up all night screwing Caley.'

'What, are you serious? You fucked Robert Caley?'

'Yes, yes, I did.'

'I don't believe it,' Rosie said, astonished.

'Well, it's true, and it was a dumb move to make, but . . .' She gave a glum smile, and lifted her shoulders in an apologetic gesture. 'Couldn't help myself. So the next day I was so determined to find out if he was a suspect or not, I went at it like a bat out of hell.'

'Nick was right then? He suggested you do it, and it got results.'

Lorraine turned away. 'No, Bill, Nick was wrong. I didn't fuck him for information, I did it because I wanted him. Now excuse me, I need a shower.'

She closed her bathroom door, and Rosie snatched up her notes, her face set rigid. Rooney reached for his jacket and made for the door.

'That's it, is it?' Rosie said angrily.

He turned surprised. 'What?'

Rosie put her hands on her hips. 'We just accept it, say nothing? She sleeps with our client. The guy hired us, Bill, and she gets fucked by him. Oh, that is really very professional, really good work. Gets laid so hard that the next night she crashes out early and Nick goes it alone and gets killed?'

'Rosie,' Rooney warned, glancing towards the bathroom.

'I don't care if she does hear me, I am disgusted, disgusted!'

'Don't be.'

'Why the hell not? Now she's going to see his wife, what if she finds out, what do you think will happen? We'll lose that bonus. I am through taking orders from that slut.'

Rooney opened the door and walked out into the corridor. 'Come on, Rosie, she got the information on the trust fund and she might not have if she hadn't gone through that connecting door.' He stopped and turned back with a half-smile. 'We don't have one, do we?'

'I beg your pardon?' Closing the door with a bang, she caught up with him at the elevator. 'Was that a cack-handed come-on, Bill?' Rosie glowered.

'Hell, no. It was just a joke.' He stepped into the

elevator. 'I wouldn't make an indecent proposal to you, Rosie, I've more respect.'

The elevator door closed, and he pressed for their floor. They stood in silence as the elevator stopped and they stepped out into the hallway. Rosie's door was first, and she was determined to open it without even looking at Rooney, but he placed his big hand on the handle.

'Unless you wanted me to?'

She looked at him, refusing to allow herself to smile. 'I haven't had an indecent or a decent proposal made to me for a long time, Bill, but right now, with Nick gone, I don't think I am ready for either. See you later.'

She turned the key and entered the room. Not until the door was closed behind her did she allow a small smile to break through. 'The old buzzard's really got the hots for me,' she said to herself gleefully.

Lorraine dressed with great care, with the fan running overhead so she wouldn't break out in a sweat before she'd finished admiring herself. She had one of her new suits on, a silk shirt, high-heeled sandals and a single strand of cheap but good-looking pearls. She picked up her briefcase, having washed everything inside and just about managed to get rid of the smell of the doll.

In reception, she passed Rooney, who turned and gave her a smile. 'Looking good.'

'Thanks. Was that you or Rosie who slammed the door?'

'Me, getting worried you might have blown our million. Do you know if Mrs Caley has found out?'

'If she has, I'll sort it out. You won't lose because of me, Bill. I know what I did was unethical, but at least I didn't lie. Saying I'm sorry I did it would be a lie too. I liked him. Liked him a lot.'

368

Rooney turned away. 'What about Nick? You liked him too?'

'You know I did.'

'Then we split three ways now, huh?' he said sadly.

'I guess so. What's that you've got there?'

He held a folded sheet of paper. 'A list of Nick's possessions. His clothes, he had nothing else. His cowboy boots, his wallet and driving licence were missing.'

Lorraine sighed. Her heart sank, but then she remembered something. 'What about the necklace? That gris-gris thing he had round his neck, that listed?'

'Nope, but we don't know if he was wearing it or if it was also stolen.'

'Well, check his room and I'll come straight back here as soon as I'm done at the Caleys'.'

'They know you're coming?'

'No, best to keep an element of surprise! Mind you, they might refuse to let me in, but I doubt it. They must know by now about Tilda Brown, it was in the papers.' Lorraine started for the doors, and stopped. 'Bill, the newspaper wrapped around that voodoo doll. It had a date on it, February fifteenth, but no year. Could you check with the newspaper printers and see if they can date it by some of the articles? It's just too much of a coincidence, the date. Anna Louise disappeared on February fifteenth, so if it was last year's paper it means Tilda Brown kept that thing for a long time.'

She strode out through the heavy front door to meet her driver. Rooney remained staring at the pitiful list of Nick Bartello's possessions, and he couldn't help hearing his voice and that smoky laugh he had had. 'No coincidences, Billy Boy. Never believe in them, just good detective work.'

Rooney sighed, a lump in his throat. He couldn't

actually remember if it had been Nick or Jack Lubrinski who'd said that. They had been so alike and now they were both dead. Rooney became aware of his own mortality and was scared; no son, no wife, but maybe, just maybe a future with financial security beyond his meagre pension. And maybe there was also Rosie.

Elizabeth hurled the pot of Lancaster neck cream at Caley's head but it missed by yards and smashed against the wall of her bedroom in the beautiful Garden District mansion in which she had grown up.

'How could you, how could you fucking do this to me?'

Caley side-stepped the brushes and the silver-backed mirror that followed, and waited until she hurled her body down on to her velvet day-bed, her arm resting against her brow in classical fashion.

'Go away from me, I hate you!'

He applauded. 'Bravo, none of your performances deserved an Oscar more than this one, Elizabeth.'

'*Fuck you!*' she screamed.

'Why don't you just calm down? Why work yourself up into such a state that you're gonna need to call your dealer for something to space yourself out into oblivion? That is what you usually do, isn't it?'

She dived across the room and glared. 'Calm down? You have stolen, *stolen* from your own daughter's trust fund!'

'Correction, she's not my daughter.'

'*You were paid to treat her as one!*' Her face was red with anger, but even as she said it she wished she hadn't as she saw the pain on his face. She immediately resorted to tears. 'How could you steal from Anna Louise, Robert,

370

and why? You know if you ever needed anything I always gave in to you in the end, you know that. So why?'

He sat sullenly, hands clasped in front of him. 'Because I was sick and tired of coming to you for hand-outs. Sick and tired of playing the same charade, of forever needing you to bail me out. I didn't want to touch one more cent of your fucking money. I just wanted for once to stand on my own two feet, prove that I could do it. Maybe get back my self-respect. That's all there is to it, I didn't want to ask you.'

She smiled. 'Why not? You have for the past twenty years, and it's not that I don't have enough, for chrissakes!'

He felt exhausted even trying to explain, but he felt he owed her that much. 'Because I knew it would work. I knew it, and it would have made me independent. Don't you understand? It would have been my own show, not yours, not even associated with you.'

She smirked. 'But you couldn't pull it off, could you? Just like you could never have got the time of day from any one of your so-called partners without me – without my being who I am.'

He sighed, shaking his head bitterly, and his voice had an undercurrent of sarcasm. 'True, everything I am is because of you, you've given me everything. What do you want me to do, kiss your feet? Jesus God, Elizabeth, I've been on my knees too often, taken too much of your shit to do it again.'

'My shit? You think I like being married to a failure? You think I wouldn't have liked someone I could lean on? Someone who would take responsibility?'

'What? *What did you say?*'

'I need, I always have needed . . .'

He was hardly able to contain himself. 'You and *your*

needs are all I have been taking care of since the day I agreed to marry you, and that, as you fucking well know, was also part of the deal, taking you on, your drugs, your booze and Lloyd Dulay's illegitimate child. *Don't you tell me about your needs.* When have you ever, *ever* at any time considered mine? Huh?' He dragged her towards him, scaring her. 'Yes, look at me, Elizabeth, you look real good, because whatever I was paid to marry you, whatever contracts you had me sign to keep my mouth shut, were regarding Anna Louise. Now she's dead, so that contract is now null and void.'

She tried to wriggle away from him, but he gripped her wrists, pulling her towards him. 'Yes, *dead*, she is dead, and you just won't face it.'

'She isn't, she isn't, how can you say it? You don't know for sure.'

He wanted to slap her but all he did was release her, moving as far away from her as possible. 'It's been nearly a year, Elizabeth, if she's not dead, where in Christ's name is she?'

She started to cry, and he began to walk out but she screeched at his back. 'Juda said she felt her presence, she told me.'

He stopped and pointed his finger. 'That goddamned woman is nothing but a leech.'

'Takes one to know one, Robert.'

He took four fast steps towards her and back-handed her across the face. She stumbled, and then he went after her again, this time gripping her by her hair.

'You have spent thousands on that fucking fake bitch. Even when I barred her from the house you still saw her, you even took Anna Louise to her, a fat, stinking pig of a woman who just greases your vanity to get what she wants. Well, how much did she make from you for her so-called psychic feelings on Anna Louise? How much, Elizabeth?'

'Nowhere near as much as you have taken in one week, never mind twenty years. Juda and I . . .'

'Oh please, not that again, not the old friend from the past, because it makes me puke. She's a con artist, and what kind of vice she's gripped you in for twenty years is beyond me, unless it's blackmail.'

'Don't be ridiculous.'

'Ridiculous?' He sat down, shaking his head. 'You don't have a life, Elizabeth, you spend your days and nights in a drunken or drug-induced haze, and Lorraine Page . . .'

He hesitated. Just saying her name hit him hard. 'Mrs Page told me you were now injecting a drug that could give you a thrombosis. Do you even remember me getting you in the ambulance, this time, to save your life? How many more clinics, Elizabeth? How much more punishment can that body take, how many more times can it be surgically put back together again? Well, it's no longer any concern of mine.'

'What do you mean?' She looked scared.

'It's over, I quit. I want a divorce,' he said calmly and matter-of-factly.

'I'll have you arrested for using Anna's trust, Lloyd will call the police.'

Robert Caley laughed. Deep inside, he felt good for the first time in days, perhaps years. 'Really? Well, go ahead, and you know what I will do? I will tell everyone you lied to me, that Anna Louise was not my child. I'll demand they give Dulay blood tests, and that means the very thing you are so terrified of, Elizabeth, your blood will be tested too. The gloves will come off, and if you want it dirty, it will be dirtier than you ever believed. I will expose your drug addiction and your freak friendship with that fat bitch.'

'STOP IT!'

He smiled, now ticking off on his fingers. 'I will give details of your plastic surgery, the face lift, the body tucks, the liposuction. So much for your big star status! The only place you are still a star is here, out in the real world you were forgotten fifteen years ago.'

'*Stop this!*'

'No, Elizabeth, you stop this sham right here and now because there's no need for it to continue. Without Anna Louise, there's nothing. Consult your lawyers, but there will be no contest.'

'Don't do this, Robert. I mean it, don't do this or you will be sorry. I'll make you so sorry.'

'Will you?' He was walking out now, smiling all the while. 'You've made me sorry, Elizabeth, from the day we married. Now I'm going to make you pay for it and you *will* pay for those twenty years. Believe me, that mega-fortune is going to be sliced right down the middle.'

'I'm warning you,' she said furiously.

'No, I am warning you, because this time I mean it!'

She glared, her mouth a thin tight line. 'You do, and I will fight you, tell them you even had sex with your daughter!'

'That deserved a punch in the face, Elizabeth, but I will never strike you again. You will never hold that against me, and as you know, she was not my daughter.'

'You adopted her.'

'I gave her my name. I also loved her like a daughter, and she loved me. You can't take that away. There's nothing you can do to harm me. It's over. Goodbye.'

'She was a cheap slut, you didn't know that, did you?

The precious *daughter* you loved so dearly was a cheap whore.'

'Don't do this, leave her be.'

Elizabeth smirked. 'Ask Mrs Page, get her to show you the photograph of your beloved sweet daughter.'

He walked out, closing the door quietly behind him, and she stood in a blind fury, wanting to scream after him, kick him, punch him, scratch his eyes out. But she walked to the window and looked out, her arms and hands clenched round herself. Her voice was hardly audible.

'I will make you bleed, Robert Caley. So help me God, I will make your life a living hell, just like mine.'

Lorraine stared out of the car window at the ranks of gracious colonnaded houses which the new American arrivals in New Orleans had built for themselves in the Garden District when cotton, sugar and slaves had begun to make them rich: street after street offered the same vista of dazzling white columns, black iron-work fences and the dark green of shade trees and glossy clipped shrubs. Much of the area dated from the decades before the Civil War when the natural wealth of the whole region had poured into New Orleans, and it was as though the magnificent Italianate and neo-classical houses had been erected to show the world that the South was an empire to rival any that had been seen upon earth.

'Nice area,' said the driver. He was slowly warming to Lorraine; he liked the fact that she never felt the need to patronize him or involve him in some inane conversation, and that she didn't hide her moods. He liked it that sometimes she was really attractive as a woman and

375

sometimes she was not. Tonight she was. She looked sexy and classy, and it made him straighten up in his seat. When they arrived at the tall, double-galleried mansion on one of the most exclusive streets in the district, he was out of his seat fast to hold open the passenger door. Lorraine held her hand up for a moment, took a swig from a can of Coke, which she had brought with her, then tucked it back against the seat. The soft drink was laced with vodka, and she had already bought another bottle back at the hotel.

'Okay, just hang in there, pal, 'cos I don't know if they are gonna let me over the door-mat.' She looked up at the great white house, framed between two chestnut trees behind an austere spearpoint fence, and straightened her jacket.

'Right, ma'am, I'm here, no place else to go, ready and waiting.'

She turned and stared at him for a moment. 'What's your name?'

'Frankie, short for François.'

She touched his shoulder lightly. 'Keep your fingers crossed, François.'

He liked it that she didn't call him Frankie; François sounded cool.

Missy, one of the Caleys' maids, ushered Lorraine into the drawing room.

'Will you please wait just one moment while I inform Miss Elizabeth you are here. I think she is resting a while.'

'Thank you, and would you stress that it is very important that I speak to her?'

*

Elizabeth hung up the phone and smiled; she hadn't even had to persuade Juda, she agreed instantly. She then called Edward to tell him to return to LA immediately and collect Mrs Juda Salina – it was imperative that she arrive as soon as possible.

She felt more confident now – she'd get Robert put into his place, she'd make him pay. She smiled at her reflection in the large gessoed and gilded mirror above her bureau, and the feeling of compressed rage lifted until she was almost light-headed just thinking about taking revenge. Robert Caley was no more than a cheap con man, he'd been one when she met him. He was very attractive, that had helped, and he'd taken the bait even faster than she believed he would. But it had had to be fast because she had already been three months pregnant, and neither she nor Lloyd, who was already married, had wanted any scandal. And after Caley had signed the pre-nuptial agreements, and the various other deals for a considerable amount of money, Lloyd and Elizabeth had toasted each other with chilled champagne.

'He's a good find, Elizabeth,' Dulay had said admiringly.

'Well, we didn't have too much choice.'

Dulay had leaned over and patted her belly. 'Con men are easy enough to control. Never let him handle the purse strings, my darling, I'll always oversee all that, and I'll get trust funds set up for you and my baby.'

'If it's a boy, Lloyd, what then?'

'Screw the scandal. You get rid of the creep, I'll get a divorce, and we'll get married.' They had toasted each other again.

They had even decided that they would call him Louis if it was a boy. She had wept when a girl was born, and Anna Louise was named after the son Lloyd had wanted so badly. But he had been true to his word and made watertight financial settlements, hiring advisers to handle the money and trust funds, for both herself and Anna Louise. But his visits grew further and further apart, until she only saw him once a year at Mardi Gras. Anna Louise never knew who her real father was because Caley had kept his side of the bargain, had brought her up as his own, and was named as the father on the birth certificate.

Missy peeked in. 'A Mrs Page downstairs asking to see you, said it's important ma'am.'

Elizabeth frowned, irritated at the interruption of her daydreaming, but then felt guilty. 'I'll be right down, Missy, just powder my nose.'

She opened one of the drawers of her satinwood bureau and stared at the rows of pill bottles, then she slammed it shut. 'Now don't, Elizabeth, don't get it started all over again,' she said sharply to her own reflection. 'Just stay calm.'

Lorraine waited downstairs, looking around her at the double parlour whose elegant proportions and furnishings exhaled restraint and grace as unmistakably as those of the Dulay house screamed for attention. Whatever impulses Elizabeth had towards movie star glamour she had kept in their place in the Los Angeles house, while here little had changed since the inventory taken by her great-grandmother. The ceiling frescoes painted shortly after the house had been erected had never been covered, while the Russian carpets, the piano and music box, and the delicate chairs and side tables had been part of the young bride's dowry: curtains that fell straight and plain to the floor did not try to compete with the magnificent plasterwork of the cornices, and for fifty years the walls had been a deep and quiet Nile blue. The two fireplaces were unashamedly empty of dried flowers or fake logs;

above one hung a family portrait, above the other, a Corot.

It was a quarter of an hour before Elizabeth Caley came into the room, looking stunningly beautiful in a cream silk suit.

'Mrs Page. I am so sorry to have kept you waiting.'

Lorraine smiled. 'That's all right, really.'

'Now, what can I offer you? Champagne, or wine, or maybe a real Southern sloe gin?'

'I don't drink, Mrs Caley.'

'Oh, well, maybe an iced tea?'

'That would be fine.'

Elizabeth rang for the maid, drew up one of the chairs and sat opposite. 'You wanted to see me?'

She was bright-eyed, not a hair out of place, groomed and manicured and more confident than Lorraine had ever seen her before.

'You look very well,' Lorraine said quietly.

'Thank you, I am. Ah, refreshments.'

Missy passed them both tall fluted glasses of iced lemon tea, with slices of lemon and lime. It was refreshing, bittersweet.

'Mmm, delicious,' Elizabeth said, putting down her glass. 'Cigarette?'

Lorraine took out her own pack and lit Elizabeth's first before her own.

'Have you any results, any news?' She could have been asking about a movie contract from an agent, she showed no emotion whatsoever. She was clearly in control of herself.

'Well, I have certainly been kept very busy,' Lorraine opened her note-book and took out her pen. 'You know the Polar bears on Anna Louise's bed, did you give them to her?'

Elizabeth's eyes widened in surprise, but knew it was

not a joke question. 'No, I think Robert gave her three or four. She used to call him Polar because sometimes he can be very frosty, you know.'

'Did he also give one to Tilda Brown?'

Again, Elizabeth seemed slightly fazed by the question. 'I really don't know.'

Lorraine looked at her directly. 'Did you hear about Tilda Brown?'

'Yes, I did, they were the first people I called on when I arrived. Tragic, just terrible.'

'Yes, it is. I interviewed Tilda, just to go over her original statements, but she confirmed that she never saw Anna Louise.'

Lorraine paused while Elizabeth sipped her iced tea, patting her lips with a folded white linen napkin.

'Do you know a man called Fryer Jones?'

Elizabeth blinked and then shook her head. 'No, I don't think I do.'

'He was the only person the police arrested for questioning, an eye witness said he saw him on the night of the fifteenth talking to Anna Louise close to his bar near the French Quarter, not far from your hotel.'

'I didn't even know they had arrested anyone.' She sounded surprised.

'Well, it wasn't put out as they released him the same evening. He had a number of alibis from people who stated he didn't leave his bar the entire evening. There was a Jesse Corbello, his brother Willy, and young sister Sugar May, plus . . .' Lorraine passed the handwritten sheet Rooney had jotted down from the police files. 'Do you know any of these people at all?'

'No, no. I'm sorry, I don't.'

'Do you know Edith Corbello at all?'

'No.'

Lorraine seemed to concentrate on her note-book,

380

but she was watching Elizabeth closely, she had hardly given the list a glance. 'But you know Juda Salina.'

Mrs Caley was tensing up now, small signals of her unease showing. Her knees pressed close together, her arms twitched slightly. 'Well, you know that I do.'

'She is Edith Corbello's sister, they used to be known as the Salina sisters.'

Elizabeth suddenly gasped. 'Of course, yes, I do recall her. I don't know her but I remember Juda mentioning her sister, she's married to Fryer Jones, I think.'

Lorraine looked up, taken by surprise. She paused a moment before continuing. 'There is also another son, Raoul Corbello, he was working for Juda in Los Angeles.'

'I don't recall the name.'

'And also a second daughter, she's eighteen, Ruby Corbello, she is about to be crowned.'

'Not debutante of the year, surely!'

'No, she is queen of a new black krewe in the Carnival, it's apparently a great honour, and a big ceremony.'

'Yes, yes, it is. More tea?'

'No, thank you.' Lorraine picked up her glass, she had only taken a few sips, and watched Elizabeth pluck at something on her skirt. 'And what about Lloyd Dulay, do you know him?'

Elizabeth's head shot up and she stared wide-eyed at Lorraine. 'Of course I know Lloyd, he's a dear old friend.'

'Anna Louise was his daughter,' Lorraine said flatly.

Elizabeth looked away, her cheeks flushed. 'You have been busy. I hope you have been equally discreet, that is a very personal and private matter. Did he tell you or did Robert?'

'It will remain private, Mrs Caley, I assure you, and Mr Dulay told me himself.'

'Good heavens!' She sighed and then said she felt

tired, and if Lorraine had no further questions would she mind if she excused herself?

'I saw your film *The Swamp* and I enjoyed it very much.'

Elizabeth laughed, a little theatrically. 'Oh, goodness me, where on earth did you see it?'

'Mr Dulay kindly lent me a video. I noticed in the cast-list that both the Salina sisters and Fryer Jones were in the film, not large parts, basically extras.'

'I didn't mix with the extras, Mrs Page.'

'But you saw a lot of Juda Salina.'

'Yes, but not during the filming. We met up years later at some function here, and if you don't mind me saying so, I really can't see how that old film has got anything to do with you tracing my daughter. Good heavens, I was almost her age when I made it, so it was a long time ago.'

'Do you believe in voodoo, Mrs Caley?'

Her hand flapped. 'Oh, really, I can't answer that, no, no I can't answer that.'

'Did your daughter?'

'I very much doubt it, she was a very sensible girl.'

'So are many of the thousands of worshippers here. Do you know if Tilda Brown believed in it?'

'Tilda? I wouldn't know, but then one never knows what children get up to.'

'She was hardly a child, she was the same age as Anna, almost nineteen . . .' Lorraine wondered whether or not she should mention the doll. She knew Elizabeth was lying, her tic had become far more pronounced, as she brushed her skirt one moment, then picked at the flecks of the raw silk, then scratched with her long red fingernail.

There was a long pause, and then Lorraine went for the kill. 'I found a doll in Tilda Brown's tennis racquet

382

case. It was a disgusting, stinking, hand-made doll encased in excrement and urine. It was made, although crudely, to resemble Tilda, and even had a cut-out photograph of her face stuck on to the head. Human hair and, I think, possibly blood was matted on the top of it and there was a long pin sticking through the left eyeball out to the back of the head.'

Elizabeth Caley stared at the toe of her sandal, very still now. There was another long pause before Lorraine continued, 'Because of their distress, I have not been able to discuss my findings with Mr and Mrs Brown, but my partners are taking the doll to the mortuary, hopefully to get samples of Tilda's hair and blood to see if they are a match.'

'This has nothing to do with Anna Louise,' Elizabeth said sharply.

'Perhaps not, but do you know what that doll represents? According to a book I have on the voodoo culture, it is a terrible curse. It is, Mrs Caley, a death doll.'

Lorraine flicked through one of the handbooks Rosie had bought from the museum. She found the page and pressed the book further open. '"Put hair of the person you want to affect in the side of the doll, use black pin where you wish to induce pain", you will see a diagram—'

'No, I don't want to see it, take it away from me, please.'

Lorraine closed the book. 'This might have no connection to Anna Louise, but on the other hand, I must—'

'Stop this right now, and do not for pity's sake show the Browns anything so repellent. It is just appalling that you should even think that poor little Tilda would have—'

'She wouldn't have made the doll for herself.

383

Somebody must have made it and given it to her. Maybe whoever did is guilty of manslaughter at the very least!'

'No, she committed suicide.'

'I know that, Mrs Caley, but Tilda was Anna Louise's best friend and I am simply trying to ascertain if they played around, went to any ceremonies.'

'No, absolutely not. No.'

'But you are very close to Juda Salina, at one time a high priestess, as was her sister. Edith Corbello is apparently less active now, but still runs a spiritualist group and a similar practice to her sister's in LA. Juda Salina doesn't mention the voodoo connection, but hands out leaflets to her clients advertising that she is a psychic medium, reads tarot cards, specializes in trances and hypnotism, spiritualism and . . . voodoo. I have a copy of her leaflet—'

'No, I do not know anything about this.'

'But as Anna Louise went to Mrs Salina on a number of occasions with you, might she not have seen this? And being young and impressionable she may have started messing around with the occult.'

Elizabeth pushed her chair back, scraping the beautiful antique rug. 'I do not want to repeat myself, Mrs Page, but this has gone far enough. I do not wish to discuss this element in any way whatsoever. In fact, if you believe Anna is dead, then I see no point in your continuing.'

Lorraine stood up. 'No point? I am trying to find out if your daughter was murdered and at the same time who is responsible. She has been missing for eleven months.'

'I *know that!*'

'So why say there is no point in pursuing this angle?'

'Voodoo is *not* an angle, Mrs Page, it is a way of life, and you probably would not understand the complexities of it. It is taken very seriously here and is not, as you have implied, similar to the occult or black magic. It is not used for curses or evil, but the reverse, it is practised as a safeguard against sickness and is spiritually uplifting.'

'I am trying to learn, Mrs Caley, and if you have any information I would be grateful.'

'What do you mean, information? I don't have any information, why do you think I hired you? And as I did hire you, Mrs Page, I am now dismissing you. I will fully reimburse any costs you have accumulated to date, but I no longer wish you to continue this investigation.'

'I am sorry, but I can't walk away from this.'

'Of course you can, you're only hired, you have no personal ties to keep you.'

'I'm afraid I do. You see, my partner was murdered working on this case, so I have strong personal reasons why I would like to bring it to a conclusion.'

Elizabeth hesitated, but did not ask any further details about the murder, dismissing it. 'You seem to have forgotten what that conclusion was, Mrs Page.'

'Not at all, it was to find your daughter, dead or alive.'

'But you have not found her.'

'And my time is not up. I still have over a week to go, we have an agreement.'

'And I am paying you off, finished. Phyllis will send you a cheque. Now, if you will excuse me.'

'One million, Mrs Caley, you can pay off the final week now or whenever, but the contract still stands.'

'Don't be silly, it was a verbal—'

'No, it wasn't. We have it in writing, one million dollars. So even if you did pay me off, I wouldn't leave, not until I had covered every possible avenue. I'm sorry.'

Elizabeth's hands were clenched tightly, her face set in a hard, furious glare. 'You don't know what you are getting into, Mrs Page.'

'One never does on a case, Mrs Caley. That's what makes it so interesting, the unexpected twists and turns.'

Elizabeth's voice was hushed, threatening. 'You might just get something unexpected here, and believe me, you will wish to God you had walked away.'

Lorraine felt drained as Elizabeth Caley left the room, her footsteps echoing on the black and white chequer-board tiles of the hall as she called out, 'Missy, Mrs Page is leaving, show her out!'

The maid appeared at the door.

'No need, Missy, I'll do that.'

Lorraine replaced her note-book in her briefcase and turned as the door slammed shut and Robert Caley stood there.

'You've got a fucking nerve coming to the house.'

She snapped her case closed, her legs shaking at seeing him so unexpectedly. She took a hold of herself and looked up, meeting his eyes.

'I owe you an apology. I said things I shouldn't have without verification. I am sincerely sorry.'

He stuck his hands into his trouser pockets. 'Sorry? You bad-mouth me to my partners, you pass around scurrilous, disgusting accusations about myself and my daughter, you remove details of private papers from my desk and—'

'I have said I am sorry.'

'It's not good enough. I want a formal letter of retraction sent to Lloyd Dulay.'

She blushed and could not meet his eyes. 'But you were using Anna Louise's trust find illegally.'

'You don't back off an inch, do you, Mrs Page? That one-million-dollar bonus must be a big incentive.'

'Maybe as big as your daughter's trust is to you?'

'Touché!'

Lorraine picked up her briefcase. 'I am not scoring points, Robert.'

'Aren't you?'

She sighed. 'No, I am not. I am trying to do my job, that's all.'

He was so angry he wanted to throttle her. 'Does that include fucking someone for information the way you used to for a drink?'

She wanted to say that it had meant so much to her, she wanted to drop her briefcase and go into his arms. Instead she froze him out, her eyes without a flicker of emotion, so direct and cold it was he who broke the moment, turning away from her.

'Did you give Anna Louise toy white Polar bears?'

He shook his head in disbelief. 'What?'

'She had a row of white bears on her pillow, you gave them to her?'

'Yes.'

'And your nickname, or pet name was Polar?'

'Yes, yes, it was.'

'Did you also give one of the same white bears to Tilda Brown?'

'No.'

'Do you recall how many you gave to your daughter?'

He had to sit down. She was snapping out the questions as if he was some suspect held on a rap in a police station.

'It's important, Robert, how many?'

'Five, for her thirteenth, fourteenth, fifteenth, six-teenth and seventeenth birthdays. I then said there was no more room for them, they were to mark her teenage years, for her diaries.'

'Her diaries?'

He rubbed his head. 'Yes, the bears unzip, they have a sort of secret pocket where she used to keep her yearly diary.'

Lorraine could feel the buzz. 'Did the police ever see them?'

He shook his head. 'No . . .'

'Why not?'

'They weren't there. Maybe she grew out of them, I don't know.'

Lorraine's buzz went flat fast. 'Shit! Okay, now can you try and remember if on that flight, the one on the fifteenth, Anna Louise carried or packed one of those bears?'

'I have no idea.'

'It's very important, Robert, think.' He shook his head, and she came closer. 'When you went into her bedroom at the hotel did you see one of the white bears?' He sighed, and she moved even closer. 'Shut your eyes and think, Robert. You said her purse was in the sitting room and her new dress was laid out in the bedroom, so you must have looked at the bed.'

'Why? What's so important?'

She was close enough to bend down and touch him but she remained upright. 'When I went into Anna Louise's bedroom in LA, I found four bears lined up on her pillows. Four, Robert, not five, *four*.'

He reached out, not looking at her, and stroked her calf, her leg so slim he could almost slip his hand right around it. 'No, there wasn't one in the hotel.' He eased her round to stand in front of him and leaned forward, his head pressed into her crotch. 'Why did you not even answer one call, Lorraine, why?'

'I wanted to, Robert, but I was too guilty. I was all out of kilter that day, tired from being with you. And I suppose when Tilda hinted about you and Anna, and Dulay told me about the trust fund, maybe I was jealous, or plain angry, but I have no excuse, I should not have said the things I said without . . .'

She could feel his breath, his lips pressing through her skirt, but a part of her mind was working by itself. She

388

remembered Phyllis saying she packed the day they left, or was it Elizabeth?

'I have to go, Robert.'

He dropped his hands and rested back in the chair, looking up at her. 'What's so important about the bear?'

She had picked up her briefcase and was already crossing to the door. 'Tilda Brown said Anna Louise did not see her on the fifteenth, but what if she was lying? What if the bear was a peace offering, because they'd had such an argument? It was over you, Robert, do you know that? Your daughter was jealous of the attention you gave Tilda.'

He stood up, hands wide. 'Jealous? She was jealous of little Tilda?'

'On that day, before you went to work, you passed Tilda on the tennis courts, remember? You kissed her because she was crying, and Anna Louise saw it.'

'It was harmless, I swear before God!'

'I know that, but Anna Louise didn't, and I think it sparked off a jealous rage, which resulted in—'

'Tilda leaving . . .'

She nodded, then looked at the phone. 'Can I make a call?'

She didn't wait for an answer, dialling the Caleys' home in LA. Phyllis answered, and before she could even enquire how Lorraine was, she was asked if she recalled seeing Anna Louise packing, on the fifteenth. Phyllis fell silent.

'Phyllis, are you still there?'

'Yes, I am, I'm thinking. You see, I never did any packing or anything like that, but I remember Mrs Caley asking if I'd check to see if Anna Louise had packed any nice dresses as she would be invited to a lot of parties and—'

389

Lorraine interrupted. 'Did you see what was in her bags?'

'Well, yes, and so did Mrs Caley, they were full of T-shirts and sneakers.'

'Anything else?'

'I don't think so. They had a bit of a tiff about it later because Mrs Caley told Anna to go and repack. But I never saw what was in the bag and I don't think Mrs Caley did. Was it something important?'

Lorraine said it wasn't, and thanked Phyllis. As she replaced the receiver, Missy appeared at the door.

'I've brought all your cases down, Mr Caley.'

Lorraine frowned. He waited until Missy had gone and then said quietly that he was moving back into the hotel. 'Can I call you?'

Lorraine went up to him and kissed him. He slipped his arms around her and they were embracing when Elizabeth Caley appeared in the doorway. Lorraine caught sight of her watching them and quickly broke away.

'Shit!'

He now saw Elizabeth hurrying back up the stairs. 'It's all right, I'm leaving her, it's true. I've had enough, I am leaving for good. Come on, I'll walk you to your car. You going back to your hotel?'

'You're leaving her?'

'Yes, I should have done it years ago.'

Robert kissed Lorraine again as she got into the car. 'Maybe have dinner tonight?'

'Yes, I'd like that.'

She smiled up at him, wanting him to kiss her again, and he touched her cheek. 'Elizabeth said something about a photograph, you showed her a photo of Anna Louise. Did you?'

'Yes, it was taken at a night club.'

'Do you have it with you? Is it something I should see?'

She hesitated. She had it with her but decided against showing it to him now. 'I'll talk about it with you tonight.'

He kissed her again and shut the car door, watching her smiling and waving to him as François drove off.

François flicked a look at Lorraine from the driving mirror, and smiled. 'Well, they certainly let you over the mat!'

She laughed, a big, loud bellow. He was getting to like this lady a whole lot.

'Back to the St Marie?'

She leaned back on the seat and closed her eyes. 'No. Tilda Brown's.'

She felt guilty about feeling so good and couldn't help smiling. Robert Caley was no longer a suspect and he would also be free if he left Elizabeth. And she looked forward to spending another night with him. Lorraine drained the last of the vodka and Coke, reassuring herself constantly that she was in control: the craving had stopped – she didn't crave the drink, she was just slaking a normal thirst. Everything was under control.

Elizabeth Caley watched the car drive out from behind the old lace curtains of her bedroom. She didn't know how she was going to deal with everything and she needed Juda badly. It was all falling apart, and the pills in the drawer drew her like a magnet.

Lorraine sat forward, chewing her lip, flicking through her note-book to her early jottings. They had all said it, how odd it was that Anna Louise actually ordered that dress, the one she saw in *Vogue* and then had been so determined to get. She had called from the plane to ask Phyllis to get it for her. So maybe she had not repacked anything at all after her conversation with Elizabeth, but put the Polar bear inside her bag. Lorraine knew she was making erratic assumptions and wild guesses, but maybe all the fuss about getting the dress sent out had a reason, because everyone had been in a good mood when they got to the hotel the night Anna Louise went missing.

Lorraine was so intent on working everything out to a rational conclusion that she did exactly what she had agreed not to do: she forgot to call in to check with Rosie and Rooney and inform them she had left the Caleys and was now on her way to Tilda Brown's home. Something else she had no intention of telling them was that she asked François to stop at a liquor store, where she bought herself a six-pack of Coke and another bottle of vodka. It was all right, she told herself, nobody would know, and as long as she kept doing the top-ups in the can, no one could even suspect. It helped too, it helped a lot to forget Nick Bartello's voice, his smile, made it all go away. Most of all, it made her feel certain she was in control.

CHAPTER 15

AT FIRST Mrs Dubois refused to let Lorraine into the house; preparations were being made for Tilda's funeral, so it was hardly a suitable time for either of her parents to speak with Lorraine.

'I just need to go into Tilda's bedroom. Please, Mrs Dubois, it is important, or I would not intrude at this very sad time. I think when I was last here I left my key, it may have fallen from my purse. It'll take no more than two minutes.'

Mrs Dubois agreed and asked the maid to show Lorraine upstairs.

The maid remained by the door as Lorraine started to search the room, itching to get to the bed and to the white Polar bear, still left on Tilda's pillow. When Mrs Dubois called for the maid to help her with something below, leaving Lorraine alone, she picked up the bear immediately. It was too light, and she knew there was nothing inside, but she found the hidden zipper and checked just in case. She was disappointed, not even bothering to pretend she had been looking for a key when the maid returned, tapping on the open door.

'Thank you, no luck!' she said, walking towards the hovering maid; the girl seemed nervous. 'How did you get along with Miss Tilda?' she asked.

'Fine, ma'am, just fine, but she kept to herself. I just used to clean her room, press her clothes. She didn't act

393

up or nothin', not like she used to. I been asked to show you out as Mrs Dubois is busy.'

'How do you mean, not like she used to?' Lorraine asked, still very casual and friendly.

'Well, the maid before me was fired, they didn't get along, an' I was told by Mrs Brown that I was not to interfere with Miss Tilda's personal things. She didn't like me even tidying up her room, but then she was real neat and tidy.'

'When was she fired, the maid before you?'

'Oh, last year, I only worked here since then.'

Lorraine kept on smiling. 'What date would that be?'

The maid really was eager for Lorraine to leave, looking down the stairwell to the hall below. 'Well, I was interviewed mid-February, 'cos Ruby had already left.'

'Ruby?' Lorraine followed her down the wide staircase.

'Yes, miss, the previous maid here was a girl called Ruby Corbello, she got a job in a hair salon after.'

'Thank you very much.'

One minute depressed, the next Lorraine was buzzing again, and to the maid's relief hurried out without even asking to speak to Mrs Dubois.

Lorraine sat in her car thinking it was too much of a coincidence, then she sighed. Maybe it was the lead she needed. She checked her watch and told François to take her back to the hotel, realizing how late it had got and remembering her own instructions that they should all keep in touch.

Rosie and Rooney sat at the garden table in the courtyard of the St Marie with their cups of frothing café au lait.

'I dunno, she tells us to call in, and then she goes her own way. I mean, where is she now? Mrs Caley said she left over an hour and a half ago,' Rosie said, irritated.

Rooney looked at his watch and said nothing. He'd done what Lorraine had asked, checked at the cop shop, but there had been no gris-gris necklace on Nick's body or listed along with the rest of his personal possessions.

'Maybe he didn't have it on,' he said.

'What?'

'The necklace.'

'As far as I can remember, he was wearing it when we last saw him, he kind of liked it. I miss him, Bill.'

'Yeah, me too, he was a good guy.'

They sipped their coffee in silence, then Rosie took out her note-pad.

'What we going to do about Edith Corbello? It's a shame to waste time. I got her address but her phone number's not listed, so we'll just have to turn up.'

Rooney pushed his coffee aside. 'You're right, I'll leave my notes under Lorraine's door and we'll go see this Mrs Corbello. Might as well be doing something!'

Lorraine found the torn pages from Rooney's note-book under her door. She sat on the bed, reading the scrawled writing. No necklace was found on Nick Bartello's body. There was also a brief outline reiterating what the cops had said about Fryer Jones and his alibis. In brackets he added that Fryer Jones was married to Juda Salina. Coincidences! Lorraine underlined Raoul's name, remembering him from LA.

What Rooney had not mentioned was the fact that he and Rosie were going to see Edith Corbello. He had been going to, but Rosie suggested they just go ahead and see what they could come up with and tell Lorraine

395

later. Lorraine waited around for a while, got a sandwich and Coke and sat outside in the garden. She checked over her notes, wondering what she should do next, deciding not to follow the Ruby Corbello lead until she had talked to Fryer Jones.

François was a little apprehensive about taking Lorraine to Fryer Jones's bar. He watched her in the driving mirror, drinking the Coke and topping it up with vodka, but she didn't seem in any way intoxicated.

'I'm not a tourist, François. But you wait right outside and if I'm not out in half an hour, you come in and get me! So just take me there!'

'Okey dokey, we're on our way.'

The cab drew up outside the tiny dilapidated house in the old Irish Channel.

'You sure you want this address?' the cabbie asked.

'Yep, but if you wait you got a return fare,' Rooney said, passing over the money and an extra ten-dollar bill.

'Sure, be right out here for you, sir.'

Rooney and Rosie looked at the battered front door, its glass panel broken and blocked out with a piece of board. The top four panes of a French door had also been broken at some time and replaced with an almost opaque frosted glass, so that it was impossible to see into the house. Rooney took a few steps down the alleyway between the house and its neighbour and saw a broken fence enclosing a yard out back with old wrecked cars and a string hammock strung between two leafless trees. Bits and pieces of rusted car engines were scattered amongst ripped tyres, inner tubes and bags of bursting garbage.

396

'If we got the right address, you leave the talkin' to me,' Rooney said, hitching up his pants.

'You said that three times already,' Rosie said petulantly.

'Fine, then make sure you do, no interruptions.'

The door-bell didn't work: Rooney banged on the front door and it creaked open.

They stood on the porch and waited before knocking again, peering into the dingy hallway.

'Yeah, what you want?' Sugar May called out from the kitchen.

'Mrs Edith Corbello?'

'She's busy right now, you got an appointment?'

Rooney looked at Rosie and said quietly, 'Okay, now we do as I said, see what we can come up with.' Rosie nodded as Rooney looked towards Sugar May, smiling broadly. 'Hi, there. We came on spec, recommended by Fryer Jones,' he said.

Sugar May wrinkled her nose, strolling down the dark, dirty hallway. 'She don't like being interrupted, best wait see what she says.'

Sugar May pointed to a room off the hall and disappeared back into the kitchen.

Rooney and Rosie sat on a sagging sofa whose broken springs bulged beneath them. The carpet was threadbare, cigarette butts ground into the pile, and there were beer stains on every available surface. The doorway had an old beaded curtain tied up.

'What a dump,' Rosie said quietly, then turned as a high-pitched scream from the room down the hall made her sit bolt upright.

In the room was a table covered with a cloth, a mirror propped up behind it reflecting a figurine of the Virgin and a picture of Marie Laveau on the wall behind. Incense and three blue candles smoked in front of the statue, surrounded by saucers of rain-water, a dish of bread and apples and others of special grasses and oil.

Edith had made the young girl lie on a cot-bed while she bathed her head with an infusion of herbs: now she pressed down on the girl's temples with both hands, her eyes shut tight, chanting to invoke the spirits' healing powers.

The girl's head wobbled at the pressure of Edith's strong hands pressing down hard on it. It felt like her neck was going to break, and it was worse pain than any of the blinding headaches she'd been having every month.

'Oh my, we got tension in here. We got such tension. Sit up now, girl, and put your head forward so I can feel your neck.'

The young girl moaned, and Edith closed her eyes, rubbing and kneading the vertebrae down the girl's neck until she felt a click. She twisted the girl's head quickly and there were two more loud clicks. Edith smiled.

'Yes, that got it, you feelin' easy now, honey?'

Rosie looked at Rooney as the moans stopped and a soft laugh could be heard, but he was immersed in an old magazine.

'Listen to this. Voodoo came with the slaves from West Africa in the sixteenth century and in New Orleans the name of Marie Laveau is legendary. She is said to have been the daughter of a wealthy planter and a quadroon girl. She was part Indian, and she married a Jacques Paris, who mysteriously disappeared after the marriage, when she began calling herself Widow Paris.

Holy shit! Marie Laveau had fifteen children and she lived in St Anne's Street between North Rampart and Burgundy Street. She is said to have eliminated all other queens by her powers of the gris-gris, literally voodooing them all to death. And today the doctors of respectable medical schools have consulted voodoo doctors for treatment of paranoid schizophrenics.'

Rooney was about to continue reading from the magazine when the door farther down the hall opened, and although they couldn't see who was coming out, they heard the deep throaty voice of Edith Corbello.

'Don't you worry yourself about payin'. Get well, and get employment, and then you come back and see me, Tulla.'

Sugar May yelled from the kitchen. 'Hey, Mama! You got clients in the front room, you hear me, Mama?'

Edith Corbello walked in to see Rosie and Rooney, and whatever they were expecting didn't quite add up to the large, stout woman in an apron and old slippers, frizzy greying hair surrounding a big, round, sweating face.

'Yes?'

Rooney stood up. 'I am Bill Rooney and this is my friend Rosie.'

Edith sighed. 'Mmm, what you be wanting?'

'Can we talk to you? You are Edith Corbello?'

'Sure I am, but I don't see strangers. Who sent you to me?'

'Fryer Jones.' Rooney said.

Edith nodded, and walked back to her room. 'Come on in, but I got an appointment in fifteen minutes.'

The room was darkened by old drapes drawn across the window, and besides the bed and the altar table, it contained a large old trunk and a row of hard chairs.

Even in the dim light, it was noticeably cleaner and more orderly than the rest of the house and there were a variety of masks and pictures on the walls.

'Sit you down, get a chair for yourself,' Edith said to Rooney. Moving behind the desk, she opened the trunk, took out cards and a stack of leaflets. 'These my prices.'

She passed two leaflets which were torn at the edges and the print faint. They listed rituals, consultations and readings that would reveal the future, as well as healing bathing with a long list of oils and herbal remedies for health and vitality. All the treatments offered cost between twenty to fifty dollars. Underlined in red pen were the items that would be extra to the cost of the session – herbs, teas, candles and incense, plus any necessary home visits.

Rooney opened his wallet and laid out two fifty-dollar notes.

'You want a reading?' Edith said, indicating the deck of tarot cards.

Rooney leaned over to Rosie and held her hand. 'We need advice.'

'You come to the right place.' Edith stared at Rooney and did not touch the two fifty-dollar notes.

'Well, Mrs Corbello, Rosie and I, this is Rosie . . . we want to get married.'

Rosie almost fell off her chair, and turned to Rooney with her mouth open. He planted a kiss on her cheek.

'We're in love,' he said.

Rosie remained speechless: Bill needed to have no further worries about her interrupting, as his words had put her in a state of shock.

'Mmm.' Edith folded her hands over her big belly, looking from one to the other, and smiled, but her eyes remained suspicious and wary. 'A lot of people want the same thing, marriage. If you want this lady, and she wants you, where's your problem?'

'I'm already married.'

'You get a divorce.'

'She won't give me one.'

'Ah, so you got a troublesome wife?'

'That's right.'

'Mmm, mmm, I been one of them.' She chuckled.

Rooney released Rosie's hand. 'I have offered her a good settlement and she has refused, point-blank, and she won't move out of the house, and we got no children. She is just refusing to release me out of spite.'

'That's sad, children make a house into a living thing, they also wreck it something bad.' She chuckled again.

This wasn't what he had expected. There were no evil spirits or drum-beats, just a big woman who seemed, if anything, amused by him. He was unsure how he should approach what he was working his way round to asking, when Edith leaned towards him.

'You are not impotent, are you?' Edith said, and started to flick the tarot cards with her big, raw hands.

'No, I am not, most definitely not. But I feel like I am with a wife that won't give me a divorce. I got to wait, maybe two years or even longer, and then she—'

'How long you married to this other woman?'

'Er, twenty-five years.'

'Long time. An' she been a good wife?'

'Yes.'

'So, she no longer good, huh? Because she is no longer wanted?'

'Yes, that's right. So, what we were thinking about, what we've been told is that you might help us?'

Edith nodded her head, and stifled a yawn, her hand resting on the tarot cards that she only brought out for the types like these that came to her, white tourists.

401

Rooney coughed; the room was stiflingly hot and claustrophobic. 'If this voodoo works, like we've been told it does, then we're here to ask you to do something for us. Voodoo is what we want.'

'Mmm, mmm.' Edith stared at Rosie and after a moment she asked, 'Don't you talk?'

'I agree with Bill, he is speaking for both of us,' Rosie said sweetly.

'Does he now? And so, Bill, what is it you want exactly, huh? Voodoo covers a mighty big area, you want to tell me specifically what you are wanting from me?'

'My wife to die, Mrs Corbello, can you do that? Make us one of those voodoo dolls that make people—'

Edith slapped the table hard and she gave them a wide grimace. 'You want me to make you a voodoo doll? Make your wife afraid of her shadow? Make her think she is cursed? Make her so frightened of the spirits that she lies down and just wastes away? All her limbs to go stiff and her thoughts twisted so she gets to be like a zombie? Huh? That what you are asking me for?'

Rosie began to get scared and looked at Rooney.

'Yes, now if that is more than fifty dollars, I am prepared to pay,' Rooney said.

Edith leaned back in her chair, her big hands clasping the arms. 'You believe that I can do this for you?'

'Can you?' Rosie asked.

'You want this doll too, do you, Miss Rosie cheeks?'

Rosie nodded, and then almost fell backwards out of her chair as Edith let the lid of the trunk bang back down, scattering the cards on the bare floor. For a second they both thought she was going into a trance as she rose up on her feet, her big body looming over the pair of them.

'Get out of my house, pair of you, *get out right now*!'

'But Mrs Corbello . . .' Rooney said.

She moved towards him, her finger digging him in the chest. 'You know my name, but you don't know me and I don't know you. You take your evil thoughts out of my house and you *take your money with you*!' She threw the two fifty-dollar notes in their faces and yanked open the door. 'Sugar May, *Sugar May*! These two people are leaving, an' they are never coming back.'

Rosie and Rooney were shoved out on to the doorstep by the little girl in pigtails and rubber flip-flops. The broken front door slammed hard after them and then swung back open. It was no wonder it didn't have any glass left in it.

'Well, I left the talking to you!' Rosie said as she walked down the path.

'I just tried it on,' he said grumpily. 'I tried it on because of that doll Lorraine found. I mean, maybe we could have got her to talk.'

'We? You did all the talking, Bill Rooney, and it didn't work, did it?' Rosie said as they looked up and down the street for the taxi driver. He had gone, and she shrugged. 'He must have seen us coming, Bill. That was a nice tip you gave him, ten bucks more than the cab ride,' she said, and linked her arm through his.

'Never mind, we can walk,' he said, feeling dumb and inadequate; he had blown it and wondered if he had lost his touch. That really got to him. 'We should've waited for Lorraine,' he said.

'We did, and she didn't show,' snapped Rosie. She was getting sick and tired of having to wait for Lorraine, but nevertheless they made their way back to the hotel like two naughty school kids who knew they were going to get bawled out.

*

Edith was at the upstairs window, watching the two squat bodies walking down the street, furious at Fryer for sending people like that to her. She opened her dressing-table drawer and took out the telephone. She always hid it because she hated it, loathed the intrusion of its jangling ring, especially when she was working.

The telephone rang at the side of the dingy bar by the door leading up to Fryer's room. The barman was just coming on duty and picked it up. 'Fryer's.'

'You get that bastard on the line,' said Edith in a fury.

'What bastard are you referring to?' he asked, grinning.

'Zak, you son of a bitch, this is Edith and you know it, so you get him to the phone. You tell him he never sends me over scum like I just had to deal with. They had cops written all over their big fat faces, and I knew he didn't have no wife, she's already buried six feet deep. He could get me in a whole lot of trouble.'

Zak placed the handset on the bar, saying he'd just go check if Fryer was around.

'I know he's there, that son-of-a-bitch don't ever move his ass outta there!' Edith shouted down the phone.

Zak moved up the narrow staircase, shuffling his feet on the bare boards. 'Eh! Man, Fryer, it's Edith on the telephone, she's all steamed up about you sending some cops to her place.'

'*What?*'

'Just repeatin' what she's yelling on the telephone. She's mad as hell.'

The door at the top of the stairs inched open. 'Tell that fat bitch I never sent nobody over there. She's raising bad spirits like she's raising bad fucking kids.'

Zak shrugged as the door closed and returned to the bar.

'Hi, Edith,' he said into the phone.

'You get that lazy son-of-a-bitch to talk to me,' she yelled.

Zak took a deep breath. 'Fryer said to tell you that he would never waste your precious time sending nobody to you he didn't know or trust like a brother. He's not feelin' so good right now, but said he'd call you later. If you need him to come over he'll drop whatever pressing things he's got on, because you are a very important woman in his life.'

'May God forgive the lies that spew out of your lips, Zachary. That no-good son-of-a-bitch probably never even lifted his hungover head.' She slammed the phone back down.

Zak laughed, and then turned as the door opened at the far end of the bar by the main street entrance. Lorraine Page squinted to adjust to the darkness and then slowly began to walk the full length of the room. Zak never took his eyes off her as she hitched her skirt up and sat on a high bar stool.

'Diet Coke when you're through checking the price of my suit,' she said softly, and flipped open her pack of cigarettes. 'You got a light?'

Edith stashed the phone back in the drawer. She hadn't paid a bill for years. The boys had done something with the wiring on the telephone cables outside their house and connected their line to someone else's. Nobody called in except maybe Juda. Nobody ever made appointments over the telephone because Edith wasn't listed in the book and she never paid any taxes on her earnings, meagre as they were. A bit of thieving never bothered her. What did was strangers coming to her parlour, especially strangers that smelled like cops and asked for bad work. She'd have it out with Fryer. All the years she'd known him, he'd never understood, never believed in her. That was his problem, he wasn't a believer in public but in private she'd scared him a few times, even if he refused to acknowledge it.

Juda travelled luxuriously in the Caleys' private plane, and their car was waiting at the airport to drive her straight to their mansion. She wondered what Elizabeth needed her so badly for and felt tired just at the prospect of having to deal with her. But she would have to, she always had to pay for the 'luxuries', and this was heavy – first-class all the way.

Missy opened the imposing front door, looking scared.

'Oh, Mrs Salina, I sure am glad you're here, she's acting up bad. She's crying and shouting up there, she's thrown her tray at me and she's in such a rage. Mr Caley packed all his things and walked out, saying he's never coming back home.'

'All right, Missy, don't you get all excited now, make us a nice pot of tea, the kind Mrs Caley likes, and bring it straight on up.'

Juda began to walk slowly up the gently curved staircase. Her legs pained her, her feet were swollen from the flight, and she clung to the bannister rail as she heaved her body up stair by stair.

'She got some medication in her bedroom, Missy?'

Missy looked up fearfully. 'I don't know what she got up there, Mrs Salina, but she's acting crazy, saying there's people there with her and there's things inside of her.

Got me to shut up the shutters, then open them again. She makes me shiver, she does.'

Juda could now hear the furniture being hurled around, and Elizabeth's hoarse voice talking loudly to herself.

'Get away from me, stay away from me, *don't touch me*!'

Juda took a deep breath before she opened the bedroom door. Elizabeth Caley was dishevelled, her long hair loose as she staggered from bed to window to bureau, the beauty and dignity of the room making her behaviour seem even more grotesque. She appeared to be half dancing, half trying to control the body spasms that made her look as if she was working up to some kind of fit. Spittle formed at the side of her mouth, but as soon as she saw Juda she sighed with relief, stretching out her arms.

'Thank God, Juda, help me. Please help me, they've come for me. They're here again, the snakes are inside me again.'

Robert Caley unpacked his clothes, almost high on his own adrenalin. He'd done it, he'd finally done what he should have done years ago.

He called Lorraine at her hotel but was told she was not in her room, and then checked with the desk downstairs to make sure the adjoining suite was still retained for her. He called Lloyd Dulay and asked to see him. He wasn't going to grovel, not ever again. Doubloons had not been awarded the gaming licence; it had gone to a huge leisure combine from another state which no one had even known was in the running. Clearly the Governor had made some new friends, but he hadn't forgotten his old ones either – the land, of course, was still Caley's, and the Governor had announced that Caley, Doubloons and the new group should get round a table and hammer out a partnership agreement. Caley's financial future was safe.

Just hearing the tone of Caley's voice, Dulay didn't argue, agreeing to see him that evening. Caley then called his other partner, arranging to meet with him next day. He felt confident, knowing he now had enough on Lloyd Dulay to ensure that he wouldn't give any trouble. It felt good. But the one person he wanted to share his new-found freedom with was still not at her hotel. He left a message at the St Marie, saying he wished to see her urgently, and left his mobile number on which he could be contacted at any time that evening.

Lorraine was beginning to feel uneasy as a few more people entered Fryer's bar and sat as far away from her as possible.

She had asked to speak to Fryer, but the barman had said he was resting. She smoked four cigarettes, getting more and more edgy and impatient as she waited for him: she eyed the rows of liquor bottles, needing another drink, but disciplined herself not to ask for one, telling herself again and again that she didn't need it. The telephone rang and the barman asked the caller to hold, and disappeared through the doorway at the end of the bar. She heard him call up to Fryer and a gruff voice yelled down.

'Shit, man, what you wake me for? Tell him to come by tonight.'

Lorraine moved off her stool and walked the length of the bar. 'He's awake now, okay? So I am going up to see him whether you like it or not.'

Zak reached for the phone to speak to the caller, at the same time looking at Lorraine. 'Don't you go up there, miss.'

'You try and stop me,' she snapped back, and disappeared.

Fryer Jones had one hell of a hangover, more than his usual, and he sat up, angry at the yelling from below. He leaned over his bed, picked up a bottle of bourbon, and took a long swig before he flopped back on his dirty stained pillows. The door opened, and Lorraine looked in.

'Mr Fryer, my name is Lorraine Page.'

'What?' he grunted, and then eased up on his elbow. She stepped into the room but could hardly see him in the darkness. He could see her and he liked what he saw. 'Well, come into my parlour, said the spider to the pretty pushy broad with a briefcase in her hand and all.'

There was an overpowering smell of urine, tobacco, stale booze and body odour. A ragged curtain hung over the small window behind Fryer's single bed, a broken armchair with stuffing coming out of it was stacked with sheets of music, brown with age. The walls were covered with posters, old photographs and masks. Shelves hung lopsided with books and magazines.

'You wanna sit?' Fryer asked, scratching his crotch. He was barefoot and his denim shirt was open to the waist, the thick leather belt of his dirty jeans unbuckled and the flies half open, but he behaved as if he was seated in some draped boudoir, and added an elegance to his gestures that lifted him above the squalor.

'Sit down, miss. What you say your name was?'

'Lorraine Page, Mrs.' She passed him a card and

looked hesitantly at the only chair that was not under a mound of rubbish. The rocking chair was covered by a knitted shawl, and as she sat down it creaked ominously, moving backwards so that her feet left the ground before she rocked forwards uneasily and put her briefcase down beside her.

'*Mrs* Lorraine Page,' he said softly, and then flicked the card away. 'Uh huh, a private investigator.'

'Yes, Mr Fryer, I have been hired by Elizabeth and Robert Caley to trace their daughter Anna Louise.' The rocking chair creaked again and she held on to the arms, trying to keep still. She couldn't help but notice that one of the posters, peeling off the damp wall, was from the movie *The Swamp*. It was a garish picture of Elizabeth Seal with a snake entwined around her body, arms reaching up to the sky.

Lorraine opened her briefcase and took out her notebook. 'You mind if I ask you a few questions?'

'For a lady that walks into a gentleman's bedroom with a whole lot of purpose in her stride, I'd say I don't have much option. Why don't you set that nice tight little butt you got next to me?'

'I'm fine where I am, Mr Fryer.'

He smiled, and then let out a rumble of a laugh. 'I guess you are, Mrs Page, but I don't see as how I can help you in your investigation.' He saw her glance at the old movie poster. 'I was in that movie, *The Swamp*, the one your eyes keep straying to, with your employer, Mrs Caley.'

'Yes, I know. And you were arrested on February sixteenth last year and questioned regarding the disappearance of Anna Louise, Mrs Caley's daughter.'

'I was, but I was released with no charges. I also had a full bar of customers who all stated that I never set foot outside my establishment the entire evening.'

'Yes, I know, but most of them were your own relatives.'

He eased his legs over the edge of the bed to sit upright, staring down at his toes. 'Is that so? Well, maybe you should talk to the police about that, because they got a list as long as your lovely legs that says not only my relatives was drinking and making music in my bar that night, but a lotta mah friends.'

'Did you see Anna Louise Caley that night, Mr Fryer?'

He reached for some skins and a tobacco pouch. 'No, but some motherfucker says he saw me talkin' to that poor child, and in this town, Mrs Page, there are a lot of them. Motherfuckers. But when the police of this mighty fine city take you in, you do not argue, you got no option. They beat you up on the way to the cells, they beat you up in the cells, and they beat you up some more just for somethin' to do when they release you. It's a kind of custom we got in New Orleans.'

He sprinkled tobacco, or what she presumed was tobacco, on to the paper and licked it. Her eyes were becoming accustomed to the dark, dingy room, and to him; there was a kind of magnetism to Fryer Jones. He seemed not to care she was there, he was so laid back and casual, his deep, throaty, smoky voice quite attractive.

'But you were held until the following morning,' she said.

'That I was, but they had to check out that what I was saying was true, and it was the truth, Mrs Page. I never saw Miss Caley that evening. In fact, I ain't seen her for a long, long time. Maybe four or five years.'

'But you knew her?'

'Sure I did, and I knew her mama.'

'Mrs Caley says she does not know you, Mr Fryer.'

'Well, she don't, I know of her, maybe she knows of me. Don't make us friendly now, does it?'

411

He lit up and inhaled deeply. He took three more deep drags, letting the smoke swirl into his lungs, sucking it in with a loud breath before he sighed, releasing it. And then to her astonishment he held it out to her.

'You want a hit?'

'No, thank you.'

'How about a drink?'

He brought out his bottle of bourbon.

'No, thank you, I don't drink.'

He laughed, watching her, and then gulped two big shots down before he screwed back the cap. Lorraine took out her cigarette pack and, as she had forgotten her lighter, had to cross to him for a light. He struck a match, looking up into her face.

'Oh yes, you got nice eyes too, I like the way you look. Like the way you hold yourself, Mrs Page, you are a classy lady, mmm, mmm.'

Lorraine returned to her precarious perch. 'You were married to Edith Corbello?'

'Close, but not quite right. I was married to her sister, Juda Salina.'

Lorraine chewed her lip. He dragged on his joint, his eyes mocking her as she tried to think how she should lead up to what she wanted to ask him, thrown slightly by the fact that Elizabeth Caley had given her incorrect information.

'So you are married to Juda Salina?'

'Yes, ma'am. We met on that movie, best money I ever earned in my life. They hired a whole bunch of us as extras. We was due to film for 'bout a week but it got to two and then three, man, I was sitting around for more'n a month. They paid for it though, paid well. I got this bar outta the proceeds, I never earned such easy money.' He chuckled again.

'And Juda and her sister?'

412

He nodded, his face almost obscured by thick smoke as he dragged again and again on the joint.

'The Salina sisters was brought in because of the problems, you know, to kind of quieten things down. It was gettin' outta hand, but I didn't care, I was being paid. None of us had employment.' He lay back, smiling at her. 'You know, it's hard to believe but those two sisters were beautiful, man, they was glorious to look at. But then nature has its way, and they blow up and get so bloated it's hard to believe that once they was a force. A beautiful force, yess, yess, I didn't know which to fuck first.'

He stared vacantly at a spot on his filthy, stained ceiling and sighed, rubbing himself.

'She was beautiful too, Elizabeth Seal,' Lorraine said softly.

'No, Elizabeth Seal was just a pretty little thing. I used to feel for her, locals was against her, she was white and she was rich, and she was not Marie Laveau. Never could be, so they thought. Marie Laveau is a goddess, she is worshipped in these parts, and to get a pretty little white girl to play the part was creatin' bad feelings. Real bad feelings.' He curled up his legs and lay on his side. 'So they bring in the Salina sisters to kind of calm the waters, you know, to act as spiritual advisers, because folks here think they are related way back to Marie Laveau, and if they give their blessing, well, it's theirs to give.'

Fryer looked at the burning stub of his joint and dropped it into the filled ashtray at his bedside. 'I am getting very stoned. It's age, takes less and less now. Do I have another drink? Yes, I think so. You sure you won't join me, Mrs Page?'

He drank from his bottle again, and replaced the cap, then started to make another joint. 'You know why

413

Elizabeth Seal is crazy, Mrs Page?' he asked, his attention on his joint. Lorraine's was on the bottle: she wanted a drink badly now.

'No, I don't.'

'You want for me to tell you?'

'Yes.'

'Then come and sit near old Fryer, come on, sit close.'

'I'm fine where I am,' she said.

'Are you now? Well if you say so, but I have never had a woman complain. I may be old but my snake never lets me down.'

'Tell me more about Elizabeth Seal,' she interrupted him.

'Then will you sit by my side?'

Lorraine shrugged, wanting to get him to talk, not ramble. 'Maybe I will.'

'Ohhh, then lemme think, Elizabeth Seal. Well, she was a girl with big hopes, big dreams, and they was all falling down because she was beginning to wonder if the film would ever get made. There was a whole lot of trouble, folks gettin' drunk and not turnin' up for work, an' if an' when they did they started fighting. Then Juda found out something about Elizabeth, don't know how, but Juda could find out anything. Nobody ever had secrets from the Salina sisters.'

'Found out what?'

Fryer chuckled, taking much longer to roll up the joint as his movements were so slow. 'Marie Laveau was a woman of mixed race, and Juda finds out that little Elizabeth Seal has black blood in her veins. Way back obviously, but it was there, like a sleeping cobra. So Juda gets paid a lot of money and she gets everyone together and says they got to stop the threats, stop the curses.'

'What do you mean?'

'Hell, they had been laying coffins and conjure balls

414

outside her trailer, beatin' the drums so she couldn't get any rest, making that child's life a nightmare with their chanting and their curses. It was rumoured they'd even done some kind of sacrifice so that she'd be unable to walk or talk, or speak the shit-filled lines they was calling the script. And then one night a whole bunch of the motherfuckers took her out to the swamp, saying they was just wanting to show her rituals. Well, they done a lot more.'

'Like what?'

Fryer hesitated, taking yet another hit from the bottle, and Lorraine could see from his difficulty in screwing the cap back on that he was getting drunk as well as stoned. He rocked backwards and forwards for a moment, sucking his teeth.

'She was what they call a zombie, you understand what I am saying? They had scared her so bad she was wild-eyed and stiff, no life inside her. Scared the shit outta me, scared everyone that saw her, 'cos they was supposed to be taking care of her. She was no more than fifteen, sixteen maybe, and it didn't look like she could work no more. And . . . oh yeah, they got this big scene all set up and they was runnin' this way an' that, wonderin' if they should get a doctor in to see her.'

'I don't follow.'

Fryer licked his paper and rolled up another joint. 'Then they brought back the Salina sisters, and paid them even more money. Miss Seal was locked up with her for two days. Then Juda got to a meeting, well, all the black people, called us into an old church, and they locked them doors, and Juda stood up on the pulpit and she screams and she goes into a kind of fit, and she tells everyone they done a bad thing, a very bad thing. She says Elizabeth Seal had every right to be Marie Laveau because she was as much black as she was. And she held up her picture, and her voice went real quiet and she says . . .'

Lorraine had to wait as he puffed his joint alight.

'Look on the face of your Queen, look on her face and tell me if you don't see the likeness.' He began to chortle, curling his legs up again. 'I said to myself, I'm gonna have a piece of that beauty. She was so good, so powerful, an' she shut every mouth up, made them get so scared. She says every hex laid at Elizabeth Seal's door is gonna come back doublefold on them. They screamed and hollered, man, they screamed that church down. Like the windows shook from their yelling like crazies themselves.'

'Was it true? Was what Juda was saying the truth?'

He turned on her and his face suddenly became angry. 'Who knows what is truth and what isn't? Those two sisters was being paid more'n me, more'n any of us, on the condition they got that film moving. I dunno what is true an' what ain't.' He sighed. 'All I know is that the only scene in the film that's any good is that little girl dancing with the snake. She sure as hell didn't look white, didn't act white, and from then on Juda and her sister stayed in her big fancy trailer until they finished the film.'

Fryer opened his bottle again and drank. His big black eyes were becoming unfocused.

'What do you think happened to Anna Louise Caley?'

He lifted his hands up. 'Hell, I don't know, but I'd say something bad. A girl don't disappear round here unless they want to, or something bad took place.'

Lorraine opened her briefcase. 'I want to show you something.'

He rubbed himself and leered at her. 'I'll show you something if you'd come and sit by me.'

416

Lorraine took out the voodoo doll wrapped in a towel.

'I found this at Tilda Brown's, she was a friend of Anna Louise's. Do you know what it means? More importantly, do you know who would make something like this?'

Fryer stared at the doll nestled in the towel. He sniffed and sat back. 'Where you say you got this?'

'Tilda Brown, she committed suicide. This was hidden in her room.'

Again he sniffed, and then covered the doll up. 'Mrs Page, I am not a believer but I don't play with this kind of thing. You get it outta here, and you go with it. Go on, get out, *get out*!' He sprang from the bed, scaring her, pointing his gnarled finger at her chest. 'Take that shit outta my place. I don't believe, Mrs Page, but that's not to say that I don't get uneasy, understand me? I don't meddle with them, and they leave me alone.'

'No, I don't understand.'

He leered at her. 'No, I don't expect you do, no white does. You all try to take it apart, try an' understand, but you never will. Just as black is black and white is white. You want some advice, throw that thing away, burn it because—'

'Because what, Mr Fryer? Why don't you tell me what this thing is?'

'I'd need a lifetime, honey.'

Lorraine picked up the doll, rewrapping it carefully. 'I have only a few more days to try and trace Anna Louise Caley. I need all the help I can get.'

He pointed at the doll. 'Somebody is trying to frighten someone. Whoever gave that to that little girl wanted her to hurt long and bad, so bad that destroying it would make it worse. That is one bad, bad thing: that's terror.'

She snapped her briefcase closed. 'Maybe that's what it did, frightened a young eighteen-year-old girl into taking her own life.'

'I seen worse.'

'What could be worse?'

Fryer pulled the poster down from the wall. 'What they did to Elizabeth Caley, slave to the drums, slave to the drums.' He sat down on his bed and picked up his trombone. 'You know, it's all about being a slave. I am a slave to this instrument, it dominates my life, I am only a whole man when I am playing. Losing myself, feeling the sounds, like that little Elizabeth Caley feeling the earth beneath her feet and dancing herself into a trance until she felt the blood she had denied flowing like juices, and she could dance. Do you dance, Mrs Page?'

'No, no, I don't think so.'

'That's sad. But then you have a sadness to you. I feel something from you, Mrs Page, sit by me. Come on, now, share a drink with me.'

She did, not wanting to, but drawn to him and to the bottle. He unscrewed the cap, wiped the bottle neck with his sleeve and passed it to her, no longer being sexual towards her, just kindly. The bourbon hit hard on the back of her throat, warming her, and she smiled at him as she took another swig.

'You know when they brought the slaves here, they dragged them from their roots and their religion by their chains. They buried their dead in big open graves with cats and dogs. They were confused and frightened, seeing their loved ones without food and water to travel to the other side. They were fearful because they believed that if the dead did not have sustenance for that journey, their souls would forever walk the earth. And superstition, brewed with fear, is a powerful weapon.'

He replaced the cap on the bourbon and picked up his battered trombone.

'You give that thing you brought here to someone who is not afraid, it means nothing but a bad smell. But if you give it to someone who believes, it burns the nostrils and it becomes a terrible thing, a curse. Do you understand what I am saying?'

She was trying to follow what he said, wondering if Tilda Brown would have known what it meant to receive such a hideous curse. 'Do you think that Juda or her sister could have made it?'

He stared at her, and she had to look away from his dark, unfathomable eyes. 'No, no, they would never abuse what they believe is a gift from the spirits. They do good work, Mrs Page, not bad.' He touched the centre of her forehead. 'They have the sight right in there, they can see the past and the future.'

'But you don't believe?' she said softly.

He closed his eyes, his hands stroking his trombone. 'I have seen them working themselves up into trances, plucking out evil, healing pain. But I never wanted to be a part of it, because I could never be. I'm not like them, my soul is young, my soul lives in my music and I am a happy man. I never wanted all that pain, never could deal with it.'

He pursed his lips and blew two low blasts on his trombone. Then he looked at her with a smile, his gold teeth gleaming in the faint light. 'Find the maker of the doll, Mrs Page, and you'll have the evil, or stay beside me and we'll make sweet music.'

Lorraine smiled back, unafraid of him, liking him, and he knew it because he laughed.

'That's my evil, I am a ladies' man. I sure do love the ladies, and I can tell you, I have had many, and not one went away unhappy.'

419

She stood up, laughing with him. 'You sure about that?'

'No, I ain't ever sure about anything but this.' He held up his trombone. He didn't look up when she walked out, but started to polish the instrument with the edge of his shirt, seeing his grizzled face looking back at himself. He knew he had said too much, but that was always the way with him when he was stoned. He rested back on his pillow, and frowned.

Something scratched at his neck and he slipped his hand beneath the pillow to feel the necklace. He hadn't worn it since the boys had returned it covered in sticky blood. It had unnerved him, scared him a little, and he would never wear it again. But he sure as hell wanted it close when he slept because it could have been his throat those crazy kids had cut open. It had been given to him by Juda. She had loved him then and never wanted any harm to come to the man she cared about. She'd even warned him never to part with it as it warded off any evil coming his way. So far he'd been lucky, unlike that poor limping son-of-a-bitch.

Lorraine was walking very unsteadily by the time she got back to François, but she had another drink on the way back to the hotel, telling herself she'd sleep it off – once she got some black coffee inside her she'd be fine. She was feeling pretty laid back now, smiling, but as they got closer to the hotel her mood began to plummet, and she hurled the Coke can out of the window, swearing and muttering under her breath. François saw it all in the rear-view mirror, saw her run her hands through her hair and lurch from one side of the seat to the other as he took the corners, not even at speed.

'Maybe you shouldn't drink no more, Mrs Page.'

She leaned forward, her face contorting with anger.

'Fuck off, who the fuck you think you are, tellin' me what to do? Just drive the fucking car, that's what you're paid for, you son-of-a-bitch.'

'Sure, lady, we're almost there.'

He saw her stumble as she walked towards the hotel, saw her stop, smooth down her skirt and put on dark shades. She looked like she was taking deep breaths before, straight-backed and head held high, she walked into the courtyard and disappeared behind the palms.

Lorraine found Rosie and Rooney sitting under the palms in the hotel courtyard.

'Where the hell were you two?' she snapped.

'We could ask the same of you,' Rosie replied angrily.

Lorraine sat down, kicking off her shoes. 'Working, that's what I've been doing.'

'Well, maybe we have as well,' Rosie said, prodding Rooney under the table for him to say something.

Lorraine leaned her head in her hands and told them briefly what she had been doing, then stretched her arms above her head, yawning. 'Fryer's right, we got to find out who made that doll.' She signalled to the waitress. 'You want another beer, Bill, or are you pissed enough already?'

Rooney looked away, pissed off by Lorraine, but by no means pissed. Rosie watched Lorraine carefully: she hadn't been sure at first, but now she was, she could smell the drink. Lorraine scanned the terrace from behind her dark glasses, her voice just a little too loud.

'Ruby Corbello is first on my list tomorrow. She was sacked from the Browns' same day as Anna Louise arrived in New Orleans. Maybe, just maybe, she got the diary out of the Polar bear, and that diary is very important. It might be all we've got, it might also give us a clue as to who gave her that doll. And we got to find out when she was given it. Did you check out that newspaper date, Bill?'

The waitress appeared and Rooney was thankful; he hadn't checked it out, and judging by Lorraine's mood there would have been trouble. She ordered a black coffee and a sandwich.

'So, Rosie, you get the Corbello address?'

Lorraine listened and lit a cigarette, her foot tapping on the table leg in mounting anger as Rosie told her what they had done.

'I don't recall telling you to fucking go and see Edith Corbello, or make up some stupid story about wanting a doll made. Jesus Christ, I've never heard anything so dumb! Gonna make it tough for me going there now. Why? What made you do it, Bill? I'd have thought you, of all people, would have known better. You're supposed to be the professional, for chrissakes.'

'You mean like you?' Rosie said quietly.

'What?'

'I can smell it, Lorraine.'

Rooney frowned, looking first at Rosie, then at Lorraine.

'I had some liqueur chocolates.' Lorraine laughed, humourlessly, too loud. She peered over her shades. 'You fouled up, Bill.'

'Sorry.' He shrugged.

'It's not good enough!' Lorraine snapped.

Rosie was getting really uptight.

'We waited here for you, and when you didn't show, as we had agreed, and we found out you'd left the Caleys' house, we didn't know what to think. So don't you get uptight with us, it's you that should have come to the hotel and told us what you were doing.'

422

'Piss off, Rosie, go on, just fuck off, will you? You're getting on my nerves.'

Rosie pushed back her chair.

'I'll do just that, and maybe when you've sobered up we can have a proper conversation, like professionals.' She marched off. Rooney looked after her, then back at Lorraine.

'She's talking bullshit, so come on, what's the matter, Bill? Lost your tongue as well as your touch?' Lorraine asked sarcastically.

Rosie was still within earshot and spun round. 'Leave him alone,' she snapped.

'Oh, you talking for Bill now, are you? Well, tell me, Rosie, did he find out about the newspaper the doll was wrapped in?'

'Shit, I knew there was something,' Rooney said uncomfortably, noticing that people at other tables were beginning to look at them.

Lorraine stared at him. 'You search Nick's room for the gris-gris?'

Rosie looked at him and then at Lorraine. 'We should get her back to her room, Bill.'

'I asked him a fucking question,' Lorraine cut in. 'Well, did you find it or didn't you?'

'No, no, I didn't.'

Lorraine slapped the table. 'Why don't you go up there right now and search? They'll be renting it out any day, they might already have done, so ask if they found anything at reception.'

Rooney pushed his chair back. 'Right, whatever you say, but keep your voice down. Everybody's looking at us.'

Rosie stepped closer to him. 'Don't take this crap from her, Bill, she's drunk. Can't you smell it? Look at her!'

423

Lorraine had now got to her feet, knocking over her chair as she pointed at Rooney. 'It is what I say, Billy, and I wish the two of you would stop fucking it up. From now on, please just do what I tell you to.'

Rooney walked away from the table. He seemed depressed and heavy, and Lorraine knew it, but let him go. She hadn't finished, and she couldn't find her shoes. Now she turned on Rosie. 'You know, you got to stop play-acting at this investigation business. It isn't a game, it's serious!'

'Oh, is it? That why you fucked Robert Caley? That was very professional! Now get yourself together and get up to your room.'

'At least I got developments, which is more than I can say for you two, bumbling around like amateurs. You've both just tipped off Edith Corbello.'

'But you said Fryer Jones—'

Lorraine slapped the table again, this time with the heel of her shoe.

'Rosie, I don't take everything he said as gospel. He's a stoned old bastard I wouldn't trust as far as I could throw him. What I do take very seriously is that Rooney, as my back-up, *just blew it*.'

Rosie pursed her lips. Sometimes she really loathed Lorraine, but before she could say anything, the waitress brought the coffee.

'He fucked you yet?' Rosie blushed. 'Oh, come on, what's all this? Being coy doesn't suit you, Rosie, and the sneaky little glances that pass between you both, plus the pats and the sniggers, get on my nerves.'

'Maybe you're jealous,' Rosie snapped, meeting the curious glances of their fellow guests as Lorraine sat down again and reached for the coffee pot.

'Where's my sandwich? I ordered a ham and cheese sandwich.'

The waitress tightened her lips and said it would be right there. Lorraine slurped at her coffee.

'I'm jealous, *jealous*? Got to be kiddin', Rosie. But you didn't answer my question. Has he? Can he?' She laughed, adding sugar to her coffee and spilling it down the front of her shirt. Rosie leaned close.

'That is my business, not yours, and you should apologize to him for speaking to him the way you did. In fact, you should take a good hard look at yourself, Lorraine, because what you are is a hard-nosed, drunken bitch.'

The slap came so fast it made Rosie stumble back. She clenched her fist to give one back but held back. She could hear people murmuring all around her: everyone was staring at them.

'Now you'd better apologize to me, because we don't need you.'

'No, just the cut of the one million bonus that I'm doing all the work for.'

'Don't worry, Rosie, we'll split it three ways, as agreed. That's if we get it.'

Rosie couldn't stop herself: she punched Lorraine in the shoulder, having meant to hit her face, but missing. Lorraine took the punch and then slowly fell off her chair to the floor. Rosie made no effort to help her get to her feet.

'Yes, *if*. Anyone blowing our chances was you falling for Robert Caley.'

Lorraine took hold of the table to help herself up: she was beginning to feel sick.

'But even if we don't get the money, it won't matter to us, because we've got something else going for us, and it's something I doubt you will ever have. We're getting married, Lorraine.'

Rosie walked away, leaving Lorraine holding on to the edge of the table. Everything was spinning, blurred and unfocused, and as the waitress returned with her sandwich, Lorraine passed out.

Rooney saw Rosie standing by reception and walked over to join her.

'I carried her up to her room, well, me and the bell-boy. She's out cold,' he told her.

Rosie nodded and passed him a computer print-out of their account. 'She's been putting it on the bill, look at it. Vodka, bottles of it.'

'Shit,' Rooney mumbled.

'We're going to have to dry her out, maybe try and find a meeting,' Rosie said impatiently, taking her anger towards Lorraine out on Bill. 'Why did you let her talk to you that way?'

'Well, in some ways she was right, and, I mean, I knew something was wrong with her.'

'I could smell it as soon as she sat down,' Rosie fumed.

'Well, I guess we just let her sleep it off and talk to her when she's got herself together.'

'What if she doesn't get herself together?' Rosie snapped.

Now it was Bill's turn to turn on Rosie. 'Then I take over and I mean take over, because I've had just about enough of her crap. I'm not prepared to lose my cut of the one million, even if she is.' Before Rosie could apologize, Rooney had walked out, letting the swing doors into the lobby bang behind him.

Lorraine had been violently sick and now had a headache to end them all. She had soaked a towel and packed it with ice, and was lying flat out on the bed, hardly able to raise her head from the pillow. She sighed, not knowing why she'd been so hurtful, so cruel. She'd make it up to Bill and Rosie tomorrow. Tonight she was too tired.

She tried, too, to digest all that she'd been working on that day: she must find out who made the doll. Find that out, and she'd know who gave it to Tilda Brown. She winced at the noise as the door opened suddenly and Rosie barged in and banged down a tray of sandwiches and a pot of black coffee.

'You are going to sober up,' she said, pouring out a cup. 'You are going to get in that shower, drink all of this coffee, eat these sandwiches, and you are then going to accompany me to a meeting. I got an address and there's one in an hour's time.'

Lorraine began to cry, sniffing and wiping her face. 'Leave me alone, I'm not feeling well, it's just something I ate.'

'Yeah, liqueur chocolates, you said. Lies won't work, Lorraine, I know you were as drunk as a skunk, in fact, the whole hotel knows. I'm surprised they didn't ask us to leave. Now, SIT UP.'

'No.'

Rosie hauled Lorraine to her feet and shoved her fully clothed into the shower. Lorraine howled as the jets of ice-cold water hit her, yelling that she would kill Rosie, knife Bill Rooney, twist his testicles off. Her threats became more and more ludicrous, but eventually she stopped trying to fight Rosie off.

Afterwards, Rosie helped her into a nightdress and forced her to finish the coffee and sandwiches, refusing to allow Lorraine to go to sleep until she had promised that she would attend a meeting next day and sworn on the hotel Bible that she would not touch another drop of alcohol and that she would call Bill or Rosie if the thought even entered her head. Lorraine was apologetic now, weeping like a chastised child.

'I didn't mean to do it, Rosie, I swear before God I didn't, it was just Fryer offered me something at his place, I thought it was Coke. I give you my word I won't touch another drink, all I need is sleep, please.'

Rosie sighed, cleared up the mess in the room and checked there were no more liquor bottles. By the time she was through, Lorraine was drowsy, and Rosie sat beside her on the bed for a moment.

'You also got to apologize to Bill, you hear me? He really liked Nick and he took his death very hard. So first thing tomorrow you make up with him – me, I'm used to it, but he isn't. You were downright rude.'

'I'm sorry.' Lorrraine's voice was like a child's.

'Yeah, you should be, with all we got at stake.' Rosie stood up and Lorraine held out her arms.

'Give me a hug, Rosie, please, I feel so bad about this.'

Rosie hugged her, then gave her a warm smile as she fluffed up her pillows. 'You sure test your friends, Lorraine Page.'

'But I'm a lucky lady to have them,' Lorraine answered softly.

Rosie left her, thinking she was sleeping, but sleep wouldn't come. Eventually Lorraine got up and looked at her messages – several of them were from Robert Caley. Part of her wanted to call him because if he asked her to she would go. It wasn't enough to be hugged by Rosie, by a friend, she wanted to be really loved by someone – by Robert Caley. Why could Rosie and Rooney find comfort with each other when she could find none? But she kept on making lame excuses why she shouldn't call Robert Caley.

She opened her briefcase, taking out the soiled towel and opening it to stare at the grotesque doll. Someone had stuck the photograph of Tilda Brown's face over the plastic doll's head. Someone had glued blonde hair to the cloth body, covered it in excrement and urine, and then that someone had taken a long thin pin and pierced it right through Tilda Brown's face. That someone had to have access to a photograph. That someone had to know the curse would terrify anyone who believed in spiritual evil and its powers. Lorraine wondered if that person might be Elizabeth Caley, or even her missing daughter, Anna Louise. It might perhaps be Juda Salina or Edith or Ruby Corbello, or even, and she didn't want to accept the possibility, Robert Caley.

The unease remained as she changed and got ready to go to bed. The telephone ringing made her physically jump, but she didn't answer. When it stopped she called down to reception; the call had been from Robert Caley. She closed her eyes and felt it again, the warm rush of feeling she'd had when he had kissed her again, told her that he was leaving his wife. She was falling in love with him, and it scared her. She couldn't help but remember the pornographic magazine, the Valentine cards she had found in Anna Louise's bedroom, all from Caley using the nickname 'Polar'. Who had taken the diaries, if there were any, from Anna Louise's Polar bears? He had said none had ever been found. But he knew their hiding place, so he knew that if Tilda Brown had a diary it would have been hidden in the same place. Round and round in her mind went all her suspicions until she felt like weeping from tiredness.

'Please don't let it be him,' she whispered.

CHAPTER 16

ROONEY HAD had to wait for more than an hour as the printers took away the shreds of newspaper wrapped around the voodoo doll. It was almost eight when eventually a small crumpled man with ink stains on his hands and apron emerged from a back room, holding a full sheet.

'You know there is a price for this?'

Rooney nodded. 'How much?'

'Well, I've had to go back into the files and double check the photographs for you . . . say, fifteen bucks.'

Rooney smiled, he'd expected to be asked for a lot more. 'Sure, that sounds fair to me.'

He took out his wallet and laid out fifteen dollars. The printer pocketed it, and gave a furtive look around: he had, as he'd said, gone through a lot of back issues, but it was on his employer's time.

'Okay, this newspaper issue was out on February fifteenth last year, 'cos of the casino pictures and the—'

Rooney interrupted, taking the sheet. 'That's all I wanted to know, thanks.'

He stood outside the printers, folding the single sheet of last year's paper into a small square. The evening was hot and clammy, and he was sweating all over, so he trudged down the street until he saw the streetcar, and stepped up inside. He sat on the bench seat close to the entrance, hoping for a bit of a breeze, but the air was hot and sticky. He ran his finger around his collar, not sure if it was the heat that was getting to him or the fact that he had made up his mind to propose to Rosie.

Shaved and showered, he tapped on her door. She opened it, wearing a big bath towel around her plump body.

'How did it go?'

'Well, it was the date we all wanted, Feb fifteenth last year. Can I come in?'

'Sure.' She stepped aside, drawing up her towel. 'I just had a shower.'

He sat on the edge of one of the many beds in her room, waiting as she dressed in the bathroom. He told himself he was a lonely old fool, and tried to make himself back out of what he wanted to ask Rosie.

'You divorced?' he blurted out as she returned.

She looked surprised. 'Yes, I told you, years ago. Why?'

He took a deep breath. 'No reason,' he said grumpily, unfolding the newspaper print-out and passing it to her.

'That's a lie, there is a reason.' She was looking at the double-folded centre-piece. 'What?'

'You want to get hitched to me, Rosie?'

'You bet I do.'

'What?'

She sat next to him and took his big hand. 'I said yes, I do . . .'

'Shit, you do?'

'Yes . . . you worried about that?'

'Hell no, that's what I wanted you to say.'

There was a moment of silence and they slowly looked into each other's face.

'So, we're engaged?' she asked coyly.

'Yeah, I guess we are,' he said flatly. It had all gone as he had hoped, but a fraction too fast!

'We'd better tell Lorraine,' Rosie said, and he hesitated.

'Maybe don't rush it, wait until we both get used to the idea, okay?'

She nodded, smiling. 'I meant about the newspaper article, Bill!'

Lorraine was deeply asleep when Rooney called to tell her the newspaper date coincided with the day Anna Louise had arrived in New Orleans. She refused to go and dine with them, saying she needed a good night's rest. It was after nine and she couldn't get back to sleep for a long time. She thought about going to see Robert Caley but decided against it. Instead she tossed and turned, pushing him from her mind, going over what had happened during the day – with the exception of her lapse back into drunkenness.

She got up, feeling restless, and began to pace the room. She came to the conclusion that only one person could have hated Tilda Brown enough, and that person was Anna Louise Caley. But how in the hell could she prove it without Anna or Tilda alive? And Tilda Brown's suicide must not be given priority over tracing Anna Louise, unless they were linked. And Lorraine intuitively knew that they were . . . but how?

She wanted a drink and searched round the room for any bottle that Rosie might have overlooked, still convincing herself that she was in control, and that the problem had been caused by the bourbon at Fryer's bar, not the dilute vodka she had been drinking all day. She knew though that she was going to have to be a lot smarter, as Rosie and Rooney would be watching her every move. She couldn't call down to reception for a bottle, as she was sure that Rosie had found out about

432

that, perhaps had even warned them not to send anything up to her room, and she didn't have the energy to leave it.

She didn't realize that energy was nothing to do with it, but she was moving into another phase of the addiction – that of fear. She was frightened to leave the hotel room, frightened to face Rosie and Rooney, and her confidence in her ability to analyse the case was wavering badly. The more she sorted through her notes, running over details, the less confident she became, not knowing what the next move should be. It was later, when the sweats began, that Lorraine knew she needed something to get her back on her feet: she called down to ask the receptionist to see if her driver, François, was outside the hotel, and if so could he be directed to her room.

It was over half an hour before François was tracked down, and by the time he had seen Lorraine, agreed to buy her a bottle of vodka and brought it back to her, more than an hour had passed. She called down then to reception for a six-pack of Coke, assembling everything she needed, but didn't open the bottle immediately. Just knowing it was there was enough: she'd be all right now.

But still sleep eluded her as she continued to turn the case over in her mind for hours, and she eventually fell asleep planning to see Ruby Corbello first thing next day. In the morning, she told herself, everything would be all right again.

Robert Caley left the city that night and drove up the coast to a casino in Gulfport, Mississippi, where he and Dulay had often played in the private rooms. High-stakes gamblers rarely bothered with the riverboat casinos in New Orleans, but once the casino in which he would now be a partner was open, all that would change. A lot

433

of things were going to change for him now. By 9.30 he had lost more than 10,000 dollars, but that didn't matter now: he was going to be rich. There was no limit to demand for gambling, and he knew he would never have to worry about money again. Dulay came in after ten o'clock and it felt good to see him smile warmly, falsely, a cigar clamped in his mouth. Even Dulay had not succeeded in cutting him out in the cold because he had put his money where his mouth was: the leases that had been such a millstone round his neck had saved his skin.

'Hey, Robert, how are you doing?'

Caley smiled. 'Fine, I'm doing fine.'

'Well, looks like we're both in the money . . . after the announcement, I mean.' Even Dulay's polished manner betrayed a trace of awkwardness. 'We're all on the same side now – the way it ought to be, hey Robert?'

Caley smiled; the man was a snake. There was no reason why the Doubloons group should have been cut in on the deal, but clearly pushing the Governor's golf cart was a useful skill. Still, it felt good to come out a winner, and he was sure, very sure, that at long last he had played with a full deck.

'Yes, Lloyd,' he said with equally false graciousness. 'It seems like we are. You'll excuse me now, I was just on my way out.'

He checked his watch, wondering if Lorraine had called. He wanted to see her, wanted her to know and to celebrate with him. He drove back to New Orleans, thinking of the new world they would share. He wanted her tonight, because it was all going to be different now – he was dependent on no one, he was free. He had been trapped for years, caught in Elizabeth's Caley's secret nightmares, but that was over. Besides, they were nightmares he had never understood or cared to find out about.

Caley called Lorraine but was told she wasn't taking

434

any calls so he left a message to say he had returned to his hotel and had arranged for her usual suite to be waiting. He called again at midnight but the message was the same – Mrs Page was not to be disturbed. He let the receiver fall back on to the cradle, confused. He would wait for her to come to him, he would make no further calls.

Early the following morning, before Rosie and Rooney had even come down to breakfast, Lorraine had left the hotel. She had got herself dressed and out with just a couple of shots of vodka and half a pot of coffee: she'd been shaking badly and had a hell of a hangover, but at least she was able to get out of the room. She sat in the parked car, looking out of the window at the Corbellos' house.

'Wait here, François.'

She knocked three times before the door was opened.

'Hi, I'm looking for Ruby Corbello.'

The young girl was wearing a barely decent slip dress and rubber flip-flops.

'You from the festival organization?'

'No, but I need to speak to her, and if necessary I can pay.' Lorraine took out a twenty-dollar note.

'She's getting her picture took for a magazine this afternoon. She's not seeing nobody unless it's press.'

'I'm a reporter,' Lorraine lied.

'She's in the back room.'

The girl skidded past Lorraine, snatching the note, leaving the door wide open.

'Ruby? Ruby?' Lorraine called out.

'Who wants her?' came a high-pitched voice.

'I'm from the Mardi Gras press organization,' Lorraine called.

Ruby Corbello had a sheet wrapped around her when she came slowly down the narrow staircase. She was stunningly beautiful.

'Who are you?'

'My name is Lorraine Page, can I speak to you?'

Ruby glided down the last steps and hung on the newel post, suddenly kittenish.

'I don't want mah picture took until I got make-up on.'

Lorraine looked at the room off the hallway. 'Can we talk?'

Ruby nodded, gathering the sheet around herself. 'Sure, but no photographs until I'm wearing my gown.'

She indicated the old worn sofa, and posed beside it. The torn sheet could have been draped by Yves Saint Laurent; anything on this girl would look classy.

Lorraine opened her note-book. 'You used to work for Mr and Mrs Brown as their maid?'

'Uh huh, that I did, but I don't no more, that is all behind me now.'

Lorraine smiled. 'Tell me about Tilda Brown.'

'Miss Brown?' Ruby asked, irritated.

'Why did you leave the Browns' employment, Ruby?'

Ruby's perfect face puckered. 'Why you wanna know? They been saying things about me, huh?'

Lorraine sighed. 'Well, in a way, and if I am to do this profile of you for the newspapers—'

'I didn't get fired or nothin' like that, I left, I walked out because that young woman was crazy and I wanted me a proper career.'

'You mean Tilda?'

'Uh huh, she was always jabberin' at me and she made my life a misery, because she believed she was so high and mighty. But she wasn't that high or that mighty. I know that, I know all about Miss Tilda Brown.'

'Do you know she committed suicide?'

'Uh huh, I know.'

'Why do you think she would kill herself?'

Ruby shrugged, and perched on the edge of a chair. 'I don't know.'

'Do you know Anna Louise Caley?'

'Mmm, I met her, and they was as alike as two peas in a pod, she was another Miss High and Mighty.'

'Did she come here?'

Ruby threw back her pretty head and laughed. 'Lordy, no, those white girls wouldn't dare come here.'

'Did Mrs Caley come here?'

Ruby drew back. 'What? You joking me? The famous Elizabeth Caley come here? No way, ma'am.'

Lorraine chewed her lip, wondering how she should play it. Ruby tossed her thick hair over her shoulder, as if ready for a movie camera.

'I was told you were fired from the Browns' residence for stealing.'

'WHAT?' She jumped up and danced around, asking over and over who had said that about her. Then she stood in front of Lorraine and pushed her face close. 'Who dare say that about me?'

'I can't tell you, Ruby, but I have to ask everything because if we are going to put you on the front page of the newspaper, we have to be sure that there can be no repercussions. You are one of the queens in this year's Mardi Gras, and the whole of America will be watching.'

Ruby slumped into a chair. 'I done nothing wrong, nothing at all, and it was by accident anyway 'cos she was cheekin' me.'

'What was?'

'That I found it.'

'Found what?'

'Tilda's diary. It was in this silly toy she had on her

437

pillow, you know, a bear. I felt something inside it, so I looked.'

Lorraine felt her knees tremble as she leaned forward. 'You have Tilda Brown's diary?'

'Hell no, I don't have it.'

'But you did.'

Ruby nodded, sucking at the end of the sheet. 'She screamed at me and accused me of a whole lot of things, like her jewellery gone missing and I never took nothing, I swear on the holy saints I never stole nothing, but her parents just told me to go. I got angry and I went up to her room, I didn't mean to steal nothing, just mess it up maybe, and then I found the diary. I was gonna give it back.'

'When was this exactly, Ruby?'

'Day she come back home.'

Lorraine took a deep breath. 'You were fired on the day Tilda came home, that would be February . . .'

'Fourteenth, St Valentine's Day. Yeah, she fired me day she got back. An' I remember it was that day because I had so many hearts sent to me and even Errol Bagley sent me a little posy of flowers, an' I said to her that I was going anyways. I believe she was jealous of me, an' all my cards an' my posy of flowers because she didn't get nothing at all.'

'Ruby, are you sure it was the day before Anna Louise arrived in New Orleans?'

'I don't know when *she* came, all I know is I was no longer working for Mr and Mrs Brown. They give me a week's salary! One week! They should've given me a month's.'

Lorraine asked Ruby how long Tilda had owned the bear but she couldn't recall exactly, only that it had been a while. When she asked what Ruby had done with the

438

diary, she became evasive, flopping back and sprawling in the chair, chewing at a corner of the sheet. She wouldn't look at Lorraine.

'Did you read it, Ruby?'

'Sure I did, most of it anyways.'

'What did you do with it?' Lorraine asked again.

Ruby slunk lower in the chair. 'It wasn't nothing bad, nothing illegal, and we hadda put a downpayment on my dress for the ceremony. My gown is costing almost one thousand dollars, you should make a note of that.'

Lorraine scribbled in her note-book, worried that she was pushing too fast for information, so she asked a few questions about the style and cut of the gown, and gradually Ruby became more eager to talk.

'It's blue handloom silk and it's got gold stitching all over it. I'd show you only it's at the dressmaker's still.'

Lorraine smiled encouragingly, feigning interest. 'It sounds as if it's going to be magnificent, Ruby.'

'Yes, yes it is, and, and I got shoes to match!'

'Can I see the diary?'

Ruby was already floating round the room, the bed sheet trailing. 'Oh, goodness me, why you keep asking me about that thing? I don't have it.'

'Who has it, Ruby?'

Ruby stared from the window, examining the fresh lacquer of her nails for smears. 'I don't know about that, don't know nothing at all. Why you asking me about that diary? He said no one would ever know, so who been talkin' to you?'

Lorraine's blood went cold, because she knew who Ruby was talking about. 'How much did Robert Caley pay you for it?'

'Two hundred dollars,' Ruby said quietly.

'Do you remember when he gave you this money?'

439

Ruby nodded, and then sighed. 'Next day, I went to his hotel. He'd only just arrived at the hotel and was going for a swim. Be the day after I was fired, I guess.'

Lorraine took a deep breath. 'Was it last year, February fifteenth?'

Ruby nodded.

'How did Mr Caley know you had the diary?'

She pursed her lips and stared blankly.

'Did you know Anna Louise went missing the same night?'

Ruby nodded. 'He told me not to say to anyone that I'd called him, and I didn't.'

'You called him at the hotel?'

'Sure, yeah. Well, not exactly. There's a bell-boy there I know, Errol, he's got this crush on me and he sent me the posy of flowers I just told you about. Anyways, I asked him to give Mr Caley a message, that I was outside waitin' and needed to speak to him on an urgent matter.'

'What time was this, Ruby?'

'Oh, 'bout sixish. See, I knew they were coming. Miss Tilda was supposed to travel with them but she came back a day early.'

Lorraine's head throbbed trying to keep Ruby on track; trying to assimilate it all and piece it together was draining. She took a deep breath and smiled again at Ruby who was growing bored by now.

'Why would he pay you so much for Tilda Brown's diary?'

Ruby yawned, and stretched her arms above her head. 'I guess, he didn't want his wife to find out.'

'About what?'

Ruby giggled. 'Him and that Miss High and Mighty was screwing. Mr Robert Caley was banging Miss Tilda Brown, that's what!' She put her hands over her mouth and shrieked with laughter like a little girl. She thought it was so damned funny.

Lorraine sat with her head resting against the seat of the car. François looked at her, presuming Lorraine had been at Edith Corbello's house for a reading.

'Love not going smooth, huh?'

'No, François, not smooth at all. Can you stop at the next liquor store?'

As they drove off, Edith Corbello trudged past with two big plastic carrier bags full of groceries. She'd been out shopping to get supper in for Juda and half expected to see her when she went into the house.

'Ruby, is Juda here yet? *Ruby?*'

Ruby's head appeared over the broken bannister rail. 'If she was here, Mama, she'd tell you herself.'

'She not called or nothing?' Edith asked as she trudged into the kitchen and dumped down her heavy bags.

'No, she's not called, but I just had a long interview with the lady from the noospapers, they're doin' a profile of me for the front page.'

Edith turned as Ruby sauntered in and posed in the doorway. 'You see a reporter half naked, girl?'

Ruby rolled her eyes to the ceiling.

Edith sighed and began unloading the groceries. 'If that's the clean sheet for Aunt Juda's bed, get it off and make up Jesse's room like I told you! Go on, get up those stairs.'

Ruby sauntered out as Edith continued stocking up the old humming fridge. She was hot and exhausted and one look around the dirty kitchen made her want to weep. She was going to have to spend hours cleaning up the house. Juda was real particular, and as she was paying for most of their keep, Edith always had to get everything nice and tidy. But it was becoming such an effort. What with trying to control her boys, and Ruby and Sugar May never helping out, the house was falling down around their ears.

Ruby walked in just as her mother's head rested on her bosom as she fell asleep. She banged the table, making Edith's head shoot upwards with shock.

'I got these from under Jesse's pillow, Mama, he's been thievin' again. It's somebody's wallet, drivin' licence and . . .'

Edith snatched the leather wallet and flipped it open.

'If it had any money in it, it's empty now,' Ruby said.

Edith saw the old worn ID with Nick Bartello's address, and thudded to the back door, kicking it open.

Jesse was sprawled in an old moth-eaten hammock, writing on his arm plaster with a felt-tip pen. He hit the ground hard when Edith kicked him out of it.

'You get your butt in that kitchen *right now*, an' bring your no-good brother with you.'

'Why? What I done, Mama? I just been sleepin', you near broke me other arm, for chrissakes.'

Edith waved the stolen wallet under his nose. 'I warned the pair of you not to do no more stealin', an' so you'd better get in that kitchen or I'll call the cops.'

'I found it,' Jesse said backing away.

'Oh, did you now? Then you won't mind me callin' up the police then, an' sayin' so, right? *Right?*' She boxed his ears and he ran like a scalded cat, shouting for his brother.

Ruby was furious, standing with her hands on her hips. 'They get into trouble, Mama, and then it's gonna get in the papers and with me having my big day it's just not fair. They're gonna spoil everything.'

Edith turned on Ruby, wagging her finger. 'Nobody is gonna do anythin' to ruin your crowning, Ruby Corbello.'

'Only maybe herself,' Fryer said as he sauntered through the back gate and stood there, squinting at Edith.

Ruby shrieked. 'I never done nothing Fryer Jones, an' you're a fine one to talk, letting Sugar May drink in that bar of yours an' she just a kid. Next thing she'll be strippin' off like them whores you got working for you.'

'Get your butt inside!' Edith stormed, shouting for her to finish cleaning up the bedroom for Juda. A very disgruntled Ruby slammed into the house. Edith sat heavily on the steps outside the back door and stared at the old wallet.

'They're out of control, Fryer, I get tired out just waking up of a morning these days.'

Fryer leaned on the rail, looking down into Edith's face. He reached for the wallet and flicked it open. 'This is bigger trouble than you ever had, Edith. Your boys killed this guy.'

'No, no, they wouldn't do that!' she said firmly.

Fryer squashed in beside her and put his arm around her shoulders. 'They did, Edith, they were high and shooting their mouths off down in my bar, and Jesse had a gun. They get up to all things when you're sleeping, but we can take care of it. You're gonna let me handle it my way.'

Edith nodded, Fryer helped her to her feet and they went into the kitchen. Ruby was flinging dirty crockery into the sink.

Fryer opened a beer sitting at the rickety table. 'We burn that wallet for starters. As far as I know nobody saw them do it an' the police don't know nothin'. I'll say they was in my bar all night if they come askin'. They

443

already had one good thrashin' from me, now I'd better give them another.'

Edith nodded as Fryer eased his old leather belt from his trousers. Ruby ran the tepid water into the sink. The pipes gurgled and clanked as she half-heartedly rinsed the dirty dishes, trying not to chip the varnish on her nails. Edith seemed weighed down by it all, fanning herself with an old newspaper and staring out of the window.

'They're comin' through the back gate now,' she said flatly.

Fryer fingered the beer bottle neck. 'There's a private investigator going round askin' all kinds of questions, she been here?' Edith shook her head. 'Well, you be warned about her, she's been hired by the Caleys to find that girl of theirs. Tall blonde woman, kind of fancy-looking, with a scar down her cheek.'

Ruby dropped a plate, it smashed to the floor. Fryer turned a baleful look on his niece.

'You know anythin' about this woman, Ruby, called Lorraine, Mrs Lorraine Page?'

Ruby held on to the sink. 'No, I not seen her.'

Edith picked up the broken plate and tossed it into the garbage pile as the two boys appeared in the doorway.

'Right then, Edith, and you, Ruby, get out the kitchen.'

Ruby was scared, tucking in the sheet on the small cot bed, listening to the thrashing being given to her brothers, as they howled like dogs. It went on for at least fifteen minutes.

Edith had begun to hoover with an old upright machine that billowed more dust out of its packed bag than it sucked up, but it covered the screams of her boys.

The brothers were wiping their eyes with their shirt sleeves as Fryer eased back his old belt into his trousers.

'I'll keep my mouth shut but you got to pay me, that's the bargain, boys. As from now, you work for me. You clean up my bar and you do like I tell you to or I will take this to the police.' Fryer held up Nick Bartello's wallet. 'First you start with your own kitchen, I want this sparkling and swept, not a thing out of place, you hearing me?'

They nodded their heads like glum children.

'From now on you both working for me until I say you're free to go find employment elsewhere.'

They began to carry out the garbage as Fryer opened another bottle of beer. He'd burn the wallet but he wouldn't tell the boys.

Sugar May appeared with a carton of chocolate milk, teetering on a pair of high-heeled silver shoes. She sniggered as they began getting out the brushes and mops and fetching buckets.

'What you find so funny, Sugar May?' Fryer asked.

Sugar May giggled. 'I heard the whoopin' and hollerin' like squealin' pigs.'

'Did you now? And where you been for the morning?'

Sugar May shrugged. 'Oh, walkin' around.'

Fryer looked at her shoes. 'Uh huh, you been strolling around in them platform soles, have you?'

She flicked her hips and drained her chocolate milk, sucking on it loudly before she tossed the carton towards where the rubbish bags had been.

'Lemme see those new shoes of yours, Sugar May.' Fryer held out his hands and Sugar May balanced on one foot and swung the other up into his crotch. 'You steal these, Sugar?'

'I did not, I bought them.'

'Where d'you get the money to buy leather shoes of this quality?'

'I was given it by a reporter lady that came to see Ruby, twenty bucks, and that's God's own truth.'

Fryer watched as the skinny girl sashayed to the door, the shoes making her feet look ridiculously large.

'When did this reporter lady come here?'

'This morning. You ask Ruby, I'm not lyin'.'

Fryer drained his beer and pointed the bottle towards Sugar May. 'You go help your mama clean up the house, you got company coming, your Aunty Juda's arriving for supper.'

'I don't make any mess so why should I?' she said pouting in the doorway.

Fryer stared at her, and then wagged his finger. 'Because I am telling you, an' if you don't you'll get just as bad a thrashing as your brothers. You want that?'

She was about to get lippy with him, but something about his mood made her change her mind and she teetered back to the sink to finish off what Ruby had begun.

Fryer passed Edith, now hoovering in the hallway. 'Ruby upstairs?' She nodded. 'You no need to worry yourself about those boys of yours, Edith, they'll behave well for a while.' He moved slowly up the stairs, then leaned over the bannister rail and looked down at her big, sweating body. Hard to believe she had, like her sister Juda, been as beautiful as Ruby.

'Growing old is a tough business, isn't it, Edith?'

'Uh huh, sure is when you got two boys unemployed. Ruby don't give me nothing much.'

'But you're still working, aren't you?'

'Sure, but you know, Fryer, half the poor souls that come here ain't got a pot to piss in. They all as hard up as we are.'

Fryer wasn't hard up, he'd got money, just hated to part with it, but he dug into his old torn jeans. 'Edith,

446

go get some nice fresh flowers for Juda and maybe a new dress for yourself.' He tossed a thick wad of money down the stairs, which landed in the hall, and Edith switched off the hoover.

'You're a good man, Fryer.'

He continued up the stairs. 'No, I'm not, Edith, I never was and I never will be, but I ain't no sucker either.'

Ruby was half-heartedly clearing junk off the dressing table, taking the opportunity to stare at her own reflection. She glared when Fryer walked in, closing the door behind him and slipping the bolt across.

'Don't go sitting on the bed, I just made it,' she said sullenly. Fryer sat squarely in the centre, and never took his eyes off her pretty, angry face.

'You had a visit this morning, Ruby. Woman said she was a reporter, is that true?'

'Uh huh, gonna put me in the papers.'

'Well, you might get into the papers, Ruby, but not the way you think you're gonna be in them. Be a big picture of you being arrested, maybe in handcuffs.'

Ruby was about to snap back at him, but she didn't. She wasn't afraid of Fryer Jones like her brothers were; he was nothing but a dirty old lecher who had pawed her since she was a little tot.

'So, Ruby, you want to tell me how much you were paid for that doll you made?'

Ruby's mouth fell open. 'I never made nothing.'

Fryer smiled, resting back on his elbows on the clean white pillow. 'Yes, you did, child, but you had better tell me who you made it for, not that I don't already know.'

'If you know, why you askin'?'

He sat up and now his face was angry. 'Because you

447

played with fire, honey child, and you might have to pay for it. You tell me, and from the beginning, just what you been up to, Ruby Corbello, or do you want me to beat it out of you?'

'You lay one finger on me and I'll make you regret it.'

He couldn't help but laugh. She was so beautiful when she was angry, she turned him on just looking at her. She reminded him of Juda, that same fire in her loins, those same wondrous snake-coloured eyes. He turned away from her, and sighed, but he got up fast when she tried to get out of the room. He dragged her back to the bed by her hair, throwing her down hard, and he leaned over her.

'You got death on your hands, Ruby.'

She looked up into his face, unafraid. She began to unbutton her cheap white cotton blouse, licking her sweet full lips.

'Want to play with me, Fryer?'

He placed his hand over her throat and pressed hard, making her gasp. 'No, Ruby, I don't want to play, I'm here to save your soul, so you tell Fryer what you've been up to! And if you lie, then I'll squeeze the breath out of you.'

Ruby rolled away on to her side, and he waited. She didn't seem to care or worry about his threats, twisting a strand of her thick hair into curls round and round her long slim fingers.

'That Tilda Brown accused me of prying into her private things when I done nothing but work like a slave for her and her family. She had no respect for me and I cheeked her back, told her she was being high and mighty to the wrong person. She said in that high-pitched voice of hers, "Oh, am I? Well, you just got yourself fired, Miss Ruby Corbello."'

Fryer sat with his head slightly bowed, listening to her

448

soft voice rise and fall like music. He felt her body roll over and move closer to him, her fingers no longer twisting her curls but gently stroking his back. She told him, almost playfully, that when Tilda Brown's parents had taken their daughter's side and asked her to leave she got angry and went up into Tilda's bedroom. She hadn't planned to steal anything, she had intended to piss over her nice frilly white clothes. She giggled at the thought. But then she had found Tilda's diary.

Fryer listened in astonishment as Ruby told him how she had read the diary and knew she had something worth money, so she had contacted Errol at the Caleys' hotel and asked to have a meeting with Robert Caley in private. She sighed, saying she now realized she could have asked for so much more money, but at the time she had thought two hundred dollars was a good price.

'I should have asked for thousands. I was dumb. He paid me there and then, told me never to say a word of this to anyone, never to admit to anyone I'd had a meeting with him, and he wouldn't ever mention it to nobody.'

Fryer still felt her fingers smoothing his back, making him stretch upwards, and she giggled.

'Go on, Ruby.'

She explained that she had gone to the dressmaker's and asked for gold stitching on the dress but the dressmaker had said that with just two hundred dollars they could only do the front of her bodice. 'I wanted gold all over, Fryer. I wanted to shine like I was the sun.'

She rolled away from him and he turned to face her. 'Anyways, Errol had given me this cute little posy for Valentine's Day, so I went back to the hotel to thank him and we were standing in the courtyard when Anna Louise Caley called down to me. She wanted me to see her in her room, said it was urgent.'

449

She'd had a moment of worry in case she saw Robert Caley, having just given him Tilda's diary. So Errol had sneaked her in through the staff entrance and she had gone to Anna Louise's bedroom.

'I made a mistake, Fryer. You see, I thought maybe she had seen the diary somehow and I started saying that I had nothing to do with it, just like I promised Mr Caley. But she got all crazy, Fryer, you ain't never seen anyone go so white-raged in your whole life. She was spittin' anger and asked over and over what had been written, and so I told her.'

He gently touched her cheek with the back of his gnarled hand. 'Go on, honey, then what did you do?'

She sucked on one of his fingers and smiled. 'She wanted me to make a voodoo doll, she gave me a photograph and a little envelope with some of Tilda's hair, skin and blood. But I don't know, they was just funny little black bits and pieces.'

Fryer could feel his heart thudding as her sing-song voice described how she had come back home and sat stitching and making up the doll. She giggled like a child when she told him she had crapped and pissed all over it before wrapping it up in newspaper and tying it with string.

'She give me another three hundred dollars, Fryer, an' I saved it all up. That's what I been usin' for my gown, now I got gold all over the skirt.'

'How did you get the doll to her?'

Ruby smiled, describing how Anna Louise had lowered some string and she had tied the doll to it and then Anna Louise had pulled the string over her balcony at the hotel. Ruby had then gone home and never thought any more about it.

Fryer's head ached, and he moved away from the bed. When he saw her reflection in the dressing-table mirror, she was leaning up on one elbow, her mini skirt eased up round her crotch, her blouse half open and her legs spread wide.

'You must never tell this to another soul, Ruby. You hearing me?'

She cocked her head to one side. 'I never told anyone but you, Fryer, I'm not stupid. But you know something kind of strange?'

'What?'

Ruby swung her legs from the bed and bowed her head. 'Well, Anna Louise was full of hatred, she was all deep down angry. She said she wanted Tilda Brown to hurt bad, to cause her pain. When I was making up the doll, I got one of the pins from my dressmaker and I looked at this doll, and I closed my eyes and I let my fingers feel the little head and then I stuck that pin in hard. As it went in, I said, "This'll hurt her bad." I wanted to hurt her too for being so mean to me. Getting me fired like she did. So I did an extra twist just for me.'

Fryer watched as the young girl lifted her head. As her hair parted from her face her eyes glittered, and he got the feeling he was looking into the eyes of a dangerous snake.

She whispered, smiling, 'And then she hanged herself. Now ain't that funny?'

Fryer walked into the kitchen where the boys were now scrubbing the floor and Edith was frying up a pan of chicken. It all looked so ordinary, so domestic, so innocent.

'I'm going back to my bar now, Edith. You give Juda my regards.'

'I surely will, Fryer, and Sugar May's out buying a nice bunch of fresh, sweet-smelling flowers for her room.'

'That's good.'

Edith wiped her hands on her apron. 'You gonna

451

come to the ball with us, Fryer? It's gonna be something special and Ruby is gonna look like a dream when they crown her.'

He nodded, knowing she would, and knowing just how much that dream had cost made him uneasy. He had always felt uneasy round the sisters when they were younger. All their potions and their visions, all the trail of people coming to them for guidance, weeping and wailing, treating them like they were royalty, and in a way they had been. Now Ruby was grown, and contrary to what Edith and Juda believed, that their powers stopped with them, he knew they hadn't. The Marie Laveau legacy would live on. Upstairs in that tiny bedroom was proof, and it unsettled him, just as it always had done.

'You watch over Ruby, Edith. Maybe you and Juda sit down and talk to her, make sure she don't abuse what God given her. You make sure of that now.'

Edith frowned, not fully understanding his concern. 'She's just a pretty girl, Fryer . . . Fryer, why you actin' this way?'

'I'm not actin' any way, Edith honey, just watch over that child. Maybe it's time she learned to have some of your big heart.'

He had gone before she could ask him any more questions, and she went back to stirring the pan of fried chicken, the beads of perspiration rolling off her big, round face. Someone rapped on the back door and she banged down the slatted spoon and crossed to the door.

The woman had a small child in her arms. She looked up at Edith, her face strained. 'Please, Mrs Corbello, my youngest is so sick, it's some kind of fever.'

Edith ushered the frightened woman into her altar room. She was about to close the door, when she

452

hesitated and called up the stairs, 'Ruby honey, will you come on down to me now?'

Ruby peered over the bannisters. 'I'm busy fixin' mah hair, Mama.'

'Well, you do that later. I want you down here with me.'

Ruby blinked; her mama had never asked her to come into the back parlour before.

'You want me in there with you?' Ruby said hesitantly.

'Uh huh, come on, we got a sick child in here.' Edith's tone of voice was not going to take no for an answer.

Ruby came down the stairs, buttoning up her blouse and straightening her skirt, a little frightened.

Edith was sitting behind her table, the woman was weeping, rocking the sick baby in her arms.

'How long has he not been feeding from your breast?'

'Days, Mrs Corbello. He just gone all listless on me and vomitin' up all night. Now he just lies still. I got him a bottle to try and feed him, but he won't take it.'

Ruby watched as Edith took the child and unwrapped his blanket and eased off his clothes, while the mother wept, rocking backwards and forwards in her chair. Edith beckoned Ruby to her side.

'Hold him up real gentle, Ruby, lay him flat on his blanket.'

Edith walked out of the room and hurried into the kitchen. She put a pan of milk on the stove and examined the bottle, sniffing at it, then she boiled up a big pan of hot water to sterilize the bottle and the teat. She turned as Ruby walked in, holding the child in her arms, just the blanket around him.

'Mama, this little one's been bruised bad, all down his belly and his back.'

'I know, we got to talk to her easy, see what she says. We'll use some herbs and oils on his hurt body and keep him cool. I'll need an iced cloth and fresh water.'

'He should go to a doctor, Mama.'

Edith busied herself at the stove, testing the milk.

'She got no money for a doctor and she scared what she's done to the child. She'd be arrested if a doctor saw that, that's why she's come to me. So do as I tell you, Ruby.'

Edith talked quietly to the weeping woman as Ruby tended the baby. He was still listless, but the soothing creams lowered his temperature. The mother eventually admitted she had hit the child after days of sleepless nights when she could no longer cope with his crying. Edith examined her breasts and then told her that as she was dry of milk her child was crying for sustenance, and they must begin to encourage the baby to suckle from the bottle. She never admonished the woman, but was gentle and understanding throughout.

Ruby held the bottle to the baby's lips as the woman held on to Edith's hand and watched as her mama said she would ease her mind so she would be able to cope with her child. Her big hands massaged the woman's head and shoulders until her eyes drooped, and then she worked on her neck and back, a rough, hard massage. She then sipped from a cup of liquor, and Ruby's mouth dropped open as Edith hissed out the water in a spray, covering the woman's face and head. She drank and hissed the liquid three times before leading the woman to the cot bed in the corner of the room and helping her to lie down. She was in a deep sleep almost as soon as her head rested against the pillow.

Ruby looked down at the child. She said nothing, but Edith saw her gaze deep into the child's eyes, no trace

454

now of the sneering teenager in her manner, but a quiet intensity. The child's eyes opened and he looked back at Ruby, not listless now, drinking in her eyes. Then suddenly his lips puckered and he began to suck from the bottle in Ruby's hand.

Ruby looked up at her mother as she felt the child's pulse, and it was as if this was the first time in many years she had really seen her – not overweight and irritating, but almost regal, someone to be admired, and it made Ruby feel humble and ashamed. She couldn't stop the tears filling her eyes. Edith kissed the top of her daughter's head and caught the tear that trickled down her cheek on her finger. For a second it was a shining clear crystal.

'They don't come for tears, Ruby, just your love and a little of your strength. Mine's fading now, but . . .'

'I'm strong, Mama, I'm strong.' Even Ruby's voice had changed; it seemed quieter, more melodious.

Edith nodded. 'I know you are, Ruby. You purify your heart, because maybe you are stronger than you know.'

Lorraine was silent on the drive to Elizabeth Caley's home. François had tried to make conversation, but receiving no reply fell silent, watching her through his driving mirror. She clutched a bottle inside a brown paper bag. He'd seen her go to open it on two occasions, and then stop. She acted like a woman who had just got bad news. She had, and it took all her self-control not to want to go and face Robert Caley out there and then, but even more not to take a drink. She had to find further proof of Robert Caley's guilt. Yet again, he was their number one suspect, and this time she would not allow herself to be side-stepped by her emotions. She wanted to nail him.

Lorraine stood in the hall at Elizabeth Caley's mansion. Juda Salina came slowly down the sweeping staircase. She was as tired out as her sister had been.

'Well, she almost did it for real this time. They been an' pumped it all out of her, and now she's sleeping like a baby.'

Lorraine waited until Juda reached the bottom step. 'It'd be a pity if your golden goose died, wouldn't it?' she said sarcastically.

Juda gave her a scathing look. 'I earn every cent I ever made from her, Mrs Page, believe me, I earned it.'

Missy brought them some tea in the double parlour and then left them. Juda sipped her tea; she seemed truly exhausted and her thick make-up had run on her big, round face.

'I never thought I'd be seeing you again.'

'Why?' Lorraine asked.

'No reason,' Juda said, and then smiled to herself. 'Powers dimming, get confused and too tired now days. Anyone close to you with the initial L?'

'No.'

'That's good. I had a bad premonition about someone, I thought maybe it was you.'

Lorraine shrugged. 'Well, as you can see, Mrs Salina, I am fine. Where is Robert Caley?'

'I dunno, maybe at his hotel, maybe not. I left messages but he never came here, so I guess he really don't care any more.'

'About Elizabeth?'

'Uh huh, she thought maybe he'd come, you know, if I said she was in a real bad way, but I guess she done it once too often.' Juda clasped the arms of her chair. 'You know, Mrs Page, it may be hard to believe, but Mrs Caley is one sweet woman. Just, she got demons inside her. I've tried to help her for twenty years but they get so strong that she just goes crazy and sometimes she frightens even me. Maybe she should let out who she really is, but she won't, she keeps it hidden away, so she has to use anything that'll ease the pain, anything that'll stop the demons.'

Lorraine stared. 'You keep them alive, Juda, don't you? I know about her, I know she is too scared to admit she's got black blood, but I can't believe that is all there is to it!'

Juda smiled. 'Oh, you been talking to Fryer, he's the only one that knows. I'm right, huh? You been to see Fryer Jones?'

Lorraine nodded. 'He told me that he knew, but I don't know if he was aware that Anna Louise was not Robert Caley's child.'

'Oh, he knows. But, Mrs Page, maybe half of what he said was just him piecing things together. Old Fryer likes to be in on things, always hated not knowing.'

'Were you, or are you, blackmailing Mrs Caley about her past?'

Juda laughed softly, closing her eyes. 'No, Mrs Page, I wasn't doing nothing like that, I wouldn't stoop so low.'

Lorraine half-raised an eyebrow; if Ruby could contemplate getting money out of Robert Caley, she was damned sure that Juda or Edith had shown her the ropes.

'You don't believe me?'

'No, Mrs Salina, I don't. What I have seen is your apartment and limo – are you telling me that fancy address on Doheny Drive is paid for from your business?'

Juda stared at Lorraine. 'She pays me, I admit that, and she pays me well, but it's not the way you think.'

457

'What is it then, Juda?'

Juda sighed and looked away. 'Mrs Caley was hexed, a long time ago. Because she played Marie Laveau in that movie she got to believe, and as a believer she needed me. That's all I ever been to her, someone she could talk to, someone who knew her secrets and could soothe her fears. She is a woman who is very fearful.'

'That's it? Elizabeth Caley was fearful, of what?' Juda shrugged her big shoulders, refusing to look at Lorraine. 'What about Anna Louise Caley, Juda?'

Juda sipped her tea. 'She was obsessed with her father, nothing more to be said, she wanted him to herself.'

'Did he want her in a sexual way?'

Juda smiled, shaking her head. 'No, honey, the girl was just infatuated. He is a real handsome man, and a nice strong body to him, and Anna was just going through a stage in her young life. But she kept on coming to me, begging me to help her, wanting love powders and herbs and gris-gris bags. I just let the child talk.'

'Did you give them to her?'

Juda looked away. 'I have to earn a living, but I never encouraged the girl, always told her that no good would come of it, that it wasn't natural for a girl to dote like that on her father.'

'But he wasn't her real father, and you knew it. Did you tell her?'

Juda shook her head. 'No, ma'am, the child didn't know, that was a big secret we all kept close. Mrs Page, all I could do was tell her not to go after something that was unobtainable, but she was kind of crazy, you know. Asking for potions, things she'd been reading about, anything that would make him respond as a man to her. You got to remember Anna Louise spent a lot of time here in New Orleans when she was a little one, she was

458

often at this place by herself for months on end. The help was black, she had a sharp mind, she took everythin' in, a real inquisitive little girl she was.'

Juda sighed, and closed her eyes. 'I told her over and over what she wanted was bad work and only evil would come of it, but you know, she kind of liked that. There was a side to that girl, a bad side. I hate to speak of it now, but there could be a look to her face that was mean-spirited and bad. She was spoiled, used to getting anything she wanted, but the one thing she couldn't get was her own father on top of her! It was sick all right.'

'What do you think happened to her?'

Juda opened her eyes and stared hard at Lorraine. 'If I knew, honey, I'd be in line for that one million dollars you are trying to get.'

'How do you know about that?'

Juda sucked in her breath. 'Honey, there is little connected with Miss Elizabeth Seal that I don't know about. Truth is, all I know is that child is dead, an' she's been dead a long, long while.'

'Like eleven months?'

Juda nodded. 'Yes, she's been gone a long time, I don't get any feeling that she is alive, so now you know. But I got to earn a living, I got a big family to feed, and sometimes it helped Mrs Caley to have something to hope for.'

'Even if it was a lie?' Lorraine asked coldly.

'I wasn't going to be the one to tell her I felt no feelings, no heart, because I knew she'd start up those bad drugs again. All I did was try and keep her steady.'

Lorraine rubbed her head. 'So let me ask you again, what do you think happened to Anna Louise?'

'They didn't bring me down here until she'd been gone awhile. By then it was too late, I got no response.'

'What about Ruby?'

Juda gave a tight-lipped smile, and suddenly Lorraine could feel that she was very tense.

'Well, Ruby is Ruby. She's my niece. Why you ask me about Ruby?'

'She worked for Tilda Brown's family.'

'Mmm, mmm, she did. In fact I got her the job. Anna Louise told me her friend was needing a maid, so I rang Edith, and Ruby called by their house. Be about three years ago. Work is hard to come by in these parts, a lot of unemployment.'

'But Tilda Brown came to you, didn't she? With Anna Louise?'

Juda pursed her lips, the deep shiny lipstick running up the lines around her mouth like cracks in baked red earth. 'Once or twice, I read the tarot cards, looked in her hand, but nothing serious. They was just young teenagers, it was harmless, and they paid me fifty dollars!'

'Did Tilda believe, like Anna Louise, Juda? I mean, they were close friends, they may have thought it was fun, or interesting. Did they both come to see you together always?'

Juda sighed. 'One time Miss Brown booked an appointment by herself, encouraged by Anna Louise, I think. If anything little Tilda seemed frightened, and when I next saw Anna Louise I said to her not to weave stories, that she was giving her friend nightmares. You got to understand, Tilda was born in these parts too, she would have been brought up by black servants, and children hear things, get things distorted.'

Lorraine was tick-ticking again. She got to her feet and started to pace up and down.

'What kind of nightmares?'

'Oh, she couldn't sleep in the dark, silly things. She

460

asked if somebody hexed you what you should do about it, that kind of thing.'

'Who was hexing her?'

'I don't know. When I asked her she said she'd been reading some book, that's all.'

'Did Anna Louise ask you to make something special for her, Juda?'

'Yes, I told you, love stuff.'

'Not a death doll? A voodoo doll in the image of Tilda?'

Juda gasped, and clenched her hands. 'No, no, and I would not play with that kind of thing, Mrs Page. I would not be a part of it, no matter what money was offered.'

'Really? No matter what money? Anna Louise was rich, she could have offered a lot, couldn't she?'

Juda stood up angrily, planting her big fat feet wide apart. 'I don't have to sit here listenin' to you saying that stuff. I would never, so help me God, abuse what powers I have, not for a child, not for anyone. I don't play with darkness because if I do, I got to go into it too, maybe you don't or can't understand what I am, but it's not a gift I would wish on anyone, it's a vocation. I help people – I don't play with fire.'

Lorraine raised her eyebrows. 'You sure about that, Juda? I mean, you don't seem to be doing too badly. How about your sister? These powers you are supposed to have, do they weigh heavy on her?'

'You joke on, honey, we don't expect you whites ever to understand. When you do come to us, it's not for good, or for helping others. It's not for spreading joy or healing or loving, but for evil. That's the only time you people want to believe, when you want something from us, and it's been that way for centuries.'

461

Lorraine laughed softly. 'Come on, it's not us wringing the neck of chickens and drinking blood. Or was it new-born babies they used to slaughter for their joyful "love thy neighbour" ceremonies?'

Juda pursed her lips, her whole face as shiny as her lipstick, her blue eye-shadow running into a smudge from her black mascara-ed false eye-lashes.

'You won't make me angry enough to say something that'll go against me, Mrs Page, because I have done nothing.'

'What? Don't kid me, you have withheld evidence, Juda. You have stated to me, and to the police, that Anna Louise did not visit you, nor did her friend Tilda Brown. You have also been blackmailing Elizabeth Caley for years. You say you haven't, but I don't believe you. But right now all I am trying to do is find out what the fuck happened to Anna Louise Caley, because I think she made *this*! And I think she gave it to Tilda Brown.'

Lorraine took out the voodoo doll wrapped in the hotel towel and thrust it at Juda. The big woman's large melon-like bosoms heaved as she slowly unrolled the towel on a side table, her breath rasped and Lorraine saw that her black wig had shifted slightly, and her own short fuzzy grey hair showed through. Juda was drenched in perspiration, her curls wet around the nape of her neck and across her forehead. There was a dark V down the back of her dress, the underarms of her dress were damp, and her ankles were swollen, her feet puffy in her tight court shoes. Lorraine watched as Juda looked over the doll, noted how she too sniffed it as she had seen Fryer Jones do, then pushed it away.

'This is not made by a professional voodoo practitioner: it's more likely to be a conjure ball here than a doll if someone wanted to do bad work. This is an amateur thing, disgusting. The pin's just a dressmaker's pin too, not the right kind. Whoever made this didn't know what they were doing.'

Juda flipped over the towel, covering the doll. 'I didn't make this thing, Mrs Page, and I honestly don't know anyone who would. I'm getting old now, like Edith, we get real tired doing trances and rituals. They're all taken over by the young, me and Edith are tired old women now.'

'What about Ruby? Does she have the powers, as you say you have?'

Juda chuckled. 'I say I have them, Mrs Page, and if you get off your high horse you kind of know I have them, and you are just that little bit scared yourself. Took a long time, Mrs Page, but you are beginning to believe.'

'No, Mrs Salina, I am not.'

Juda shook her head, took out a paper tissue from a pocket and dabbed around her mouth. 'I don't care either way, but maybe you should ask my golden goose, as you rudely describe Mrs Caley, whether I am black-mailing her or not. You ask her, honey.'

'Perhaps I will.'

Juda put her hands on her wide hips. 'I don't want to go back to LA, Mrs Page, I want to stay here with my relatives. I'm one tired old woman and I pray what powers Edith and I have end with us, I think they do. Little Ruby don't have the sight, and you know something, I am glad, because sometimes the pain is so bad. We don't say what we feel when we have somebody crying at our tables, but we always know. Knowing is an affliction we were born with.'

She came up close to Lorraine and pinched her chin in her fingers, staring into her eyes. 'You're a clever woman, Mrs Page, sharp-eyed like a pecking bird, an' you don't miss nothin' with those sharp bird eyes o' yours, but I can look at you and say you are hurting right

463

now, hurting for some love, and it is tearing you apart. You been a woman with no love for a long, long time, and you ain't gonna find it in the bottom of a bottle.'

Lorraine blushed and Juda laughed softly. 'I'm right, huh, but you know what I don't understand – why can't I tell when my own nephew is gonna rob me of all my savings, eh? So what good is having this extra vision for every poor bastard that comes to me? How come I can't know things that'd warn me? Life is not easy, is it?'

Lorraine sat forward, not wanting to ask, but unable to stop herself. 'What do you see for me, Juda, in the future?'

Juda laughed softly. 'Honey . . . it'll cost you fifty bucks.'

Lorraine went to open her wallet, but Juda put her hand on Lorraine's head.

'No . . . don't. You got to walk away, you make your own future, sweetheart, believe me. You don't want to know what's in store for you. Besides, I don't have the energy to get into it.'

Missy appeared. 'Mrs Salina, she's askin' for you, she says you got to stay here, she doesn't want you to leave.'

Juda nodded, and pointed to the door. 'I'm keeping her alive, Mrs Page, and if she pays me for it, who am I not to take it? I got a niece set her heart on being a queen in a fancy dress and a dressmaker asking for more money than is decent. So if you want to go up and see her, you go do it. I need to wash, freshen up.'

Lorraine watched Juda walk to the door. She seemed weighed down, not just by her bulk but something else, a sadness. And Lorraine remembered Fryer saying that once she had been beautiful.

*

Lorraine tapped on Elizabeth Caley's bedroom door.

'Juda, is that you?'

The voice was like a frightened child's, and when Lorraine eased open the door she saw the room was in semi-darkness, the shutters closed. Even in the gloom it was clear that Elizabeth's stricken face was as white as paper, so pale that Lorraine was alarmed.

'It's me, Lorraine Page, Mrs Caley. Are you all right?'

'Go away, I want Juda, I need Juda. I can't see anyone else right now, go away. Juda, Juda!' Elizabeth was curled up hugging the pillow, her voice barely audible. 'Please, please get Juda, I need her – I am sick, very sick.'

Lorraine took a couple of steps further into the darkened room as Elizabeth moaned and then uncurled her body. Her hands were clenched into fists, and she began to make deep, guttural sounds, her body thrashing as if she was having a fit.

'Juda! Juda!' she screamed, and her eyes rolled back into her head, showing only the whites. It frightened Lorraine, who didn't know what she should do, but then Juda appeared behind her. She'd changed into a big tent-like dress and a blue silk turban, and was barefoot.

'I'm here honey, rest easy now, Juda's right here.'

Lorraine watched as Juda ran water over a cloth in the bathroom and then dipped it into an ice bucket by the side of the bed.

'You want to ask Mrs Caley something? You go ahead. You ever seen anyone act like this, huh? Take a good look, Mrs Page, these are her demons.'

Lorraine looked over to the bed. Elizabeth moaned and thrashed around the crumpled sheets but Juda seemed unconcerned.

'She's been like this for thirty-five years. Started on that movie she made. They hexed this poor child, made her think the spirit of the snake was inside her, and sometimes it takes her over. Right now that's what is screaming out. Not the drugs or the booze, but her fears. This is what evil can do. This is what comes of playing with the spirits, Mrs Page. This poor woman was cursed.'

'I don't understand,' Lorraine whispered.

'No, your kind wouldn't. Now, if you got nothing to ask her, leave me to calm her. This is what I am paid for, an' I do it because she can't trust no one else.'

Lorraine took one more look at Elizabeth Caley and walked out. She closed the door behind her, still not fully understanding what was going on. But she didn't want to see any more because it was unnerving to see someone so out of control, as if in a fit. By the time she had walked to her car, that is what she believed was wrong with Elizabeth Caley – she was suffering from some kind of epilepsy.

Juda sat by Elizabeth Caley's bed, rinsing out the cloth and gently wiping her sweating brow. She would never cease to be in wonderment at Elizabeth's beauty, it always touched her soul, just as the demons inside Elizabeth wrenched and exhausted her. All those terrible curses laid on little sixteen-year-old Elizabeth Seal's head had created such agony, such fear, that she had lived inside of it all of her adult life and there would never be an end to it. Juda knew that all she could do, all she had been able to do, was calm her and stop her sinking into such a state of terror that it froze her mind and body. She eased that terror now, talking in a soft voice, whispering that it was going to be over any moment. Juda felt the evil, sometimes had taken it through her own body, just as she had felt the loneliness inside Lorraine Page. When she'd looked into Lorraine's face she had seen deep insecurity, and it made Juda feel compassion – not a lot, but some.

'Juda,' murmured Elizabeth.

'I'm here honey, like I always am, right up close, you can reach out and hold me, I won't leave you.'

Juda felt Elizabeth's nails cutting into her palm as she clasped her hand tightly. Her body heaved as she retched, but there was no vomit; it was as if she was releasing something from inside herself, her mouth frothing and the spittle trickling down her chin as she heaved and her tongue hung out. Then she lay still and her hand slowly released Juda's. It was over.

Ten minutes later the wondrous eyes opened and the fear had gone. Juda saw the sweet, innocent smile of thanks.

'Everyone leaves me Juda, but not you. I love you Juda, I love you.'

Juda kissed the perfect cheek. 'I know. You're nice and calm now, no fears, nobody will ever hurt you, Marie. My own little Marie Laveau.'

Elizabeth closed her eyes and sighed. 'Tell me some more about her. Tell me how strong she was.'

Juda smiled. 'Well, you remember the day I first met you with that snake and you said to me, "Juda, I can't let that thing wrap around my body." And I said, "Come on now, if Marie Laveau could, then so can you. What's more you're gonna dance with it, fall in love with it, feel its body inside yours," and you said—'

'Dance with me, through hell and back.'

Juda was rocking her gently in her arms. 'That's right, honey, you showed you weren't afraid. You want to dance now, sugar, or are you too tired?'

Elizabeth eased away the bedcovers and helped by Juda stood up, her crumpled chiffon nightdress hardly hiding the outline of her glistening, sweat-soaked body.

'I want to dance, Juda.'

How many times she had had to watch this she couldn't count, but she watched again as if it was the first time, still whispering encouragements as Elizabeth Caley stumbled round the room, her arms undulating like snakes and her thin white gown swirling around her. And Juda wanted to weep, weep for the exotic beauty that had once been Elizabeth Caley, who for one moment had allowed her real blood to shine through, caught on celluloid as the reincarnation of the greatest voodoo queen of all time.

It had not been Juda alone, but many others who had sworn they saw Marie Laveau come to life for a few brief moments: the cameras had kept rolling, the director said nothing, none of the crew spoke as the big voodoo scene began to take on a life of its own and young Elizabeth Seal danced herself into a state of total exhaustion. It had not ended there, nor had it ended when Juda helped her back to her trailer. She had not come out of the trance, and Juda had been unable to stop the men coming in, unable to stop them encouraging her into a night of debauchery. Even when the crew and director had packed up for the night and left, the 'dancing' continued until the men had carried Elizabeth Caley into the swamps. Juda had been barred from going and Elizabeth was not brought back until dawn: she had been repeatedly raped, blood covering her gown and face. Whatever terrible things had been done to her left such a mark on Elizabeth Caley that thirty-five years afterwards she was still living in fear and was sometimes transported back into the shadow world of that night.

Elizabeth Caley believed she was cursed for playing the famous Marie Laveau, and when she had been given the opportunity to admit she had the right to do so, because black blood flowed in her veins, she had refused, publicly denouncing the allegation as scurrilous lies. To this day she was still scared that it would be proven, but as both her parents died shortly after the film of *The Swamp* there was no one who could betray her, only the sun. Elizabeth Caley was not allergic to the sun. It did not burn her delicate, whiter-than-white skin – it showed her heritage. If this had been known in the days when Elizabeth was a star in Hollywood, she would have lost her contract with the studio. The birth of her daughter, Anna Louise, had quietened the gossip – the child's blonde hair and blue eyes buried Elizabeth Caley's secret deeper, for Anna Louise took after her real father, Lloyd Dulay. Blond and blue-eyed, he was the man Elizabeth had loved for more than twenty years, but like everything else in her sad life, even that had been forced into secrecy.

CHAPTER 17

R OSIE REPLACED the receiver and looked at
Rooney.
'Caley's maid said she just left.'

He sighed. 'Well, maybe you're getting youself all
worked up over nothing, honey.'

'No, I'm not, Bill, you didn't see the way she was.
You don't understand, she's an alcoholic – one night off
the wagon won't be the last.'

'Hell, she was up and out before you or me, maybe
she's more resilient than you give her credit for.'

'Yeah, and maybe I know her better than she knows
herself, Billy, and if you want to know, it's because I've
got the same addiction. There's been plenty of times I've
thought I could control it, you know, just a few drinks,
it won't matter, but believe me, it matters, and I'm
worried.'

'You care a lot about her, don't you?'

Rosie looked at him in surprise. ''Course I do. I mean,
we may yell at each other, but underneath it all she's the
best friend I ever had.'

'Doesn't look that way to me. She's got a tongue like
a viper, I know, because she's stung me with it pretty
good.'

Rosie sucked in her breath. 'Same time, Bill, you and
me are both here because of her. You and me could also
have one hell of a nest-egg because of her. You said it to

470

me often enough, she was one of the best – well, when she was sober.'

'I know, and maybe, Rosie, what I am facing is that I'm not. She pushes me, and she can work stuff out and get on to it quicker than me, and I feel tired lately, you know? I don't know if it's just I don't have the incentive any more, but I'm not a number one, never was . . . didn't really know it until now.'

'Yes you were, and you still are – look at the way you got that cop to open up.'

He gave a lovely chuckle. 'No, Rosie, I belong to the old school, a dying breed, and you know something? I've even been scared to admit it to myself, but it's the God's honest truth – I've spent my whole life among the dregs of humanity, and I'd like to spend the next part breathing good clean air. I've done a lot of thinking about this.'

Rosie suddenly felt frightened: was he saying that he wanted this new life without her? Her heart lurched in her chest as Rooney continued.

'You may not be interested, but Rosie, if we do get this big cash bonus, we should have us a good time, go on trips, maybe as far afield as Europe. I always wanted to see Vienna – that's somethin' else I never admitted to anyone.' Rosie hugged him tightly. 'Bill, I'd go anywhere with you, Vienna, China . . .'

'China?' he said, looking down into her upturned face.

'Yeah, I've always wanted to go there, don't ask me why. I'd like to go some place exotic, stimulating, you know what I mean?'

He beamed. 'China it is. But first, you think we should look out for a ring, you know, make this official?'

Rosie was brimming over with happiness and kissed him passionately in the middle of the hotel lobby, oblivious to the group of old ladies passing by. Nobody paid much attention – there were a lot of things more interesting to see in New Orleans than an old couple kissing.

Lorraine was parked just outside Tilda Brown's home, draining her second can of vodka and Coke and trying to think of the best way to go about things – whether to confront the parents and demand that they speak to her, or go to the back door and talk to the servants. She instructed François to head up the Browns' manicured drive, and tried to get up the energy to open the car door, but she felt empty and tired out. Robert Caley was now in first place yet again as the prime suspect, and it hurt. Just as thinking about what Nick Bartello had said hurt, his death hurt, everything hurt. She couldn't get out of the car.

'You okay, Mrs Page?'

'No, François, I'm not. I'm thinking about a nice guy who died, and another man who I thought was a nice guy but wasn't. If I go in there this afternoon, I have to come out with a result or I may not be allowed in again.'

François leaned over the front seat. 'You want some advice, Mrs Page?'

She half laughed. 'Why not?'

'Well, my advice is to come back tomorrow. You're not strong now, I can feel it. Whatever you need from this house can wait.' She smiled and then agreed.

'Yeah, you're right. We'll come back tomorrow, François, and tomorrow I won't be drinking.'

He gave that wide smile, half gaps, half gold.

'Okey dokey, Mrs Page.'

Juda stood in the kitchen and just smelling that big pan of hot chicken made her feel good. The small house was spick and span, cleaner than she had seen it for as long as she could remember. They had carried her bags into one

472

of the boys' rooms and she had been touched by the beautiful, fresh, sweet-smelling flowers. The boys, wearing smart suits, and Sugar May, wearing a clean print dress, were laying the table for supper.

Edith had changed and was truly happy to see Juda, embracing her warmly, almost forgetting the terrible thing Raoul had done. They didn't speak of it right away because Ruby's dressmaker had arrived for a final fitting, so there was a lot of excitement emanating from the front room, Ruby screeching that nobody was to enter until the dress was fixed up.

Edith opened some beer, handing Juda a frothing glass.

'You able to stay a while?'

'Maybe, all depends. I got to be on hand for Mrs Caley, she was took bad tonight again, but she's got the resilience of a wild bronco, that woman. I see her so bad, so bad, Edith, but she picks herself up again.' Juda sipped her beer. Edith drew out a chair and sat opposite her sister.

'You know there is always a place here for you.'

'I should sure as hell hope so, Edith, as I've been paying for this house since I can recall!'

Suddenly there was the muffled sound of the telephone, hidden in a drawer, and Edith looked at Juda in confusion.

'It's the telephone, I'll get it. I dunno who can be calling, as you're the only one knows we got a number.' Edith opened the drawer and lifted out the telephone, which was still ringing. 'It's Fryer, maybe, he got the number.'

She picked up the receiver gingerly. 'Hello?' There was the sound of bleeps and static. 'Who is this please?' Edith said nervously, always frightened that one day the telephone exchange would call.

'Mama? I'm on a mobile,' came Raoul's voice. Edith had to sit down, her body breaking out in a sweat.

'Where are you, boy? *Where are you?*

Raoul laughed and said he was calling her from his automobile. 'I want to come home, Mama, but I ain't coming if I'm gonna get a whoppin' or you start hexing me. I know I done wrong, I know that, but I wanna come home see mah little sister crowned, Mama.'

Edith passed the receiver to Juda. 'It's Raoul, you deal with him, I am havin' nothing to do with that thievin', no-good boy.'

Juda grabbed the phone. 'He's speakin' from a mobile in a car,' Edith explained.

'An' I know whose money bought that mobile,' said Juda, her face turning red with fury. 'This is Juda, you hearing me, Raoul Corbello? You get that snake ass of yours back here, and you bring me mah money – you got mah money?'

'I have, Aunt Juda, minus a few dollars, but I ain't comin' back if you're fixin' to do bad things to me. It was a madness that took over me, and I will return all I got left. All I want to do is be with my family and get your forgiveness and see my sister crowned.'

'You all drugged up, boy?'

'Hell, no, Aunt Juda, I'm clean, I don't do drugs no more, not since they made me do somethin' as wicked as to steal from you, my own flesh and blood.'

Juda pursed her lips. 'You got a free and easy grease tongue, boy, but you come on home. You bring me my money, and maybe we'll sort this out real amicable, no whippin', but so help me God, if you disappear then I'll set the devil hisself on you.'

'I'll be home soon, Aunt Juda, bye now.'

Juda slammed the phone down. She would have liked

to have told him that she personally would whip him until he bled, but she wanted her life's savings back first.

Edith prepared herself for an onslaught about Raoul, but before it came there was a holler from Ruby that they should come and see her. Juda heaved herself up on her feet and Edith reached out and caught her hand.

'She's changed, Juda, it happened so quick. You'll see, you won't hardly know the little girl you last saw running around.' Juda drained her beer and carefully put the glass down.

'She a good girl, Edith?'

Edith nodded, and linked her arm through Juda's. 'She looks just like we used to, Juda.'

Juda held on to her sister's arm. She spoke softly, not wanting Jesse and Willy to hear. The pair of them, dressed in their best suits like choirboys, were afraid to so much as take a Coke from the fridge without permission. Fryer's thrashing had instituted good behaviour, for a while anyway.

'How much like us, Edith?' Juda asked.

Edith stared into Juda's eyes. 'In every way. I didn't think so, but she helped me today and there was something there, I felt it.'

Edith pushed open the door, Juda just behind her, and both of them felt for each other's hands because of the emotion of seeing Ruby. Even the bad-tempered old dressmaker was close to tears, pressing against the far wall, smiling with pride.

Ruby turned slowly to face her mother and aunt. There was only one lamp lit and its radiance surrounded Ruby like a faint halo, the dress so richly embroidered in golden thread that it seemed to glow. The skin-tight bodice displayed the girl's slim waist perfectly, while the neckline, surrounded by exquisite garlands of embroidery, revealed the smooth brown skin of her bosom and throat. The cut, though, was modest, and the long blue sleeves were full-length, fastened with a dozen tiny golden buttons between elbow and cuff. At Ruby's hips, the dress was gathered at the back in an effect which could have been worn only by a girl who was as slender as a gazelle, reminiscent of an old-fashioned bustle and train, the skirt almost filling the floor space of the room.

'Look Mama, look.' Ruby smiled, lifting the hem at the front to show the dress's silk lining and net under-skirts, then her own delicate ankle and high golden shoe. She swished her skirts and the embroidery danced and sparkled like the gold of sunlight on water. Edith wiped a tear from her eye.

'There's a mantle too,' Ruby cried, beckoning to the dressmaker, who unfolded a blue silk cloak, lined with the same golden silk, and fastened it on Ruby's shoulders with two scalloped golden clasps while Ruby reached behind her head and skilfully wound her long dark hair into a sleek knot.

'Here, girl, put these on before your headdress,' said the dressmaker, unfastening the gold hoops that hung on her own ears. 'Just try how they look with your hair.' Ruby slipped the rings through her ears, her eyes cast modestly down.

'Oh, my, my, my,' whispered Juda.

'You approve, Aunt Juda?' Ruby asked softly, and only then did she lift her eyes, the colour of night, to meet her aunt's, and they were eyes that held secrets, that would see into nightmares and dreams.

Juda whispered, almost in awe of her niece, 'Oh, I approve, I approve. Now you are ready to be a real queen, Ruby. You got a light inside your eyes now, child, you feel it glowing? Don't you abuse that now, honey, never abuse it, for it's very precious.'

476

And then it was gone: the dressmaker fastened the headdress of tall ostrich plumes on Ruby's head and she was the laughing, posing, teenage Queen of the Carnival again. But Juda knew what she had seen, and looked at her sister, and they did not need to exchange a word – both knew that the sight was precious, just as they knew it would exhaust and weigh the young girl down. But they would be there when the darkness felt like it was dragging her into oblivion, just as their mama had been, and their grandmama and great-grandmama.

Lorraine sat at the cheap veneered table in her hotel room, updating their information. There had been a note from Rosie and Rooney to say they had gone out to dinner, telling her the name of the restaurant and how to get there. There was also the number of an AA meeting, and a special note, underlined, from Rosie saying that if Lorraine had any sense she would go. Despite the suggestion that she should join them at the restaurant, the note made Lorraine feel excluded, and guilty about the fact that she had been drinking all day, but moderately, so that she was sure that even someone who knew her as well as Rosie could not have detected it. She hid the bottles she had bought – with so many beds to choose from, there were plenty of mattresses under which they could be stashed – before ordering some more cans of Coke, a hamburger and fries.

She finished her notes, making sure they were all neat and intelligible. Nothing must give her away, nobody must have any inkling that she was drinking again: she didn't even admit it to herself.

*

It was late, after midnight, and Fryer Jones rocked in his chair, looking from Juda to Edith, a half-smile on his face. Sometimes he'd forget which sister he'd married, and he couldn't be absolutely certain it wasn't both of them. He'd had them both on numerous occasions, which was the reason Eddie Corbello had taken off, and he was unsure which of Edith's kids were in fact his. He wasn't all that sure if he was actually divorced from Juda. He wasn't about to break their good-humoured drinking session, as once again they refilled their glasses. Now they drank to the most powerful queen of voodoo, Marie Laveau, whose light was still shining now in Ruby Corbello's eyes. As the wine took hold, they determined in slurred voices that no one would ever destroy the past that belonged to their people. Juda and Edith touched glasses for yet another toast as Fryer got to his feet; he'd had enough.

'Goodnight, y'all. Watch over that little tinderbox Ruby, an' if she gets into trouble you call me. You two witches may not appreciate this, but I play a major part in this family.'

He walked down the alleyway between the small crumbling houses, looking forward to playing some music that evening, the way he always looked forward to it. He reckoned he had covered all his tracks, and Ruby and the boys, be they his or not, were safe. Soon he'd have his old cracked lips round the most kissable thing on earth, his trombone.

Lorraine ploughed on through her note-book, checking back on information and jotting dates and names into a new book, and it was after twelve when she fell into bed. There had been no calls from Robert Caley, but she had told the desk to tell him she was not in her room. She was to be woken at seven in the morning, and a message relayed to Rosie and Rooney that she wanted a breakfast meeting at 7.30.

Lorraine was so exhausted she fell asleep as soon as her head hit the pillow, but she was awake before the alarm call, already showered and changed. She checked her notes once more before heading down to the dining room. She had taken only a small slug of vodka from the bottle, and had then performed her usual routine, emptying some of the Coke out and then topping the can up. Nothing in her manner, she was sure, could give her away.

Rooney and Rosie were already seated, even though it was only 7.25.

'Morning, thanks for making it so early, we got to get moving.'

'That's what we're here for, standing by, ready and waiting, boss,' Rooney said, pouring her coffee.

Lorraine put down her can of Coke and opened her note-book, not even bothering with small-time chit-chat.

'Okay, did you find that gris-gris necklace of Nick's in his hotel room?'

'Nope, not in his room,' Rooney replied, and Lorraine chewed her pen tip.

'You sure he had it on when he went out?'

'No, I never saw him leave, but he had it on earlier in the day. In fact, he hadn't taken it off since Fryer Jones gave it to him.' She made a note and then looked at him.

'Newspaper, you got written confirmation it was dated February fifteenth last year?'

Rooney nodded and pulled the folded copy of the page from his pocket. 'Means the doll was given to Tilda on that date or maybe the day after. Reason being, if someone was wrapping up something, they wouldn't use

479

the fresh morning papers, but maybe the previous day's was lying around? So we more or less know when Tilda was given the doll.'

'Mmm,' Lorraine said, sipping her coffee. She flipped her note-book closed and picked up the menu, then tossed it aside. She had no appetite for anything but the can of Coke, and reached out for it again. Rosie looked quickly at Rooney, and then at the can. She interrupted as Lorraine began to outline the developments of the previous day in matter-of-fact fashion.

'What did you just say, Tilda Brown was screwing Robert Caley?'

'Yes, well, she wrote it in her diary, may have been lies, but if he paid off Ruby Corbello, I doubt it. There must be some element of guilt, and more reason for Anna Louise to get so heated about seeing him kissing her, maybe she found out. I dunno, but I was wrong about the bear, she'd had it for months, so Ruby said, and it doesn't matter now anyway. I doubt the diary will still be intact.'

Rooney squinted at the menu, and looked at Rosie. 'Maybe you order? Nothing too fattening.'

Rosie nodded and signalled to the waitress, who took their order for more coffee and fresh fruit.

'You not eating?' Rosie said, turning to Lorraine as the waitress moved off.

'Nope, nothing for me, coffee's fine.'

Lorraine's foot kept kicking at the table. She listed on her fingers what she had discovered about Elizabeth Caley, and about Juda's involvement, breaking for quick sips of coffee and Coke before she continued.

'Ruby Corbello, Juda or Edith made that doll. Maybe even Fryer Jones? But one of them did, I'm sure of it, that doll was made to scare the pants off Tilda Brown. But Tilda didn't kill herself when she was given it, so what made her wait so many months and why didn't she destroy it?'

Rooney poured himself more coffee. 'You think Anna Louise gave her the doll?'

Lorraine snapped. 'Yes, obviously. Question is how and when she got it, and when did she take it to Tilda?'

Rooney scratched his head. 'I go for the evening she disappeared, maybe thought she'd be back in the hotel before dinner, and something happened to her either at Tilda Brown's or on her way back from there.'

'Yeah, right,' agreed Lorraine, 'I've been over and over what I said to Tilda on the afternoon I interviewed her and I still can't think that anything I said would have made her kill herself, or anything she said to me that gives me any insight. The only thing I said to her was that if Anna Louise had been having sex with her father, then that might have been a reason for her disappearance. Since then I've discovered that it wasn't Anna Louise having a relationship with Caley but Tilda, so maybe knowing that I would talk to Caley, she might have been scared it would all come out about them and hanged herself. Plus the fact I had the photo of Anna Louise at the Viper Room and she was scared *that* would all come out as well, because in her suicide note she wrote something like, "God forgive me" . . .'

Breakfast arrived, and the waitress set up a trolley, placing a big bowl of fruit and another pot of coffee on it, and throughout the nervous tapping of Lorraine's foot never stopped.

'You interview the bell-boy at Caley's hotel, Errol, scare him up a bit, Bill. He showed Ruby Corbello in, delivered a message for her, and he's not opened his little pill-box hat about that to me or to the police.'

Lorraine drained her can of Coke, then spooned some sugar into her black coffee.

481

'Don't you want honey?' said Rosie. 'All you got to do is ask.'

'Sugar's fine.'

Rosie was watching Lorraine closely: maybe she was wrong, but somehow she was sure that Lorraine was drinking. She was searching her packet of Marlboro Lights as if she thought there was a stray one left inside, then suddenly threw the empty pack aside.

'You need a fresh pack?'

'Later,' Lorraine said, her foot still kicking. 'Okay, this is what goes down today. You stay well clear of Caley, Bill. I don't want to go near the hotel because I don't want to confront him yet! Okay, Rosie, job for you. Check all taxi firms and see if they got a log-book of cab rides the night Anna Louise went missing.'

Rooney nodded and looked at Rosie.

'We know they've been questioned and they have come up with fuck-all, so this time give them the date, February fifteenth, the time, about seven o'clock, and Tilda Brown's address. Maybe one will remember if you say a purse was found and has never been claimed, and a cabbie handed it in to lost property. Fat chance in this place, but see what you can get, Rosie, say you're looking for the guy to pass over a reward, I dunno, make something up, but don't mention Anna Louise Caley or anything to do with our case.'

Rosie nodded: she liked it when Bill let the old Captain Rooney show, even though she had never known him when he was on the Force. Lorraine flipped over her notes as Rooney tapped her elbow.

'Maybe I should see if the police have searched Fryer's place for that necklace.'

'Yeah, good thinking. If they haven't, ask them to, or maybe you take one of them with you. That guy you paid the five hundred bucks to might help out, an' if necessary pay him more. But don't you go on your own, Bill, it's in a bad neighbourhood.'

'You did!'

She nodded. 'Yeah, I know, and it was dumb, but somehow I think they're such a bunch of male chauvinist bastards around here I'd get away with it. Big guy like you might not, and they got barmen in there like snakes, and a few with muscles, so just do like I said, don't take risks.'

Rosie smiled and pushed her chair back. 'Lemme go get you some smokes, won't take a second. They got packs at reception.'

Lorraine looked up at her and smiled. 'Thanks, Rosie.'

Rooney started to peel an apple. 'So, anything else on the agenda? I mean, I know what I'm doing, what about you?'

Lorraine frowned.

'We're moving,' Bill went on, 'but ... you know we're still no closer to finding Anna Louise Caley, no matter how much information we've come up with. Getting as far as we have has been time-consuming, and time is one thing we don't have. Without that diary, without proof there was some sexual thing going on between Caley and Tilda Brown, it'll be his word against yours, and that won't look good in a transcript of the investigation. Like when did you discuss this possible sexual motive? Oh, when I was being screwed by the defendant.'

Lorraine sucked in her breath and turned away. 'You hit below the belt sometimes, Bill.'

'But all the same, you know I'm right.'

Lorraine nodded. 'Come on, Bill, it's not that bad, and maybe we'll get some joy with cab drivers.'

Rooney munched on the apple. 'You think so? Well, have a look over the old case sheets, every cab driver from every district was questioned and shown photographs of Anna Louise Caley. Nobody admitted picking her up, seeing her. It was the first part of the investigation by every private dick hired and all the cops, here and in LA. They got nothing. You want a slice of apple?'

Lorraine smiled and opened her mouth like a fledgling in a nest. 'Sure, I like it peeled, always tastes different, doesn't it?'

Rosie had told reception that she wanted to collect something from Lorraine's room, and as the girl behind the desk knew they were all friends, she handed Rosie Lorraine's room key. Rosie was fast: she knew the places she used to hide bottles, so it didn't take her long to find Lorraine's hidden stash. She left the bottles where she had found them and walked out.

'One pack of cancer sticks,' she said as she tossed the cigarettes on to the table, and watched while Lorraine picked up her note-book and rose to go.

'We should talk some more,' Rosie said quietly.

'I'm all talked out, Rosie, we haven't got the time to sit around gassing.'

'You need to go to a meeting, Lorraine.'

Rooney patted Rosie's hand. 'Maybe let that go for a while.'

'We can't let it go, Bill. We can't, can we, Lorraine?'

'Sure we can. I got more important things on my mind right now, Rosie, and so should you.' Rosie picked up the empty can of Coke, smelt it, then held it lightly in her hand.

'Maybe you can pull the wool over Bill's eyes, and maybe even over your own, but you can't pull it over mine. I know Lorraine, and this . . . here, Bill, smell the

484

can, it's been laced with vodka. One of the biggest myths in history is the belief that vodka doesn't smell . . . it does, believe me, it does.'

'What's she talking about?' Rooney asked.

'Tell him, Lorraine, why don't you tell him how much you had to have to get yourself down to breakfast? Not that you ate anything.'

'Get off my back, Rosie.'

Rosie smashed the can down. 'For chrissakes, Lorraine, don't be such an idiot, you can't get away with it, you maybe think you can, but you can't.'

'What the fuck is going on?' Rooney asked.

'Tell him, Lorraine, go on, tell him!'

'Leave me alone,' Lorraine snapped.

'No can do, we've got too much at stake. She's drinking, Bill, she's started up drinking.'

Rooney sat back. 'Oh shit, this is all we need. For chrissakes, Lorraine, are you out of your mind?'

Lorraine wouldn't look at either of them, but fumbled with the new pack of cigarettes, trying to unwrap it.

'She's got bottles stashed in her room,' Rosie said flatly.

'Is this true?' Bill asked, sadness in his voice.

'Do you think I'm lying? I've just been in her room,' Rosie snapped, and Rooney looked at her sharply.

'Rosie, do me a favour, just leave us a second, will you? I mean it, go on, go wait in the lobby.'

Rosie pursed her lips, then pushed back her chair. 'Fine, but I'm not waiting long. Like she said, we're running out of time.'

Rooney struck a match and lit Lorraine's cigarette: she inhaled deeply.

'You need it that bad, huh?'

Lorraine let the smoke drift from her nose. 'I need it,

Billy, but it's under control, I promise. I just need something for a while, then I'll go to one of her fucking meetings.'

'Can you control it?' He reached for her hand, but she withdrew it. When she spoke her voice was low and husky.

'Please don't bring up that kid I shot, please don't. All I need is a stop-gap, just to keep me steady. If I don't have it I'll fold, because I feel so bad inside.'

'Is it Caley?'

She nodded, then sighed.

'Yeah, it's him. I really liked him, Billy, and to be honest, I felt that maybe, just maybe I could have some love in my life. Then there was Nick – he was such a good guy. Sometimes it feels like whenever somebody is nice to me, loves me just a little bit, I foul it up, or it gets fouled up some other way, and I get so lonely . . .'

'You know,' he said softly, 'Rosie and me both love you. She really cares, and I just don't want to see you fuck up.'

She gave him that rare, sweet smile. 'I promise that if you just let me get through this, at least until the time runs out on the case, I'll keep myself steady. In fact, I'll try not to touch the fucking stuff, I can't say more than that.'

Rooney nodded. 'Okay, but if you do foul up, then . . .' He sighed. 'Don't destroy yourself, Lorraine, because you're too good, too smart, and you're one hell of an investigator, better than I could ever be, better than most I ever met.'

'Thanks. Now you go and talk to Rosie, we've got a lot to be getting on with.'

He leaned over and kissed her cheek. 'Just promise

486

me you'll talk to us when you need to, because we're here for you.'

She watched him walk away, ashamed, but unable to cry. She'd already done too much of that.

Rooney joined Rosie in the lobby as Lorraine shot past: she smiled, but didn't slow her pace.

'Any chance you telling us where we can reach you? Just in case we come up with something,' Rosie blurted out, and Lorraine turned.

'I'm on my way to Tilda Brown's home and then I'll be back here, dunno how long it will take.'

The doors swung after her as she disappeared and jumped into her car. Rosie would have gone after her, but Rooney held her arm.

'Let her go, Rosie, let her go.'

She glared at him. 'I hope you know what you're doing, she's back on the booze, Bill.'

'I know,' he said sadly, tilting Rosie's chin up to make her look at him. 'We can try to take care of her, but we can't stop her, she's got something inside her neither of us has.'

'Oh yeah, well let me tell you—'

'No,' he said firmly, 'let me tell you. She feels more guilt than either of us ever will, and if she needs liquor to get her through this, then we will just have to let it go and look after her as best we can – we don't have much time left as it is. She's aware of it all, Rosie, believe me, she knows, and I trust her.'

Rosie shrugged. 'Okay, but if she carries on this way Vienna and China won't happen because she won't be able to function.'

He straightened up.

'But we will, and we got a lot to do, so let's get moving.'

Robert Caley was now becoming angry at Lorraine's silence, it just didn't make any sense to him. Then he began to get a little uneasy as to why she had not called, so he tried to contact her again. As he was dialling her hotel number, there was a light rap on his door. He opened it, and the bell-boy hovered.

'Yes?' Caley snapped.

Errol looked down the corridor and back at Caley.

'What do you want?'

'Er, can I come in, sir? It's just, someone's been asking me questions and I'm not sure what to say.'

Caley sighed and opened the door wider. 'What is it?'

Errol took off his pill-box hat. 'I'm a friend of Ruby Corbello's, Mr Caley, it was me that brought you the note that night last year.'

'I don't know what you're talking about, what note, what night?'

Errol stepped from one foot to the other. 'Night you first arrived last year, Mr Caley, Ruby give me a note for you and I passed it to you and then you met her down by the pool, sir.'

Caley took a deep breath, and reached for his wallet. 'No, I don't recall ever speaking to you or Miss Corbello, in fact I have no idea who she is. Now, how much do I owe you?'

Errol licked his lips, peered to the half-open door. 'You see, there was this guy stopped me on my way in to work and asked me about it. I said I never passed no note, and—'

Caley's eyes were like ice. 'You didn't, and I never received anything that night. Now here's a hundred bucks, get out and stay out, or you'll lose your job. And when my casino opens I am going to need employees with good recommendations and experience, do you understand?'

'Yes, sir, thank you, sir.'

Caley kicked the door shut after Errol, not too worried. If it ever came to it, it would be his word against the boy's. But he knew he would also have to make Ruby Corbello understand that she too had better keep her mouth shut. There was no diary, that had been destroyed immediately, but he just didn't like any loose ends, especially now when everything was looking so good. At no time did Caley connect the diary and Tilda to his missing daughter. She was gradually fading from his mind, and she hadn't been his own daughter anyway, but she had been useful.

Lloyd Dulay had not liked it one bit when Caley had said that if the accusations that he had had a sexual relationship with Anna Louise were not publicly retracted, he would sue, and obviously it would have to come out that Anna Louise was, in fact, Dulay's daughter. He was merely threatening, but Dulay had taken him seriously and suggested that if in place of a retraction of any stupid gossip he demonstrated full cooperation with Caley in the new partnership negotiations, that would be advantageous on both counts. On the one hand it would dismiss the allegations and prove they were simply ridiculous, because if a man of Lloyd Dulay's standing considered entering a business deal with someone he had accused of having sexual relations with his young daughter, then it couldn't be true. And on the other hand it would not be necessary to bring up the fact that Anna Louise was actually Lloyd Dulay's child. And he used the fact that poor Elizabeth was of such a nervous disposition he did not wish her to be put through some awful scandal in the papers. Dulay had come round all right – and he hadn't taken much pushing.

Caley did not use his own driver, but walked a short distance from the hotel, then took the streetcar a few stops before flagging down a passing taxi to take him to Edith Corbello's.

Lorraine had returned to Mr and Mrs Brown's home. They had been talking quietly for almost half an hour and it had been a testing, drawn-out time. They could not remember when they had last seen Tilda with Anna Louise or with Robert Caley. As far as they knew, their daughter had no problems, none. That was why they were finding it so difficult to come to terms with her death.

'So during the time Anna Louise has been missing, you never saw anything faintly suspicious about Tilda's behaviour? By that I mean, did she change? Did she become moody or uncooperative in any way?'

Mrs Brown was so pale and washed out that Lorraine felt almost cruel questioning her. She wept constantly, wiping her tears away with a handkerchief, unfolding it to blow her nose, then refolding it again to wipe her eyes.

'Well, of course she was very, very upset. Anna Louise was her best friend, she was inconsolable about her, and for her to disappear like that was just dreadful for Tilda. They had been very close since childhood and I think what made it worse was that they had argued the day before, so Tilda never had a chance to make it up with Anna Louise. That's what upset her most of all.'

Lorraine looked at Mr Brown, who sat straight-backed, his face bearing a pained, quizzical expression.

'Do you think Tilda did what she did because she was

490

still upset about Anna Louise?' Lorraine asked, her voice hushed and sounding, even to herself, excessively conspiratorial.

'We don't know, we had thought she had got over it all, but she obviously had not, and quite possibly, Mrs Page, your visit might have made her sink into a depression. We do not know, just as we really do not know why you came out to see her.' He looked at Lorraine almost accusingly, and he was becoming agitated, his hands clenching and unclenching, though he tried to hide it by pressing them into his thighs. 'We had interviews for many weeks after Anna Louise disappeared, and poor Tilda, on top of losing her dearest friend, was questioned more than anyone. What did you ask her, Mrs Page? Why don't you tell us if she became upset, because we would dearly like to know, *need* to know what made our only daughter do such a terrible thing? She has broken our hearts.'

Lorraine lied for a further half-hour, making up chit-chat questions and answers regarding her interview with Tilda about Anna Louise. It was all so emotionally tense that Lorraine felt they were draining her energy from her.

'I need to see any friend of Tilda's that she saw on a regular basis, and where she went. I need to build up a picture of your daughter prior to the tragedy.'

Mr and Mrs Brown whispered to each other, and Mrs Brown nodded her head. She then excused herself and left the room.

Mr Brown sighed and looked towards the wall of glass through which the pool and tennis court were visible.

'We have tried to come to terms with it, Mrs Page. We know Tilda was so worried about what had happened to Anna Louise. There were such stories about kidnap and rape, or even, pray God it is not true, that she might

491

have been murdered. And as a result, Tilda kept very much to herself for the past few months, but my wife will give you details.'

'Thank you.'

He stared down at his shoes, and then bit his lip. 'Although I do not see why you are taking such an interest. I believe Mr and Mrs Caley hired you to keep up the search for their daughter, and rightly so, but I do not understand why you would spend so much of your time on Tilda. In fact, I feel quite guilty that we are taking you away from your investigation to talk about Tilda.'

Lorraine smiled. 'Please, Mr Brown, I think in the end it will only help me. You see, they were such dear friends, the more I find out about Tilda means I am also finding out about poor Anna Louise Caley.'

'Ah, yes, I understand, well . . .'

Lorraine opened her briefcase and took out the doll, still wrapped in the towel. He seemed not to be paying any attention, staring vacantly towards the window. She crossed to a dining table near the window, and unwrapped the doll.

'I didn't want your wife to see this as it is so upsetting, but I think you should.'

He joined her at the table, and then gasped. 'Dear God, where did you find this?'

'In Tilda's bedroom, hidden in a tennis racquet cover.'

His hands were shaking as he reached out, not to touch the doll but hold the edge of the table.

'It was in my daughter's bedroom?' he said, aghast.

'Yes. As you can see, it has her picture on its face, and . . .'

His fist banged down on the table. 'It must be one of the help, but why? Dear God Almighty, what would any one of them make this for? It's disgusting.'

492

'It's a voodoo doll, Mr Brown.'

'I know what it is,' he snapped.

'So you see why I am here. I know a girl who worked here, Ruby Corbello, was fired, and I think perhaps she made it out of spite, to frighten Tilda.'

'I'll have her arrested.'

'But I don't have the proof that she did, Mr Brown. Also, the newspaper it was wrapped in was dated February fifteenth last year, the day Anna Louise went missing, so your daughter had this doll for a long time.'

He was staring at the doll, and suddenly his shoulders began to shake, and he sobbed, awful dry gasping sobs.

Mrs Brown walked in, carrying a sheet of violet notepaper. 'I've jotted down all the people I can think of.'

Mr Brown straightened trying to control himself, but he was obviously very distressed. 'I'm sorry, so sorry, please excuse me, I'm sorry.'

He rushed past his wife as Lorraine quickly covered the doll and looked after him. Mrs Brown tried to touch him, but he hurried out, closing the door.

Mrs Brown joined Lorraine at the window and sighed. 'I think I know what upset him, they used to play in there for hours on end when they were children, Tilda and Anna Louise. We should take it down.'

Lorraine looked out in the same direction as Mrs Brown but could only see a gardener clipping hedges, and a small white building, the size of a shed, close to the bushes. Even at this distance Lorraine could see that there was a large padlock on the door.

'My husband built that little playhouse for her and she would never let him take it down. She used to say she wanted to bring our grandchildren here to play in it when she got married, so seeing it must have reminded him. We loved our daughter so much, Mrs Page.'

'Yes, of course, I understand.'

Mrs Brown passed Lorraine the neatly folded sheet of note-paper. 'These are some of the friends I know she visited, plus the pastor and group she went to church with. And this is her doctor and the girls she went horseback-riding with, and this is the list of the people she knew at college. I've put down their addresses and phone numbers, or the ones I recalled and were on the Christmas card lists. Most of them came to her funeral, well, not the ones from her college.'

'Thank you, I do appreciate this.'

'She didn't go back to Los Angeles after Anna Louise went missing, said she couldn't face it there. She said she wanted to be here, just in case she called, or made contact.' Mrs Brown drew out the sodden little handkerchief again. 'She had been doing so well in college, it was such a shame, but she said she just could not think or concentrate until she found out what had happened to Anna.' Mrs Brown shrugged her shoulders.

'I'm sorry, it must have affected her deeply.'

Mrs Brown nodded. 'Yes, it affected us all. Now, well, nothing will ever be the same again.'

Lorraine slumped into the car and wound down the window.

'Jesus Christ, they say they don't know why their daughter fucking hanged herself when it's so obvious she was going nuts in that house because her best friend disappears and . . .' Lorraine leaned forward. 'She doesn't go back to college. She stays home most of the time and is nervous and worried. She's got a fucking death doll in her tennis racquet case. Holy shit, they must really have been blind not to pick up the fact their daughter needed professional help! And added to that, the poor kid had also been fucked royally by her best

494

friend's father. No wonder she tied the knot. I think I'd maybe do it under the same circumstances.'

François waited as Lorraine checked over Mrs Brown's neat list of so-called friends. He had no idea what she was talking about, but he nodded his head.

'Okay, François, I want the Pastor first. Then we've got to get to the first two addresses on this list.' She passed him Mrs Brown's note.

'Yes, ma'am, church it is. Pastor Bellamy is a mighty fine man.'

'You know him?'

'No, ma'am, but he's well known for preachin' a good sermon.'

Lorraine smiled. 'Do you all lie, François?'

'Who do you mean by all, Miss Lorraine?'

She laughed. 'Cab drivers, François, cab drivers. What do you think I meant, all blacks?'

He gave a big, gap-toothed grin that showed an inch of pink gum. 'I didn't think a fine lady like you would make a racial remark like that. We hear and see things in a cab, Mrs Page, but we say nothin'.'

'Unless there's money in it for you,' she muttered.

'Unless there is money in it,' he giggled.

They drove out through the front gates, Lorraine turning the interview over in her mind; she was sure it hadn't been the playhouse that had so disturbed Mr Brown, but the foul-smelling doll she had shown him. She sighed. Maybe she shouldn't have shown it to him, it didn't do any good in the end, just added to their grief.

By 10.30 Rosie had decided that the amount she was offering was too little. The first cab company seemed not the slightest bit interested in whether or not they had a

495

possible reward on offer for something left in a taxi maybe eleven to twelve months ago, which would entail hours of leafing through old record slips from the previous year. So she rethought her approach, and this time took a cab to the Hotel Cavagnal. She asked if they divided up the territory, cruised, or picked up fares by phone call, and was told that they did all three, so that was not much help. What was also not helpful was that the town was filling up rapidly as the preparations for Mardi Gras began in earnest. Bunting and flags were hung, large floral displays were being watered, and every shop window was being decorated. Posters of forthcoming events were being plastered on every available section of wall space, and the streets were beginning to throb with visitors arriving early for the parades.

Rosie got out at the hotel but did not go into the closed courtyard. Instead she walked a block up the street. Anna Louise had not booked a cab via the hotel, that they knew, so did she walk to the main intersection and flag one down? Rosie began to note all the different cabs passing backwards and forwards. A few even slowed down and asked if she needed a ride. Eventually she flagged down a persistent one which had passed her three times.

'You look like you're lost, ma'am,' the driver said politely.

'Nope, not lost. I'm looking for a special taxi cab. I'm from an insurance company, and whoever this driver is, could be in line for . . .' She hesitated, wondering how much would be a good incentive. Then she stopped because she remembered Lorraine saying in one of their note sessions that Robert Caley had seen his daughter's purse on the bed. So, did it mean she did not have any cash on her? If so, maybe someone from the hotel gave her a lift to wherever she went that night.

Rosie waved on her persistent cab driver and looked around for a phone box, she needed to talk to Lorraine.

She called the Browns' house to find that Lorraine had already left. She then called the hotel, but neither Rooney nor Lorraine was there. She returned to the Cavagnal and hovered outside for a while, trying to make up her mind what she should do and watching two bell-boys carrying new guests' luggage into the hotel, departing guests' luggage out. For a smallish hotel there was a lot of activity. She heard one bell-boy shout over to the other as he struggled with a set of Hermès luggage.

'The second-floor blue suite for those, Errol.'

Rosie sauntered across to the sweating Errol, wondering if Rooney had already questioned him.

'Hi, I wonder if you could help me out?' she said, smiling warmly.

'Anything you need, ma'am,' he said with a slight bow.

Rosie said that she was not a hotel guest, but needed to have a private conversation, and that she would pay for it. If he was unable to talk right that minute she could wait.

Errol pushed his pill-box hat up and gave a look around. 'Well, what do you want to talk about?'

Rosie tried the direct approach. 'Anna Louise Caley.'

He threw up his hands, and shook his head. 'Lady, I been asked about that girl more times than I had wages slips. I don't know nothin' about her, and that is the truth.'

Rosie looked away, something she'd learned from watching Lorraine. 'Fine, it's just that I got five hundred dollars cash for a little bit of information.'

'How little is this bit?' he asked, toying with what Robert Caley had said, what he'd given him, and what the future might hold. But a car drew up and he had to get back to work.

'I got a break in fifteen, why don't you come back?'

Robert Caley asked the cab driver to stop about halfway down the street from Ruby Corbello's house. He paid him off and told him if he wanted double his fare he should wait. He then walked down the road to the Corbellos'.

'Why, Mr Caley!' Juda said, and it pained her because she had such a hangover she could hardly lift her head.

'Mrs Salina,' he said, but without the surprise he felt at seeing her.

'Come on in,' she growled, and he looked from the doorstep to see if anyone was watching, but there was no one.

Caley sat in the kitchen, refused any refreshment, his mind ticking over as to whether or not he should ask after Ruby.

'My sister and niece, Ruby, are out visiting a sick baby. I am here alone, and it's good because it gives me an opportunity to talk to you straight.'

He nodded, wondering how much she knew and if she was about to try and blackmail him like her niece. It was all becoming too much, too heavy, and he loosened his collar.

'I know you don't like me and you never have,' Juda said, as she poured a glass of root beer. 'But now I am asking you to help me.'

'You want me to help you?' he said with a smile.

'Yes, sir. I've just lost my life's savings, my nephew stole it and I have come back here as penniless as I left over twenty years ago.'

Here it comes, he thought, wondering how much she wanted.

'I want to stay on here, Mr Caley, I don't want to go back to LA, I don't belong there, this is my home.'

He looked at the stained wallpaper. This is going to cost heavy, he thought to himself, but he would not show that he had any indication. He'd just act innocent.

'I can't take care of your wife no more, Mr Caley, she drains me, she uses up everything I have, but I care for her and I don't want to let her down. I feel guilty. I feel that she is my responsibility, and that has been the rope that has hung round my neck. I used to feel that in some way I was to blame, but I no longer believe that.'

'Are you asking for money, Mrs Salina?'

'No, sir, not money, I don't want your money. I want you to get someone else for Mrs Caley because I am tired out and I want to stay here, move back in with my sister. I want to sell my lease on the apartment in Doheny Drive. I don't want to go back there, Mr Caley.'

He coughed and ran his finger round his collar. 'I'm still not sure I follow what you are asking from me, Mrs Salina.'

'No, maybe you don't, because you never took much interest, but you should know a lot from what Miss Elizabeth does. The way she behaves is because she can't help it.'

'I'm sure she can't,' he said brusquely, irritated by Juda, and then leaned across the table. 'My wife takes drugs and alcohol like it is going out of fashion, she has an addictive personality.'

'No, sir, she has a fear inside her that she is trying to obliterate. Now, you may not believe it, and you have that right, but she needs someone to control her demons. If she does not get help she will go out of her mind.'

499

He smirked. 'So you are saying that she isn't right now?'

Juda turned on him. 'I am saying that you refuse to understand that your wife needs help, not from your clinics but from—'

'People like you?'

She pushed her face closer. 'Just what do you think I am, Mr Robert fucking Caley?'

He didn't back off but leaned closer. 'You blackmail my wife and hold her in some kind of terror, that's all I do know.'

'You are wrong. I am forced into trying to control the terror and what I am saying to you is that I can't do it no more. I am old and I am tired out. She is your wife, you fleece her more than I never even begun to know how, but that is not my business. Mine is to help her, because unlike you, Mr Caley, I love her.'

'Do you?'

'Yes, sir, I do, but like I said, I am too old, so I am asking you to go back to her. I'll find someone she can hold on to to help her in the way she needs helping.'

'You mean someone who'll feed her drugs?'

Juda sat back, shaking her head. 'No, sir, I mean help her spiritually, that's the only help I have ever given your wife.'

'I am never going back to my wife, Mrs Salina.'

Juda stared at him and she felt cold, icy cold. The chill moved from her big, bloated feet up through her body. 'Then why did you come here? To tell me that?'

He shrugged, he had come to see Ruby, all this was irritating and now all he wanted was to leave.

Juda stared at his handsome face; she saw his weakness and smiled. 'You will never have the woman you want, Mr Caley, your heart is frozen over by greed. I think you

500

should leave, I don't want anything more to do with you.'

He eased back in his chair, about to stand up, when Ruby walked in. She gave him a nonchalant look, crossing to the fridge to take out a root beer for herself.

'Why, if it isn't Mr Robert Caley,' she said as she banged open a drawer for the bottle opener.

'You know each other!' Juda said, surprised.

'Sure we do, this is Anna Louise's daddy. Am I right?'

Juda looked from Caley and back to Ruby, who opened her bottle and drank it down thirstily.

'I used to work for Tilda Brown, Aunty Juda, you forgettin'? She was Mr Caley's daughter's closest friend. Isn't that right, Mr Caley?'

'Yes, that's right,' he said, staring at Ruby, unable to fathom out what was going on and how much Juda knew. From irritation he had slid into fear.

'Mr Caley is opening up a big casino, Aunty Juda, gonna be a rich, rich man.'

Juda watched her niece, then Caley. She was confused as to what the undercurrent was about, but she could sense it, and see the hold Ruby seemed to have over him.

Ruby sidled up to Caley and flicked her hips at him. He moved away.

'Mr Caley is a very sexy man and he likes them young and fresh, 'bout my age, is that not so, Mr Caley?'

He got up, moving as far away from Ruby as he could in the small kitchen. Juda could smell his fear, and she caught hold of Ruby as she passed her.

'Mr Caley, would you wait in the hallway for a few moments if you please? I can see you want to talk to my niece.'

Caley eased past Juda and went into the hall. The kitchen door slammed shut behind him as Juda kicked it closed.

'What's going on, Ruby?'

Ruby sat on the edge of the table, sipping her root beer and enjoying outlining what she had found in Tilda Brown's diary about Robert Caley. She gasped when the punch knocked her to the floor. Her beer bottle broke into fragments and she hunched up, terrified, as Juda picked up the damp dishcloth and began to swipe it at her so hard it made her eyes water. She covered her head, screeching, but then came the kicks and the slaps. It was as if Juda had gone crazy, and she kept up the onslaught until she had to sit down, exhausted. Her breath came in short sharp rasps.

'You made that doll for Anna Louise Caley, didn't you?'

Ruby began crying, scared of her aunt.

'You shouldn't have done that, Ruby, you did a terrible thing, you raised up evil.'

'He's evil, he was fucking that girl Tilda Brown.'

Juda kicked her so hard she crunched into a tight ball. She then ran the cold water and filled a tumbler full to the brim. Ruby didn't see her swallow, all she saw was this massive looming figure leaning over her and spitting out a jet-spray of water. She tried to inch away, but Juda grabbed her hair and then pressed her hands tightly round the girl's skull.

'You got evil in you, girl, an' I got to get it out.'

Caley stood in the dank hall, waiting. He couldn't help but hear Ruby's screams and sobs, and the strange high but deep voice of Juda Salina calling out words that he couldn't make out. Eventually Ruby appeared, her hair wet and clinging to her face, and she was weeping.

'Mr Caley, please don't go.' She knelt before him and clasped her hands together. 'I am sorry I came and asked

502

you for money, I meant no harm, I have never meant any harm. I will never ask you for anything again, I give you my word. Please, don't you say anything about what I did, just as I won't ever repeat what was in that poor girl's diary.'

Caley was nonplussed as Juda walked out from the kitchen.

'You go away from this house now, Mr Caley, Ruby will never bother you again, she has more important things to do with her life. We want no money from you, we don't want anything from you.'

'Is this true, Ruby?'

Ruby remained on her knees, nodding her head, and after a moment he left. Juda stood behind her.

'You never do anything that'll cause such pain again, Ruby, you hear me?'

'Yes, Aunt Juda,' she whispered.

'You take in evil and it will possess you, do you understand? You got power, child, and it must not be used for the darkness, or darkness will seep into your soul and you will become its slave. You hear me?'

Ruby nodded, and then watched as her aunt eased her bulk on to her knees beside her.

'You ask forgiveness now, Ruby.'

Ruby clasped her hands together. 'What if we could get so much money, Aunt Juda, that'd help so many?'

'We don't ever want devil's money because he's sly and he always wants to be repaid. You must never be in debt to the devil. I've seen a woman who owes him, I don't ever want that to happen to you. You got a future ahead of you, but you have to obey the spirits and take care of our own, just like Queen Marie.'

Ruby clasped her hands tighter, and whispered to Juda that she was afraid.

'We all are, honey, every living soul is frightened at

some point in their lives, but you can help guide people through that fear. You got to respect that power, never abuse it; love it and it will do good. Mr Caley will pay his own dues, you care only about your own, Ruby.'

Errol was rubbing his head, his bell-boy's hat in his hands. 'I love Ruby Corbello, I have loved her since high school, but she don't seem to know I exist. Sometimes she walks past me on her way to Fryer Jones's bar, swishing her hips, smiling that smile. I know she's out of my league, I know that, but it won't stop my heart fluttering like I was having some kind of attack. That is what she can do to me, make my heart beat faster than it should.'

Rosie nodded. 'I know how you feel, I felt that way about someone for a long time. In fact I never would have believed he would love me, that's how low my self-esteem was, Errol, but you know, two nights ago he asked me to marry him.'

'You jibing me? Someone wants to marry you?' He was wide-eyed with astonishment, not realizing the insult. To his mind, Rosie was so far removed from his beautiful Ruby Corbello it was hard for him to accept that anyone could love the fat woman who sat beside him. It made Rosie laugh.

'I am telling you the truth.'

'Maybe, Miss Rosie, it's different for you, you maybe don't understand about *desire*.'

'Errol, you believe me. Fat, thin, ugly or beautiful, everyone finds their partner, and he or she becomes the most beautiful creature in the whole wide world,' Rosie said with good humour.

'You don't understand, do you? You see, Ruby Corbello really is the most perfect woman God created. She's a goddess.'

'That worked as a maid for Mr and Mrs Brown until she was fired for thieving, and now is sweeping up hair off some floor. Some goddess, Errol.' Rosie paused. 'All I want to know is if you somehow helped Ruby Corbello pass over a package to Miss Anna Louise Caley, and if you knew what was in the package. You can be real honest with me because right now there are no police involved.'

Rooney returned to the hotel. He'd not been able to contact his cop as he was on patrol duty, but was told to call after lunch when he would be back in the office. Nor had he had any joy with the bell-boy, who'd been tight-mouthed, so it had been a pretty tedious morning so far. There was a message at the desk for him to call up to Lorraine's room.

Rosie opened Lorraine's hotel room door. She had a smug look on her face, so Rooney guessed she'd found out something, but she remained silent.

Lorraine came out of the bathroom looking worn out. 'Right, I'll start. My morning so far has been heavy, and pretty unproductive. Tilda Brown's father broke down when he saw the playhouse he'd built for her to which she was going to bring her children to play – and that was the high point. The rest has been downhill, but I've still got a few more "close" friends to speak to. I hope they are more forthcoming than her local bible-thumper who said, and I quote, "Tilda Brown was an example to every young teenager. She was joyful, enthusiastic and ready to help anyone in need." That this joyful bundle tied her own dressing-gown cord to the curtain rail and hanged herself seems to have escaped him. Only one kid, part of the choir that Tilda Brown used to sing in, boy called Eddie Mellor, said she had changed over the past six months. She used to be much more outgoing and friendly, but she had hardly spoken a word to anyone, and seemed to him to be in a very nervous state.'

Rooney coughed. 'You mind if I say something?'

'Sure, go ahead.'

'Well, we're hired to trace Anna Louise Caley, and you seem to have got side-tracked by this Tilda Brown girl.'

'You saying I'm wasting my time, is that it, Bill?'

'No, but we seem to be side-tracking, that's all.'

Rosie told them how she had gone to the hotel, and had questioned Errol.

'I did that too,' Rooney muttered.

'I know, I'd hoped I'd see you there,' Rosie beamed at him.

'I just got better results than you, because me and Errol had a good long conversation. He admitted that he had passed a note to Mr Caley, so he was lying about swimming, or maybe not exactly lying, just using it to cover up the fact that he was meeting Ruby Corbello. He said she had a conversation with Mr Caley, and after Caley had gone back to his room, Anna Louise saw him and Ruby talking in the courtyard; she beckoned to Ruby to come up, and Ruby asked him to smuggle her up the backstairs. This was, he said, around six o'clock. She was with Anna Louise for only ten minutes, and left the same way she had come in. And he said she was in a mighty hurry. Something we didn't know before is that Errol saw Ruby Corbello again later that night, the night Anna Louise went missing, and it'd have been about seven-thirty, so she returned to the hotel.'

506

Lorraine flicked through her old note-book. 'The Caleys said they went down to eat around that time, in the hotel restaurant.'

Rosie nodded. 'Ruby, he said, was ducking and diving round the palm trees in the back of the courtyard. He's in love with her and so he gets all angry as he thinks she's meeting up with one of the other boys working at the hotel. Errol follows her, and she's looking up at Anna Louise Caley who is bending over her balcony. Which means she was still in her room at seven-thirty.'

'Yes, and?' asked Lorraine impatiently.

'Well, by the time Errol got to the balcony, or was standing underneath it, there was no sign of either of them, and he was on duty so he had to get back out front.'

Lorraine sighed. 'That's it?'

'Yep. Now, this is just supposition, but Anna Louise could have also used the servants' stairway, just like Ruby Corbello, to leave the hotel. That would mean she never passed the front desk, never took the elevator. It exits right round the back of the hotel near to the garbage collection, and a car could have been waiting for her.'

'Mmm,' Lorraine said, frowning as she crossed to her desk and searched around the top. 'Need to know how long it takes from the hotel to Ruby Corbello's house.'

Rooney and Rosie glanced at each other.

Lorraine was flicking through the maps and guides, chucking them aside, hunting for the street map she'd seen of the tourist attractions.

'If Ruby Corbello left that hotel at six-fifteen, then returned at seven-thirty, that gives her just over an hour to make that doll, wrap it up, and take it back to Anna Louise.'

'Unless she made it at Fryer Jones's place,' Rooney said.

507

Lorraine found the map and squinted over the small print. Then, tracing the route with her finger, she tapped impatiently on the table.

'Maybe she did make it at Fryer Jones's. If she didn't, it was quite a schlep to her house unless . . .'

'Somebody drove her there,' Rosie suggested.

'Yes, somebody drove her.'

All three of them stood by the trash cans outside the staff entrance of the Hotel Cavagnal. Rosie was to take the route to Fryer Jones's bar and return, Rooney was to do the run to the Corbellos'. They both asked Lorraine the same question.

'What are you going to do?'

'Talk to security. Okay, check watches and *move*!'

She was smiling as she watched them both charge off like kids at a sports day event. She noted how many people came and went via the staff entrance. Then she slipped inside and walked down a narrow corridor. A small staircase led off to the right at the far end, and she moved up the stairs until she came to a door marked, 'PRIVATE – NO ENTRANCE TO ANY UNAUTHORIZED PERSON'. Lorraine opened the door; standing in front of it was a security guard. He didn't even hear the door close behind him, as Lorraine continued up another flight of stairs till she reached Robert Caley's floor. She had seen no one, had not been stopped at any point, and she did a U-turn back the way she came. Again she saw no one, but when she opened the door to leave, a security guard turned, frowning.

'You staff here?'

'No, I'm a guest,' Lorraine said briskly, and gave the number of the suite she had used. He held up his hand, asked her name and dialled reception. When it was confirmed that the suite had been booked for Lorraine Page by Mr Robert Caley, he apologized but warned her that she should not have used the private staircase, it was for staff only.

'I'm very impressed with the hotel security,' she said, smiling.

He gave a small nod of his head.

'Is this exit covered at all times?'

'Yes, ma'am.'

'Day and night?'

'Yes, ma'am.'

'How many officers are on security?'

'Three, ma'am, we work in shifts.'

'How long have you worked here?'

'Five years.'

She nodded and kept smiling. 'You were here then when Anna Louise Caley went missing?'

'Yes, I was.'

'I am employed by Mr Caley to trace his daughter, you were obviously questioned, as I believe most of the staff were.'

'Yes, I was.'

Lorraine turned to face the staff door. 'Maybe she left the hotel this way, that is why no one saw her leaving. Do you think it possible?'

He shrugged, not committing himself.

'You have to take the odd break, so it could have happened?'

'Guess so. Like you said, we take breaks, but usually we try and cover for each other.'

She smiled, and turned to face the small yard. 'Do cars ever park down here?'

'No, no parking allowed. If anyone parks here they get towed.'

'But you could get picked up from here easily.'

509

'Yeah, picking someone up is not parking, and some of the women working at night like to be met. There's a lot of drunk guys in the French Quarter.'

'I'm sorry, what did you say?'

'The women like to feel safe.'

'Is there a particular cab firm they use?'

'Yeah, Gordon's Cabs, staff use Gordon's Cabs.'

Lorraine nodded. 'But not the guests?'

He smiled. 'No, ma'am, they not very luxurious. Just two brothers, one of 'em used to work here. You want their number?'

'Thank you,' Lorraine said pleasantly, and passed him ten bucks. He pocketed it fast, then took out a biro and jotted down a number on the back of a hotel card.

'Thank you, I'm expecting two friends shortly. A plump woman and a big, red-faced man. Could you tell them to come up to my suite?'

Lorraine walked out on to the street and then round to the front lobby of the hotel. She had been lucky that Robert Caley had booked the suite for her. She got her key from reception, asking if Mr Caley was in his suite, and was very relieved to be told he was not. She then took the elevator to her floor. The room was wonderfully cool, and she sat on the bed and ordered some tea and cakes, then called Gordon's cab firm. There was an answer-machine on but she left no message, deciding she'd call again. Her eyes kept drifting to the closed door to the adjoining suite, her body remembering the night she had spent there. She walked slowly towards it, knowing she would have to face Caley sooner or later. It was locked, and she pressed her face against the white glossy wood door with relief. But she couldn't just forget their closeness, dismiss it, because it had been real. She had felt so loved for that night. Then she felt scared because she remembered Juda's words about her being

510

without love, and having been without it for a long time, and the sadness welled up inside her. That night had not been anything to do with love, but lust, and she was sure that Robert Caley had used her because he had been protecting himself, covering his tracks so she could not unearth the truth of how he had killed his daughter. She stepped briskly away from the door. She had said it to herself earlier, now she said it out loud, pointing to the adjoining bedroom door.

'I am going to nail you, Robert Caley.'

CHAPTER 18

ROSIE HAD returned and was surveying the suite as the tea Lorraine had ordered arrived.

'My, this is very nice, I could move in here,' Rosie said admiringly, looking from the hangings over the bed to the luxurious bathroom.

Lorraine poured tea for them both. 'How long did it take you?'

'I walked there in forty-five minutes. If I'd been running I could have done it in less. Bar was jumping by the way, great music and a group outside drinking beer, kids mostly. This town's hotting up, an' I don't mean the weather.'

Rooney did not appear for another twenty minutes, and he was hot and sweating. He sank on to the bed with a moan, paying no attention to the decor of the suite.

'Fucking hot out there. Knock off ten minutes trying to flag down a cab, streets are crowded, and Mardi Gras's not even started yet. They got clowns walking around passing out leaflets, and there was a couple of jams, but I'd say if Ruby had a clear night she could get there and back in just less than an hour.'

'Which does not give her long to make the doll,' Lorraine said moodily.

'So she did it at Fryer's,' Rosie said, passing Rooney a cup of tea.

'It wasn't exactly well made,' Rooney said.

Lorraine sighed. 'You know, we're just kind of grasping at straws, trying to make the jigsaw pieces fit together.'

'You're trying to get her to Tilda Brown's house, right?' Rooney said, and she nodded.

'But nobody saw her there either, just like nobody saw her leave here, no cab firm picked her up, she didn't have a purse on her.'

'We've got a possible.'

'Possible what?' Rosie asked.

'Cab firm. The staff use these two brothers for late-night pick-ups, but they're not listed in Information, I've checked. I think they're just two guys with a couple of cars, so they're probably working without a licence. You want to check them out, Rosie? Maybe see them face to face. And when you've finished your tea, Bill, call that cop and get over to Fryer's. Check out the necklace and put a feeler out about whether or not Ruby was there on the night of the fifteenth.'

Lorraine yawned, she felt tired and depressed, as if they were going round and round in circles. Time was moving, they had only five days left, and they all knew it. Bill and Rosie took off without complaint.

Lorraine hadn't meant to fall asleep, she meant to let it all run by in her mind, sift over everything they had come up with so far. She didn't hear the key turning in the connecting door, which opened so silently she was unaware that Robert Caley had walked into the room.

He stroked her cheek with one finger, and she woke with a start.

'Hi! I was beginning to think I'd never see you again.'

She eased herself up, blushing.

'You never return my calls, do you know how many times I have tried to see you, talk to you? In fact, the receptionist at your hotel knows me so well I don't even have to say my name.'

'I'm sorry, but I've been caught up.'

He sat on a chair opposite the bed. He was wearing a white collarless shirt and jeans, with the loafers she liked.

'I wanted to take you to one of the riverboats, I've wanted to take you to a whole lot of places.'

'Well, I am here to work you know, Robert.'

'Oh, I know that, but if you don't want to see me, why don't you come out and say so?'

'Things keep on getting in the way.'

He cocked his head to one side. 'How about dinner tonight?'

'I don't think so.' She wouldn't look at him.

'You don't think so? Do I take it that you have other engagements? What do you mean, you don't think so?'

She chewed her lip. He stared at her, trying to fathom her out, and then leaned forward. 'It would be nice to celebrate with someone.'

She looked up. 'Celebrate?'

He nodded. 'Casino development's going ahead. An out-of-town group got the licence, but because I had the land I'm in as a partner. Dulay switched sides, but I've got him and his group eating right out of my hand. So the big bucks are going to start rolling in.'

'How is Elizabeth?' she interrupted.

'I don't know. I told you the last time I saw you – I've left her. I've been here since then, waiting for you behind that connecting door!'

'Have you?' Lorraine eased her legs from the bed and pressed her feet into the carpet, staring down at her toes. She took a deep breath and slowly raised her head to meet his eyes. 'You are a very good liar, Mr Caley, one of the best I have ever come across.'

'What?'

514

'You heard me, you are a liar.'

He leaned back, turning his palms up. 'What have I lied about?'

She eased herself from the bed and walked to the dressing table. He reached to touch her but she side-stepped his outstretched hand. She began to brush her hair, keeping eye contact via the mirror. 'What have you lied about? Well, let's try Ruby Corbello for one.'

He leaned back again slightly but he didn't take his eyes off her face.

'She got a message to you, via the bell-boy Errol, for you to meet at the swimming pool. That would be on the night of February fifteenth last year, and in case it has slipped your memory, that was also the night your daughter, or adopted daughter, went missing.'

He looked away, showing no emotion at all.

'Ruby had a diary, didn't she? Tilda Brown's diary, and in this teenager's diary it gave explicit details of her sex life with you. *You*, Mr Caley! So that kiss on the tennis courts wasn't quite as innocent as you made out, was it?'

He shrugged his shoulders and then leaned on his elbow, his hand partly covering his face, but his eyes were steady and didn't flinch from her angry gaze.

'What have you got to say to that?'

'Not a lot, Lorraine, but if you want me to go into details then I will. Tilda Brown was not under age, she was eighteen years old. In fact, she made all the moves, and as you are more than aware of my wife's physical problems, not to mention her mental state, having a young, pretty and nubile girl creeping into your bedroom at night is hard to ignore, let alone the hard-on she gave me. So I fucked her. She liked it, I liked it, and there is no more to be said.'

'She also committed suicide,' snapped Lorraine.

'I know, and I am deeply sorry about it, but I don't

see that my sexual relationship with her can have anything to do with it.'

'Don't you?'

'No, I don't, but you obviously do. So if you have something to say, say it.'

Lorraine threw down her hairbrush. 'Your daughter was fighting Tilda Brown for your affections, and you knew it. What happened, you get a kick out of that as well? As you pointed out to me, Anna Louise was not your daughter anyway, so were you also fucking her?'

'No, I wasn't. Just Tilda and a few other lady friends, you want their names?' He sprang to his feet, and now she could see how angry he was. A small muscle at the side of his neck was twitching. 'I lied to shield Tilda. She was already deeply distressed by Anna Louise's disappearance, and I wanted to protect her from further unnecessary questions by the police and investigators.'

'To shield Tilda or yourself?'

'Does it matter?'

Lorraine snapped open her briefcase and took out the towel with the doll in it.

'Unwrap it, have a look, I think your little blackmailing friend, Ruby Corbello, made that for your daughter to give to your girlfriend Tilda. Go on, open it, Robert. As you said, she was eighteen, she knew what she was doing. What you didn't say was just how long you had been having a sexual relationship with her. She was your daughter's childhood friend, wasn't she?'

He slapped her face, and she picked up the brush and swiped him across the cheek. He stepped back. 'My, that was a nice left hook, but then you're a tough lady, aren't you? And you have the scars to prove it. A whore, a drunkard . . . I should have asked for a blood test before I fucked you, shouldn't I?'

'You bastard!' she snapped.

516

'Am I? And what are you? At least I know with someone as young as Tilda she's unlikely to be diseased.'

She kicked him hard in the groin. He gasped and clutched at himself, leaning forward. 'I can also take care of myself, Mr Caley. You want to say shit to me, you'll get it back, which is something else maybe a young innocent kid couldn't do. Now look at the doll.'

He was wincing with pain, still bent forward, as she flipped open the towel to show the voodoo doll.

'Do you know if Ruby Corbello made this for your daughter?'

''Course I fucking don't, it's disgusting!'

'So are you. I found this in Tilda's bedroom, hidden in a tennis racquet case.'

He turned back to sit on the bed. 'Anna Louise wouldn't do something as sick as that. Her mother, maybe. In fact, if you know who made it I'll order one for Elizabeth.'

'You think it's funny?'

'No, I don't, I don't know what the hell to think, and with this burning fucking pain in my testicles it's tough thinking about anything right now. What the hell did you kick me in the nuts for?'

Lorraine rewrapped the doll. 'You've got away with stealing from her trust fund. You're a thief, Robert Caley.'

He laughed. 'Bullshit, I'll be able to pay every cent back. I've even offered to, but Lloyd Dulay wouldn't hear of it, and it's his cash, Lorraine. So who's stealing from whom?'

'You stole Tilda Brown's innocence.'

He threw his head back, laughing. 'Did I? So what was that you told me about her and Anna Louise getting gang-banged at some club? Lorraine, you are thrashing around trying to find something, anything, to prove that I am . . . what? What are you trying to prove I am?'

'A thief.'

517

He laughed. 'I admit it. Right, what next? Oh, of course, a child molester, right, that's the second thing, anything else?'

'A murderer, maybe.'

He straightened up, still nursing himself between the legs. 'Who did I murder, Lorraine? Anna Louise, is that what you are trying to prove?'

She folded her arms.

'I didn't kill my daughter, I know no reason why she disappeared off the face of the earth unless it was to get away from her fucking mother, like I am doing. I admit I used Anna Louise's trust fund, but I had every right, I had given the best years of my life to Elizabeth, and to her daughter. I looked out for that child from the day she was born, and I had to be satisfied with that bitch doling out money as if I was a hired hand. It was me that built up her properties, worth fuck-all when I found them, now valued at millions. It was me that covered for her drinking, her drugs, me that saved her life, not once but Christ knows how many times, and I was never shown an ounce of respect. I have been cross-questioned, interviewed, interrogated by cops and people like you, that in the end are all pursuing the investigation for money. But you, you win the prize. You're so desperate for that one million bucks my crazy wife offered, you will try anything, and I know why. You have only five more days to crack this case. You even fucked me to get more information. You, sweetheart, are the lowest of them all. Now get your stinking piece of evidence and get out of here before I throw you out on your ass, you whore!'

He was so angry he was panting, but she didn't back down, instead she smiled at him.

'Takes one to know one, Robert.' She threw a right upper cut, and he stepped back and let go with a body punch that made her gasp and totter backwards, but she

518

pushed herself off the wall, ready to go at him again. She walked into his fist, catching her right eye. He froze, not wanting to brawl with her, and that was his mistake. Lorraine brought her knee up, crunching him yet again, and then she punched him in the face so hard she felt her knuckles split open on his teeth. He sank to his knees, unable to make a sound.

She picked up her briefcase, shoved the doll inside and snapped it closed. She tossed twenty bucks on to his moaning, huddled figure. 'That's for the tea.'

She was shaking her fist – it hurt her more than his punch to her eye. As she opened the door, the telephone rang. She hesitated and picked up the nearest extension to the door.

Rosie was so excited she was gasping. 'We got lucky. Nicky Gordon picked up a girl outside the staff exit of the hotel, he had just dropped off a regular.'

Lorraine interrupted Rosie, partly because Robert Caley was slowly getting to his feet, and partly because she was eager to know where the luck came in.

'Where did he take her?'

'Tilda Brown's.'

Rooney laid the steak over Lorraine's eye, which was now really swollen.

'Hey, if you think I look bad, you should see the other guy.'

Rosie was bandaging her knuckles, which were swollen, the skin split open. 'You might have a cracked knuckle, Lorraine,' she said.

'Bullshit, it's okay, I'm okay.' Lorraine struggled up and wove to the mirror, she took one look and felt as if she was going to faint; her right eye was closed and already dark bruising was showing above and below.

519

'Well, I look really good, didn't think it was this bad. Anyway, let's not waste any more time.'

Rosie flipped open her book. 'Reason he never reported it, or has never been questioned, is because he thought the girl was staff and she wore a head-scarf and dark glasses. She came out of the staff entrance as he dropped Mimi Lavette, a fifty-year-old chambermaid, off for the late shift. He was doing a U-turn when we think Anna Louise waved him down, gave him the address, and got impatient with him when he had to double-check it. He got all nervous, even talking to me, just for the so-called reward. You were right, he hasn't got a taxi licence, and judging from the look of the vehicle I'd say that it's not taxed or insured neither.'

Lorraine pressed the steak to her eye as the telephone rang. Rosie answered, told the caller to hang on, and for a moment Lorraine thought it might be Robert Caley, but it was the cop, Harris Harper. He couldn't see Rooney until the morning.

Lorraine suggested they leave visiting Fryer's bar until the following day. Returning to Tilda Brown's home had to be their first priority.

Rosie remained in the car as Rooney and Lorraine went up the steps and rang the bell which echoed through the dark hallway. Lorraine peered in through the glass as Rooney rang again. A maid turned on the hall lights and opened the door.

'I need to speak urgently to Mr or Mrs Brown.'

''Fraid they are not at home.'

'When will they be back?'

'They is dining with friends.'

Lorraine, Rooney and her driver François sat in the

520

car for over an hour. At last they saw the headlamps of a car heading towards them.

'Here they come, I hope.'

They watched the car slow down and swerve past them to take a left-hand turn into the drive. Lorraine dug François in the back. 'Go after them, we don't want them to refuse us entry.'

Mr and Mrs Brown turned, startled, as Lorraine got out of the car.

'Mr Brown, I'm so sorry, but I need to speak to you.'

Half an hour later, Mr and Mrs Brown were still adamant that Tilda, on the night of 15 February, had remained in her room watching her own TV. She had not eaten with them but had had a tray sent up at 7.30. They had both gone up to say goodnight at 10.30. She had not left her room, no one had called by and no one had telephoned. All this had been stated over and over many times and Mr and Mrs Brown were tired and becoming irritated.

'Could I just go to her room, please?'

Rooney and Lorraine stood in the centre of the dead girl's bedroom as Mr Brown opened the doors on to the low, metal-railed balcony. Mrs Brown had started weeping again, and her husband was angry at the intrusion, but Lorraine refused to leave. Rooney was embarrassed at the couple's obvious distress, and he was very uneasy. Lorraine looked bad, her bruised eye had swollen and was still closed.

'Maybe we leave it until the morning,' he had said quietly.

'No. If that cab driver was telling the truth, then Anna Louise Caley came here that night.' Lorraine stepped out on to the balcony and pointed to a narrow metal stairway

521

leading down to the garden. 'You don't have a dog, do you?'

'No, we don't.'

She looked across the garden. 'So if someone did come here at night and crossed the lawns, they could easily walk up to this balcony?'

'Yes, I suppose so, but why would they want to?'

'If they didn't want to be seen, Mr Brown, and if they also knew the layout of the house, knew by looking up at this window that Tilda was here, someone could have come and gone?'

Mr Brown pursed his lips and then suddenly rounded on Lorraine. 'What exactly are you trying to suggest? That my daughter had someone up here, someone she didn't want us to see?'

'No, Mr Brown, maybe that someone did not want to be seen. Could you leave us alone for ten minutes? I'd appreciate it.'

The Browns left Rooney and Lorraine alone, but it was quite obvious they did not approve, and said they would wait in the drawing room for ten minutes and no more. As the door closed, Lorraine turned to Rooney.

'What you thinking?'

He sat down on the dead girl's bed. 'Not a lot, so Anna Louise came here and left. We got almost four missing hours before Robert Caley and his wife contacted the police, so she could have met with Tilda Brown, but after that God only knows what happened to her.'

Lorraine picked up the white Polar bear, and tossed it back on to the bed. 'If she left, she didn't take a cab, no record of her doing so, and the taxi she came in had already left. Bill, what if she never left here?'

'What?'

Lorraine walked out on to the balcony and stared across the gardens. Just to her right was the playhouse, the place where the two girls had played as children, now locked up, and suddenly Lorraine knew. The hairs on the back of her neck prickled.

'I don't think she did.'

'What?' It was Rooney's turn now.

'Come on downstairs, Bill.'

Mr and Mrs Brown sat in their drawing room in subdued but angry silence as Lorraine walked in, but before they could ask her to leave she pointed to the window with its expensive slatted blinds.

'The playhouse in the garden, I noticed it was padlocked, can you tell me why?'

Mrs Brown looked at her husband in confusion, but he only frowned in response.

'Did you padlock it, Mr Brown?'

'Not that I can recall. Did you, honey?'

'No, I thought perhaps you had done it. Maybe Tilda did.'

He stood up. 'I didn't, in fact I avoid looking at the thing, it brings back such memories. Are you sure? Padlocked?'

Lorraine shrugged. 'Well, I saw the chain when I was here in daylight, maybe I'm wrong. Do you have a flashlight?'

Rooney plodded after Lorraine, Mr Brown walked ahead with the light.

'Can you tell me what the fuck we're doing, Lorraine?' Rooney whispered.

'You tell me. Everybody else on this street has security cameras, they don't, they leave their gates open and put a padlock on a kids' playhouse? Doesn't make sense.'

The faint beam of the flashlight showed there was a padlock, and quite a heavy one.

'Perhaps the gardener is storing equipment in there?' Mr Brown suggested.

'Do you have bolt-cutters or something we can get the lock open with?'

'Why?' asked Mr Brown.

Lorraine hesitated. 'I want to see inside.'

It was another ten minutes before they had prised open one of the links in the thick chain. Lorraine eased back the child-size door and stooped low to enter.

'Can you shine the light inside, please?'

Two chairs and a small matching table set with plastic tea cups and saucers, and a tiny cot-like bed with two dolls tucked under a blanket were all that could fit inside.

'There's nothing here,' Rooney said.

Lorraine took the flashlight from Mr Brown and shone it around the house, then down to the plastic sheeting that covered the floor.

'Can you smell anything, Bill?'

Rooney sniffed, leaning in from the tiny door. 'Just mildew.'

'I'm rather cold,' Mr Brown said, standing outside, behind Rooney. Lorraine suggested he return to the house, and after hesitating a moment he walked away. She shone the yellow beam slowly over the interior, sniffing, until she got down on her knees and sniffed closer to the ground.

'Mildew, you sure?'

Rooney sighed, and bent low to get inside. He sniffed. 'Yeah, mildew, like moss or mould or something, but that's natural. It must be hot as hell when the sun shines inside here, it's all plastic and it'll sweat with the heat. What you doing?'

'Hold the goddamned light, Bill, I'm gonna pull back the ground-sheet.'

'For God's sake, Lorraine, why don't we come back in the morning?'

'Because we're here now, so do as I say.'

Rooney was on his hands and knees, shining the flashlight as Lorraine began to pull back the plastic ground-sheet. She pushed the little chairs and table aside, and crawling on all-fours, dragged back the sheet. She sat back on her heels, reached over to the table and took one of the small plastic plates.

'What you doing?'

'Digging, what do you think it looks like? Keep the light up for chrissakes, I can't see.'

Rooney crouched down, watching as she scraped the earth away from beneath the ground-sheet.

'Ground would be dry in here. It was February, right? So if something was buried under this sheet it'd stay dry, and being inside, you said it stinks of mildew. Well, if a body was hidden under here we'd expect a lot of mould, same smell as mildew.'

Rooney held up the torch, then moved its beam to spread further over the tiny floor space, leaving Lorraine in darkness.

'What you doing?'

'Looking for droppings, rats'd be clawing their way in here if there was a body, and there's nothing, Lorraine. Plus they got raccoons in these parts, they'd have torn the place apart.'

She continued digging with the plastic dish, her hands and nails filthy, and Rooney shone the torch, watching. One inch down, two inches down, and still she shovelled the earth, making a deep hole. Then the beam from the flashlight began to fade.

'Batteries are running out,' he said.

Lorraine began to scratch and dig the earth with her bare hands, and then she sat back. 'There's something here, come closer. For God's sake, get closer, I can't see. And it'd help if you gave me a hand.'

Rooney crawled towards her, the flashlight beam now just a faint yellow. 'What is it?'

'I dunno, I can't fucking see. You dig, I'll hold the light.' She leaned back and took it from him as he began to dig harder. He used one of the plastic cups, scooping up the earth. Soil sprayed over Lorraine, and she brushed it aside.

'Shit! You're right, there is something.' Rooney dug for a few more minutes and then squinted at the hole. They could just see a corner section of a black plastic trash bag. Rooney lifted up his hand; white maggots were clinging to it, covering the cuffs of his jacket. 'Aw shit, there's millions of them, maggots, fucking white maggots.'

'Gimme the flashlight, I can't see a damned thing.'

Lorraine passed the light over and he shone it down into the hole he had sliced through the black plastic. As he carefully inched it aside they could see part of a skull in the yellow beam, the skin completely decomposed, but there was a portion of long blonde hair and what looked like a head-band.

'I think we just found Anna Louise Caley,' Rooney said softly.

'We also maybe just got one million dollars,' Lorraine added.

Rooney looked at her face, a black eye on one side and her scar running down the other. She looked like a prize fighter coming up for round ten.

'You don't give in easy, do you?'

526

'Nope, but then life's not that easy. Least, mine isn't.' She stood up, still having to bend as the roof of the house was so low. 'I'll go and see the Browns.'

They were still there at dawn, as the police put up their cordons and arc lamps. It took two hours for the entire body to be dug up. The corpse was wrapped in four layers of black garbage bags, sellotape wound round and round the bags, virtually mummifying the body. All that was left were scraps of rotting cloth. The corpse had been buried almost a year, judging by the extent of the decomposition. Beetles and maggots were lodged in the eye sockets and the inside of the skull. There had been no terrible odour of death because all the gases had evaporated and the mummification of the body, wrapped tightly with no air, had dried all the body tissues. There was little left as a means to identify the body, but the dental records and possibly the fine, almost waist-length blonde hair. They would even find it difficult to determine what had caused the death.

By eleven o'clock the next morning, the dental records had been flown to the forensic laboratory from Los Angeles. The body was formally identified at 12.30. Anna Louise Caley had died approximately eleven months ago. She had been killed by a single blow to the back of her head, probably inflicted by a rounded, blunt-edged instrument.

Elizabeth Caley was informed at 12.45 p.m. that the body of her daughter had been recovered at Tilda Brown's home. She was also told that it had been discovered by Lorraine Page and her partner, Mr William Rooney. It was just after two the same afternoon that Lorraine and François drove back through the Garden District to the Caley residence.

'You want your bonus?' Elizabeth asked coldly. She looked as elegant as ever, and Lorraine was impressed at the woman's resilience.

'I will have all my reports typed up and sent to you, either in Los Angeles or here, whichever you prefer.'

'How did she die?' Elizabeth asked, lighting a cigarette.

'It's difficult to give you details at this stage, but she had a deep indentation on the back of her skull.'

Elizabeth inhaled. 'They brought a head-band, the police asked if I could identify it as Anna Louise's. It wasn't hers, it was mine.'

Lorraine checked over all the receipts of their expenses which Rosie had meticulously kept and clipped neatly together.

'I will send our details of costs for the trip to New Orleans to Phyllis, unless you would like them left here? Mrs Caley?'

Elizabeth stared out of the long window at the fig orchard. 'Send them to Phyllis, she'll pay you.'

Lorraine replaced the documents in her briefcase.

'Who killed her, Mrs Page?' Elizabeth asked quietly.

Lorraine hesitated. 'This is just supposition, because without her statement obviously we will never know exactly what happened.'

'So what do you think happened?'

'Well, your daughter was very jealous of Tilda Brown. Did you know she was having a sexual relationship with your husband?'

Elizabeth arched one fine eyebrow, 'Well, I suppose he needed to get it someplace. It certainly wasn't from me.'

528

Lorraine looked away, Mrs Caley sickened her, there seemed no emotion in her whatsoever, she was calm, almost sarcastic.

'Go on, please. I'm paying you for this, so I might as well hear what you have to say.'

'Anna Louise seemed to be very jealous because she was in love with her adopted father, and the fight the two girls had before you and Anna Louise left Los Angeles was because your daughter had seen Tilda kissing or embracing Mr Caley.'

'The cheap bastard,' Elizabeth said bitterly, stubbing out her cigarette.

Lorraine licked her lips. Her head was throbbing and her eye, although now less swollen, was still painful; moreover she had been up all night.

'Go on, Mrs Page,' Elizabeth snapped.

'Well, after you arrived at your hotel that afternoon of February fifteenth, Tilda . . .'

Elizabeth crossed to the window and stood gazing out at the trees as Lorraine continued.

'I know that your husband met with a Ruby Corbello, a girl that used to be a maid at Tilda Brown's. She was trying to blackmail him.'

'What?'

'She had found Tilda Brown's diary and she wanted to get money for it. The diary contained confirmation that Tilda and your husband were having a relationship.'

'You read this diary?' Elizabeth asked.

'No, I did not. I have not seen the diary, but your husband has admitted that he did meet with Miss Corbello, and she did give him the diary. He paid her two hundred dollars for it.'

Elizabeth laughed. 'Cheap at the price, silly child could have asked for a lot more. Go on, Mrs Page.'

'Ruby Corbello was then led via the staff entrance up

to Anna Louise's suite. She left the hotel after ten minutes, but was seen back at the hotel, in the courtyard beneath your daughter's balcony. I think your daughter asked Ruby Corbello to make her a doll, a voodoo doll in the shape of Tilda Brown. She possibly passed over a photograph of Tilda to use as its face, and may have paid Ruby Corbello, but she has not admitted that she did make the doll, and without your daughter's statement, it would be difficult to prove.'

Elizabeth lit another cigarette. Lorraine noticed her hand was shaking, but otherwise she remained impassive, gesturing for Lorraine to continue.

'I traced a cab company, not a licensed company, but one used by the staff at the hotel to ferry them back home when they were working late. A driver recalls collecting a young woman from the hotel and taking her to Tilda Brown's house on the night of February fifteenth last year.' Lorraine reached over and sipped some iced tea that had been brought in when she arrived. 'That was the last sighting of your daughter, nobody ever saw her again. I think she knew Tilda's house so well that she did not enter via the front door but climbed up on to the balcony which is only on the first floor, and saw Tilda there. Her parents have stated that Tilda never left her bedroom that night, so possibly they met at around seven forty-five.'

Elizabeth sat down, running her hand down her slim-fitting skirt, crossing her ankles. 'Go on, please.'

Lorraine sighed, her head really throbbing now. 'How do we know what exactly happened? They were young, angry with each other, jealous, and both had been to Juda Salina on numerous occasions for tarot reading or whatever. Both girls, having been brought up here, were obviously aware of voodoo, Anna Louise perhaps because of your connections.'

'My connections?' Elizabeth said sharply.

'You did play Marie Laveau, you even have a portrait of yourself in the role in the house in Los Angeles. So Anna Louise must have been aware of the voodoo culture. Perhaps they were both afraid of it, I don't really know, but I think Anna Louise wanted to scare Tilda, wanted to frighten her badly. Perhaps she showed her the doll and that started it, who knows, but they had fought before. In fact, when I interviewed Tilda she described how Anna Louise had struck her and punched and scratched her. So these two girls had fought before – perhaps that night they did again, and perhaps Tilda picked up something, a tennis racquet maybe? And struck out at Anna Louise.'

As Lorraine opened her cigarettes and lit one, Elizabeth remained silent, head bowed slightly.

'Perhaps Anna Louise was leaving, facing the balcony, and Tilda struck her from behind. There were stains on the carpet in that area, but after Tilda's suicide the carpet was cleaned so we will never know if there had been blood there or not.'

Elizabeth looked blankly to the window.

'I think Tilda went down to the kitchen for some plastic bags straight away because the body was wrapped very tightly soon after death. She then used reels and reels of sellotape to seal the bags around the body. She may have hidden it in her room, waited until the following morning, and could have dropped it over the balcony and dragged it to the playhouse. At some point she dug the grave, and buried Anna Louise, then put a padlock on the door and . . .'

'Left my baby rotting,' Elizabeth said softly.

'Yes. She did not return to college, she remained with her family, and from people I have interviewed I understand she became nervous and withdrawn, probably

531

living in a state of terror that the body would be found. I think my visit to her must have scared her very much because someone new was making enquiries after all that time. I think I was the only one who had discovered not only the two girls' sexual permissiveness, but also their jealousy. Tilda became very upset when I interviewed her but did not give me any indication she had played a part in Anna Louise's murder.'

'Played a part? Dear God, she killed her!'

'I would say the surrounding pressures and the—'

'Please don't excuse the girl, she murdered my daughter.'

'Yes, she did.'

Elizabeth stood up, pressing her hands down her sides, then brushed one across the crease in her skirt. 'So, it's over.'

Lorraine also stood up. She swayed, feeling faint, and had to hold on to the arm of the chair.

'Are you all right?' Elizabeth asked, looking directly at Lorraine for almost the first time since she had arrived.

'I am very tired.'

'What happened to your face?'

'Oh, I bumped into a door, it's nothing, but I would like to leave now.'

Elizabeth crossed to an escritoire and opened it. She sat down on one of the delicate English chairs and drew out a cheque-book. Lorraine collected her jacket and picked up her briefcase.

'Do you still have the doll, Mrs Page?'

'Yes, yes, I do.'

'You didn't give it to the police?'

'No.'

'Would you leave it here? I don't think it is necessary for it to be seen by anyone else.'

Lorraine opened her case again.

'Why didn't you give it to the police if I might ask?'

'Well, it is only circumstantial evidence.'

'My, my we are so professional, aren't we?'

Lorraine put down the doll, still wrapped in the hotel towel.

Ellzabeth ripped out the cheque and blew on it to dry the ink. She then held it out at arm's length. 'Your bonus, Mrs Page.'

Lorraine walked the few paces towards Mrs Caley and took the cheque. She glanced at the amount: one million dollars.

'It won't bounce,' Elizabeth said as she closed the lid of her desk. Then, without turning back, she picked up the doll and walked to the door.

'The maid will show you out, Mrs Page. Thank you very much.'

Lorraine remained standing, staring at the cheque as the click-click of Elizabeth Caley's high heels died away on the hall tiles.

Missy appeared and gestured for Lorraine to go with her to the front door. By now Elizabeth was almost at the top of the sweeping staircase, but she didn't look back as Lorraine left.

Elizabeth watched her depart in her car with her driver, and then let the curtain fall back into place. She crossed to the bureau. The head-band was still in the plastic bag the police had brought it in, and she touched it with one delicate finger, before picking it up and tossing it into the wastepaper basket. She crossed to the bed where she had placed the doll and slowly unwrapped it, staring down at the hideous face with Tilda Brown's photograph, the pin stuck through the doll's left eye. She picked it up, carried it to the old wide fireplace, bent down and set it on the bars of the empty grate. She emptied an entire bottle of nail varnish remover over it before she struck a match and set it alight. She stood there as the flames caught and burnt it quickly; last to blacken and melt was the small plastic doll's head with Tilda Brown's face.

Elizabeth waited until all that was left were charred ashes and the acrid smell of burnt plastic. She then went to her bedside and picked up Anna Louise's photograph and held it to her chest. She lay down, clutching the picture, her face impassive, but gradually her eyes filled with tears and they trickled down her cheeks, until she sobbed quietly, saying her daughter's name over and over again, whispering that she was sorry, so very sorry.

Robert Caley had asked to see the body or what was left of it, but nothing had prepared him for the blackened, decomposed corpse. He was shocked and distressed, staying no more than a few moments. Like his wife, he wept for Anna Louise. He also asked for her forgiveness, knowing that he had in many ways been to blame. He was now on his way to accomplishing everything he had dreamed about, and he would without doubt be a very rich man, but he felt empty, drained and ashamed. Two young girls had died as a result of his foolishness and selfishness. The woman he could love had seen him for what he was, and he knew the damage was irreparable. Just thinking of her made him look towards the connecting bedroom door, and his heart thudded as it opened.

'Excuse me, Mr Caley, but the manager has asked if you will still be requiring the double suite as . . .'

'No, no, I will also be leaving by tonight.'

'Shall I tell the manager then, Mr Caley? Only with Carnival coming up . . .'

'Yes, please, thank you.'

The maid shut the door and locked it, and he packed his bags, wanting to get out as soon as possible.

The bell-boy was carrying them to his car when Saffron Dulay drove up in her convertible Rolls Corniche.

'Honey, you're not leavin', are you?'

He looked at her as she slid out of the driving seat and sashayed towards him, arms held out for a hug. Golden-brown, golden-haired, she reminded him of Anna Louise.

'Daddy, give me a hug, give me a big bear hug and tell me you love me lots, lots and whole lots.'

Caley wrapped his arms around Saffron; he was crying.

'Shush now, honey, I know, I know they found her,' Saffron cooed, stroking his head.

He turned away, embarrassed by his tears, and she drew him close.

'Now, you're not leaving, are you? Not when I have come all this way to see you, and Daddy and you being in business together, you are not upping and leaving, you have to celebrate.'

Saffron had already dismissed Anna Louise's death. That was over, that was all in the past. She saw him waver, hesitate, and she turned to the bell-boy.

'Put Mr Caley's bags in my car, would you?' She gave him that wide, frosty smile. 'Hey, we are going to have a ball, it's just starting, it's Mardi Gras!'

She walked around to the driving seat as his luggage was placed in the trunk, slipping on her dark glasses as she started up the engine.

'My daddy says you've gone and left that lush you been tied to for more than twenty years. That true, Robert?'

He nodded, getting in beside her, and like her he

535

slipped on his dark shades as they eased out into the traffic. They headed towards Esplanade, Robert with his arm lying loosely along the seat, his hand stroking Saffron's slender neck.

'Oh yes, that is so nice.' She laughed.

Caley smiled, a sad smile, because he knew his life from now on would be filled with Saffrons. Money breeds money, breeds bastards.

Lorraine stared from the window of François's steaming hot car. She was sure Caley had not seen her, and she was glad, not because she looked bad, but because she might not have been able to hide her expression. Saffron's blonde head was tilted back, laughing, Robert Caley's hand resting at the nape of her neck. A golden couple, seemingly with no remorse, no pain and no grief. She was more than glad, because it made her angry that she had been such a fool to have felt something for him, even for a moment. He was not worth it, not worth another thought, and whatever she felt would soon pass. He would soon be forgotten, just like poor misguided Anna Louise, whose skeleton lay covered in the morgue.

Lorraine walked in as Rosie snapped her last case shut on her pink, frilled, nylon bedspread.

'Right, that's me packed. You know they want us out as soon as possible as they're booked out?'

'How long did you book the room for?'

'Well, I did tell you we got a special rate so long as we leave before the hotel fills up. Mardi Gras is their busiest time.'

'I know that,' Lorraine snapped.

Rosie crossed to the writing table. 'I did a provisional booking at a place way out of town in case we needed to stay on, but we don't, do we?'

Rooney barged in and dumped down his bags.

'So, how did it go?'

'Cheque's in my wallet, one million!'

Rosie whooped, and Rooney hit the flimsy wall with his fist. 'Yes, yes. One fucking million.'

Lorraine folded her arms. 'So you're both leaving?'

Rooney frowned. 'Well, we all are, aren't we? I mean, did you want to stay on for Mardi Gras?'

'Nope, I'm not crazy about the idea of being elbowed around the streets, but . . .'

'But what?' Rosie said as she opened Lorraine's wallet and took out the cheque.

'But, well, you think we're all done here?'

Rosie passed the cheque to Rooney.

'You mean we should see if it's good? I doubt if she'd bounce it on us,' he said, squinting at the cheque.

Lorraine had that edgy feel, sort of shifting her weight from one foot to the next.

'Nick's room rented, is it?'

'What?'

'I said, is Nick's room rented out?'

'Yeah, well, we stopped paying for it,' Rosie said, becoming suspicious.

'His body collected by his sister?'

'Yes,' Rooney said, frowning.

'You know it was, we told you it was, he'll be buried by now.'

'And forgotten, just like that? Forgotten like that pitiful skeleton in the morgue? Well, for your information I have not forgotten Nick Bartello, I have not forgotten him in any way.'

'Shit, Lorraine, nor have we. If this is leading to us giving his relatives something from the one million, I don't mind,' Rooney said.

'We don't need to give anybody else a cut of the one million,' Lorraine said, slumping into a chair and leaning forward, her head in her hands.

'So what's up?'

She shook her head and then leaned back, closing her eyes. 'What's up is some piece of shit killed Nick, and that shit, whoever he is, is just walking, and nobody is doing anything about it, that's what's up.'

Rooney sighed, he could feel the carpet being tugged from under his big flat feet. 'Lorraine, the cops have nothing, we got nothing. What do you want us all to do now, stay on here and start up another investigation?'

'I want us to finish off what we started, I said I wanted you to visit Fryer Jones's bar, I said I wanted his place searched with that cop you palmed five hundred bucks to, because some fucker got his necklace. Some bastard killed Nick Bartello and I just want us to check out a few things before we all piss off back to Los Angeles and buy our own condominiums, okay?'

Rooney sighed, lifting his hands up to calm her. 'Okay, just stay cool, I'll contact him right now, we can do it straight away. But, Lorraine, if we come up with nothin' then I don't care what you say, I'm out of here. What about you, Rosie?'

Rosie nodded. 'Yes, I'll leave with Bill.'

Lorraine stood up. 'Fine, but I might hang around until I am satisfied we gave Nick a run for his cut of the cash. So, we'll keep one room for us all, make it mine as I haven't started to pack.'

Lorraine slammed the bathroom door shut hard, and Rosie sighed.

'When she gets into these moods, I could punch her,

538

I really could. I mean, how can we come up with something if the police got nothin', huh? You tell me that? She just gets obsessive.'

Rooney rubbed his chin. 'If she wasn't so obsessive, Rosie, we'd never have found Anna Louise Caley or be looking at a cheque for one million. So we get off our backsides and do like she says because we got to keep her sweet. I don't want her suddenly saying she's got a right to a bigger cut.'

'She can't do that!'

Rooney dangled the cheque. 'This is made out to her, Rosie. She's gonna have to put it in her account, then pay us our share, so I'd say we do whatever she wants us to do.'

Lorraine showered and changed but didn't feel very fresh or energized, just angry, and she knew it was connected to seeing Robert Caley. She glared at her reflection in the mirror.

'Hey, chill out of this one. Remember, he's not worth one more second of your time, so stop this!'

Rooney tapped and she opened up. 'You got someone in here?'

'No, I was talking to myself.'

'Oh well, this cop's downstairs, you want to talk to him?'

'Yep.'

Rooney held open the door. All their bags were littered around the room. 'Lemme warn you, he's no Burt Lancaster, he's kind of a bit freaky-lookin'.'

'Oh yeah?'

'Yeah, his neck is as wide as his ass!'

*

Harper sat with Rosie, well beamed herself; they made a good couple. He had a beer in his fat pudgy hand, and lifted half a cheek of his ass as Lorraine joined them. They were sitting beneath an umbrella on the blue and white plastic furniture of a cheap sidewalk café, its neon signs glowing weakly in the daylight. The pavement in front of them was thronging with people.

'This is Lorraine Page.'

'Hi, how you doing?'

'Fine, thanks for coming over.' She looked across at him over her dark shades. Rooney was right, the guy was obese.

'No problem, you want a beer or . . .'

'Coffee,' she said, and lit a cigarette.

'Place is hotting up. Pity you aren't sticking around for Carnival.'

Lorraine stubbed out her cigarette. 'Okay, can we get down to why we wanted to see you?'

'Sure, fire away.'

Lorraine spoke quickly, detailing the events that led up to Nick Bartello's death and mentioning the fact that he had been in Fryer Jones's bar the previous night, and might possibly have returned.

'Look, I know he was your pal, right? But he was crazy to go to Ward 9 late at night and to get involved with anyone there. Now, I know we investigated this, we asked around, because he was found close to the bar, you know, about a block away down an alley, but nobody there saw him. Nobody saw him down the alley either.'

Lorraine leaned forward. 'Okay, so you're sayin' with Mardi Gras comin' some poor fucker is gonna walk off the main drag by accident, go into Fryer Jones's bar, have a few beers, walk out and get his throat cut? And all the cops are gonna say is that he shouldn't have been in that district? You got notices up there saying, "Beware, you could end up fucking dead"?'

Harper wrinkled his pig-nose, annoyed at being spoken to by a woman in that tone.

Lorraine ticked off on her fingers. 'We know he went there, we know he pissed off some kids because they were shooting a pistol and shoving it up Fryer Jones's nose. We know he made them look dumb, we know all of that. We know that Fryer Jones gave Nick a necklace, a gris-gris, which wasn't on his body when he was found, nor were his wallet or his driving licence. He used to keep them in separate back pockets.'

'Uh huh.' The fat face wobbled.

'Fryer Jones admitted to me that he had met Nick, and I want to know who was in the bar that night. I want to know who was in the bar the following night – in other words I want to know if Nick Bartello went back to Fryer Jones's bar and somebody there cut his throat. So if it means getting a search warrant, if it means—'

Harper shook his head. 'You are an impatient lady, that's for sure.'

'Well, we only got the room booked for one more night,' she said with a tight-lipped smile.

'Okey dokey. This area that your friend went into is well known as the wrong neighbourhood for whites to go drinking in the early hours, unless they are known or trying to score dope. Your friend use dope, did he?'

'No, he didn't,' snapped Rooney.

'Okay, so he was acting dumb. But we don't like going into bars like Fryer Jones's without real good evidence. We don't like doing that, because Fryer is an informant.'

Lorraine leaned back. 'Is he? That's why you arrested him on the night Anna Louise Caley was missing?'

'Yes, ma'am, we did arrest him and we hadda knock

541

him around a bit. We needed to ask old Fryer if he had heard anythin', you know, if he knew where she might have disappeared to, because there is nothing down in that section of town that Fryer Jones don't know about. But we have to always make it look real good, because if it was known, then it'd be old Fryer with his throat cut like your friend.' Harper rested back in his chair and burped, he thumped his chest with a curled fist. 'Better out than in.'

Lorraine lit another cigarette and looked up and down the street, inhaling the smoke. Okay, let's try this another way. You're telling me you couldn't get a warrant to search that bar, maybe haul a couple of guys into the station? That is what you are saying, isn't it?'

'I guess so. We don't like to rock the boat.'

'Right, so what would it cost to rock it?'

'I'm sorry?'

'Come on, you heard me. I am asking you what it would cost to get maybe four or five of you to back me up, get yourselves armed with more than your wooden bars. They can be cops, or they can be cops not acting as cops, if you follow me?'

Rosie could feel the non-alcoholic beer churning in her stomach. Rooney turned to stare down the street but the sweat was trickling off his face.

'How much?' Harper asked.

'You tell me,' she said softly.

Rooney flicked a glance at Rosie. Her face glistened with perspiration, and she was twisting a bit of the tablecloth round and round one of her fingers.

Harper caught a drop of water running down the neck of his cold beer bottle. He licked his finger. 'Are you gonna be around until this afternoon?'

'Back at the hotel, sure, we can wait for you to contact us.'

Harper pushed back his chair. 'Be in touch. Been nice talkin' to you, Mrs Page, Bill, and nice to meet you, Rosie.'

He waddled off, seeming to make a wave through the people in the street, his girth not something to push around but to bounce off, his thick neck giving him a thuggish quality accentuated by the thin black moustache on his baby's lip.

'How much do you think he'd want?' Rosie asked.

Lorraine stood up. 'Why, you worried about parting with your hard-earned money, Rosie?'

'No, just being cautious. And you should put that cheque in the bank before you lose it.'

Lorraine laughed, and swung her purse round her shoulder. 'Sure, and I guess you both want a cheque for your cut, but you mind if I wait until it's actually in my account?'

She walked off, and Rosie reached over for Rooney's hand. 'I didn't like him and I'm getting to not like her.'

They both looked towards Lorraine. She was standing on the pavement, slowly turning to face them as on the opposite side of the road she saw a red convertible Mustang cruise past. It was driven by Raoul Corbello, one hand trailing down over the door, the other lazily holding the white steering-wheel. Rap music blared out, and his eyes, hidden behind the mirrored shades, were checking out a young black chick selling postcards. He drove on, he could do a lot better for himself than a street vendor, and he needed to get to his uncle's bar, Fryer Jones's place. Raoul was hyped up on crack and needed to get easy, chill out for a while so he could face his family and see his precious Ruby crowned. That's what he'd come home for: Mardi Gras.

CHAPTER 19

RAOUL CORBELLO snuck into his uncle's bar, and stayed near the doors, just where the old wooden counter ended. He leaned back against the windowless wall as the barman sauntered down towards him.

'Mexican, and a shot of bourbon on the rocks,' he said, collar turned up, his shades still on.

'Sure, Raoul, but let's see your money.'

'Fuck you, Zachery Blubber.' But he slapped twenty bucks down.

Zak opened a beer, banged it on to the counter and sauntered back for the bourbon. 'So how's LA, man? You get all that fancy gear there?'

Raoul shrugged. His nose was running and he sniffed as Zak leaned against the bar, sliding the bourbon glass forwards.

'Cool, it's cool.'

'You look like you need to chill out.'

Raoul knocked back the bourbon and reached for the beer.

'Your brothers are workin' out back.'

'Uncle Fryer around?'

'Sleepin', like always at this time. Place was jumpin' last night, he played so much he got his big old lips swollen up, but he sure as hell can play that beat-up bugle o' his.'

Raoul sniffed again, wiping his nose with his shirt cuff. He took out a thick roll of notes and peeled off another twenty. 'Same again, have one yourself.'

Zak eyed the wad, and slowly moved back along the bar. 'Don't mind if I do, brother, don't mind if I do.'

Raoul had to wait a while as a couple of customers needed refills. He was beginning to get the shakes and wondered why the hell he'd come back. He'd get more than the shakes when he showed his face back home. What had seemed like a good idea was now beginning to pale.

Zak passed another beer and bourbon along, holding up a glass to indicate he'd taken his drink and started to chinwag with two old boys huddled at the far end of the bar.

'Zak, eh, Zak man, come on down here a second, will ya?' Raoul said loudly, gulping down his beer.

'What you want?' said Zak, handing out beers and tossing the empties into a crate beneath the bar. He kind of knew, so he opened a drawer under the till and took out a packet. 'This what you want, bro?'

Raoul put his hand over the plastic bag. Zak leaned forward, whispering that it was good home-grown gear, he could vouch for it.

'You got any skins?' Raoul asked, peeling off fifty dollars.

'Shit, man, what you want me to do, smoke it for you?' He reached into the back pocket of his pants and tossed down a squashed pack of rolling papers.

The two Corbello boys were filthy from stacking all the crates, ready to load up the truck, when Raoul appeared in the back doorway of the bar. They yelled and flung their arms around him, and then sat in the outside john as he rolled up three big joints, one for each of them.

'How come you workin' out back here?' Raoul asked. They were hesitant to begin with but after a few drags they told him that Fryer was getting heavy. They giggled as they said that when their Aunt Juda got hold of Raoul he'd get some heavy-handed activity. Raoul laughed, saying he was cool, and started telling them about his Mustang, his dealin' and his thievin' of their aunt's hoard of cash from under her bed. She could try beating it out of him, but he wouldn't tell her where he'd stashed what he hadn't spent. They were both in awe of their older brother, and the more stoned they became the more they got to bragging about carvin' up a whitey. Raoul listened, his eyes drooping, not really believing their stories, not really caring. They rolled up some more joints, and started messing around as Raoul took a leak, having to prop himself up against the shack wall to piss straight.

'Eh! How's Ruby?'

'Oh man, she's gettin' so in with Mama and Juda she don't have time for us.'

'She getting into all that voodoo shit, huh?'

The two boys, now hurling empty bottles against a wall, didn't really pay any attention. Fryer Jones looked down from his dirty window, pulling the sacking curtain aside. He could see his three nephews that might even be his own sons, but he sure as hell didn't like what he was seeing. They were whooping and hollering and smashing up bottles. He drew on his dirty old jeans and had a good scratch before he made his way down the stairs. He was well hungover. It had been a good night, too good, and he was still buzzing.

'Eh, Zak, gimme a pick-up, will ya?' he shouted down, and Zak was waiting for him with his usual glass of snake's eye.

'That Raoul's turned up,' he said.

Fryer knocked back his pick-me-up in one, and kissed his swollen lips. 'Yeah, I see him, and I had enough o' my fucking relatives to last me a lifetime. Give us another, I need something to waken me up before I get my belt off to those little no-good shits.'

Lorraine was washing her hair: she'd had a good few hours' sleep and was feeling, if not a hundred per cent, at least a lot better. She had stopped drinking, and hadn't had a drop since she'd been at Caley's hotel, but she wasn't congratulating herself, just hoping she'd be able to keep it up. All around her in the room was Rooney and Rosie's baggage, but where they were she had no idea. A second later, though, Rosie banged on the door.

'It's us, Lorraine,' she shouted.

'It's open,' replied Lorraine, still rubbing her hair dry.

Her partners came in and Rooney sat heavily on the bed – unlike Lorraine, he hadn't caught up on sleep from the night before, and he yawned, resting back on the pillows.

'I banked the cheque, the teller said it would take a couple of days to clear. Where have you two been?' Lorraine combed her hair and began to dry it with the hair-dryer.

'With Harper,' Rosie answered.

'He's got five guys, plus him makes six, and you and me. He doesn't want you to go in, Lorraine.'

'I want to be there. Did he get a search warrant?'

Rooney shook his head. 'He didn't say, but I doubt it. They're all ex-cops, two grand each.'

'What?' Rosie said, astonished.

'For twelve thousand dollars, it's worth it,' Rooney said.

Lorraine switched off the hair-dryer. 'And Nick Bartello's dead. If he was alive, Bill, he'd get a hell of a lot more from his share of the one million bonus, so quit beefin'. And you, Rosie.'

'I never said anything!'

'Right, but you were thinking about it,' Lorraine said, checking her hair. The ends were still damp, so she turned the dryer on again and began to curl them over a brush. She watched Rosie and Rooney in the mirror: both looked exhausted, Rosie yawning and Rooney's eyes drooping as he leaned back on the pillow.

Nobody spoke, and Rooney nodded off and began to snore. Eventually Lorraine switched off the dryer and went back into the bathroom to dress. When she came out, Rosie was also fast asleep. Lorraine smiled: sometimes the pair of them were like two kids, and she felt worried about the idea of involving them in the scene at Fryer's bar. She didn't want anything to happen to them, not now that they'd found one another at last.

She stared at them, and then sat down and wrote a note. She left it on Rooney's big heaving chest, packed her bags and carried them out, closing the door quietly behind her. Neither woke. The note said: 'Don't stay for Mardi Gras, see you back at *my* new place. Good luck. L.'

Lorraine left her cases at the desk and walked out to pay off François. He was still hovering, even after she settled his bill, asking if she needed him to take her to the airport, astonished she wasn't going to stay on for the Carnival.

'Thanks, but no thanks François. You take care now.'

She walked off, and he counted out the dollars. She'd given him a bonus, fifty dollars more than he'd asked for. He grinned, a happy man.

Lorraine walked out into the French Quarter. It was a muggy evening and the street was crowded as more and more tourists flooded in. Purple, green and gold were everywhere and there was already a carnival feeling in the air, but she didn't feel in a festive mood.

The six men were waiting in two patrol cars down a side street. They were smoking, wearing dark glasses, all the car windows open. Lorraine got in beside the obese Officer Harper, and smiled as he introduced her to the men squashed in the back seat.

'Cash up front, Mrs Page.'

She opened her purse and took out an envelope. 'Twelve grand, right? Half now, half when we're through.'

Harper turned to look at the officers behind him, they shrugged. He got out of his car and waddled to the car behind him, leaned in the window, had a brief conversation and then returned.

'Okay, but you'd better not try to put anything over on us.'

Lorraine smiled. 'You think I would really try it on with you guys? Come on, I know you're taking a big risk.'

It seemed to do the trick. He nodded, his cheek jowls wobbling.

'So how do we work it?' she asked quietly.

Rooney grunted, and his body jerked. He lifted his head. 'Shit, what time is it?'

Rosie murmured as he eased himself off the bed. The note fluttered to the floor and he picked it up. The room was in darkness so he turned on the bedside lamp.

'Rosie, wake up, girl. Rosie!'

She blinked and swallowed, and then sat up with a start.

'She's gone. Read this.'

Rosie took a moment to adjust to the light, and then read the note. 'What should we do?'

Rooney hesitated, then crossed to the bathroom. 'Check if there's a flight out of here. If there isn't, we'll stay.'

'We're going to leave her?'

'Just see if there's a flight, sweetheart.'

Rooney splashed cold water over his face and patted it dry with one of the damp towels Lorraine had used. It smelt of shampoo, and he lowered it from his face, staring at himself in the mirror. He felt old and tired, wondering what the hell he was thinking of doing, getting himself engaged at his age. Had he really suggested she move in with him? He sat on the edge of the bath, wishing he'd taken his shoes off before he fell asleep; his feet felt swollen.

Rosie called out that there was a flight in an hour and a half.

'Gimme a second,' he shouted back. He didn't know what to do. Not knowing what the hell Lorraine had arranged with Harper or when they were going to do it, or for that matter why. What did she expect to gain? He sighed.

Rosie was brushing her hair when he walked out. 'I gave them your credit card number, that okay?' She watched him plod across the room, and she turned. 'Bill? You want to leave or not?'

'I'm thinking about it, Rosie.'

She'd been thinking about it too, and virtually asked him the same questions he had just asked himself.

'I mean, what does she expect to find at the end of it?'

'I dunno, Rosie, maybe someone scared enough to

say they saw Nick, who knows? I think she's throwing away good money, but that's just my opinion.'

'It's mine too. I liked Nick, of course I did, but it's a long shot, isn't it? We don't even know if he was in Fryer's bar the night he got killed. Even if she was to find the gris-gris, even if whoever did kill Nick was dumb enough to hang on to it, they wouldn't have it in the bar, would they?'

'I don't know, Rosie.' He hadn't meant to snap at her, it just came out that way.

'Listen, if you feel guilty about going, we'll stay.'

'I don't feel guilty.'

'Fine, then we'll leave, yes?'

He sat down, said he needed a drink, and Rosie flung the brush on to the dressing table.

'We can't hang around, Bill, the flight goes in an hour and a half.'

'I heard you the first time, Rosie.'

'So, I am repeating it.'

Rooney stood in the lobby as Rosie checked out, looking at Lorraine's suitcase waiting behind the desk.

'Bill, if you want to wait, you'd better say so, they got people wanting her room. Which means if we do check out and stay on we'll have nowhere to stay for tonight. It's Mardi Gras, Bill, the hotels are all filling up.'

He suddenly made up his mind. 'You stay with the bags, I'll go over to Fryer's bar.'

'But what about the plane?'

He turned on her angrily. 'We fucking miss it. Hell, if we have to we'll hire a private plane, okay? Just wait here.'

Rooney walked out. Rosie felt near to tears; he'd

551

never been angry at her before, never snapped at her the way he just had. But then she understood why – he was worried about Lorraine. For all his complaints about her, he really cared about her, and if Rosie thought about it, so did she.

'Excuse me, is Mrs Page checking out or not?'

Rosie glared at the receptionist who was getting more frazzled by the day. It was always the same at Mardi Gras; she hated it.

'Yeah, I'm checking Mrs Page out, but we need to leave the bags here, is that all right?'

The receptionist sighed; she was knee-deep in people's luggage as it was. 'I guess so, but the hotel can't take any responsibility for them.'

'Fine, I'll take the goddamned things out with me.'

Rooney tried in vain to flag a cab down. The pavement was crowded, there were people walking arm-in-arm down the streets. More jugglers and clowns had appeared on the scene, passing out leaflets for all the forthcoming events, people already getting into the spirit. Fireworks were going off in all directions, they whizzed and banged overhead, and lit up the dark sky. A Dixieland band was playing, or rehearsing, stop-starting. It was like he had stepped on to a fairground Ferris wheel and couldn't get off. He pushed and jostled his way along the street, eyes peeled for a vacant cab, and he couldn't stop the feeling of panic rising. He didn't know what he was getting so het up about – his personal life or Lorraine. Or maybe it was just the memory of Nick Bartello, but he had a hideous feeling of something coming down, and his frustration at not being in control of it made it worse. She was somewhere with a bunch of guys, and probably bad ones. She was alone, and he shouldn't have let her

552

go without back-up. He was her back-up man, her partner now, and he'd never be able to live with himself if something happened to her, because for all her faults and her headstrong ways, he cared about her, more than he ever dared admit. And one thing he knew, she was one hell of a cop, in the Force or out. Lorraine was in a class all her own.

'Taxi!' he yelled.

Rosie sat outside the hotel on the small terraced area. She was not the only person sitting by a sea of luggage. There were a lot of back-packers and families, some licking ice creams, some becoming irate with their tired-out kids, and the persistent noise of the fireworks was giving her a thudding headache.

François tooted his horn and waved over. Rosie jumped up and waved back frantically. He grinned, then realized she was gesturing for him to join her.

'Can you get all these bags on board?'

'Sure, you want to go to the airport?'

'Yeah, eventually, but first can you get me over to Fryer Jones's bar in Ward 9? Lorraine's there.'

He jumped out, opened the trunk, and began hurling the bags inside.

Rooney was sweating. He had got into a near fist-fight with a drag queen who had flagged down the same taxi, but as he or she was a good foot higher than Rooney, he'd walked away. Now he turned as he heard his name shouted out, and he looked this way and that. Then he heard Rosie's voice and he pushed his way through a crowd of people before he saw her waving to him from across the street in François's car. His panic rose as he

nearly got knocked down by a kid on a bicycle with three
other people somehow balanced on it as well.

'What's happened? You heard from Lorraine?'

'No, get in and shut up,' she said.

Rooney sat beside her and she nudged François to get
a move on.

'We going to the airport?'

'No,' she snapped. 'Fryer Jones's bar, all right?'

He grabbed her hand and pulled her closer. 'She's my
partner, Rosie.'

'She's mine too, in case you've forgotten.'

Boom went another firework, and a rocket exploded
over their heads. 'Carnival getting started!' shouted
François gleefully. 'Man, this place hots up, don't you
just feel it all coming down all around you? This place is
crazy, man, it goes wild, real wild.'

Ruby placed the steaming bowls of crawfish stew on the
newspaper that served as a tablecloth. Juda, Edith and
Sugar May dug in. They had chilled beers and big chunks
of bread, and they ate hungrily as they had been working
all day on the float. Baskets and baskets of fresh flower-
heads had been delivered, and each one was to be placed
around the throne to make a sea of colour for the Queen
to step over as she was led to her throne.

Ruby was barefoot, wearing just an old underslip. Her
hair was pinned up off her face as she'd worked up a
sweat. They were tired but they would all be up and
working the following morning. It took a lot of time and
loving care to get the floats ready, and all the hard work
only built up the excitement until it was like being drunk
with it all.

Juda dunked her bread and sucked on it; it was good
to be back home, good to be free. She had decided not

to go back to LA, even if Elizabeth Caley offered her a fortune. She was not leaving home again. She broke off a piece of bread and was just about to dip it into her bowl when she saw the newspaper article.

'Missing Movie Star's Daughter – Body Found!'

'Move your plate aside, Sugar May.'

Juda inched the newspaper around to read it. 'They found her, they just found Anna Louise Caley.' She pulled the paper from the table and wiped off the crumbs. 'Oh, my Lord, she was buried in . . . Oh my, oh my.'

Edith looked at her sister. 'What's that, Juda?'

Juda folded the paper into a roll, staring at Ruby.

'They found poor little Anna Louise Caley buried in a garden, under suspicious circumstances, it says.'

Ruby continued to eat, sucking her bread loudly.

'Where, Juda?'

Juda kept on looking at Ruby. 'In Miss Tilda Brown's back yard. You know who she is, don't you, Ruby?'

Ruby looked up and her eyes were glittering, her voice soft, almost purring. 'I know who she is, Aunty Juda, she tied a dressing-gown cord round her neck and hanged her little self.'

Sugar May put her hand over her mouth and giggled, and received a slap across her head with the newspaper. Edith now looked in confusion at Juda, who slowly pushed her chair from the table and stood up. She wasn't wearing her wig or false eye-lashes, just an old smock dress, her cropped grey hair thinning at the crown.

Ruby tried to be nonchalant, still dipping her bread into her bowl, but she would not look up, did not want to face her aunt. She was scared of her, even more so when her big body loomed over the table.

'Ruby, remember what I told you, play with the devil and he'll come for your soul.'

'No he won't. And whatever I done, Fryer's taking

care of, like he's taking care of my brothers. Nobody is ever going to know nothing.'

Edith was still confused, looking from her sister to her daughter. 'What you two talking about?'

Juda walked to the door. 'She knows, Edith, Ruby knows, and Fryer never took care of nobody but himself. That is the way he lives. He sold to the devil a long, long time ago.'

Edith was really worried now, and she pushed her half-finished supper away, following Juda out.

'What you done?' Sugar May asked in a whisper.

Ruby had just taken a mouthful of water, and she turned on Sugar May, hissing, and the water sprayed from her mouth like a jet.

'I just used my powers, Sugar May, I just used my powers.'

Sugar May scuttled out after her mama, and Ruby sat alone. Then after a moment she reached for her mama's bowl, and tipped it into her own. She continued eating, delicately dipping her bread into the bowl and sucking it. She felt no guilt, no remorse for what she had done, or what she had begun. After all, she had only given them what they had wanted.

Elizabeth Caley sat at Lloyd Dulay's side, looking composed and as beautiful as ever. She wore black, out of respect for her daughter, and everyone there had whispered their condolences. The Dulays were old money, and the whole of New Orleans society had accepted the invitation out of curiosity, wanting to see Anna Louise's grieving mother with their own eyes. Elizabeth did not let them down. She was composed and distant, as if frozen with grief and shock. She was starring in another movie, and she acted the part to perfection. She knew

Robert would ask for a massive settlement, but she didn't care. She had more money than she knew what to do with. Money had never been a priority for Elizabeth, she had grown up with it, always had it and never considered being without it. She was going to be invited to every Mardi Gras ball and top-level function in New Orleans, as she had since she was a child. She was famous, now even more so because of her tragic daughter. She was sitting next to Lloyd Dulay, the man she had always loved. She was his prize guest of honour, but tonight she didn't relish it – tonight she no longer cared. She had determined there would be no more secrets, all she was waiting for was the right moment. It came when Lloyd rose to ask everyone to lift their glasses to Elizabeth Seal.

There was a polite murmur, none expecting her to speak, but she stood up like a queen. She held her glass in her right hand, lifting it a fraction.

'A long time ago, I was given the lead role in a film called *The Swamp*. I was sixteen years of age and excited at the prospect of becoming a star. I paid no heed to the fact that I was to portray the great voodoo queen, Marie Laveau. I did not consider the culture that Marie Laveau brought to her people, it was just a movie, and I was going to be a star.'

Elizabeth gave the performance of her life, but it wasn't scripted, it came from her years of torment, from the nightmare during filming when she had been taken and raped, curses written in blood on her body. She told them all about the doll she found in her trailer, a doll bearing her face, cursing her and any offspring that she might conceive to live in the hell of the living dead, and condemning Elizabeth Seal to spend the rest of her days feeling the weight of the great queen's coffin lid pressing on her heart. And as those gathered became frightened by her driven, emotional declaration, they knelt before

557

her as she at last admitted, 'I am black and I have hidden behind a white skin. I have been punished and cursed for abusing the great voodoo goddess, Queen Marie Laveau. Every child my womb conceived was also doomed to live under her shadow.'

It was all so clear to Elizabeth what she should do, exactly what she should say, and the impact her words would have made her feel stronger than she had ever felt in her wretched life. She was going to free herself, she would be free. No need for Juda anymore, no more nightmares, it was all over.

Elizabeth still held the photograph of her daughter Anna Louise, as the drugs distorted her mind so that she truly believed she was there, dining alongside Lloyd Dulay, and that it was all taking place. He was in fact waiting impatiently downstairs when Missy came running from the bedroom, unable to wake Mrs Caley. She had screamed to him that something bad had happened.

Lloyd Dulay felt for Elizabeth's pulse; it was very weak. She opened her eyes only once, and smiled at him, saying that everything was all right now, it was all over. Her black gown was laid out in readiness for the dinner, with matching shoes and sequined purse. By the time the doctor arrived, she was dead. She looked peaceful and calm, a sweet innocent smile on her lips. He sat down in a chair close to the bed.

'Oh, Elizabeth, my little queen.'

Harper looked at his men. He was sweating as he listened to the radio and then rehooked it back on the dashboard.

'They're standing out back ready. We go in via the front, let's keep this as tight as we can, no shooting unless . . . Well, we done it before, so here we go.'

He looked at Lorraine. 'Stay back, once we got the

558

place quiet you can come in, but not until I give you the word. Let's go!'

Fryer Jones was sitting with Raoul at the far end of the bar, trying to get him straightened out enough to take him home and face his Aunt Juda. His two brothers were out in the yard lying stoned among the beer crates they were supposed to have been stacking. There were only the usual regulars dotted around the bar, it never hotted up until after midnight. Sugar May had crept in, and was hiding out down the back, talking to one of the hookers, thinking she was someone to emulate, when it happened.

Fryer looked in astonishment as the big motherfuckers charged in from the back yard and through the front door. Even Zak gaped. Nobody had bust them for years, they paid a high price for it not to happen, so nobody was sure what the hell was going down. Glasses were shattered, mirrors cascaded into jagged pieces as the thugs came in, screaming and shouting for everyone to back up against the wall. It was a raid. Customers raised their hands in terror as they were thrown up against the wall, others ran for cover under the old bar tables.

Fryer turned on his bar stool and yelled in fury, 'What you motherfuckers doing, for chrissakes?'

Batons clipped heads, boots kicked groins, as everyone inside the bar tried to disappear into the walls. The more the cops yelled and hit out, the more Fryer Jones screamed abuse. The cops were laying into the customers, asking between fists and batons what their names were. One of the thick-set cops had virtually thrown the Corbello kids on to the floor and they lay curled up as the boots went in, screaming and shouting they hadn't done anything.

559

Raoul was hauled by his hair from his bar stool next to Fryer, but not one cop touched Fryer himself.

'You better have a fucking good reason for this, you motherfuckers,' Fryer screamed.

Lorraine couldn't wait any longer and walked into the bar. It was mayhem, screaming and shouting, people huddled in corners, crying and hunched up as the boots and batons still went in.

Lorraine shouted, 'This is for Nick Bartello, *Nick Bartello*!'

Fryer squinted in the darkness down to the end of the bar.

'His throat was cut down an alley, one block from here.'

Fryer shook his head and pointed. 'You are a crazy bitch, you know that?'

As they spoke, cops were hurling the drugs taken from the drawer beside the till on to the bar. Two more moved up the narrow back staircase to Fryer's private quarters.

Rooney walked in as Fryer Jones spat a spray of his beer over Lorraine. 'You gonna pay for this, you fucking whore. Nobody come in here and takes over my bar. Nobody!'

'You want to bet, Mr Jones? I wouldn't bother, we already took it over.'

Rooney edged closer and said to one of the cops kicking the shit out of a guy caught between the tables, 'I'm with her, I'm with Mrs Page.'

Lorraine turned, and seeing Rooney she gave a quick grin before turning back to Fryer.

'We will all walk out, Fryer, when you give us the names of whoever cut Nick Bartello's throat. That's all we want, all I want, no charges, you all hear me? No charges, but we want who cut my friend's throat.'

One of the cops searching upstairs appeared in the doorway behind the bar. 'Mrs Page?'

Lorraine turned to the cop, who gestured for her to come closer, and chucked Nick Bartello's wallet on to the bar. Fryer looked, and then pursed his lips, swearing. He had fucked up, he had meant to destroy it. But he kept smiling. 'This is gonna cost, you motherfuckers, this is gonna cost.'

Lorraine moved closer to him, and then reached out. He had on the necklace or a similar necklace to the one Nick had been wearing.

'This is yours, Mr Jones, is it?'

Fryer looked at her, and laughed. 'Sure is, honey, we make 'em for the museum, how many you want, huh? You fuckers are not even here on a warrant, are you?'

The second cop walked in from the backstairs. He held up Nick Bartello's licence in a small plastic bag and tossed it down.

Harper looked over the wallet and the licence, then at Lorraine. 'These your friend's?'

Lorraine fingered the empty wallet, looked at the licence, and said, 'Yes, these belonged to Nick Bartello.'

Harper held his hand up. 'Okay, back off everyone, come on, quieten down in here. Quiet!'

He turned to face Fryer Jones and took out his handcuffs. 'Okay, Fryer, you overstepped yourself, this is one you won't wriggle out of.'

'I never saw them before in my life!' Fryer said calmly.

Harper clipped on the handcuffs, roughly pulling Fryer's hands behind his back.

'Well, they was under your pillow, Fryer, and they may very well have your prints all over them. So let's walk out nice and quiet, shall we?'

Fryer Jones bowed his head. He could see Raoul shaking in one corner, his brothers huddled under a

561

table, and Sugar May crying with the hookers. Fryer eased off his stool, his hands cuffed behind him. He was pushed past Lorraine, and he stared at her.

'You got the devil in you, lady.'

Fryer Jones leaned back in the patrol car and closed his eyes. He could never name his own kin, maybe one of them even his own blood, so he sighed, and asked if they could bring him his trombone. It made Harper turn and stare, because he had reckoned in all honesty that Fryer had nothing to do with this Nick Bartello. He leaned out of the window and shouted to one of his pals, 'Get this old buzzard his fucking trombone.'

Lorraine sat in the back of François's car and wept. Rooney one side and Rosie the other. They just held her tightly between them, she didn't need to say anything. In fact, they all felt tearful as François asked if they still wanted to make it to the airport.

They got there with five minutes to spare, bags and baggage intact.

Fryer Jones played his trombone in his cell until other prisoners asked for him to shut up, as they couldn't sleep. He sat there in silence, staring up at the small window of his cell. He wouldn't name the Corbello boys or Ruby or any of them. He guessed it was time he took responsibility, time he paid his dues, so he admitted to killing Nick Bartello. He didn't ask to talk to a lawyer, the only call he made was to Juda Salina. She came, as he knew she would, all done up in her turban and false eye-lashes.

562

'Elizabeth Caley's dead.'

'Uh huh.'

'Anna Louise Caley's body was found.'

'Uh huh.'

She sighed, not meeting his eyes. 'Ruby is ready to be crowned, no guilt, no remorse. That girl worries me – she'd better straighten out.'

'Uh huh.'

'Raoul's back, with only half my savings.'

'And I'm goin' away for a murder I did not commit.' He gripped the bars with his gnarled hand. 'I'm doing it for you, Juda. You take over my bar, you keep those two young ones in line.'

She gently stroked his hand. 'Why are you doing this, Fryer?'

He gave her that gappy gold-toothed smile. 'Because once you were young and beautiful like Ruby. Nothing stays young or beautiful, Juda, only memories. Take care now.'

Juda wanted to cry, but she just walked away. She could hear him playing his trombone a long time after she left. She could still hear it in her small bedroom at Edith's. Life played tricks on you like that, hearing things that weren't there, seeing things that were about to happen. Life was full of strange things, especially in New Orleans and always just before Mardi Gras.

Rosie stood with her bags all packed, and two big boxed crates. Her apartment seemed suddenly bare.

'Well, I got everything,' she said sadly. She looked around again – stripped of her things, the place looked bigger. 'If you are staying on, Lorraine, you should get a better kitchen put in.'

563

Lorraine smiled. 'I intend to, Rosie, I'll get the place done up. It's a waste of money moving somewhere else, this will do me fine.'

Rosie chewed her lip. 'You can always call me if you need someone in the office, you know, part-time. I'll always be willing.'

'And able. Yeah, I know, you told me four, no, five times. Now, the cheques, you got the two cheques?'

'I certainly have,' Rosie said, patting her purse.

Lorraine smiled. 'You know, I never thought I'd be writing out cheques for that amount, and from my own bank account. We're rich, Rosie, we all got over a quarter of a million, so, you feeling happy?'

Rosie nodded. 'Well, not quite up to the brim, but I guess we'll make it work. I'm gonna give it a try, and you try to keep up the meetings, won't you? Keep on going, because I'd hate to see you blow this chance, Lorraine.'

'Rosie, I know I almost lost it, but I promise you I'm off the stuff now, and if it makes you feel any better, I give you my word that I'll keep going to the meetings. I'll contact Jake to be my sponsor, how's that?'

Rosie kissed her, and then hugged her tightly. 'Oh, hell, I'm gonna miss you.'

Before Rosie could become tearful, Rooney arrived and tooted from the street. Rosie began to take her bags and boxes and cases down, and he appeared, moaning as he helped her carry all her bits and pieces.

'I don't know if this is gonna work, Lorraine, but at least . . .'

She laughed. 'You'll give it a try? And you know there will always be a job open for you at Page Investigations, I've told Rosie that too. Office will be open Monday morning – you got the number?'

'Right, thanks.'

Eventually it came to the real goodbyes; it was a bit awkward. They didn't really know what to say to each other because for all the offers of work in the future, Lorraine knew it was the end of their partnership. Neither Rosie nor Rooney had actually said it, but she just knew. They all knew.

'We might sort of go on an extended honeymoon,' he muttered.

'Great, you do that, but I will be invited to the wedding, won't I?'

'Hell, don't be stupid.'

There was nothing left to say, but it was the last moment and they hung on to it. They seemed not quite to know how to walk out of the door, so Lorraine pushed them through it, saying that when they were settled they would all have a big celebration dinner, but until then they should just piss off and leave her alone.

Rosie started to cry, so Rooney told her to go on ahead, then turned back to Lorraine, half closing the door.

'You know, if you need me for anything I'll always be there for you, any time you feel, you know . . . if this drinking problem rears its head. You call me, call us, and we'll be right with you.'

Lorraine reached out and held him close. 'Bill, I'm okay, but I appreciate what you just said.'

He stood holding her for a few moments more, then turned abruptly and walked out, the screen door banging shut behind him.

Lorraine slumped down on the sofa bed, which she would now no longer have to sleep on. She would have Rosie's room all to herself, and she suddenly felt good, looking around the room. Her room. Her apartment. She would start to redecorate the next day, and lay on the old sofa thinking about colour schemes, and drapes, and then she sat up sharpish, swearing. She'd forgotten him, in all the excitement of returning home and banking the million dollars, she'd forgotten him, forgotten her promise.

The kennels were just closing when she arrived. She'd made the promise, and she wouldn't go back on it, but she began to doubt it when the kennelmaid started saying that he'd been a packet of trouble from the day he'd been left. He had attacked every one of the helpers and every canine they had in residence, and was now kept in solitary confinement.

Tiger didn't greet her, he sat at the far end of his wire meshing, his blue eyes beady and angry.

'Hi, kiddo, it's just me, I'm afraid. Nick's not gonna be able to take you home.'

He still sat, and then he bared his teeth.

'Listen, man, it's up to you, but I am the best bet you got. I walk away and it's the lethal injection, know what I mean?'

The beady blue eyes froze, and she bent down.

'Come on, Tiger, they want to close up, and I'm tired.'

Tiger slowly got to his feet, his head hung low as he padded towards her. Then his big bushy tail started to wag slowly.

'Okay, man, we're out of here.'

COLD SHOULDER

ACKNOWLEDGEMENTS

I sincerely thank Suzanne Baboneau, Gill Coleridge, Esther Newberg, Patty Detroit, the real Lorraine Page whose name I borrowed, Hazel Orme, Clare Ledingham and Liz Thorburn. To everyone at the Pasadena Police Station and Sheriff's Office, thank you for your time and expertise. But above all my thanks to a very admirable lady who brought me the story of her life.

LOS ANGELES, CALIFORNIA, 12 April 1988

I T WAS dark, the alley lit only by neon flashes from the main street; not a single bulb above the many exit doors leading into it remained intact. The boy was running. He wore a black bomber jacket, a bright yellow Superman stripe zigzagging down its back, shiny black elastic knee-length pants, and sneakers, flapping their tongues and trailing their laces.

'Police officer – freeze.'

The boy continued to run.

'Police officer – freeze.'

Half-way along the alley, the boy sidestepped a trash-can like a dancer. The flash of a pink neon light gave an eerie outline to his young body, and the Superman stripe appeared like a streak of lightning.

'Police officer. *Freeze!*'

The boy turned, in his right hand the stiff, flat metal of a 9mm pistol, and Lieutenant Page unloaded six rounds from the long-barrelled .38. Bam-bam-bam-bam-bam-bam. The boy keeled over to his right, in a half spin, his head jerked back, his arms spread, his midriff folded, and he fell face forward. His long dark floppy hair spread over his gun arm, his body shuddering and jerking before he was still.

Lieutenant Page approached him, automatically reloading the .38. The hoarse voice of Sergeant William Rooney barked out to back off, to put the gun in the holster.

1

Pushing past, his wide ass hid the body as he squatted down on his haunches.

'Get back in the patrol car, Lieutenant.'

Page did as requested, snapping the shoulder holster closed. The car doors were open. A crowd of people, hearing the gunshots, had started to press forwards. Two uniformed officers barred the entrance to the alley.

Sergeant Rooney was sweating as he carefully wrapped the weapon before easing it away from the boy's bloody fingers. He stared at the young dead face, and then walked slowly to the patrol car. Leaning inside, he displayed the weapon, cushioned in his snot-stained handkerchief. 'This the weapon, Lieutenant?'

The 9mm pistol was a square, flat silver Sony Walkman. Inside was an old Guns 'N Roses tape. Axl Rose had been blasting out 'Knock on heaven's dooowarrr . . .'

Page turned away. Rooney's fat face was too close, sniffing like an animal, because he knew, and he could smell it. 'Get back to base – and fucking sober up.'

The locker room was empty, stinking of feet and stale sweat; the vodka was stashed under a tote-bag. Just feeling the coldness of the bottle gave Lieutenant Page's jangling nerves instant relief. Page leaned on the sink, not even attempting to hide the bottle, drinking it like a man in a desert until it was empty. Suddenly the sink was slippery and the floor uneven, moving, shifting, and the long bench against the nearest wall was a good, safe, secure place to hide beneath.

Fifteen minutes later, Sergeant Rooney kicked open the door. 'Lieutenant? You in here?' His fat feet plodded down towards the washbasins. 'Captain wants you in his office. Now!'

*

She was hunched against the wall beneath the bench, her skirt drawn up, one shoe on, one off, knee poking through laddered tights. Her head rested on one arm, the fine blonde hair hiding her face. The other arm was spread wide across the floor. Rooney tapped her upturned hand with the toe of his black crêpe-soled shoes. 'Lieutenant!'

He bent down slowly, and yanked her hair roughly away from her face. She was unconscious, her lips slightly parted, her breathing deep and laboured. A beautiful face, the fine blonde eyelashes like a child's, the wide flattish cheekbones, and perfect straight nose almost enhanced by her flushed pink cheeks. Out cold, Lieutenant Lorraine Page was still a class act.

Rooney stood up, then with his foot pushed her arm closer to her body. She moaned and curled up tighter. He wandered over to the washbasin, picked up the empty bottle, then returned to Captain Mallory's office.

'You find her?'

'Yep! She's out cold on the floor, bottle must have been in her locker.'

Rooney stood it on the Captain's desk and just shrugged his shoulders. 'She's a lush, been coming down for a while. I reckoned she was in control, I've talked to her . . . She always had an excuse – you know, marital problems, et cetera, et cetera . . .'

Captain Mallory stared out of the window, then sighed. 'Get her out of here, will you? Get her badge, her gun, and tell her to stay out of my sight.'

Lorraine didn't even empty her locker: it was done for her, everything stuffed into the regulation tote-bag. The key was taken, her weapon and badge signed out. She was helped from the station, too drunk to comprehend what was happening. Rooney had gripped her by the elbow, pushing her roughly through the corridors. The zipper on her skirt

3

was half undone, her slip showing, and if Rooney hadn't held her tightly she would have fallen more than twice. He even banged her head, as if she were a prisoner, warning her to dip low to get into the rear of the car. She had laughed, and he had slammed the patrol car door so hard the vehicle rocked.

'You think it's funny? I hope you can sleep tonight, Lieutenant. Sleep as deeply as that kid you took out. Now get her the hell out of here . . .'

As the car drove out of the station yard, the mother of the dead boy, weeping hysterically, was being brought in. All she had been told was her son had been shot while escaping from a drug bust.

Two weeks later, Lieutenant Lorraine Page was officially out of the precinct. No disciplinary action was taken. She lost her pension, her career, but her forced resignation was quietly glossed over and it never reached the press. Tommy Lee Judd's family never knew the name of the officer who shot their fourteen-year-old son six times. At the inquest it was stated that the boy had ignored three police warnings to stop. He had been charged with crack dealing two years previously but the statements from his probation officer that he had been clean for the past six months were glossed over. His death was recorded, and the record filed away. No one mentioned that he had had no weapon, and had been mistaken for another suspect – or that the officer who opened fire had subsequently been released from all duties and was no longer attached to the force.

In fact, Lieutenant Page might never have existed, and, as word passed, no one who had worked alongside her spoke to her again. She was given the cold shoulder. She had betrayed their badge, her rank and position: she had been drunk on duty, and a fourteen-year-old boy had died.

They closed ranks – not to protect Lorraine, but to protect themselves.

Twelve years' service, two commendations, and a service record that any officer, male or female, would have been proud of, was over. No one cared to find out what would become of ex-Lieutenant Lorraine Page.

After the shooting, when she had been unceremoniously dumped outside her apartment, she had stumbled inside and collapsed onto her bed. Mike, her husband, knew she was on night duty and had already dressed, fed their two daughters, and driven them to the school. Their babysitter, Rita, collected them and took them home where she checked the details of Lorraine's duty times. According to the rota, she was due for two days' leave. Rita would have stayed to make the girls their lunch, but little Julia, only six years old, was calling, 'Mommy, Mommy,' as four-year-old Sally began collecting her toys to play with her mother.

'Is your mommy home?' Rita asked, surprised.

'Yes, in bed,' piped Julia.

Rita tapped on the bedroom door and peeked into the room. Lorraine was lying face down, her head beneath a pillow. 'Mrs Page? Is it okay if I shoot off now?'

Lorraine eased away the pillow. 'Yeah, yeah, thanks, Rita.'

Julia climbed up on the bed. She had already delved into her toy box, bringing out puzzles and something that made a pinging sound that cut like a knife through Lorraine's blistering headache.

'Mommy, can we go to see the puppets?'

'Mommy, I want pee-pee.' Sally pulled at the duvet.

'*Mommy*, can we go to see the puppets?' Julia repeated, as Lorraine slowly sat up.

'Mummy, I want pee-pee *now*.'

Lorraine had to hold onto the edge of the bedside table

5

to stand upright. She took her younger daughter into the bathroom and helped her up onto the toilet. 'I not got my panties down,' the little girl howled.

After a good belt of vodka she found in the freezer, she was not so jumpy and strung out. Once she'd settled the girls in front of the TV, Lorraine had another few nips of vodka with three aspirin so she could bathe and clean herself up. By the time Mike returned from his office, the kitchen was in order, their bed remade and Lorraine, with her face made up, looked presentable. Wearing a long cotton wrap, she was checking the fridge for what she could cook for dinner when she heard the front door slam and Mike's usual, 'Hi, honey, I'm home.' He dumped his briefcase and, smiling, came to stand behind her, slipping his arms around her and cupping her breasts in his hands.

'We got time for a quick one before they come?'

Lorraine eased away from him. 'Who?'

He returned to the table and picked up his briefcase. 'Donny and Tina Patterson. I said we'd eat here and then go to the movie. Rita said she could babysit.'

She closed her eyes.

'You haven't forgotten, have you? I wrote it down, it's on the board.'

'Fine, yeah. Did you get groceries in?'

Mike pursed his lips. 'You said you'd pick up dinner on the way back from work this morning.'

'I'm sorry, I forgot, I'll go get something now.'

'Don't bother,' he snapped, and went into the bedroom. She followed.

'It's no bother, for chrissakes, it'll take me two minutes. I'll get dressed and—'

He began to loosen his tie. 'Send out for something. There's a list by the phone of takeouts, they'll deliver.'

She rubbed her arm. 'Anything you don't make a list of, Mike?'

He glared. 'Yeah, and you know what that is. I haven't

6

slept with you for a month – you want me to start putting that down? Like, when it suits you?'

She walked out, not wanting to get into an argument as the two little girls hurtled into the bedroom to fling themselves at Mike. He swung them round, tickled them on the king-sized bed to their delight. Then he showered and changed, bathed each girl, combed their hair and put them into their pyjamas. They were tucked up in bed, each with their own special toy, when he returned to the kitchen. Lorraine was sitting with a mug of black coffee.

'You want to say goodnight to them?'

'Sure.' She got up and bumped into the edge of the table, and gave a little smile. As soon as she was out, he checked the freezer. One look at the bottle was enough.

'Did you call for some takeouts?'

Lorraine was cuddling Sally. He repeated the question and she sighed. 'Yeah, yeah, there's some pizzas coming any minute.'

'Pizzas?' he said flatly. Donny Patterson was his superior in the law firm, so Mike had wanted something more special but he went to lay the dining table. He could hear Lorraine reading to the girls, who were giggling loudly – she was good at funny voices. He took out the best cut glasses and the best mats and even gave the cutlery a quick polish. Then he went into the kitchen and began to make a salad. He was neat and methodical as usual, carefully slicing each tomato, washing the lettuce and the celery.

'You going to get dressed?' he called out, one eye on the clock.

Lorraine was lying on their bed, eyes closed. He opened the wardrobe and began to choose a shirt, a pair of slacks. He took great pride in his clothes, which were expensive, stylish, proof of his new-found success. He was hoping to be made a partner in the firm, and knew it was on the cards.

'What you working on?' she asked, stretching her arms above her head and yawning.

7

'It's the Coleridge case. It looks like he'll divorce his wife without too much aggravation, and it's more than likely he'll get custody of the children.'

'Really?' she said, without any interest, as she watched him holding up a shirt against himself.

'Do you like this shirt?'

'Yeah.'

'What are you going to put on?'

She swung her legs over the side of the bed. She didn't feel like seeing anyone, let alone going to a movie or having dinner with two self-important, wannabe-wealthy middle-class snobs. 'Oh, maybe the Chanel or the Armani. I dunno, Mike, and I've got a headache.'

'You want an aspirin?'

'Nope, maybe I'll take another shower.'

He held her close. 'The Pattersons are important to me, sweetheart, okay?'

She kissed him and rested her head against his shoulder. 'I'll be a good girl, promise.'

He touched her cheek. It never ceased to amaze him that she could arouse such passion in him. He loved the way she looked, her tall slender body. 'You okay? Did you have a bad night?'

She pressed her face into his neck. Did she have a bad night? The painful blurred memory physically hurt, and she moaned softly, a half sob which he took to be con-firmation that she wanted him. He began to slide her robe off her perfect shoulders, kissing the side of her neck.

'I better change.' She stepped away from him.

'What's the matter, Lorraine?'

She sighed, shaking her head. 'Nothing, Mike. I guess I'm just tired.'

He heard the shower running and slowly got dressed. As he reached for his cufflinks, he saw the photograph of Lorraine and her former partner, a dark, tousle-haired,

8

moody-looking guy. Lorraine always referred to him as Lubrinski. Since his death, she had been different, unapproachable. Mike had tried unsuccessfully to get her to talk about it but she seemed loath even to hear Lubrinski's name. Mike had not said a word when the silver-framed photograph appeared after the man had been shot. He had tried to persuade Lorraine to take a few weeks' leave but she refused. Instead, he knew, she had asked for more overtime and specifically night duty.

Lubrinski's laconic half-smile seemed to mock him yet he was sure there had been nothing between them. She had admired him, Mike knew that. He had seemed shy, hardly speaking on the few occasions Mike had met him.

Lorraine came out of the shower, wrapped in a towel with another round her wet hair. 'You want some aspirin, sweetheart?'

'Yeah, yeah, thanks.'

The hair-dryer felt leaden in her hands. All she wanted was to lie down and sleep. Mike handed her a glass of water and two aspirins. He kissed the top of her head; her hair fell in a soft pageboy style, flattering her heart-shaped face. 'I'll maybe get a partnership soon,' he said, as he sat on the edge of the bed. 'It'll mean a lot more money and you not having to work.'

She slowly rubbed foundation cream over her cheeks, a small dop on her nose. 'When will you know?'

'Well, this Coleridge case is good for me. He's an influential guy – he's even said he'd recommend me to his friends.'

'All getting divorces, are they?' He laughed as, dipping the thick brush into the face powder, she dabbed it over her face. 'I thought you wanted to specialize in criminal law.'

'Yeah, I did – maybe I still do but it's good to get a grounding in all aspects. Besides—'

'Divorce pays better, doesn't it?'

9

Mike's expression was sharp. 'Is that such a bad thing? Do you like this place?'

'Yes, of course I do.'

'Well, I'll be making a lot more soon. Next we'll have a house in Santa Monica, right on the beach.'

'Oh, business is that good, is it?'

He laughed again. 'It'll take a few years but Donny seems to think I'll go places. When I look around here, it's hard to believe what we came from.' He slipped his arms around her. 'And I'll never forget how I got it. If it wasn't for you . . .'

She smiled, now brushing on a light blusher. Those days when he was studying day and night, when he worked at any odd job he could get, those days were a long, long time ago.

'We'd have more time together as well.'

Lorraine put down the brush. 'If I was at home with an apron on and a casserole in the oven?'

'I doubt if you'd ever be that, sweetheart, but you know we should think about it and also, maybe, about a holiday. When will you know about your next vacation so I can work it out with Donny?'

She carefully outlined her lips, her pale blue eyes staring back at herself. 'I'll talk it over with Rooney.'

The doorbell rang and Mike charged out. It was the pizza delivery. She should get a move on. She heard him on the phone, confirming with Rita what time she was to come over. Mike the methodical! Upwardly mobile Mike was so different nowadays, she seemed to be losing him.

Lorraine stared at the blurred picture of Lubrinski. She touched his face with the tip of her forefinger. His face seemed to crease into a smile – but that was impossible, he'd never smile at her again. Lubrinski was dead; he had died in her arms. Sometimes she felt as if *she* was dead. Nothing seemed real any more; this apartment, all the new-fangled equipment Mike filled it with, all the new furniture.

10

Mike had organized the move down to the curtains. She'd liked their old place even if you did have to lug the strollers up and down three flights of stairs. She missed the neighbours. Sometimes Mike's energy drained her and lately she was always tired. She never spoke to anyone in the building and didn't even know who lived on her floor.

The doorbell rang again and she could hear Mike welcoming the guests. Still she sat, unable to muster enough energy to join them. She pulled out the bottle from the bottom drawer of the dressing table. Just a few nips, that's all she needed.

Donny and Tina were chattering in the kitchen while Mike uncorked the wine. Tina Patterson looked as if she was heading out to a premiere rather than the local cinema. She kissed Lorraine on both cheeks and Donny gripped her tightly in a firm 'trust me' handshake. Mike ushered everyone into the dining area and proceeded to pour the wine. He was doing everything – seating his guests, bringing in big platters of pizza, apologizing for the informal dinner, explaining that Lorraine had only just got home from duty.

She sat sipping her wine. She couldn't look at the pizza: its bright colours made her feel like vomiting. They discussed the Coleridge case. Donny constantly gripped Mike's shoulder in another 'trust me' gesture that irritated Lorraine, just as she found Tina's delicate hands with their red-painted nails annoying. They made clicking noises on the plate as she picked up a minuscule slice of pizza, popping it into her collagen-enhanced lips. 'To look at you, Lorraine, you'd never know you were a cop, it's just amazing.'

Lorraine forced a smile as Mike reached over and held her hand. 'I'm so proud of my wife. You know, she's been commended for bravery twice.'

He sprang up from the table, went to the side cabinet and returned with two framed photographs. Lorraine in uniform with President Reagan and in a group picture of the year's most decorated officers. 'Lorraine caught the killer of that little girl, you remember the one that was found in a drainpipe? The caretaker had done it, she was the one that caught him.'

Tina made the right noises, shaking her head and rolling her eyes – with admiration, Lorraine supposed. She drained her glass; she needed another drink. 'I'll put some coffee on,' she said, leaving the table. She took out the vodka from the freezer and drank from the bottle. She had only just slipped it back when Tina appeared carrying the dirty dishes. 'Men's talk in there. Can I help?'

Lorraine laughed. She was feeling better, eased by the vodka and wine. Tina began to stack dishes in the dishwasher.

'Do you get involved?'

'Pardon?'

'When you have to do these murder investigations, do you get involved?'

'Yep.' Lorraine was fixing the coffee percolator.

'Does it affect you?' Tina enquired, running her hand under the tap. 'I always know when Donny's on a tough case – he's so moody. He works out at a gym to get rid of the anxiety, you know, but . . . that case of the little girl . . . That must have been terrible.'

Lorraine fetched a tray. 'She was only six, her name was Laura Bradley. She'd been raped, tortured, and she had a face like a little angel. Yeah, it hurt me.'

Tina hunched her shoulders. Lorraine set the tray, placing each cup in its saucer with deliberate precision. 'For a while afterwards, I got possessive about the girls, scared they'd be picked up. It never leaves you. You think it'll go away but it never does.'

Tina had left the kitchen. Lorraine could hear her next door.

12

'Okay, you guys, no more business, this is movie night. We're just gonna enjoy ourselves.'

The movie programme had so many previews that Lorraine excused herself, saying she wanted to go to the ladies. She needed another drink. She reckoned if she just slipped out to the nearest bar and had a quick one, she'd be back before the film had started.

When she hadn't returned half-way through the movie, Mike went to look for her. He called Rita to see if she had gone home; she hadn't. Back in the cinema, he told the Pattersons that Lorraine sent her apologies but had felt ill, and rather than spoil their evening had gone home. It was after eleven when Mike got back. He checked Lorraine's duty periods; as he'd known, she was on a two-day break but he called the station in case he'd got it wrong. He was put through to Bill Rooney.

After the call, Mike paced the apartment, sat in the kitchen, then in the living room flicking the TV from channel to channel, waiting. He checked the girls. He waited until he fell asleep on the sofa. He was woken by shrieking laughter. He got up and crossed to the window.

Lorraine was standing on the pavement outside, paying off a taxi. Two people were inside it. He watched her drop her purse and fall against the wall before she reeled into their building.

The front door was open as she walked from the elevator. She took a deep breath and, with a fixed smile, peered inside. Mike grasped her by the elbow and drew her into the kitchen. He kicked the door closed. 'Where've you been?'

'Oh, I hadda do something.'

'What?'

'Just interview somebody.' She was trying to keep her

voice from slurring; her eyes were unfocused. He pushed a cup of coffee towards her. 'I'm tired.'

'Drink it and sober up.'

She rested her head in her hands. Mike drew out a chair and sat opposite her. 'I know, Lorraine.'

'Know what?'

Mike told her he had spoken to Rooney. She sighed, looking away, and shrugged. He leaned over and gripped her hand. 'I know about the shooting. Why didn't you tell me?'

She tried to pull away her hand. He wouldn't let go. 'Why won't you talk to me?'

She pushed him off and hunched up, clasped her hands together. He had to lean further forward to hear her. 'There's nothing to say, Mike.'

He got up and paced the kitchen. 'What do you mean, nothing to say?' He wanted to slap her. 'You were drunk on duty and you're telling me that you have nothing to say about that?'

She gave a soft laugh. 'No complaints.'

He gripped her hair and drew her head back. 'You killed a boy, Lorraine.' She made no effort to release herself and he shoved her forwards, disgusted. 'You shot him.'

She nodded.

It was impossible for Mike to know what she was thinking; her eyes were glazed, and she seemed to be half smiling.

'You're out, don't you understand? You're out of the force. *They've kicked you out!* Rooney told me they took your badge.'

She shrugged again. 'Well, that'll make you happy, I'll get some nail extensions and some Carmen rollers and make myself into a Tina clone. That what you want, Mike? *Is that what you want?*' Her face was ugly with rage. She had no shame – and worse, no remorse.

'Go to bed, Lorraine.'

14

She stumbled against the doorframe, and fell face down on the bed. Mike didn't bother to undress her. He was almost out of the room when she said something, muffled by the pillows. She was repeating it, over and over. 'I don't remember, I don't remember, he's dead, he's dead.'

Mike never heard the plaintively whispered, 'Don't go.' Instead, he sat in his study until dawn, compiling notes for his case.

The next morning, glass of whisky in her hand, Lorraine sat at the kitchen table. Nothing meant anything any more.

Mike joined her and sat opposite. She held up the glass. 'Hair of the dog.'

'What are you going to do?'

'You mean work?' she asked.

'No. Will you be on trial or what?'

'I don't know.'

'I blame Lubrinski. You've not been the same since you started working alongside him.'

'Lubrinski's dead, for chrissakes.'

Mike watched as she refilled her glass. Suddenly he sprang to his feet and yanked away the bottle. 'That's enough.'

She held out the glass like a dirty diaper. He snatched it. 'It's nine thirty in the morning. How long has this been going on?'

'What going on, Mike?'

Holding the bottle, he almost felt in need of a drink himself.

'I just wanted something to ease me up a bit. I've been kind of tense lately.'

He was speechless.

'I don't have a problem, Mike. It's just . . . lately things have got to me.'

He felt as if someone had punched the air out of his

15

lungs. Lorraine looked at her bare feet. 'I feel all strung out and I can't remember what happened the other night.'

He swallowed. 'You killed a kid, Lorraine. They've taken your badge, you're out, don't you understand?'

'Oh.' She said it lightly, still staring at her feet.

'I'm gonna talk to Rooney again. I don't know if they're pressing charges.'

'Have you talked to Rooney, then?' she asked.

'Yes,' he snapped. 'I told you last night. How the hell do you think I know about it? And what do you think Donny is gonna say about this if it gets into the press?'

'Donny?' she said, confused. 'What's he got to do with me?'

'He's got a lot to do with *me*. I'm in the middle of a big case right now. How do you think it's gonna look if they find out my wife not only opened fire on a kid but was drunk on duty as well?'

She rubbed at her neck. 'It's none of their business.'

Mike closed his eyes. 'No? You think the press won't have a field day with this?'

She took out a cigarette, hands shaking. He watched as she tried to light it. She inhaled deeply. 'You remember that day, Mike?' He sighed. She looked at him, tilting her head to one side. 'Best day of my life. You'd just qualified and . . . what happened, Mike? I feel like I don't know you, like I'm drifting in some kind of sea. I hate what you're becoming and I've gone along with it, never felt I could say anything to you but it's all changing between us. You want success more than you want me.'

Mike poured himself two fingers in the tumbler she had used and drained it. It was as if someone was pulling the rug from beneath his feet. Suddenly everything he had been striving for was ragged at the edge. He sat down, cradling the glass in his hands. 'Nothing has changed between you and me, nothing. I love you. I always *have* loved you. Okay, maybe I've had to put in more hours lately, but then so

16

have you. You know I wanted you to give up work, you think I didn't notice the strain you were under, but you'll never talk to me.'

She knelt down at his feet and wrapped her arms around him. 'I want things to be the way they were when we both had nothing.'

'You had your career. It was me that had nothing,' he said petulantly.

'But you know why? I worked hard so we'd have a home and you'd have your chance.'

He kissed her forehead. 'Maybe you haven't noticed that I'm earning good money now – you haven't needed to work for years and you're missing the girls growing up.' She leaned against him and he slipped his arm around her. 'Whatever happens, we'll come through this together.'

They went to bed and made love for the first time in ages. That evening, Lorraine began to prepare dinner, even putting candles on the table. Then it started, the panic. It swamped inside her, beginning, as always, with fast flashes of faces. Lubrinski, then Laura Bradley, and now the boy? A boy running with a yellow stripe down his sweater. All she could think of was to get just one drink; then the panic would stop and the pictures would blur into oblivion. She wouldn't feel so uncomfortable, so trapped. Just one drink would do it and she'd be all right. She went on with the dinner, having just one more, then another and another.

Mike didn't come home until after midnight. He saw that the table had been laid for some special occasion; the candlewax had melted over the cloth. In the kitchen he found two wine bottles and the Scotch bottle, all empty in the trashcan with the remains of dinner.

Lorraine was asleep, still in her dress. He didn't wake her, not even to tell her that Donny had offered him a partnership. He pulled the quilt from beneath her and laid it gently over her. He went round the apartment and threw every liquor bottle he could find into the garbage chute.

Not until he slid into bed next to her did he see that Lorraine was cradling the picture of Lubrinski in her arms. When he tried to take it from her she moaned and turned over. Maybe there had been a lot more to their partnership than he had realized.

Next morning, Lorraine was up early, cooking breakfast for the girls. Mike could hear her laughing and talking. By the time he went into the kitchen, they were ready for school.

'I'll drive them,' she said. 'You haven't had breakfast yet!'

He snatched up his car keys. 'I'll drive them, okay?'

'When will you be home?'

'I'm in court today so I'll be late.' He walked out without kissing her goodbye, slamming the front door.

She was making the bed when he called. He'd booked her a doctor's appointment.

'You did what?'

'Listen to me, sweetheart, he's somebody you can talk to, friend of Donny's—'

Lorraine interrupted, 'I don't need a god-damned shrink, especially not some asshole friend of Donny's. There's nothing wrong with me that a few days' rest—'

Mike was adamant, not wanting to sound angry but unable not to. 'Yes, you do, Lorraine, listen, don't hang up—'

Her voice was icy, calm and controlled. 'No, Mike, I don't need anybody, I am not sick, okay? That's final. I'll see you tonight.'

Lorraine made no contact with the station. She checked the newspapers for articles on the case, but was afraid to read about herself. She was afraid, too, to be seen on the street and for the next few weeks she led a double life. When Mike left in the morning she did some housework and ordered in groceries. When Rita brought the girls

18

home, she played with them, read to them and cooked dinner for Mike. He knew she was drinking but she denied it and he never saw her with a glass of alcohol in her hand. He had no idea that she spent her days sitting in front of the television with a bottle of vodka. She appeared sober, keeping herself at a sustained level, and every night he would look for empty bottles. Mike hid from himself that she was drinking consistently, partly because it meant less tension between them. He asked Rita to tell him if she ever saw Lorraine drinking, especially in front of the girls.

It was only a few weeks later that Rita called him. 'You'd better come home, Mr Page. I don't know where she is – she left the girls by themselves – anything could have happened.'

Mike drove like a madman back to the apartment. The children had been alone for most of the day. After Mike had calmed them, he asked Rita to stay with them, and went out in a blind fury to find his wife. After searching in vain for three hours, he called home. Rita was in tears: Lorraine was back, she was drunk, unable to stand upright. A cigarette in her hand, she apologized, telling him that she had had an important meeting. She seemed barely to hear him when he talked to her, and if he touched her she screamed abuse at him. Then, as if terrified of something or someone, she begged him to hold her tightly.

Next morning, shame-faced, she promised him he would never see her like that again. Never again would she touch a drop.

Mike coped as best he could. He instructed Rita never to leave Lorraine alone with the girls until he was at home. But the situation grew worse. Time and again he confronted her with empty bottles he found hidden around the apartment. She would swear she hadn't had a drink and even accused Rita of planting the bottles.

Mike was at breaking point. He tried to understand Lorraine's frame of mind by putting himself in her position – she had shot an innocent boy and had lost the job she had always been so proud of – but all he felt was shame and guilt, of which she showed none. She seemed more intent on blaming his success for her failure.

'You spoiled it. You wanted us to move up and we were happy where we were.' The continual goading made him feel she was pushing him physically to hurt her. 'You were the housewife, but I was out on the streets. You were the mother, but I had to earn for both of us, out on the streets with my breasts still full of milk for my babies.'

No matter what he said she twisted it against him. If he had any guilt about those years when she had kept him and the children, it was soon dispersed by her venomous onslaughts. She exhausted him; night after night he would come home in dread to find her ready for a row. At other times, she would kneel at his feet and beg his forgiveness, pleading for him to carry her to bed. And yet she seemed incapable of tears.

In the end Mike went to Donny's doctor friend. He needed to talk it over with someone. The doctor warned him that unless Lorraine sought help Mike would be dragged down with her. He encouraged him to leave her and thus force her into taking medical help. But Mike's own guilt and his awareness of how much Lorraine had done for him, held him back. When his daughters became scared of their mother, though, Mike made one last attempt.

Lorraine finally agreed and he accompanied her, quiet and sober, to the doctor. She spent two hours with him, talking first with Mike present and then alone. After the appointment she had appeared almost triumphant, admonishing Mike for wasting money. There was, as she had said to him over and over again, nothing wrong with her.

Mike returned the following day and was told that Lorraine had insisted that she was perfectly all right and able to cope with no longer working. She had refused to give a blood test.

But the drinking carried on and the rift between them grew deeper. Lorraine adamantly refused to admit anything was wrong: she had her drinking under control. She was becoming sly; apparently sober, she continued to dress well but rarely left the apartment. Mike continued to find empty bottles hidden away.

Only six months after Lorraine had left the force, he filed for divorce. He refused to make her leave the apartment, and signed it over to her with the contents. She protested when he insisted on custody of the girls but otherwise seemed not to care. He gave her five thousand dollars and promised three thousand a month in alimony. She was strangely elated when he brought the papers for her signature, which made him suspect that she didn't believe he would go through with it. But she signed with a flourish and smiled.

'You do understand what you've signed, don't you, Lorraine?' Mike asked quietly.

'Yes.'

He gripped her tightly. 'I'm leaving and taking the girls but call me if you need me, and I'll do whatever I can to help. You need help, Lorraine, all I want is for you to acknowledge it.' He felt wretched. She helped him pack, kneeling to lock the suitcase. She was wearing a pale blue denim shirt and her feet were bare. Her hair shone as she bent over the cases. Mike wanted to hold her, to make love to her. This was madness.

The Pattersons came to help with the cases. The girls, clasping Tina's hands, thought they were going on holiday. It had taken only the afternoon to get everything packed and out, such a short time after all the years they had been together.

'Tina's going to take the girls in their car. Do you want to say goodbye to them?' Mike asked.

'No. I don't want to upset them.' She heard her daughters asking if they were going to see their granny and why was Mommy staying behind? She heard Tina reassuring them that Mommy would be coming to see them. She heard Donny call out that everything was in the car. She heard Mike say he would be out in a few minutes. She heard Rita saying goodbye, her voice breaking as if she was crying.

Mike walked into the kitchen. Lorraine turned and held up the glass. 'Just milk.'

He leaned on the table. 'I don't want to go, Lorraine.'

'Doesn't look that way to me.'

'I love you.'

She tossed her hair away from her eyes. 'I love you too, Mike.'

There seemed nothing left to say. He crossed to her, reached out and held her in his arms. She rested her head against his shoulder, the way she always used to. He could smell lemons, a clean, sweet smell of freshly washed hair, and he tilted up her face and kissed her. She had the most beautiful clear blue eyes he had ever seen. She seemed to look straight through him, yet her lips had a soft sweet smile.

'Promise me you'll get help?'

'I'll be okay. Don't worry about me, Mike.'

Donny Patterson sat in the car. He watched Mike walk slowly down the path, looking as if he was crying.

'You okay, partner?'

Mike got into the car and blew his nose. 'I feel like such a prick. She doesn't seem to understand what's just happened.'

Donny put his arm round his friend. 'Look, buddy, I been through this three times. It's not easy, but, Jesus, now it's over you're gonna feel such relief. She's got problems. You tried every way to help her, Mike.'

'Maybe we'll get back together,' Mike said.

Donny gripped Mike's knee. 'Christ almighty. When are you gonna face facts? She's a drunk and she was dragging you down with her. If she won't get help, you're gonna have to forget her, act like she's dead. Believe me, it's the best way. Say to yourself she's dead, be a hell of a lot easier.'

Mike nodded. His heart felt like lead. He closed his eyes. 'I loved her,' he said softly.

Lorraine sat on the sofa, flicking the TV from channel to channel. There was no need now to hide the half-bottle of vodka that lay beside her. She could do what she liked, she was on her own. She didn't deserve anyone's love or respect, she knew that. She was deeply ashamed that she didn't have the guts to slit her wrists. Or was it because she didn't deserve to die so easily? She was her own judge, her own jury. She had to be punished.

Lorraine finished the vodka and went in search of more. She looked around the bedroom, seeing the open wardrobe doors, the empty hangers where Mike's clothes had hung, and backed out of the room. She discovered another bottle hidden in the kitchen and had drunk most of that before she wandered into the children's room. She was humming tunelessly. She got into Sally's tiny bed, holding the bottle to her chest. She could smell her daughter on the pillow; it was as if the little girl was kissing her face, she felt so close. She reached over to the other bed for Julia's pillow and held it to her cheek. She snuggled down clasping the pillows. 'My babies,' she whispered, 'my babies.' She looked drunkenly at the wallpaper, with its pink and blue ribbons threaded round children's nursery rhymes. 'Run rabbit, run rabbit, run, run, run . . .'

She could feel a lovely warm blanket begin slowly to cover her body, a soft pink baby blanket, like the one tucked round her when she was a little girl, like the one she had wrapped round the dead child's body. She felt her chest tighten with panic, her body tense. She could hear him now. Lubrinski.

'Eh, how ya doin', Page?'

'I'm doin' okay, Lubrinski,' she said aloud, startled to hear her own voice. 'I'm doin' fine, partner.' She frowned. Who was screaming? Somebody was screaming, the terrifying sound going on and on and on, driving her nuts. She rolled out of bed and ran from the room. She tripped and fell to her knees until she was crawling on all fours into the bedroom. The screaming continued. She heaved herself up and caught sight of a figure reflected in the dressing-table mirror. She clapped her hands over her mouth, biting her fingers to stop the screams. *She* was the woman, it was *her* screaming. The terrible sweating panic swamped her.

It was Lubrinski's smiling face that calmed her, looking up at her from the dressing table. She snatched up the photograph. 'Help me, Lubrinski, for chrissakes help me.'

'Sure, honey, take a shot of this, then what say you and me go and rip up the town? You wanna hit the bars?'

'Yeah, why not, you son-of-a-bitch?' Lorraine gave a tough, bitter laugh, and felt herself straightening out as the panic subsided and she was back in control.

That was the first night Lorraine went out to drink alone in one of the old downtown bars. She never knew who she ended up with, she didn't give a damn, and they didn't mind when she called them Lubrinski. A lot of Lubrinski lookalikes came and went, and there were many more drunken nights when she didn't care if Lubrinski was with her or not. All she cared about was getting another drink to keep her away from the terrified woman who screamed.

The downward spiral began the night after Mike left her. It was a long road she travelled, searching for oblivion. It was frighteningly easy. People were real friendly in the bars but they used and stole from her. When the money had gone she sold the furniture, and then the apartment. It was good to have a big stash of money, never to worry where the next bottle came from, and still she kept running from the woman in blue whose terrible screams frightened her so much and dragged her down so far. She could take the fights, and the taunts of prostitutes and pimps. Hell, she had arrested many of them. They pushed her around and spiked her drinks but drunk, she didn't care. Drunk, the screams were obliterated. Drunk, the men who pawed her meant nothing. Drunk, she could hide, feel some comfort in slobbering embraces, in strange rooms, in beds where the little rabbits didn't creep into her mind and she didn't hear the children singing, a high-pitched shrill voice that turned into a scream.

'Run, rabbit, run rabbit, run, run, run . . . RUN.'

CHAPTER 1

CALIFORNIA, 11 April 1994

S HE HAD almost died that night. The hit-and-run
driver had probably not even seen her, and Lorraine
could remember little. She had been taken to hospital
with head injuries. The following weeks were a blur, as she
was moved from one charitable organization to another;
she had no money and no medical insurance left. Eventually
she was institutionalized and preliminarily diagnosed as
schizophrenic. To begin with, she was not thought to be an
alcoholic as so much else was wrong with her. She had
severe abscesses, a minor venereal disease plus genital
herpes, skin disorders, and poor physical condition from
lack of decent food. Eighty cigarettes a day had left her
with a persistent heavy cough. She contracted pneumonia,
and for a few days it was doubtful that she would live.
When she pulled through, the hallucinations, screaming fits
and vomiting made the doctors suspect severe alcohol
withdrawal symptoms.

A string of psychiatrists and doctors interviewed her and
prescribed various medication. After two months she was
transferred to the nightmare of Ward C, Watts City Mental
Hospital where LA County sent only their worst cases, the
drop-outs and no hopers. Drug-crazed kids, deranged old
ladies, suicidal middle-aged women – every fucked-up
female soul who walked the earth seemed to be marooned
with Lorraine. They added chronic alcoholism to Lorraine's
list of ailments. Her liver was shot, and she was warned that

if she did not give up drinking she would be dead within the year. Eventually she was transferred to the White Garden rehabilitation centre.

Rosie Hurst was working as a cook at the centre, one of those women who gave their free time as part of a rehabilitation programme. Rosie, a big, plump, sturdy woman, with short, frizzy permed hair, was a recovering alcoholic with six months' sobriety. She worked hard and was as friendly as she could be with the inmates, a there-but-for-the-grace-of-God attitude never far from her thoughts. Some of the saner inmates were allocated menial jobs in the kitchen and that was how Rosie got to know Lorraine Page.

Lorraine didn't want to live. She had been waiting to die, wondering hazily why she wasn't already dead, and then musing that, perhaps, she was. And this was hell. It wasn't such a bad hell – the drugs made her more relaxed – but she wanted a drink. It was the only thought that occupied her dulled senses. Her mouth was thick and dry, her tongue felt too big, and she drank water all day, bending down to the small fountain in the corridor, hogging it, mouth open, hand pressed down on the lever for the water to spurt directly into her swollen mouth. Nothing dulled her thirst.

'How long you been an alcoholic?'

Rosie had been watching her in the corridor. Lorraine couldn't say because she had never admitted it to herself. She just liked to drink.

'What work did you do?'

Lorraine could not recall what she'd been up to for the past few years. All the weeks and months had merged into a blur, and she could hardly remember one year from another. Or the bars, dens, seedy, run-down clubs where she had been drunk alongside girls she had once picked up and locked away. They had liked that. And the pimps she had hassled and booked in her days as a vice squad trainee, liked being able to sell her so cheaply. She was known to go with anyone, as long as they kept her supplied with a steady flow of booze. Hotels, bars, dives, private parties . . . Lorraine would be cleaned up and sent out. It didn't matter how many or who they were, just as long as she made enough money for booze. She had been arrested, not just for hooking but for vagrancy, and released, pending charges, but had never made her court appearance. She had simply moved on to another bar, another town.

At the time of the hit-and-run accident, Lorraine had reached rock bottom. So far down in the gutter she couldn't even get a trick, and no pimp wanted her attached to his stable. So many truckers, so many different states, she was unaware she was back in LA. She owned only what she stood up in, had even sold her wedding ring. She was such a wreck that the prostitutes didn't want her hanging around them. She was even out in the cold from the street winos, because she stole from them. She had become incapable of caring for herself or earning a few cents for food.

No one remembered her as Lieutenant Page, it was all so long ago. The human flesh trade moves on and changes fast. Many of the young vice-patrol cops who saw her falling down in the streets had no idea who she was. Sergeant Rooney had been promoted to captain. He didn't know if she was alive or dead, and he didn't care.

No one cared, not even Mike or her children. Mike had tried often, over the years, to help her. He heard from her occasionally on the girls' birthdays and at Christmas, but she was incoherent on the phone and lapsed into strange silences apart from asking him for money. The calls stopped when Mike moved house. He remarried, and the children settled into a new school, a new life. They no longer asked

28

about their mother; they had a new, better one. Lorraine made no attempt to contact Mike again. She seemed almost satisfied that she had at last severed every tie.

Only Rosie, because of her own problems and her open friendly nature, wanted to help Lorraine, so thin and pale, with that strange waif-like blonde hair that hung in badly cut, jagged edges. Her fingers were stained dark brown with nicotine, and she had lost a front tooth. She also had a strange way of looking at people, her head tilted as if she were short-sighted, an odd, nervous squint, made more obvious because of a nasty scar running from her left eye to just above her cheekbone. The shapeless regulation blue hospital gown hung loosely on Lorraine's skinny frame. She wore overlarge brown shoes – like a ballet dancer's; someone had passed them on to her and they flopped at her heels as she walked.

Rosie and Lorraine worked side by side, helping to dish out food and make up trays. As the weeks passed, Rosie realized there was more to Lorraine than appeared on the surface. She never had to be told twice which inmates required a special diet but passed out the food to the right women.

'You must have had a job once. How old are you?' Rosie was trying to make conversation.

'I guess I must be around thirty-six. D'you have a cigarette?'

Rosie shook her head. She'd given up smoking when she gave up booze. 'I used to work on computers. What sort of jobs did you do?'

Lorraine was delving among the food scraps in the trashcan, looking for a butt end. She gave up and dried her hands. 'Rosie, you wouldn't believe me if I told you . . . I'll go an' see if I can steal one.'

Rosie watched as she shuffled over to Mad Mona, who really was out-to-lunch, but always had a guarded packet of cigarettes. She watched Lorraine searching Mona's pockets,

29

pretending to tickle her, and then the screaming started as she caught Lorraine with her precious packet. But Lorraine got one, because she came back puffing like an asthmatic on an inhaler.

'Do you have any family?' Rosie enquired, as Lorraine leaned against the door, eyes closed.

'Nope.'

Rosie remarked that she had a son somewhere, but hadn't seen him or his father for years. She busied herself at the sink, and was about to resume her conversation but she saw Lorraine had gone. Rosie took off her overall and went to collect her wages, a pittance, considering the number of hours she put in, but she was only part-time, and most of the staff were Mexican. Probably they were paid even less. She smiled at the receptionist as she buttoned up her baggy cardigan. 'I'll see you in a couple of days.'

The receptionist nodded. 'It's hot out. You won't need that on.'

Rosie shrugged – she had arrived so early that there'd been a chill in the air. She asked how long Lorraine was being kept on the ward.

The receptionist checked on the clipboard behind her. 'Oh, she's due to be released. May not be here when you come back Thursday. The doctors haven't signed her out yet, but she's down to leave. Has she been okay in the kitchen? You know the way they are – steal anything . . .'

Rosie's shopping bag suddenly felt heavy: the chops, the half-chicken she had removed along with the sugar, potatoes and carrots meant she'd be fired if she were caught. She hurried off, saying she wanted to catch her bus.

Lorraine, however, was still resident when Rosie returned two days later. She looked even paler, and coughed continually. According to the receptionist, she had developed a fever, so they were keeping her in for observation. Rosie was concerned, but did not have time to talk as she had to prepare lunch.

It was not until later, when they were washing up, that she could ask Lorraine how she was. She seemed reluctant to talk and didn't bother helping Rosie with the trays, more intent on guarding her position at the water fountain. Her need for alcohol was becoming more desperate each day; she craved sweets and nicotine, stealing treasured hoards of chocolate bars and cigarette packs from the unwary.

With no money and no place to live, she decided she'd have to turn to Rosie who might have somewhere she could stay – and something worth stealing. That was her sole motive for talking to Rosie. Lorraine wanted a drink, wanted money, wanted out of the crazies' ward. All Rosie wanted was a friend.

'You know, I could help you – if you want to help yourself. If you tell me, say, "Rosie, I want to help myself", then I will do everything in my power to help you. I'll take you to my meetings . . . We have counsellors, people you can really talk to, and . . . they'll help you get work. You're an intelligent woman, there must be something you can find . . .'

Lorraine had given her that odd squinting look, smoking a cigarette down to its cork tip. 'Yeah. Maybe I could get my old job back.'

'What did you do?'

'I was a cop.'

Rosie chuckled, rolling out pastry. She jumped when Lorraine stood close behind her, so close and so tall she had to lean over.

'I am arresting you on the charge of molesting that pastry, Rosie. Anything you say may be taken down and used in evidence against you . . .'

Rosie laughed, and Lorraine tickled her, just like she tickled Mad Mona. Far from stupid, Rosie was beginning to suspect that Lorraine was after something. She wondered what it was. She dropped heavy hints that she was broke

31

just in case Lorraine had thought otherwise and was after money . . .

Three weeks later Lorraine was given her marching orders. While she waited for Rosie to arrive, she cleaned the kitchen. Then she helped Rosie all morning, but it was quite late before she mentioned that she was leaving. To her surprise, Rosie told her she already knew. 'I've been thinking about all the things you've been telling me, Rosie. And, well – you're on. I'll come to one of these meetings 'cos I want my life back.' Her voice was hardly audible. 'I'll tell you a secret. I really was a cop, a lieutenant.'

Rosie looked up into the pale face. 'Is that the truth?'

Lorraine nodded. 'Yeah. Look, can I crash on your floor until I get a place of my own?' She reckoned if Rosie knew she had been a cop she would trust her. It worked.

Rosie gave a wide grin, concealing her hesitancy. 'Sure you can, but it's not much of a place. Do you have a lot of gear?'

Lorraine lied, telling Rosie that her belongings were with a friend she didn't want to see because she was another drinker – and she wanted to stay clean.

Rosie understood, knowing it was a mistake for a drinker to return to old friends and old habits.

'Okay. You can stay at my place.'

At the end of the day, Rosie waited for her outside the hospital. Lorraine was wearing an odd assortment of clothes. Nothing fitted – sleeves too short, the skirt waistband hanging around her hips. She carried a clean set of underwear in a brown paper bag, and seemed even taller, thinner and stranger-looking than she had in the safety of the rehabilitation clinic. Someone had given her a pair of pink-framed sunglasses, the lenses so dark they hid her eyes. Seeing her in the bright sunshine, Rosie had severe doubts about taking her in. She wished she had not been so friendly.

Lorraine was silent on the long journey, as they changed buses four times. She didn't like going back to her home territory, Pasadena, but then she didn't really know any place any more. She was glad to have Rosie – even felt a strange desire to hold her hand, afraid she would lose sight of her.

Eventually they were walking along a wide road with small dilapidated bungalows, past a four-storey apartment block. Rosie pointed to a grocery store. 'I shop there and live above that garage just a few yards along. It's very convenient.'

Lorraine nodded. Even from this distance she had seen the liquor section in the store. Her body broke out in a sweat, her mouth felt rancid, and she licked her lips. As she stood at the counter next to Rosie, who was buying bread and salads and coffee, she felt like screaming. Her eyes constantly strayed to the bottles: she wanted a drink so badly she felt faint.

'Here we are, now, you go up ahead. It's so narrow, this staircase, I'm always tripping down . . . watch how you go, the fifth step is loose . . .'

They climbed up the wooden stairway and Rosie unlocked the screen door, then her front door. As she pushed it open a cat screeched and dived out between Lorraine's legs.

'That's Walter. Go in, you first.'

Rosie's tiny apartment was stiflingly hot, even with the blinds down. She turned on the air conditioning, which whirred noisily. There was a living room and one cramped bedroom with a tiny shower room attached. The kitchen was a messy corner of the living room. Rosie busied herself unloading the groceries, pointing out the couch for Lorraine to sleep on, bringing sheets and pillows.

'Now, do you want some tea, or coffee, or something cold? I think I've got chilled Coke – or lemonade?'

Lorraine rested back on the sofa, rolling an ice-cold Coke can across her forehead. She was still desperate for a real drink. She gulped at the Coke, draining the can quickly.

Rosie held up a packet of cigarettes. 'I thought you'd be needing one, so here.' She tossed it over. 'Now you clean up and run a comb through your hair, and then we should go, the meeting's due to start in about an hour.'

Lorraine closed her eyes and sighed. 'Maybe I'm a bit too tired today.'

Rosie loomed over her. 'Today is when you really need to go, and I can arrange that you go every day for the first few weeks.' Lorraine managed a weak smile and hauled herself to her feet, crossing through Rosie's dusty bedroom into the small bathroom, which was crammed with jars of creams, tubes, and a vast array of worn toothbrushes and half-squeezed toothpaste tubes. Old tights were hung up to dry, large faded panties and a greyish bra pinned on a piece of string, so large Lorraine stared in disbelief.

She ran the water and bent down to drink it, gulping it down, then she splashed her face and reached for a thread-bare towel. She looked at herself then, really studied herself, no drugs and stone-cold sober for the first time in years. The image that stared back was of a stranger. Her eyes were puffy, washed-out, red-rimmed, and her nose had small, white-headed spots at each side. She caught sight of her yellowish, stained teeth, the gap in the front. The scar stretched her cheek slightly, an ugly reminder of a past she wanted to obliterate. She traced the outline of her cracked, swollen lips and then ran her hand through her thin hair, strands of it coming away. It looked as if someone had hacked it haphazardly, any way but straight. Maybe she'd even done it herself, she couldn't remember. There were not just days or weeks or months she couldn't remember but whole years.

Rosie rapped on the door. 'What are you doing in there?'

Lorraine took a deep breath. 'Just washing. Won't be long . . .' As she dried her hands she gazed at the stains along her fingers, the nails jagged, bitten and dirty. Everything about her was hideous: she was revolting, she disgusted herself, she *was* disgusting. And deeply angry. She didn't know this person. Who was she?

Rosie looked up from the sofa and smiled. 'You ready?'

Lorraine looked around for the pink-framed sunglasses. She pushed them on, as if to hide behind them. 'Thank you for taking me in like this. It's very good of you.'

Rosie, searching for her keys, wafted her hand. 'I made a vow, because somebody helped me out when I was down. I promised that I'd help someone else if I could. I guess that person is you.'

Lorraine sat at the back of the meeting, hands clenched, face hidden behind the sunglasses. The other people there had greeted her with such warmth that she had wanted to run out of the building. Gripping her hand, Rosie had found her a seat. She was introduced only as Lorraine. Nobody gave their last name unless they wanted to. As the meeting began, Lorraine was able to look at the others. None looked in bad shape though a few had a lost air about them, as they sat with their heads bowed, or stared into space. Slowly she began to pay attention to those who told their stories.

One woman recalled how she had not known who she was for fifteen years, because those years had merged into one long, blurred binge. Now she was smart, and positive, and proud that she had been dry for four years. She had met someone who had given her love and stability. Soon, she hoped, she would have the confidence to tell him that she was an alcoholic. He had been so embarrassed for her when, sober, she had tripped over a paving stone and fallen flat on her face. She laughed then, saying that she hadn't had the heart to tell him she had been face down on the floor more often than she had been upright. She grew emotional, lifting up her arms as if she were at some Baptist church meeting. Lorraine sighed with boredom. 'I'm standing upright now, and I intend to remain this way, just as, when I get a little stronger, I will tell him that I am an alcoholic. Hopefully he will come to one of our meetings so he can fully understand my illness and that I believe, at long last, I am in recovery. I want to recover – just as I know I will always be an alcoholic. I am an alcoholic. Thank you for listening to me, thank you for being here. God bless you all . . .' She burst into tears and many people clustered around her, hugging her, congratulating her.

Lorraine remained at the back of the hall, embarrassed by the show of emotion. She was glad when the meeting ended, refusing to hold other members' hands as they prayed together for strength and guidance. Rosie, on the other hand, was very into it all, her eyes closed, clutching the hands of two elderly women.

Later, back at the apartment, Rosie was full of enthusiasm and energy. 'Those meetings saved my life. Some people have been going for ten or fifteen years. When you face what you are it doesn't stop. You will always be an alcoholic. One drink, and you're back at square one. What you've got to understand is that you have an illness, and it kills you. If I hadn't stopped drinking I'd be dead now, as would most of those people there tonight.'

She set the table, splashed water into glasses, clanking ice cubes. She was sweating even more than usual from the heat of the stove. Even at seven in the evening, the air conditioning was so half-hearted that the temperature in the apartment was nearly eighty degrees.

Lorraine played with her food, drank three or four glasses of water. Rosie reached over and scraped the remains of her meal onto her own plate, ploughing through the leftovers as if she were starving. Her mouth bulging with food, she waved her fork in the air: 'Now, what are we going to do about finding you some work? You've no money, right? As soon as we've finished supper, we can catch a bus, go to another meeting across town, see if maybe anyone has any work, just to tide you over, nothing too strenuous . . .'

Lorraine couldn't face another meeting, let alone another bus ride. 'Maybe I could just sleep now? I'm really tired.'

Rosie nodded – perhaps they were pushing it. Instead, she chatted incessantly, about her job as a computer clerk in a banking firm. She took out her family albums, displaying her parents' home, her ex-husband, the son she hadn't seen for five years. She talked until her eyes drooped from tiredness. 'I lost so much, Lorraine, but I'm hoping to see my son soon. My ex said that I could have a day out with him. I want him to get to know me as I am now. The most important thing is that I take every day on its own, I count every day as precious, because it's a new day without a drink.' Lorraine smiled, but inside she wished Rosie would leave her alone. She yawned in the hope that Rosie would take the hint and go to bed but she went on for another hour, delving into the pages of her beloved AA manual as if it was a Bible, reading snatches aloud.

At last she stood up and wagged her fat finger at Lorraine. 'I am responsible,' she said. 'Keep on telling that to yourself: *I am responsible*.' She went into her bedroom and closed the door.

Lorraine flopped onto the couch with relief. She lay there for about fifteen minutes, listening to the air conditioner, the cat lapping its milk . . . and all she could think about was how she could get a drink without Rosie finding out. Eventually she drifted into sleep. She slept without pills, without alcohol, a deep, dreamless sleep.

*

Lorraine was awake before Rosie, and started brewing coffee. It was only five, and still reasonably cool. She felt hungry, too, and ate some bread and cheese, followed by a bowl of muesli. She'd had four cups of coffee and five cigarettes before Rosie appeared.

'Good morning, coffee's made . . .'

Rosie grunted, poured some and returned to her room. Lorraine sat by the window, smoking. A new day. Would she make it without a drink? Could she make it? Most important, did she *want* to make it? She didn't answer the question – she was too aware of the rich smell of coffee, and that it was a beautiful day.

Rosie was not at her best in the morning. She remained grumpy, uttering low, growling complaints as Lorraine took a shower. She was in the small bathroom for a long time, scrutinizing herself. Scars covered her thighs: small round marks like cigarette burns dotted all over her white-bluish skin. Her feet shocked her: they looked like an old woman's, reddish toes and heels all blisters and corns, with hideously long toenails – she was surprised they hadn't been cut at the hospital. She scrubbed herself almost raw, using up all the hot water. She oiled and massaged herself with Rosie's lotions, cleaned her teeth gently, and creamed round her mouth so her cracked lips felt less painful. Finally she used Rosie's shampoo and hair conditioner, searching the cabinet for nail scissors and a manicure set.

Rosie was seething. Lorraine had been in her bathroom since half past seven and it was now almost nine. When she emerged, swathed in Rosie's towels, Rosie pushed past her and banged the bathroom door shut.

'Well, thanks a bundle!' She stormed out. 'You've taken all the hot water! Now I gotta wait an hour, maybe more. I always have a shower in the morning.'

'Sorry,' Lorraine muttered. The floor shook as Rosie thudded into the sitting room.

'Would you come in here a minute, please!' Rosie boomed.

Lorraine sighed with irritation and followed the voice. Rosie, like some irate sergeant-major, stood with her hands on her hips.

'Okay. This is not a hotel, not the goddamned hospital. When you get up in the morning, put your bedclothes away and it'd be a nice gesture if you tried washin' a dish when you used it. This is my home. It may not look much but it's all I got an' I work my butt off to keep it.'

Lorraine watched as Rosie dragged her sheets and pillow from the couch and hurled them towards her. They landed at her feet. She was picking them up when the floor shook again and Rosie thrust a dirty ashtray under her nose. 'And all this smoking – it's not good for me. Please try and cut down or at least open the window and wash out the ashtray.'

Lorraine couldn't get a word in edgeways. Rosie slammed into her bedroom and two seconds later charged out again demanding that Lorraine go back in and clean the bathroom.

'It was a shit-hole when I went in there!' Lorraine screeched. 'You like it so fucking much, *you clean it*!'

Rosie glared. 'No fucking way! Get the vacuum from the closet, *and clean up in there*!'

Lorraine sat down and rubbed her hair. 'I've just got clean, I don't want to get all dirty again.'

Rosie charged to the closet, yanked open the door and dragged out an old-fashioned vacuum cleaner. Her fat body wobbled under the pink nylon nightdress, and she wore the most extraordinary bedroom slippers, like boats, but with the face of Pluto on one and Mickey Mouse on the other. The faces were old and food-stained – Pluto was minus one ear.

Lorraine watched as the immense beam bent over to fit

39

in the plug. 'You've not had that out for a while, you should run it over the carpet in here. It's full of cat hairs. Are you working at the hospital today?'

Rosie switched on the hoover and glowered. 'No, I am not. Why? So that you can have a good rummage through my things? I only work part-time, in case your memory fails you. Mondays and Thursdays.'

Lorraine nodded, uncertain what day it was, and fazed by Rosie's personality change. Rosie continued to complain, bellowing above the machine's whirring, which made Lorraine's head ache. Peace came when she departed for her shower, but only for a moment: more thuds emanated from the bedroom as Rosie dressed. Closet doors squeaked, drawers banged open and shut, until Rosie appeared with an armful of clothes which she tossed onto the floor. 'Here, something might fit. If it doesn't, chuck it out. I dunno why I kept that lot, maybe because I hoped I'd shrink . . . Help yourself.'

Lorraine looked through the odd assortment of garments, all in dreadful colours and a mixture of sizes, ranging from a ten to a sixteen. Nothing fitted. A few items were vaguely clean, but there were no shoes or underwear. Finally she chose a print dress three sizes too large and tied a belt around the waist. At least it would be cool. She put on her panties from the day before, turned inside out. She had no bra, no stockings or tights. She looked around for the brown paper parcel she had brought from the hospital, but couldn't remember where she had left it. Her hair was dry now, and she tied it back with an elastic band, then folded the rest of the clothes and put them into a black plastic garbage bag. She tipped the contents of the trashcan into the bag, and carried it outside for collection.

It was such a beautiful morning that she walked to the deli at the end of the street, and stood staring in the window with all the bottles on display. The windows were barred, and Lorraine threaded her fingers through the meshing, longing to go inside. She didn't have so much as a cent so, unless she robbed the place, there was no way of getting a bottle. Reluctantly she walked back to Rosie's, climbed up the wooden staircase, then hesitated. She could hear Rosie talking on the telephone, and she sat on the steps, listening.

'Well, I was hoping as I've got a few days off this weekend if we could make it Saturday? I can get the bus over . . .'

The call went on for a while longer, then Lorraine heard the thudding footsteps, and a door slamming. She went inside and opened the fridge. Rosie appeared dressed in a white blouse and circular cotton flower print skirt. Her frizzy hair was wet, and she tugged a comb through it.

'Water was still cold! And you had the last Coke yesterday. I'm not a charity, you know. Now, we'd better see which meeting you go to . . .?' Rosie began making a series of phone calls and talked at length to someone whom she described as her sponsor. Eventually she hung up.

'Jake figures I shouldn't be your sponsor, but since I've taken you on, I'll give it a try. Any time, day or night, if you feel the need for a drink, or someone to talk to, then you just tell me. Have you wanted a drink this morning?'

'What do you think?'

Rosie sighed irritably, and warned Lorraine that she did not have enough money to ferry them both all over LA. 'Don't you have any money at all?' she barked.

'No, but I'll manage . . .'

Rosie pushed past her, into the tiny kitchen area, took cereal and fruit, and began to munch noisily. Slowly, the warm, friendly Rosie began to surface. She complimented Lorraine on how she looked, and started counting dollars from her purse. Lorraine watched, trying to work out how much money it contained. As soon as she had a chance, she would steal it and get the hell out of the apartment.

'How about social security? Can you claim any benefits?'

Lorraine shrugged. Said she couldn't recall any social security numbers, but declined to admit to Rosie why she didn't want to – the skipped bail, court appearances, debts ... If she tried to apply for financial assistance she'd be arrested. Rosie gulped her coffee and began to make a long list, chewing the end of an already gnarled pencil.

'Okay. We got enough here for a few days, but we'll look around for jobs, see about taking you to the social security to see if they can trace your numbers and maybe you'll get some benefits. Not that you can live on what they dole out, I know, I'm on it—'

'We? I can manage on my own.'

'No, you can't. I can't go off to the hospital and leave you, well, not until I can trust you. So here's some suggestions ...' She had jotted down waitress, cleaner, mostly menial jobs, and then listed all the addresses of AA meetings. Lorraine wondered idly if all this effort was to help Rosie keep on the wagon, never mind herself.

'I thought you said you were something to do with computers. Can't you get a decent job?' Lorraine enquired.

Rosie looked up. 'Oh, yes. I can get into any bank and they'll make me head cashier! I lost my job, my respectability. I've got no references, not even a driver's licence, they took it away. I thought you'd know that – if you were a cop like you said. If you were, why can't *you* get a decent job?'

Lorraine began to chew at her nails. She'd finished the pack of cigarettes; now she craved not only a drink but a cigarette, too. She suddenly felt tired, and yawned. It was as if she had been up for hours, which indeed she had, but it was still only ten o'clock.

'Can I use your toilet?'

'You don't have to fucking ask me to go to the john, for chrissakes!'

When Lorraine didn't show for fifteen minutes, Rosie went to check on her. She was curled up on her bed, deeply

42

asleep, her hands cupped under her chin. Rosie studied Lorraine's sleeping face, and realized that she must once have been beautiful. You could still see glimpses of it: in repose, Lorraine's face lost its hardness. Her mouth was closed, so you couldn't see the missing tooth, and the deep scar was hidden by the pillow. For the first time Rosie really wondered about Lorraine's past, still certain that the cop line was just that – a line.

She crept out, then searched through Lorraine's belongings. Nothing. The brown paper bag was empty of any personal mementoes. No letters or cards, no make-up – and the plastic purse they had given her was empty, she hadn't lied about that. But Rosie was sure she had lied about having no family; a girl who had been as attractive as Lorraine must have had someone – had maybe even been somebody.

Rosie let Lorraine sleep for almost the entire day. She read, made some calls, cooked lunch for herself. Food was one of the few pleasures she had left in life. At four o'clock the phone rang. She snatched it up, afraid it would wake Lorraine.

'Hello, is this you, Mommy?' The high-pitched voice tore at her heart. At last he had called. It was her son.

'Yeah, it's me. How you doin', Joey? We gonna meet up? I kinda thought maybe this weekend?'

'I can't, I got a big game, I'm on the second division basketball team, and so I can't. I gotta go now.'

Rosie started to panic. He was going to put the phone down. She wanted to tell him she would drive across LA to see him play, but she stuttered, 'Wait, Joey, what about you gettin' a bus out here to me? I can meet you at the depot, Joey? You still there, Joey?'

'I'm goin' to Florida. Me and Dad are movin' there, we got a place sorted and everything.'

43

'Florida?' Rosie screeched.

There was an ominous silence. She could hear Joey whispering. 'Is that woman goin' with you, Joey? Is – put your dad on the phone, Joey, you hear me? I wanna speak to –'

Rosie was shaking, she knew that cheap bitch was there, knew she must be putting her ten cents in. Her hand clenched round the receiver as she heard her son calling his father, and then the phone being put down. 'Hello? Hello?'

Her ex-husband came on the line – she could even hear his intake of breath as if he was preparing himself to speak to her. It always got her so mad, the way he talked to her, all calm and coming on like he was a shrink, or as if she was ten years old. 'Rosie?'

'What's all this about Florida? You never said anythin' to me about Florida, takin' my kid to Florida.'

'Rosie, just calm down.'

'I'm calm, for chrissakes. I'm angry too.'

'When we're settled we'll write. This is a good job for me, a lot more money.' The voice was smooth, saying each word too slowly.

'I wanna see Joey. I'm not interested in what you earn – you never paid a cent to me, anyway.'

There was the sound of heavy breathing and then he repeated slowly and painstakingly that as Rosie had not been awarded visitation rights, never mind custody, she had little say in where her Joey lived. That was up to him and he was making the best decision for his son's welfare and if she didn't like it then she should hire a lawyer.

'Oh, yeah? And where do I get that kind of money?'

'You got it to buy booze, Rosie. Maybe you're stewed right now – you usually have been in the past when you've called. It's been six months since your last call and Joey doesn't wanna know, Rosie. It's not me and don't think it's Barbara either, he –'

'You bastard.'

44

Again the heavy breathing. 'Rosie, I'm sorry, let's not be like this. We'll write, we'll be in touch and I'm hanging up now because I don't want to get into an argument. I'm hanging up, Rosie.'

She looked at the receiver as she heard the line go dead and replaced it gently on the cradle. She patted the phone with the flat of her hand, wishing it was her boy's head. She didn't even know how big he was now, it had been such a long time . . . One day, she told herself, she'd hold him in her arms and he would forgive her. She felt so empty she wanted to cry, for all the lost years.

Hours later, Lorraine woke up, heart pounding. There had been a violent crash, as if the front door had been knocked down. Music thumped out, the volume on maximum. She sat up, and eased herself off the bed. She didn't recognize the screeching, confused voice, and the sound of breaking glass topped even the music.

Lorraine pushed open the bedroom door, and gasped. Rosie was reeling around the room, falling into furniture, drinking from a quart bottle of bourbon. She leered at Lorraine, and waved the bottle. 'You wanna drink? Come on in, sit down, have a drink with me!'

Lorraine watched, incredulous, as Rosie crashed into the kitchen, smashing glasses as she attempted to get one from the cupboard. She swore and kicked at the jagged pieces. Her eyes were unfocused, her face bright red and sweating. She swayed as she poured and held out a half-full tumbler. 'Have a drink, skinny!'

Lorraine was about to take the glass when the front door opened. She had no idea who the short, squat man was, who knocked the glass out of Rosie's hand, snatched the bottle from her and began pouring the contents down the sink. Rosie screamed and lunged at him with a punch, missed, and fell into the closet. Brushes tumbled around her as she slumped on the floor, weeping. Her sobs came louder as he ran water into the sink, making sure every drop of liquor was gone. Rosie's head fell forward onto her chest and her breath came in terrible, heaving rasps.

'Help me get her into the bathroom and *turn that fucking music off*!' Lorraine did as she was told, and between them they dragged Rosie into the bedroom then the bathroom by both arms, like a beached whale, and inched her into the base of the shower, before the man turned it on full blast. When Rosie finally came to, she began to vomit. The man held her head up, getting soaked himself in the process. He snapped out instructions for Lorraine to pass him towels and a pillow. When the vomiting subsided he stuffed a pillow under Rosie's dripping head, and stood up. 'She'll sleep it off now.'

Lorraine followed him into the sitting room. He was attempting to dry himself with one of the kitchen towels. 'You started her on this binge, huh?'

Lorraine shook her head. He began to brew coffee, and fetched cups, treading warily over the broken glass. 'What brought it on, then?'

'I dunno.' She folded her arms. The smell of the bourbon hanging in the air made her swallow because it smelt so good. 'You got a cigarette?'

He tossed over a squashed packet, and rubbed his shoulder. 'She must weigh a ton. I'm getting too old for this – she's put my shoulder out before now, and my back. Once she knocked me out stone cold . . . So, if you didn't bring the bottle in, did she get it herself?'

Lorraine lit the cigarette and pocketed the packet. 'I dunno. I was asleep.'

'Oh, yeah?' he sneered. 'Sleeping one off, were you?'

Lorraine was annoyed by his aggressive, punchy manner. His neck was short, his greasy black hair thinning, even his hands were podgy. 'You her boyfriend or something?' she asked.

46

'Her what? You kiddin'? Need a bigger man than me to take that rhino on. I'm her sponsor, but I dunno for how long. They called me from the liquor store – little arrangement we have, saves them from one of her visits. You get her started, did you? Then she went for a bottle? After she's finished one bottle she's only after the next, and those bars they got up may have kept them safe from the riots but they wouldn't from Rosie.' He helped himself to coffee, and poured some for Lorraine. 'I'm Jake Valsack.'

'Lorraine.'

Jake eased his square backside onto the sofa. 'Well, you made it through a night, then? And . . .' He looked at his watch and smiled. When he smiled, his face changed from something that resembled a chimpanzee into a cute pixie. 'You been dry almost a whole day. We'll go to the meeting – she won't be round for a while yet.'

Lorraine had no desire to go to another meeting, so she said she'd stay with Rosie. Jake hooted with laughter. Once again she grew increasingly irritated with him.

'So, Lorraine, what kind of work did you do before drinking?'

She crossed to the kitchen and poured more coffee. 'I was a secretary.'

He swivelled round. 'So you can type, huh? You got a job? Rosie said you'd need one.'

'You going to give me one?'

Jake hooted again. 'What you think I am – nuts?'

Lorraine sat on the sofa arm. 'So what did *you* do before drinking, Jake?' she inquired sarcastically. He looked up at her from round, dark eyes – he was a dead ringer for a chimpanzee.

'I was a doctor. Still am a doctor only I can't practise any more. Now I help run a clinic for junkies and alkies and anybody who needs help, like Rosie.'

Lorraine looked away for she could read the pain in those animal eyes. Maybe Jake could see something similar

47

in her own because he seemed to relent. He opened his wallet and passed over a card. 'You can call me on that line. I know somebody who needs a bit of clerical work done, be a few bucks in hand – or you can work for me. I'm a glutton for punishment. We need as many helping hands as possible, but there's no money in it.'

As she pocketed the card, she felt Jake's cigarettes. She didn't dare bring one out in case he asked for them back. He stood up and glanced at the broken screen door. 'Tell Rosie I'm around.'

Lorraine watched his stocky figure strut off down the road. Then she searched for Rosie's handbag. She was opening the purse when she heard moaning from the bathroom. Rosie was trying in vain to stand up. Lorraine looked at her, in no way disgusted by the spectacle: she'd seen and been in a lot worse states herself. 'I guess I just tied another one on, didn't I?'

Lorraine laughed. 'Yep, you sure did. Your pal was here – Jake.'

'Was he? Well, are you gonna stand there gloating or are you gonna help me get up off the fucking floor?'

Lorraine tried to pull her up but fell forward on top of her. Rosie felt like a mammoth blanket. Eventually, after much tugging and heaving, she managed to get into a sitting position, where she held her head in her hands and groaned. Lorraine fetched a glass of water and held it out. Rosie gulped it down, and then demanded another. She drank four full glasses before she rested back against the shower. 'Did you say Jake was here?'

Lorraine nodded, and Rosie began to cry, guilty and morose. She sobbed and sobbed, a jumbled, incoherent stream of adoring phrases about the chimpanzee man, blowing her nose and wiping her eyes.

'I'm off to see if I can find a job, Rosie. Did you hear me?'

48

Rosie hauled herself slowly to her feet. 'Sure. Do what you like.'

'Can I take a few dollars?' she called from the sitting room.

'Sure, honey, if there's any left. I dunno how much I spent . . .' Rosie dragged herself unsteadily to the chair by the telephone and sat down. 'I'll wait a while, then call him. I need to talk to him. I'm sorry, but I guess you'll do better without me. I knew I'd make a lousy sponsor. Jake was right about that.' She leaned back with her eyes closed. 'You must be proud of yourself. You didn't have a drink with me, did you?'

'Nope, guess I didn't.' Lorraine emptied Rosie's purse, and walked out.

She had no intention of seeing Rosie again. She felt almost lighthearted, a strange new confidence in herself: she had not taken a drink. She might have finished the bottle if Jake hadn't walked in when he did but, as it was, she had not had a drink.

The late-afternoon sun was brilliant, blistering down, and she could feel the pavement scorching through her cheap second-hand shoes. The feeling of being in control of something as simple as her own feet, of walking in a straight line, made her confidence jump a tiny notch higher. She took off the elastic band from her hair, and shook it loose. It smelt of lemons, just like the old shampoo she used, how long ago? Lorraine reached the corner, and stopped to light a cigarette. Tossing the match aside, she inhaled deeply and let the smoke drift slowly out of her mouth. She sucked again at the cigarette, watching the lit rim of tobacco move up the white paper before she exhaled. She didn't want to think about the past, about what or who she had been.

A car crawled to a stop just ahead of her. She'd seen it

out of the corner of her eye even before it passed: a dark blue Sedan. She could even describe the driver – linen jacket, blue open-necked shirt, cropped blond thinning hair, round, rimless glasses, and a wide, wet mouth. That was all she focused on as he leaned out of the window. He smiled, running his thumb around his shiny wet lips as he asked if she needed a lift any place. Lorraine stepped closer, inclining her head, making sure the jagged scar couldn't be seen, keeping her lips half closed. She didn't want to scare him off, didn't want him to see too much of her teeth – or lack of them. She was an old hand at this and knew that if he was a cop he would try to get her to name a price. She bent lower, down to his level.

'You lost?' She said it softly, her hand reaching out to the door handle. 'You need me?'

He stared at her as if sizing her up, then looked past her both ways before he jerked his head. 'Get in.'

Lorraine went round to the passenger side and climbed in beside him. He drove off fast like they always did, acting flash. Acting stupid. He said quickly, licking his wet lips all the time, that he wanted oral, he wanted it public. Did she understand? Lorraine leaned her arm along the back of the seats, but as she touched his neck, he jerked away. He didn't want to be touched, he said, he hated being touched. He kept on driving, passing every car on the highway until he wheeled into a supermarket car park. The ground level was almost full, people staggering to and from the store with bulging bags of groceries, their hatchbacks open wide as they loaded up.

He bypassed the first level, then the second, tyres screeching as he drove round and up the narrow entrance lane. In the fourth-storey parking area, he pulled into a space. He had hardly switched off the engine before he unzipped his trousers. Lorraine put her hand out. He swiped it aside. 'I told you, I don't want you to touch me!'

50

'Okay, chill out, man, want me to talk dirty, you like that? That what you want?'

His body was tense, his hands clenching and unclenching.

'No, I reckon you want to be sucked off, right here, like with maybe someone close enough to catch you at it, that's exciting, isn't it, bad boy? You're a very bad boy, aren't you? Well, you got lucky because that's my speciality. I give the best head. Come on, you want to ask me for it, yes? That's what you want, isn't it?' His lips twitched, his eyes darting round the gloomy parking lot. She kept her voice low, whispering, making sucking sounds, and he closed his eyes. 'Like I said, I'll make you feel good, real good, and this is a real public place, but we got to sort out my dough. Can we sort that out? Yeah?'

He looked out of the window, getting more excited as a few customers stashed away their groceries, their voices echoing in the concrete building. He loosened his belt, as if he hadn't heard her, pulling at his pants. 'Just do it, bitch.'

Lorraine's back pressed against the passenger door and her left hand felt for the door handle. If he played games, she was out. 'Twenty dollars.'

A woman with her husband and two kids parked directly next to them. As they headed towards the elevators, Lorraine's john started to jerk himself off, his mouth stretched in a weird wet smile of pleasure. His erect pink penis burst up from his crumpled flies and he began to pant, leaning his head back, as his left hand flicked the switch for his seat to recline.

Lorraine tried again. 'Twenty dollars.'

He lost his erection and gave a half sob. She swore, realizing he was one of those half-a-minute stand-up-for-America and then the weeping impotent syndrome.

Fumbling in his wallet, he took out a thick wedge of bills, peeled off a twenty and tossed it at her. 'See what you

51

can do for it, bitch!' He reached over and grabbed her by the hair, forcing her face onto his pink flaccid worm. Lorraine could smell him, smell his trousers, even the cotton of his blue striped boxer shorts. His hand on the back of her neck was holding a strand of her hair as he pressed her further down onto his crotch.

Was it the sweet lemon smell of her freshly washed hair? Or that she was stone-cold sober? She knew exactly what she was being paid to do, she'd done it too many times before. But never sober. Face down between a john's legs, having just been paid twenty dollars for a blow-job in a shopping precinct car park, the ghost of Lieutenant Lorraine Page resurfaced and fought back for a tiny fraction of respectability. She couldn't suck him off.

'I'm sorry. You can have your twenty dollars.'

He held onto the back of her head, forcing her down. She pushed up with her hands trying to free herself. He was much stronger than she was now and, leaning over the seat towards him, she was vulnerable, incapable of getting away. He was able to hold her down with only one hand, and her head was stuck under the steering wheel. She heard the click of the glove compartment being opened but couldn't see what he had taken out. She forced herself to relax, to try to get into a better position so she could move off him, but he still held onto her hair.

The first blow stunned her for a second – it glanced off the back of her scalp – but he had hit her with such force that he had automatically released his hold. She pushed upward with all her strength, propelling herself against his chest. He slipped back in his reclining seat, and it was then she saw the claw hammer. As he tried to raise it to strike her again, she knew he could kill her if he wanted.

Lorraine twisted her face towards his, and bit into his neck. She held on ferociously, her teeth breaking the flesh. He screamed, now more intent on getting her off than on using the hammer, but she wouldn't release her bite.

The family loading their groceries looked over to the Sedan parked next to them. Its windows were steamed up, but the screaming made the woman push her kids inside their car. She even shouted for her husband not to go across, but he took no notice, and as he reached the driver's door, he called out: 'You all right in there?' He turned back to his wife, who gestured for him to walk away, but he bent down, his hand tentatively reaching for the handle on the driver's door. 'You all right in there?' he repeated.

As he opened the door, Lorraine fell out, face forward onto the cement floor, almost knocking him off his feet. The family started to shriek as they saw the back of her head covered in blood, and blood streaming from her mouth.

The Sedan jolted backwards, dragging Lorraine with it – her dress was still caught on the reclining seat lever. The man who had come to her assistance made a grab, almost had the driver by his sleeve, but he too fell, as the car swerved to make a turn. The door slammed shut, and with burning rubber tyres the blue Sedan shot down the exit ramp.

The woman was bending over Lorraine as she struggled to stand. At her feet was the wallet: it must have fallen from the john's jacket in the struggle. She snatched it up. 'He tried to rob me, he stole my bag and –'

The woman shouted for her husband to call the police, but Lorraine shook her head. 'No, no, it's okay – I've got my wallet. I'm fine really –'

'But you've been injured, look at you.'

Lorraine backed away from their concerned faces. She touched her head. 'It's nothing, I'll report it to security. Thank you very much.'

By now the woman's husband had run back to them, red-faced and shaking with nerves. 'I'll get the police. Are you okay?' The woman suddenly became suspicious of Lorraine, and caught her husband's arm. 'Get in the car,

53

just leave her. She said she doesn't want any help. *Get back to the children!*'

He looked from his wife back to Lorraine, who managed a half-smile. 'I'm okay, thanks for your help.'

Still he hesitated, but his wife called him again, and as he hurried across to her, Lorraine could hear the shrill voice. 'Can't you see what she is? Didn't you see her face? She's a whore, she was probably trying to steal from him. Just get in the car!' They continued to argue, even as they drove out and he stared back at Lorraine, confused and shocked.

In the ladies' room Lorraine soaked a handful of toilet tissue, and held it to the back of her head. She had lost a shoe, her dress was bloodstained and she couldn't stop the flow of blood from the back of her scalp. Her mouth, too, was bloody, and she panicked. Had he hit her in the mouth? But it wasn't her blood, it was his, from the bite she had given him. She was shaking now, her legs jerky, and she had to sit down on the toilet seat to stop herself fainting.

With trembling hands she opened the wallet. A driving licence plus a photograph – but not of the man inside the car. There were odd ticket stubs and dry cleaning receipts, and more than three hundred and fifty dollars. She folded the money, and stuck it into her panties. Then she stuffed the wallet into the trashcan.

She remained at the washbasin for another fifteen minutes, using more tissue soaked in cold water as a pad. When she had recovered enough to make her way slowly outside, she still felt dizzy and faint, so she hailed a passing cab and gave him Rosie's address.

Lorraine hardly had the strength to get out of the cab and the driver was blazing when he found his seat was bloodstained. Jake, who had returned to check on Rosie, was watching the display from the apartment window.

Thinking her as drunk as Rosie had been, he nevertheless helped Rosie to carry her upstairs. When he spotted the wound on her head he insisted Lorraine go to the hospital. She refused. She didn't want any hospital or police reports – she was fine. And she had not had a drink.

The wound was still bleeding freely, so reluctantly Lorraine agreed to go with Jake to his clinic to have it stitched. By the time they arrived she was subdued. She lay on the couch as Jake examined the gash. He doubted her claim that the wound had been caused by her falling on a loose paving stone. It looked to him as if someone had struck her from behind; if the blow had landed an inch further up, her skull could have been shattered. She'd been lucky.

Lorraine returned home with Rosie and Jake, her head bandaged and with a cropped haircut. Rosie put her in her own bed, and gave her the sedatives and antibiotics Jake had prescribed. Once she was asleep, Jake began to quiz Rosie. 'What did she tell you that you think is lies, then, Rosie?'

Rosie shrugged. 'Oh . . . just that she used to be a police officer.'

Jake smiled, his eyes concentrating on unscrewing the hinges of the damaged screen door. 'Well, that may be fantasy, of course. *I* think she's a whore and that's why she didn't want to go to the police. Someone nearly killed her today, though. But my worry is you – because you are my main concern, Rosie dear, and you were doing so well before she came on the scene.'

'I don't think she had anything to do with me tying on a load, Jake. That was down to my husband.'

Jake squinted at the hinge. 'Maybe, but you're vulnerable right now, sweetheart, and it won't take much to make you fall off the wagon. How long has she been dry? Not long. Right?'

Rosie knew he was right and that he meant well, but she

couldn't keep calling him just for social reasons – even though she had every right to call him when she was in trouble. 'I get lonely, Jake. I need a friend.'

Jake held up the new hinges. 'Who am I to say what you should or shouldn't do? I'll have to come back and fix this tomorrow. These aren't the right screws.'

Rosie sighed and looked to the bedroom. 'I think we'll be okay, for tonight anyway. It'll take my mind off things looking after her.'

Jake put on his jacket. 'Up to you, but keep your eye on her. I don't trust her.'

He had made no mention of Lorraine's reaction when he had seen the thick wad of notes fall out from under her skirt. Her expression was angry and when he asked about the money she had told him to mind his own business; it was just her savings. Jake was sure she had a police record, he could tell by her face: that hardness. She must be as tough as any man to have taken such a crack and still be able to walk around.

Rosie started to make some chicken soup, even though it was eighty degrees outside. She was feeling a bit wobbly and had almost eaten the entire pot before taking a small bowl in to Lorraine. She had been awake for quite a while, but kept her eyes closed, wincing as Rosie collapsed onto the bed. Her head ached, a sharp nagging pain that pressed into her eyes.

'Soup,' barked Rosie, holding up the bowl and a large spoon. Lorraine smiled. It was the last thing she would have thought of asking for on a warm clammy evening but when she tasted the first spoonful, it hit the right spot – as her mother always used to say. She took the spoon from Rosie, and fed herself, dunking the fresh white bread into the remains, and finally wiping the bowl clean.

'I'd offer you some more but I made a pig of myself,' Rosie admitted as she took away the bowl.

Lorraine snuggled down. 'I'm full and it tasted so good

'. . . and I don't mind you sleeping with me – you'll never fit on that sofa out there.'

Rosie laughed. 'Well, thank you very much! I thought I'd take the cushions off and put them on the floor. I'd kick you out, but Jake said you should watch it, you know, not roll about or bang your head. I'll manage out on the sofa – but only for one night.'

Lorraine listened to the plodding feet moving around. Her hand had slipped up her panties to feel the money, afraid that maybe Jake had mentioned it to Rosie. It was still there, and it acted as a comforter. She had more than three hundred dollars, enough to get away from Rosie.

The bedroom floor shook as Rosie reappeared with some hot chocolate, slipped the mug onto the bedside table, turned on the night light, and straightened the duvet. It was the caring that did it, simply being tucked in like when she was a little girl, that made Lorraine's heart ache.

'Rosie . . . you still there?' Lorraine whispered.

'Yep, hovering like a hot-air balloon. Don't forget to take your antibiotics.'

Rosie watched Lorraine slowly raise herself on her elbow, her face twisted. 'You want an aspirin?'

Lorraine nodded, and Rosie fetched two tablets and held the mug of hot chocolate to her lips. Lorraine felt the thick sweet liquid slip down her throat.

'I'll be right outside if you need me.'

Lorraine flushed. 'Rosie, I, er . . . well, I guess I do want my life back and if it means going to those meetings, well, then we'll go together.'

Rosie nodded. 'I should fuckin' hope so. G'night, sleep tight. Tomorrow you're back on the sofa.'

Lorraine gave a soft laugh, and nestled down. She hadn't heard the sound of her own laugh for so long that it warmed her now, and made her feel good, as did the soft duvet and big, squashy pillows. Nearly four months, she calculated, and she had not had one drink. Could she – did

she really *want* to stay on the wagon? The money was a
hard lump in her panties. She eased it out and tucked it
under the pillow, keeping her hand on it, feeling drowsy,
wondering vaguely why the driving licence had a different
picture from the guy who had picked her up. The car was
probably stolen, she told herself, the wallet must have
belonged to its real owner. She sighed deeply as she recalled
the incident. The claw hammer kept in the glove compartment. Very convenient. The position he had forced her into
on his lap, the reclining angle of the seat . . . as if he had
done it before? Jake had said she was lucky to be alive,
another fraction of an inch higher and he would have
cracked her skull open. If she hadn't bitten his neck she'd
be dead. She knew she had marked him – the bite was deep.
Should she call the LAPD in the morning, give them an
anonymous tip-off? Describe the attacker? She yawned,
maybe. Maybe she should just get some sleep, take it all day
by day as Rosie said.

Rosie pulled the cushions off the sofa, turned the TV set
down low and, from her reasonably comfortable position
on the floor, propped herself on her elbow to see if there
were any more game shows scheduled. She used the remote
control to move from channel to channel, paying only a
moment's attention to the local news item that showed the
photograph of Norman Hastings, whose body had been
discovered in the trunk of his dark blue Sedan. He had been
beaten to death with some kind of hammer. His wallet was
missing. Anyone with any information regarding the dead
man was asked to contact the local police, and a number
was flashed onto the screen. Fifteen minutes later, she
switched off the TV and settled down, with a regretful sigh.
Tomorrow was another day, another meeting when she
would have to admit she had slipped. She began to recite

the twelve AA traditions. She rarely got beyond the sixth or seventh and tonight was no exception. By the third she was soundly asleep. 'The only requirement for AA membership is a desire to stop drinking.'

CHAPTER 2

THE NEWS bulletins about the discovery of Norman
Hastings's body were repeated on the early-morning
television shows, but now included footage of the
abandoned blue Sedan and a further request for anyone
who had seen him or his vehicle to come forward. The
officer heading the murder enquiry at the Pasadena Homicide Division was Captain William 'Bill' Rooney.

Directly after the morning shows, Rooney's department
received a phone call from a Don Summers. He was not a
hundred per cent certain, but he thought he had seen the
blue Sedan in a Pasadena shopping mall car park the
previous afternoon.

Rooney did not get around to questioning Summers
until the following day. He doubted if Summers's evidence
could help, since he could not be positive that he had seen
the exact car, and had not made a note of the registration
number. Neither had he had a clear view of the driver, only
the woman who had been in the vehicle with him. Rooney
was able to ascertain that at the time of Summers's possible
sighting of the blue Sedan, Hastings, according to the
autopsy report, was already dead. Rooney also had details
of the dead man's missing wallet, and knew that it contained
a few hundred dollars which Hastings had withdrawn from
his bank on the morning of his death. He suspected that
robbery was the murder motive as they had failed to come
up with any other reason. Hastings appeared to be a happily

married man, well liked at his work and without enemies or anyone with a grudge against him.

Rooney did not review Summers's call-in statement until he had further evidence from Forensic and the full autopsy report. Although the interior of the Sedan had been cleaned and no prints found – not even those of the dead man – Forensic had discovered two further blood samples, one on the driver's seat, the other on the inside of the glove compartment. What prompted Rooney to question Summers personally was the woman's shoe found rammed beneath the front seat. It did not belong to Hastings's wife.

Rooney sat with Mr and Mrs Summers, as Summers repeated his statement of how he had seen the blue Sedan parked, heard the man screaming and gone to investigate. He was now more sure that it was the one in the photographs shown to him by Rooney. His wife was convinced that if it was not the same car, it was the identical model and colour.

'Okay, now, can you tell me about the woman? The one you stated was in the car?'

Summers gave a good description. Tall and thin, she was wearing a bloodstained flower-print dress. She was injured, her mouth was bleeding, and he thought she had a head wound. She was also clutching a purse. She had told him the man had tried to rob her. Summers's wife interjected that she had thought it was a lie, because when they offered to call the police or for some assistance the woman had refused, insisting that she was all right.

Rooney asked for a more detailed description of the woman. Summers was hesitant, but his wife wasn't, recalling the thin, wispy, badly cut blonde hair, that the woman was about five feet eight inches tall, but exceptionally thin and sickly-looking. She remembered remarking to her husband that the woman might be a prostitute.

'What made you think that?' Rooney asked.

Mrs Summers bit her lip. 'I don't know, just something

about her, a toughness. She was very rough-looking, sort of desperate – and, of course, she was covered in blood.'

'That doesn't mean she's a whore,' said Rooney.

Don Summers glanced at his wife. 'Maybe she wasn't. All I can say, and I got a closer look than my wife, was that the woman was terrified – and she was really hurt, blood all over her dress.'

Rooney showed them the shoe found in Hastings's car and they confirmed that the woman had been wearing only one.

'We need to find our Cinderella,' Rooney joked, but the Summerses didn't find his comment amusing. They were overawed by the massive new Pasadena police station, a high-tech palace, the holding cells below computerized.

The building was so spacious that Rooney himself felt uncomfortable. He wasn't used to so many corridors, rooms and sections, so many clerks. The old days, when a guy could pass a pal in the narrow, paint-peeling corridors, have a chat, smoke a cigarette, were over. Nearly every office had no-smoking signs; some officers had even stuck them on their computers. Only Captain Rooney continued to work in a haze of cigarette or cigar smoke. If the truth was told, he didn't quite fit the new high flyers who surrounded him, but retirement was looming shortly. He reckoned the Hastings murder would be his last case and he hoped to crack it fast, get a good retirement bonus and then be put out to pasture. The prospect made him uneasy, but then so did the new station. He was unsure about life outside the police, which had been the only world he had known since he was eighteen.

By the time Rooney returned to his office there had been another call in connection with the Hastings homicide. This time the caller was anonymous and refused repeated requests to divulge her name. She did, however, give a detailed description of the man she thought was driving the car belonging to the deceased: around a hundred and eighty pounds, possibly about five feet ten, though she wasn't sure, blue eyes, rimless gold-framed pink-toned glasses, a straight nose, thick-lipped mouth, wearing a linen jacket and shirt. She described a bite wound in his neck that would be visible above shirt collar level, close to his jugular. It would be deeply inflamed as the teeth had broken the skin and drawn blood. Furthermore, the man was in possession of a claw hammer, which he kept in the glove compartment.

Rooney looked at the duty sergeant's notes. 'She said all this over the fucking phone?'

'Yes, Captain. Then she hung up.'

'So, you get a trace on it? Shouldn't take more'n a second with all this new-fangled equipment.'

The call had not been traced, partly because it was felt to be a 'joke' call, and when it had been deemed genuine, she had already hung up. Rooney plodded back into his office. He waved the anonymous statement at his lieutenant, Josh Bean. 'You fuckin' read this? Whoever she is she wants him caught – she's even described the weapon. What's odd, though, is that the only thing she seems unsure of is the guy's exact height. Everything else, clothes, hair, glasses, mouth, even his weight, she gives it all. But not her name! And the stupid sons-of-bitches didn't trace the call.'

Bean took a look at the statement. She hadn't given the car registration number, he mused, as Rooney deposited his overweight frame behind his desk in his precious old leather swivel chair.

'I reckon that Summers woman was right – she was a whore, that's why she doesn't know how tall the guy is. Maybe he never got out of the vehicle, just picked her up on the sidewalk . . .'

Bean nodded agreement. 'Unless both the Summerses and this caller got the wrong guy. Maybe he just drives a blue Sedan.'

Rooney leaned on his elbows. 'Possibly, but it's the

hammer, a claw hammer. If you read Forensic on the type of weapon used to kill Norman Hastings, they say: "A blunt-edged hammer-type head, one inch in diameter, with a claw section one and a quarter inches long".' He sifted through his files until he found the Forensic photographs of the dead man, close-ups of the blows inflicted to his skull, cheeks, and chin. If the anonymous caller was right, they were looking for a killer with a big bite taken out of his neck.

Rooney looked at Bean and grinned. 'This shouldn't take long then, should it? We got Dracula out there now – but at least we can check all Hastings's associates. No bite, we'll eliminate them.'

Lieutenant Bean frowned, unsure if Rooney was joking. Suddenly he barked at Bean to get cracking.

'I thought you were joking, for chrissakes!'

Rooney picked at his bulbous nose. 'Fuck off. We got to take that call seriously, it's too detailed not to. Go on, move it! And, by the way, the shoe we got could also be the whore's. The Summerses sort of thought she only had one shoe on *but* they weren't certain.'

'Right. I'll take the shoe with me – get everyone to try it on, maybe find the owner.' Bean was joking but Rooney looked as amused as the Summerses had been by his Cinderella crack. He carried on, working through the file, yawning. Something was nagging at him – the description? Was it too pat? Some kind of hoax? But the fact that they had found bloodstains in the glove compartment where the anonymous caller claimed the man kept the hammer was just too close a coincidence. Rooney guessed the caller was the woman the Summers couple witnessed leaving the car – and that Mrs Summers had been correct. She probably was a whore.

*

Lorraine had the worst headache she had ever known. No hangover had been this painful. She was dizzy if she stood up, if she moved she felt sick – and she had vomited the first time she sat up. Thanks to the antibiotics and the aspirin, however, the splitting pain behind her eyes eased a fraction. She had made the phone call then, while Rosie was out getting ice from the grocery store. She had been brief intentionally as she didn't want a trace made, and she was back in bed when Rosie returned.

The torn old sheet crammed with ice was soothing, but there was no way she could get up and go to the AA meeting. Rosie was uneasy at leaving her alone, but needed to go to the meeting herself. Lorraine just wanted to be left alone. Her whole body ached, but the pain across her eyes was torture, so bad she couldn't even think of a drink, let alone getting up to pour one. All she wanted was for the pain to go away.

She remained in Rosie's bed for more than a week, had to be helped to the toilet, for even that small amount of exercise exhausted her. She found any noise unbearable – no TV, no radio. She could eat, and Rosie waited on her hand and foot. She enjoyed being needed; it occupied her mind and, like Lorraine, she didn't give a thought to booze.

Two weeks went by. Jake never got round to contacting his friend at the clinic to ask about Lorraine. In fact, like Rosie, he had grown quite fond of her because, sick as she was, she didn't complain, and often made him laugh. Her pain was obvious, however, and he had told Rosie that if Lorraine's condition did not improve she should be taken to hospital.

Almost half-way through the third week, the headache subsided and Lorraine was able to shower by herself. That afternoon, Jake took out the clamp stitches. The wound had healed well, but he was doubtful about his prowess as a hairdresser. Lorraine had almost a crew-cut at the back of her head and crown while the front was long and jagged. It gave her an almost boyish look, and she made them laugh when she tied a ribbon around the front strands to keep them from flopping in her eyes. She read a lot, magazines at first, because even flicking through the newspapers gave her a headache but gradually she began to plough her way through Rosie's spartan collection of bodice-ripping blockbusters.

She kept the money stashed beneath the mattress. Sometimes she had qualms of guilt when Rosie paid for everything, but didn't know how she could hand out money if Rosie believed she was broke. Afraid of being questioned too closely about its source, she decided against mentioning it. And Jake made no reference to it either.

Four days later, she saw a way round it. When Rosie returned from work, Lorraine presented her with fifty dollars. 'You can be proud of me, Rosie. I went over to my friend, then to a pawnbroker's. Here, this is for you. I sold off my things.' Rosie had no idea that Lorraine had never left the apartment, but she did remark that it was time they discussed the sleeping arrangements. She assured Lorraine she didn't want her to leave, it was just that Rosie needed a good night's sleep in her own bed. That night, Lorraine moved back onto the sofa.

Months had passed since Lorraine had last touched alcohol, had been stone cold sober; it was six weeks since the attack. Curled up on the uncomfortable sofa, she began to plan what she should do next. On the positive side, she was sober. She had no craving, yet, but would it develop as she regained her strength?

Money she had, almost three hundred dollars. It seemed like a fortune, but she knew it wouldn't last long. She wanted to move on, but the question was, where to? And what would she do? Two more days and it became obvious, not just to Rosie but to herself, that she could no longer hide out in the small apartment. Rosie was already hinting that the fifty dollars had been swallowed up in groceries.

Lorraine felt incapable of making major plans for her future; it was the immediate that occupied her. Marooned in the apartment she watched a lot of TV and could follow the murder inquiry. The news showed an artist's impression of the woman seen in the blue Sedan, which she found almost amusing; it bore no resemblance to herself, and Lorraine felt no guilt in not making further contact. The police were making inquiries in all the cab ranks, trying to trace if anyone answering the blonde woman's description had hired a cab that afternoon. They had drawn a blank at all the hospital emergency departments. It seemed no one had seen either the woman or the deceased's blue Sedan on the day of his murder. Lorraine's phone call was becoming more and more important to the investigation.

Jake, now a frequent visitor, was disturbed by her inertia. In an attempt to motivate her, he suggested that, if she was interested, his friend could do something for her teeth. They needed treatment badly, and the missing tooth didn't help her looks. If she could find thirty dollars or so, he said, she could get it capped.

'Know a laid-off dentist, too, do you, Jake?'

Jake laughed, but she was right – his friend was AA and only just starting to rebuild his practice.

Lorraine spent four days in agony, but the end result was two front teeth capped, all her cavities filled, her gums cleaned and the rest of her teeth bleached. Her mouth was swollen and sore, but the exercise had been a success. She used the lie about selling off her belongings again, and paid the thirty dollars. She also gave Rosie another twenty, adding that now she had nothing more to sell or pawn. Rosie believed her: Lorraine was a good liar.

She went to the local hair salon to have her hair streaked, cut and blown dry. Jake's pitiful attempt at styling limited her choice – the back was so short where the scar was still visible – but the salon made a reasonable job, taking the back and sides even shorter and the front into a low fringe, like a twenties crop, which accentuated her cheekbones, while the highlights gave body to her thin hair. She was by no means transformed into a beauty: her nose was crooked, flattish from where it must have been broken, and the white jagged scar on the left side of her face remained. Nevertheless a new, more confident, Lorraine was emerging.

Rosie was astonished and full of admiration as Lorraine presented herself, and Jake was equally complimentary in a back-handed way. He had whistled, then said, 'Honey, you must have been a cracker!'

Rosie became a little envious. Nothing she could do to her frizzy mop would ever change her much – and it rankled that Lorraine could have an expensive haircut, yet not pay a cent towards the rent. Money was short, and Rosie's salary plus her benefits was hardly enough to keep herself, never mind two.

It also irritated Rosie that although she went to AA regularly, Lorraine made excuses to stay in the apartment and read. Eventually she made it clear that she was not a charity, and it was time Lorraine got off her ass . . .

But Lorraine was scared to leave the safety of the apartment. Even Jake's presence was comforting. He was always so dependable and calming. She still made no mention of her hidden stash: it was her only security and it meant that she could, if she wanted, go on a whopper of a binge. The idea of drinking remained an avenue of escape for her but she no longer woke up with booze on her mind. Far from it: some days she relished the simple pleasure of waking up and knowing where she was. But that was soon replaced by fear – fear of being let loose and alone.

Lorraine never hinted at her inner turmoil. To Rosie and Jake she appeared confident and composed. She was meticulously clean, often taking two or three showers a day, scrubbing her body until it felt raw. She examined her teeth and gazed at her face in the mirror, studied her scars, as if she was trying to find out who she was, where she had been the past six years.

She drank bottled water all day and ate so well that her skin took on a freshness and her fingernails grew. She sat for hours polishing and filing them, totally preoccupied with herself. She never did any housework, looking on as Rosie changed sheets and went alone to the laundromat. Not once did Lorraine cook or wash up; she ate whatever Rosie banged down in front of her, and ignored the heavy hints about outstaying her welcome.

Finally, Rosie turned to Jake. She wanted him to ask Lorraine to leave.

'I thought you liked her?' he mused.

'I did, I do, but she just *takes* from me, Jake. And I'm not just talking about money. She uses all my hot water, all my things, and now she doesn't even talk to me, never says thank-you, just sits looking at herself, cleaning herself. Sometimes she reminds me of my goddamned cat. She's got to leave, she's driving me nuts!'

Jake came round when he knew Rosie was out. He tapped on the screen door and let himself in. Lorraine was sitting by the window, reading. She looked up, acknowledged him, then returned to her book. 'We got to have a little chat,' Jake said, sitting on the sofa. Lorraine didn't look up. He crossed his fat legs. 'I know you're maybe scared of leaving here, you feel safe, feel like you're getting back to some kind of normality. But it's an unreal normality, Lorraine. This is Rosie's home, and she's broke – caring for you and herself . . .'

Lorraine snapped the book shut. 'Okay. I'll leave.'

'You don't have to do that – but you got to get a job, put some money into the housekeeping, help out around the place. Then, when you've found your feet, maybe you can get a place of your own.'

Lorraine stared at her manicured fingers and looked out of the window. 'I dunno about that . . .' She turned to him. Her eyes were washed-out blue, wide apart, without expression. He couldn't tell what she was thinking. 'It's been a long time since I worked, Jake. You know – with sane people . . .' She half smiled. 'Maybe I'm not ready to take on any responsibility. I'm kind of living day to day, but I hear what you're saying, and I'll leave.'

'Where will you go?' Jake asked.

She shrugged. 'I dunno. I'll make out. What do you care?'

'I care a lot – especially after all that dental work you got done! Hate to see you go and start the rot again, because if you walk out of here with no purpose you'll be back on Skid Row pretty soon.'

She sighed; she felt tired and it hurt to think. She ran a finger along the scar at the back of her head. 'Skid Row. That where we met, huh? Joke, it was just a joke . . . Look, Jake, I'm real tired, so if you don't mind leaving . . .'

He got up and went to the kitchen. 'I'll make us some coffee.' He saw the way her face tightened. She wanted him to leave, he knew, but he hadn't finished. 'Let's talk some more, Lorraine, throw a few ideas around. Like I said, you got to find a purpose.'

She picked up the book again. Jake walked over and snatched it away. 'You can fuck around with Rosie, Lorraine, because she's weak and desperate. She needed you in some sick kind of way – it took her mind off her own problems. But now you got to put a bit back, understand me?'

She smirked at him. 'Why don't *you* put it back, Jake? Give her a screwing, she needs that more than anything else! She hasn't been laid in five years.'

He could have slapped her sullen face, but he didn't. He just held the steady gaze of her washed-out eyes. 'You been screwed lately, then, do you? Remember it?'

'I've had enough to last me a lifetime.'

'I bet you did. A lot of drunks whore for booze – that what you did?'

'Fuck off.'

Jake gripped her skinny wrist. 'I fuck off – and you're fucked. You need Rosie, you need this place, because it's all you've got – but you've used her. I'm just trying to help. You're already helping yourself.'

'Am I?' she snapped.

'Yes. You look a hell of a lot better than when you first arrived – and you can keep on looking and feeling better – but you have to want a future!'

Jake had to hand it to Lorraine: she still didn't give an inch, still showed no sign of what she was feeling. She did, however, drink the coffee he made and even though she didn't speak to him again, she seemed to listen, chain-smoking his cigarettes, staring at the wall. Eventually he could think of nothing more to say. He wrote down a few contact addresses for jobs and went away, feeling depressed and disappointed. She didn't say goodbye or thank him for the extra pack of smokes he had left.

By the time Rosie returned, however, the apartment was tidier, and Lorraine had vacuumed and cleaned the kitchen. Rosie's bed was made, the shower room was clean. Even the cat had been fed.

Rosie muttered thanks and put down a grocery bag full of cans of Coke, oven-ready french fries, and a cooked chicken. She began cooking dinner as Lorraine watched television, shrugging in reply to anything Rosie said. They ate in silence, Rosie glancing at Lorraine as she sucked each chicken bone, eating with her hands, polishing the plate clean with her bread. Rosie shifted onto the sofa for a better view of the TV as Lorraine cleared the table and washed up. Not until she had dried all the dishes and put them away did Lorraine begin a conversation.

'Jake was here.'

'Yeah, I know.'

'I'll go an' see if I can get a job tomorrow, start payin' some rent.'

Rosie nodded. 'Okay. You want to come to AA tonight?'

Lorraine hesitated. 'Okay.'

As before, Lorraine sat at the back, playing no part in the proceedings. As she checked over the list of jobs she'd try for in the morning, her head throbbed. Then, without any warning, the sweating began, and she slipped out into the corridor where she found the water fountain. She had gulped down several cupfuls before she was steadier and her mouth stopped feeling like sandpaper. The fountain was close to a large bulletin board: there were lists of contacts, jobs, AA meetings, white elephant and garage sales. Lorraine noted down an address for second-hand clothes.

Rosie appeared, looking concerned, but seeing Lorraine squinting up at the bulletin board in that odd way she had, writing down information, she relaxed.

Lorraine looked over to her. 'I guess I'll need some clothes for work. There's a yard sale on. You want to come?'

It wasn't until they got there and Lorraine began to stack up suits, shirts, shoes, that Rosie wondered how she was going to pay. When she asked how much they'd cost, Lorraine told her fifteen dollars for the bunch – the woman wanted to get rid of the stuff quickly as she was moving. She had actually paid a hundred and fifty and was now down to less than a hundred bucks in her stash. The fact that she had broken into it for something other than booze, was – even though she didn't realize it – another step forward.

Rosie sat draining a can of Coke as Lorraine inspected her new clothes, trying them all on, mixing and matching. Her face wore a studied, concentrated expression. She muttered and nodded, running her hand through her hair. 'Mmmm, nice, not bad . . . yes, I like it.'

She felt jealous as she watched Lorraine parade up and down like a model on a catwalk. The clothes were good, anyone could see that, tailored skirts and jackets, a particularly nice cream silk shirt, and a black crêpe one, tasteful walking shoes and a pair of brown slingbacks that had never been worn. 'I doubt if you'll need that gear for the jobs Jake's got lined up for you,' Rosie pointed out, burping from the Coke.

Lorraine was looking at herself in the long wardrobe mirror. 'Maybe I'm gonna try for a real job. There were quite a few listed at the meeting.'

Rosie pouted. 'Like what?'

Lorraine turned round. 'Receptionist – got to look smart for that – nice and easy, sittin' down all day. I might get lucky.'

Rosie sniffed. 'You might not.'

Lorraine hardly slept. The sofa was uncomfortable at the best of times, but constant worrying about the next day made her toss and turn. Four times she had to walk through the bedroom to the toilet, but she didn't disturb Rosie, who slept as always like a beached whale, snoring loudly. Lorraine's thirst seemed unquenchable. She finished all the Coke, all the bottled water, sweating and shaking, flopping up and down on the old sofa. Then it started – the craving. She badly wanted a beer. Would it be so bad to have just one?

She slipped into Rosie's old dress, and inched open the screen door. The need consumed her; she could think of nothing else. She got as far as the bottom step before she saw the patrol car moving slowly up the road, the two officers inside staring at the buildings as they cruised along. She watched for a few moments before returning to the apartment, where she looked out from the window as they passed on down the road. By the time they had disappeared she didn't feel so desperate. Still fully dressed, she got back on the sofa.

She had been expecting them. They must have contacted the cab ranks by now, but because she had seen no sign of police interest, she had been too wrapped up in herself to give it a second thought. Now she remembered . . . but instead of focusing on the present, Lorraine recalled her own days in uniform.

The only female in the precinct, she hadn't even had a place to piss in privacy until they designated a toilet for her. She would do anything rather than go into the john and even when she had her own there was always a cop leering, presenting his dick for her appraisal. Her partner would throw fits because she was always asking him to pull over at public conveniences. It got so she wouldn't drink during the day so she didn't have to piss. They nicknamed her the Golden Camel, because no matter what temperature blistered the paint off the car, rookie Lorraine Page never accepted a drink. Later, she sure as hell made up for it, and when she had moved on, and upwards, she could drink most of her colleagues under the table. It had started as an act of bravado, to show she was as good as any man on or off duty. She could hold it. And then she got a new nickname: 'Hollow Legs Page'.

Half dreaming, half awake, Lorraine recollected times she had not thought of for years. In these sequences she was always in uniform, and what hit her hardest was the persistent humiliation to which she had been subjected. A woman in a man's world, a woman none of them wanted or encouraged to become part of their close-knit group. She had clawed every inch up the ladder – she had always had to prove herself tougher than any man. She was not better educated, she had no special qualifications, and if her father had not been a police officer she doubted that she

74

would ever have joined up. She'd enrolled almost as an act of perversity.

Lorraine had hated her father because he had no time for her while he had doted on her brother, Kit. Whatever Kit had wanted Daddy made sure his precious son got. Kit was the pride of the family.

Lorraine's mother had been an alcoholic, a frightened, pathetic woman who drank in secret, who remained inside the house, afraid of her own shadow until she had drunk enough confidence to go out. To everyone's embarrassment, she would be picked up and brought home in a squad car by one of her husband's colleagues. She was never charged with being drunk and disorderly, whatever she did. If she stole money or became abusive, it was quietly glossed over, and she would be locked in her bedroom to get over yet another binge. Poor Ellen Page, sober and regretful, apologetic and weepy. Lorraine used to hide from the sound of her sobs by covering her ears with her pillow. When her mother was sober, the house would return to order and routine – until the next time.

Lately Lorraine had not given her mother much thought. Now, she could picture her pale face, her white hands always twisting the thin gold wedding ring. Her red-rimmed eyes, her lank blonde hair. Lorraine was the image of her mother: perhaps that was why her father had so little time or love left for her.

She never discovered what had started her mother's drinking. She used to search for the hidden bottles and, under instruction from her father, pour the contents down the sink. At first she always told him when she found the tell-tale bottles, but it seemed to Lorraine that the awful fights that followed were always directed at her – as if the blame was somehow partly hers. In the end, the pale, thin look-alike daughter protected her mother, and simply poured away the booze without saying anything.

Lorraine's mother died quietly in her sleep. She was only

forty-two, and Lorraine thirteen, but from then Lorraine ran the house. She cooked and cleaned up, waited on her father and brother. She would watch them leave for ball games, always together, like pals rather than father and son.

Kit was killed in a car accident. Two kids joy-riding in a stolen car mounted the pavement and ran him down. She could see him clearly, it was strange, she hadn't given him a thought in she couldn't remember how many years. Now she could even hear his voice, the way he always called out when he came into the house: 'Hi, I'm home, anythin' to eat?' He had never talked about their mother's 'problem' – if anything he refused to acknowledge there was one. When Lorraine was forced to clear up her vomit, wash her like a child, he shut himself in his room and played his records. Loud, louder than ever if Ellen was weeping, or if she was stumbling around the kitchen trying to get supper ready.

That night Kit hadn't come home for supper, and her father got the phone call, just as she was about to serve him steak. She could smell it, all these years later, the steak, the mashed potatoes, and the mint peas. She knew it was something terrible because of her father's expression and the way he let the phone slip from his hand as he pressed his face into the old flowered wallpaper. Then he punched the wall twice before he walked back and collected his jacket.

'There's been an accident. It's Kit.'

Lorraine was left alone with a father who never came to terms with his grief. He hadn't been affectionate before the accident, but afterwards he showed her no warmth whatsoever. If he felt any pride in her being accepted into the police academy, he kept it to himself, and he was dead three weeks before she graduated.

Lorraine sold the house and prepared to move into an apartment. It had been while sorting through his belongings that she had found pictures of her mother. She had once been so beautiful, with a fragility that took Lorraine's breath away, but the sweet smile, even in her youth, was a little frightened. She also found albums of photographs of her brother, every achievement recorded for posterity. But there were few pictures of herself, and those she did find had been left in an envelope.

Lorraine burned most of the memorabilia, and sold all the furniture along with the house. She kept a photograph of her brother and one of her parents on their wedding day. She would have liked one of them all together, as a family, but there hadn't been one – there hadn't really been a family. Now she had nothing – not even a photograph of Mike or the girls. She pictured them in her mind, little Julia and sweet-faced Sally . . . and Mike. The feeling of loss swamped her. She forced their faces from her mind and found solace in counting the specks of dirt on the wallpaper – anything rather than think of the past.

She woke up as Rosie thumped into the kitchen. She felt stiff from the cramped position in which she'd finally fallen asleep.

'I'm going to be late,' Rosie muttered, in her usual bad-tempered early-morning mood. She stood to shovel in her cereal, milk trickling down her chin. Lorraine stretched.

'Will you feed the cat?' Rosie barked.

Lorraine joined her in the kitchen. 'Do you think alcoholism is hereditary?'

Rosie rammed her cereal bowl into the sink. 'If you came to a few more meetings you'd know, wouldn't you? But they say it is. Why don't you read the leaflets I gave you?' She continued spouting as she returned to the bedroom, and Lorraine uttered a silent prayer that she had not gone out for that beer. Another day over, sober.

Rosie plodded down the road and turned the corner, just as the squad car drew up. Two officers checked the address and glanced up the rickety wooden stairs. The cab driver had not been sure of the number he had driven the woman to, but he had known the street and the date his fare had flagged him down. His description of her matched that of the other two witnesses, and he had picked up the fare a short distance from the shopping mall car park. He was able to add one more detail: the woman had a front tooth missing.

Lorraine examined herself: the suit jacket was a fraction too large, the skirt band a couple of inches too wide, but she bloused up the jacket, a safari-style fawn cotton, and with the cream silk shirt beneath, it looked good. She borrowed a pair of pearl stud earrings from Rosie's jewel box, and used her mascara, a little rouge and powder and, as the lipsticks were all a violent orange, rubbed on lip balm instead. When she heard a rap on the door she hesitated: maybe she should have asked Rosie about the earrings. If she was back, she might get into one of her moods. She heard a second rap; knew it couldn't be Rosie, who would have used her key, and assumed it was Jake.

She stepped back in shock as the two officers lolled at the door. One remained outside while the second came in to 'ask a few questions . . .' She lit a cigarette and sat on the edge of the sofa, thankful she had cleared away the blankets and pillows.

'Do you live here?'

'Yes, I do.'

'What's your name?'

'Laura Bradley. Actually I'm just staying here, I don't own this apartment.'

'Who does?'

Lorraine gave Rosie's name. He asked for a description, and she said Rosie was dark-haired and in her late thirties.

'Is she fat?'

Lorraine half smiled. 'No. Why? Has something happened to her?'

'No. Were you here early evening on the seventeenth of last month?'

Lorraine nodded.

'Did someone else come here? Did a taxi cab bring someone else to these premises?'

'No. Not that I can recall . . .'

The officer stood up, walked towards the bedroom, and pushed open the door.

'Just the two of you live here? Nobody else? Short, dark-haired man?'

Lorraine laughed. 'No. It's a small place. Why are you so interested?'

The photograph was not the same as the one in the wallet but much larger. Yet Lorraine knew at a glance that it was the owner of the vehicle licence – the owner of the wallet.

'Do you know this man?'

'No, I'm sorry. What has he done?'

'He was murdered, ma'am. Haven't you read about it? Local man.'

Lorraine looked suitably shocked, then stood up. 'Maybe he lived here before I came to stay – I can ask my friend.'

The officer slipped the photograph back into his jacket. 'Thanks. Truth is, we're only interested in tracing the woman – cabbie reckoned she was dropped off around here.' He relaxed, smiled at Lorraine. 'As you don't fit the description we must have got the wrong place, but thanks for your help, been nice talkin' to you.'

Lorraine followed the young officer to the door. 'Was she murdered as well?' she asked innocently.

'No, but we think she may have known the man driving the deceased's vehicle. We have two witnesses.'

'They saw her coming here?' asked Lorraine.

79

'No. In the local shopping mall car park, and we were told she may have been brought here by cab. We're asking everyone in the street if they saw her. She must have been hard to miss – she was covered in blood.'

Lorraine opened the front door. 'I'll ask Rosie when she comes home if she saw her. Do you have a number? Somebody I can call?'

The officer told her to contact her local station or sheriff's office and they would pass on any information to the department handling the homicide.

After they had gone, Lorraine leaned against the door. Her heart was beating so rapidly that she felt dizzy. She began to talk herself down for being so stupid. She was not involved in any murder. All she had done was tip off the cops with the description of the man who picked her up. There was nothing to be afraid of – except that she had taken the wallet. But she'd got rid of it and nearly all the money was gone. They had not been new notes so she doubted they could be traced. Why was she worrying about something so inconsequential when the officers hadn't even recognized her as the woman they wanted for questioning? She ran her tongue over her newly capped teeth. She had come a long way since that attack, physically and mentally, and she congratulated herself on the way she had handled the cop.

She even mentally castigated the police for being so slow in finding the cab driver who had driven her home that afternoon. If she had been on the case it would have been the first thing she'd have checked.

Self-satisfied, she left the apartment, her pace quickening as she walked towards the bus stop. Nothing in her appearance resembled the woman the police had described: her hair was well cut. She looked elegant, though the shoes were a bit tight and she was without a purse, but she was more confident than she had been for years. She caught a glimpse of her reflection in the grocery store window as she passed and didn't even notice the rows of liquor bottles, so intent was she on admiring herself. It was another day, and she had moved on faster than she could ever have anticipated or believed possible.

CHAPTER 3

CAPTAIN ROONEY looked over the reports and statements from the various officers. They were, as he had half expected, of little use. The cab driver had given them a bum address and nobody had located the bloodstained woman with only one shoe. She had disappeared – could even be dead. The Summerses had been questioned again to see if they could match the description from the anonymous caller. He was similar, they said, but they were not too clear about the driver of the vehicle. When shown a photograph of Norman Hastings, they were sure that it was not him. Rooney doodled over his notebook.

He wondered again if they were looking for two killers, the man and the blonde woman working together. They had killed Hastings and then had an argument – maybe they had come to blows inside the car at the shopping mall. The woman subsequently made the anonymous phone call describing her partner, husband or lover . . . But if that was so, she would have known the killer's height and could even have given his name, although that might have incriminated her, too. Rooney concluded that the woman was probably not involved in the murder and did not know the killer's name or height because she was, as he had first thought, a prostitute the driver had picked up.

The missing blonde woman had become a vital witness to the murder of Norman Hastings. Somebody out there knew who she was. A man and a woman had helped her out of the cab; the man had even paid her fare. Rooney instructed his officers to step up the search for her, and called in the two officers Lorraine had met earlier.

He checked over all the statements they had taken. They were convinced that no one had lied. They thought the cab driver might have been mistaken. 'We saw only one blonde woman, Captain – but she'd got all her teeth, her hair was short and she was real smart, just staying with her friend. She didn't look like a whore or the type to know one.'

Rooney told them to question everybody once more. Seeing them exchange covert, bored looks, Rooney snapped, 'Get the cab driver to go with you, if needs be. Go on, get moving!'

The two men had just reached the office door when Josh Bean walked in. 'You better look at this, Captain.'

Rooney reached out his podgy hand for the internal fax sheet. Bean gave the nod for the two men to leave the room, but to wait outside. Rooney looked up. 'We'd better check this out. Looks like our missing girl.'

He snatched up his jacket, told the two officers they could go off duty. If the new information panned out, they had just found their star witness.

The run-down apartment block was a graffiti jungle. Burned-out cars littered the disused yard and every window was smashed. The Paradise Apartments billboard, showing palm trees and a semi-naked girl sunbathing, was peeling and covered in daubed slogans.

Rooney stepped under the obligatory yellow tape to join the group gathered round the covered corpse. There were five patrol cars, lights blinking, and a horde of officers assembled to protect the men in this notorious down-town area. Groups of kids were hanging around watching avidly. This wasn't unusual in the middle of the day as most of them never bothered to attend school for more than one or two days a week, if that. This was crack-dealer territory. The kids on their BMX bikes more than likely had shooters stuck up their fashionable jackets.

'Who found her?' Rooney asked as he neared the corpse.

'That kid over there, one with the red hat on, but he must have had help to drag her from the trunk of the car. That's been there for weeks, by the way, the car not the body.'

Rooney stared at the kid, who was no more than six or seven and laughing as he pointed to the dead body, nudging his pals.

'She was in the wrecked car, nearest the tapes. He dragged her out here, said he thought she was alive – but if she had any jewellery on her, she ain't got it now.'

As he crouched down, Rooney took out his handkerchief to cover his face – the stench was of a body at least two days old. So much for the kid's story about thinking she was still alive. She was wearing a floral patterned dress, with a belt and flat black shoes. Rooney noted they were the same size as the one they had found in Hastings's car. Her thin legs were bare, and one stretched out at an odd angle. Her arms were by her sides, the back of her dress undone. The thin blonde hair was matted with dark congealed blood; a wound gaped at the base of her skull, so deep, he could see white bone. Slowly they turned over the unwieldy corpse. Her face had been hammered out of all recognition. Blood obliterated the brightly coloured flowers that had once patterned the front of her dress.

There was nothing Rooney could do; he couldn't tell if it was their witness or not. His only option was to wait for the report to come in, and for her to be cleaned up so he could see her face.

'Any of her teeth missing?' he asked as an afterthought.

An officer peered down into the mass of blood hiding her face. 'I can't tell, her nose has been flattened so bad . . .'

Rooney returned to his office with Bean. They opened a bottle of Scotch, and both had a heavy hit. No matter how many you see, it's always the smell that gets to you, stays in your nostrils. The sweet, sticky, cloying smell of rotting flesh.

'I think it's our witness. Cinderella,' Rooney said flatly. 'Fuck it! Really needed to talk to her.' He sighed.

'Yeah.' Bean knocked back his drink.

Rooney looked up as his secretary peered in. A message had come through from the city morgue: the corpse wouldn't be ready for viewing until at least the following day, maybe longer. Did he want to speak to the scene-of-crime officers? Rooney jerked his head for Bean to go and do the leg-work; he had some paperwork to finish. Bean raised his eyebrow, knowing Rooney always said that when he wanted to take himself off home. But he was wrong this time: Rooney spent the next hour making phone calls to different precincts. It was something one of the officers had said – or he might even have said it himself. She had been hammered in the face and at the back of the head. He wanted to know if anyone else had a similar homicide – weapon used probably some kind of hammer, that was all . . . In reality he passed more time chatting to old buddies, in no hurry for the facts. He knew he wouldn't get them straight away, if at all. Old files would have to be sifted through, and checked out on computer. Probably wasting everybody's time, but he caught up on gossip, arranged a game of billiards and agreed to have a drink with Colin Sparks, an old poker-playing pal he'd not seen for six months.

Sitting on a bar stool in Joe's Diner, his fat ass bulging over the red plastic stool top, Rooney had downed two beers and a chaser by the time Sparks walked in, but promptly ordered another round and a fresh bowl of peanuts.

Sparks whacked him on the back, then produced a dog-eared file. 'I'm late because I got interested in that! It happened before I got transferred – it's been around for four years. Dead hooker. Go on, read it.'

Rooney grinned at the young, fresh-faced lieutenant, and cuffed him like a father would his son. 'Looking sharper than ever, Colin. How you keeping?'

'Fine, new baby on the way – everythin's good.'

Rooney opened the file. He looked at the prostitute's face, her dyed blonde hair scraped back from her head showing at least an inch of dark hair growth. Half Mexican. Maria Valez, aged thirty-two. The next page had a photograph of her body when it was discovered in the trunk of a wrecked Buick. Like the dead woman that afternoon, Maria's face had been virtually obliterated by heavy blows. There was an enlarged shot of the back of her scalp, showing the deep wound. Type of weapon, possibly a claw-sided hammer. No witness, no arrest, no charges, case closed for lack of evidence, but authorized to remain open on file.

Rooney closed the file and tossed a handful of peanuts into his mouth. 'Can I keep this? There's a few details on blood groups I'd like to check out with my case.'

'Go ahead.'

'Thanks,' smiled Rooney, as he waved at the waitress for another round. 'An' I'm gonna treat you to the best curry in Pasadena!'

Rooney, well toasted, and Sparks, soberish, left Joe's Diner to head for the Star of Asia curry house. Rooney's crumpled alpaca coat flapped. The file was stuffed under his arm and he was sweating in the early-evening heat. He upped his flat-footed pace to get into the air-conditioned restaurant.

*

Lorraine emerged from the health club Fit as a Fiddle feeling like a washed-out rag. Her heels were blistered, her silk blouse creased, tears of sweat dripped from her fringe, and her hair was wet at the nape of her neck. So far she had applied for ten different jobs to discover either that the position had been filled, or that she didn't have the required experience. At Fit as a Fiddle she had snapped back at the Cher-with-muscles lookalike: 'How much fucking experience do you want to pick up a phone and book an appointment?'

'Cher' had wafted a hand adorned with fake nails. 'Maybe I was just bein' polite. You look like death warmed up for starters – and you're too old, okay? That real enough for you?'

Lorraine had slammed out and was about to throw in the towel and go home, when she realized she was standing outside Seller Sales, the next job prospect she had noted down. She pulled at her jacket, using the sleeve to wipe the sweat from her face, and walked into the run-down office. A moment later and she would have faced Captain Rooney as he and Sparks went into the restaurant three doors down the street. As it was, she almost walked straight out of Seller Sales: no one was in what she supposed passed for reception – a counter, a bowl of wilting flowers, two posters for Gay Liberation, and a faded breakfast cereal ad. She opened the door, which buzzed, and a man shot round from a room at the back. 'Thank God! Come on, come on, hurry up. I'm Art Mathews. I've been getting desperate.'

Lorraine hesitated and closed the door, following Art round the screen and into the back room. He was about five foot four, tight, muscular little body, shown off by a close-fitting white T-shirt, skintight white jeans, white sneakers and white socks. His dark eyes were too large for his face behind huge glasses – round, thin, red-framed bifocals – and made even more striking by his complete baldness.

The room was cluttered with paints, trestle tables, stacks of canvases, ladders and rolls of carpet. Art walked in small, mincing steps, side-stepping all the paraphernalia with a dancer's precision.

'Now the phone is somewhere, and the lists. Oh, Jesus, where did I put the lists? I'm so behind – and they said you'd be here hours ago . . .'

Lorraine looked around. 'I think there's a misunderstanding.'

Art stood, hands on hips, his little rosebud mouth pursed. 'Seller thingy closed down months ago, I've taken the shop lease over. I'm opening an art and photographic gallery here tomorrow, would you believe it? My God, if you knew what I've been through . . . WHERE'S THE FUCK-ING PHONE!'

Lorraine spotted it beneath a table. Art dragged it out, swore because it was off the hook and sat cross-legged on the floor. Lorraine watched as he arched his body to enable him to drag out a card from his jeans pocket, and punched out some digits.

'What are you here for?'

She coughed. 'Receptionist.'

He looked at the card, then back to Lorraine, his eyes darting like a demented frog's. He pursed his lips as his call was connected. 'This is Mr Art Mathews and I was prom-ised a . . . hello? FUCKING ANSWER MACHINE!'

He sprang to his feet. 'I need someone to call my guest list, there's over a hundred people, and I need it done by tonight. I need someone here to help me open this up. I've got to get that paint on the walls, hang those canvases and photos—'

Lorraine unbuttoned her jacket. 'I'll do it. How much you paying?'

Art clapped his hands. 'Ten bucks an hour – I love you. What's your name, darling?' She told him. 'Right, Lorraine, here's the phone, grab a seat, I'll find the list and you start with the calls. I need to know how many are coming so I can order the wine . . .'

'Have they been invited already?' Lorraine asked.

'They have, dear, but not to this address. I had a problem with my last place. Now if I don't open and show all the canvases and the photographs then I'll be fucked – I'll lose my credibility and it's hanging on a thread as it is . . .'

He alighted on a bulging Filofax. 'Right, darling, here you go. Be charming, be distant, but get an answer.'

Lorraine put down her cigarettes and lighter, and studied the guest list, detailed in a neat fine scrawl, in pinks, greens and blues with red stars drawn against some names. 'Does the red star mean they're important?'

'No – just a good lay!' Art shrieked with laughter. He almost did a triple spinning turn as the buzzer sounded in reception.

Lorraine could hear a lot of shrieking and raised voices, then Art returned with a massive floral display – and two extraordinary-looking transsexuals, carrying a basket of food, a crate of distilled water, and two more floral displays. 'These are my dearest friends, Nula and Didi, they're going to help me. This is – what's your name again, dear? She's going to make all the phone calls, and be Girl Friday.'

Nula and Didi began to put down their goods as Art moved to clear the back of the room. Lorraine pulled out a clean page from the Filofax, and started making calls. She looked up gratefully as Nula placed a paper cup and a bottle of spring water by her side. Didi was inspecting some tapes, then crossed to a ghetto blaster and slipped in a tape. Lorraine expected some ear-shattering music to interrupt her call, but she was surprised by Mahler's Symphony No.9, the volume almost restful. Didi laid out a neat row of tapes, choosing each with studied concentration. She turned to Lorraine, her husky voice half whispering: 'Do you like opera?'

She nodded as Didi selected the next tape. She had never listened to opera in her life.

The pace at which Art and his two friends worked was astonishing. They had painted all the walls with a quick-dry rough white, swept the floors, stacked the rubbish, torn down the screen partitioning at the front of the shop, and were now painting that area, using big roller brushes on sticks.

Lorraine remained at the table, making calls and listing acceptances and refusals. She now had her spiel down to a bare minimum: 'Good evening, I am calling on behalf of Art Mathews's new gallery, Art's Place ...' She gave the address, time of the show and mentioned that wine and canapés would be served from seven o'clock. Most said they would try to make it, but only twenty would definitely be there.

The strains of Puccini floated into the room, and Lorraine downed two bottles of water as she continued her calls. Nula slipped her some home-made banana cake wrapped in a napkin, a little bowl of fruit salad, and some crispbread with home-made pâté. Her big hands were rough from scrubbing, her overall covered in white paint splashes but she had the sweetest of smiles. Didi paid Lorraine hardly any attention as she was intent on finishing the work. When they did take a short break the three huddled together, admiring the gallery, discussing where the paintings and photographs would look best.

Art occasionally leaned over her to see the list, but on the whole behaved as if she weren't there. It was almost ten o'clock when Lorraine made the last call to a Craig Lyall. The deep, rather camp voice enquired if it could speak to Art. She covered the mouthpiece. 'Art, it's a Craig Lyall, he wants to speak to you.'

Art passed his brush to Nula. His whiter-than-white outfit was filthy, his round glasses speckled with paint. 'This is he,' he lisped into the phone.

Lorraine got up and stretched. Her back ached, and her mouth was dry again. She wandered towards the main room where Nula and Didi were unwrapping canvases and stacking them against the walls.

Art rang off, came across and put his arm around Lorraine. 'Well that, my dear, was good news. Craig Lyall, sweethearts, is coming.' He peered up into her face. 'You can go now but I insist you're here tomorrow. What on earth did you do to yourself? Car crash?'

Lorraine stepped away from him, her hand automatically moving to her scarred face. 'Yes.'

'You should have it fixed, dear. I know the best surgeon if you want his name . . .' Art put his arm back around her waist and gave her a little hug, beamed, then released her to dig deep into his pants and took out a thin leather wallet.

Lorraine felt embarrassed as he counted out thirty dollars in ten-dollar bills, but she took the money and pocketed it fast. 'See you tomorrow, then,' she said, hovering at the doorway. All three smiled and Art accompanied her to the main exit. He unlocked the door, which buzzed as she stood on the mat. He tutted, 'I'll have to get this fixed.'

Lorraine turned back to see him inspecting the faulty buzzer, his bald head shining in the street lights. She intended to get a bus and was heading towards the bus stop, when a car travelling in the opposite direction tooted its horn. Lorraine looked over, and was relieved to see Jake at the wheel. 'You want a lift?' he called. By the time she had crossed the road, Art had closed the door and returned to Nula and Didi.

Nula looked at Didi and nodded. 'Tell him.'

'Tell me what?' Art asked, his attention focused on the paintings.

'I think I've seen her before though I can't put my finger

91

on where. I've been trying to remember all evening. How did you find her?'

'She just walked in off the street. I thought she was from that agency I use, but she was looking for work at Sellers Sales.'

Nula studied her nails. 'That's been shut for months.'

Art said, 'Didn't you like her?'

Didi shrugged. 'I've just got this funny feeling about her.'

Art wished they would pack up and leave as he liked to hang the paintings alone, taking his time to choose where each would go. 'Isn't it time you two left?'

Nula gave a camp, 'Well, thank you . . .' and started to put her stuff together.

Didi was almost ready, giving a last look around. 'It looks good – be even better when I bring some more knick-knacks tomorrow.'

Art kissed them both, almost tearful with gratitude. 'You'll be here in the afternoon, won't you? Are you working tonight?'

They both chorused 'yes' and he watched them walk off, arm in arm, high heels, tight skirts, only their rather broad shoulders giving any indication of their former masculinity.

As soon as they were out of earshot, Nula snapped, 'I think you should have told him.'

Didi pouted. 'Why didn't *you*? It's always me. We'll have to sort it out between us. If he finds out he'll go ape-shit, so we'll sort it.'

Art watched them hail a cab then closed and bolted the door. He took out a tiny square envelope from his jeans pocket and carefully laid out a half-inch line of ice. This would see him through his all-night session. He snorted, blinked back tears as the ice burned his nostrils, then took a few deep breaths. No rush, nothing immediate like cocaine . . . he'd given that up. It would be a while before he felt any real benefit, so he placed the canvases around the room, then sat cross-legged in the centre of his little white gallery to appraise each painting. They were awful and he knew it.

Nula had showered and changed. She wore an overtly sexy outfit: stacked heels, tight leather mini skirt and, as she was well endowed, showed off her tits with an outrageous low cut bodice. She heard the door opening and turned from her make-up table. Didi dangled the car keys. 'Ready, sweets? You'd better go and get on the pitch, I've got to change.'

'Well, another night, dear. I'm ready and I'll be waiting.'

The prettier of the two, Nula pouted at herself and dipped her fingers into thick moisturizing cream. She hated her big hands which, even with nail extensions, looked too large and mannish. 'Funny the way I keep on thinking about her, that Lorraine. Do you think she's a prostitute?'

Didi teased her hair. 'I suppose you could always ask her. She said she'd be there tomorrow. You look lovely, now go on, get out or I'll never be ready.'

Half an hour later Nula was on their patch, hustlin' her tricks, duckin' and divin' down to the cars that cruised past. Most drivers knew she and Didi were trannies – the area was known for it. Both had their own regular customers and both paid off a regular lookout. Curtis wasn't actually a pimp, more of a minder, but he took a cut of every trick and seemed to know how many johns came and went. But Nula and Didi paid up without argument. It wasn't worth the aggravation to protest. Besides, at times they were glad of his tips as he seemed to know in advance when the Vice Squad were in their area.

Tony de Savoy – nicknamed Curtis because he had an old-fashioned haircut like Tony Curtis used to have – strolled up smiling warmly. He kissed Holly, his special sweetheart, tapped her tight little ass for her to get moving, then turned to Nula.

'Hi, how you doin'?'

Nula shrugged. 'Bit quiet tonight. Tony, you know a broad called – oh, I can't remember her name – Lorraine Page. Big tall blonde with a sort of beat-up face?'

'She's not one of mine, why?'

'I just met her tonight, remembered her from some place.'

Holly folded a piece of chewing gum into her tiny mouth and chewed hard. Curtis looked at the wrapper. 'Put it in the trash-can, slut.'

Holly pouted and bent down exaggeratedly to retrieve it, sashayed past and flicked it into a bin.

Curtis nudged Nula. 'She's a looker, isn't she? And with a figure to match. Eh, Holly! Shake that tight ass.'

Holly giggled and twisted, showing off her tits, then flounced off, teetering on her high heels, swinging her ass.

Nula saw a car cruising and took off as Curtis slipped a comb through his slicked-back hair. 'See you later. You just missed a trick – nothing gets by my sweet Holly.'

He laughed as she started to cross the road towards the john. 'I'll be at the Bar Q,' he called out as she sidestepped an oncoming car and gave the finger to the driver.

Nula watched him stroll on down his territory, stopping to chat to his girls. It still needled her that she couldn't remember where she knew Lorraine Page from. Holly was starting to get into the john's car and Nula hurried across the road after her, giving a quick look back to see if Curtis was still watching. But he was chatting up two black chicks, laughing and still flicking his comb through his grease-mop hair.

'This is mine, Nula baby. He wants a real woman, see ya.' Holly laughed as she got into the passenger seat.

Lorraine sat in Rosie's bedroom, telling her about Art and the gallery. She even gave her ten dollars towards the rent.

'Will you go back for the show, then?' Rosie asked.

Lorraine pulled off her creased shirt. 'Well, he wanted my phone number in case he has some more work, so I think I'll go.'

Rosie bashed the pillow. 'Put my earrings back in the box! And ask next time – they happen to be real pearls. About the only thing my ex-husband ever gave me . . .'

Lorraine made a show of removing them and replacing them. Rosie watched her every move, irritated yet again by Lorraine's confidence. She seemed to be getting herself back together, but instead of feeling pleased, Rosie felt jealous.

'Maybe I'll come with you.'

Lorraine switched on the shower. 'Don't force yourself. What's the matter with you?'

Rosie sat up. 'Nothing – but didn't you think I'd be worried? Jake was, too.'

Lorraine unzipped her skirt. 'Did you send him out to look for me?'

'Of course I did. I didn't know where the fuck you were – no note, nothin' to tell me what you were doing.'

Lorraine stepped out of her skirt, and Rosie turned away, not out of embarrassment but with the shock of seeing just how thin and scarred Lorraine was. 'What the hell happened to you?' she asked softly. 'All those scars . . .'

Lorraine wrapped a towel around herself. 'I got them when I was too drunk to feel I was getting them. Some of them are cigarette burns – maybe I did them myself . . .'

Rosie sighed as she heard the shower running. She'd meant to tell Lorraine, and Jake for that matter, that she'd lost her job at the hospital. It was nothing she'd done: they were cutting back on part-time staff.

By the time Lorraine emerged from the shower, however, Rosie was fast asleep. Lorraine turned off the light and went into the lounge to make up the sofa bed. She sat, still wrapped in her towel, with the TV turned down low, smoking a cigarette. Another day without a drink – and a day when she felt she had done something positive. But what did it all mean, anyway? She closed her eyes as she leaned back. Was every day going to be like this? Tramping from one place to another looking for work? She got to thinking of how much Art and his two helpers had achieved in one evening. They had transformed that shitty little place, not into anything fantastic, but he was going to be able to open a gallery – maybe even make some decent money. What was *she* cut out to do? She wondered what Nula and Didi did. Maybe they worked in another gallery or a night club. She'd liked them, Art, too, and the music – maybe things *could* get better . . . Maybe the key was to do as Rosie and Jake said and take each day as it came, not try to think of any long-term future, just another day – and one without a drink. She was so tired she fell asleep almost immediately before any pictures of her past had time to squeeze across her mind. She had no reason to think that her past would catch up with her the longer she remained sober. Old memories long forgotten would resurface to haunt her, like her dead brother's face. She had been able to deal with Kit, but there would be more, much more and she was not ready for it. The closer the past inched towards the present, the sooner she would have to face what she had obliterated by drinking.

Nula met up with Curtis for breakfast. She hadn't seen Didi for hours so presumed she had scored either a hotel john or an all-nighter. Curtis was edgy. He'd been looking for Holly and kept asking everyone who came and went if they'd seen her. Nula said she'd seen her score but not since. She could tell he was pretty coked up so she downed her coffee, paid what she owed him and took herself off. It was almost five thirty and she was feeling strung out, worried that Didi hadn't turned up.

Didi was at home, lying prone with an ice pack on her head. Nula leaned over her, concerned. 'You okay?'

Didi removed the ice pack to show a bruised eye. 'What do you think? Look at me, I got a black fuckin' eye and my foot, I twisted my ankle when I got out of the car, it's all swollen up.' Nula brought more ice and wrapped it in a tea towel to place on Didi's foot. She was concerned: the bruised face could always be taken care of but if Didi couldn't walk, that blew it for picking up customers and people would start asking questions.

Didi sighed, shifting the ice pack on her head. 'Oh, I remembered where I saw that Lorraine . . .'

Nula was creaming her face. 'Where?'

'AA meeting, we were both there, few days back.'

'So, that's that, then.' Nula wiped the tissue over her chin, looking at the blur of grease and make-up removed from her stubble-free face. She touched the soft skin lovingly. Odd that she hadn't remembered Lorraine from the AA meeting. She was usually good with faces.

'I'm gonna look terrible for the opening,' Didi moaned. 'Art won't let me in, I'll look so bad – you know the way he is.'

Nula looked at her. 'I wondered where you'd got to. I was worried, then I thought you might have scored. Curtis was strung out, lookin' everywhere for Holly.'

'I couldn't walk, could I? And my face, Jesus Christ, look at my face. Be hard pushed to score anything looking like this.'

'You'll be fine. I'll cover those bruises and your foot'll go down. I remember once I had a john punched me straight in the nose. I thought I was gonna die, two black eyes, but I got a real cute nose afterwards.'

Didi stared at her as if she was crazed and then eased the ice pack over her face. She started to cry but Nula said nothing. She put Didi's discarded clothes in the wardrobe with distaste. They were stained, and would have to be laundered. Suddenly she saw the car keys on the dressing table and whipped round. She began to panic. Why had she brought the car keys back?

'Where's the car?' she asked and Didi slowly removed the ice pack. 'What did you do with the car?'

'I just had to leave it outside, I couldn't walk back.'

Nula swore. She could have slapped Didi but instead she snatched up the keys and walked out slamming the door. Didi flopped back onto the pillows. Sometimes Nula really freaked her – she had no feelings. She cuddled down under the sheets, feeling sorry for herself. Then she felt beneath the pillow for the big topaz ring and slipped it on her finger. It made her feel better, more secure. At least she'd kept that safe.

The morning was bright and clear with the sun bringing a deep low orange glow that seemed to pinpoint the beige, highly polished metal of the Lincoln. A police car drew alongside it, as the two officers noted it had been left in a no-parking zone. That was the only reason they stopped. One officer got out and looked at the front of the car: he noted down the licence plate and returned to his car. He glanced back, which was when he noticed the pink material sticking out from the trunk.

The car had not been reported stolen but both officers walked over to it. One tried the doors. They were unlocked. He peered inside as the second officer pressed open the trunk.

She lay curled up on her side. One glance was enough. Her face was grotesque, beaten so badly that hardly a feature remained intact, and there was a gaping wound at the back of her skull. No one could have recognized her easily, but the tiny anklet she wore with a name engraved in gold letters made them think she was possibly called Holly.

CHAPTER 4

LORRAINE WAS up and cleaning the apartment before Rosie was awake. She put some coffee on to brew while she stacked and folded her sheets and bed linen. She had a plastic bag full of laundry ready to take to the laundromat, and was mentally compiling a list of groceries.

Rosie eventually surfaced, glowered and established her usual early-morning gloom. Lorraine's hyperactivity served only to increase it.

'You want any laundry done?'

'Jesus! I don't know at this hour, do I?' Rosie banged open the cupboards as Lorraine started up the vacuum.

'Can you just *leave* that until I had my breakfast?'

Lorraine picked up the laundry and walked out. She had it spinning when she took off for the nearest grocery store, the same shopping mall where the attack had occurred. She didn't give it a second thought – all that seemed far in the distance and, in any case, she wasn't anywhere near the parking lot.

It had been a very long time since Lorraine had shopped or bothered to choose food. She wandered up and down the avenues of goods, and the effort of concentrating on what she wanted to buy became more and more difficult as the Muzak attacked her in one ear while a bubble-gum voice belted out 'sales of the day' in the other, enhanced by the high-pitched *ping* of computer cash registers, a clicking

99

she couldn't identify, bells ringing from check-out assistant to floor manager as prices were asked, or assistants screamed conversation and the *peep-peep* of each article as it was passed over the automatic price scanner.

It seemed to Lorraine that only she was aware of the sounds. She noticed all the other shoppers were moving like lightning – it seemed that their sole intention was to get from A to B at the fastest possible rate. Carts collided, there was heavy breathing from a customer if she took too long weighing food. Not until she got to the freezer side did it occur to her that maybe the customers were moving so fast in the grocery section because they had just suffered frostbite in arctic temperatures. Nothing was familiar; had it really been so long since she had done something as ordinary as going to a grocery store?

No matter how hard she tried, Lorraine could not get the polythene roller bag open. Her tomatoes were still on the scales as she battled with her bag that – she felt sure – was only a single strip of plastic. 'Excuse me, could you show me how to get this open?'

The pink-gingham-clad shelf filler didn't look up from her task of stamping the canned peas, with what looked like a small Sten gun. Now Lorraine knew what the *click-click-click* noise was and she waited until the gun had ceased firing before she wafted her unopened bag. 'Is there a trick to this?'

The assistant stuffed her gun into her pocket, and without uttering a word took the bag, licked her forefinger and thumb, rubbed them over the serrated edge, shook it open and returned it to Lorraine.

'Very hygienic. Thank you!' Lorraine turned back to her scales with the waiting pound of tomatoes only to discover someone else had tipped them out.

She bought salad, yoghurt, fresh fruit, oranges for juice, some wholewheat bread, cereal and nuts. She was picking up some cherries when it started. She steadied herself, and pushed her cart over to the freezer section. Her whole body began to shake and she could feel perspiration breaking out all over. As she opened the ice-cream freezer, the gust of chilled air reminded her of the morgue and the first time she had had to take prints from a corpse. She had not shown any disgust, or emotion, but had clung to the fingerprints card, the black ink roller.

'Get the prints, Page, and bring 'em up to records.'

Lorraine had lifted the stiffened hand. She was a black woman, about fifty years of age. Lorraine didn't look at her face, but forced herself to concentrate on taking the prints. No sooner had she uncurled one dead finger than it recurled, the woman's hands tightening like fists. Lorraine was unaware that the team were all watching her, giggling like schoolboys as they saw her struggle. Eventually she had forced the woman's hand to lie flat, palm upwards, but just as she began to roll on the black ink, it had taken on a life of its own, curling so tightly around Lorraine's fingers that she could not release them. The watching men broke up, and only one of them had the decency to feel sorry for her. He was not much older than she was, but the team had shown him the ropes – unlike Rookie Lorraine: she was to be their entertainment. She watched as he hit the elbow of the deceased, which opened up the fist long enough for prints to be taken. She had laughed, treating it all as a big joke. But she'd had nightmares for weeks of being trapped by the dead in that hideous vice-like cold grip.

'Please shut the freezer doors,' snapped a gingham-garbed floor manager as she marched past. Lorraine rested her head against the fridge door, as the sweating subsided, but her hands were shaking. She didn't understand why she had suddenly remembered that incident.

When Lorraine got home, Rosie was sorting through the help-wanted ads, checking the possibles. By mid afternoon, she had made a few calls, but found no work. She sat watching television, and eating the nuts Lorraine had brought home. She paid scant attention to the announcement that a seventeen-year-old girl, Angela Hollow, nicknamed Holly, had been found brutally murdered.

Lorraine blew dry her hair, then rubbed moisturizer over her face and neck, and into her hands. She was sitting on Rosie's bed, smoothing cream into her fingertips when Rookie Lorraine Page appeared again. The rubber gloves she wore to examine a corpse always made her hands dry, and she kept lotion in her locker. The others teased her about it, but it wasn't just the dryness – it was the stench. No matter how fresh the corpse, there was a sickly sweet smell to it. Lorraine never wore perfume, so the moisturizer not only felt good, but smelt clean and fresh. As she massaged her hands, it started again. She was powerless to stop the memories.

They say your first homicide is the one you remember most clearly. Lorraine had been summoned to a domestic and her car had been first on the scene. The small house had looked so neat from the outside, so normal, so quiet that she and her partner had radioed back to base to double-check the address. A neighbour had called to say they had heard screaming and gunfire.

Lorraine tried the front door. It was open. The woman's throat had been slashed, as had her arms and chest. She was wearing a cotton shift, nothing else, and there was so much blood that the material was a bright vermilion red. They found her husband in the front bedroom with his head blown apart, the gun still in his hand. Blood had sprayed over the walls and soaked into the blanket on the bed where he was lying. The third body, that of a twelve-year-old girl, was in the back bedroom. She had been killed by a single knife wound to the heart. She was tucked up in the bed, the covers up to her chin, one arm around a doll, as if peacefully asleep. Subsequently they discovered pornographic material and videos of the child and the dead man. Lorraine never forgot viewing those wretched home-made films, just as she never forgot how innocent the little girl had looked with her doll. She learnt from that incident never to judge by appearances: the family with no previous criminal record, the suburban couple with their respectable jobs, played out in secret a despicable game of perversion on their own child. It was a hard and brutal lesson for a twenty-year-old rookie cop. Worse followed, but sitting in front of Rosie's dressing table, the memory of that first suicide came back. Lorraine felt icy cold, as if she was standing in the morgue, as if the child's murder had just happened, as if the little girl was calling out to her.

Rooney stared at the body, moving around the stretcher, pulling at his nose. The hammer blows to her face had broken both cheeks, her nose, and the right side of her jaw. The wound to the back of her head would have killed her, as it had cracked open her skull. She had no other body scars, no new skin abrasions or bruising, and her fingernails were intact, but there was evidence of previous beatings. At seventeen years old, Angela Hollow, blonde, about five feet seven, with a good figure, had three previous arrests for prostitution.

Rooney thanked the morgue attendant and returned to his office. Bean was waiting. He had interviewed Holly's pimp and four other girls who had seen her on the evening of her death. No one had seen the man who had picked her up, but one witness remembered the metallic beige car. They had not glimpsed the driver as he had been on the far side of the road. All they remembered was seeing Holly cross the road at about nine thirty. She had not been seen since.

Rooney looked through the statements and tossed over the file he had been given by Colin Sparks. 'Have a look at that, Josh. I want the blood group checked out against that girl we got and on the Hastings guy.'

Bean left the office, but returned immediately with a lengthy internal fax. 'You better look over this, it just came in.'

Rooney nodded. 'Angela Hollow. It's a fucking hammer again.'

As he went out, Bean heard Rooney swearing. The fax sheets were the result of his previous evening's calls. Three more girls, in different areas over a period of seven years, had all been killed by hammer blows to the back of the head, and suffered severe facial injuries. All were hookers of different ages, their bodies left in the trunk of a stolen vehicle. No witnesses. Each case left open on file. Three murders, Angela Hollow made it four and Maria Valez five, the woman from the wreck, still unidentified, six, and if the killer had also murdered Norman Hastings it was now seven. If they had all been killed by the same man, as Rooney began to suspect, he had better start gathering the evidence to link them together. He was now about to launch a multiple murder inquiry.

Later that afternoon he got the first verification. The blood found inside the stolen Hastings car matched the retained blood sample from the murder case handed to him by Sparks. The killer of Maria Valez had left no other incriminating evidence behind, but Rooney made a note that she had, like the woman in Hastings's car, put up a struggle. According to the autopsy reports, she had clawed and scratched her assailant: blood samples had been taken from beneath her fingernails. None of the other women had struggled: they had been killed by the blow to the back of their heads.

Rooney summoned Mr and Mrs Summers again, hoping they would be unable to identify the corpse from Paradise Apartments as the woman they had seen in the mall car park. If it were not her, then what they had witnessed in the car park, the woman in Norman Hastings's car, was a failed murder attempt, possibly by the same killer. It also meant that Cinderella was still alive and, once again, a vital witness – or accomplice.

As they had been throughout, Mr and Mrs Summers were eager to give every assistance. They had never been to a morgue before or played a part in any criminal investigation let alone a murder inquiry. Rooney decided they should see the body together, and he accompanied them into the viewing room.

'Okay, she's behind the curtain. We can turn her around, get any side you want to see, right or left. You just take your time . . .'

He pressed the buzzer for the curtain to move away from the screen window.

The dead woman had been cleaned up, her hair washed and combed, and they had also had her face repaired, covered and filled in by a qualified cosmetic mortician. A little trace of make-up served only to enhance the deathly pallor and her eyes were closed.

Mrs Summers let out a gasp. She stepped closer, but her husband remained where he was, staring through the window. It was the husband Rooney concentrated on; he had been close to the woman for longer and had spoken to her.

'Yes,' said Mrs Summers.

'I don't know . . .' said her husband.

'It's her – look at her hair, it's the same hair.'

'Maybe.'

Mrs Summers turned to Rooney. 'I'm sure it's her.'

Rooney nodded, then looked at Mr Summers. 'What do you think? We can turn her round if you like?'

'No, no, I think my wife is right. She's the woman I saw.'

Rooney asked if he was positive that it was the woman he had tried to help in the parking lot that afternoon.

'Yes,' Mr Summers said firmly.

Rooney returned to his office. Bean was waiting for him: he had received confirmation via police records, and they now had an ID of the victim. The dead woman Mr and Mrs Summers had just identified was Helen Murphy, aged thirty-nine, a prostitute, mother of three children, all in care. Murphy had been reported missing three weeks before she was found.

The Summerses' mistaken identification left Lorraine in the clear yet unaware of how valuable a witness she was, just as it meant that Rooney and his team were no longer looking for her. Instead they focused on trying to find a link between the dead women and Norman Hastings.

But Rooney was still not satisfied. He looked over the report and asked if dental records were available, remembering that the cab driver had said the woman had a front tooth missing. Helen Murphy had false teeth. Rooney was anxious to bring the cab driver in to view the body. He was not as positive as the Summerses: she was similar and had the same colouring, he said. Eventually he agreed that it was probably the woman he had picked up. Rooney conceded that Helen Murphy was the woman from the car park, which meant there would be no further visits to Rosie's address. That line of inquiry was now closed.

It was five o'clock when Rooney faced his team. He had requested extra officers and an incident room. They waited patiently as he shuffled his papers. 'Okay, this is Helen Murphy,' he began. 'Prostitute, blonde, aged thirty-nine, body found in the vicinity of the derelict Paradise Apartments in the trunk of a wrecked car, she had been there for approximately two to three days.'

The men stared at the blow-up pictures. Next to appear were Angela Hollow and the stolen vehicle, then Maria

106

Valez, and three more unidentified females. Lastly there was a photograph of Norman Hastings and his car.

Rooney paused as the men murmured and made notes. 'Okay. Obviously the Norman Hastings killing is different because he's male. Maybe the car was stolen and Hastings managed to see or catch the thief. Either way, he was killed with a similar weapon to that used on each of the others: a claw hammer. We know it's not the same weapon – some of the impressions taken from the women are of different dimensions, but all of them have been hammered in the face, and the claw section used for one blow at the back of the skull, near the base. When the victim is face downwards, the claw hammer strikes and gets drawn upwards, leaving – as you can see – one hell of an open wound.'

Rooney waited as they took it all in, then began again. 'The women are all prostitutes, all with records, obviously all blonde. No witnesses. Nobody has ever come forward with any motive, and so far we haven't found a link between the women, apart from their line of business and the fact they were tall, blonde and – apart from the last girl, Angela Hollow, nicknamed Holly – all dogs.'

Rooney continued for another hour, explaining the Summerses' part in the inquiry and Hastings's missing wallet. He concluded with the description of the man driving Hastings's stolen car. The man they were hunting, he pointed out, would have a bad bite mark on his neck, close to the jugular, according to Helen Murphy.

'Our first hammer killing comes in 1986, the next 1987, then 1988, 1991, which was Maria Valez, and the last two, Helen Murphy and Angela Hollow, plus Hastings, are all within months, if not days of each other. We've got a gap between '88 and '91, unless more come to light. Let's hope to God they don't – and let's give this all we've got.'

One young, eager-faced officer asked where they were going to start and Rooney, unsure himself, snapped that as the victims were hookers, they should start by asking on the streets, in the brothels. To begin with he wanted it kept low key and, until they had more evidence, he wanted the press kept out for as long as possible.

Rooney returned to his office feeling worn out and hungry. Bean looked up as he barked out, 'You feel like some curry?'

Bean didn't, but agreed to accompany Rooney, because he didn't think they should keep it from the press.

As they got into the car, Rooney gave him a sidelong look. 'What's the problem?'

'Well, I don't think we should keep this quiet. We could have a multiple killer on the loose! Those gaps between the murders, what if our man was in prison?'

'Whoever the fuck he is, he's on the loose now.'

'That's my point, Bill. He killed Norman Hastings, Helen Murphy, Angela Hollow within weeks of each other. Even if it's hookers he's taking out, the street girls should be warned.'

As Bean expected, Rooney dismissed this. 'We get the fuckin' press on this, they'll blow it up out of all proportion. This way it's giving us time to make some headway, because we have fuck all but—'

'A pretty tight description. Somebody somewhere knows a guy with a fucking bite out of his neck.'

Rooney started the engine. '*That* we never put out, else we'll have Dracula and his uncle wastin' our time . . . The guys on the street can put the word out to the whores but, you know as well as me, nothin' stops them. They'll keep on trading no matter who we say is out there.' He turned the car and prepared to drive out of the police pound.

'Who do you think is out there, Bill?'

'Someone with a hatred of tall skinny blonde whores – how the fuck do I know? You got his description, what do you think?'

'I dunno.'

'Right, you don't know, nobody knows. They may give us all the psychological profiles from so-called professors, why he kills, what he gets out of it. But when you say: "Okay, where do I find the guy?" they don't fuckin' know. The truth is, Josh, they can pinpoint or direct us to a psycho, because he's obvious. But our man, he's not obvious. He's cool, it looks like he's been getting away with it for years. It don't even run to a pattern because of Norman Hastings, who was a straight, decent guy.'

They drove out of the yard in silence. Then Bean sighed. 'Killer obviously has a thing about hookers . . .'

Rooney snorted. 'So maybe his mother or his wife was one. Then you can say he's killing *her*. Bullshit. I hated my mother but that don't make me want to kill every square-faced, red-haired tyrant, now, does it?'

He drew up outside the Star of Asia and switched off the engine. He was beginning to wish he'd not asked Bean along. 'That means he's just taking out his hammer whenever he feels like it. Now shut up, I'm hungry and I don't wanna talk about it.' Rooney got out, locked the car, and caught sight of Art's Gallery. 'Christ, how did that spring up? It was an old real estate agency yesterday.'

He wandered over to look: inside were a lot of people rapping and drinking, arty types, not his sort. A cab drew up and more guests began heading inside. A good-looking coiffured man in a pale blue denim outfit paid off the driver, adjusted his shades, and followed his two tanned friends into the gallery as Rooney walked into his favourite curry restaurant. Art screamed out a welcome to his friend Craig Lyall and drew him into the throng.

Some time later Jake arrived with Rosie and Lorraine. They drew up and parked behind Rooney's car. Jake was wearing a cheap suit with a nylon shirt and wide flowered tie, Rosie a tent-type dress that accentuated rather than hid her bulk, various bead necklaces that clicked as she walked, and a pair of leather sandals. Lorraine had on the same fawn skirt now pressed, the black crêpe blouse, and the safari-style jacket draped around her shoulders. This evening she wore sling-back high heels, and appeared taller and thinner. Her make-up was as sparse as ever, and, as Rosie had refused to let her borrow the pearl studs, she had no jewellery. Art made a great fuss of her when she walked in, telling her she looked simply wonderful, and that her friends were more than welcome.

A camp young man was drifting around with a tray of wine. Lorraine was about to accept a glass when Jake asked loudly for mineral water and she quickly withdrew her hand. The three of them stood a little self-consciously at the doorway to the main room which was crowded with guests.

'Do you want to see the paintings?' asked Lorraine.

'Are there any?' Rosie couldn't see a single canvas as they edged further inside.

Nula beckoned Lorraine and took hold of her hand. 'I remembered where I had seen you – at a meeting!'

Lorraine was puzzled, then she understood. She looked at her glass of water, noting that Nula had one too. She asked about Didi and Nula told her about the twisted ankle.

'Oh, I'm sorry, after all her hard work, too. Have many pictures been sold?'

Nula shrugged. 'I hope so. Art is broke, but then, aren't we all?'

Lorraine looked across at Rosie and Jake standing exactly where she had left them. 'Come and meet my friends?'

Jake was polite, but Rosie stared, looking at Nula with such obvious fascination that Lorraine felt uncomfortable, but Nula didn't seem to mind. She chatted on about the gallery, how much work she and Didi had done and how marvellous Lorraine had been. 'Were you an actress?' she asked Lorraine suddenly.

Lorraine smiled. 'No, I wasn't.'

'What do you do?' asked Rosie bluntly.

Nula cocked her head on one side and smiled. 'Anyone who hires me, dear.'

Rosie wasn't sure what she meant and didn't care, she was hot and her feet hurt. She caught Jake's eye. 'Look, I don't think this was such a good idea, why don't we leave?'

Jake looked at Lorraine. 'Okay by me. Lorraine?'

They were about to walk out when Art caught Lorraine's hand and drew her towards some of his friends. Rosie and Jake waited for ten minutes beside the car before Lorraine appeared. 'You two go on, I'll stay for a while longer. Art needs me to help out a bit.'

Jake opened the driver's door, and was about to get into the car when a big pot-bellied man walked out of the Star of Asia, accompanied by a fresh-faced, square-jawed younger man. The older man was deep in conversation while searching in his pockets for his car keys. Yet he couldn't help but see Lorraine, who was only yards ahead of him. Jake saw the way Rooney looked, then looked again. He stopped talking in mid-sentence, as if surprised, or shocked. Jake couldn't make out which.

'Lorraine?' Rooney said loudly.

She half turned and took a sharp involuntary step back, bumping into Rosie.

'It is Lorraine, isn't it?' Rooney stepped closer.

Jake noticed the way she straightened her shoulders, clenched her fists.

'Lorraine,' Rooney repeated again. He couldn't stop staring – it was like seeing a ghost. Was it her? Or was he mistaken? Then she tilted her head, gave that sidelong look and he knew for sure. He said emphatically, but flatly, 'It's Lorraine Page.' She gave a barely detectable nod and hurried back inside the gallery. Rooney watched her go, then stared directly at Jake and Rosie. 'Evening.'

Rosie heaved herself into the car. Jake slammed his door, still observing Rooney as he walked around to his own car.

'What was that all about?' Rosie asked.

Jake shrugged as Rooney drove away. 'He's a cop, so is the guy with him. That Indian diner's a known hangout for 'em. But that's Bill Rooney, a real mean shit.'

Rosie was astonished. 'My, I have never heard you talk like that!'

'Well, maybe there's a lot about me you don't know. I guess there is about your room-mate, too. That fat prick busted me, maybe he arrested her too. Looked like he knew Lorraine from some place she didn't want to be remembered bein' in.'

He drove a few yards, then stopped. 'Maybe I should go back, see if she's okay. She looked a bit shook up.' He was about to reverse when Lorraine walked out of the gallery with Nula and hailed a cab.

Jake set off again. 'You know any more about her? She ever mention some money she had? Remember that night she came back, when she said she'd fallen? She had a lot of money on her then.'

Rosie looked out of the window. 'She told me she sold off some things a friend was keeping for her. Jake, I think I'm gonna ask her to leave. There's something about her – I dunno, but she's . . .'

'Tough?' said Jake.

'Yes, with a selfish streak, too. I mean, I kind of admire the way she's getting herself together but I know as much about her now as I did when I first met her. Sometimes I get the feeling she doesn't want anyone to know her.'

'That cop knew her. He knew her very well.'

Rooney pulled on the handbrake outside Bean's apartment. 'She was picked up for prostitution. Last they put her in a straitjacket, she was that crazy.'

Bean had his hand on the door handle. 'She looked straightened out tonight.'

Rooney nodded. 'Yeah, she sure as hell did. Mind you, I

112

didn't get that close a view, but she was one hell of a looker back then – never fooled around, well, not that I knew of. I think she even had a couple of kids, married a lawyer, but whatever she was, she blew it. That lady sure as hell hit the skids.'

Bean opened the door. He was barely interested in ex-Lieutenant Lorraine Page, but Rooney seemed eager to continue. 'Killed an unarmed kid.' He shook his head. 'Six bullets, emptied the fucking .38 into him – and you know what sickened me? She was laughing, no kidding, meant fuck all to her. She was pissed – she was a lush. I kinda thought she must be dead by now . . .'

'Goodnight,' said Bean, stepping out of the car.

Rooney remained deep in thought. He could still picture her curled up on the washroom floor, skirt up round her thighs. That was the last time he'd seen her, so drunk she couldn't even stand. That half-smile on her face had been the same half-smile she had given him tonight.

Lorraine looked round Nula's strange apartment with its outrageously theatrical living room: drapes and frills, mock leopardskin sofa and chairs, fur rugs, and huge paintings of nude female couples with male genitals displayed in semi-grotesque poses. Just as she was wondering idly if Nula and Didi had been totally transformed or if they still had their cocks, Nula came out of the bedroom. 'Something terrible happened to a friend of ours.'

A limping, red-eyed Didi appeared, dressed in a scarlet silk kimono, a clutch of tissues in her hand. 'She was a friend, only seventeen. They found her locked in the trunk of a car. She'd been hammered to death, not a feature left intact, dear . . . Now what pig-shit bastard could do a thing like that?'

Nula sobbed loudly. 'We saw her last night – I was standing talking to her. Holly was so cute, so nice . . .'

Lorraine listened as they wept and wailed. She didn't know who they were talking about. She tried twice to interject and ask if they'd like her to leave, but they seemed unaware she was in the apartment. Of the two Didi seemed more upset, and it was Nula who eventually turned to Lorraine. 'I'm glad you're here, help take our minds off it, she was only a kid . . . Didi, we gotta keep busy. Let's feed this babe – come on, get that apron on.'

Didi scurried into the kitchen, and Nula sighed. 'She'll be okay now. She's really upset, but I can always cheer her up.'

They cooked a delicious dinner, and the initial shock of Holly's death subsided. Their conversation centred on their friend Art: that he was a genius photographer, his boy-friends, his bankruptcy, his inability to stay in business.

Nula gestured to their apartment. 'This was his, then he made a stack of bread and he *gave* this to us and even when he's been broke and desperate, he has *never* asked us to leave.'

Lorraine nodded. The place was a nightmare, but that was just her taste, and she was enjoying the outrageousness of the pair, swapping stories, jokes, about old times when they'd been dancers. They didn't speak of the present, but out came albums and programmes. Eventually they seemed to talk themselves into silence. The subtle music, playing throughout, was switched off, and Lorraine took her cue to leave. She stood up, smiling her thanks.

'How long have you been dry?' asked Nula.

''Bout four and a half months.' Nula laughed and told Lorraine that she had been dry eight years, Didi four. She looked at Didi, and then pursed her lips. 'I suppose we should tell you we're whores – you've probably put two and two together anyway. It's just that we'd prefer you to hear it from us rather than anyone else – and we'd like to see you again.'

114

Lorraine was taken aback when Nula, sitting close, slipped an arm around her shoulders. She was wearing a heavy scent and, close to, it was overpowering.

'Listen, I got contacts who could put some work your way, straight decent johns, all you gotta do is ask.'

Lorraine did a neat sidestep, saying that she had some work lined up, thanked them again, and they insisted she take a cab home. She hadn't meant to sound so cool, be so distant, but they were touching on that hazy part of her life that remained unreal, which she hadn't yet faced up to. At the same time, she couldn't help but feel angry that they seemed to know she'd been a hooker. Somehow she had felt that no one could or would suspect that.

Nula kissed her cheeks. 'You come by any time and, keep it in mind, if you need cash to tide you over, we can always get you a few clients.'

'I'll think about it.'

Lorraine was relieved to get away from them, from the cloying perfume. Yet they had, unknowingly, helped her over a hurdle she had dreaded. Seeing Bill Rooney again had been like a punch in the stomach, so totally unexpected that she had been unable to speak, or even acknowledge him. The humiliation of the meeting made her feel physically sick. The cab fare took the last of her earnings from the gallery but she didn't care. One thing she knew for certain, she couldn't turn tricks again.

Each step up to Rosie's apartment was an effort, and the last person she wanted to be confronted by was Rosie sitting like a Buddha watching a mind-numbing game show. Lorraine shut the door and headed for the bathroom. The television was clicked off, ominously.

'We got to talk.'

Lorraine hesitated. 'Yes, I know, but I need a shower first.' The television clicked back on. When she returned to the sitting room, wrapped in just a towel, off went the

115

television. 'Just let me get a drink.' Lorraine slammed the fridge shut. It was empty. 'Thanks! Thanks a fuckin' bundle!'

Rosie smirked. 'Now you know what it feels like!'

'So you did it on purpose? You great fat pig, I bought enough to last days—'

'Oh, yeah!' Rosie sniggered. 'Well, who the hell do you think has been filling up that fucking fridge since you arrived?'

Lorraine turned on her. 'Jesus Christ, I've *given* you money!'

Rosie pulled herself up. 'An' I gave you a roof over your head, and my bed when you were sick. I fed you, washed you – and not once did you have the decency to say thank you!'

'So now you want me out of here, is that it?' Lorraine sighed.

'Why don't you get off your high horse and be real?' Rosie retaliated. 'I'm honest with you, when are you going to level with me?'

'Level with you about what?'

'Who you are for starters!' Rosie shouted.

Lorraine lifted her arms in exasperation. 'You know who I am! I've fucking told you who I am! *I am Lorraine Page!*'

'That's not enough. I knew your name at the hospital. It's like I live with somebody I don't know and I can't take it.'

Lorraine lit a cigarette and closed her eyes. She sat on the edge of the easy chair. 'Rosie, I can't tell you much because I don't *know* who I am. I am trying to find out who the fuck I am so if *I* don't know, how am I supposed to tell you?' She got up and paced the room, taking long drags on her cigarette. 'I look in the mirror and I don't know if this is the way I always looked. I see scars all over my body, and I don't know who inflicted them. I don't even know how I got *this*!' She pulled her hair away from the jagged scar on

116

her face. 'I got marks all over my body. I can see them, you can see them – but what about the ones inside my brain? There are whole years of my life missing, and sometimes I just don't know if I *want* to find out everything.'

Rosie nodded, suddenly concerned. 'How about tonight? You seemed pretty shook up.' Rosie waited but there was no reply. 'That man this evening, the fat guy, he said your name three times. Do you know who he was?'

'Yeah.'

'So why don't you start telling me? No? Okay, I'll make it easier. He's a cop, Jake knew him. Now if you've been in prison, it doesn't worry me – just tell me, 'cos I'd like to know.'

Lorraine gave a soft, humourless laugh. 'You see, you didn't believe me. I told you back at the hospital, Rosie. I told you what I was.'

Rosie stared as Lorraine sat down, rested her head against the chair and closed her eyes. 'I was a cop, Rosie. In fact, I was a lieutenant, and that fat man you saw tonight used to be my sergeant. His name is William – Bill – Rooney. He looked surprised, huh? Seeing me? Maybe because he thought I was dead, probably hoped I was . . .'

'Why did you leave?' Rosie asked.

'I was kicked out, Rosie. Because I was a drunk.' In a low, expressionless voice she began to tell Rosie about her husband, her two daughters, Sally and Julia, the divorce, her husband's remarriage, his custody of the girls whom she had not seen for almost six years. 'After the divorce I went on a binge. It kind of lasted until you found me, Rosie. I sold everything – apartment, furniture. The car was taken because I was caught drunk-driving. I got off with a fine. I got away with a lot of things, I guess, for the next few years. I don't remember much of it, just that eventually all the money ran out and when I had nothing left to sell . . .' She coughed, a heavy smoker's cough that made her body shake and her eyes run.

Rosie waited, watching as Lorraine lit another cigarette from the stub. 'So, go on, when you had nothing else to sell, then what?'

Lorraine gave her that odd, tilted, squint look. 'I sold myself, Rosie – to anyone, anything, any place, just so long as I got a drink. I worked for the pimps I'd arrested, and got drunk with the whores I'd booked. I ended up in shit-holes, bars, and flop houses. And I don't remember hardly a day of it. I got arrested for whoring, I got picked up for vagrancy. Sometimes the craving for drink drove me into a kind of deranged madness. By the time I was hit by the truck – when I was taken to the hospital – I think I had reached a sort of dead end hell. That's it. That's who I am, Rosie. Now you're as up-to-date as I am.'

Rosie began to make Lorraine's bed. It was a sickening story, but not one that she hadn't heard before: everyone she knew at the meetings, including herself, had a similar story of loss and desperation. What was different about Lorraine, however, was her complete lack of emotion when relating it.

Lorraine slipped into the freshly made bed and sighed contentedly, laying her head on her arm. 'I'm thinking . . .' she said softly.

'What about?' asked Rosie.

'Well, I'm not sure about bothering to get myself back together. Who am I doing it for? Be okay if I felt good, or if I felt I was doing it for a reason. But there's no reason.'

Rosie stood, elephantine, in the bedroom doorway. 'Maybe because it's your life. Or perhaps it's those two little girls.' Lorraine said nothing, so Rosie continued: 'My mother died when I was ten and there's a hell of a lot I would have liked to ask her – like who the fuck in my family did I inherit this fat from? My dad was skin and bone. And I'd like to know if she loved me. She took an overdose, you see, killed herself.'

Lorraine propped herself up on her elbow. 'You know, Rosie, sometimes I sort of loathe you, especially in the mornings, but if I forget to say thank you, then I'm sorry. I've no one else who gives a shit about me, no other place to go. So thank you for being my friend.'

Rosie flushed. 'Goodnight, Lorraine.'

Lorraine heard her move heavily into the bedroom, and then lay back staring up at the ceiling. Her daughters had had a new mother for five years, and they probably weren't even little any more. They probably wouldn't want to see her. She didn't even know where they lived.

It hurt to remember, physically hurt, as if each memory was so tightly stored away she had to squeeze it out. It was strange, because instead of being able to conjure up her own daughters' faces, she saw only the little girl she had been assigned to trace. Laura Bradley, six years old, who had last been seen waiting outside school for her mother. Lorraine, the officer in charge of searching the school outbuildings and cellars, had found Laura's naked body stuffed into one of the big air-conditioning pipes. Like a rag doll, so tiny, so helpless, yet her body had felt warm and Lorraine had tried mouth-to-mouth resuscitation. But nothing brought her back to life; even when she had felt the small ribcage lifting, it was not Laura breathing, it was Lorraine's own breath.

Lorraine got out of bed and began to pace the room. Why? Why was she suddenly remembering this child? Laura had been brutally sexually abused, her internal organs ripped by a blunt instrument. Not content with having sexual intercourse, the rapist had continued to torture the defenceless child. Laura Bradley's injuries were so horrific that all the officers on the case were sickened; Lorraine recalled seeing even the big, blustering Bill Rooney weeping. Obsessed with catching the killer, she worked day and night and had no time to spare for her own daughters. She had shouted at her husband that the girls were never to be left alone for an instant, and even hired a baby-sitter to collect them from school.

She poured herself a glass of water. She remembered yelling in fury at Mike, 'I'm trying to find Laura Bradley's killer. You may not think that is important, but you didn't hold her dead body in your arms. I did. And I will not sleep until I have that bastard locked away so my daughters and every kid in this neighbourhood can be safe.'

Mike had tried to make her rest but Lorraine had kept up one hell of an investigation and she wouldn't let it go. She visited Laura's parents and swore to them that no matter how long it took, she would bring in their daughter's killer. Her dedication paid off. From day one she had been suspicious of the school janitor and, as this was before the time they had DNA testing to assist them, she kept up the pressure. Intuition told her she had the right man.

Even her chief hinted that perhaps she should back off, but she refused, returning time and again to the scene of the crime and to the janitor's home, until, in yet another confrontation when she had shown him Laura Bradley's clothes, all her photographs, when she had interrogated him for more than six hours, she finally broke him. He admitted his guilt. She had been so proud, and she had been promoted. Laura Bradley could at last rest in peace.

Lorraine felt chilled now, remembering the visit of the young uniformed officer to Rosie's apartment, asking about the night she had returned after the attack in the parking lot, how she had substituted the dead child's name, Laura Bradley, for her own. She had uttered it without a moment's thought. Now she realized just how often in that long distant past she had placed her work above the needs of her own children and husband. Mike had been right. She had become obsessive. She had also become addicted to the adrenalin, the excitement, the tension and the pressure – until she had found it impossible to relax.

She returned to bed and sat for a moment staring at the wall. Maybe Rosie was right, she should try to contact them again. She would like to explain to Sally and Julia, perhaps even ask for their forgiveness. Yes, her life *was* worth bothering about, even if it was just to make peace with her children and Mike. Feeling calmer, she turned off the lamp, snuggled down and was asleep within moments.

This was the first time she had dealt with a section of her past without getting the shakes. She had talked it over in her mind and remained calm. Forced herself to hold on, remain distant from it. She reckoned it was another step forward in rehabilitation.

But she had spoken to Rosie about her past as if she was talking about another person, another Lorraine. She hadn't cried or, to Rosie, appeared to feel remorse or guilt. Instead there was a cold confidence, a control, that seemed to be getting stronger around her, as if she was divorcing herself from the past. What she was not doing, Rosie had surmised, was facing the full reality.

Rosie knew how harsh that reality was. Unlike Lorraine, she couldn't sleep. Instead, she was mulling over what she had been told. At some stage in her own recovery Rosie, like Lorraine, had asked herself if remaining sober, facing what she was and what she had lost, was worth all the trouble and the pain. Sober, she felt, she had nothing to live for. It had been Jake who had said her life was worth fighting for, for the sake of her son. She had tried to contact Joey, and she had felt really positive – but it had been a disaster. Rosie had been, and was still, unable to cope with the emotional strain of seeing Joey, of knowing there was another woman her son called Mother. She could not cope with talking to her ex-husband, or seeing the new home he had made for himself and their boy. As it all swept over her once more, she began to feel guilty about opening up the same terrible emotional road for Lorraine.

She crept out of bed. If Lorraine was awake she would

tell her that she should take more time before she tried to confront her lost family. She was wrong to push her, she wasn't experienced enough, and maybe this wall of control Lorraine was building around herself was good, and safer for her than allowing anybody like Rosie or Jake to break it down. But Lorraine was sleeping, one hand tucked under her chin, only the strange, jagged scar running from her eye to her cheek marring her look of innocence. She seemed peaceful, a half-smile on her lips.

Rosie made a vow. She would not ask Lorraine to leave the apartment: it was important for her to have a sense of security. Lorraine was her friend. That settled, Rosie went back to bed, swiped at her pillow and, within seconds, passed into a deep sleep.

CHAPTER 5

THE FOLLOWING week Lorraine got a job in a
florist's shop. It was only short term, replacing an
assistant who was on holiday. She also did four
nights at Art's gallery, as he remained open until ten in the
evening. He was rarely there, and she was often alone
waiting for the odd customer. A number of paintings had
been sold, but business was not flourishing. Art was out
looking for new pictures, but whenever he saw her, he
greeted Lorraine with affection.

The week was good because she was occupied, and with
the little money she earned she bought two more outfits
from a garage sale. Nula and Didi dropped in for chats, and
always brought some home-made banana cake with them.
Didi was still limping but she refused to see a doctor. The
two transsexuals admired Lorraine's taste in clothes and
discussed second-hand bargains they'd bought. Because of
their size they often found it difficult to get really stylish
clothes, and especially shoes. Lorraine was looking better
and feeling stronger every day. The sweatings were less
frequent and she had put on weight.

Rosie had started doing clerical work at home and had
hired a computer and printer so she was always in. They
began a routine of sharing the cleaning and laundry. Lorraine
contributed towards the rent and groceries. It meant that at
the end of the week, after she had bought her cigarettes and
clothes, she had little left. But what was left, she saved.

When the florist job finished, Lorraine asked Art if he could use her for a few more hours. As more paintings had been sold, and he had discovered a new artist, he took her on for two full days a week, plus the four evenings. There were few customers, and she didn't know how the gallery paid for itself let alone paid her salary. On her way to and from work she had to pass Fit As A Fiddle, now called Fit 'N' Fast, and decided to join one of their classes. She only managed the first ten minutes of the step aerobic session before she felt her energy give way. However, she began to practise in the empty gallery with a stack of telephone directories and slowly built up her strength, stepping up and down until her legs felt like jelly.

Lorraine used Art's telephone daily to try and trace her ex-husband. She called a number of Mike Pages but so far she had been unsuccessful. He had disappeared. Rosie surprised her by suggesting that she call the Bar Association: if he was still practising, they would know his address.

Mike Page was living in Santa Monica. Lorraine had not spoken to him directly, but to a secretary, who confirmed that he had two daughters, Julia and Sally. Before she could ask any further questions, Lorraine hung up. Then she stacked up the telephone books and stepped until she was exhausted.

It was a Friday evening, two weeks since Lorraine had found Mike's office number. She had put off getting in touch, always making the excuse that she didn't have enough money to get the bus to Santa Monica – and she was still in need of better clothes. She arrived home with a banana cake made by Didi and some fresh fruit. She was flushed from walking. It had been a full day of exercise: she had done a light workout with Hector, the owner of Fit 'N' Fast, who had put together a beginner's programme, starting with small weights, to build up the atrophied muscles in her arms and legs.

Rosie peered up from a mountain of brown envelopes and watched as Lorraine removed from her bag boxes and boxes of vitamins. Hector had taken to giving them to her free because most were samples. He suggested she took vitamins E, C, D and B12, and with her past record of alcohol abuse, he said, zinc. They all knew about Lorraine's drinking problem – Nula had told them – but Lorraine didn't mind. It was easier that everyone knew, and besides, as none of them drank she was never tempted.

'I see we've been to the hairdresser's – or did Hector turn his muscular body to that, too?' Rosie smirked.

'No, I had it done at the local.' She still had the short cropped cut, but she'd had new streaks put in.

Rosie licked a few more envelopes, slapping them down. She didn't say how good Lorraine looked because she was jealous. Lorraine was changing before her eyes. She was lightly tanned from all her walking back and forth to the gallery and whereas before she had seemed to shuffle, head bent forward, shoulders rounded, now she was straight-backed and looking fit.

Lorraine counted her money, putting some aside for Rosie. Then she went into the bedroom and opened the crammed closet. She took out her shoes, and stuffed the money inside with the rest of her savings. She sniffed gingerly: Rosie's clothes stank of body odour. She wished she had her own closet.

'You comin' to a meeting with me tonight?' Rosie asked, lolling at the door. 'Only I got to deliver these so I thought I'd maybe go straight on.'

'I said I'd go over to see the new paintings being hung.'

Rosie pursed her lips. 'Hector helping out, too, is he?'

Lorraine sighed. 'Hector's gay, Rosie, okay?'

125

'Maybe he swings both ways – some of them do, you know . . .'

'Rosie, don't start. Go mail your letters, I'll make some supper.'

Rosie banged out and Lorraine went into the kitchen. She cleaned up, then sat down by the telephone. She knew it was after office hours, but she just felt like making another of her calls. Mike Page's answering machine was on. This time she heard his voice, which gave an emergency number where he could be reached. Lorraine jotted it down and waited a moment before she dialled.

'Hello.'

The high-pitched voice was obviously a child's.

Lorraine hung up. She lit a cigarette and smoked it before dialling again. This time Mike answered. She had to swallow hard before she could speak.

'Mike, it's Lorraine.'

There was a pause before he spoke.

'Well, long time. How are you?'

'I'd like to see you . . . and the girls.'

Another long pause, and then Mike coughed.

'Yeah, I understand that, and it's fine by me. When do you want to come?'

Lorraine's hands were shaking. She couldn't answer. Mike asked if she was still there. 'Maybe this weekend?' he said.

'You mean tomorrow?' Lorraine could hardly get her breath.

'Or Sunday.' He suggested twelve thirty. They could have lunch, maybe walk on the beach together.

There was another pause. Then Lorraine said, 'Twelve thirty Sunday, then,' and hung up before he could say anything else. She stared at his address. Her mouth was dry. She mentally repeated every word they had said to each other. They had not spoken for so long.

She sat cupping a mug of coffee in her hands. She had

finally done it. Slowly she calmed herself down. She'd be able to cope, she'd coped so far, and she was looking good. More important, she was sober.

Bill Rooney sat opposite his chief, Michael Berillo, leaning forwards, which made his squat backside spread even more. 'Nothin'. We've not got a single witness—'

'But there was a witness, Bill.'

Rooney nodded. 'Yeah, but that was Helen Murphy. We reckoned he must have tracked her down again after the attack, right? And made sure the second time.'

'But before she died, this phone call . . .'

Rooney nodded. 'That's what we've been going on – all we've had – and it was a pretty good description.'

'What about the bite?'

'By now it'll have healed, or scabbed over, I dunno.'

Chief Michael Berillo was a big, glowering man. No matter what hour of the day or night, he always had a dark, five o'clock shadow. As he leaned back in his chair, his expansive chest almost burst the buttons on his sweat-stained shirt. 'Any of this Helen Murphy's associates give you anything?'

'Nope. She was a real old dog, though, hard to believe anyone'd pick her up, let alone screw her, and most of the people we talked to don't have a lot to say about her. Nothin' complimentary – she was trouble with a major T. She's also moved around. We can't trace her husband – he's a trucker, nobody seems to know where he is – and she's got three kids in care.'

'Irish?'

'What?'

The Chief yawned. 'I said, was she Irish? With a name like Murphy . . .'

'No, that's her husband and he's from Detroit. We talked to a woman she roomed with, a real dive, and she said

127

nobody had seen the husband for at least six or seven months. But we got him circulated so as soon as he's traced we'll question him.'

The two men remained silent, each wrapped in his own thoughts.

'Six.'

Rooney nodded. 'Yeah. Six – seven if we attach Norman Hastings. We've interviewed everyone he worked with, everyone he knew. He's got – or had – a real nice wife and two kids, nobody seems to have anything against him. He was a well-liked, ordinary guy, played poker with a few pals, went to ball games, good steady worker, and—'

The Chief banged his elbows on the desk. 'No connection to any of these women. Did he pick up hookers?'

Rooney shook his head. 'If he did, his wife didn't know it, and none of his friends did either. Unless they were lying.'

The Chief thumbed through the massive dossier which represented the hours and hours of interviews and statements, the lists of officers assigned to the investigation. 'Okay, we'll open it up further. Let's see if any other states have anything on record. Reason is, to keep this on the boil I'm going to need more. We got a hell of a lot of men with their thumbs up their asses and we'll have to open it up to the press.'

'Shit! You do that and we'll have our job cut out for us – you know what a circus starts when there's a whiff of a serial killer on the loose.'

'You've had it all to yourself, Bill, and you've drawn a blank. We got a fucking maniac out there and I can't hold this back any longer. We'll get in a psychological profiler.'

Rooney snorted, and the Chief rapped the desk. 'Get all the help you can, Bill, and get it fast. If you and your team don't get a result soon, I can't let you sit on this – and you know it. Bring in that Helen Murphy's husband.

So far he looks like the only possible suspect and you need one.'

'What's that supposed to mean?'

'You dumb? I'll have to bring in more than a fucking profiler. Don't you understand? I'm under pressure. That last kid might have been a hooker, but she was only seventeen years old. And Norman Hastings was, as you've laid out thick and clear, an upright citizen. You think his family don't want a result? It's not just old tarts. One dead bitch like the one you dug up from your pal Sparks can be put on ice. Hastings can't. A pretty blue-eyed angel called Holly can't. You with me?'

Rooney felt the carpet being tugged from under his feet. If they wanted a profiler then he'd get one. If they wanted Clint Eastwood they could have him too. Anything, so long as they didn't give him the side-step just before he was due to retire. 'I hear you loud and clear, Chief.'

'Good – and, Bill, any other bright ideas you get, run them by me first. You started the ball rolling, now it's out of control.'

Rooney got out fast.

Unfortunately, Bean was in his office sitting in his chair. It was a bad omen and Rooney yelled at him to shove his butt off. 'Get onto one of those profilers – and by tonight. And *don't* say one word. Then I want every man on this fiasco in the main incident room in one hour. We want Helen Murphy's fuckin' husband found and brought in.'

Bean coughed. 'There's another one.'

'What?' Rooney's face flushed a deep puce.

'I said there's another one come in, from a Brian Johns, Santa Monica, details on your desk.'

Rooney reached over and picked up the fax sheet. Prostitute murdered 1992, found inside the trunk of a Cadillac, face and skull beaten. Mona Skinner, aged forty. Possible murder weapon: a blunt instrument, some kind of hammer.

Bean shut the door as Rooney thudded into his chair. It creaked ominously, the springs taking the strain of his eighteen stone. Mona Skinner was an ugly, square-faced woman with long, frizzy, bleached-blonde hair and her mouth was turned down in a thin scowl. Her mean, aggressive eyes stared back at Rooney with a 'fuck you' expression. She had been charged with soliciting more than nine times over a period of fifteen years. She had also served four years for assault and battery, and receiving stolen property.

Rooney leaned back and swivelled around. He was angry with himself for opening the can: the worms were certainly wriggling out and all over him. He ran a check to see if there were any links between Mona Skinner and the others. He struck lucky: Mona Skinner and Helen Murphy had both served time together at the same women's prison, had once lived in the same motel. Rooney stepped up the order to find Helen Murphy's husband who now became his main suspect for real.

Rosie ate the spaghetti, waded through the garlic bread and, filled to bursting point, heaved herself onto the sofa. Switching on the TV, she paused briefly to watch the news, then flicked on to find a game show.

'They've still not found that guy that bumped off that local fella. You know what always amazes me?'

Lorraine was washing up. 'No?'

'Well, you know when they put all these ads out for people to come forward if they saw anythin'? That murder happened weeks ago. How do they expect anybody to remember? I wouldn't be able to remember if I saw a guy in a metallic blue car this morning, never mind weeks ago.'

'You'd be surprised,' Lorraine said, wiping round the sink. 'I was working on a case once, and we were up shit creek without a paddle, and then this boy was hypnotized

130

and he gave not only the car's registration number, but about four or five others as well.'

Rosie switched channels again. 'I wouldn't have that done, you know why? Because it means they always got you in their power.'

Lorraine sat down beside her, her mind miles away. She thought again about the wallet, the man who had attacked her. She was vaguely surprised that he hadn't been traced yet. She closed her eyes, conjuring up a mental picture of him, the way he had picked her up at the roadside, how he had wanted her to give him a blow-job in a public place. She saw him as clearly as if it had been yesterday. She remembered his hands: long, thin tapering fingers. Had he worn a ring? She concentrated hard, no, she was sure he had no ring, but then she saw his cuff, his jacket sleeve, and the cufflinks. She leaned forward, frowning in concentration, and then shook her head. It was no concern of hers, she had enough to think about, and besides, the further removed she was from it the better.

The following morning Lorraine went off to the gallery, pausing on the way to buy a newspaper. The headlines shrieked in big bold letters: POLICE HUNT SERIAL KILLER. Sitting in the gallery, she read the entire article, then folded the paper. It seemed almost comical that Captain Bill Rooney should be heading the investigation. From her own past experience with press releases, they had trouble on their hands. She could tell they were covering up, the old phrases they all used to churn out about 'making headway', 'confident of an arrest'. But the biggest giveaway was the police request for any member of the public having further information to make contact. It meant they had zilch.

The buzzer sounded and a flushed, excited Art rushed in, carrying a small gym bag ready for his workout next door. 'I think, my dear, I just made a killing. Last night I had a friend over who knows a big dealer out of New York. He saw the new stuff and went ape-shit! He's back tonight and he's not just interested in one or two but the whole show!'

Lorraine was genuinely pleased as it also meant more money for her. Art had promised that as soon as business picked up she would get a better wage. He danced around, checked the mail, and then said he would be next door if anyone wanted him.

She took another look at the canvases hanging on the walls, still not impressed with the daubs of colour and squiggles that the new Art discovery had supplied.

Later, Nula dropped by. She put her arms around Lorraine. 'You know, I think you're looking even better. As soon as your hair grows a bit more, ask Didi to style it – she's an artist. She can colour as well – she does mine, and she does Holly's—' She froze, and covered her mouth: 'Oh, God, I forgot.'

'There's a big article in the paper this morning, and a photograph.'

Nula looked at it. 'She was much more beautiful than that, a real stunner. You know, the cops have been out every night. Terrible for business, but they reckon this maniac only does whores, so everybody's a bit uneasy. First time they came round, hardly any of us out, but you know business is business. And I doubt if he'd come our end of the street, we just have our usuals and a few that have been tipped off.'

Lorraine smoothed her skirt. 'All the same, you two should look after yourselves. Take the vehicle registration of the johns you're wary of – or better still, don't go with them.'

Nula cocked her head to one side. 'That's just what the cops told us.'

Lorraine smiled. 'Well, make sure you do it.'

Nula opened her tapestry bag and took out a packet. 'Give this to Art for me, would you? It's just some more postcards, and our rent. See you soon.'

Lorraine put the packet in the desk drawer and was just about to shut it, when she noticed a thick wad of notes secured with just an elastic band. She looked to the door, then back to the open drawer. She took the money out and flicked through it. There was at least two or three thousand dollars. She held it a moment, tapping it in her hand, then replaced it.

About an hour later Art returned, pink from his workout, his bald head gleaming. He dropped his gym bag and fractionally adjusted a canvas.

'You mind if I say something?'

He turned, and smiled. 'Oh, you sounded so stern, why should I?'

'There's a lot of money in the drawer, Art, and it's not locked or anything. Anyone could just walk in and take it.'

Art danced over and banged open the drawer. 'I meant to put it in the bank this morning but I forgot and I didn't want to leave it in the health club.'

Lorraine watched as he tossed the money into his gym bag.

'Right, I have to go. Will you lock up, leave the keys with Hector next door?' Then, pursing his lips, he delved into his pocket, dragged out his wallet, and started counting out ten-dollar bills. 'Whoops . . . I'm a wee bit short. Can I give you the rest on Monday, darling?'

Lorraine flushed. 'I need it all today, Art. I have to go somewhere this weekend.' She couldn't help but flick a look to the gym bag.

'That belongs to a friend.'

She shrugged. 'Monday will have to do.'

'Okay.' Art smiled. 'Is that your paper? Have you finished with it?'

She passed it to him. He glanced at it and then held up Holly's photograph. 'I didn't know her but she was a friend of Nula and Didi's.'

He waltzed out, and the door slammed behind him.

Remembering Nula's package she hurried after him, only to see him driving away in a cab. She felt pissed off: she needed her money to buy a little something for the girls. She put the package away, then opened the drawer again, took it out and looked at it. Nula had said that her rent was in it; maybe she could just take out what she was owed and leave a note.

Lorraine eased open the package, pulling the Scotchtape away, making sure she didn't rip the paper. As well as some postcards wrapped in a sheet of paper, there was a brown manilla envelope. She crossed to the kettle, and turned it on to steam open the flap. Inside was a big pile of notes. She was surprised by the amount – unless they were behind with their rent. She counted out sixty dollars for herself, and was about to replace the rest and reseal the envelope when she wondered if the postcards were meant for the gallery, so she opened the paper.

Lorraine sat down. She felt sick. It wasn't that she hadn't come across pornographic material when she was on Vice, but each of these was especially revolting because they featured Nula and Didi. Maybe if she'd been more together, she would have realized when she visited that they used their apartment for photographic work – there were certainly enough props. She sighed, looking intently at each disgusting picture, sad that Nula and Didi could subject themselves to such degrading acts, displaying their genitals, their heavy breasts. They featured together, just the two of them, on the first few cards, and then they were joined by various animals and masked figures, and on four cards a pretty sweet-faced blonde girl appeared, her face childlike but her breasts over-large and her curved body taut and firm. Her eyes unfocused, she looked as if she had been drugged, but Lorraine recognized her immediately. It was Holly. No wonder Didi and Nula had been so upset. They knew her because both had screwed her. If the cards had been just of Nula and Didi, even with Holly, Lorraine

134

would perhaps have been less upset, but the rest showed obviously under-age boys committing homosexual acts.

Lorraine lit a cigarette and inhaled deeply. She was no innocent – in fact, it was more than likely she herself had taken part in some perverted session in the past to make a buck. She paced the gallery and kept on returning to the postcards, picking them up and putting them down. She was uncertain what, if anything, to do. Her first thought was to send them to the police, let them sort it out – especially as they featured Holly. She asked herself if the girl's murder could be connected to the pictures. She doubted it – it could just be coincidence. But one thing was for sure: Holly was no innocent and already on the game, so she would have been fully aware of what she was doing. Then Lorraine looked again. *Had* Holly been drugged? If so, had she been forced into the pornographic session against her will, or agreed to do it because she was drugged?

'It's not my business,' she said aloud. She was angry with herself for opening the package. It changed everything. If she sent the contents to the police, they would question Nula and Didi. They might come to the gallery, too. Art was involved, so she would also be questioned – by Bill Rooney. So much for feeling safe and secure. The thought of having Rooney barging into her fragile existence made her feel weak. She was caught, trapped first by stealing the wallet from the man who had attacked her, and then because, as it turned out, it wasn't his wallet after all but Norman Hastings's. She even remembered the dead man's name, could picture his face on his driving licence. 'What a fucking mess!'

Lorraine lit another cigarette, sat at the desk propping her head on her hands. She steadied herself. She knew the wallet was of no great importance to the investigation. More to the point, and this she knew, too, was that her attacker had been in possession of it. It was obvious he had to have taken it from Hastings's body. If the newspaper

135

reports could be relied on, and Hastings's body had been discovered in his own car, then it was surely the same vehicle driven by the man who had attacked her. So it meant that all the time she was in the shopping mall car park, the dead man had been in the trunk of the car.

The officers who had come to the apartment had been trying to trace her, but had never returned. Were they still looking for her? She swore, wishing she had kept the newspaper, but she was certain there had been no mention that the police were looking for anyone seen in Hastings's car that afternoon. She had given them a good enough description, they even repeated it in the paper, so they must be taking it seriously. There was nothing else she could do.

'This is all I fucking need!' she said aloud, as she stubbed out her cigarette, immediately lighting another. Her neck felt tense, her whole body was strained. She began taking everything out of the drawer – leaflets, notes, letters – without knowing what she was looking for. There was no diary, and nothing of any particular importance. She flicked through the supposed sales ledgers, noting the prices Art had paid for his canvases. They were all low. According to the sale-or-return memos, most of the paintings she had presumed sold had been returned. She started to replace the papers, and then stared hard at the money and the photographs.

'Shouldn't open people's private property.'

Lorraine gasped. She hadn't heard him return – the buzzer again! Picking up the photographs, Art began to shuffle them, stacking them, clicking them against the desk as he straightened them to stuff back into the envelope. 'I've been watching you sifting through my desk. What were you looking for?'

Lorraine flushed. 'I don't know.'

Art replaced the photographs, folding the envelope into a tight packet. 'Well, Lorraine, did they turn you on?'

'No, no, they didn't.'

'Takes all kinds, dear.'

'I suppose it does . . .'

Art unzipped his bag, tucked the photographs inside. 'I only came back because I felt bad about not giving you your money. Lucky I did. I'd forgotten Nula was delivering these.'

Lorraine moved out from behind the desk, gesturing to the gallery. 'This is all a front, isn't it? A sham.'

Art glanced around. 'Not all sham, dear. Sometimes I sell some, but I've been ripped off so many times, I keep it on as a kind of pastime. Maybe one day when I've made enough dough I'll be able to find some real talent. This stuff is from Venice Beach, I buy it for peanuts.'

Lorraine shook her head. 'The porn sells, does it?'

Art looked at her, his eyes so enlarged by his glasses that they seemed like a gargoyle's. 'How else do you think I've been able to stay open? I have regular customers, you met most of them. In fact, if I recall, you called them.' He picked up the cash and peeled off a fifty-dollar bill. 'Here, it's a bonus.'

Lorraine didn't take it. 'The pictures of Holly, the girl who was murdered . . .'

'What?'

'There are pictures of Holly.

Art shrugged. 'Well, they won't bother her, will they?'

'Maybe the police would be interested, though.'

He pursed his lips. 'I don't see why, she was obviously enjoying herself and nobody forced her. In fact, I didn't even know the girl.'

'Who takes the photographs?'

He sighed, hands on his hips, then looked back at Lorraine. 'None of your fucking business. Now, let's just forget this, shall we?'

She stared at him, forcing herself to keep her voice steady. 'Why don't you make it worthwhile for me to not make it my business?'

'What?'

'You heard me. You've got under-age kids on those pictures – so pay me. And . . . like you said, it's not my business.'

Art hesitated. He picked up the money, seemed to weigh it in his hand before he made the decision. He threw it at Lorraine. 'You know what my big problem in life is? I trust people. I make friends with people, I give them a break, and they always fuck me over it. Take it, you scrawny, ungrateful bitch!'

She picked up the money and stuffed it into her pocket. As she reached over for her cigarettes and lighter, Art gripped her wrist. 'Just one thing, sweetheart. I want you to sign for that cash, just as a safeguard for me. Just in case you want to rap about me and—'

Lorraine released her wrist and rubbed it. He was strong and he had hurt her. 'You'll never see me again, I promise you that.'

Art didn't speak another word. Lorraine signed for the money, walked to the door, opened it, and the buzzer shrilled. She turned, a half-smile on her face. 'You should get this fixed, you know, Art.'

As the door closed quietly behind her, he kicked at the desk. He was – and always would be – a shit-head when it came to sniffing out people.

Lorraine did some shopping. She was feeling quite high and kept on touching the thick wad of notes in her pocket. She bought two dolls for her daughters, some cans of paint, brushes and a small wardrobe. She bought some tights, underwear, a shirt and, finally, a nightdress for Rosie. Laden with goods she caught a taxi home.

Rosie's jaw dropped as Lorraine staggered in. 'Jesus Christ! What did you do? Win a lottery?'

Lorraine laughed. 'We sold four paintings and this is my bonus!'

Rosie peered at the cans of paint. 'Who's gonna do all this, then?'

'You and me!'

Rosie snorted, but by now she was busy unwrapping her gift. She took out the white cotton nightdress. 'Oh, wow! This is pure cotton, *and* it's new!'

She saw two boxes. 'What's this, shoes?' She opened one, and looked at Lorraine. 'Wow! I might act like a mental nine-and-a-half-year-old, but . . .'

Lorraine took back the box, closing the lid. 'They're for my daughters.'

'So you made contact, then?'

Lorraine walked out without answering. She had left more bags piled outside on the steps and yelled for Rosie to lend a hand. Jake arrived, unannounced, and was immediately recruited to carry in the rest of the paint, trays and rollers. He began to wish he hadn't dropped by as he was cajoled into shifting furniture to clear the room ready for painting. He promised to return later in the evening to help out some more. Lorraine didn't say goodbye – she was carefully putting the two doll boxes under a cushion in case they got damaged.

She and Rosie had a snack and then, draped in old nightdresses Rosie was now prepared to throw out, set to work. After seeing the way Art, Didi and Nula had transformed the gallery, Lorraine imagined it would be easy, but she had underestimated the threesome's expertise. By the time Jake reappeared they had covered only one wall.

He and Lorraine finished the main room and by the time they had pushed all the furniture back into place, it was after midnight. Jake promised he'd return in the morning so they could start on the kitchen and maybe get around to the bedroom.

Lorraine showered and combed the flecks of paint out of her hair. It was good to feel so tired – it meant she didn't have to think over what had happened during the day. She felt stiff from painting, and her back ached, but when she flopped onto the sofa she was too tired even to work out what she was going to do the following morning. She had a bus schedule, a street map of Santa Monica; she had even decided what she should wear. The two dolls were packed in a carrier bag: one blonde the other dark-haired. She didn't think about the future, about having to find alternative work. Tomorrow, seeing her daughters, was all that mattered.

CHAPTER 6

ROSIE WOKE up with a start, and then flopped back. Lorraine was in the shower. She squinted at the alarm clock: half past eight. She couldn't go back to sleep, so she got up and went into the freshly painted main room. Lorraine's bedding was neatly folded, and a pot of coffee was on the stove. Rosie toasted some muffins, then went out to see if the Sunday papers had arrived.

Lorraine emerged, made up and in her new blouse and the safari suit. She also wore the high-heeled slingbacks and skin-tone tights. She no longer needed to raid Rosie's make-up or jewellery box, as she had bought her own cosmetics and a pair of fake pearl earrings.

Rosie gaped, and then sniffed. 'My God, you look good and you smell terrific. Are you working today?'

'Yeah, there's a big art dealer coming so I've got to open the gallery early. I'm sorry if I woke you.'

'No problem. You want a muffin . . . coffee?'

'No thanks, I've had breakfast. I'm off now.'

Jake arrived about an hour later. Rosie was still reading the papers. 'Morning. It's baking out already. Where's Lorraine?'

'Gone to the gallery. You want some coffee and muffins?'

'Wouldn't say no.'

Rosie bustled around getting him a cup and plate, then sat and ate another muffin, washing it down with more coffee. She divided up the paper and they sat opposite each other, reading.

'They found another body,' said Jake. 'Prostitute. Reckon she was killed the same way couple months back, this time in Santa Monica.'

Rosie slapped down the paper. She looked at Jake. 'She's lied. She's not gone to that gallery, she's gone to see her kids in Santa Monica. She's so secretive . . . but I know she's traced them 'cos I saw the address on a note by the telephone and I know she's gone because she's taken the dolls she bought. Now why does she lie?'

'That's maybe just the way she is,' said Jake, folding his paper. 'Why don't we surprise her? Let's get the kitchen started.'

Rosie pulled a face. 'I was hopin' you'd forget all about it, I hate painting, it gives me a backache, and then my arms ache from the brushes. Even Walter's done a bunk – paint gets to cats, you know.' She glared at the bedroom door. 'This is bloody Sunday morning, for chrissakes, a day of rest!'

Jake began to clear the kitchen. It was so small it wouldn't take long, and then maybe they could do the bedroom, really surprise Lorraine.

Rooney was sweating. Ten o'clock and it was way up in the seventies. He hated losing his Sunday: there was nothing he liked better than sitting in the yard with the papers. He had them all stuffed under his arm as he plodded along the corridors towards his office. He saw Bean up ahead with a balding man.

'Morning, Captain.'

Rooney glowered, and waited for Bean to join him. 'That's not him, is it?'

'Yep, he's been working from home, seems a nice guy, real low key.'

Rooney snorted, and together they went into his office. Andrew Fellows was younger than Rooney had first thought. Prematurely bald, his rather handsome face was marred by a pair of enormous ears that constantly caught the attention – they moved up and down when he talked. The more animated he became, as Rooney was to discover, the more the ears worked overtime – and Professor Fellows was an animated man. He used his hands like a conductor, and his trim body in its pristine white T-shirt and tight jeans seemed incapable of staying still for a second. Rooney took him into the 'Hammer Killings' incident room. Photographs of all the victims had been posted up on the walls and rows of computers installed. He looked up expectantly at Fellows. 'So, you come up with anything for us?'

Fellows nodded, his ears waved, and he opened a worn leather briefcase. 'I've spent three days studying all the evidence to date, and I've tried to assimilate the most important aspects so we can cut through the dross. Much of the evidence you gave me was of no use, so I concentrated on this detailed description apparently given by an anonymous caller . . .'

He began to pace up and down. 'The caller gave a concise and exceptionally clear picture of the assailant – apart from his actual size . . .' Rooney sighed, looked at Bean and raised his eyes to the ceiling. Fellows flapped his hands. '. . . leading me to believe she had not met the man before. He was in the car when he picked her up, so she may have been a stranger to him. Let's give him a name rather than have to keep calling him the assailant or killer. Why not – for want of better – "the Teacher" . . .' Fellows laughed. 'Sorry, it's just that the description fits an old college professor I had.' Rooney gave a faint grimace that was supposed to be a smile.

Fellows moved to the row of victims' faces. 'Now, we're led to believe that all these women and Norman Hastings were killed by the Teacher – and this woman, Helen Murphy—' Fellows pointed to the wrong picture, and Bean corrected him. 'Ah, sorry, the body of Helen Murphy was found in the trunk of a car, so we are to presume the Teacher first attempted to kill her, failed, then traced her once more, or knew where she lived or the area she worked, whatever, and killed her, using the same method, claw hammer blows. Am I right so far?'

Rooney sighed. 'Yes, but, frankly, you're wasting time. What we need to know – what *I* need to know – is what sort of man is this bastard?'

'That's obvious. You've been given a remarkably clear description, but don't get me off track. Something's wrong, you see. When I went over the information regarding Helen Murphy, I was confused.'

Rooney coughed. 'What *we* got from that description, Professor, was that he's probably got a good income, a good job and—'

'Yes, yes, but let me get round to that. What's bothering me, as it doesn't make any logical sense, is, if a woman is badly beaten – as witnessed by, er, that couple, Mr and Mrs Summers – and, assuming that it was the same woman who subsequently gave you the killer's description – going so far as to report the incident to the police, describing the hammer – would she go with him again? He had to pick her up again, correct? Now, she was found in a car that had been left unattended, a wrecked vehicle, abandoned for possibly two or three months. Not like any of the other vehicles used. All of those were reported stolen shortly before the crime was committed. So that means our Teacher had to pick her up in another vehicle, kill her, and then dump the body. So Helen Murphy's murder does *not* follow the same pattern as the others.'

Rooney frowned. He'd given this a lot of thought himself and was about to say as much when Fellows continued, pointing at Bean. 'Whoever took the call said the woman was precise, articulate, and spoke fast in an almost clipped tone. She refused to give any details about herself, and they were unable even to ask her name because she continued to talk so quickly, but they jotted down almost the entire conversation, and then she hung up. Yes?'

Bean nodded. He felt almost guilty, as if he'd done something wrong, because Fellows was glaring at him.

'You took statements regarding the victim Helen Murphy, correct?'

'Yes,' Bean said, 'but I didn't do them all, a few of the statements were taken by—'

Fellows interrupted, his arms swinging like windmill sails, 'Who was Helen Murphy? Previously Helena, Helena Dubjeck, an alcoholic, drug abuser, persistent brawler, and . . . I can't recall all her previous charges. And she had false teeth. Also, according to the pathologist, a possible malformation of her upper lip, which you can even see on her photograph . . .' He paused. Rooney was rising slowly to his feet, when the windmill arms waved again. 'One moment. Didn't your anonymous caller say that the assailant, our Mr Teacher, was possibly around one hundred and eighty pounds? Odd, don't you think? Not "fat" or "thin, skinny, well-built" – but she gave you his possible weight? Doesn't that strike you as an odd thing for this kind of woman, Helen Murphy, to say? And you make *no* allowance for the fact that she might have had a speech defect, might even have had – and you must ask those who knew her – the trace of a foreign accent. She was not born in America, was she?'

Fellows ran his hand over his bald head then pulled at one of his ears. 'Do you see what I'm getting at? I would say that whoever made that call describing her attacker was someone familiar with police procedure, familiar with short-cutting a description. Am I right? It was *not* made by Helen Murphy.'

Rooney sat back, transfixed by the information that Fellows spouted out like bullets.

Fellows faced the wall lined with photos. 'These women were all prostitutes, but none of them had been penetrated at the time of death. No sexual intercourse took place. So why did he pick them up? What was he wanting them to do? I doubt he wanted intercourse – perhaps he wanted simulated sex, or to be jerked off. Or I would say he has a sexual problem, probably impotence. They get into his car or stolen vehicle, he drives them to some location. If they are bending over his groin, then it's simple for him to strike the back of the head. Again, go back to Mr and Mrs Summers. The woman they saw was bleeding badly, but also bleeding from her mouth. Correct?'

Rooney nodded. 'She also said she'd bitten the man in the neck.'

'But she also said she'd broken the skin, *his* skin, I presume, so the blood on her mouth could easily have been his blood, not her own. She was facing the Summerses who saw no wounds to her face apart from the bloody mouth – but the back of her head was bleeding. Nevertheless she was quite capable of flagging down a cab, giving an address. *Now*, would that woman, just a few days later, go with the same man again? And be caught the same way, yet again, with a hammer blow to the back of her head? Unless she knew him or was an accomplice to the other killings I doubt it. If she was an accomplice and made that call, then she could or would be arrested.'

Rooney felt inadequate. This big-eared windmill of a man, after just a few days' thumbing through their files, was throwing out mind-blowing stuff. He half expected Fellows to have another pull at his ears and then name the killer. But Fellows had become silent, and was sitting staring down at his sneakers.

'He is a sick man, a tormented man, deeply disturbed, and I think he has killed regularly. I don't think he's been

146

put away or locked up. On the contrary, he's walking around confident, *very* confident, because he's gotten away with it for years. Now, with this press coverage, will it make him stop killing? Possibly. I hope so. But it may make him irrational. You see, he'll want to prove, even more, just how clever he is. You won't catch him unless he makes mistakes. On the other hand, the press coverage could also make him stop, for a while anyhow. But he won't be able to stop completely, because, I would say, these murders are the only way he's able to get sexual gratification.'

Fellows got up again and marched up and down the wall of victims, peering at the faces, turning to retrace his footsteps. 'He must be in full employment, possibly some kind of travelling sales executive. He's moving around a lot of areas. He could even be a car salesman – he certainly knows about cars and how to steal them. I would say he might have a garage, or a storage place where these cars can be hidden. I doubt if he has a family – no wife or children. This man has a hatred of older women, a terrible hatred—'

Rooney interjected to ask about Angela Hollow. Fellows took a deep breath. 'Yes. She was young – and the most recent victim? Prostitute, working the streets the night she was killed?' He looked at the picture of Holly. 'Find out if, on the night she was killed, any other girl or woman was next to her. Maybe Holly crossed to him when he was really after another girl close by, it's possible. Because I have to admit she makes my theory wobble, as she's not in the same category as the others. This worries me . . .'

He tapped the picture of Norman Hastings. 'There's something odd about him, too, if we talk it through. He leaves his car, I can't recall the exact location, our Teacher steals it, or is even in the process of stealing it, and is caught red-handed. Hastings calls out, may even try and stop Teacher so, in that case, why the wound to the back of his head like the women? Unless Hastings was actually opening his car, Teacher, ready for the kill, simply walks up and strikes him?'

Rooney hitched up his pants. 'He went to the bank and—'

Fellows wafted his hand. 'That's immaterial – Teacher's not after money, he even left the victims' jewellery on their bodies. No, he's not after something as mundane as that, he's not a robber. He's a sex killer, he wants sexual gratification, nothing more.'

Rooney waited, almost afraid to interrupt. Fellows sighed, and sat down, looking at the picture of Hastings. 'It's possible they knew each other. I could be wrong, and nothing in all the reports gives any indication, other than that Hastings was an unfortunate man who was simply in the wrong place at the wrong time. What is not clear is what was that place? Outside his bank? In a car park? No one has come forward to say they saw Norman Hastings on the day of his death, so where did it happen? We don't know.'

Fellows went silent, chewing at his lower lip before he returned to the photo wall, to the graphs and memos. He stared at the photographs of the vehicles in which the dead women had been found. A Lincoln Continental, a Chrysler Le Baron, a Saab, a Mercedes, an Eldorado Cadillac – the latter the burned-out wreck where Helen Murphy had been found. Then he looked over the charts of the locations. Beverly Center on Melrose, Shopping Mall Van Nuys, West Hollywood, Santa Monica Boulevard, Century City and lastly the Santa Monica shopping centre. He stood for at least three minutes, his eyes roaming the photographs, the locations. There had to be a link between them, a pattern beyond the method of the murder itself. He needed to know as near as possible the times of, one, when Helen Murphy was killed, two, when the attack on the woman in the Van Nuys shopping mall occurred – the one they had wrongly presumed was Helen Murphy – and, three, Holly's murder.

The three were of interest because Holly's was the last, the failed murder attempt would have been between the last two.

'How close are these, time wise?' Fellows flicked his hand to Helen Murphy and Holly.

Bean crossed to the information section and looked up. 'The reported attack on the woman in the Van Nuys shopping mall was on the same day Hastings was killed. This woman, Helen Murphy, was, as close as we can get from the labs, murdered about three days before we found her.'

Fellows nodded. 'But they can't be exactly sure, can they? I mean, it could be a day either side. Her body was pretty high, wasn't it? Already decomposing?'

Bean nodded and then checked the information on Holly. Fellows had taken a small black leather diary from his pocket and was flipping through it, licking his fingers as he pushed the small pages over. 'And, Lieutenant, Holly was killed on what date?'

Bean looked at Rooney. 'Fifteenth of this month.'

Fellows pursed his lips. 'You got dates for all the others? See if it's always around the same time. I know some of them are four to six years old, but I'd like to get a calendar made up. Would you do that for me?'

Bean nodded. Fellows turned to Rooney and gave a glum smile. 'I'm sorry, but that's about it for today. It's not much because I need more time, and I'll hopefully come up with something else. I expect you've already come to the same conclusions yourselves. Basically, a lot of what I do in the end is simply common sense.'

He picked up his briefcase. 'You're not going, are you?' Rooney asked anxiously. 'I mean, all the team is coming in today to talk this over—'

Fellows snapped his case shut. 'I'm sure you can repeat everything, and I have a game of golf waiting. If you just keep me informed of any new developments, I'll get back to you.'

149

'What did you think of him?' asked Bean when Fellows had gone.

'I take back everything I said. How's that for starters?'

Bean grinned. 'Odd character, wasn't he?'

'Big ears.' Rooney sighed. 'We're almost back at the starting gate, aren't we? From what he's said, we're off by a long way with Murphy's husband. Nobody's found the fucker anyway.'

He flicked at the blind on his office window. 'You know, way back I was on a case, a missing kid – long time ago – but we'd all given up, we just had nothing. You remember that woman I saw that night when we went to the Indian?'

Bean raised an eyebrow.

'Well, she was on the same case, a little girl missing. She found her body at the school. She was such a cute little kid, and . . .' Rooney sighed, seeing the little girl's face again. 'Anyway, Lorraine – that was her name, didn't I tell you about her?'

'Drunk on duty, right?'

'This was before she became a lush, years before, and she was a good cop, dedicated – well, as much as a woman can be. Anyway, she wouldn't let go, she was so sure it was this janitor, but we had nothing on him. He even had a strong alibi for the afternoon the girl went missing. We'd all scrapped him as a suspect – she was even warned off from visiting the school and his place. Did it in her own time. She just wouldn't back off him. And we had not one shred of evidence, it was just her intuition . . .'

Bean yawned and looked at his watch, he could hear all the men starting to arrive outside, and he wondered where the story was leading. Rooney too seemed uncertain, still flicking at the blind with his fat stubby finger. 'She broke him down, I don't know how, none of us did. She brought him back into the station for maybe the tenth time, questioned him over and over, and meanwhile there was the Captain going ape-shit, saying we'd be accused of harassment. Then she walked out, and she had this look on her face like some prize fighter. She lifted up her fist, said he'd admitted it, that he'd just broken down and admitted killing the little girl . . .'

Bean wasn't listening, his attention on the doorway as he looked at the men that passed. 'Everyone's gathered. You want to go in?'

Rooney hitched up his pants. 'Maybe we try again with Hastings's wife, maybe we've been going too softly-softly, maybe he wasn't such a good, upright, honest citizen. And we start trying to trace that missing witness again. We don't back off, but keep on going – okay?'

Bean sighed. 'You know, even if we do find her maybe all she knows is what she told us and that won't help.'

Rooney jabbed at him with his finger. 'Wrong. She never said where he picked her up from. She probably knows a hell of a lot more than she let on. Now, let's get fucking cracking before the entire Sunday's up the spout. We got to trace that bitch and all leave is cancelled as from now . . .'

The cab drew up outside a narrow, three-storey house facing the ocean that didn't look much but, Lorraine knew, would have to be worth outside three million dollars. Mike Page was certainly doing a lot better for himself nowadays. The cab driver, who had been watching the clock, now turned to face Lorraine. 'You want to drive around some more or are you getting out?'

'Drive around a while longer.'

He sighed. 'Okay. Anything you want, lady, this is your ride.'

They did another tour of Santa Monica, then returned and parked in exactly the same place as before.

'This is it, lady. I got an account customer I need to pick up, so, if you don't mind . . .'

151

He was lying, she knew, he just wanted her out of his cab, probably because it was Sunday and he wanted to get home. She paid the fare, and stepped out. Hardly had the cab door shut behind her before he drove off. She felt marooned, afraid to walk the few yards to Mike's front door, yet unable to turn and walk away. She stood there, frozen.

'Lorraine?' The voice was unmistakable. It was Mike. She turned and shaded her eyes. He was wearing an open neck shirt, white slacks and flip-flops. A big dog with long scruffy hair padded beside him. Her heart was thudding and she knew she must be flushed a bright red and her whole body broke out in a sweat. Mike had a deep sun-tan and his teeth gleamed; his dark brown eyes had lines at the side, crow's feet, but apart from that he didn't seem much older than when she had last seen him.

'Hi!' He stood about a foot away from her. 'I wasn't expecting you until later.'

'I got a taxi.'

He smiled, reached for her bag and she let him take it.

'I got something for the girls, I don't want you to think I'm staying over . . .'

He took her elbow, about to draw her towards the house, then he stopped. 'They're out swimming but they won't be long, so we can have a chat, catch up.'

She followed him towards the front door, but he went down some steps to enter the house through large french windows which opened onto a verandah.

'This is nice,' she said lamely.

'Yep – and it's breaking me financially, but the kids love it.' He paused. 'Oh, maybe you don't know. I've got two sons – they're with the girls and Kathy.'

Lorraine nodded, presuming Kathy to be their step-mother. She stepped into the big open room, where toys and newspapers, even breakfast dishes, had been left on a huge round table facing the ocean window.

'Sorry about the mess but Sundays we just let everything hang out. Now sit down and I'll get some coffee going.'

Lorraine sat on the wide sofa. She looked slowly around the room, at the paintings, the throw rugs, the grains of sand that sparkled on the floor. 'Can I smoke?'

Mike cleared the table, and looked up. 'Sure, I'll find you an ashtray.'

She lit up, her hand shaking so much that she glanced over to see if he'd noticed, but he was carrying a stack of dishes into the kitchen. The door closed and she inhaled deeply, letting the smoke fill her lungs. She got up and stood by the open window, taking deep breaths to calm herself.

Mike held onto the edge of the sink, shaken. Nothing had prepared him for the way she looked. She had aged so much – she was skin and bone, her face scarred so badly she seemed to squint. He shook his head, wishing he had more time to prepare the girls. Then he heard Sissy calling, and before he had time to warn her not to come down, she was in the drawing room. He listened at the door.

Sissy was wrapped in a cotton kimono. She was deeply tanned and had waist-length, ash-blonde hair. She was as tall as Lorraine, but full-breasted, her legs muscular and taut. Her long arms and perfect hands immediately pulled the kimono closer as she had no belt and was naked beneath it. 'I'm sorry, I didn't know anyone was here.'

Lorraine bowed her head. 'I'm, er . . . well, I guess you knew I was coming. I'm Lorraine.'

'Oh, yeah, I'm sorry. Where's Mike?'

Lorraine swallowed. 'He's making me some coffee.'

She wondered who the beauty was, but Sissy seemed totally at ease, striding to the kitchen. 'Darling, you should have said, or yelled up that Lorraine was here. I'll go back up and shower, leave you two to have a chat . . . Mike?'

He walked out of the kitchen and slipped his arm around Sissy. 'Well, you've met. This is my wife, Sissy.'

Lorraine forced a smile as Sissy walked out and up the stairs. 'She's very beautiful,' she said quietly.

Mike nodded. 'The girls adore her, and – well, lemme get the coffee.'

Lorraine looked out onto the verandah and lit another cigarette from the stub. Then she started to cough, one of her awful, chesty, phlegmy coughs that made her feel weak and her eyes run. She gasped, tried to control it and Mike appeared with a glass of water.

'You should give that up!'

She shrugged, still coughing, and took the glass. Mike returned to the kitchen, and Lorraine remained outside on the verandah, sitting on one of the wooden bench seats. She drained the glass and set it carefully on the table. At least her hands were no longer shaking.

Mike carried out the tray of coffee and set it down. He poured a cup, and she smiled. It was the first time she even faintly resembled her old self: Mike noticed that she still had the palest of blue eyes.

'So. It's been a long time, hasn't it? I've often wondered how you were, hoped you'd get in touch.'

He waited for her to reply but she stared ahead. He could see the deep scar down her cheek, and her body shaking slightly. He'd sometimes wondered how he would react to seeing her again. He'd expected to feel anger, or perhaps attraction, rather than this deep sadness. He had worried that she might have some custody query, or have become financially secure enough to want the girls to live with her. But the worn, old-fashioned safari suit, the cheap shoes, everything about her looked seedy and worn. Worse still was Lorraine herself. She had always been so positive, arrogant even, now all he could see was a pitiful shell of what she had once been. That was what he felt more than anything: pity, and an overwhelming relief she was no longer part of his life.

'I don't drink any more, Mike.' Her voice was smoky from too many cigarettes, deeper than he remembered.

'Good, that's good . . .' he said, hesitantly.

'But I sure as hell could do with one now!'

CHAPTER 7

LORRAINE SAT on the verandah shading her eyes, waiting for the first glimpse of her daughters. Mike stepped out carrying two photo albums, and came to sit beside her. Momentarily her shoulder rubbed against his.

'These are my boys – Chip, whose real name is Charles, and this is Mike junior.' They were both blond, both as beautiful as their mother. She quickly turned the pages back to the beginning, barely interested in Mike's sons. The first photograph was one she remembered: they were sitting side by side on a piano stool, Sally with a front tooth missing.

Mike looked up, hearing a shout from the beach. 'Here they are . . .'

Lorraine stood up and leaned on the rail. Sissy had one boy by each hand, and behind her walked a dark-haired teenager – but running up ahead were the girls. Sally and Julia, torn jeans, faded T-shirts, as suntanned as Sissy, they shouted and waved. Lorraine was stunned. They were both so tall, so different . . . she would have passed them in the street and not recognized them. 'My God,' she murmured.

Mike laughed. 'Yeah, they grow up fast, don't they?'

Sally was ten, Julia twelve. Six years was a very long time. Their initial exuberance faltered as they reached the verandah, and they turned to Sissy as if they needed her to be with them, but Mike called for them to come on up.

Julia was tall for her age, as slim as Lorraine had been at twelve.

'Hello.'

Lorraine smiled. She would have liked to put her arms around her daughter, but she wasn't sure if that was what she wanted. Sally wouldn't come close; she hung back as if afraid. Sissy slipped her arm around Julia's shoulder. 'Now, why don't you three show Lorraine the photo album, and I'll make some lunch?'

'Okay,' said Julia.

Sally sat beside Lorraine, but Mike followed Sissy into the lounge and pulled the doors half closed behind him. He watched for a moment before joining his wife in the kitchen.

The three sat in uncomfortable silence. Lorraine knew the dolls were a mistake – certainly for Julia, who seemed sophisticated and grown-up. Sally sat with her head bowed.

'I'm sorry not to have kept in touch with you both . . .' Lorraine said haltingly.

Julia gave her a strange, furtive look. 'That's okay. This is me winning a swimming prize at school.' Lorraine leaned forward to look at the photograph, and the tension eased slightly.

Lunch was served inside because it was cooler, and Julia showed Lorraine where the bathroom was so she could wash her hands. Lorraine crept from room to room, peeking in at each door, until she found her daughters' bedroom. It was full of posters and rugs, old teddy bears and a wardrobe bulging with clothes. Untidy comforters lay on their unmade beds, but it was a room any girl would covet. The last door she opened revealed Mike's study, the walls covered with pictures of the family, and some of himself on fishing trips. There was a large modern desk with stacks of files and papers, and Lorraine was just closing the door when she caught sight of a picture of herself, with the girls. It surprised her that he would have it, and she edged into the room, afraid that anyone should hear her creeping around.

She leaned across the desk to get a better view of the photograph and then froze as she inadvertently knocked some papers onto the floor. They were business letters, and as she glanced disinterestedly over them, the letter heading of one document caught her eye. The company was a vintage automobile reconditioning firm, specializing in imported cars. The letter confirmed that leather upholstery had been installed in a Mercedes sports car, circa 1966, and the client had refused to accept the costs. It was not, however, the contents of the letter that caught Lorraine's attention, it was the small black and green oval raised letters of the company logo: S & A. She was almost certain she had seen it before . . . not on a letter . . . It was on a pair of cufflinks.

'Lorraine? *Lorraine?*' Mike was calling her, and she quickly slipped the letter back and hurried out.

At lunch, the conversation – strained at best – turned to the subject of cars.

'What do you drive now?' Lorraine asked.

Mike grunted and prodded one of the boys. 'I have to have a coach for this crowd, it's an old station wagon. Sissy, however, has an MG – it's an English sports car.'

'I do know what an MG is,' Lorraine said.

Sissy flicked a look at Mike and then smiled. 'That was more for my benefit – it's always in the garage, not because I've damaged it, but because of the spares.'

'Is there a good garage near you?' Lorraine asked innocently.

Mike nodded. 'Yeah, there is. It specializes in vintage

and foreign cars, big money in it. They've got Rolls-Royces and Bentleys and Mercedes Benz—'

Lorraine interrupted, 'Is it a big company?'

'Pretty substantial.'

'How many people does it employ?'

Mike looked a little puzzled, but said, 'Maybe sixty, seventy, I don't know. Why?'

Lorraine smiled. 'I'm sure a friend of mine bought a car from a garage around here – maybe S and A?'

Mike nodded. 'Well, that's the company's logo all right – in fact I'm doing some business with them. Have you got your licence back, then?'

Lorraine flushed. 'No, but I can't afford a car.'

'Not from S and A.' Mike laughed.

'Does your friend live around here?' Sissy asked.

'No, I just heard the garage mentioned.'

Julia got up, cupping her hands to whisper in Sissy's ear. She frowned and shook her head. 'No, you can't, now sit down.'

Julia pouted and slumped back at the table. The room grew silent. Sissy shrugged her perfect shoulders. 'She wants to go play tennis.'

Julia snapped, 'I always play tennis on Sunday afternoons.'

Mike wagged his finger. 'Not this Sunday. Now, help your mother clear the table and—'

Lorraine stood up. 'No, that's okay – you go play tennis, Julia. I don't mind, I have to go in a few minutes anyway.'

Mike stacked the dishes, anything to cover his embarrassment. 'Well, it's up to you, but as you've come all this way—'

'I can come again – if you don't mind . . .'

'Where's Rufus?' Sally demanded, and suddenly they were all calling the dog. It seemed they all wanted to find an excuse to leave the room. Lorraine went over to the bag

159

she'd brought, and took out the box with the doll. 'Sally?' She went out to the verandah. 'I brought you this – maybe it's a bit childish for you, I just thought you'd kind of like it.'

Sally opened the box and looked at the doll. 'Does it talk? My friend Angela's got one that talks and sleeps and cries, and you feed it with a bottle and it wets itself.'

Lorraine looked at the moody-faced child. 'This one drinks and then if you press its stomach, it spits in your face.'

Sally's mouth trembled.

'It was just a joke!'

The child ran into the house, past Mike. Lorraine laughed at his worried expression. ''Sokay, Mike, I was never very good with them anyway. I got to go.'

Mike sat on the edge of the bench seat. 'I'm sorry. Maybe they'll take a while to get used to you – that is, if you're planning to make this a regular—'

'Would you mind?'

'No – well, maybe . . . I don't know, it's kind of taken us all by surprise. I think they're scared you've come to take them away.' He stared at her. 'You haven't, though, have you?'

Lorraine hugged her arms round herself tightly. 'I wouldn't want to do anything that'd upset them. Besides, I kind of don't know them any more – and you've changed. She's got you domesticated, carrying dishes back and forth.'

Sissy came out, overhearing the last remark.

She put down the coffee pot, and went back into the house.

'Can you call me a taxi?'

Lorraine was relieved when the cab arrived. She kept the doll she had bought for Julia, because she didn't want Julia to know that she had still thought of her as a little girl; she noticed that Sally hadn't even taken hers out of its box. Sally wouldn't kiss Lorraine goodbye, but hung on to Sissy. Mike kissed her cheek, and Sissy shook her hand – she had a strong, firm grip. She stared coldly at Lorraine as she said, without any warmth, 'Do come again.' Seeing them grouped together, waving, Lorraine knew she would never come back.

She asked the cab driver to take her past the S and A garage. Two massive showrooms were filled with vintage cars, but it was closed. Lorraine got out and walked along the showroom window, peering inside, and shaded her eyes to look at the counter. Dinky toy cars and memorabilia were displayed, but she couldn't see any cufflinks. By the time she returned to the cab, she was sweating again. It was three o'clock, the sun was blistering, so she asked the driver to stop at the next grocery store as she needed a can of Coke.

At ten o'clock Rosie called Jake to say that Lorraine still hadn't come home, and she was worried. Perhaps she was staying over, he suggested. If she was really worried, why not call? She had the number. Jake was exhausted: they had decorated the kitchen and the bedroom, and all the furniture was back in place.

Rosie waited until eleven before she called Mike Page, and was told that Lorraine had left around three. She called Jake. Already in bed, he was tetchy at being disturbed again. 'Rosie, what do you expect me to do? I'm not her keeper. I'm not responsible for what she does or does not do. Now lay off me, okay?'

Twelve o'clock, and Rosie went to bed. The smell of fresh paint made her feel sick, and she couldn't get to sleep, so she got up, made herself some iced tea, and sat by the window. Then she watched some late-night television and eventually, at two thirty, went back to bed.

Monday morning and Lorraine had still not returned, so Rosie called Jake again, but he had left for work, and she didn't want to pester him there. She told herself she was overreacting, but when Lorraine had still not appeared at four in the afternoon, she went along to the gallery. It was shut so she squinted through the window and saw that all the canvases had been removed. The place looked deserted, so she went home.

For want of something better to do, and to take her mind off Lorraine, Rosie began to clear her bedroom cupboards and drawers, tossing out junk she had hoarded. A new wardrobe kit had been assembled in a corner of the now tidy bedroom. Rosie pushed it into position and began to fill it with Lorraine's few possessions. Lastly she put in the shoes – and that was when she found the roll of money. She was amazed at the amount, then felt guilty because it would look as if she had been searching through Lorraine's personal belongings. She had, of course, but not with any ulterior motive.

Jake dropped by at seven o'clock. There was still no word from Lorraine. Rosie was upset. Jake took her to a meeting; he had a good idea that Lorraine would eventually come home, and he refused to borrow his friend's car to go on a street search. If she had started out in Santa Monica, God alone knew where she was.

They came back to Rosie's just after ten, and ate some takeaway food. Midway through the meal, they heard a screaming, hoarse voice. Jake gestured for Rosie to stay at the table and crossed to the window, peered out, and sighed. 'She's home. I'd better go and give her a hand.'

Rosie could hear the sound of breaking glass, and went to the window.

Lorraine was standing in the middle of the road, swinging a doll by its arm. Her blouse was torn, her skirt hanging off and she was filthy. She swiped at Jake.

'Fuck off! *Fucking leave me alone, you shit!*'

Jake backed off, arms raised, and Lorraine kicked out at him, swearing. A woman with a shopping cart was passing by and Lorraine caught her stare. 'What you fucking looking at, you cunt? *Fuck off – go on!*'

Jake had to coax and cajole her to come to the stairs leading up to Rosie's apartment. It took him fifteen minutes to get her up them. She took two steps up and fell down three. She screeched with laughter, then slowly crawled up, only to insist on going down again as she had dropped her doll.

At last Jake got her into the apartment. She stood by the door. 'Hi, Rosie. He fucked you yet?'

Rosie went into the kitchen as Jake tried to get Lorraine onto the sofa. Halfway there she pulled out her shirt, stripping it away from her skinny body: she fumbled with his pants. He swiped her hand aside and dragged her to the sofa, she fell, and slithered onto the floor.

'Run the shower, Rosie,' Jake said.

Lorraine stank of booze, vomit and urine. She had no jacket. She refused to release the doll even when they half carried her into the shower, ran the cold water over her, and between them stripped off her clothes, Jake paying no attention to her naked body, apart from glancing at Rosie when he saw the fresh red bruises and the old scars.

Rosie wanted to weep at seeing her friend like this, but she fetched towels and soaped Lorraine clean. Lorraine became subdued and listless, but she would not let go of the doll. Washed, with a clean nightdress on, she lay down on Rosie's bed.

'Best let her sleep it off,' Jake said, and ushered Rosie out of the bedroom. They picked up the filthy clothes and tossed them into the trash-can. Lorraine fell into a deep, coma-like sleep, with no idea where she was.

Rosie checked on her throughout the night, in case she vomited and choked to death. Jake left, depressed, though it was hardly unexpected. He'd seen it all before with Rosie – but at least Lorraine had been easier to get up the stairs.

Rosie slept on the sofa. She was woken by Lorraine stumbling out of the bedroom. Her face looked pale green, and there were deep, dark rings beneath her eyes.

'Coffee,' was about the only word she could squeeze out. Her head felt like someone had attached a chunk of concrete to it, with a bolt hammered into her skull to keep it steady. She needed Rosie to help her back to bed, and she moaned in agony as she lay down. Ice packs were prepared, and gently Rosie rested them on her forehead. Lorraine slept for the remainder of the day, rising in the early evening for a shower. By then she was able to move around more easily. 'What day is it?'

'Wednesday evening.'

'Wake me Friday.' Lorraine gave a wan smile and lay down on the sofa.

Rosie shopped, using Lorraine's hidden savings: she would tell her when the time was right, but she couldn't work with Lorraine as she was, and the rent was due. So Rosie kept dipping in.

It was Friday before Lorraine's hangover lifted. She was quiet, staring into space, unable to hold a conversation. Every time she attempted to explain herself, her voice trailed off mid-sentence. Rosie stroked her head. 'Honey, you don't have to explain, because I've been there. Just get better, then we can talk.'

Lorraine clasped her hand. 'Thanks.'

Rosie smiled, dipped into the savings again and went out to buy some fillet steak: Lorraine needed her strength building up. She also paid the telephone bill, the electricity bill – dip, dip, dip – but she'd admit it when Lorraine was better. It wasn't stealing, she told herself – what was hers was Lorraine's, after all – it was just that, right now, she was short of cash.

At the weekend when Jake came round, Lorraine greeted him warmly.

He cocked his head to one side. 'Back in the land of the living now, are we?'

Lorraine flushed. 'Oh. Were you here?'

'Who do you think carried you up the fuckin' stairs? You really went for it, didn't you?'

Lorraine gave him that odd lopsided, squint-eyed look. 'Christ only knows what I went with – my crotch feels like I been sittin' on hot coals.'

Jake turned away: he was never sure about her, she had a filthy mouth one minute, the next she came on like a real lady. 'If I was you, I'd get down to a clinic and get checked out. You smelt like a sewer.'

She was unable to meet his steady gaze. At least she could still be ashamed, he thought, that was something in her favour. 'Rosie's been taking good care of you so you make sure you say thank you.'

'I don't need you to tell me to do that, Jake.' Her voice was so husky he had to strain to hear what she said.

'What?'

'I said I'd go and have a medical, *okay*?'

'Good. I suggest you come to a meeting, and keep on coming for a few days, unless you got to go to work. You still think you got work at the gallery? Only I passed it two days ago and it looked all shut up.'

She walked into the bedroom. 'Soon as I feel fit enough I'll be out looking for another job.'

Rosie banged open the screen door, her arms bulging with groceries. Jake took the loaded bags from her. 'You've been spending a bit freely lately haven't you?'

'Let's just say I got a bit of a windfall. Now, will you stay for dinner? I got fillet steak and salad and I'll make jacket potatoes.'

Jake put the bags on the kitchen table. 'Sounds good!'

He continued, whispering, 'She should have herself checked out at a clinic.'

'She's only got a hangover, Jake.'

'She could also have HIV, venereal disease and Christ only knows what else, so have her down to a clinic.'

Rosie looked towards the bedroom wondering if Lorraine had heard, then started unpacking the groceries.

Lorraine had heard, and rested back on Rosie's bed. She was sober. She had little or no recollection of what she had done or where she had been. She dimly remembered stopping off in the cab, going to buy a can of Coke and coming out with two litres of vodka. She had a vague impression of having been thrown out of the same taxi, thumbing a lift from a trucker, and then – blank.

She sighed. Maybe it was better this way. She didn't know why she was getting herself straightened out again. Now she knew she didn't have anyone to do it for. She closed her eyes, making a silent decision that as soon as Rosie and Jake left the apartment, she'd pack up what she'd got, get her stash of money and go. Go and get so drunk she would never get sober again. Her resolution to blow it all – blow herself – made her feel light-hearted, and she sat up, wrapped her robe around her and went into the kitchen.

'This smells so good. We having a party?'

Rooney looked round the tastefully furnished room, and at the pictures arrayed on a bookcase. Norman Hastings with his wife, Norman Hastings with his daughters, his dog, his car, Norman Hastings smiling. Norman Hastings the nice, ordinary husband and father. Rooney could smell baking, mixed with polish, or some kind of lavender room spray. He could hear Hastings's dog out in the back yard with the kids, barking as the creaking swing swung backwards and forwards. The little girls were calling to the dog, to each other, and the sound of their voices added to the air of normality. The only thing missing was their father.

Mrs Hastings came in with home-made cookies and a pot of coffee. She was a pretty woman, nice-coloured hair with a sweet-faced smile. She perched rather than sat on the chair opposite Rooney. She had good hands, square-cut nails without any varnish.

'I'm sorry not to have any news,' Rooney said. She bit her lip, trying not to cry. Rooney hated having to do it, but he couldn't put off what he was there for, and she seemed to sense he wanted something.

'Mrs Hastings, I'm sorry if this seems like going over old ground, but I just want to ask a few more questions.'

She began to nibble a cookie.

'Tell me about a normal, everyday week – where your husband went, who he saw, that kind of thing.'

The familiar story unfolded. Norman Hastings got up at the same time every day, even at weekends. He took his kids to school, he went to work, he came home, he had supper with his family. Two nights a week he went bowling or played poker with his friends. Weekends were kept for the family.

'Did he have any other hobbies?'

'Just taking care of the garden, that kind of thing. He did all the decorating and he built the kitchen and the girls' wardrobes.'

'Nothing else?'

She shook her head, then hesitated. 'We did join a country and western club two or three years ago. We went to four or five nights, but he didn't really enjoy it. I did, but he said they weren't his type.'

'Did you continue going?'

'No. You need a partner, you see, for the square dances . . . I'm not being much help, am I?' she asked.

'Was there anyone you didn't like among his friends?'

167

She shook her head.

'Would you show me over the house?'

She seemed surprised, but stood up, and walked to the door. Rooney trailed after her. She was like a tour guide, pointing out what Norman had done – the extensions, the custom-built closets. She was boring him and he began to feel faintly irritated. The last room they went into was Hastings's den. Its walls were painted the identical colour to three other rooms, the pictures indistinguishable from those in the living room. Norman with his wife, his kids, his bowls-playing pals, his poker pals. Four men standing, hands in their pockets, staring at the camera. Rooney moved closer, peering at the photographs, half hoping he would see a man with wide lips, glasses and a bite out of his neck, but they were all pot-bellied, jovial types with just a faint glimmer of enjoyment on their faces. Rooney sighed and turned away, but as he did he noticed a faint mark on the wall where another picture had hung. 'What was there?'

Mrs Hastings blinked. 'I can't remember.'

He knew she was lying, the house was too orderly for her not to know every inch. 'Was it a photograph?' Rooney asked, relaxed and casual.

'I can't remember. Norman must have taken it down.'

'Do you mind looking for it?'

She hesitated, then crossed to the desk. As she opened a drawer, they heard a crash outside, and one of her daughters started to cry loudly. 'I won't be a minute – I think she's fallen off the swing.'

'Can I look through the desk?'

She paused in the doorway. 'I'd prefer it if you didn't.'

He lifted his hands in apology. Stepping back from the desk he sat down in Hastings's chair. 'I'll wait for you.'

As soon as she was out of the room Rooney looked over the contents of the drawers. Tax forms, house insurance, life insurance, dental and medical checks, they were like the rest of the house, orderly. He drummed the desk top with his fingers. There was yet another photograph of Mrs Hastings, a daughter on either side. Rooney picked it up and stared at it, then he turned it over. There was a hook, and a stand. He looked to the space on the wall, then back to the photograph. When he placed it against the faint dust outline, it matched.

He crossed to the window. Mrs Hastings was examining her daughter's leg, so he returned to the desk and picked up the photograph again. He pushed open the small clips at each side, and opened the frame. There was nothing beneath. He swore, replaced the clips, and was about to stand it upright on the desk when she walked back in.

'She's all right, just a grazed knee.' She stared at Rooney, then at the photograph.

'Pretty photograph – in fact they're all very nice.'

She prodded the frame into exactly the same position as before. 'Yes. He's a professional photographer.'

'Ah, just goes to show – you can always tell!' Rooney paused. 'Mrs Hastings, that photograph was the one off the wall, wasn't it? Was someone else's photograph in it? Is that why you took it down?'

She pursed her lips: she didn't seem quite so pretty now – there was a steely quality to her. 'Yes, it was, now I come to think about it.' She folded her arms. 'I'd like you to go, please.'

Rooney remained where he was. 'Mrs Hastings, your husband was found brutally murdered. Now, I have no motive, no reason why anybody should have done that.'

'Robbery. You never found his wallet. It was robbery. That's what the papers have said and the television news.'

'And you can think of no other motive?'

'No. He's buried now anyway. It's all over. I'd like you to leave.' She pointedly held the door open and Rooney walked past her.

He stopped as they reached the front door. 'The photographer. Do you have his name and address?'

'No, I'm sorry I don't. Norman always arranged the sittings.'

Rooney scratched his head. 'Was he local?'

She coloured. 'I can't remember.'

'But you had them taken every few years, you told me so yourself. Surely you must remember?'

'I don't.'

She had the front door open when he leaned close. 'Why are you lying?'

'Please leave me alone.'

Rooney shut the door with the flat of his hand. She pushed against him, and then backed down the hallway. *'I don't want to talk about it.'*

Rooney followed her. 'What don't you want to talk about, Mrs Hastings?'

Her hands were flailing, her face bright pink.

'Why don't we go and sit down?'

'No.'

Rooney gazed at the freshly painted ceiling. 'Don't make me get a whole bunch of officers checking out every photographer, Mrs Hastings, don't waste my time . . .' His voice was low, flat and expressionless. 'Seven women have been killed in the same manner as your husband – a blow to the back of the head with a hammer, and their faces battered beyond recognition. If you have anything – *anything* – that will help me find the killer, you had better tell me!'

She stood with her arms wrapped round herself, her whole body shaking. 'I said if I ever caught him doing it again, I would divorce him – I'd tell his parents, his boss, his friends—'

'Doing what, Mrs Hastings?'

She turned round and her face was ashen. 'He was dressed in women's clothes.'

Rooney didn't show a flicker of distaste or surprise.

She had come home from one of the country and western

nights – when Norman had said he didn't like it, she went alone. She started to cry. 'I was only there a few minutes and I felt stupid all dressed up in cowboy boots, and I just thought he was right, it *was* stupid, so I came home. But he didn't hear me coming in. I knew he was in the bedroom because I saw the light on, and I thought I'd surprise him.' She gave a strange, bitter, high-pitched laugh. 'I don't know who was more surprised, him or me. He was all made-up, with a blonde wig, a cheap awful frilled dress, high heels . . . I – I just couldn't believe my eyes.'

She broke down and sobbed, and Rooney remained silent, waiting. 'Anyway . . . a long time after, because I ran into the bathroom and wouldn't come out, he was on his knees outside the bathroom sobbing, and I was scared he'd wake the girls, so I came out. He'd taken everything off, but he still had traces – his face . . .'

Norman Hastings, on his knees before his wife, had sworn on the Bible that no one else knew, that he had never done it before. But she knew he had, because of all the clothes. She found more in the garage, more wigs and shoes. She had burnt everything.

Rooney asked, 'This photographer . . . do you think he might have had the same inclinations?'

'He was homosexual, but after I found Norman, I refused ever to go to him again.'

Rooney took out his notebook. 'What's his name?'

She wrung her hands. 'Dear God, this won't come out, will it? His parents are elderly – all his friends, his daughters – please tell me this will never come out?'

Rooney promised he would do his best to keep it from being disclosed to the press. He was lying. The photographer's name was Craig Lyall; she even supplied his studio and home address.

Rooney walked down the immaculate path from the tidy little house, and crossed to his car. The big-eared wonder had been right – now he had a lot more to go on. He suddenly remembered Lorraine Page again, and the Laura Bradley case. He recalled how shocked she had been at the normality of the house and family of the brutalized, abused child. He looked back at the Hastings house, and suddenly it wasn't so neat or tidy and homely. He felt deeply sorry for the man, trapped in that perfect little prison. For the first time he also felt an odd compassion for Lorraine Page; she had been a crack officer all those years ago. What a terrible waste.

'Lorraine! *Lorraine!* We're leaving, did you hear? *Lorraine!*' Rosie bellowed.

'Okay, I'll see you later.' She was desperate for them both to go, wanting to take her savings and get the hell out. She was so impatient that as soon as the screen door closed she ran to her closet, and wrenched it open, falling to her knees to search for the money. She found the shoes, and then stared in disbelief at the pitiful remains of her hoard. She began hurling things out of the closet, convinced there must be some mistake. Then she sat back on her heels and punched at the door.

'Rosie!' she snarled.

Rosie and Jake were at the bottom of the steps when the screen door flew open. Lorraine hurled herself down the stairs, her hands splayed like claws. She grabbed Rosie by the throat. *'Where is it?'*

Jake tried to haul her off, but she thrust him back so hard that he crashed into the garbage cans. She dived at Rosie again, who was screeching at the top of her voice.

'My money! *You stole my money, you fucking bitch!*'

Rosie reeled back as Lorraine punched her in the face, tripped over a paving stone and fell. Lorraine sprang at her, pulling at her hair. 'You fucking bitch! That was *my money, my money* – you two-faced cunt, you piece of shit . . . *you fucker!*'

172

People were coming out of the grocery store to watch. Lorraine was on top of Rosie now, hitting her. Jake was trying to drag her off, but nothing he did could stop Lorraine. She swiped and spat like a wild cat, and then she collapsed, kicking and pounding the road with her fists.

Rosie's nose was bleeding, her face was scratched, her dress ripped and she was shaking with terror. She had never seen anyone so crazy, well, not when they were sober.

Jake had handled crazies and drunks, but Lorraine's immense strength surprised him – she'd almost broken his jaw. He now hauled her to her feet and dragged her over to the steps. He turned on two gawping onlookers: 'Show's over, okay?'

Lorraine didn't resist. She let Jake propel her up the stairs, and a trembling Rosie followed slowly, keeping a good distance.

Jake sat Lorraine on the sofa, then squatted back on his heels in front of her. 'What the hell was that all about?'

Lorraine glared at Rosie. 'Tell him!' she shrieked.

Rosie started to cry, dabbing at her face, and Lorraine swung back her fist and caught Rosie another blow, which started her screaming. Jake prised them apart, pushing Lorraine away. Abruptly she raised her hands. 'Okay, okay . . . but if she won't tell you then I will. Every cent I've saved and fuckin' worked my ass off for – she has stolen. I've got no more than twenty, thirty bucks left from over a thousand.'

Jake frowned. 'Where did you get a grand from? Rob a bank, for chrissakes?'

'What is this? An inquisition? It was my dough. *She's* the one who stole it. Why not interrogate her?'

Jake stood up, ran his hand over his thinning head. 'How much is left?'

Lorraine closed her eyes. 'Not enough to drink myself to death, which is what I intended doing.'

'So, you want to die. Fuck you – and your attitude.

173

Anyone that can make a thousand bucks in less than a week gotta have somethin' goin' for them – unless you did pull a heist, but somehow I doubt it . . .'

Lorraine gave her odd squint-eyed look to Jake. 'Okay. You want to know how I made it? Blackmail, I blackmailed a little queer bastard . . .'

Jake grinned. 'Can we all have a go at him – or is it just you that's got the information on him?'

'It was Art, at the gallery, he's into porno – no paintings – porno, with kids.'

Rooney walked into his office and beamed at Bean. 'Guess what? Norman Hastings was a cross-dresser!'

Bean gaped as Rooney displayed the photographs from Craig Lyall's studio. Norman Hastings in a blonde wig, dressed up and in full make-up, smiled with thick, glossy red lips into the camera lens. 'Jesus Christ, I don't believe it!'

Rooney was pleased with his efforts. He told Bean to bring in the pictures of the dead women, and Rooney held up Hastings's photograph.

'What if Teacher picked up Hastings? Maybe thought he was a hooker?'

Bean deflated Rooney by reminding him that Hastings was found in male clothes, so that theory was out of the window.

'Maybe he knew him? Maybe they dressed up together?'

They were going down the maybe road again, but at least they now had a road. All Hastings's friends would be requestioned.

'What was the photographer like?' Bean asked.

Rooney picked at his nose. 'Campy, queer, probably a cross-dresser too. Best get him back in, you have a talk to him. I got so excited when he showed the photos I might have missed something.'

'Fellows was right, wasn't he?' Bean mumbled. They had begun walking towards the exit when he stopped. 'Bill, what if Helen Murphy is or was not the woman who had been attacked? Maybe we should have another interview with that woman Laura Bradley, go over everythin' again.'

'What did you say?' Rooney snapped. 'The last thing, Laura Bradley?'

Bean explained again about the two uniformed guys who had interviewed a woman at the address where the cab driver thought he had dropped off the injured woman.

'Laura Bradley? That her name?' Rooney stood in the corridor, blinking. He could picture that little girl, see rookie Lorraine Page's face. 'Check her out.'

Lorraine told Jake and Rosie the entire Art, Nula and Didi story, and described her visit to Mike. She felt drained, by them, by everything.

Jake gently touched her head, fixing a stray strand of hair. 'You gonna come clean about that time you got a crack over the back of the head? You had money that night, too.'

'You really are grilling me tonight, Jake, what's with you?'

'I just know it helps to talk things over. You still want to slit your wrists?'

She smiled. 'Maybe not quite so much.'

'Good. So, how did you get that crack on the back of your head?'

Lorraine yawned. 'Well, you know the grocery store? At the end of the road? The crossroads just at the side of it? I walked across there, up along the road, and you know the traffic lights at the end of that block?'

'Yes,' Rosie and Jake said together.

'That's where I tripped and fell.'

Their faces made Lorraine giggle and suddenly they

broke into laughter too. They were all laughing when they heard the footsteps coming up the wooden staircase. Rosie looked out of the window.

'It's the cops.'

Jake caught Lorraine's expression. She was drained of any colour.

CHAPTER 8

LORRAINE DIDN'T panic. She calmly picked up her cigarette pack and headed for the bedroom.

'Jake, if they ask for a Laura Bradley, she's not here. She stayed a while and then left.'

'They coming for you?' Rosie asked.

'Yeah, but I swear I've done nothing wrong. I just got a lot of outstanding violations, and—'

Jake took her by the elbow, pushing her even further into the safety of the bedroom. 'Why Laura Bradley?'

'Because they came here, that friend of mine must have told them where they could find me. Please, Jake, get them off my back and I swear I won't kill myself!'

'It's a deal,' Jake said as he closed the door.

Rosie hardly said a word, just gave her name. Jake did the rest, smooth-talking, open and friendly. Sorry he couldn't help them, but Laura Bradley had left. The young uniformed cop smiled, tipped his hat: with his shades and suntan he could have come straight out of a movie. He returned to his partner, waiting below in the car, and Rosie watched them draw away.

The cop car cruised one block up and parked. The cab driver had said a short dark-haired guy and a fat woman had helped the injured woman, so they radioed in for further instructions.

In some ways Lorraine knew they'd be back – even wished she hadn't played games and had come forward, rather than involving Jake and Rosie. They heard the cops returning, and Lorraine gave a long sigh. 'Okay. Remember that night I cracked my head? Just tell them we were all at an AA meeting, agreed? That's what you say and you stick to it.'

'Why do we have to lie?' Rosie gasped, the footsteps almost at the screen door.

'So I don't get arrested for non-appearance in court. I got traffic violations. I also blackmailed Art Mathews, and you, Rosie, spent the dough – you need any more reasons?'

There was a rap on the door and Lorraine opened it. She'd got her jacket and purse and cigarettes, and made a joke of it. 'Okay, guys, I'm Laura Bradley.'

Rosie and Jake were driven off in one squad car, while Lorraine travelled solo with two officers in another. She was taken straight in to see Josh Bean, and admitted straight away that she had lied, that she was Lorraine Page. He seemed to accept her excuse that she didn't want to get involved, because – as she presumed he already knew – she was an ex-cop. As they spoke, from the corner of her eye, she could see her details rolling off the fax machine. But she was relieved that Captain Rooney was not around. Just being inside the station had brought her out in a cold sweat.

Bean elaborated as to why they had asked her to accompany the officers. He told her they were investigating a murder and asked where she was on the night of the seventeenth of last month.

Lorraine said she was at an AA meeting and gave the address. Bean was quiet, almost too friendly and apologetic for any inconvenience they had caused. 'You see we're searching for a witness, a woman we believe is a very valuable witness.'

Even as he spoke she could see him scrutinizing her, and

it was obvious he doubted that she could be the same woman as described – she had all her own teeth, for a start. Lorraine remained in control, smiled and joked. 'Well, we sure get a lot of riff-raff in the street. Only the other night there was some drunken woman out there, screaming the place down.'

Rosie and Jake kept to the AA meeting story. Rosie told how she had met Lorraine in hospital, how long she had been staying. When they were asked if they had assisted a woman from a taxi on the night of the seventeenth, a woman with injuries to her head and face, both repeated that they were not at home that evening. But they kept glancing nervously at each other.

'You ever see a blue Sedan parked in your street, like this one?'

They were shown a photograph of Hastings's car.

'No, not that I can recall.' Rosie peered at the picture. 'This has been on the TV, hasn't it?'

'Do you know or did you know a Mr Norman Hastings?' Rosie shook her head.

'He was the guy that was murdered, right?' Jake asked.

'I didn't know him,' Rosie said, 'but I seen all the papers. What's this got to do with us?'

Rosie and Jake were released, but were told that they should inform the police of any change of address in case they were required for further questioning. Jake asked if Lorraine was also free to go, and was told that she was still being questioned.

'We'll wait.'

They huddled together to review the officers' questions. They were confused. It seemed a lot more serious than traffic violations but they were in too deep and the spacious waiting room made both feel small and conspicuous. It was to be a long wait.

Four hours after Lorraine had entered the station she was led into a line-up. She had remained calm, accepting a tepid coffee and an extra packet of cigarettes. When she heard that her friends were waiting for her, she asked for someone to tell them they could go home unless they were required for the line-up. They were not: to arrange for a line-up with twelve fat women, and twelve short, squat men in one afternoon was too much to hope for. So Rosie and Jake left the station. They had no idea why Lorraine was still being detained. But Jake had been around too many cops, in too many stations not to know that this was something a lot heavier than traffic violations.

Lorraine knew the procedure backwards, and made it clear she was more than willing to co-operate. She waited patiently, knowing what a runaround would be going on behind the scenes. Captain Rooney had still not made an appearance and for that she was grateful.

The line-up corridor annex was like all the others she had dealt with years before, but larger and with better equipment. The more she looked around the Pasadena station the more impressed she was with the massive building. She wondered how Rooney fitted in, his squalid old office, his grimy-walled, smoke-stained room far removed from the white, neon-lit, airy offices with the red 'no smoking' signs on every door.

She chose place number seven, for no particular reason except to avoid being dead centre or at either end, which were not good positions. The other eleven women carried in their cards and lined up on the small, narrow platform. Some were prisoners, and others Lorraine could not imagine where they had been dragged in from. Probably a couple of hookers, housewives or canteen workers, who were always willing to make a few bucks.

When Mr and Mrs Summers arrived, Bean told them to take their time, to look at each subject closely, without making contact. If they recognized the woman they should

180

walk out and give the number. If they wished her to speak they must ask the officer at their side to repeat whatever they wanted the prisoner to say.

Mr Summers walked slowly down the line first, staring at each woman in turn. Then he left the room. Next came his wife. She, too, took her time, but she was confused as she and her husband were sure they had already identified the woman. They also felt slightly guilty. Had they made a mistake earlier? Both had been so certain that the deceased Helen Murphy was the woman they had seen in the parking lot.

'Could they all smile?' Mrs Summers asked nervously. 'I want to see their teeth.'

Captain Rooney walked into the viewing room. There was Lorraine, at number seven, taller than any of the others. It was strange to see her, chin up, holding the card in front of her, her face expressionless. He moved closer to the glass and stared at the deep scar running down her cheek. She looked different, meaner, harder and yet there was still an attractiveness about her. Her clear eyes seemed to stare back at him, through the one-way glass, almost as if she knew he was there.

The third person to be led across the line-up was the cab driver, unshaven, having been ordered out of bed as he was now working night shifts. He was bad-tempered, asking over and over if he was getting paid for all the time they had used up. He had already identified the woman, hadn't he? In some ways he'd half expected a row of corpses.

Rooney turned to Bean. 'Anything?'

'Yeah. The Summerses both said it could be number four – she's from Records! And the cab driver said it was the skinny woman, number two. She's a hooker, but she was banged up on the seventeenth for breaking into a car.'

'Great.' Rooney sighed.

Lorraine was asked to wait in reception. She had stood upright in the line-up – that was another little tip: never slouch, makes you look guilty, always meet their eyes. Never smile, just look. They can't deal with a straight confrontation.

Rooney sat at his desk, swivelling his chair from side to side.

Bean was looking over Lorraine's charge sheet. 'We can hold her if you want. You had a look at this? Vagrancy, prostitution – she's got twenty-five traffic violations, five non-appearances for court hearings . . .'

'Yeah, I know,' muttered Rooney.

'She said she was at an AA meeting, so did her friends. We can check it if you want.'

Rooney shrugged. Lorraine didn't fit their description, she looked to him to be doing okay for herself – and she was sober. 'I can understand why she didn't want to be brought in.' He held out his hand for the sheets. 'I'll talk to her, you can take yourself off home. Get some rest while you can, this is gettin' out of control an' you got no leave until we get results.'

As Lorraine was led along the corridor towards him, Rooney leaned against the wall. He gave a noncommittal nod and held the door wider for her to pass into his office. She sat in the chair opposite his, and waited. Rooney walked slowly round to his chair, sank into it heavily, then rested his elbows on the table.

'Laura Bradley.'

She smiled. 'Yeah. I dunno why I said it, just came into my head. Maybe the little kid's always there, I don't know . . . I'm sorry I wasted your time.'

He stared at her charge sheets.

'I guess whoever you were looking for must have used my address – old ploy. You tried the apartments either side? There's a lot of oddballs live around that street, and then there's the liquor store on the corner—'

Rooney interrupted, 'I know the area. How long have you been sober?'

'A year,' she lied.

Rooney sighed. He hadn't revealed to Bean why he'd not been around when they'd brought in Lorraine. He'd been with Chief Michael Berillo and he'd been hauled over the carpet . . . 'I'm being really pushed on this one. Chief inferred I'd be off it if I didn't get a result soon.'

'What's the case?' Lorraine asked.

'Seven hookers cracked over the skull with a claw hammer. One of 'em's only seventeen, rest are real dogs.' Rooney smirked. 'Maybe some of 'em are your friends. You want to take a look?'

'Cunt.'

'What are you doing now?'

'Work in an art gallery, go see my kids – pretty boring but it keeps me. Can I go?'

'No. I need someone to talk to. What do you think of the new station – well, be about five years old now. It wasn't built when you left, was it?'

She lit a cigarette, and was surprised when he slumped forward, clasping his head in his hands. 'I'm fucking coming up for retirement, and what happens? I get a case that's . . . I keep on going up one blind alley after another. Nothing makes sense.'

He suddenly looked up, and then got to his feet. 'Come on, take a look, maybe you did know one of these whores.'

She glared at him, and he laughed. 'Hey! You be nice to me. I could have you locked up. You know how many violations you got outstanding? Twenty-five, sweetheart, so move your butt.'

Lorraine followed Rooney into the incident room. The officers in there turned and stared. Rooney announced loudly that she was an ex-cop, and there followed a few strange glances and a whispered exchange between two females who knew that she'd been in the line-up. She lit a cigarette from the butt and heard someone say it was a no-smoking zone. She paid no attention.

Rooney took her over the photographs, pointing out each woman in turn, where they were found, the dates. She looked closely at Hastings. Pinned next to it was one of him in drag.

'How about that for a turn-up? Drag artist in his spare time, I found that out,' Rooney said, as if he expected her to applaud.

She remained with Rooney for two more hours. Back in his office, he talked on and on. She knew he was running everything by her, for no other reason than that he wanted to run it all by himself. She let him ramble on with barely an interruption and wondered if at the end of all this he was going to book her. Then came: 'You ever think about that kid? The one you took out?'

She turned away. She didn't think of him, and she suddenly felt guilty. But Rooney continued, 'You were good, you know. I wish I had someone here with your dedication. If you'd not got on the bottle, you'd be somewhere now. A lot go the same way – well, not quite as low as you. You hit the skids, didn't you? Worked the streets?'

'Yes. Look – can I go?' She stood up.

'No, you can't. Fucking sit down.'

She sat down, and then he blew her away. 'I want you to do something for me.'

She stared.

'Make you a deal.' He picked up the charge sheets between finger and thumb and dangled them. 'See what you can come up with for me. Ask around the whorehouses, the—'

'You kidding me?'

He shook his head, his voice suddenly low and unpleasant. 'No, I'm not kidding. The deal is I'll clear these,' he indicated the long list of charges, '*if* you help me out. Somebody's got to know these hookers, somebody's got to

184

know something, maybe where Murphy's hiding out. We're trying to trace Helen Murphy's husband but so far no joy and I doubt if it's him. If you find anything, any link, you got a clean sheet.'

Lorraine laughed. 'I got a job, Bill.'

He leaned closer to her, and she could smell his stale breath. 'This is not a job, sweetheart, this is a deal. You get a clean slate for helping me out or I'll bust you.'

'Then I'll need a car—'

'Fuck off, Lorraine! Look at this. You've been charged on eight counts for driving without a licence, without insurance and under the influence. No way can I get that cleared. The other stuff, yes – the no-show for court appearances, prostitution.'

'What about expenses?'

He laughed, shaking his head. 'You sure try it on.'

'I got to eat, pay rent. I walk out of my job, and—'

He sneered, 'Do what you did before, Lorraine, sell your little ass—'

She leaned over the desk. 'Screw you. Take those charges and shove them up your ass – it's big enough to take the entire filing cabinet.'

He roared with laughter and slapped the desk with his hand. 'Okay. Fifty bucks.'

'A day?'

'A week.'

'Fuck off. I know how much you pay informers, I also know you'll have a nice little stash that you'll divvy out between you and your pals at the end of each month, filling in fictional names and places. I know, Billy. Fifty bucks a day. I can go on the streets, into the bars, the clubs. I'll find someone with information. Like you said, I was good.'

Rooney got up and crossed to his window. He stood playing with the blind. 'How long you been sober?'

'I told you, a year. Call my husband, he'll tell you. Call my room-mate, she'll tell you. I'm straight, Bill.'

He picked at his nose – it was a habit. No wonder it was always so red, Lorraine thought.

'You'll call in every day?'

'I'll call in on the hour, if that's what you want.'

'Yeah, it is,' he said quietly, and opened his wallet.

Lorraine couldn't believe it: he was going to pay her there and then. 'Is there any way I can get copies of the statements you got to date?'

Rooney nodded, counting out a hundred bucks. 'This is it, Lorraine, and believe me when I say I'll have you brought back in here so fast if you mess me around. I need information.'

'I'll also need photographs – everything you got so far.'

Rooney looked at her, suddenly uncertain.

'I got to know what's going on, Bill.'

'Yeah. I guess you do.'

Rooney watched Lorraine walk out of the building and flag down a taxi before he let the blind flip back into place. He told himself he must be nuts, especially as he'd not even got her to sign for the cash. Added to that, he'd handed over copies of the case files. He had a moment of blind panic: if she was to take it to the press he'd be screwed to the floor. Then he relaxed; he was almost nailed there already. He checked the time and put in a call to Andrew Fellows.

'Ah, Captain, I'm so sorry not to have got back to you since you gave me this new stuff on Hastings. Reason is, I've not had too much spare time, I'm on a lecture tour.'

'I'd appreciate your input as soon as possible,' Rooney rumbled.

'I'll get back to you soon as I've got a moment to go over the file, but I'm up to my ears right now.'

Rooney listened to the drawling voice, half smiling at the 'ears' line, waiting for what he suspected was coming. It came.

'I don't suppose there's some way you could finance me, is there? Only it does take up a considerable amount of my time.'

Rooney said he would run it by his chief and dropped the phone back on the hook. The chief would, no doubt, arrange payment – it had been his idea to bring Fellows on board, so let *him* budget for him. Rooney was stretched and he was not about to pay Fellows out of his own pocket, not like Lorraine.

He remembered finding her on the floor in the old precinct, looking into her face in the patrol car when he held that poor kid's Sony Walkman under her nose. She'd given that half-dazed smile. He remembered that moment now. That kid would've been alive if it wasn't for that bitch. He wanted to be deeply angry, but he couldn't, and it confused him. She had to be pretty tough to have survived, to have got herself back together. At least he hoped she was: that she wasn't right that moment walking into a bar with his case file in one hand and his cash in the other. If she was, then he would make sure, no matter what else he did, that she paid a high price.

Lorraine read through the files all night. Her concentration blanked out Rosie and her television shows. When Rosie went to bed, Lorraine continued working, sifting through every statement, studying each photograph, jotting down notes. It was four in the morning when she stretched and got up. She had sat with her legs tightly crossed, just the way she had when she was working in the old days. She massaged her thighs, easing out the cramp, then sat staring into space. Rooney was right, they had nothing: no witnesses but herself. If only he knew! Lorraine had seen the killer – had almost gone down on him, had almost got herself killed. And she also had a clear memory of the killer's cufflinks. She wondered if Norman Hastings had ever

187

bought or owned a reconditioned vintage car. From what she had read so far, she doubted it – but, then, everyone had been wrong about him being the perfect family man.

Lorraine didn't go to bed until almost five, and by then she was so wired up she was unable to fall asleep. The sofa bed was uncomfortable and too soft, her back ached and her legs still felt as if they were going to cramp up. She was in the half-dream state when suddenly she had a vivid image of the boy. She saw him running, saw the flash of the Superman striped jacket.

'Freeze!'

She sat up, wide awake now. She didn't want to see him, didn't want to see herself, didn't want to see the boy's jerking body as the bullets tore into him. She flipped over the sheet, got up and drew back the curtains. She forced herself to think about the murderer, remembering exactly where he had picked her up. Was he local? Somehow she doubted it – he was too flashy, too well dressed. Again, Murphy, the only suspect, did not tie in. Lorraine closed her eyes and visualized his face: the rimless, gold-framed glasses, the blue close-set eyes, the sharp nose and the wide, wet, thick-lipped mouth. She conjured up a picture of his hands, went over exactly what he had said, how he had picked her up, how he had reached into the glove compartment. She wasn't scared, she just let the killer move into her mind. And just as she had done with the Laura Bradley murder, she repeated to herself, over and over again, her voice a soft whisper: 'I'll get you.'

CHAPTER 9

ROSIE WAS so immersed in the horror of the statements and pictures she didn't hear Lorraine walking into the bedroom.

'That was private, Rosie, you shouldn't be reading it.'

Rosie looked up and hunched her shoulders apologetically. 'It's those mortuary shots that get me – really close up, aren't they? I didn't know you looked like that when you were dead, how they can clean them up . . .' She held up Helen Murphy's photograph. 'This is her when they found her, and this is her at the morgue and this is her – I mean, she looks like she's sleeping.'

Lorraine walked into the bathroom. 'They had her face fixed up with plaster for an ID. Made-up, that's all. The only suspect they got is her husband, a trucker, but they're way off, he's not the killer.'

Rosie shut the file. 'I doubt if anyone'll grieve over these women, they look like they're all pretty shot up – in fact some of them look happier dead, know what I mean? Well, not the little blonde girl, she's sort of cute.'

Lorraine leaned on the bathroom door. 'Yeah. She doesn't fit in, does she? All the others are older, worn out, hard . . .'

'You know what I think?' Rosie licked her lips. 'I think he picked *you* up. You were hit on the back of the head but somehow you got away from him. The taxi brought you back here and . . . I remembered it was the seventeenth of

189

last month.' Then she shrugged her heavy shoulders. 'It couldn't have been you, though, could it?'

'Why not?'

'Because that was the day Norman Whatcha-call-it was done – they found him in his own car, right? So he wouldn't have been whacking you over the head and killing somebody else, would he?'

'I fell on the pavement, Rosie.'

'Yeah – and I'm Sharon Stone's lookalike.'

Lorraine walked into the shower and pulled the curtain round her. Rosie surprised her – not that she had said anything intelligent, or especially intuitive even: Lorraine had been cracked over the back of the head in exactly the same manner as described not once but eight times in the files. But it was the simple dismissal of the possibility that the man could have killed Hastings and then an hour later attempted to kill again. Lorraine made a mental note to check through the exact times and dates of each murder.

Lorraine felt tired, but a good sort of tired. She'd worked hard last night just assimilating all the evidence and, although she didn't like to admit it, she had liked chatting over it with Rosie. That's what had surprised her: that she had, for a few brief minutes, felt like a player again. 'Marking out the jigsaw' was the way she used to describe it to Mike.

The water jets sprayed into her uptilted face. Mike and she had talked over her cases to begin with, but gradually he'd become uninterested, telling her that he didn't want to hear about the whores or the details of the murders, he had to study. She had no one to talk it out of her system with: she had just bottled it all up inside.

She gasped, turned the taps to cold. She didn't want *him* to come back into her life, not now, please not Lubrinski, she couldn't deal with him. It had been Lubrinski who realized she was bottling up all the horror, anger, disgust. It had been Lubrinski after a particular heavy night when they had found two teenagers in a boarding house, stiff from death, stiff from drugs, stiff and stinking, but they were so beautiful, like frozen angels the pair of them, who had insisted they go to a bar, insisted they get smashed. And drunk she had suddenly broken down and Lubrinski had gripped her tightly, had even cried with her as he said it was okay to let go, to let the poison out, rather than have it seething inside her. Lubrinski.

Rosie was eating muffins with a jam smear across her cheek and also over the file, which Lorraine promptly snatched away from her. 'You don't get it sticky with jam!'

Rosie washed her hands in a great display, and then returned to reading the files and statements. 'This Andrew Fellows is something else, isn't he? You read what he came up with about Helen thingy? The killer really likes them in bad shape, doesn't he?'

Lorraine couldn't help but be drawn in. 'Apart from Holly.'

'Oh, yeah. Well, maybe he just got lucky that night.'

Lorraine dressed and made up her face. When she came back into the room Rosie was still engrossed in the files.

'Could you borrow that car from Jake's friend?'

'What do you need a car for?'

'I need to go to Santa Monica. A bit of investigation work. Maybe you could help me.'

Rosie's face lit up. 'Do I get paid?'

'Yeah, you'll get paid, Rosie.'

They eventually found 'W-rent W-rent Wreckers' where Lorraine had to pay a hundred bucks down in case there were any further dents to the Mustang. The man was not overly interested in the licence Rosie waved at him, but the car cost fifty bucks for a week, plus gas, with the hundred-buck deposit. Rosie drew a diagram of all the dents to avoid them being conned on their return, and in a cloud of exhaust fumes, bangs, and the engine clacking at an alarming rate, they bombed out of the yard.

The roof was down – it could not go up – and as it was a bright clear day, Lorraine rested back on the torn seat and considered how they – she, she corrected herself – would go about interviewing the men working at the vintage car garage in Santa Monica. All she wanted to know was if they sold cufflinks; if so, how many, and how many men they employed. And she needed to know if they had someone fitting the description of the killer. With Rosie at the wheel, Lorraine relaxed for the journey, as much as Rosie's driving style would allow: she was an incurable horn tooter, thrusting an abusive finger up to anyone who cut her up. Yet, and again Lorraine found herself surprised, she was a competent driver, even if she did cut across lanes. But she did it so positively that it didn't make Lorraine nervous.

Rosie sighed as they turned into yet another road, Lorraine shaking her head. She simply could not remember where the place was, or which route the cab driver had taken. She knew they were close, but she didn't want to ask directions. Instead she told Rosie to drive to Mike's address: maybe she would recognize landmarks, and as Mike's house was along the shore, she was confident she'd be able to direct Rosie from there.

With a screech of tyres Rosie did a U-turn and headed for the beach.

'Keep going, we're almost at Mike's house now.' They drove on until she spotted the house. She hadn't meant Rosie to stop, especially not so close, but she jammed on the brakes hard. Lorraine felt the confidence draining from her. 'That's it, just across the street.'

Rosie peered over the road. 'Very nice. Worth a few dollars.'

'Just drive on, Rosie.'

'But you don't know where we're going!'

'Just drive, will you? I don't want him to see me.' As they set off, Lorraine tried to concentrate on the road ahead. But all she could think of was Mike and the girls. She closed her eyes, and then jerked forward as Rosie hit the brakes again.

'You're not even looking, for chrissakes! We carry on at this rate and we'll run out of gas.'

Lorraine yanked open the door and got out of the car.

Rosie sighed heavily. 'We lost again?'

Lorraine didn't answer, but walked over to the railing and stood looking out to the ocean. Rosie sat in the car for a few moments, then joined Lorraine. 'You okay?'

'Not too good, Rosie.'

They stood side by side, like something out of a comedy duo: one so tall and slim, the other so round. A female Laurel and Hardy, but nothing was funny.

'I've lost my girls, Rosie, I know that. It wouldn't be right for me to see them. They're happy, settled, they call her Mom. They've forgotten me – but, then, I wasn't really worth remembering.'

'Don't say that. Everything's worth remembering, the good and the bad, and things *are* gonna get good for you. You never know, maybe next time you see them it won't be so bad.'

'You think so?'

'I know so.'

Lorraine looked down into the plump, concerned face. 'You're the eternal optimist, aren't you?'

'Yep. That's why I got myself so together.'

Lorraine slipped her arms round her, gave her a squeeze. 'I'm glad I found you, Rosie.'

'Me too,' Rosie said.

Lorraine released her and turned to face the road. She remembered the cab took a right at the next junction. 'Okay, let's go. I think I know the way.'

'You sure you want to do this?'

Lorraine threw up her hands in frustration. 'Why do you think we came here? Now get in the car, I've been working out exactly what I want to say. I'll draw a picture of a cufflink and you show it to the salesman. You say your husband has lost one, and you want to replace it – are you listening? Left, take a left here!'

Five miles later they pulled up in the forecourt of the building next to the vintage car showroom. Rosie got out carrying the sketch, and armed with the questions she had repeated four times to Lorraine.

Lorraine watched her disappear as she passed between the cars on display on the forecourt. When she slid up to sit on the back of her seat, she could see Rosie inside the big glass-fronted showroom, waiting at the long mahogany counter. Then she lost her as Rosie accompanied a man to the far end of the showroom. Lorraine dropped back into her seat, and lit a cigarette, never taking her eyes off the showroom entrance. Had she asked too much of Rosie? She was about to go in after her when she appeared.

'Christ, what have you been doing? Do you know how long you were in there?'

'Sorry, but the guy never stopped talkin'. You want the good news?'

'Yeah, yeah. Come on, tell me.'

'Okay. They sell the cufflinks, or they used to. They were originally part of a promotional thing, started in 1990. You know, spend hundred and eighty-five thousand dollars on a vintage car and they'll throw in a set of cufflinks.'

'Shit!' Lorraine hit the dashboard with her fist. But Rosie wasn't through. She had the number of workers, fifty-eight in all, each of whom had been given cufflinks with their Christmas bonus. Around two hundred and fifty sets had been made up – that was the bad news. Further good news was that the first batch had been made in cheap silver, which had proved so popular that they had had a second batch made. These had been handed out last Christmas –

and only to their executives, the difference being that these were made in nine carat gold. Rosie beamed. 'There's a board showing the top salesmen and the directors, listing their offices, so I presumed they'd be the executives, right? Eight in all.' She fished around in her purse and dragged out a dog-eared Mickey Mouse notepad and a felt tip pen. She sucked the end and then scribbled down as many as she could remember. Lorraine watched in astonishment. Rosie chuckled as she underlined the last name: she'd remembered all eight, even their titles.

'I always win every time! Those game shows where they show you a sort of runner thing with articles and you gotta remember each one! Now, were the links you saw gold or silver?'

Lorraine couldn't remember. 'You see anyone with blondish hair, rimless glasses, wide wet mouth?'

'Nope. The guy was short and fat and looked like he got a sack of potatoes in the back of his pants . . .'

Lorraine grinned, and then looked over the list of names, wondering about her next move. Fifty-eight workers, all with cufflinks, eight executives all with gold ones – and a few hundred vintage car owners with God knew how many more.

'He also said that the silver ones were crap and most of them broke after a few outings. He gave me a set for free.'

Rosie revealed the box and Lorraine snatched it from her. She opened it and knew at a glance that the man who attacked her had worn gold cufflinks. She snapped it closed. 'Rosie, you are a fuckin' marvel!'

Eight names, eight men with gold cufflinks. Now she would work on eliminating each one. She knew she had to be careful: if she confronted her attacker she could be in danger. At the same time she had to be sure; if she gave Rooney bum information he could arrest her, charge her, and have her locked up. She wouldn't put it past him because he had brought up the shooting incident. It must still sit heavy on him, maybe he felt the guilt he wanted her to feel. Lorraine knew she couldn't make any mistakes — there was too much at stake.

CHAPTER 10

THE FOLLOWING morning Lorraine could not summon any energy and had no idea how to progress, so at eight o'clock she took herself off to Fit 'N' Fast.

'I just feel so tired all the time,' she complained to Hector.

He shrugged. 'Bound to feel that way, you've punished the hell out of your body for years, right? You can't suddenly force it into feeling fit. Nothing happens overnight, it takes time and dedication.' He agreed to make out a diet and a tough work-out programme for every other day, including weights, a strict high-carb diet, and a high-protein drink. Armed with a boxful of new vitamins, Lorraine went home.

Rosie looked over the array of cans and pills, and the charts Lorraine was pinning up. 'I'd join you, but I've got a built-in resistance to all of this kind of stuff.'

Lorraine laughed. 'Well, you're so full of energy you don't need it. Do you have a camera?'

'It's in the pawn shop – been there about seven months.'

'Can I get it out?'

'I dunno where the ticket is, and it'll cost a few dollars. It's a very expensive model.' Rosie started sifting through her papers and eventually found the pawn ticket: there was a hundred and fifty dollars to pay. Lorraine wondered if she could buy a cheap camera instead.

'Has it got a zoom lens?'

'I dunno, there's all kinds of attachments for it. I never used it so I dunno what it's got.'

'Okay, go get it, I'll wait here for you. You'd better take this – it's the last of my stash.'

Rosie departed, moaning about being used as a gofer but when Lorraine asked if she had anything better to do, she said, 'I guess not but why do you need it?'

'To take photographs.'

Lorraine worked through the telephone directory, matching the names on Rosie's list. She called each one, checked if they worked at the garage, and slowly narrowed down all the wrong numbers. She was still busy when Rosie returned two hours later.

The camera was a professional fast-slide action with zoom lens. Rosie watched in fascination as Lorraine quickly checked over all the accessories, testing out the viewfinder, attaching the different lenses and grinning in triumph because it even had a laser night shutter: she could photograph at night.

'How come you know so much about cameras?' she asked.

'Part of my job. On surveillance we used high-tech equipment and I went on a couple of courses—'

The phone rang. It was Rooney. 'You out on the streets? What you doing?'

'Gimme time, for chrissakes. Like I said, as soon as I have anything, I'll be in touch. One thing, this Fellows guy, can I get in touch with him?'

'Why?'

Lorraine could hear his chesty breathing down the phone. 'Just like to talk to him. I won't if you don't want me to.'

'Maybe stay away from him, okay?' Rooney said flatly. 'Call me. I need anything you can come up with.'

Rooney hung up. Why did she want to talk to Fellows? He remembered how intuitive she was. Perhaps she'd come across something he'd missed – or was she just ripping him off?

Bean reminded him that the second shift team were waiting for the morning's briefing. Rooney slowly stood up. 'Be right with you.'

Bean joined the men in the incident room. When he saw Chief Michael Berillo pass, he hoped he wasn't going to see Rooney, as that meant keeping everyone waiting, but Rooney appeared right behind the Chief.

He snapped out orders to his men to begin spreading their inquiries to drag clubs and transvestite hang-outs. 'I want everyone, and this is priority, to check out Norman Hastings's contacts. Hastings is our main link to the killer because out of all the murders he's the odd man.'

There was a loud guffaw, and when Rooney saw the funny side, he snorted. He also divulged that he now had a reliable informant working on the streets, who he hoped would soon bring in some information.

The Chief hitched up his pants, and jerked his head for Rooney to follow him to his office. 'Who's your informant?'

'She's a hooker, been arrested a number of times, she owes me a favour. She's asking round the street girls, the pimps. Some of them won't talk to us, so she'll be useful.'

The Chief nodded. 'That's it then, is it?'

Rooney attempted to bluff his way out, saying there'd been the breakthrough with Mrs Hastings. 'Not enough, Bill. I can't let this continue, I'm under pressure, I've had the Mayor on to me, City Hall. I need an arrest, Bill. There's seven fucking women dead.'

The desk phone rang. The Chief picked it up. He listened and scribbled on a notepad which he passed to Rooney.

'They just got Brendan Murphy, bringing him across State today.' He underlined the word State three times, his face darkening, and then he repeated the name 'Bickerstaff', and put the phone down.

'Good news, they picked up Murphy, your number one suspect. Bad news is it's now FBI business as they've had to get the documents to bring him back to us. He's in Detroit. Looks like you're gonna have to hand over the entire inquiry to a guy called Ed Bickerstaff, you know him?' Rooney swore under his breath. 'I don't like it but I've no option. I've even been asked if you're capable of controlling the case. I've gone out on a limb for you, especially as I know you'll be retiring soon. Bill, if you don't pull the stops out, you'll be taking retirement even earlier than you anticipated.'

Back in his office, Rooney opened a fresh bottle of bourbon and poured himself six fingers, downing it in one gulp before he repeated the dose. Not until his third hit did he relax and begin to think straight. What possibilities had he missed, or glossed over? The FBI would go through everything with a fine-tooth comb. It pissed him off, even more so as he was sure Brendan Murphy was not their man. He rubbed his chin. This was the most complicated inquiry he had ever been on and he was nowhere. He had so little that he was almost depending on that whore Lorraine Page to come up with something. He reached for the phone to call her again. There was no reply.

Lorraine sat with Rosie in the car outside the address of Suspect One from the S and A garage, a Sydney Field. When he pulled up outside his house, Rosie got out and asked if he was a Mr Sam Field. He shook his head. She carried a clipboard. 'I'm doing some market research, Mr Field. Do you work in computers?'

200

'No.' He was surly.

'But you are Mr Sam Field, aren't you?'

'No, Sydney Field. I'm a mechanic, you got the wrong man.' Rosie turned to leave and gave an almost imperceptible nod to Lorraine, who took two photographs. They spent the rest of the evening checking five more names listed from the vintage car garage. It had been a long, tedious afternoon and an even longer night. Six down, two more to go, and Lorraine had not yet seen the man who had attacked her.

The cost of the car rental and payment to get the camera out of hock meant she was already out of pocket, so the next morning she called Rooney. 'I need some more money, Bill.'

'Give me something first,' he snapped.

'I'm checking somethin' out. I'll have it by the end of the day.'

'Drop by, I'll give you a hundred bucks but this is out of my pocket and I'll be out of here in forty-eight hours. FBI taking over.'

'I'd prefer if we didn't meet at the station.'

He swore and then agreed to see her near his Indian restaurant.

Lorraine replaced the receiver and turned, knowing Rosie had overheard.

'What's going on?' Rosie asked.

'Just trying to get us some more cash.'

Lorraine chewed her lips. 'I'm doing this work for an old cop friend, that's all.'

'That why we're taking photographs?'

Lorraine had underestimated Rosie's dogged persistence. 'This cop, he wouldn't be the one you saw outside the gallery? Captain Rooney? Only he's on these murders, isn't he?'

Lorraine made no answer. It'd be dark soon and if they

were to make the most of what daylight remained they'd better leave.

They drove into the outskirts of Beverly Hills and parked outside a neat row of bungalows on Ashdown Road, a heavily gay area. Men were already parading up and down or gathering on street corners talking. A blonde woman was tap-dancing on a small square piece of cardboard, tap-tapping away, her flowered hat on the pavement beside her.

A car drew up and Rosie got out with her clipboard. Lorraine suddenly felt the adrenalin pumping. She knew he was not the man, which left only one to go. Who had to be the man, if – *if* – she was right.

Rosie returned to the car, smiling. 'This is better than sticking down goddamned envelopes. Where to next?'

The final address was on the other side of town, on Beverly Glen. With a screech of tyres, Rosie took a sharp right, directly across the traffic.

'Bastards, it's my right of way!' Lorraine clung to the side of the car as Rosie swerved across the road, and steered onto Sunset Boulevard. She peered over to Lorraine. 'You sure we're on the guy? This is movie-star territory.'

'Yeah, it's off to the right.'

They drove past the Bel Air Gates and took a left onto Beverly Glen. They headed up the winding road, passing the signposts to the Bel Air Hotel. Rosie veered from one side of the road to the other as she glimpsed the magnificent properties on either side of them.

Eventually she pulled up outside a secluded, three-storey house, surrounded by a high wall, a barred gate, and signs warning of guard dogs and electric fences. It was here that Steven Janklow lived, the last name on the list. Rosie got out and crossed the road to look through the gates. A Buick was parked in the drive, alongside an old Mercedes SL 180. She rang the intercom bell at the side of the huge gate. 'Hi,

I am doing market research into computer users and we have a query for a Michael Janklow. Could I please speak to him a moment?'

The phone went dead. Rosie rang again and repeated as much of her rehearsed speech as she could before the phone went dead again. A gardener tending the well-kept lawns walked towards the gates. Rosie smiled and waved at him. 'Can you gimme a minute?'

He didn't speak very good English, so she had to ask two or three times if a Michael Janklow was at home.

'No, no, his name not Michael.'

'Does he work in computers?'

'No, he work in big garage, you have wrong man, go away.'

Rosie returned to the car. 'I think he's the last guy.' She repeated what the gardener had said and gave the car registration numbers.

They waited over an hour but only saw the gardener drive out in an old truck, the gates closing automatically behind him. Then they saw a German shepherd dog sniffing and prowling around inside the gates.

Lorraine told Rosie to go home and that they would come back early next morning. She didn't want Rooney to meet Rosie and it was nearly time for their appointment. She made the excuse that she wanted to work out, so Rosie dropped her off at Fit 'N' Fast.

Fifteen minutes later Rooney arrived. 'What you got for me?' he asked as soon as Lorraine had got into the car.

She hesitated. 'Well, I've been questioning a lot of the hookers. So far nothing much but a couple of them remembered a guy picking them up, real edgy, and I'm trying to find Holly's pimp to see if he can help. You got anything on a vintage car garage, Santa Monica?' She talked about one of the girls seeing the cufflinks, that she, herself, had discovered that fifty odd workers might have a pair. 'What I'm doing is narrowing it all down, taking shots of the workers, taking them round to the girls. It might be your man, then again it might not. It's costing, though, I had to get a good camera and I gotta pay a friend to drive me around, hire a car.'

Rooney took out his wallet. Lorraine leaned closer. 'I'd like to talk to this profiler guy. Can't you swing it for me?'

'Why do you want to see him?'

Lorraine ran her hands through her hair. 'Maybe I just want to talk to him. I was always good at piecing jigsaws together and he sounds like he knows what he's talking about.'

He folded a hundred and fifty dollars and passed it to her. 'Take it, but I want those photographs, and in the meantime I'll do a quiet check on the men who work at this garage, see if there's anyone with a record.'

'Do it quietly, Bill. If your man works there, you don't want to tip him off.'

He grunted.

'I'll call you.' She had her hand on the door handle.

Rooney hesitated, and then muttered grudgingly, 'I'll give this Fellows a call. You can see him if he agrees. I'm up against it. Anything, Lorraine, anything, for chrissakes get it to me fast, you know what snot-nosed bastards those FBI agents are.'

She got out of the car and he watched her walking down the street, long legs, tight ass. All the guys had tried to get into her pants but she had never, to Rooney's knowledge, got it on with anyone of the old team. It pissed them all off that she refused to have a scene with any of them and they had made her life as unpleasant as possible. To her credit she had treated it as a joke, but then she had always been tough.

'You got any complaints?' Rooney had asked.

'No, no complaints,' she had said, quietly and firmly. She never complained or put any man on the line, even when she found out they were having free fucks from the hookers.

She was so tough no one would have believed she would plummet out of control. Rooney wondered now just how long she had hidden her drinking. He had liked Lorraine, admired her tenacity. She had proved her guts too. As he drove Rooney remembered how he and his partner had been called out to an affray in a down-town bar. Neither was prepared to confront the young Mexican holding a waitress by the throat. He'd already knifed two men, everyone was hysterical, and crowds were gathering on the pavement outside.

Rooney called for back-up which arrived in the shape of the young rookie Page, and her beer-gut partner, Brian Dullay. Dullay waddled over to Rooney, bellowing for an update. Suddenly there was a single terrible scream from inside the bar. They needed a decoy: someone to go in the front, distract the Mexican, so they could unarm him from behind. No fucking way, Dullay said. Just as Rooney was about to order him inside, Lorraine stepped forward. 'I'll do it. We can't leave that girl in there.'

While Dullay and Rooney's partner headed for the escape at the back, Lorraine opened the door to the bar. The terrified girl was held by the deranged barman, a knife already cutting through her neck, blood streaming down her dress. Her legs were buckled, she had pissed in her pants with terror, and her face was stricken, frozen, her mouth open wide.

Lorraine walked in holding her hands above her head. 'I'm alone, Roberto, just let her go and you and me can talk.'

The man pushed the girl down to the floor and stamped on her head, holding her firm with his foot. He grinned crazily as he lifted the knife. 'It's too late, no talk now, no more talk.'

Lorraine held her gaze, never flinching when he switched the knife from his right to his left hand. Then he snatched a gun from his belt and pointed it at her. She stood still, without taking her eyes off him. 'It's never too late to talk. Why don't you tell me what's been going on?'

'They kick me out my place, they take my kids, they got no right to do that, I work hard, I pay my taxes, they got no right, I been to the right people, weeks I been goin' an' they say it's okay, nobody can take your place, but they—'

Rooney fired first, then Dullay. The bullet blew the back of the Mexican's skull apart, his blood and brains splattering Lorraine, his body falling over the sobbing waitress.

The girl clung to Lorraine. Even when the ambulance came she wouldn't let go, so Lorraine sat with her until the sedatives took effect then slowly stepped out of the ambulance.

Rooney was talking to Dullay as Lorraine approached him. 'There was no need to kill him,' she said flatly.

Rooney had glared at her. 'He would have used this. You got a complaint?' He had shoved the dead Mexican's gun under her nose.

'No,' she said quietly. 'No complaint.'

Rooney was still thinking about her when he let himself into his home an hour later. He remembered Lubrinski. He was sure there had been something going on between them. They were real close, used to drink together after duty. Thinking of the dark, handsome officer Rooney felt sad. He was one of the best he'd ever come across, bit of a loner but a real man's man. When Rooney had partnered Lorraine with him, he had expected fireworks but instead she and Lubrinski had formed one of the strongest teams he'd ever had. He wished he had a twosome like them with him now but they only come once in a blue moon. Page and Lubrinski, chalk and cheese and yet . . .

Lorraine kept on walking after seeing Rooney. Then she took a bus to Sunset and set off towards the hookers' hang-outs and on until she got to the gay quarter. She stopped outside a coffee bar with a few tables planted on the dirty street. She was looking for Nula or Didi but couldn't find them so asked around for Curtis and was told he would be in the Bar Q further along the stretch. The bar was dark, with music so loud it was deafening. There were only a few customers dotted around, none Lorraine knew, so she sat at the bar and ordered a Coke.

'How you doing?' smiled the black bartender. 'Not seen you in a long while.'

Lorraine grinned. 'Is Curtis out back?'

'Yeah, he's got a game going.'

Lorraine could see a few men in the small pool room. She strolled in and stood sipping the Coke, watching Curtis play with three other dudes in snazzy suits and flash ties. Printed silk was the rage among pimps, reminiscent of Micky Spillane. She knew better than to interrupt, but Curtis looked up suddenly. 'You want me, sugar?'

'When you got a second.'

Curtis chalked his cue. As she moved away, he asked one of the players, 'Who's that?'

The man couldn't put a name to the face. Curtis continued the game.

Lorraine went back to the bar and ordered another Coke. A few more customers had drifted in and a bleached blonde with heavy breasts was perched on an end stool, talking to a boy in leathers. She was all of forty, her tight leather skirt up round her crotch. He leaned forward as if hanging on her every word but his eyes were focused on her deep cleavage. Her breasts were pushed up by a wired bra and burst through the clinging Lycra. Lorraine was almost amused to watch the old pro at work. Every move was sexual – she didn't even reach for her drink without the carefully orchestrated swing of her hips, or opening her legs further, constantly touching her breasts, and licking her thickly painted lips. The boy moved closer, desperate to touch her, and Lorraine waited, knew Blondie would talk money any second. Sure enough, she saw her whisper, then lean back, resting her elbows on the bar, and the boy was hooked.

He passed some bills and the come-on act dropped. Blondie downed her drink, slid off the stool and, arm in arm, they walked out. Lorraine reckoned she'd have a room in one of the motels close by and that the boy was probably a college kid high on grass and desperate to get his rocks off. Well, he would, but he would probably not have reckoned on it being so fast.

Curtis leaned on the bar next to Lorraine. He ordered a beer.

'You know some friends of mine, Didi and Nula. I'm lookin' for them, but they're not on the strip,' she said.

'Bit early for them. What do you want?'

'I'm a friend of Art's.'

'You want some videos?'

'Maybe.'

Curtis suddenly moved close to Lorraine. 'So you know Didi and Nula.' He stripped her with his eyes, then focused on her crotch. 'But you're not one of them. You want to turn a few tricks?' he asked casually, as if offering her a drink.

'No, I want to see them and I don't like goin' to their place in case I interrupt a session.'

Curtis tilted his head back and laughed. 'Not party to that, girlie, not with kids, not my scene.'

Lorraine smiled back. He was relaxing, trusting her, and even more so when a skinny black hooker, Elsa, breezed in and saw Lorraine.

'Hey, how you doin'?' she screamed across the bar, then wiggled over and slipped her arms around Lorraine. 'Long time no see, an' you cleaned yerself up. Baby, you're lookin' great.'

Lorraine was entwined in strong skinny arms and the thick black curly wig tickled her face as Elsa kissed her on the lips. Curtis looked on, as Elsa, still clasping Lorraine tightly, told him how many good times the two of them had had together. She traced the scar on Lorraine's face with her thumb, its long, hooked, bright-red nail like a claw. 'Oh, Jesus, do I remember that night.'

'More than I do,' said Lorraine.

The barman summoned Curtis to take a call and Elsa perched on a stool next to Lorraine. 'So, what you been doin', sugar? I thought maybe you were dead.'

'No, I'm alive. You want a drink?'

'Sure, Coke an' bourbon, if you're buyin'.'

They carried their drinks to a booth, but Elsa's attention flitted constantly to the entrance, waiting for a customer.

'Did you know Holly?'

'Sure, sweet kid, one of Curtis's. He's been cut up bad about it.'

Lorraine led the conversation round to which was Holly's pitch but Elsa couldn't remember: she moved about because some of the girls could get nasty and they reckoned Holly was hedging in on their territory. Curtis was small fry: he only had a few girls and was too weak to get heavy with any of the other pimps. He mostly had trannies because nobody else wanted them – trannies and a few young chicks that he screwed more than any john. Holly was his girl.

'The night she died, did you see her at all?'

'Nah, I was in the Long Down Motel. I got a room there now.'

Lorraine tried to ask as much as she could about Holly without it sounding suspicious but Elsa would only say that on the night of the murder, it had been real slow for business and any john was picked up fast. 'You get good nights and bad nights.'

'Yeah,' murmured Lorraine, but then Curtis returned and Elsa moved off to a prospective client.

He leaned on the back of the booth. 'You still want

videos? I can maybe get some in a couple of hours, I got business right now. Come back later.' The barman waved him over to take another call. Curtis did his video and drug trade in the bars, just small stuff. His girls made the drops for him. Lorraine gave him an uneasy feeling. He watched her walking out. He didn't believe the line she'd fed him about wanting a porno video.

'Elsa!' She sauntered across and Curtis covered the phone. 'Who was the blonde?'

Elsa looked back to her john, and scratched the front of her wig. 'Hooker, used to hang round the pool halls, did a few tricks with her way back. She was something else, man, a real sleaze lady, but boozed out – Lorraine. We called her Lazy Lorraine. She'd never score a john, just waited until she was so smashed she wouldn't have known if she had one or not. She went with some weirdos, didn't give a fuck.' She hesitated a moment and then leaned closer. 'Maybe don't trust her too much, okay?'

Curtis gripped her wrist. 'What you mean?'

Elsa twisted free, pissed off because he'd hurt her. 'Word was she used to be a cop, that's all.'

Lorraine walked along the strip, stopped at two more bars and then spotted Nula paying off a cab. She called, Nula turned, was puzzled for a moment, and then recognized her.

'You got time for a drink?' Lorraine smiled.

'No, I just come on, I'm late.'

'How's Didi?'

Nula shrugged and they walked down the strip together. 'She's still got problems with her foot but she won't see a doctor – hates them.'

Lorraine asked again if she had time for a drink. Nula looked at her watch and agreed, but only a quickie. They went to a small coffee bar and sat with two espressos. Nula was edgy, constantly looking out at the strip.

210

'I wanted to ask you about the night Holly was murdered. A friend of mine was picked up by a real creep. He had wet slobbery lips, rimless glasses, quite middle America, not beat up . . . and she was uneasy about him. She figured she'd seen him the night Holly died – maybe it was him picked her up. Anyway, she did the business and got the hell out of his car.'

Nula stirred her coffee. 'Never saw nobody like that the night she got it. I tell you somethin' though. Didi, right, she was duckin' and divin', she sees the guy cruisin' down the road, right, she reckons she's scored but little Holly beat her to the punch.'

'Wait a minute. Are you telling me Didi saw Holly being picked up?'

'She said it was a guy in a sort of beige-coloured car.'

'Have you told anybody this?'

'No, why should I?'

'Because he might have been the guy who killed her.'

'Yeah, he might not. It was early, just after I come on, so . . .' Lorraine didn't like to push too hard. She started asking casual questions about how they worked it, the trannies and the straight chicks, but Nula wasn't interested.

'You think the john that picked up Holly might have been wanting Didi?'

'Jesus, I dunno. Why you askin' all these questions?'

Lorraine lit a cigarette. 'Just curious. Is Didi workin' tonight, then?'

Nula said she was at a motel with a regular, but she'd be around later. 'I gotta go. With Art gone, we're short of cash.' Nula rested her hands on the table. 'I said I'd not talk to you again because of Art. That was a bad thing you did, Art was a decent guy.'

'Come on, Nula, he was getting kids screwed. I saw the photographs, even saw Holly in a few of them.'

Nula leaned in close. 'How come you're so interested in Holly? What's she to you?'

'She's dead. Maybe I feel sorry for her – she was only seventeen.'

'So was I once! We had cops around – some fucker gave them a tip-off. We haven't done any photographic work for weeks – that's because of you, isn't it? You know, I been trying to place your face, like Didi says, we was at an AA meeting but . . . I don't trust you. Stay away from us.'

She walked out and Lorraine took the tab to the counter. As she turned to leave, she saw Curtis outside with Nula, who pointed to the coffee bar. Curtis pushed her, they seemed to be arguing, and then he turned to look in at the window. Lorraine saw the sign to the toilets and walked out. Curtis came in, asked for Lorraine and the waitress pointed.

Lorraine stood on the toilet seat. She heard the door creaking open, then footsteps and the other cubicle door pushed open. As there were just the two, she knew he would try the next door, and find her, but just as his footsteps stopped outside her door, the waitress walked in and told him to get out. Lorraine waited fifteen minutes before she eased open the door and peered into the coffee bar. Curtis was standing directly outside and there was no back exit, or none she could see, so she decided to front it out.

He turned fast when she came out. Suddenly his arm shot out and he grabbed her elbow. 'You askin' questions about Holly an' I wanna know why. What you askin' questions about my little baby for?'

She could see in his face he wasn't going to hurt her. He wasn't scared, just upset.

'What's it to you?' she asked.

'She was my girl.'

Lorraine pulled her arm free. 'Maybe for no reason but that I liked her.'

'You knew her?'

212

'Yeah, not well, but I knew her.' He made to move off. 'Curtis, wait a minute.'

He looked at her. 'I dunno what you want but stay away from here.'

She took a chance. 'Maybe I'm askin' for the cops.'

He stepped back fast, his face altered, his hands tightened into fists. Suddenly she knew that if they were alone he would hurt her, really hurt her.

'Not in the way you think, Curtis – come on, I was a hooker. All I'm doin' is feedin' back a bit of information, they got nothin' on her killer. Don't you want him caught? She was your girl, you just said so, she was beautiful, real beautiful, and—'

'She's dead, right, so fuck off.'

Curtis walked away and Lorraine followed. He turned into an alley and stopped. Now she no longer had the safety of other people around her.

'You got a fuckin' nerve, lady. Back off me.'

She stood four feet from him, far enough to keep out of range of a swinging fist. She held him in a steady gaze, not afraid, showing him she was on the level, letting him look at her.

'I'm bein' paid under the counter, fifty bucks. I'm not paid to do anythin' else, just see if there was anyone who saw her that night, saw the john that picked her up. I don't want to know anythin' else. Help me. Why don't you help me? Come on, man, she was your girl.'

Curtis leaned against the wall and, to her astonishment, started to cry. Lorraine moved closer. 'She was picked up last time you saw her near Didi and Nula's patch, that right?' He nodded. She asked if he had seen anything, asked why Holly had been working the transsexual patch. He sniffed, wiping his face with the back of his hand. 'She'd had a fight further up the strip, that's all I know. She'd had this fight and we'd been talkin', she said she wanted to

213

move further down the strip, I was sortin' it for her. I never got to tell her I really cared—'

'Now's your chance to make it up to her, Curtis. If you hear anything, know anybody that saw anything, will you contact me?'

'I don't work for cops.'

'I'm not a cop.'

She made him write her telephone number on the back of his hand. Then he walked off down the alley.

Lorraine sighed. She was about to walk back the way she came when it hit her.

'Freeze.'

The boy ran on, his Superman stripe lit up in the neon lights.

'Freeze.'

He didn't turn because he hadn't even heard her, because it wasn't a gun in his hand but a Sony Walkman.

Sweat broke out all over her body. Her mouth felt dry and rancid. All she could think of was getting a drink. She started to run, back up the alley, along the strip, banging into passers-by, her whole body aching, her brain screaming for a drink. '*No, no, I won't, don't do it, don't do it, just keep walking, keep walking.*' A lethal, whispering voice repeated over and over, 'You killed the poor kid, he wasn't involved, you emptied your gun into a little kid's back. How does that make you feel, you drunken bitch? You killed him.'

Lorraine walked until the panic attack subsided. She sat on a wall, gasping for breath, waiting for her heart to slow down. She knew what she had done, but refused to face it. She had never faced it.

'You okay?' Didi limped towards her. 'You ran right past me like you'd seen a ghost.'

'I did. I was just running from a drink.'

Didi laughed, understanding. 'Well, if you're okay I guess I'd better get a move on.'

'No, please, I need to ask you something, about the night Holly died. *Please* just wait.'

Didi hobbled closer. 'Listen, I don't know nothin', I didn't see nothin' and I don't know why I'm talkin' to you. We had cops asking questions, we can't get a shoot together, we're broke, all down to you.'

Lorraine faced her out. 'I'm not a cop. I was once but so long ago even I can't remember it. I've been hookin' for years and drunk for as many, you know that.'

Didi pursed her lips. 'Once one, always one.'

Lorraine caught hold of Didi's sleeve. She gripped her hand, feeling the heavy ring on Didi's finger. 'Please just tell me about the guy. The one Nula said you saw. He picked her up right on your patch.'

'I don't remember nothin', not even that night, they're all the same to me.'

'Come on, Didi, it was the night you got beat up. Did you see the john that picked her up, see his car?'

Didi shrugged. 'Maybe. Nula's been talkin' to you, has she?'

'Yeah, and Curtis. They both want to help me, so please, just tell me what happened that night.'

Didi told Lorraine almost the same story as Nula – how the car had cruised down the road, stopped, driven on, how Holly had run across the road and got into the passenger seat.

'You think he really wanted maybe you or Nula?'

'If he did we're lucky then, aren't we?'

'Close your eyes and think, Didi. Was he dark, blond, balding? Think about him.'

Didi tried but her mind was blank.

'Did he wear glasses, kind of rimless, pinkish-lensed glasses?' Lorraine prompted.

'Yeah, yeah, maybe he did.'

'Was his mouth wide, wet? Did he have a crew-cut? Short-haired, blondish hair?'

'Yeah, yeah, that's right.'

'He never cruised by you before?'

'I remember anyone that's near to a regular, darlin'. I'd never seen this guy.'

Lorraine cocked her head to one side. 'You're not holding anythin' out on me, are you? You're not just saying, yeah, yeah, because that's what I said?'

'Why would I do that? He kind of fitted the description you said but it was a while ago. Listen, I knew Holly, and like everybody else round here, we'd like that piece of shit put away, right?'

'If you think of anything, will you call me?'

Didi nodded and limped off to earn her night's cash.

Lorraine arrived home to find a note from Rosie saying Rooney had called and she had gone to a meeting. Rooney was not at the station so she called his home. When she got through he sounded hoarser than ever, she could hear his heavy rasping breathing. 'You can go see Fellows now, he's expecting you – and I'm expecting somethin' soon for my dough, understand?'

Lorraine fixed some food, stuffed vitamins down herself and, a little refreshed, left the apartment.

Rosie, meanwhile, had returned to Janklow's house on Beverly Glen. At night it was easier to park and remain semi-hidden. She pulled out the camera, double-checked the instruction manual and then took a few practice shots. She heard a car come up the hill behind her and stop in front of the barred gates. It was the Mercedes. Crouching, Rosie inched up over the front seat. 'Come on, you bastard, get out of the car, lemme get a good shot.'

The driver opened the gates by remote control, never looking in Rosie's direction. She could see the glint of his glasses but nothing more – the top of his head was hidden by the roof of the car. The gates closed behind him as he drove up to the house. Rosie got out and, still carrying the camera and keeping close to the hedges, made her way cautiously towards the gates, hoping to get a second shot as he got out of the car to go into the house. She fiddled and muttered, the zoom lens was loose, and by the time she had it tightened the man was inside.

Rosie returned to the car. She'd tried, she told herself. As she turned on the ignition, the engine coughed and died. She tried again, it coughed, spluttered and then died again with a low, whirring sound. 'Oh, fuck it!' She tried another three times to start it but the ominous whirring sound grew fainter and she was miles away from the main road. She got out and started to walk.

The road she was in was badly lit, so she kept to the centre as much as possible. Two cars passed her going down the Glen and, even though she stuck out her thumb, they didn't stop. Her feet were aching and she was working up quite a sweat. She wished she'd locked the camera in the trunk; it was heavy and the strap cut into her shoulder.

When Rosie reached the main road, she was past caring about Janklow or anything else. She was hungry and it was getting chilly. She heard a car behind her and looked up to the traffic light. The 'Walk' sign was blinking and she reckoned she'd never make it across the wide road before it blinked off, so she hovered at the kerb. The Mercedes paused at the red light just as Rosie realized it was the car. She fumbled with the camera and made out she was taking a shot of the sign 'Hollywood Stars' Homes Maps Here'. She had the bonnet of the car in focus just as the lights changed to green, and then the car moved off. It was not a man driving, but a blonde woman, wearing dark glasses, a silk scarf wrapped round her throat.

Rosie got two, possibly three, reasonably clear-angled

shots before the car disappeared out of sight. She caught a bus and got off at Sunset, called home, but when there was no reply decided she'd take the film round to the all-night Photomat Snap store, and get a set of prints made up while she waited. She also had to arrange with the rental company to collect the car. Suddenly being busy rather than in limbo, as she'd been for so long, made it all okay again. She handed over the roll of film and settled down outside the store with an ice-cream cone. She had half finished the big strawberry and chocolate ice cream when she saw the Janklow Mercedes passing. The blonde woman was alone, hunched over the driving wheel and wearing black gloves. She reminded Rosie of an old movie star, with her thick make-up, black sun-glasses, or maybe someone else, but she couldn't put her finger on it. Rosie sucked her hand, sticky with ice cream. She was good at remembering faces. She could match those puzzles, the jigsaw faces of stars, faster than a bat of the eye. Julie Andrews's lips, Goldie Hawn's eyes, Jane Fonda's nose. She concentrated and then remembered. She was sure she'd seen the blonde woman at the art gallery, the one Lorraine had worked at. Confident she was right, Rosie returned to the store and collected the photographs.

As she waited for the bus back to Pasadena, she ripped open the envelope and sifted through the pictures. On the whole they were disappointing, especially the ones she had taken up in Beverly Glen, but there was one clear set of the blonde woman. She couldn't wait to tell Lorraine but, to her disappointment, the apartment was still empty when she got home. It was way after ten and she began to worry. She fed the cat, and then sat by the phone but when Lorraine didn't call she started to lay out the photographs on the table. She turned the one of the woman round, held it up, studied it from every angle, and then it hit her. It was not a woman at all, but a man. When she squinted at the photograph of the driver who had first pulled through

218

those gates in the Mercedes, even though it revealed only half his face, Rosie was sure that the blonde woman, and the man they presumed to be Steven Janklow, were one and the same.

CHAPTER 11

AT THE University of California, Lorraine paid off the cab and headed for the main entrance and reception. She went up to a janitor who was polishing the floor.

'Excuse me, I've come to see a Mr Fellows.'

He switched off the noisy machine. 'He's not here, was he expecting you?' Lorraine nodded. The janitor checked in the visitor's book. 'He's not in the laboratory but I think he's over on the squash courts.'

No one paid her any attention as she approached the entrance. A group of students wearing tennis whites passed her, laughing and talking loudly; young tanned limbs, healthy fresh-faced kids, gleaming teeth, shiny hair. They made her feel old, unclean and uneasy.

Professor Fellows was on court six with a partner called Brad Thorburn, according to the booking card on the gate. The sound of the squash ball was like cracking thunder and more thunder emanated from court six than any other. Lorraine slipped into a seat at the end of a row overlooking the court. As neither player looked up to acknowledge her, she was able to watch both men and wonder which was Fellows.

She leaned forward, her concentration on the man she thought must be him, red-faced and sweating profusely as he lunged and hurtled round the court. She was sure Red-face had to be Fellows, hoped it was, because his partner attracted her. She had not been attracted to any man for so long that it threw her slightly, but it was not until she had sized up Fellows that she slowly turned her attention to Thorburn. He didn't yell but gave small grunts of satisfaction, like a man fucking somebody well, those short hard grunts. He snapped out, 'Yes, yes, yes,' every time he did a good shot and gave a smile of recognition when he missed one. It was his smile, a half parting of his lips, that attracted her. He was much taller than Fellows, she reckoned about six two, maybe more. His body was perfectly proportioned with long, muscular legs, dark-tanned with not too much hair, though she knew he would have a thick thatch around his genitals – a man with black hair always had. Because he was sweating, his hair clung to his head, thick, short hair, and she knew he would have a chest to match – she could see it, just, through his high-sleeved, fashionable T-shirt. This man was very different from Fellows. He kept hitching up his shorts as he swung his racket back and forth, bending forward as Fellows lined up a shot, and dragging his wristband across his forehead. His hands were strong and big. Lorraine inched further forward to get a better view of his face. His dark eyebrows were fine and his eyes . . . He turned and looked up. They were dark greenish-blue.

Fellows looked up and waved. 'Are you Lorraine Page?' She nodded. 'Won't be long.'

The game continued for another ten minutes and then she presumed Fellows won as he yelled his head off and flung his arm around his partner, who picked up a pristine white towel and wiped his face, arms and neck before draping it round his shoulders. He didn't acknowledge Lorraine as he walked out of the court. Fellows, however, gave a wide grin and shouted that he would meet her in reception in five minutes.

She sat for a few moments. She pressed her crotch. It shocked her just how attractive she had found Brad Thorburn. She hadn't wanted a man since she could remember

221

and this one had sneaked up like the hard black ball they had been thrashing around the court. It felt as if it had hit her in the groin: she ached, she was wet, and she was scared to walk out and face him. Not until she felt the old Lieutenant Page surface, the one that didn't give a shit what any man said or made her feel, did she leave her seat.

Lorraine waited in the main reception. An even pinker-faced Fellows finally emerged with his kitbag, now wearing slacks and a shirt with a sweater tied round his neck. 'Sorry to keep you waiting but Captain Rooney didn't give me an exact time.'

'That's okay.' She looked past him, half hoping his partner would come out, half hoping he wouldn't. He didn't. Fellows took her by the elbow and walked her out into the cool night. He continued to chatter in an open, friendly manner as they crossed the courtyard and returned to the main hall. He hoped she didn't mind having their discussion at his apartment as the main laboratories and his office were closed for the evening. He picked up his car keys from the janitor and, still with a light gentlemanly touch to her elbow, guided Lorraine to the staff parking lot where an English MG sports car, like Mike's wife's, Lorraine remembered, headed towards them. Fellows waved and Lorraine purposely didn't look as she knew it would be Brad Thorburn. Instead she kept her attention on Fellows, saying how kind it was of him to see her. When she was seated in the passenger seat of Fellows's odd little Japanese car, she clenched her buttocks, angry because she was still sexually aroused. She had wanted to see Thorburn, wanted to see a man that had made her feel like a woman again.

'It was a very interesting game,' she said rather lamely.

'Yes, first time I've beaten him this year. He's an old friend – we were at Harvard together.'

'Does he teach here too?'

'Good God, no. He's rich as Croesus. He's a writer, but he runs a big vintage car garage out in Santa Monica. He imports the cars, has them refurbished and then sells them at immense profit. It's just a pastime really, because he's got a garage full of his own. He started up to keep them in good condition and now it's a flourishing business. Anything that man touches flourishes. He's got the Midas touch but you'd never know it. He's a charming, unassuming man. I'm sorry I didn't have time to introduce you but you didn't come to meet my old college buddy, did you, Miss Page?'

Fellows chatted on about real estate and how his property had lost its value. Nothing he said was of any importance but he was trying to work out what had suddenly made her so tense and distracted. He wondered if she was uncomfortable being driven to a stranger's home but she didn't seem the type who couldn't take care of herself, especially after what Rooney had told him about her. As if she had read his mind, she suddenly asked what Rooney had said to him.

'That you used to be a lieutenant, and a good one.'

She laughed and he found it attractive, a low, soft gurgle more than a laugh.

'Was that all?'

He paused at traffic lights. 'Yes, well, he implied that you made a mess but he didn't embroider.'

'So what did he tell you?'

Fellows drove on, turning into Marmont Avenue. 'Something about a drinking problem.'

Before they could continue, he turned into a driveway. The house was as neat as Fellows, a swimming pool taking up most of the garden. Lorraine calculated the property would be worth around one and a quarter million dollars, perhaps more.

Fellows opened Lorraine's door for her and waited for her to get out. The front door opened and a pleasant, rather plump woman waved from the porch. 'Dilly, this is Lorraine Page. She's working on the case I told you about.'

Lorraine felt an immediate warmth towards Dilly, short for Dylisandra. The interior of the house mirrored her generous personality – open plan, comfortable, not ostentatious. The sitting room was filled with deep, inviting sofas and thick Moroccan-style coffee tables, big lamps, spotlights focusing on large, bright canvases. The one that hung over a stone fireplace was of a man reclining, stark naked. The painting was impressive: no matter where you sat in the room you couldn't help but be drawn to the figure, or, more specifically, to his large penis and balls that were over-prominent.

Dilly worked in the kitchen, opening wine, talking nineteen to the dozen as she listed who had called and left messages. Fellows took himself off to his study and his answer machine, excusing himself.

The meal was simple – tossed salad, steak – but served beautifully. Lorraine was relaxing and enjoying their company, when Dilly brought the conversation round to Brad Thorburn. 'Now there's a man I could go for,' she said to Lorraine. 'That's his portrait over the fireplace, by the way. I know it doesn't look like him – that's because he refused to sit still long enough for me to get his head right, but I think I got everything else okay. Well, Andy says I've been a little optimistic about the genital area but I'm not. I just painted what I saw and, to be perfectly honest, at times it was very difficult to hold my brushes straight.' She laughed loudly, tossing her head back.

Fellows smiled adoringly at his wife, without a hint of jealousy. 'I've tried to introduce him to more girlfriends than you could imagine. They all fall for him but he's a real choosy guy.'

He suddenly stood up, ruffling his wife's hair. 'We've not come here to talk about Brad Thorburn. Can you bring coffee into the den?'

'Sure. How do you take it, Lorraine?'

'Black, honey if you've got it.'

Fellows said, 'I thought you'd take it that way. It fits with how clean-cut you are, direct.'

Dilly snorted. 'Don't pay attention to him, he's always saying things like that! It used to be his big pulling trick, now he just does it for effect!'

Fellows's study was lined with books and photographs, many of them featuring Thorburn. Lorraine walked round the room, with its leather armchairs and wide stacked desk. She looked at a photograph of Fellows and Thorburn together on a fishing trip. Fellows stood behind her.

'Where does he live?'

'Up in the Canyon. It's the family home, he's got them littered all over the world but that's his sort of base. He had quite a strange upbringing. His father left his mother when he was just a toddler and remarried God knows how many times.'

'Is he an only child, then?'

'No, I think there was an older brother but Brad was left the money.'

Dilly appeared with the coffee and bade them goodnight. Lorraine liked her and Fellows too. He was a man she felt she could talk to, a man she *wanted* to talk to, but not about the murder. She felt he would be dependable, honest, a man with no ulterior motive, a rare creature. Fellows briefly outlined his interest in the murder. She listened intently, knowing much of what he was saying because she had read the files, but she liked the reassuring sound of his voice.

'I hear there's been a development with Norman Hastings – cross-dresser. Well, I said Rooney would probably find something. Interesting, huh?'

He had thrown the ball neatly into her court.

'Yes, it is.'

'You asked to see me. For what reason?'

'To see if you knew more.'

'You think I do?'

'I don't know.'

'I think *you* do.'

She met his steady gaze. Lorraine was the one to break the look. 'Why do you think he kills?'

Fellows leaned back. 'Lorraine, nobody knows what makes a man kill, if not in the armed forces or under pressure or supreme emotional strain. I don't believe any man simply kills. There is always a reason.'

'What reason is behind our killer?'

'I don't know because there is no cohesive pattern. They are not all hard-faced prostitutes. One was a cross-dresser, one a seventeen-year-old.'

'What if the seventeen-year-old was a mistake?'

'What do you mean?'

Lorraine repeated what she had discussed with Nula and Didi, and Fellows leaned forward, frowning. 'So you're saying our killer was after one of your friends. Is she blonde?'

'Bleached. She said the driver stopped and Holly ran across the road to him, got into the car. I think Hastings knew the killer,' Lorraine continued, 'and that the killer is a cross-dresser or a transvestite.'

'Why?' Fellows asked.

'Because he seems to hate women, maybe women his own age. I think he hates the woman he becomes, the woman he attempts to be when he's dressed up.'

Fellows closed his eyes. 'Where does Hastings fit in?'

'Hastings may have known him and been suspicious. Perhaps he was about to expose him to the police . . .'

Fellows tugged at his ears. 'There is one person who must be found, the woman he attacked, the one in the parking lot. I don't think the police realize the importance of this witness. She saw him, his face, smelt him, he attacked her and, according to the witnesses, she was covered in blood. Both they and the cab driver have described her – tough, hard-faced, tooth missing, scrawny, lank-haired . . .'

Lorraine's heart was thudding.

'I don't think she was a whore, though, or at least not like the other women. I think this one was different. She was educated, knew enough to . . .' He looked directly at Lorraine. 'Did you read the transcripts of that phone call she made? Clear, concise description. I told Rooney it was almost like a professional description, as if she had been attached to the police in some capacity.'

Lorraine coughed. He was bloody good – did he know? 'I agree but I don't think they'll find her.'

He shrugged. 'Then they're not looking, are they? Because she's still in this area.'

'Why?'

'Because she wouldn't give her name. She wants to remain anonymous.'

'That doesn't mean she didn't pick up a trucker and is out of town. Just because she didn't give her name doesn't mean anything.'

'She wanted him caught! If she was moving on, why bother calling the police? I think she's still around.'

'Will he kill again?'

'Of course, when the mood takes him. He must be feeling good – he has to know that the police have nothing. Even the press has died down.' He paused, then went on, 'This is his sex life, his action, and it's connected to his own sexuality. He will get no pleasure from masturbation, he's probably impotent so his masculinity is warped. He is both male and female, and he is killing as a man. We know this because the anonymous caller gave a good description of what he was wearing. So we're not looking for a man who dresses as a woman and then kills. We're looking for a man who consistently wants to kill. Just as you said, I too think he wants to kill the woman inside him.'

Fellows sat on the arm of his chair, swinging one leg. 'You killed a boy, Rooney told me. He said you were drunk on duty.'

Lorraine felt as if she'd been punched. She didn't like the way he was looking at her.

'Do you remember what it felt like?'

He had to strain to hear what she said. 'I had to kill a number of people in the line of duty and you never forget one of them.'

'You did not answer the question. I asked if you recalled what it felt like to kill that boy.'

'Yes,' she said quietly, 'of course I remember.'

He stared at her intently, knew she was lying but he was astonished at the way she held his gaze and didn't flinch away.

'But you were intoxicated.'

'Yes.'

'But you remember.'

She broke his gaze and he knew she was in trouble. Lorraine stood up, pulling her skirt straight. 'It's not something I'm likely to forget.'

'Why?'

'Because it must be fucking obvious why. The boy was innocent and I was drunk.'

'Even though you were intoxicated, you remember. As you said, you never forget. What exactly don't you forget?'

Lorraine sighed and lit a cigarette. 'I don't see the point of this.' She inhaled deeply, let the smoke drift, was about to take another drag when she paused and, without any emotion, described the boy's jacket, the yellow Superman stripe, the way he fell, as if in slow motion, the way his body folded, the way his head rested against his out-stretched arm, the way his soft hair fanned out, the way his body jerked a few times before he became still. Once she had begun she couldn't stop, remembering Rooney pushing past, ordering her into the patrol car, displaying in his filthy handkerchief the boy's Walkman, the tape still in the deck. That there had been no gun, that she had fired six times. She fell silent. Fellows had expected her to break down and weep.

'What about afterwards?' he asked softly. She intrigued him.

Lorraine stubbed out her cigarette, becoming annoyed that he had swung their meeting over to her life rather than the killer's.

'I felt fucking angry, desperate, disgusted, and all I wanted was to forget it.'

'How did you do that?'

'With booze, of course.'

'And did it block it out?'

She shook her head. 'Yes. I suppose you want me to say no, that it was always there, that it always will be. Well, I'm sorry to disappoint you, I don't think about it.'

Fellows picked up a paperweight. 'But you were drinking before this boy. What made you dependent on alcohol?'

'I was just addicted to it, like my mother. It's supposed to be inherited, isn't it?'

'Why did you drink, Lorraine?'

'I guess I liked the way it made me feel, the confidence it gave me – not having to think or feel. Now, can we get back to the reason I asked to see you?'

'What main thing did you not feel?' He looked into her eyes, with an expression of concern, almost apologetic. 'I'm sorry, I don't mean to pry.'

She laughed. 'Can't help yourself, huh?'

He gently touched her cheek. 'You're a clever woman, a strong woman – possibly the strongest I've ever met. I'm sorry to delve into your private life but I'm trying to get you to think like him, understand him. Like you felt the compulsion to have another drink, he will feel this compulsion to kill. He will be in a kind of torment because maybe something happened to him that twisted him, hurt him,

229

and the only way he is able to live in society and carry on in a state of apparent normality is like this. When this consuming pain takes hold of him like a rage, he will control it, contain it, and release it when he hammers a victim to death. Only then does the rage subside and calm or normality return.'

Fellows paced up and down his banks of books, all of which were serial killers' histories, and slapped each in turn. 'I have pinpointed the rage syndrome in so many of these cases. It manifests itself in an overpowering need to wound, to destroy, to hurt, to inflict pain. Time and again it is sexual: stalking, peeping, watching and knowing what they were about to commit will be exquisite, relished – and enjoyed. Many collect the newspaper cuttings to gloat over. The fact they are clever enough not to be detected adds to the overall feeling of enjoyment. And when it's over they integrate back into their homes, their work. Their secret is like a lover, precious, nurtured, controlled until the pain starts again. It's a horrific vicious circle that cannot be broken until the killer is caught.'

Lorraine put her cigarettes and lighter into her purse. 'I really must go. Would you call me a cab?'

Fellows reached for the phone, and started to punch the buttons. Seemingly intent on his task, he asked calmly why, if she wanted to assist in the inquiry, she hadn't admitted that she was the woman the killer picked up.

'Because, Professor Fellows, I am not.'

He ordered the cab and stuffed his hands into his trouser pockets. 'I know you were a prostitute, I know the address you've just given to me for the cab tonight was also close to the area where the witness was dropped off by a cab driver. Ex-cop, it was you who called the station, you who gave the description. I just don't understand why you're lying.'

'I'm not.' She stared at him.

'He said you were one of the best he'd ever worked with.'

Lorraine snapped that Rooney had a big mouth, but he knew nothing about her life since she'd left the force.

Fellows became equally tetchy, opening a file and pushing it across the desk. 'I'd say this is pretty informative.'

She pursed her lips as she saw the copy of her record. 'The bastard,' she said, and then she deflated, slumping into the big leather chair. 'Does he know? Rooney?'

'No, in fact *I* wasn't sure, until I met you, talked with you. You're in a very precarious position, my dear.'

'How did you work it out?'

'I just took one almighty guess.' He snickered. 'I threw in a wild card.'

She laughed, tilting her head back, a deep, warm laugh that made him smile.

'The description in the files fits – tall, blonde – except the missing tooth.'

'I had it capped.'

Fellows sat on the arm of her chair. 'I can't see any need to tell Rooney, unless you're holding anything else back?'

Lorraine took hold of his hand, gave it a squeeze, and then looked up into his face. 'I'm not holding anything back, Prof. Just wish I had something else to get me fifty bucks a day when Rooney's off the case. I doubt if anyone else would trust me.'

'They're fools. Does that mean the FBI will take over?'

'Yes, within the next forty-eight hours. What about dates? Is there anything in the dates the killings took place?'

Fellows frowned. 'I doubt it. He just kills when he feels the urge, no specific date code.' He sighed. 'I'm sorry I couldn't be more help but if I sift through the files again, find something, can I call you?'

She nodded.

'Good, and will you call me if you find anything? It's interesting to me or I wouldn't have spent so much time on it already, and, I might add, with no fifty bucks a day.'

The doorbell rang. He walked her to the cab. 'It's paid for, so don't worry. And if you need me, call me.'

She smiled her thanks and he remained watching her until the cab turned out of the drive.

Back in the den, he picked up the dirty ashtray piled high with cigarette stubs – fifteen. He tipped it into the waste basket, then straightened the leather cushions, and went upstairs to the bedroom.

Dilly was sleeping, her arms entwined round a pillow. She hardly stirred when he slipped into bed and turned off his bedside lamp. He rested his head on his arms and thought about Lorraine. There was an arrogance about her that attracted him and a directness he admired. There was also, he detected, a deep, hidden pain which, in his professional opinion, was about to erupt.

CHAPTER 12

LORRAINE ASKED the cab driver to take her to Beverly Glen. She would meet any extra costs. By the time they parked outside Janklow's house, she was already annoyed with herself for not asking Fellows if the name meant anything to him or had any connection to Brad Thorburn. She was also confused as to why she had told the cab driver to take her there.

She stood a short distance from the gates. The dog was still loose, sleeping about ten feet inside. He woke and growled, his tawny eyes daring her to lay so much as a hand on the gate. As the rental car had been towed away, nothing indicated that Rosie had been back. The house was in darkness, shutters closed on the lower-floor windows, and the drive was empty. It seemed ominously quiet and yet there was nothing creepy about the property, quite the opposite. Lorraine stepped closer and her body set off the automatic security lights. The gardens, the lower storey of the house, the gates, even the road she was standing in, were suddenly bathed in brilliant light.

She started back to the taxi when she heard someone calling. She paused and looked back.

'Bruno must have set the security lights off again. *Bruno!*'

Brad Thorburn, wearing shorts and flip-flops, appeared at the front door. The dog ran to him, standing on its hind legs to lick his face. Brad ruffled its fur and scanned the garden for an intruder, but his voice was mocking when he clapped his hands and said to the dog, 'See them off, go on, good boy.'

Lorraine whipped round as the cab driver tooted his horn. 'You want to stay here much longer? Only I got another fare to pick up.'

She had her hand on the door when the gates opened. Thorburn looked over the road and was about to close the gates, when he looked again. 'Hey! Were you at the college earlier?'

'Sorry,' Lorraine said innocently. 'Are you talking to me?'

He nodded. 'I was playing with Andrew Fellows.'

Lorraine smiled. 'What a coincidence.'

She turned back to the driver. 'Give me five minutes.'

'You got a problem?' Thorburn asked.

Lorraine walked over to join him. 'No, not really. I was supposed to drop in to collect something for a friend of mine. I thought it was number three eight hundred but I must have been mistaken.'

'Do you need to make a call? You can use my phone.'

'I won't be a second,' she called to the driver, who gave a surly nod. She grinned at Thorburn. 'My driver's fed up as we've been up and down the Glen. I didn't like to start ringing doorbells, with all the security around here.'

Thorburn pressed the gates closed and released the dog, which immediately launched itself at Lorraine, wagging its tail and slobbering. 'He's not quite got it together yet, he's only a puppy. This way . . .'

The hallway alone took her breath away. It was an antique mixture of Baroque furniture, massive chandeliers and gilt mirrors, but it was not oppressive because the pieces were not crowded together. The hallway was of such a grand scale, it could easily have accommodated a number of vehicles parked side by side.

'Phone's on the table just through that arch. I'm Brad Thorburn.'

'Lorraine Page.'

He walked off and Lorraine went towards the wide archway. The room was sunken, with deep white sofas and a single glass-topped coffee table with a basket of flowers the like of which Lorraine had only seen in magazines. The paintings were all huge and the white telephone was the smallest object in the room. She called Rosie.

'Hi, it's me.'

Without a pause for breath, Rosie gave her a tongue lashing – how worried she was, that she was just about to call Jake and get a search party out looking for her.

'I'm sorry, I got lost. I'll come straight home now.'

Rosie tried to tell her about the photo session but Lorraine could hear the sound of the flip-flops across the white marble hallway.

'I won't bother tonight, I've got a taxi waiting. Goodnight.'

She replaced the receiver before Rosie could utter another word.

'Can I get you a drink?' He had put on a loose white caftan over his shorts.

'Ah, no, I'd better go, but thanks for the offer and the use of your phone.' She could feel herself blushing, so she dipped her head.

'Did you go over to Andrew's?'

'Yes, we had a relaxed dinner, just Dilly and Andrew.'

He smiled. 'I've offered her money to take that painting down. I know you've seen it because you won't look at me.'

She hadn't even thought of the painting, it was him she couldn't look at. They walked towards the front door, which was still ajar. As they stepped onto the porch, her taxi drove off.

'Since your transport has departed, will you change your mind?'

'No, thanks all the same, but if you could call me another cab . . .'

'Don't you drive?'

'Yes, I do but I also used to drink. The two didn't go together. Now I don't drink or drive.'

He took her elbow. 'Come and sit down. Let me fix you a soft drink, or tea or coffee, if you'd prefer?'

Brad took her into the kitchen. It was like a movie set – more appliances and high-tech equipment than she'd seen in any restaurant. He poured her a glass of iced water, then crossed to a wall phone, asking her what she did for a living. She told him she worked part-time for an art gallery. He turned to look at her. 'Anyone I'd know of?'

'I doubt it, it's not very successful.' She knew she had to concentrate on using this situation and told herself to stop acting like a tongue-tied teenager. This was too good an opportunity to pass over. Maybe she did fancy him but she had to ignore it. It was unlikely he'd have any interest in her – Dilly had said that all his women were young, perfect beauties. But she was sure, unless she was kidding herself, that – wasn't he putting out signals? She gave him a hooded glance as he picked up the receiver but he turned and caught her looking at him. He didn't smile but met her eyes and then his attention was drawn to the phone.

'The cab will be here in about fifteen minutes.'

'Thanks.' She decided to start doing the job she was there for. 'You have a wonderful home, do you live here alone?'

'No, my brother's here as well. You want me to show you around?' Politely, he led her through one vast ornate room after another. He was obviously uninterested, so they viewed each quickly and Lorraine hardly said a word. It was not until they went upstairs that his closeness made her feel uncomfortable. He touched her elbow as he showed off the master bedroom, with floor-to-ceiling white silk curtains that Barbara Stanwyck might have draped herself in. It lacked the freshness of the other rooms.

'This room's different,' Lorraine said, and walked further inside, her feet sinking into thick-piled, soft rose-coloured carpets.

'My mother's room. She likes it kept this way.'

She saw photographs in heavy silver frames, at least fifteen, clustered on the dressing table. The main one was of an astonishingly beautiful woman, pale blonde hair, elegant, a classic beauty.

'My mother.'

'She's stunning, very beautiful.'

'Yes, she is – or was. She's now made herself into a plaster cast, hardly recognizable as the same person. I don't think she has a single feature she hasn't attempted to freeze in time. She refused to age gracefully. And that was my father. I think the only reason it's here is because she looks so wonderful in the same photograph. He died a long time ago.'

Lorraine picked up a smaller picture frame. 'That's my brother, well, a half-brother. I think I was four, he'd be about twelve, different fathers.'

They heard the sound of a car heading up the drive. He replaced the picture and, crossing to the window, drew back the drape.

'Is that my cab?'

'No, they'll call from outside. It's just the staff returning.' He walked briskly to the door, impatient for her to follow, yet he remained the gentleman, holding the door open until she passed him, about to head down the stairs.

'No, come into my office.' He gripped her elbow and they walked along the landing and through another archway. 'Go in and sit down, I'll be right with you.'

He crossed to the banisters and looked down as the front door slammed. 'Don't put the alarms on, I'm waiting for a cab.'

'Are you going out?'

Lorraine was just about to go into the office. She paused. Although she had heard a man's voice, she had also heard the *click-click* of high heels.

'I've got somebody here – they're just going so stay down there.'

The *click-click* faded and a door below closed. Brad beckoned her into his so-called office, which was mostly windows with a vast array of books lining the walls. A modern desk was covered with a word processor and stacks of manuscripts.

'What kind of books do you write?'

He closed the door. 'You mean attempt to write! I haven't done it yet.'

He frowned as footsteps could be heard on the polished wooden stairs but they carried on up to the floor above them. Then he seemed to relax, pointing to a photograph of a vintage car. 'I have a collection.'

'Do you keep them all here?' Lorraine asked.

'No, I have a garage. I bought it to house my own vehicles, then I hired a mechanic to keep them in condition, and every other day somebody with a comparable car would appear and ask if my mechanic could help them repair it or where they could get a part, so I opened up a garage, dealing only in vintage imported or American cars.'

He looked up as the footsteps passed over the ceiling from the room above. 'Excuse me.'

He walked out and closed the door. As soon as it shut, Lorraine was at his desk, opening drawers, checking. She found stacks of notepaper with the S and A logo, envelopes, drawers full of magazines and more manuscripts. She looked over the bookcase – novels, theology, medicine, dictionaries, biography, autobiography – then opened a door into another room and saw the professionally equipped gym. She suddenly looked up as she heard low voices arguing. It was frustrating because she couldn't hear a word they were saying. A door slammed and then there were running footsteps. Lorraine hurried to sit down as Brad returned.

'Maybe you should call me another cab.'

He walked to the bookcase and removed a book. The entire wall fell back to reveal a large bedroom.

Brad bowed. 'There's even a private staircase leading out and down to the garden. If the cab hasn't arrived by the time we get there, I'll run you home.'

Lorraine passed him to walk into the bedroom. The king-size bed had several mirrors above it yet it didn't feel overtly sexual. The room was too orderly, everything pale oatmeal, even the polished wooden floors. The walls were covered with photographs, mostly of blonde women.

'My harem, as Dilly calls them.' Lorraine moved closer and he stood directly behind her. 'She says they were interchangeable. What do you think?'

She could feel the heat of him but she calmly looked from one girl to the next. 'I think they're lovely.'

He touched her shoulder, a light feather touch, and then slowly traced down her arm. He reached for her hand and drew it back slightly to feel his erection.

'I want to fuck you.' His voice was hardly audible.

She did not withdraw her hand but allowed him to press it against his erect cock. Her whole body seemed to catch fire, and then she laughed. 'Dilly's painting doesn't exaggerate, does it?'

She moved her hand, without his assistance, slowly over his erection and he moaned. She closed her eyes, she didn't want it to happen. He pressed closer and his right hand began slowly to unbutton her blouse, pushed beneath her bra to feel her nipples. They were hard and he knew she was aroused. He bent his head to kiss her neck. His tongue licked as he pulled her blouse further open, while her legs began to spread as if out of her control.

'No,' she whispered. 'Please don't do this to me. I don't want this, I have to go.'

She wanted to scream, wanted him to go on. She could feel herself start to pant as he massaged her nipples. She knew that if he reached down, put his hand between her legs, she wouldn't be able to resist – but she had to make it stop, walk away from him. She pushed his hands off but he turned her roughly to face him and kissed her lips. It was a sweet, gentle kiss and she craved more and pressed against him. She felt her arms lifting to hold him.

'How did you get this?' He traced the scar on her cheek. 'It drives me crazy, you know that? It's so sexy, the way you tilt your head. You have beautiful eyes. I want to make love to you, Lorraine.'

She was embarrassed about her body, her scars, and hearing his husky voice, saying things she had never expected to hear from any man, let alone one as handsome as he was, made her want to weep.

'I have to go.'

'No, not yet.'

'Yes. Just get away from me.'

He stepped back as she buttoned her blouse, pulled down her skirt. She had to keep talking because if he laid so much as a finger on her again, she'd be unable to say no. 'I don't know what you think I am but you've got a fucking nerve. Now just stay the hell away from me – go fuck one of your classy blonde college kids but don't come on to me because I'd make you pay, sweetheart. You picked the wrong lady.'

He stepped away from her, his face like a boy's in his confusion. She ran her hands through her hair and looked up to the mirrors. 'They may get turned on by this crap with the mirrors but please don't play out your fantasies with somebody you don't know, and will never know. Now, did you really call me a cab or was that all part of your pussy-suckin' game?'

'How much do you charge?' His face was taut with anger.

240

'*I* choose my clients. Now how do I get out of here?'

He grabbed her wrist and she did a quick twist, released her hand and brought it up to slap his face. 'Stay off me, rich boy.'

'I said, how much?'

She could feel her stomach lurch, wanting him to hold her, wanting him to stop her foul mouth, wanting him to kiss her just like he had a moment ago.

'Name your price!'

She looked for the door to get out. Shocking him hadn't worked. He was humiliated, angry, and even more attractive.

'I said name your price.'

She glared at him. 'You don't have it.'

'Want to bet? Five hundred? You want more? Seven fifty? You don't look like a thousand-dollar whore to me but if that's your price . . .'

He crossed to a wardrobe, opened one of the drawers and took out a wad of notes. Just as he was about to proffer them, the telephone rang. He tossed the money at her as he picked up the receiver. He listened and then let it drop. 'It's your cab. Why don't you leave me your number? Maybe we'll make it another night.'

She laughed as he opened the hidden door leading to the staircase into the garden. She didn't wait for him to direct her but headed straight down. He didn't follow, but stood, watching her.

'I meant what I said, Lorraine.'

She paused and looked up at him. 'I'm not a whore, Brad. I don't want you or your money. Goodnight.'

He waited until the door below closed, then relocked it automatically, stood to see her stride down the pathway, and pause to give the dog a few words. Then he used the remote switch on the main gates, saw her hesitate as they swung open, but she didn't look back. Maybe she didn't know he could see her.

He lay down on his bed, looking up at himself in the mirror, confused and still smarting from her rejection. He was not used to it, nor was he used to meeting a woman who excited him so much. The phone rang. He sighed with irritation and snatched it up.

'What do you want?'

'Did you switch the security lock on the gates?'

'Yes.'

Steven Janklow replaced the phone and walked into his bathroom, closing the door silently. Locked inside the house he felt safe and secure. He let his silk dressing gown fall away from his body, gazing at himself admiringly as he stepped into the perfumed water. As he slid slowly beneath the soft warm bubbles, he sighed with satisfaction.

Lorraine travelled home in style. The car was a stretch Mercedes, the driver wearing uniform. He did not say a word the entire journey. She was glad, she didn't feel like talking. Rosie, however, was still up and ready to launch in as soon as Lorraine opened the front door.

'You cut me off before I could tell you.'

'Rosie, I'm real tired. Can't this wait until morning?'

'No. I got the photographs developed. I went back to the Janklow house.'

'You did *what*?' Lorraine snapped.

Lorraine chucked her purse down. 'Listen to me, Rosie. This is not a game. You *never* – do you understand me? – *never* do anything unless you run it by me first. This is work for me.'

Rosie stuck out her lower lip like a child. 'I was only trying to help and then the car broke down. I hadda walk miles and get it towed back. I walked from the Janklow house all the way down—'

Lorraine interrupted, 'Jesus Christ, you broke down outside the house? I don't believe it.'

'Good thing I did because I saw the Mercedes and I got a good picture of the driver.'

Lorraine was hooked. 'Janklow?'

'Yeah, well, I think so. You tell me.'

Lorraine stared at the photographs, lingering longest on the blonde woman driver.

'Is that a man or a woman? You tell me.' Rosie made an elaborate show of matching the two sets of photographs, the ones with Steven Janklow driving, and the ones with the blonde woman.

'It would be hard to tell if it wasn't for the mouth.'

It was a wide mouth, a mouth Lorraine was sure belonged to the man who had attacked her. But she was concerned about Rosie, that she was becoming too involved and might do something that would get her into trouble or, even worse, get her hurt. 'We'll see if we can get them enlarged. Now, if it's okay with you, I'm going to bed.'

Lorraine slipped into her bed on the couch and drew the covers close up around her chin. She gripped the sheet tight, twisting it round her knuckles. She had wanted to be loved tonight, she had wanted to be held, kissed, but she had been so afraid because, after all this time, after so much loss, she didn't think she had any feelings left. Lubrinski's death had been the worst moment of her life. He was the only person who had given her the love she craved from her husband, who had loved her for what she was and asked nothing in return.

It began with a single, dry sob, wrenching upwards from the pit of her stomach. Afraid Rosie would hear, she bit the sheet, held it between her teeth as the second sob shook her body. She told herself to get control. 'Fucking take control of yourself, Page. People depend on you to be a rock. You start howling and you'll make us a laughing stock. There's a mother out there needing to know if her little girl is alive or dead – you show any emotion and she won't be able to take it. You want to weep, do it in your home, never on duty. You hearing me, Page?'

'Mrs Bradley, I'm sorry but we've found Laura, and I'm sorry to tell you . . . Laura's dead, Mrs Bradley.'

Rosie sat up. Something had woken her and she was afraid for a moment. Then she heard the strangled, awful sounds. She threw back the blanket and went in to Lorraine. She was rigid, the sheet clenched between her teeth, her knuckles white from the strain of gripping her fingers so tightly. The sound was like a wounded animal, a low mewing sound, as she tried to suppress the desire to scream. Rosie reached over and picked her up in her arms, holding her and rocking her. 'Let it go, Lorraine, let it free. It's only me, it's only big fat Rosie. You have a cry, let's hear you cry . . .'

The dam broke and the mewing sound erupted into gasping sobs as the tears flowed. Lorraine held onto Rosie as if she was drowning, as if she was terrified to let her go. She sobbed for almost two hours. She wept for everything she had lost, for her children, her husband, her dead mother, her brother, her father. She cried for the boy she had shot, she cried for Lubrinski and called out that she was sorry, sorry, and at long last she wept for herself, for what she had done to herself, for what she had forced herself to become.

At last the crying stopped. She was drained, so exhausted she couldn't speak. Her body still shook, and she made soft, hiccuping sounds as Rosie gently dried her face and together they walked into the bedroom. Rosie helped her into the bed, rinsed a facecloth so she could pat her face cool, and then got in beside her. Lorraine rested her head against Rosie, whose big fat arms cradled her friend as she said softly over and over, 'It's all over now, everything's going to be better now, honey. It's gonna be easy now.'

*

The ring of the telephone by the bed made Rooney's heart thud so loudly he thought he was having a heart attack. It was Bean. They had just got a report in. The body of a white woman, aged somewhere between thirty and forty, had been discovered in the trunk of a stolen vehicle. Judging by the look of the corpse, the killer had struck the victim from behind with a hammer, and she also had horrific facial injuries. Rooney flopped back, cradling the phone against his chest. His wife peered up at him, her face masked with nightcream.

'Dear God, we've got another one. He's done another.'

CHAPTER 13

ROONEY AND his lieutenant waited in the anteroom of the City Morgue. They could do little until they had further information from the pathologist. The stolen vehicle, a Lincoln Continental, had been towed to the yard and was being checked over by forensic experts. The owner of the vehicle had been traced, having reported his car stolen the previous day from outside his bungalow in Ashcroft Avenue, LA. Rooney was morose, knowing that the press would be on to the killing and had, more than likely, given it front-page coverage as he had declined to say anything to the photographers and reporters waiting outside the mortuary.

The Lincoln had been left in the third storey of a garage where it could have remained for days, along with all the other cars on long-term contracts. The only reason it had been investigated was that the alarm had been triggered off when another car accidentally touched the rear fender. According to the attendant, the ringing had been driving him nuts for almost an hour so he had gone to take a look. No long-term parking ticket was displayed on the window or on the dashboard, and he was about to return to his booth when he saw something dripping from beneath the trunk. At first he presumed it was oil but on closer inspection, realized it was blood and called the police.

Rooney sighed. 'He give a description of the driver?'

Bean shook his head. 'He said he wasn't on duty until

246

late and the car was already parked. We've got a number for the daytime attendant but we've not spoken to him yet.'

Rooney checked his watch. 'Get on to that right now.'

'I'm on my way.'

Rooney waited another two hours before the doors opened and the masked and gowned attendant gestured for him to follow. Draped in green sheeting, the body dominated the white-tiled room, whose strip-lighting gave a surreal white brightness to all the rows of instruments and enamel sinks.

'Morning, Bill,' said Nick Arnold, the pathologist, as he washed his hands at a large sink. 'You're pretty impatient for this one, aren't you? I hear you've been hovering outside – you should have come in.'

Rooney hated being anywhere near an autopsy. He'd never gotten used to the way corpses were sliced open, never been able to stand hearing the hiss of stinking gases or looking at the blood pumping out; the open, sightless eyes of the victim as their body was systematically inspected.

Arnold knew Rooney of old and understood he wouldn't want to take a close look. He appeared distinctly greenish already. 'Come and have a coffee,' he said pleasantly. 'It'll be a while before we get the photographs and tests completed.' He yawned. 'Got called out of bed for this one.'

'So did I,' muttered Rooney as he slumped into a low chair, its cushioned seat puffing loudly as his bulk made contact. 'So what you got for me?'

'Death occurred late evening – can't be more specific. Until I get my reports back, I can't pinpoint the exact time but it was evening and the last meal was banana bread.'

'That's a big help,' Rooney slurped his coffee.

'Victim's age was late thirties, may even be forty, but fit – good muscle tone.'

'Was she blonde?' Rooney asked.

'Yep, but who said "she" was female?'

'What?'

Arnold grinned. 'He was almost a she and at first glance I'd have said definitely female, heavy breasts, but he was also well endowed in the nether regions. Transsexual, Bill, one who'd been on a lot of hormone replacement treatment, Adam's apple has also been removed at some time.' He stood up and pointed to drawings. 'Hammer blow here to the base of the skull, which would have almost certainly rendered her unconscious. Her face was beaten to a pulp, nose, cheekbones and frontal lobe shattered, very heavy blows, one eye forced back into this region and the other socket split open by the force of the hammer. Not a pretty sight now but I would say she or he had at one time been quite attractive. Hair is bleached blonde, well cut. We've also got nothing from under her fingernails so the first blow was unexpected. She put up no resistance.'

Rooney went into the forensic laboratories to see the victim's clothes. They were reasonably expensive, some with well-known labels, but only the shoes would be helpful. They were large-sized, high-heeled stilettos and made in a specialist shoe store that catered for transsexuals and transvestites. As Rooney jotted down the information, he was sure he could get an identification of the victim quickly.

Bean joined up with him back at base. He had talked to the parking attendant, who had no recollection of the driver of the vehicle. He was sure the car had been parked there for more than twenty-four hours. The car's owner had been away for a week and only knew the car was missing when he returned home. Neither of the attendants could be certain of when the Lincoln had been left.

Rooney instructed officers to check out the garage. Perhaps the killer had stolen the car, left it there, then returned in another vehicle with his victim. Forensic reports from inside the Lincoln yielded no bloodstains, no fingerprints in the interior or the glove compartment, and the driving wheel had been wiped clean. They did, however, find long strands of blonde hair which were sent to be tested and matched to the victim's. All this took considerable time – time Rooney did not have. At nine thirty Chief Michael Berillo summoned him.

Rooney listened to him glumly. He was still to lead the officers in the inquiry but only until the FBI officers had familiarized themselves with the evidence. Then they would take over and, as Rooney's chief had said, 'You can start mowing the lawn, Bill.' He'd sounded gloating, even if unintentionally. Mowing the lawn was not something that Rooney pictured himself doing even if he'd retired of his own free will. Now this enforced 'release from duty' sat uneasily on his wide, sloping shoulders. 'You mustn't feel you've been ousted due to any unprofessional conduct or lack of ability. It's just that—'

Rooney leaned on the Chief's desk. 'You gotta have a scapegoat, someone to blame for not making an arrest. Sure, I understand. I just didn't expect to go out this way. I've given the best years of my life to the force but it don't matter. Somebody's got to pay for not finding this crazy bastard, so why not make me the sucker?'

'I'm sorry you feel that way, Bill.'

'At least I should have a chance to talk to this guy they brought in with them.'

The Chief coughed. 'They're with him now but I'm sure they'll let you talk to him later.'

Rooney knew they'd all been aware of the possibility he'd be replaced but his men seemed taken aback that it was happening so quickly. For all his bad-tempered ways, he was well liked. Bean, too, felt a trifle embarrassed. If Rooney was being moved, it meant that everyone on the case would be scrutinized. He repeated Rooney's request that until the FBI formally took over, they must all work double time.

No one attached to the case had yet had access to

Brendan Murphy or had seen him brought in. Bean patted Rooney's shoulder. 'Be just our luck if they walk in with a suspect and pin the whole string on him. They'll get all the glory and we'll be made to look fools.'

'We want to know who he or she is so that's our first priority.' Rooney jerked his head at the pictures of the last victim, already being pinned up, and plodded out of the incident room. He had decided to have one more crack at Mrs Hastings. The link between her husband, victim and cross-dresser, and the latest victim, was too much of a coincidence.

'Captain, should I take what we've got over to Andrew Fellows?' Bean called after Rooney. 'See if he can help us out at all?'

'Sure. I'll be interested to hear what Big Ears has to say.'

While Bean went off in search of Fellows, the rest of the team split up to make inquiries with known transsexuals, shoe and clothing stores that might recall the victim. Rooney assigned two men to run checks on the employees at the S and A vintage car garage in Santa Monica but told them to keep it low key.

Rooney stepped into the lift and went down to the basement. He proceeded along the brightly lit corridor towards the holding cells. He had to pass through innumerable security doors and left his weapon in the locker outside the last before he took the key. Then he joined the duty sergeant at his computerized board, which indicated every occupied cell and every corridor, a maze of small red and green lights.

'Where they got the suspect?'

The sergeant indicated cell fourteen.

'Any way I can hear what's going on?'

The sergeant gave him a sidelong look and flicked a switch. 'FBI been with him for hours.'

Rooney crossed to the bank of screens and gazed at the one showing the occupant of cell fourteen. Brendan

Murphy was sitting on the bunk bed, his hands held loosely in front of him. He was wearing a denim jacket and a stained T-shirt. His shoes had been removed. His beer gut, even larger than Rooney's, hung over his baggy old jeans. Rooney could not see who was in the cell with him but he heard the soft voice asking him to start from the beginning again and to take his time. Murphy seemed to stare directly into the camera and then ran his thick stubby hand over his square jaw.

'Jesus Christ, I'm gettin' confused, I'm hungry, I want some cigarettes. I dunno how many more times I can tell you I'd not seen my wife for almost ten months. I've not met the other woman more'n once or twice and that was fucking years ago. You got the wrong man.'

Rooney dragged on his cigarette. Murphy did not resemble the only description they had of the killer – nothing could be more different. He was thickset, over-weight, at least six two and, by the look of him, had never worn a jacket in his life. Murphy listed plaintively where he had been on the night of the murder and then stood up, angrily swinging his fist. 'I wasn't even in Los Angeles, for chrissakes. I told you all this in Detroit. You're gonna make me lose my job.'

Rooney had seen enough. He did not believe for a minute that Murphy was their man so let the FBI question him. The longer they were out of his hair the better.

He drove to Mrs Hastings, pausing on the way to buy some bourbon and a packet of mints. He took three heavy slugs from the bottle as he drove on, then unwrapped a peppermint to disguise the smell.

Rosie was woken by Lorraine presenting her with a cup of tea. She was dressed for a workout. 'I'll be back for breakfast,' she said brightly.

She pushed herself at the gym and Hector monitored her

weights. She also did a full step aerobic class. Then she had an ice cold shower and felt fit and sharp. She even ran from the bus back to the apartment – long, slow, steady strides, not pushing herself or working up a sweat.

Rosie had laid out all her vitamins, the protein drink, cereal, fruit and yogurt. Lorraine ate hungrily. It was still not nine o'clock but even after all her exertion she didn't feel tired. She was feeling like the old Lorraine Page used to feel before she hit the bottle.

'I met this guy called Brad Thorburn last night,' she said to Rosie. 'He knew the lecturer I went to see at the college, Andrew Fellows. They were playing squash and . . .' Lorraine stared into space, seeing him again, his handsome face, his athletic body. 'He lives at that house in Beverly Glen. He owns it. And that vintage car garage.'

Rosie pulled out a chair and sat down as Lorraine sifted through her photographs. She looked closely at the Mercedes, then at the man they presumed was Steven Janklow. All they had in focus was his chin and a bit of his right nostril. She drew the clearer photograph of the blonde woman beside it. 'I think you're right – this is the same person.'

Lorraine flipped through the files, checking for Norman Hastings's section. 'I want to go and talk to Hastings's wife. While I'm doing that, I want you to hire another car and pick me up there in a couple of hours. But first see if you can get a section of this picture of the woman blown up so we get to see more of his or her face.' Lorraine counted out some cash. It was running low again.

'Any chance you can touch that friend of yours to pay us a bit more?'

'I'll try but I doubt it.' Lorraine handed out sixty dollars, plus Mrs Hastings's address.

'You going to tell him about those photos?' Rosie asked.

'Not yet. We need more, I don't want to foul this up.'

252

Rosie picked up the newspaper from the steps outside and tossed it to Lorraine. 'See you later.'

As the screen door slammed after Rosie, Lorraine opened the paper. She couldn't miss the blazing headlines: 'HAMMER KILLER STRIKES AGAIN'. She laid the paper out flat on the table: no name for the victim, just that she was white, aged between late thirties and forties and found in the trunk of a stolen vehicle. The murder had taken place early evening, the licence plate number was given and the location where it had been found, along with a request to the public for any information that would assist the police inquiry. A suspect was being held.

Lorraine called Rooney but was told that he was not at the station. She checked her watch. It was too late to change her plans.

Rooney had been waiting outside Mrs Hastings's house for fifteen minutes. She was not in but, according to a neighbour, was probably taking her daughters to school so would not be long. He took another few swigs of bourbon, screwed on the cap tightly, then unwrapped another peppermint. He settled back, reached for one of the newspapers he had bought and broke wind loudly as he glared at the front page.

Mrs Hastings finally returned. She parked her car in the drive and carried a bag of groceries inside. Rooney figured he'd wait a while longer before paying his visit. He looked into his driving mirror and saw Lorraine walking up the road. She paused as if checking she had the correct address. As she walked past his car, Rooney lowered the window. 'Morning,' he said loudly.

When she saw it was Rooney Lorraine said, 'Hi, I was going to talk to Mrs Hastings.'

'I'll come in with you.'

Rooney saw her hesitate and then, 'Fine, but maybe I can get more out of her without you.'

'You seen this morning's paper? It's not public yet but it wasn't a she, it was a he – or an it, according to the pathologist. That's why I came here – thought I'd have another go at Mrs Hastings.'

Lorraine didn't react to the information. This was the moment she should have discussed Janklow but she didn't.

'Says they got a suspect in custody.'

'Brendan Murphy, husband of one of the victims. The suits have arrived. They brought him in from Detroit. I've not even had access to him yet but . . .'

'But?'

'It's not him, I know it. Let's talk to Mrs Hastings.'

'Let me try before you, Bill. You been checking out that vintage car garage?'

'I got two guys on it this morning.'

She could smell liquor on his breath. 'You okay?'

He shook his head. 'Nah, they gave me the fucking kiss-off this morning. Well, until the FBI are ready to roll. They want me for a briefing later today.'

Lorraine straightened. 'You mind if I say something, Bill? It's just that I can smell the booze – that and peppermints. If I was you, I'd grab a cup of coffee. Mrs Hastings sounds like the type of woman who'd report you and you don't want to give the FBI a rope to swing you on . . .'

Rooney swore and cupped his hands round his mouth, blowing into them. His jowled face wobbled childishly. 'Okay, I'll be back in fifteen. I'll grab a bite to eat. If you're through wait for me on the roadside.'

He found a deli about four blocks along and parked the car. As he waited for his order he thought how incongruous it was for Lorraine to be telling him to sober up. He'd always been a heavy drinker but now he was drinking more during working hours than he ever had. He wondered if that was the way Lorraine had started. She'd had marital problems but, then, so did all the men. He dreaded the thought of being retired and at home with his wife. It gave him nightmares, as she wittered on about them getting a trailer and travelling round the country. He could think of nothing worse. He couldn't recall the last time he had taken his wife out to dinner, or, for that matter, when he had taken her anywhere. He became more and more despondent as he ploughed through his breakfast. Everything he did revolved around his station, his men, and now it was going to end. Pushing these morose thoughts out of his mind, he tried to concentrate on the case. He wondered why Lorraine had wanted him to check out the vintage car garage. Did she have something for him, something she'd held back? She hadn't made it sound important, but in the old days Lorraine always kept her cards close to her chest. He'd reprimanded her about it, reminding her that she was not a one-woman agent but part of a team. He remembered her snapping back at him, saying the day the men treated her as part of the team, she would work with them. She had put him down hard and fast because at that time she held a higher rank. It had always needled him, needled a lot of men, that she had gained her stripes before them.

'You got a problem with the men?' he could see himself leaning against his old wooden desk as she stood straight-backed in front of him. 'You want to make a complaint?'

'No complaints, but if one of them sends me out on any more fucking wild goose chases with that Merton, who wants to open fire on any kid he sees within ten yards of him, then I will. He's a lousy back-up, he's in need of treatment and everyone on this unit knows it.'

Rooney had promised to look into it but he never did. Even when the shoot-out happened and she was almost killed he had not given her anyone decent. Just suggested she take a refresher course at the shooting training gallery.

'I'm the crack shot, Bill. I wouldn't be here if I wasn't

255

and neither would my partner. It's him that needs a refresher course.'

Lorraine had taken two weeks off for further training and her ex-partner died in a shoot-out the next time he was called out. Maybe she'd been right but no one ever bothered to make an official inquiry. Officer Colin Merton was given a posthumous medal for bravery and Lorraine a new partner. Rooney had expected fireworks from John Lubrinski when he'd been told he was to partner a woman but he'd said nothing. He wondered if it was Lubrinski that had started Lorraine on her drinking sessions. The two of them were always in the bars together, Lubrinski a famous hard drinker, and it was rumoured that she was matching him. It was Lubrinski who nicknamed her Hollow Legs.

They were partners for three years. When he was injured in cross-fire, she'd made a tourniquet round his leg with her tights. He'd taken three bullets, one in his thigh, one in his shoulder and a third in his stomach. It was the last that had killed him. She had returned to duty the next week and had never spoken about Lubrinski until the internal investigation. He, too, received a posthumous award and she gained a commendation, which many of the men opposed, insinuating that, had the officer had one of them as back-up instead of a woman, they would still be alive. She had never complained or asked for an easier assignment or taken up the offer of a few weeks' compassionate leave. She had gone straight back to work and remained on the same beat for another year. Rooney wondered if perhaps she had begun drinking alone then. Then, at her own request, she was moved from Vice to the Drug Squad. Six months later she had shot the kid. No one ever knew what she had felt on that night or why she had been drinking.

Rooney pushed his half-eaten ham and eggs across the table. For the first time he felt guilty that he, like everyone else, had given Lorraine the cold shoulder. He decided that, even though it was too late, he would talk it through with her. Maybe because he himself felt as if he could finish his bottle of bourbon and not care that he was on duty. He was past caring and he wondered if she had felt that way all those years ago. Angry. In some ways they were similar because he had never complained; he was the man who had always drummed into his officers, get on with the job no matter how tough, never complain, complaints are for losers. It didn't matter if they were male or female, nobody deserved any favours. If they couldn't take it then they weren't tough enough to gain respect. Nobody respected him now, he reckoned, and nobody had respected Lorraine Page.

'My name is Lorraine Page,' she said to a nervous Mrs Hastings. 'I wonder if I could come in and talk to you for a few moments, to iron out a few things about the inquiry into your husband's murder. It won't take long.'

Sitting in the living room, Lorraine was relaxed and complimentary about the neat house, calming Mrs Hastings's nerves.

'I've told that detective Rooney everything. I just can't understand what more there is to discuss. This only makes it worse, these constant questions.'

Lorraine opened her file and smiled. 'Well, let's get this over with as fast as possible, shall we?'

She asked if Norman Hastings had ever owned a vintage car, or used a garage in Santa Monica, which specialized in imported vehicles. She went through the different makes of car to see if Mrs Hastings reacted, but the woman shook her head and said that her husband could never have afforded anything so expensive. Lorraine asked if he owned a car before they were married.

'Yes, of course, but I've no idea what kind it was.'

257

Lorraine said nothing, seemingly more interested in her file. 'I've got a photograph of it, I think,' Mrs Hastings added.

Lorraine looked up and smiled encouragingly. 'Can I see it?'

Mrs Hastings left the room and Lorraine took out the photographs she and Rosie had taken. She then made a quick drawing on a blank sheet of paper. Mrs Hastings returned with a photograph album and began to sift through the pages until she found what she was looking for. 'I think that's it. I've no idea what make it was and I'm sure it wasn't one of the cars you mentioned.'

Lorraine looked at the snapshot taken in 1979, the date neatly printed below the photograph. Norman Hastings, in shirt sleeves, stood beside the car. It was a low sports car, a British-made Morgan – and, by the look of it, quite an old model.

'Do you have any idea where he bought it?'

Mrs Hastings shook her head again. She had never seen it.

'Your husband was a few years older than you,' Lorraine observed, about to turn the album page, but Mrs Hastings took it back.

'Yes, fifteen, but we were happy.' She hesitated. 'I suppose you know about Norman's little problem. I told that man Rooney.'

'I don't think we need discuss it. You were brave to tell Captain Rooney about it – it must have been very distressing.'

Lorraine passed over her drawing. 'This isn't very good but I wondered if your husband owned a pair of cufflinks like these? They could be gold or silver but with that distinct S and A logo in the centre.'

Mrs Hastings looked at the picture. 'They're silver, but the chain's broken.'

'Do you still have them?'

She left the room again and Lorraine leaned back in the sofa. Next she wanted Mrs Hastings to look at the photographs. It was going well but the woman was tricky, nervous and jumpy. Lorraine wanted her nice and calm. The cufflinks were still in their little cardboard box and one was broken. Lorraine examined the links, then looked at the box. No date, just the same logo and the Santa Monica address.

'What do you want to see these for?' Mrs Hastings asked.

Lorraine replaced the cufflinks, shut the box. 'We may have a possible link to the killer. We think he was wearing something similar. Can I keep these?'

Mrs Hastings agreed. She was beginning to pluck at her dress in agitation. 'Will it all come out? About Norman?'

Lorraine put the box into her purse. 'I doubt it. I always think personal details that have no connection to the case should not be released to the press, especially if the family have requested them not to be.'

Mrs Hastings clasped Lorraine's wrist. 'Oh, thank you. I've been so worried – the children – then there's Norman's parents and his friends at work.'

'He was an engineer, wasn't he?'

'Yes, yes, he was, for ice-boxes and domestic appliances.'

'Did he work on his car engines?'

'He could repair anything from a toaster to a car. The neighbours were always asking him to fix things and he was such a kind man, he'd never say no.'

Lorraine used the opening and showed the photograph of Janklow. 'Did he ever help this man out?'

'I couldn't tell, there's not all his face there, but I don't think so.'

Lorraine showed the second picture, each one taken at the S and A garage. Mrs Hastings looked at one after the other and then tapped one. 'This one. He came here once to talk to Norman about his car.'

Then she showed the photo of the white Mercedes

driven by Janklow in blonde wig and make-up. Mrs Hastings glanced at it. 'I don't know her.'

'Have you ever seen the car?'

Mrs Hastings took the photograph and stared at it. 'I don't know, a lot of people came to see him. As I said, he was always helping people out.'

'It's a Mercedes sports car, drop head. It would also have a hard top. Maybe you saw it with that on?'

Mrs Hastings frowned. 'I don't know. There's something familiar about it, it's difficult to say. What colour is the hard-topped hood?'

Lorraine took a chance, reckoning if the body was white maybe the roof was too.

'Well, no, I remember a similar car out in the drive once but it had a black top, sort of dipped.'

Lorraine began to put away the photographs, still relaxed. 'Did you see who was driving it? Who it belonged to?'

'No, they were in the garage out in the yard. Norman used to keep odd spare parts out there so that was another reason why he had so many people coming round. He'd charge them – just expenses, it was his hobby but I hated it. It made his hands all dirty, and oil on everything.'

Lorraine stood up and smiled. 'Thank you very much. You've been very helpful, and I really appreciate it. Would you mind if I come back if I get a better photograph of the man in the Mercedes?'

'No, I don't mind. In fact, I haven't minded talking to you at all.'

Rooney was just drawing up when he saw Lorraine walk out. She waved to Mrs Hastings and he saw her glance towards his car. He opened the passenger door as Mrs Hastings shut her front door and Lorraine got in beside him. 'I'd stay clear of her – she's nervous, more worried about her husband's "little problem", as she calls it, getting out to the press than she is about the murder.'

Rooney sniffed. 'You got anything for me?'

'I might have a suspect but until I'm sure I'd prefer to do a bit more digging around – maybe in a few days.'

'I need anything you've got now. I don't have a few days.'

She pursed her lips. 'Give me until the end of the day. I also need anything you've got on the latest victim.'

'I told you all I've got. Until they've finished the tests, that's it. She was a man and her last meal was banana bread.' She had her hand on the door ready to leave when he said, 'You and Lubrinski, were you an item?'

'Why do you want to know?'

'I'm just trying to figure you out.'

'Bit late for that, isn't it?'

'Yeah, I know. I was just mulling things over, and I started to think about him, he was a great guy.'

She nodded but made no reply. He reached down for his bourbon and unscrewed the cap. He drank from the bottle and she turned to look at him. 'It's the bourbon that reminds you of him. Because he always had a bottle under his seat. Why are you drinking, anyway?'

He gritted his teeth as the bourbon hit his stomach. He took another swig. 'I need it. Did you drink with him?'

'You know I did.'

'On duty?'

'Sometimes, but mostly we saved the session until we were off.'

'Did he get you started on the booze?'

She laughed. 'I didn't need Lubrinski to start me drinking, Bill, I managed it all by myself.'

'Why?'

She suddenly became tetchy. 'How about I was just screwed up, tense and scared I'd foul up, and there's nobody else to blame but myself.'

'Your husband? The kids, was that it?'

'For chrissakes, back off me. Why do you want to start on this?'

He took another swig and screwed on the cap. 'Because I'd like to know, and maybe I feel guilty. Maybe this is a conversation I should have had with you years ago.'

She got out of the car and leaned in. 'You're too late, Bill, there's nothing you can do now. What happened happened. It's over.'

'I'm sorry.' He said it gruffly, not looking at her, and she straightened up, about to slam the car door, when she bent down to look at him again.

'About Lubrinski, Bill, he was the best friend I ever had. I trusted him with my life but he was a crazy fool, he took risks, got into a lot of things that I tried to stop, but he wouldn't listen to me, he never listened to anyone and, in answer to your question, we were not an item, we were just partners.'

Then she shut the door and walked off just as Rosie appeared on the opposite side of the road. Rooney drove away in a cloud of exhaust fumes.

'How'd it go?' Rosie said cheerfully.

Lorraine told her to drive to the S and A garage in Santa Monica. Then she closed her eyes and leaned back. She could see Lubrinski's face as clear as if it was yesterday. They had got drunk together on many evenings, they'd talked about everything under the sun, always carefully skirting round themselves. But eventually it had happened. She'd been boozing heavily and he'd insisted she sober up at his place before Mike saw her and threw a punch at him. He was always joking about Mike, snide one-liners about her house-proud husband, but she wouldn't let him run Mike down. He should try and clean up his own act, his wife was no angel. They had squabbled like teenagers and eventually called a truce, that neither of them would discuss

262

their partners. They had shaken hands and Lubrinski had drawn her close.

'Does this make you a single woman now?'

She had tried to slap him but he ducked so she hit the window of the patrol car. Her knuckles hurt and she sucked her fist. He reached over and caught her hand, drawing it to his lips.

That night she had been totally smashed. Even though she had drunk as much as he had, he seemed never to show it. Not until she watched him attempting to brew the coffee did she know he was as drunk as she was. 'You're plastered, Lubrinski, talk about the blind leading the blind. Here, lemme do it.'

He lay back on his unmade bed in his one-room apartment with dirty clothes strewn all around. Lorraine offered to come by and clean it up for him. He said he liked it this way, he knew where everything was, but after they'd finished the coffee he couldn't find the patrol car keys. He started throwing things about, swearing. Then he threw up his hands and laughed his wonderful, deep bellow. 'I'm lying, they're in my pocket.' He pulled them out and dangled them. 'I just wanted to keep you here a while longer but now I'm stone cold sober I don't have the guts.'

'For what?' She was still laughing at him.

'To hold you. You ever think how much I want to hold you, Lorraine Page?'

She stopped laughing, got off the bed, went to him and gently slipped her arms round him. He held her close, he didn't kiss her, he didn't fondle her, he did exactly what he had said he wanted to do: he held her in his arms. She rested her head against his chest, could feel his heart beat, could feel him tremble. She had smiled up at him and then released herself. 'I got to get back to the kids.'

'You love him, don't you?' he asked.

She was confused. She didn't really know. The rows and

bitter arguments had been wearing her out. Mike hated Lubrinski, constantly implied that he was more than just a working partner. He also hated the way she had started drinking so much. He blamed that on Lubrinski as well. Mike blamed everything on anything and anyone but himself.

'Yes, I love Mike. Now I got to go home. We both got enough problems without starting up any new ones.'

She had never seen Lubrinski ill at ease but he was that night, pulling at his thick black curly hair. 'It is kind of different for me, Lorraine.' He shook his head, looking at her. 'You don't know, do you? You got no idea. Jesus Christ, Lorraine, I love you. Some days I don't know what to do with myself I love you so much and sometimes I get scared for you, and I know that's not a good thing but I can't stop it, can't stop loving you, wanting you. And sitting so close to you, day in day out, is driving me crazy. I'm gonna ask for a transfer. It's nothing to do with you being a good or bad partner, it's just that I want you and . . . well, now you know.'

Two nights later he was shot. When she tore off her tights to wrap around his thigh as he was bleeding to death, Lubrinski had joked that at long last he was getting her pants down – he knew he would in time. If he'd known she'd do it when he was shot, he'd have stood up months before . . .

She held him in the ambulance. His breathing became laboured, his eyes unfocused. She kept telling him to hold on, to keep talking. The last thing he said was that he loved her and the last thing he heard before he died was Lorraine saying that he was a stupid, dumb bastard because she loved him too, and if he didn't hold on and pull through she'd strangle him with her tights. She saw the light go from his eyes in disbelief. She'd seen so much death, been so close to it, but this was like losing her own soul, as if he was taking it with him.

Lorraine went back to her apartment, needing Mike more than ever, but he wasn't there. She drank herself into a stupor and collapsed on the bed. Mike came back about two hours later. As soon as he saw her he shouted that Lubrinski had got her drunk again and she had said quietly that this time Lubrinski had nothing to do with it.

'I don't believe you. I'm gonna see him, report him.'

'Try the City Morgue, Mike, but I doubt if he'll talk back to you, he's dead.'

Mike was stunned, had tried to hold her, but she couldn't stand him near her, couldn't bear anyone to touch her. All she wanted was to drink herself into oblivion. Poor Mike had tried to understand, to persuade her to take leave when it was offered, but she refused; she couldn't stand not to be busy, not to be working. She began to believe that Lubrinski had taken a part of her with him when he died. Nothing she did made any sense, neither did anything Mike said. She was irritable with the girls, she was bad-tempered and uncooperative at work, but somehow she carried on until she finally lost control and killed an innocent boy.

'We're almost there,' said Rosie.

Lorraine opened her eyes. She wanted a drink. That was all she could think about. She didn't care about anything else. 'I want a drink.'

Rosie drew up outside a grocery store and hurried inside. She returned with a pack of Coke. 'Here, you wanted a drink!' Lorraine opened a can and gulped it down. Rosie opened one for herself and then proffered a piece of home-made banana bread.

Lorraine sat bolt upright. What had Rooney said? The latest victim, all they had on her or him was that his last meal was banana bread. She felt her body break out in a cold sweat. Was it Didi or Nula that was always making banana bread? Could it possibly be one of them? Didi was blonde, the right age. He had said it was a transsexual – but it couldn't be, it was impossible.

'I got to make a call, Rosie.'

Rosie looked at her. 'Oh, yeah, like you just got to go in there and make a phone call. You think I'm dumb. I know what you'll be making, a bottle of vodka. No way.'

Lorraine had her hand on the car door. 'Shit, if you feel I can't be trusted then come in with me.'

Lorraine had Rosie right at her elbow as she placed the call to Nula and Didi's apartment. Nula answered, her voice drowsy. 'It's Lorraine, who am I speaking to?'

'It's Nula, sweetheart, how you doin'?'

'I'm great, Nula. Is Didi there? I need to speak to her.'

'Nope, she's not come in, been out all night, the dirty cow. She'll be back soonish because she's got a girl comin' to have her hair cut. You want me to get her to call you?'

'Do you know where she is?' Lorraine asked, trying to keep her voice laid back.

Just then the doorbell rang at Nula's end. It was probably Didi just coming home, she said; if Lorraine wanted to hang on and wait she'd bring Didi to the phone.

'No, I got to go, I'll call later.'

Rosie waited, head on one side. 'What was that all about?'

Lorraine shrugged. 'I thought maybe something had happened to Didi but she'd just gotten home.'

They left the grocery store and drove off to the S and A garage. This time Lorraine was going to go in. She needed to speak to the man Mrs Hastings had recognized. She also knew that Steven Janklow might be there and if he was, she was going to have to come up with a good reason for her presence.

Nula fetched her coat. The two officers didn't say why they wanted her to accompany them to the station, but she knew it was something to do with Didi because they had asked for photographs of her. If she had just been arrested for prostitution, Nula knew they wouldn't want photographs. It was something else, something bad. All they had asked was if she knew David Burrows. Nobody ever called Didi David, only the cops. Half an hour later Nula identified Didi's body. She was in such a state of shock she was unable to speak coherently. All she could do was whisper Didi's name over and over. The face didn't resemble that of her beloved friend. Only the red nails and the big topaz ring made Nula sure it was Didi. Two uniformed officers returned her home by patrol car. They helped her inside the apartment, before they asked when she had last seen Didi.

The FBI checked into the complex list of dates and pick-ups that Brendan Murphy could remember. They contacted the trucking agencies he worked for and released him. He had not lied: Brendan Murphy was not in Los Angeles when his wife Helen had been killed and neither had he been near any of the other locations where victims had been found. Deprived of a suspect, they began to study the case history. Having been brought in to trace Murphy, they were now assigned to the murder investigation.

CHAPTER 14

LORRAINE SAT with Rosie in the parking lot adjacent to S and A Vintage Cars. 'Right, here I go. You wait here and if I'm not out—'

'I'll shoot myself.' Rosie laughed.

Lorraine got out of the car, gave her jacket a quick tug to straighten the back and walked briskly towards the main reception area. No one was around and the vast stretch of the polished mahogany counter held leaflets sprayed out like fans. Dull soft music, songs from the twenties, was in the air. A number of Oscar-like statues, racing cups and awards stood in glass cabinets and everywhere there were pictures of vintage cars.

Five gleaming automobiles were lined up in front of the showroom windows: a Silver Cloud Rolls-Royce, a Rolls Corniche, a 1950s Bentley, a Bristol and a two-door Mercedes sports. The leather interiors were as immaculate as the gleaming chrome, wooden dashboards, large steering wheels, by today's standards almost fragile-looking. Lorraine could see her distorted image reflected in the hub caps. She looked squat.

'Hi, how can I help you?'

She turned to the equally polished salesman. His hair gleamed, as did his teeth, his deep tan, his eyes. He had the S and A logo on the pocket of his navy blazer and on his maroon tie. He smiled expectantly, one hand shifting his immaculate starched cuff closer to his wrist, he was all logo-ed out. She wondered why he hadn't had S and A stamped on his forehead.

'Do you have an office? I'd like to discuss something with you.'

The teeth gleamed as his lips drew slightly apart in another fake smile. 'Would you like to tell me what it's about?'

'Sure, if you have an office. I am Mrs Page, and you are?'

He stepped behind the counter. 'Alan Hunter. I am the chief sales assistant. How can I help you, Mrs Page?'

He gave her a cool, studied appraisal. Even though his eyes didn't seem to leave hers, she felt as if he was scrutinizing her from her worn shoes to her second-hand suit. 'May I ask what you're selling?'

She would have liked to hit him in the face. She used to love times like this, times when, confronted by a real smart-ass prick, you drew out your ID and said in a low voice, 'You want to check my ID, sonny?'

'I'm not selling and I'm not buying. I need to talk to you in private. What did you say your name was?'

Something in her voice unnerved him so he hesitated and repeated his name.

'Right, Mr Hunter. I don't want to waste any more time and I don't want to discuss anything in this swimming pool of a lobby.'

He touched the knot of his tie and gestured towards a glass-windowed door.

Lorraine walked across the reception area and paused when she saw a picture of Brad Thorburn. He was sitting on the wing of a racing car wearing a white racing-driver's suit. One arm clasped a helmet, the other lifted a glass of champagne. To right and left were more pictures of him posing at racetracks.

Hunter opened his office door, motioning her to enter ahead of him. 'Are you with the police?'

She placed her purse on his empty polished mahogany desk and took out her cigarettes. 'Do you mind if I smoke?'

Hunter did not demur and Lorraine surveyed the room. 'You don't appear to be very busy.'

'We are, I assure you. Most of our customers wait for us to deliver, few come to the building. We have hangars and workshops out at the rear of the showroom. Can I ask what you wanted to talk to me about? Is it traffic violations?'

Lorraine sat in the perfectly positioned chair, not too far away from the desk. 'No. It's not about traffic violations.'

'Is it connected with . . .' Hunter opened his desk drawer and withdrew a card. 'A Lieutenant Josh Bean?'

'No, it isn't.'

'He was here earlier, some kind of check on stolen vehicles.'

'That's not my department. I'm investigating an insurance claim.' She took out Rosie's pictures. 'Do you recognize any of these men?'

Hunter leaned forward, sifting methodically through the photographs. He put seven aside. She watched as he glanced at the one of Steven Janklow. He frowned, hesitated a moment, and then looked up. 'These seven men work here in various capacities.'

She tapped Steven Janklow's picture. 'How about him?'

Hunter picked up the photograph. 'This could be Mr Janklow. He's one of the partners but it's not a very good picture. I recognize the car more than the face. It's one of ours – it's actually owned by Brad Thorburn. Is it something to do with Mr Thorburn?'

Lorraine nodded, looking around for an ashtray. As Hunter passed her a silver one with the S and A logo stamped into the centre, she noticed his gold cufflinks which also carried the insignia. She tapped the ash from her cigarette and eased out the picture of the woman driving the Mercedes. 'Do you know her?'

He stuck out his bottom lip, shaking his head. 'No. It could be Mrs Thorburn, Mr Thorburn's mother, but I really wouldn't know as I've never met her. But the car is the same. It belongs, as I said, to Mr Thorburn. Has it been in an accident?'

'No.' Lorraine packed away the pictures. 'Do you have a schedule of who was on or off duty over a period of time?'

He nodded, tapping his foot. She then pulled out Norman Hastings's picture. 'Do you recognize this man?'

Hunter sighed irritably. 'His name was Norman Hastings. Is it his insurance? He was murdered, is that what this is about?'

Lorraine assented.

'Well, I'm sorry, but I never dealt with him. All I know is he was a pain in the butt. He bought a car from us, long time ago before I joined the company.' He leaned back, splaying out his hands affectedly. 'If you buy one of our vehicles at the prices we ask, we have first-class mechanics and maintenance engineers at your service. We attempt to make sure no vehicle ever leaves here without its engine having been rechecked, rebuilt if necessary. Many purchasers have the cars customized to their own specifications. Every modification is made to ensure a trouble-free vehicle, but, that said, we're not dealing in new cars. Some of these are twenty, even thirty years old, and sometimes there will be problems. But we give a six-month guarantee to every vehicle, and for the first six months we will collect and redeliver should any mechanical fault occur.'

He laughed like an actor, his speech, even his own humour rehearsed. 'We had someone here not long ago, I think he had a Bentley, and he called us out simply because he was unsure where he should put the gas!'

'Norman Hastings?' Lorraine said quietly.

'His car was a Morgan. He was on the phone almost every day wanting it collected and tested. And then we discovered that the faults were self-inflicted because he was constantly taking the engine apart and rebuilding it – or that's what Mr Janklow said.'

'Is Mr Janklow here today?'

'Yes.'

Lorraine asked if it were possible to find out who was on or off work at the time of Hastings's murder and that included Mr Janklow.

Hunter plucked at his lip. 'Why would you want that for an insurance claim? Anyway, Mr Janklow doesn't work on any schedule system. He comes and goes when he likes.'

Lorraine asked if Janklow was around on the evening when Holly was murdered but Hunter shrugged his shoulders. He stared at a wall calendar. 'I simply couldn't tell you. All I know is he arrives and leaves when he feels like it.'

'Is there a place for parking workers' cars?'

'Out back. It's like an old aircraft hangar – there's always cars there – our own, some waiting for work to be done, others that have just been shipped in.'

Lorraine opened her notebook and reeled off the car each body had been found in but to little effect. Hunter could not recall any of them. He was becoming puzzled by the dates and lists of cars. She played a wild card. 'Not even, say, Norman Hastings's blue Sedan?'

'Ah, yes, he left that here on a number of occasions.'

Lorraine felt her heart jump, like a kick of pleasure at her own cleverness. 'Would you just check the last time you saw it here.'

Hunter looked at his watch. He picked up the phone. 'Sheena, can you please check the last time Norman Hastings came in and left his vehicle? Thank you.' He hung up. 'The police asked this, and they've already been over the hangars.'

Lorraine lit another cigarette and tossed the match into the ashtray. 'Hastings sold his car, didn't he? Quite a few years ago. Do you know if he purchased any other vintage car? Did he sell it via S and A?'

'Not to my knowledge but I didn't have anything to do with him.'

'Did Mr Thorburn also know Hastings?'

'I believe so.'

The phone rang and Hunter answered it. He drew a notepad towards him, said 'yes' a few times, thanked the caller and ripped off the page. 'Hastings apparently had some arrangement to leave his car here – my secretary isn't sure who he made it with or the last time he came.'

'So he parked his own car here and yet he hadn't owned one of your vehicles recently?'

'Seems so.'

'Do you think the arrangement would have been with Mr Janklow?'

'I've no idea. My direct boss is Mr Thorburn, not Mr Janklow.'

'What do you think of him?' she asked nonchalantly.

'Brad? He's great to work for. He's firm, you know where you are with him, but he's also fun, loves a good laugh.'

'I meant Steven Janklow.'

Hunter pursed his lips in distaste. 'I have little to do with him so I can't say what he's like.'

'You could try.'

'I don't see eye to eye with him, that's all. He's volatile. One day he's friendly, the next he'll cut you dead. He's witty but it's that put-down humour, that's all.'

'Is he married?'

'No.'

'Is he homosexual?'

Hunter was shocked. 'I don't know.'

'Do you think he could be? Or could he be something else?'

'Like normal?'

Lorraine stood up. 'Fine, so you think he's a nice, normal guy. I'm sorry, but my firm insists on me completing these amazing questionnaires.'

'But I told you, he's not that nice.'

Hunter gave her a hooded look and she smiled broadly. 'How about not that normal either?' she said. She was beginning to like the Ivy League car salesman. She reckoned he was being honest with her and was green enough to have taken her at face value as an insurance claim officer. She looked through the white blind to the front yard.

'Is he suspected of something?' Hunter asked. 'The police asked a lot of questions to some of the other staff but they weren't very interested in me. I wasn't here the week of the Hastings murder.' He sounded disappointed.

Lorraine got out the photographs again. 'What about taking another look at that photo of the blonde woman? Can you tell me if it could be Janklow?'

Hunter picked up the photograph. He studied it and his voice went quiet. 'I honestly don't know, Mrs Page, and I would hate to embarrass Mr Thorburn. He's a good friend.'

'Norman Hastings's family cannot sell his car or claim any monies on his insurance until I have completed my questionnaire.'

'Is Mr Janklow under suspicion?'

Lorraine ran her fingers through her hair. It was difficult to ask what she wanted to know without getting into trouble.

'There are rumours,' he said suddenly. She waited as Hunter determined whether or not to continue. 'I don't know if I should repeat them as they are just rumours.' He came to a decision. 'He has some odd mannerisms and he can be affected. Nobody here knows much about his private life, just that a few years ago there was an inquiry. He was interviewed by the Vice Squad, arrested. Nothing came of it.'

There was a light tap on the door and a pretty girl peered

in. 'I'm sorry to interrupt, Mr Hunter, but you have a customer waiting.'

Hunter introduced his secretary, Sheena. Lorraine asked if she and Sheena could have a quick chat and look at the hangar where the cars were kept. He said he had better ask his superior.

'I'll wait here with Sheena then,' Lorraine said.

Sheena looked at Lorraine. 'You wanna know about Norman Hastings? He used to come here quite a lot. He used to park his car out back – loved to look over the new arrivals. I had to check back this morning for the police. As far as I can remember these were the dates when his car was left here. I gave the officers a copy too.' She passed over a neatly typed list. 'I was so shocked when I read about his murder. He was such a quiet, unassuming man, like my dad.'

Lorraine looked over the dates and then smiled warmly at her. 'If I were to give you a list of other cars, could you see if they were parked out in the hangar at any time?'

Sheena bit her lip. 'I've already got one list from the police but I told them it's not a garage, we just let the workers park there and a few friends. Sometimes there's no free space.'

'Could we take a look at the hangar?'

Lorraine followed Sheena across a wide yard. There were a number of outbuildings and she could see cars on ramps and mechanics working. The business seemed to be thriving and she calculated that there were a lot more employees than Rosie had said.

The hangar was boiling hot and there were rows of cars, fender to fender. Some had tarpaulins over them and seemed to have been left for a considerable time. Dust covered others waiting to be reconditioned and then came a large section of what looked like the workers' cars.

'Mr Thorburn likes the employees' vehicles out of sight, says it's not a good advertisement. We park here and

275

this is where Mr Hastings's car usually was, just for a few hours at a time, but he always left the keys. We have to leave the keys in case they need to be moved if a delivery arrives.'

They reached the back of the hangar and looked over three racing cars, all draped in protective silver covers. 'These are Mr Thorburn's specials. He used to race a lot, but not so much nowadays. One of his wives created a stink about it . . .' Sheena opened a door at the back of the hangar into a corridor. It was air-conditioned, freezing cold compared with the hangar. They passed large offices with white blinds on the windows. One was Brad Thorburn's, his name on a wood plaque cut into the door. They arrived at Sheena's where she took out a large log book to check the list of cars Lorraine had given her. 'It's the same list the police gave me. I told them there was just the one. Mr Hastings's.'

The phone rang. She answered it, listened and then said, 'I'd better go. I've got to take the sales invoices to Mr Hunter. Every week the top salesman gets a bonus.'

'Can I wait?'

'Sure. I'll tell Mr Hunter you're in here.'

Sheena gathered up a file and walked out. She left the door ajar. As soon as she was half-way down the corridor, Lorraine closed the door, picked up the log book and began to search through it. She was getting close, she knew it. She felt herself growing excited. She was sure Steven Janklow was connected to the case.

Rosie got out of the car, her dress sticking to her in the heat. A number of people had already taken a good look at her, noticing that she was parked in their yard. She walked round the car, fanning herself with her hand. She was thirsty and Lorraine had been gone over an hour. Just as she thought she would go into S and A, a mechanic walked out of the building and headed towards her. 'This is a private road, you want something?'

'No. My friend's inside.' She pointed to the S and A building.

'Why don't you wait over there? We're expecting a delivery any minute. Go on, move.'

Rosie returned to the car and started up the engine. She backed out and parked for a while in the street. Then she circled the block. She was heading past S and A when a white Mercedes passed her and drove onto the forecourt. Rosie watched Steven Janklow head round to the rear of the building and disappear before she could get her camera out. She dabbed her sweating face with a tissue. 'Come on, for God's sake, Lorraine, what are you doing in there?' she muttered. From where she was parked, opposite the garage, she could see a smart salesman talking to two Japanese men. All three disappeared inside. Still no Lorraine.

The door opened and Sheena came back in. 'Sorry, but I got held up. I haven't been able to speak to Mr Hunter yet – he's still with a couple of clients and I think they want a test drive.' A voice from one of the other offices called, 'Good morning, Mr Janklow.'

Sheena pulled a face. 'He's here. Look, I'd better go and tell Mr Hunter that you're still waiting.'

Lorraine picked up her purse. 'No, it's okay. I'll find him myself. Thank you for the coffee.'

'I hope I was of some help. It was just so terrible, poor Mr Hastings.'

'Did you see him when he was here the last time?'

'No, but when he came to see Mr Janklow, he'd pop in and leave me his car keys. I think he banked up the street, but his office isn't far away. He was always anxious about parking fines. Funny, really, worrying about something as small as that and then . . . he gets killed.'

277

'But Mr Janklow was here *then*?'

'Yes. Do you want to speak to him?'

'Maybe later. I'll just go see Mr Hunter. Thanks for everything.'

Lorraine walked out, into the blast of cold air in the corridor. Her heart jumped as she passed Janklow's office but he was not inside; through the blinds, she could see a secretary placing papers on the desk. She continued along the corridor, came into the hangar and walked quickly out into the sunshine. She stood for a moment to get her bearings and then took off towards the path winding around the building, intending to go back to Rosie. Then she saw the Mercedes parked by a car-wash area. She hugged the wall when she saw a man talking to one of the attendants. He was gesturing to the car's wheels. Then he leaned into it and pointed to the interior. She saw the attendant nod, then heard him tell two black kids to wash and vacuum Mr Janklow's car, and polish up the chrome on the hub caps and fenders.

Lorraine waited, half wanting Janklow to turn round so that she could see his face but not wanting him to catch sight of her. He was wearing a pale blue linen jacket, white slacks and sandals. Slim, immaculate, his hair cut short and tight to his head – blondish-brown hair – just as she remembered. Steven Janklow was the man who had attacked her, she was sure of it. If only she could get a good look at his face.

Hunter appeared at the showroom doors. 'We've a customer who wants a trial drive, Mr Janklow. It's the Silver Cloud but we've already got someone that asked if we'd contact them if it looked like we'd got a sale.'

Janklow walked slowly towards him and Lorraine pressed closer to the wall. They were about to enter the building, Hunter stepping aside to allow Janklow to go in ahead, when Hunter saw her and waved. 'I won't be a moment, Mrs Page, I'm sorry to keep you waiting.' As soon as they disappeared, Lorraine hurried along the wide lane, past the Mercedes, to the road, hoping that Janklow's attention would be on the customers.

As Janklow was walking towards the Japanese customers, Hunter mentioned that the police had been to speak to him that morning about Norman Hastings. He added, 'There's another insurance broker, or something to do with Hastings's car, here. She was in my office but I just saw her outside. She wanted to know about Hastings parking his car in the hangar.'

Hunter was used to Janklow's mood changes but he was stunned when the man pushed past him and walked back out the way they had come in.

'What about the Silver Cloud, Mr Janklow?'

Janklow's fists were clenched as he strode along the corridor to Sheena's office and opened the door. She gave a nervous smile at the sight of him. 'Where is this woman from the insurance company?' he demanded.

'She just left me, Mr Janklow.'

'What did she want?'

Sheena swallowed. 'Same as the other two officers. She was making inquiries about vehicles we allowed to be parked in the hangar.'

Janklow picked up the log book. 'Did you get her name?'

'I presumed Mr Hunter must have. She was interviewing him this morning.'

'What do you mean, interviewing?'

'Well, just talking to him. I don't know what he said or anything. I was only doing what I was told, Mr Janklow.'

He walked out and into his own office, banging down the heavy book in a fury. He then rang through to the showroom.

Hunter was turning the engine over, the Japanese looking on with interest, when the phone went. Hunter excused himself and went to answer it. Janklow seemed hysterical, screaming for him to get into his office immediately. He didn't care if they had customers, he wanted to speak to Hunter this second. If he valued his job he would get himself over there. Before Hunter could reply the phone was banged down.

Lorraine ran towards Rosie and climbed in beside her.

'Thanks a lot, I've been roasting alive out here. Have you any idea how long I've been waiting? I've been round the block four times and I'm dying of thirst.'

Lorraine told Rosie to get out of sight of S and A. She hit the dashboard with her fist. 'I've got him, Rosie, I know he did it. Maybe he did them all but I'm damned sure for one that Janklow killed Norman Hastings. We got an A-1 suspect for Rooney.'

Rooney was sweating in spite of the chill of his air-conditioned office. He expected the FBI any minute to talk to him and the rest of the day would be spent discussing the murders, and his lack of progress. He'd finished the bottle of bourbon, his nose was redder than ever and his eyes were bloodshot. Bean put a large mug of black coffee and a packet of peppermints in front of him. Rooney had seemed less than interested in the new victim; he'd merely glanced at the reports and photographs. 'What was she? Man, woman or what?' Rooney muttered.

'A transsexual prostitute. It's in the report, happened last night around ten thirty.'

The only thing different about this one was that she had been hammered to the side of the head first, and had no rear scalp wound but multiple facial injuries. It had not yet been ascertained if the weapon was the same as that used in the previous murders.

'Any witnesses?' Rooney asked.

'Nope. She or he was seen on the streets, then said she was going to have a break because she'd got something wrong with her right foot.'

'That it?'

Bean nodded.

'Well, let these smart-alecks sort it. Any sign of them yet?'

'Due any time. They went out for lunch. Oh, you wanted a low-key inquiry run off at the S and A garage about the workers. Well, it's all here. Hastings's car was parked there in a hangar but he removed it the day before he was killed. He used it as a free parking lot – he knew the management. Place belongs to the Thorburns.' Bean tweaked two fingers up when he said the name. 'You want to take it further?'

'If his fuckin' car wasn't parked there on the day he died then it's not much use to us, is it?'

The phone rang and Rooney motioned for Bean to leave. Out of the corner of his eye, Bean saw Rooney swivel round to face the wall behind him, the report of the morning's interviews at S and A left untouched on his desk. He hoped Rooney would get his act together before the FBI grilled him. He looked shot and stank of liquor.

Lorraine was using a public call box.

'You got something for me?' Rooney snapped.

'Yeah, but I don't want to discuss it over the phone.'

'Dunno if I can get away. There's been another one.' He gave Didi's real name and that she was a transsexual prostitute. 'She was in the car like the others, similar head wounds. Car was reported stolen a few hours after we found it.'

'When did it happen?' she asked bluntly.

'Last night, around ten. Nicknamed Didi. You ever heard the name?'

They agreed to meet in an hour and a half's time at Rooney's favourite Indian restaurant. Just as he picked up

281

the reports, the phone rang again. He was required in the Chief's office. The FBI were waiting.

Lorraine joined Rosie in the car. 'Where to now, partner?' Rosie asked.

'Didi's dead – one of the transsexuals you met at the gallery.'

Rosie switched on the engine and Lorraine told her to put her foot down: she was meeting Rooney but wanted to talk to Nula first.

'You going to tell him everything?' Rosie yelled over the noise of the car engine. 'Only you could maybe get some more dough out of him if you got a suspect.'

Rooney slipped the knot of his tie closer to his sweat-stained collar. The Chief cracked his knuckles, waiting impatiently for an answer. 'I don't need this, Bill. Who the fuck did you send there?'

Rooney shifted his weight. 'Lieutenant Bean and another officer.'

'The complaint was about a woman.'

'She used to be a cop and she's been doing some work for me on the streets.'

'This isn't on the street, Bill, this is somebody impersonating a police officer.' Rooney pulled at his tie again. He had no idea what Lorraine had been doing at the S and A, or why his chief was getting so hot under the collar. 'It's not in any report, Bill. What was she fucking doing there? That family have big connections and they're screaming about this. I want you to go there personally, iron it out. We've got enough bad press as it is and I don't intend losing my job over this.'

Rooney gave a half smile. 'Yes, sir. They that powerful? This garage a big deal, huh?'

The Chief glared. 'It's the Thorburn family, old money, big money. Fucking back off them. Go on, get out.'

'What about the suits? I thought I was having a briefing with them.'

'Sort this out first.'

Rooney knew who the Thorburns were, not that you heard much about them nowadays but their donations to police charities were legendary. Lorraine Page had better have something for him.

Nula was distraught. Her face, devoid of make-up, looked haggard, her eyes without their false eyelashes were puffy and red from weeping. As soon as she saw Lorraine she broke down again. She wore a silk kimono and bedroom slippers. In the raw light of day the apartment was claustrophobic with its drapes and stuffed animals. Rosie hovered, finding it difficult not to stare at the overtly sexual pictures that hung on all available wall space. Lorraine fetched a glass of water and sat by Nula, holding her hand.

'Tell me what happened.'

Nula wiped her face with a sodden tissue. 'She used to have a number of regulars, she often stayed out all night. When she didn't come back I thought she'd scored. It wasn't her at the door when you phoned – it was the cops to tell me.'

'Do you have a list of her regulars?' Lorraine asked.

'No, of course I don't. Nothing was ever arranged, they'd just turn up on the streets and sometimes she used that motel Roselee, but the rooms there were getting expensive. Sometimes she brought them back here, I dunno their names. I've got my own clients and she's got . . . Oh, God—I don't know what I'm going to do without her.'

'Can you describe any of her johns? Did you see any that night?'

'*No!* She was with me one minute and then she just walked off.'

Lorraine opened the envelope. 'Will you look at these photographs and tell me if there's anyone you recognize?' Nula looked at each one, sniffing and blowing her nose. Lorraine saved the blonde in the Mercedes until last. 'What about this woman?'

Nula took the photograph. It was the only one she showed any interest in, but she shook her head.

'Are you sure? Keep looking at it, Nula, look at the car – it's an old Mercedes sports car. Look at the woman . . . is it a woman?'

Nula turned away. 'I don't know, I don't *know*. I want to be left alone, please, *please* just leave me alone.'

Rosie leaned forward. 'That car was driving along Sunset last night. Did you see Didi speak to the driver – maybe get into the car?'

Lorraine gave Rosie a discreet wink. Rosie remained silent, eyes swinging from Lorraine to Nula; she was impressed with her friend, she was hot shit.

Nula scrutinized the picture of the blonde. 'Does this woman have something to do with Didi?' Nula asked. 'Do you think she had something to do with her murder?'

'She might, but do you recognize her?'

'No, I just said so, didn't I?' Nula passed the picture back.

Lorraine stood up and packed away the photographs. Nula began to sob again, burying her face in her hands.

'We'll let ourselves out, Nula, and I'm so sorry, really sorry.'

Nula hugged her kimono tighter around herself, the tissue in shreds now as she plucked at it with her long, painted fingernails. 'She was the nicest person I've ever known. I'm all on my own now, I've nobody, she was my best friend. I don't know what I'll do. I can't afford this place – I've got no money.'

'What about Art? Do you know where you can contact him?'

'He's left town. We haven't heard from him since the gallery closed. I'm not sure where he is.'

Nula waited until she heard their car driving away before she went into the bedroom and opened a drawer in the bedside table. She took out a black diary and thumbed through the pages. Just seeing Didi's childish scrawled writing made her want to weep again but she gulped back her tears, flicking over the pages until she found what she was looking for. She went back to the hallway and picked up the phone. She pressed each digit and waited.

'Hi, this is Art. I'm not in, but please leave me your name and number, and I'll get back to you, okay? And wait for the tone before you leave your message.'

'Art, it's Nula. Will you call me? It's very urgent. We have to talk.'

She replaced the receiver and went into the bathroom. She'd have a long perfumed soak, that would make her feel better, and she was going to feel better. But before she turned on the taps, she went into the bedroom and knelt down by the bedside table. Lifting the curtain, she opened the bottom drawer and withdrew a large, square manilla envelope. She pulled out a number of photographs, then sat back on her heels. The one she wanted was black and white, of a woman sitting on a bed, wearing a long fifties evening gown with padded shoulders, a bit like Barbara Stanwyck, of that era. She was elegant, exceptionally beautiful. He had wanted to look like her, had brought the photograph for Didi to match, and she had worked for hours on him. The wig had been on a stand for days as she had teased and set it, ready for him. He had paid a lot of money for the session and Art had taken the photographs, draping the room to his specifications, down to the flower arrangements. The blonde woman was the same as the one in the picture Lorraine had shown her. Nula didn't panic. She slowly got to her feet and began to search through all the stacks of photographic files.

Rosie dropped Lorraine outside the Indian and drove off.

Rooney was already sitting at a table with a glass of beer. 'This had better be good and you'd better have a fucking good reason for barging into that S and A place. What the fuck were you doing there?'

Lorraine picked up the menu, asked if he'd ordered, but he said he wasn't hungry.

'You run a check on the S and A employees like I asked?' she said.

Rooney swigged his beer, banging the glass onto the table.

'There was a vice charge against Steven Janklow. You got a record of it? Be a few years back. Picked up for pavement crawlin', I think. He part owns the garage. His brother is Brad Thorburn.'

'What's your interest in him?'

Lorraine laid her hands flat on the table. 'I think he's your killer.'

Rooney pulled at his nose. 'What evidence have you got?'

She rubbed her cheek. 'I don't, but I do know that Hastings's car was left in their hangar.'

'You any idea who Janklow's family is?'

She shrugged. 'I guess they must be important if they've got you running. Can you check if there was a vice charge? If there was, you can get him for questioning, see if he can account for himself over Hastings. It's him, Bill, I'm sure.'

'Why?'

Lorraine took her time to outline the reasons before she told him that she was sure Janklow was the man who had attacked her. It didn't sink in for a while. Then he looked up.

'You wanna say that again?'

'I said, I think he was the man who attacked me, the man that I bit a chunk out of his neck.'

He leaned back, partly in disbelief, then got out his cigarettes and stuck one in his mouth. He stared fixedly around the restaurant, feeling as if the floor was opening up, and inhaled deeply. 'You stupid bitch.'

'I'm sorry, I was scared to come forward. I picked him up—'

'Sweet Jesus.' Rooney shook his head.

'He attacked me with a claw hammer. I'm sure it was Steven Janklow.'

'You seen him face to face? Or, more to the point, has he seen you?'

'No, I've held off facing him, I don't want to tip him off.'

Lorraine's order was placed in front of her. Rooney waited until the waiter had moved off before he leaned towards her. 'Say it *is* him – say he's the guy that attacked you. You can identify him . . .'

She had picked up her fork but put it down again. 'I identify him, he denies it, he walks. It's just the word of an ex-hooker, ex-drunkard against a fine, upstanding citizen, right? All he's got to say is he wasn't anywhere near the street I was picked up in and I got to admit I was picking him up for a few bucks. It wasn't his car, it was Hastings's car and Hastings's body was in the trunk. Now who's gonna believe who?'

Rooney drained his beer and beckoned the waiter to bring another.

Lorraine messed around with the food on her plate, then pushed it away. 'I think he's a transvestite.'

Rooney ran his hands through his hair. '*What?*'

'I think Janklow's a transvestite.'

'*Think?* I need more than you fucking thinking, I need evidence, I need *facts*. Jesus Christ, Lorraine, you know how crazy this all sounds?' He put his head in his hands. The more she told him, the worse it all sounded. 'You think the guy that hit on you was Steven Janklow, right? You also think Steven Janklow is a transvestite. Is there anything else you might have just glossed over – that maybe he has two heads?'

'Back off me. All the dead women have a similar look, similar age.'

'What about Holly?'

'I think she's the mistake. Because of the last one, Didi.'

Lorraine explained that she thought the killer was trying to pick up Nula or Didi on the night Holly was murdered. She told him how they had both seen a car, had both seen Holly run across the road to a punter. Her pimp Curtis saw her – but maybe the john was trying to pick up Didi or Nula. Once he'd got Holly he had to get rid of her. Maybe he panicked.

Rooney argued that it didn't make sense. Why didn't he just kick her out, if he'd got the wrong one? His head throbbed and he still couldn't believe how she'd held out on him like this.

Lorraine banged the table. 'Wait a minute! The wrong one. What if they were all the wrong ones? What if he was looking specifically for Didi all along? They're all the same age, all dyed or bleached blondes, but he can't find the one he's looking for, the main one.'

'Are you trying to tell me that this guy clubs seven women to death because he's looking for one, and we forget Norman Hastings? Did he think he was one as well? This is dumb, Lorraine. You lost your touch, sweetheart. We're looking at someone who's bumped off these women over five years, and he's doing it because of mistaken identity? Nuts!'

Lorraine twiddled her fork. 'Okay, let's try something

288

else. Let's go through every victim, including Hastings. He was a drag artist, right? He used to park his car at S and A years after he was doing any business with them but he knew Janklow. Maybe he found out something?'

Rooney delved in his pocket for his wallet. 'Maybe I'm wasting my time. I got to go take a leak.'

'But listen to me, there's every type of tool and hammer at the S and A. Can't someone check there? Match them? What if the hammers came from there?'

Rooney jabbed the air with his finger. 'Stay away from that place, is that understood? From now on you don't go anywhere near it. I'll have the place looked over again – in fact, I'll do it personally – but you stay well away.' He squinted at the bill and looked up at her. 'I'll check out what I think fit.'

'The Vice Squad, can you check that for me? See what Janklow was picked up for?'

'For *you*? Who in chrissakes do you think is runnin' this show? I'll take it from here. If you wanna press charges for assault—'

She leaned back. 'You know I won't do that but if you get more evidence, then I can be used as a lever. We let him confront me, let him know I'm alive and can identify him, and then see what he does. Use me to catch him. I'm willing.'

Rooney hauled his bulk out of the booth. 'Lemme think on it.'

She followed him as he headed for the restroom. 'Bill, he used a hammer on me. It's him.'

He whipped round. 'I could have you for withholding evidence. I only paid you to get out on the streets to talk to the hookers, so back off. I'll contact you when I need you.'

'I need a few dollars, I'm flat broke.'

'Not my problem,' he said as he pushed open the restroom door, and let it swing closed.

When he came out of the restaurant she was waiting by

his patrol car. She gave that strange, lopsided smile and he relaxed slightly. Although he was loath to admit it, she had pushed the investigation further – had even supplied him with a suspect.

'Lemme see what I come up with – but you do nothing until you hear from me, okay? Here's a few bucks, go home, wait for me to call. If it's Janklow, leave him to me.'

She took the money and watched him drive off. She checked the time – just after two thirty. As she walked to the bus stop she was thinking over everything she had said to Rooney. She had been clutching at straws, but what if she was right? What if there was a connection between Didi and Janklow? She hailed a taxi and, instead of returning home, told the driver to take her to Nula's place.

CHAPTER 15

NULA DIDN'T answer the door. Lorraine waited for almost an hour and then went home. There she hung about in case Rooney called but when it got to after six, she decided he'd got cold feet. 'I guess he mulled it all over and decided against it.'

Rosie wondered what they should do next. Without Rooney she was worried it could be dangerous to try to see Janklow again. Lorraine grabbed her purse.

'Where are you going?' Rosie asked nervously.

'You stay put so I can call Rooney back if he makes contact.'

'Don't you need me with you?'

'I'd prefer it if you stayed put in case he calls. I've got to keep him sweet, 'cos if I don't the old bastard is quite likely to get me arrested.'

Rosie sat moodily in front of the TV. She didn't even say goodbye as Lorraine let herself out. So much for partnership – all she'd been doing was sitting waiting for Lorraine in the apartment. When she heard the rental car starting up Rosie shot to the window as fast as her bulk allowed her. She pushed up the window and was about to yell after Lorraine but it was too late, she was already at the corner.

*

It had been so long since Lorraine had driven that her knees were shaking but she talked herself down, hoping she wouldn't get pulled over.

The lights were on in Nula's apartment. Lorraine sighed with relief, locked the car and headed into the apartment block. She rang the bell and waited. Nula's voice asked who it was but Lorraine rang again, afraid if she said her name that Nula wouldn't let her in. She kept her hand on the bell, and eventually Nula peered out, the chain still on.

'Fuck off.'

'Let me in, Nula, I'll stay here all night if needs be.'

Nula eventually opened up the door. Lorraine looked around. Suitcases had been dragged down from the wardrobes. Nula was on the move.

'What happened?'

'I'm going away.'

'Why do you have to go?'

Nula hurled a cushion at her. 'Stop asking me questions, just leave me alone.'

Lorraine took out the picture of Steven Janklow in drag. 'Will you have another look at this, Nula?'

Nula picked up the cushion and hugged it to her chest. Lorraine dangled the photograph between finger and thumb. 'It won't hurt you to have a look at it. Is it Steven Janklow?'

'If you fucking know who it is, why are you asking me?'

'Because I need to be sure.'

'I don't know, do I?'

Lorraine was deflated. She didn't know what her next move should be. She flopped back on the sofa.

'You gonna leave now?'

Lorraine slipped the photograph back into the envelope and stood up, facing the big four-sectioned screen behind which the models changed for a session. It was plastered with photographs of males and females, males and males, part females. Nula looked at her, then to the screen.

Lorraine started to move out then stopped and glanced back to Nula, who hid her face in the cushion. She stared at the screen. At first she wasn't sure that she was right so she moved closer, then she bent down and peered. She straightened up and waved the file. 'You don't know him? Then why is his photograph up on the screen?'

'Because it fitted the hole.'

'Who took the photograph?'

'Why?'

'Because if you don't know who it is, then whoever took the photograph might. Who took the picture, Nula?'

'Art.'

Lorraine could feel the adrenalin pumping; it was all as crazy as Rooney had said. 'What's Art's scene apart from the porno?'

'Use your head, clever bitch. Where do you think he gets all his dough from?'

'Why don't you tell me?'

Nula stood up and leaned against the doorframe to the bedroom. 'Blackmail. Some fucking detective you are. Art blackmails everybody, he's a bleeder – you should know, you copped a few grand from one of his little leech jobs. I don't know that blonde in that photo on the screen and I don't know whoever it is in your precious folder. That's not my screen, it's Art's. Now would you get out and leave me alone?'

'Where's Art?'

'I don't know.'

Lorraine followed Nula into the bedroom. 'Was he blackmailing Steven Janklow?'

Nula kicked out at the wardrobe and screamed, '*I don't know, leave me alone*.' She began to pull clothes out of her wardrobe.

'He was blackmailing him, wasn't he?'

Nula was hurling dresses onto the bed.

'The night Didi died—'

'Yes, what about the night Didi died?'

Lorraine kept her distance. Nula was becoming increasingly hysterical, dragging things off their hangers, dropping them, kicking them. She suddenly turned to Lorraine in a fury. 'He used us. If we had a john, he was sniffing around. He never let us have any peace, but then we couldn't have any because he'd give a few dollars here, a few dollars there, he let us have this apartment, okay? He said we never had to pay rent, okay? Well, if you believe that you're dumb. Art used me, used Didi, he made us both pay. Now if you don't get out and leave me alone I swear before God I'll scream this place down and have you arrested.'

Lorraine didn't budge. 'Was Art blackmailing Norman Hastings?'

Lorraine looked over the screen at the laminated photographs. She was frantically glancing from one blonde to another in a vague hope that one or other of the dead women as well as Hastings would have been photographed. 'When did Art make this screen?'

'Years ago. He brought it here with him when he left Santa Monica – he had a place there on the beach.' Nula stood, hands on hips, smirking. She had decided to try another tactic to get rid of Lorraine.

'Did he ever own a vintage car?'

Nula rolled her eyes. 'What do you mean?'

'A custom-made car or an old sports car.'

'Nah, he had a Bentley once for about six months, then he went broke again and sold it.'

'The blonde in the photograph, the one I showed you on the screen, did you meet him?'

Nula sighed. 'No.'

'What about Didi?'

Nula was holding a long chiffon dress. 'This was her favourite. It never fitted her but she wouldn't throw it out.'

'Nula, please, did Didi know the blonde?'

'She may have, she used to do wigs, she was always good

294

with hair. Art used her sometimes for photo sessions, so she may have, I don't know who she knew.'

'Did Didi know Art before you?'

'Yes, I met him through her.'

Lorraine's mind was racing, trying to put two and two together but she wasn't sure what she was trying to come up with. There was no point in staying any longer. Her priority now was to contact the photographer who had taken pictures of Norman Hastings. She asked Nula if she could use her phone.

Rosie was still watching TV when Lorraine called. No, there had been no contact from Rooney. Lorraine asked her to check in the files for the name and address of Hastings's photographer. She hung on, waiting impatiently, until eventually Rosie found his name: Craig Lyall. She gave the address and phone number. Lorraine said she would call in again. If Rooney made contact, Rosie was to tell him that she would be back in about an hour: it was imperative she speak with him.

'Have you ever heard of Craig Lyall, a photographer?' she asked Nula.

Nula clicked the suitcase shut. 'Professional, is he?'

'Yeah, takes family shots, portraits.'

Nula shrugged. 'Name isn't familiar but then I'm never good with names.'

'What about Didi? Do you have her address book? Maybe she has his number.'

Nula took a small key and locked the case. 'No, she never kept one, and now, if you'll excuse me, I am going to take a bath. Unless you want to watch me soaping my tits I suggest you leave.'

'You need a lift? I've got a car.'

'I'll get a cab.'

'Can I ask where you're going?'

'You can, but I don't see why I should tell you.'

'Just in case I need to get in touch with you.'

Nula carried her cases to the door, dumped them and went back to pick up two more bags.

'Curtis knows how to contact me.'

Lorraine reached out to shake Nula's hand but she turned away. 'Goodbye, and thanks.'

Nula stood in the centre of the room, arms folded. As soon as she heard the front door slam behind Lorraine, she clutched the sides of her head and started to scream, ripping off her wig and hurling it across the room. She screamed and screamed.

Lorraine drove to Craig Lyall's studio. She looked around for a phone kiosk to check with Rosie if Rooney had called. He hadn't but two uniformed police officers had been there. Rosie hadn't been unduly worried when they arrived, partly because she was expecting Rooney. She even asked if they were there because of him. They did not answer her questions but moved from room to room, even swishing back the shower curtain. When they asked if there were any other ways into the apartment, Rosie started to get uneasy. She was edgy after they left because they remained outside in their patrol car and didn't look as if they had any intention of driving off.

Lorraine wondered what Rooney was playing at. She told Rosie she would call him right away and see her in a while.

'Where are you?'

'Ventura Highway. I'm gonna talk to this Craig Lyall. See you later.' She hung up and called Rooney's office.

'Where are you?' he barked.

'Oh, just having a quick coffee, then I'm on my way home.'

'Do me a favour and bring yourself to the station.'

'You got a development?'

'Maybe. I want you here where I can see you.'

'I got something I want you to check out. Photographer, guy called Art Mathews. I think he's involved, blackmailer, porno stuff. He knows Janklow . . . hello?' The beep-beep-beep of her money running out cut off the call.

Rooney let the receiver drop back on the cradle. He waited, half hoping she would call again, wandering round his office, hitching up his pants. Through his venetian blind he could see the suits working with the computer officers, sifting through the investigations. He let the blind fall back into place. He was, in some way, hiding out – he'd skirted around them all afternoon and evening.

Bean breezed in and Rooney jumped. 'Fuckin' knock, for chrissakes, you give me a heart attack. You ever heard of a porno photographer, Art Mathews?'

'Nope.'

'Run a trace on him, will you? And then bring him in. I want to have a talk to him.'

'Okay, will do. You wanted to know if Vice had anything on a Steven Janklow? There's no record, nothing . . . but the Thorburn family funded an entire section of the LAPD forensic lab and—'

'Thank you,' grunted Rooney.

'You're welcome,' said Bean as he walked out.

Lorraine moved up the wood-slatted staircase to the small photographic studio belonging to Craig Lyall. She pressed the intercom and waited. Asked to identify herself, she said she was a friend of Art Mathews. Lyall unbolted the door. Small and dapper, he was shorter than Lorraine.

'What do you want? You a cop?'

'No, just a friend of Art's.'

Lorraine followed Lyall up the narrow staircase towards his studio apartment. The TV was on loudly and he switched it off. 'I was working in the dark room. Let me sort out these negs then I'll be right with you. Make yourself at home.'

Lorraine put down her purse and remained standing, looking at all the framed photographs. She then crossed to two heavyweight albums, filled with portraits of kids and families. She turned over the heavy pages, awful smiling brats in over-colourful dresses, all much the same, similar to the pictures she had seen in Mrs Hastings's home.

Lyall returned and offered her a drink. He seemed jumpy.

'Art's told me a lot about you.'

'Really?'

'Yeah. He's in trouble, you know that?'

'He's always been in trouble, ever since I've known him.'

'Yeah, well, this time he's involved in murder.'

Lyall pursed his lips. 'Jesus Christ, it's not this fucking Hastings thing again. I've had them here, you know, asking me all kinds of questions. All I did was take some photographs – poor bastard liked to drag up, right? What's wrong in that?'

Lorraine perched on the edge of a hard-back chair. 'Can I see them? Just out of interest. I'm trying to help Art. I wasn't all that honest with you – I'm a private investigator and I need to get as much—'

Lyall jumped almost a foot in the air. 'I've got nothing to do with him! I know him, that's all, I just know him, and a few times I've taken the odd photo for him, or if he's sent somebody to me. I'm discreet, okay? That's all there is to it.'

Lyall was even more nervous now, walking up and down.

'Did you ever use a transsexual called Didi?'

'How do you mean?'

'Did you ever take photographs of her? Pornographic ones.'

'No way. I wasn't into that kind of thing. I just do straight portraits.'

'But sometimes you photographed transsexuals, or transvestites?'

'Yeah, they just wanted a photo of themselves, nothing wrong in that, is there?' He fidgeted, repeating that it wasn't against the law and that he'd answered all the questions about Hastings; the police had been to question him, he'd given them his photos.

'Did you know Didi well?'

'Yes and no. She was useful sometimes. She did their make-up and hair, that's all.'

'Did she do Norman Hastings's wigs?'

'Yeah, I think so.' Lorraine watched as he bent down to a chest and took out some envelopes. 'She was good, knew her stuff, could make even Hastings look reasonable.' He showed her two or three photographs of Hastings. Lorraine complimented each photo, and Lyall preened himself, started to take out more. She asked nonchalantly if he'd ever photographed a man called Steven Janklow.

Lyall was still looking through his work admiringly and didn't hear so she repeated the name and he straightened. 'Look, I don't always ask who my clients are. This is a private thing between me and them. I have to make them feel at ease – they get quite excited, and then when Didi has finished with them, they're almost orgasmic. It's a big turn-on for them and after the session they take away their photos and that's it.'

Lorraine nodded. She didn't immediately mention Janklow's name again but took her time, letting Lyall relax.

'Did Art help out on any sessions?'

'Not for years. He did once – I didn't have a dark room of my own and he had a big place over in Santa Monica, so I used to use his facilities. If I'm honest, he taught me a lot. Many of them have a bit of a problem – you know, the skin. Art taught me how to airbrush all that out, lines. I can make them look beautiful.'

She tried again. 'Did you photograph this Janklow?' Lyall paused. 'I really don't know. Some of them use assumed names, or call themselves by their female name. Is it important?'

'He's Art's alibi.'

'Why don't you ask Janklow?'

'I can't trace him and Art thinks he wouldn't want to come forward – doesn't want his family to know about his private life.'

Lyall repacked his photographs in their envelopes.

'Do you know the S and A vintage car garage?'

'Yes, it's in Santa Monica. I'm going back years now, but Art used to wheel around in an outrageous Bentley. He bought it from them but he's useless mechanically. It was always going wrong. Art just about knew where to put the gas in.'

Lorraine took out the photo of the blonde woman and gave it to Lyall. 'Have you ever taken that person's photograph?' she asked.

'I can't say. You've seen how many I've done and they're just the recent ones.'

Lorraine took it back, and asked if the clients took away their negatives. That was part of the deal, Lyall said, suddenly becoming evasive again. 'Look, I know what you're inferring. My clients always have the negatives. Some even wait until I've done them. I've never been in trouble with the police and I would never – Look, we all know about Art and I've always said that's his business. No way do I get involved.'

'You mean his pornography?'

'No. Blackmail.'

Lorraine nodded. 'Yes, I've warned him about it and I think that's why this witness won't come forward. I reckon Art was blackmailing him.'

Lyall groaned. 'Art's been in prison and that didn't stop him. He's always after making the quick buck but it disgusts me. These poor bastards, they come here and they're like kids, you know, shaking with excitement, and they're so harmless. I mean, who does it hurt if a man likes to pretty himself up? It's no crime but society makes them hide.'

Lorraine agreed. 'I feel sorry for the guys Art's been tapping. Poor Norman Hastings, a decent married man, scared it would come out—'

Lyall looked anxious. 'I never told that to the police – I couldn't, it would incriminate me. Then I'd have to tell them about Art.'

Lorraine asked if she could smoke. 'I get asthma but go ahead.' He fetched an ashtray and turned up the air-conditioning. She lit a cigarette and blew the smoke away from him.

'How did Art get hold of Hastings's pictures if, as you said, they always take the negatives away?'

Lyall flushed. 'I don't know.'

'You didn't give them to him, did you?'

'No, of course not, but . . . maybe his friend did. I photographed Hastings's family – I knew them and I wouldn't want to hurt them. They're not even wealthy, but that was Art, he'd even settle for fifty dollars a month – awful, I hated it.'

'By his friend, do you mean Didi?'

'Yes, I suspected it was her. She was here, she made Norman up – made a very good job of it.'

'She's dead.'

Lyall gaped. 'But you were just talking about her. When? Why didn't Nula call me? Or Art? I don't believe it.'

'Last night.'

Lyall seemed genuinely shocked, so she said, 'Will you take another look at the photo I brought, in case you might remember. I think it's a cross-dresser, don't you?'

Lyall took the photograph again and held it to the lamp.

He viewed the picture through an eyeglass for at least thirty seconds before he nodded. 'Yes, but it's a very good wig and make-up . . . It's the jaw-line, I can always tell.'

'You don't recognize him then?'

'No, I don't think so, but I do so many . . .'

'He never came here with Hastings?'

'Norman was always alone, unless he was with his family.'

A buzzer sounded from the dark room and Lyall checked his watch. 'I've got to get these ready for tomorrow. It's a twenty-first portrait.'

Lorraine was heading for the door, when Lyall exclaimed, 'Of course! Let me see that picture again.'

Lorraine watched him, almost willing him to say that he *had* taken pictures of Janklow. Instead he shook his head. 'There was a famous society hostess, very wealthy – now, what was her name? She came for a sitting, very crippled, arthritic, in a wheelchair. She had two sessions, I think, but turned the pictures down. Well, honestly, if I'd airbrushed any more of her she'd not have had any face left, not a line left, and they paid just the sitting fee. That's why I remember it, because I was out of pocket, and I'm going back a few years.' He traced his thin lips with his tongue as he tried to remember, and then he beamed. 'Thorburn, that was the name, Della Thorburn, and it must have been at least eight, maybe nine years ago. She could even be dead by now. Isn't it strange? Really weird.' Lorraine waited for him to continue. 'It's odd that I can remember her so well and from that photograph, it's just that . . . Let me have another look at it.' He used his eyeglass again. 'It isn't her – she couldn't drive, she was very crippled. But the way the scarf is draped reminds me of her. She always wore these chiffon scarves to hide her neck, and the blonde hair, that old-fashioned style, a Grace Kelly roll at the back or just flicked at the sides.'

'Did Didi do her make-up and hair?'

'Good God, no. She was Society. She wouldn't want somebody like Didi around. I'm talking old money.'

Lorraine wasn't sure where this new development was leading. She asked if Mrs Thorburn had been accompanied by anyone. 'Yes, of course, she was in a chair. Her son, if I can recollect, he brought her.'

'Did you hear his name?'

'Well, I presumed it was Thorburn.'

'Can you describe him?'

Lyall screwed up his eyes. 'God, I'm going back years, and I'm sorry I can't. But Art maybe could, he has a mind-blowing memory – he can even remember phone numbers.'

'Art was here?'

'Oh, no, it was in Santa Monica, I told you, we worked together, had our own clients. But then I left and came here.'

'Was Art doing similar photo sessions, with transvestites or transsexuals?'

'Oh, yes – in fact he started me off, sent me clients. I told you before.'

His dark-room buzzer rang loudly again. 'I've really got to go, I can't leave them soaking any longer.'

Lorraine returned to the car. She sat a while as she went over everything Lyall had told her. She now had a link between Hastings and Janklow. She even had a tentative link between Didi and both men, and Art was linked to them all. Art was blackmailing Norman Hastings, she concluded, and Hastings might have discussed this with Janklow. But what if Art was blackmailing Janklow as well?

She drove home deep in thought. What if she was wrong about Janklow and Art was the killer? But she knew that couldn't be right. Her attacker hadn't been Art Mathews. What was the link between each of the dead women who, apart from Holly, all resembled each other in age? But then she thought again about Holly's murder; according to Didi, the killer had gestured to her, had wanted her. She had even said to Lorraine that she was lucky because if Holly hadn't been picked up then it could have been her. What if it *was* Didi the killer had wanted? Just as she had said to Rooney the women were or could possibly have all been mistaken for Didi. She, Lorraine, was tall, about the same height as Didi, and blonde. Was the killer looking for one woman in particular, a woman he knew worked the streets, a woman he knew was a transsexual?

Lorraine had to pull over, her head throbbing with all the jagged sections of information. Her attempts at trying to make them all fit exhausted her. She closed her eyes. She had left Art Mathews in the gallery the night Holly had died. What had he done after she left and where did he go? Were he, Didi, Nula even, all connected to the murders? She was too tired to get it together, tired and hungry. She started the car again and headed back onto the freeway towards Pasadena.

Art Mathews had been brought in for questioning. He had attempted to run from the police, who had been about to tell him that he was not being charged with anything but was required to assist their inquiries. As they entered his new studio, though, he had dived past them, which aroused their suspicions and they gave chase. He gave himself up after an abortive run between oncoming cars, zig-zagging across the road, nearly getting himself killed. A routine search of his studio yielded a vast selection of pornography stills.

Rooney had begun to question Mathews as soon as he was brought in. He was expansive and over-talkative, as if high on drugs. He had not as yet asked for a lawyer. He admitted to mild pornography but it was not until one of the officers entered the room with a black and white photograph of Holly that the interview took an upward spiral. Art admitted knowing her; he had even taken photographs of her. Agitated and sweating, the little man tried to recall where he was on the night of her murder.

At almost every turn he incriminated himself. When he admitted that he also knew the most recent murdered transsexual, Didi, Rooney could feel the hair lift on the back of his neck. He knew they had to get legal representation for Art and fast, and suggested as much to him. If he so wished, they would be prepared to wait. Rooney had also asked for a doctor to examine him: if he was drugged up they needed to know as they would have to wait until he came down from whatever he was on.

Suddenly Art jumped up, spittle forming at the sides of his mouth. 'This is crazy! You think I killed Holly? Why would I do a thing like that? This is all a misunderstanding.'

At no time had Rooney suggested there was any suspicion that Art was involved in the murder. He had him on selling pornographic material by his own admission. Now it seemed he was about to talk himself into being accused of murder.

As the interview swung up a notch, the tension in the room grew tighter. Rooney began to ask him about each of the victims.

'What? Why?' Art began to screech, his voice getting higher and higher in his agitation. 'Why are you asking me about these women? This is insanity. You think I had anything to do with those murders? This is crazy. I've admitted I knew Holly, okay, I knew Didi—'

Rooney probed into Art's business, his background, his previous criminal record. Only then did he detect the fear. Art now demanded legal representation: he would not answer any more questions. Rooney knew that most of what he had admitted might not hold up in court, especially as he had still not been checked out for drugs. He was so wired up when they brought him in, he could have confessed to any number of crimes. But Rooney was pushing, he was excited, he felt that old rush of adrenalin. Art

Mathews was like a scared rabbit almost caught in a trap and Rooney was eager to snap the door shut on him. So much was riding on his gaining results, on grabbing them right under the FBI's noses.

When Art eventually quietened, Rooney took it as a sign of guilt. It was obvious to all in the interrogation room that he had only become uncooperative when the murders were mentioned. While they waited for the lawyer to arrive, Art continued to declare his innocence. He kept rubbing his shining bald head, looking from one man to the next. 'Just because I knew Didi and Holly doesn't mean I'd kill them. This is some kind of frame-up. Did somebody tip you off about me? Is that what this is all about? Did some piece of shit put me in it?'

He demanded to know what time Didi had been killed, as he had been with friends the entire evening, but when told and asked where he was between nine and ten thirty he suddenly refused to say where he was or who he was with until he had a lawyer present. A doctor examined him and gave him the all-clear but suggested they give him plenty to drink as he was sweating so much from nerves.

His lawyer arrived and he was allowed a private discussion. Once that had been completed, he was faced yet again with all the questions that had been asked earlier. One of the reasons he had refused to state where he was on the night Didi died was also that he had been filming a session. Having already served time for selling pornographic videos and working with under-age kids, he was scared that he'd be charged with a similar offence. He was also becoming increasingly alarmed that details of his blackmail activities might leak out. The more he was questioned the more nervous he became. When the lists of the dead women started unfolding he became hysterical, screaming that they were setting him up, and some of the murders had happened so long ago he couldn't remember where he had been living. He might even have been serving a sentence. Meanwhile, his new studio was being ransacked, and more pornography discovered.

He was taken down to the cells. It was almost three in the morning and both Rooney and Bean were still working. Rooney's head ached but he was back on form, though he was sure now that Art was not their killer. He had found out that when two of the earlier murders had been committed, Art had been in jail.

When he returned to his office, Bean was waiting. 'They still haven't brought your informant in, this Lorraine Page.'

'I think we've been wasting our time, Bean. That little bastard should be locked up but not for murder. He's just into his porno and probably the blackmail rackets again.'

Bean threw up his hands in despair. 'Does that mean Lorraine Page is into all that as well?'

Rooney sighed. 'I don't know. Maybe you should get this information ready for the suits. Lay it out on the Chief's desk, let him see we've worked our butts off tonight.'

Bean took Mathews's prison record to the FBI agents' office and Rooney glanced at his watch. In all fairness it was too late to call Lorraine but he reckoned he wouldn't get any sleep. He'd give it a couple more hours and call her after he'd shaved and washed.

He was running his small battery-operated shaver over his fat chin when Bean peered into the washroom. Rooney gave him a worn-out smile and clicked off the shaver. 'I don't suppose we just got lucky and Art Mathews admitted killing eight women and Norman Hastings?' he asked sarcastically.

Bean ran the cold water into the basin. 'No. Prime suspect is sobbing his heart out down there in the cells. Meanwhile his lawyer doesn't want us to press criminal charges if he admits to what he was doing on the night of the last murder. He has already remembered where he was when Holly was murdered and this you're not gonna believe.'

'Try me,' Rooney said heavily.

'Art Mathews was working in that gallery right next to your Indian curry place. He worked there until late, all night, and Lorraine Page is one of his alibis.'

Rooney stared at his reflection. Bean dried his hands on the roller towel. 'Any money the FBI'll release him on bail, he'll get locked up for a few years for his porno trade. Been a long night for nothing. Pity we don't have something – there's press outside. Somebody tipped them off we got a suspect.'

Rooney hitched up his pants. 'Yeah, maybe the same person who tipped us off about Art Mathews. I'm going to call that two-faced bitch now.'

Bean followed Rooney down the corridor. 'You know they got Andrew Fellows coming in to talk to the FBI later this morning? Maybe you should hang around – canteen'll be open soon.'

Rooney had been about to call Lorraine even though it was only five thirty. He changed his mind. He didn't give a shit if he woke her up or not. He was gonna go one better and do it personally. As he drove out of the station yard, he watched two new patrol cars pulling in with the FBI men all bright-eyed and bushy-tailed even if they had been hauled out of their beds at this ungodly hour. He drove away, his anger mounting. Art Mathews had been another of Lorraine's theories. She had been partly right: he *had* known Holly and Didi, but he had no connection with Steven Janklow. There was no record on him in Vice. Rooney might even force her to give him back his dough. Maybe he'd have her hauled in, spill it about her being the witness they'd been searching for. He'd like to grab her by her scrawny throat and strangle her. He was through, period. The more he drove, the angrier he became. As he headed towards Lorraine's apartment, he was ready to explode. He really needed to sound off at somebody so it might as well be her! The two-faced, lying whore.

Rosie shot out of bed when the doorbell rang. She grabbed a robe and scuttled to the door. Lorraine was sitting up on the sofa yawning. 'What time is it?'

'Six o'clock in the morning! Who the hell is ringing the bell at this time?'

Rosie opened the door and stepped back. Rooney was leaning against the doorframe. He looked past Rosie to Lorraine. 'I'm gonna arrest you.'

Lorraine drew a cardigan around her nightdress. 'Arrest me? Why, for chrissakes?'

He sauntered in. 'Art Mathews, sweetheart. You were with him the night the . . .' He couldn't remember Holly's name. 'You were with him the night she was murdered, you're his fucking alibi. *You!*'

Lorraine filled a tumbler with water and drank it straight down. 'Is that why you sent cops here? Did you do that to me?'

Rooney tossed his hat aside. 'Be the FBI wanting you next, sweetheart, time's up.'

She faced him in a fury. 'Did you tell them about me? Bill, did you tell them I was attacked?'

'You know I didn't but I sure as hell intend to because you are full of bullshit and you've lied to me right along the way. When I tried to help you out, all you did was lie.'

Lorraine glared at him. 'They still holding Mathews?'

'Far as I know. Maybe you were mistaken about this Janklow and maybe it was Mathews attacked you in the gallery when you were working together, hanging up pictures, the night Holly died.'

She sighed. 'That's stupid. He's right-handed.'

'What?'

309

'Art Mathews is right-handed. The guy who attacked me was left-handed, according to all the forensic and pathology reports and even the reports from Andrew Fellows. The killer is left-handed, opens the glove compartment with his right, holds their heads down with his left . . .'

Rooney looked at her, then turned away. 'Get dressed. We're out of here.'

'No. You sit right where you are.'

He pouted and then tugged a bottle of bourbon out of his pocket. He slowly unscrewed the cap and took a heavy pull. He dangled the bottle towards Lorraine.

Rosie eyed it and then eyed Lorraine. She was walking towards it.

Rooney watched Lorraine. 'Want a drink?'

Lorraine snatched the bottle and marched to the sink, about to pour it down the drain, when the smell suddenly hit her. She wanted a drink, everything started to crystallize, all she could think of was reaching for a glass and drinking. She didn't care about Art Mathews or Steven Janklow, she wanted a drink. She slowly lifted the bottle to her lips, closing her eyes in anticipation.

'Don't do it, Lorraine.' It was Rooney. 'Chuck it out, don't do it. I'm sorry. Here, Lorraine, give it to me.'

Rooney had to prise her hands away from the bottle. It shocked him, made him feel wretched. He leaned on the sink pouring the booze away, as Lorraine tried to wrest the bottle from him. He turned on the taps so the water splashed into the sink and over him. 'Shit. I'm soaking wet.'

'Aren't we all?' snapped Lorraine. 'Old washed-up soaks,' she said as she took down coffee cups. 'I suppose it's black coffee all round?'

There was a sudden hard tap at the front door. Rosie went to open it but Rooney stopped her. He peered out of the window and told Lorraine to get into the bedroom. She obeyed immediately, closing the door behind her as the front door was tapped hard again.

'Don't say anything,' Rooney said quietly to Rosie. 'Just leave this to me.'

The two officers framed in the doorway asked for Lorraine Page. Rosie held the door wider to reveal Rooney standing in the centre of the room with a cup of coffee in his hand. They seemed fazed by his presence and made no move to enter the room.

'Captain Rooney.'

'You come to pick her up?'

They nodded, and one passed him a warrant for Lorraine's arrest.

'I'll hang on to this. I'm staying put until she shows. Go back to base. Soon as I got her I'll call in.'

Rooney pocketed the warrant, carried his coffee towards the sofa, and sat down. 'Unless you want to hang around here.'

'We'll leave it to you, Captain.'

A few moments later Lorraine came out of the bedroom. She leaned against the doorframe, looking at the squat Rooney. 'Why did you do that, Bill?'

'Christ only knows, I must be nuts.'

She cradled her coffee cup in her hands and sat in the easy chair opposite him while Rosie hovered, uncomfortable and ill-at-ease with them.

'I'm sorry for bringing the booze in,' Rooney said.

'That's okay,' and Rosie wandered to her bedroom, feeling in the way.

'She seems a nice woman,' Rooney said.

'Rosie's great.' Lorraine got up for a refill. She leaned over the back of the sofa towards Rooney. 'You wanna hear my developments? What I've come up with this evening?'

He wanted to say no but he didn't. Instead he let her talk without interruption, listening intently as she pieced together her talk with Nula, then her meeting with Craig Lyall.

Lorraine's face was expressionless as she explained

clearly, emotionlessly, what had happened when she had
been attacked. She described walking up to the car, how he
had driven her to the parking space, how she had fought
him, bitten hard into his neck, hung on for her life as he
tried to push her away from him. He was strong, she said.
The grip on her hair had been like a vice, and it had taken
all her strength to lever up her body to turn and bite. She
was sure if they hadn't been disturbed by the Summerses,
she would have been dead. She then told Rooney that she
had also taken Norman Hastings's wallet.

Rooney closed his eyes and kept them closed. He was
scared that if he opened them he'd charge at her like a mad
bull with fury.

'There's something else. At first I didn't think it was
important. It was his cufflinks. They had a logo. I didn't
think it was important until I saw the same logo on a
letterhead. At my husband's place – Mike, you remember
Mike? He has nothing to do with this, I know that, but it
gave me the first clue to the killer.'

Rooney was fighting to control his temper. She looked
directly at him and continued. She described how she and
Rosie had gone to S and A's garage, how she had narrowed
the list of cufflink owners down and taken photographs of
suspects. None resembled the man who had atacked her.
She took the photographs out and passed them to Rooney
and leant close to him as he examined the one of the blonde
woman.

'I think this is Steven Janklow. I think he's a transvestite,
and that he had a photographic session with either Mathews
or Lyall. It could have been as far back as nine to ten years
ago, maybe when he was just daring to come out. I think
Mathews subsequently discovered who he was and started
blackmailing him, realizing he'd found the golden goose. I
think Art and Didi may have worked as a team. She was
used or hired to do wigs and make-up. She made up
Norman Hastings, fixed his hair for the photo session.

312

Maybe she even tipped off Art, as Lyall said most of his clients always took the negatives. You interviewed Lyall, too, didn't you?'

Rooney nodded. They'd come up with nothing as concrete as Lorraine. He couldn't help but give a tight smile: she was good, always had been good. Now she began pacing up and down. There was something about the way she moved, tensing, relaxing her hands, and she rubbed her body, sexually, her face becoming more and more alive. She was exciting to watch, as she became increasingly animated.

'I've got Hastings linked to Janklow – maybe they discussed the blackmail. Who knows what they discussed? Possible theory is, when Hastings went to the bank that morning, was he going to pay off Mathews? Pay off somebody? The strange thing is all his bank statements have been checked and the major transactions are accounted for.' She suddenly stopped and clicked her fingers. 'Unless Hastings was also tapping Janklow for money. It seems strange that he was allowed to park his car in the hangar. Nobody seems to know why he should have been when he no longer owned one of their cars. Did you know that at one time he owned a vintage car? Maybe that was where he could have found out that he and Janklow were the same kind of men. Whatever, we know they're linked, and linked to Mathews through Didi. She's very important. She may not have collected from Mathews's blackmailing activities, but I'm beginning to think she may have been the go-between or, and this is a wild guess, maybe she was the person Janklow believed was blackmailing him. So that brings me to the last bit of guesswork.'

Lorraine took out the victims' photographs and laid them along the sofa for Rooney to look at. 'They have one thing in common apart from prostitution. Look at the make-up, the type of clothes they wore. Now, look at the morgue shots of Didi . . . Put her beside each one. You didn't believe me earlier but what if Janklow was only after *her* – was only interested in tracking *her* down and killing her? He's a Thorburn, right? His mother was a big society hostess, his brother is holding all the purse strings. What if Janklow has been paying out blackmail money because he's scared his family will find out and it might be made public? Just as Hastings hid his private life from everyone who knew him.'

Lorraine tapped Rooney's shoulder. He edged away, annoyed by her but more angry with himself. She had run rings around him and his department, and it infuriated him. But the only thing against her that he could think of was that she had withheld vital evidence.

'You got to break Art Mathews – get him to admit this blackmail. If you do, then you got a clean motive and you've got Janklow – or at least enough to arrest him and take him in for questioning.'

Rooney's head was spinning, and as he tried to assimilate everything she had told him he felt dizzy. She added, 'And the guy has got to have some mark from where I bit him. Maybe the skin's healed, even the bruising, but I held on for grim death.'

Rooney was unnerved by her toughness. 'You faced him yet?'

'I told you I hadn't, I'm not stupid.'

'You are one hell of a witness, you know that, don't you?'

'Yeah.' She stepped back, suddenly wary of him. He was a big man and when he stood up straight instead of his usual slouch it was surprising how much it added to his size.

'You'll have to come in with me. I'm sorry, Lorraine, there's no way out of it now.'

'Come on, Bill, don't make me have to go to court, not now, not when I'm getting myself back together. I go to court, they can start throwing old charges at me, make me admit to what I was and they'll dish the dirt on me, even bring up the shooting. Don't do it to me, Bill.'

314

'You were fucking attacked! That's what you'd be in court for, nothing else.'

'I know what he did but I won't go to court. Don't make them call me out, Bill.'

'You've withheld evidence, and you even had Norman Hastings's goddamned wallet! You never even told me about the cufflinks, so what do you expect me to do? You are the only witness. You gave me weeks of fucking waste of time. If you'd been upfront with me I'd have cracked this, I'd have been—'

She yelled, 'Patted on the back and given a commendation before you retired, that's what you're pissed off about right now! Instead of moving on what I've just been spewing out for the past hour, you're gettin' the needle to me. You want me to face out Steven Janklow, then I'll do it right now, I'll go over to his place in Beverly Glen with you, with anyone you want, but I won't go to court. Bill, I'm not standing up as ex-cop, ex-alcoholic, ex-hooker so you can get a slap on the back. I won't do it, I'll pack up and walk out right now and you won't see me for dust.'

He waved the warrant. 'I can take you in, Lorraine.'

'Try it, *just try it*.' Hands on hips she glowered at him. 'Go get Art Mathews to talk, Bill, that's what you should be doing. You know it, so stop bullshitting and get on with it. I won't be taken in and I warn you, if they drag me into court, then I won't pour the next bottle down the drain.'

He pointed at her with his index finger. 'You don't leave this apartment, you hear me? If you want I can make sure. I can have a squad car out front in two minutes. I can have you watched day and night, right round the clock, have guys on your doorstep.'

She sat down. 'I won't leave, Bill, I give you my word. Maybe just to the corner for groceries but I'll stay put.'

His upright position relaxed and he resumed his habitual slouch. 'I'll call you, see what I can do, lie about you, I suppose. But don't let me down, Lorraine, I couldn't take it.'

She hugged him tightly. He smelt of cigarettes and booze and food and he grunted at her to get away from him. He walked out of the door without a word and slammed it behind him.

Lorraine slumped onto the sofa. She was hot, angry, frustrated and a little scared. She should have kept her mouth shut about Hastings's wallet. There was no need for her to have mentioned it – that had been a big mistake. She wondered if Rooney would have the balls to keep her identity secret and not make her go to court. To have all her past made public, to have her daughters and Mike read about her made her anger turn to humiliation. For the first time she faced her shame. She was disgusted with herself. Tears slid down her cheeks, but she made no sound. Had she really been stupid enough to think that she could start a new career? Who would want to hire her if her past life was splashed across every tabloid? She knew they'd love it, that she'd be hounded, and she knew they'd rake up why she'd been forced to quit the police. She saw him again, the yellow zig-zag stripe down his jacket, his face as he fell, his hair flopping.

Rosie opened the bedroom door and Lorraine heard the heavy, plodding feet crossing the room. She waited, praying for Rosie to leave her in peace. She bit harder into her hand as she felt her friend's weight subsiding on the edge of the sofa. Rosie stroked her hair. 'I listened at the door just in case you needed me.'

Lorraine sighed. She never had any privacy. She almost forgot that this was Rosie's place.

'You serious about going into the investigation business? For real?' Rosie asked quietly.

'No, I'd never get a licence, I was just kidding myself.'

'You shouldn't. I was real proud of the way you just

316

talked to Rooney, the way you were piecing it together. You're good, you know, clever.'

Lorraine gazed up at the big plump face. 'Did you hear it all?'

'Yep, and that's another thing you're good at. He was right, you sure as hell can lie better than anyone I know.'

Lorraine laughed softly. 'Yeah, I guess you just get used to it, part of a cop's life that, you know. "No cause for alarm", when a whole building's about to collapse.'

Rosie rubbed Lorraine's back, like a mother would her child's. 'Maybe if you had to go to court it wouldn't be such a bad thing. Maybe your kids *should* know, maybe they'll be proud that you're fighting back, proving yourself – proving your worth.'

Lorraine grinned. 'Rosie, you're such an optimist.'

'Yeah, but I'm looking out for me too. I think I could get used to this kind of work – being a private investigator's more interesting than sticking down envelopes – computers, even!'

Lorraine moved away from the soothing warmth of Rosie's reassuring hand. 'You don't know it all, Rosie. It's not just the drinking, the whoring, it's not just that . . .' and she told her about the fourteen-year-old boy. Rosie didn't say anything but she felt even more warmth towards Lorraine, and especially when after the telling of the story, she tilted her face slightly and gave her a sweet, sad smile. 'I'm gonna take a shower now.'

The telephone rang and Rosie answered it. It was Rooney and she knew something was wrong straight away.

'She's just taking a shower, Captain Rooney, you want me to fetch her?'

Rooney coughed. 'Rosie, I've got some bad news. Art Mathews committed suicide.'

Rosie gasped. 'My God, but how – how did he do—'

Rooney interrupted, 'I'm sorry, but you'd better warn

Lorraine. There's not a hope in hell of me keeping her out of this now, you understand?'

'How long does she have before they get here?'

'They're already on their way.'

Rosie looked at the closed bedroom door. 'She'll be ready.'

Rooney wanted to say more but there was too much going on so he hung up. Rosie opened the bedroom door: she could hear Lorraine singing in the shower. 'Run, rabbit, run, rabbit, run, run, run . . .'

CHAPTER 16

J AKE LISTENED without interrupting. When Rosie had
called him before he'd even had his breakfast, his first
thought was it was she who needed him 'urgently'. He
was relieved to find her waiting at her front door stone
cold sober. As she drew him into the apartment, she put
her finger to her lips, indicating the bedroom. She didn't
want Lorraine to hear what she was saying but she knew
she had to make it fast. 'They arrest her, Jake, and everything she's accomplished so far will be over. She'll go back
on the booze – she as good as said it.'

It was hard for him to take in everything Rosie said. Just
the pertinent facts were enough to make him break out in a
sweat. Lorraine had been attacked by the so-called hammer
killer; she was the witness the police were searching for; she
was also investigating or assisting the police in their inquiries. It was hard to believe, and even more so when Rosie
slipped in that Lorraine's 'partner' was also helping the
investigation.

They couldn't carry on the conversation as Lorraine
walked in. She was surprised to see Jake.

'You come for breakfast?'

'Nope. I was wondering if you wanted to come to a
meeting.'

'What? Are you nuts? It's not even nine o'clock. Besides,
I can't. I got to stay in the apartment.'

'I'm gonna get dressed,' Rosie said, eyeing Jake and

jerking her head towards Lorraine, who watched her go out and then started to wash the cups.

She ran water into the sink. 'So, what has she told you?'

Jake fiddled with his collar.

'Is it about me admitting I wanted a drink?'

Jake shrugged. 'You may not know it, Lorraine, but you just broke through, and you'll make it even if it doesn't look or feel like it right now. But I want you to come to a meeting with me this morning. According to Rosie you might need a morale boost.'

Lorraine put her head on one side. 'She tell you I might be arrested?'

'Is it true?'

She put down the dishcloth. 'It's true, and I think I'm gonna need a lot more than just a morale boost.'

'Then you'll come to the early-morning meeting?'

Bean strode into Rooney's office, hands in his pockets. 'Ambulance just taken his body away.'

Rooney pulled at his nose. 'How the hell did he do it?'

'Broke his glasses and slit his wrists.'

'FBI must be shitting themselves.' Rooney snorted with a half-derisive laugh and sneer.

'Yep, all in there blaming each other and patting each other on the back at the same time.'

Rooney gaped. 'What you mean?'

'Well, it's obvious, isn't it? I mean, why kill yourself if you're innocent? They reckon he must be the one.'

Rooney snorted again. 'That's bullshit. We know he couldn't have done two of them because he was inside. They got the report of his criminal record, didn't they?'

Bean said that they might have found some discrepancies over the dates. Whatever, they were not digging too deep as the Chief was putting out a press release that the suspect in custody had admitted his guilt.

'Had he?' Rooney asked, astonished, because when he'd last seen Mathews he hadn't – far from it.

'They reckon so, but they still want to question his accomplice.'

'His what?'

'Lorraine Page. I was told you were bringing her in. They've been waiting for you.'

Rooney could feel the warrant in his pocket. He took it out and passed it to Bean, his heart pounding. He felt sick, needed time to plan what he was going to do with the information Lorraine had passed him. He had already decided not to mention the theft of Norman Hastings's wallet, and would maybe tell her to leave out the cufflinks. He was even toying with trying to keep the attack on her out of his statements; now it looked as if it was out of his hands. He asked himself why he'd go out on a limb for her like this, but all he came up with was that he liked her, but if it got out that he'd used her, paid her, and had been privy to the information, he'd not only be out in the cold but his hoped-for bonus was shrinking by the minute.

The squad car drew up outside Rosie's apartment just moments after they'd left for the AA meeting. All vehicles were instructed to be on the look-out for the prostitute Lorraine Page, described as five feet nine, short blonde hair, last seen wearing a cream suit and silk shirt. She was to be arrested on sight.

Lorraine was still uncertain as to why she had let Jake and Rosie talk her into coming to the meeting. Maybe, if the truth was to be admitted, it was because she was at a loss and she was also scared.

The woman was neatly dressed in printed cotton, her hair well cut, parted in the centre and constantly falling forwards to hide her face. She spoke quietly, nervously. 'My name is Carol. Nine months ago I was sleeping rough, I felt there was no hope for me. I felt no shame, I felt nothing. I had lost my husband, my children, my home and my job. I had turned to prostitution to feed my drinking. I was a prostitute, a thief. I owned only what I stood up in, I had nothing, and no respect for anyone, least of all myself.' Carol continued to talk and Lorraine held tightly to Rosie's hand, understanding for the first time what she felt, what she had been through and that she was not alone. Everyone at the meeting, she now began to realize, had felt shame and rejection, knew loss and humiliation.

When they stood and warmly applauded Carol, when they embraced her and congratulated her, Lorraine was one of the first to leave her seat. She was shy, at first proffering her hand, but then she put her arms around her. 'I've been there too. I know how you feel,' she said simply.

Carol hugged Lorraine back. 'We've all been there, that's why we're here.'

'What was the hardest thing for you?' Lorraine asked.

'Facing myself, not being angry or ashamed. It wasn't me but the drink. I hid behind it, I know that now, and I'm determined to stay sober. I got a job today. I was scared but I told them I'm an alcoholic and now that I know that's what I am, I feel free. For the first time in years I'm not hiding.'

'You said you hid behind drink. What did you mean?'

'I was afraid of failing. I'm a nurse and I had a patient, a child, who died. I gave the wrong medication and I was never able to face the guilt or come to terms with it. I have now. It will always be with me but I can deal with it, I'm taking responsibility for myself and I want to stay sober. I *have* to stay sober or I'll go down again.'

Jake was watching Lorraine. He winked at Rosie. 'It was good we came. You were right, Rosie, it was important for her.'

'And for me too. If Lorraine had started drinking I'd have probably joined her,' Rosie replied, and Jake smiled.

Lorraine joined them. 'Thanks for bringing me. Now we should get back in case Rooney needs me.'

Rooney watched the FBI agents talking to his chief. He sat in a hard-backed chair at the rear of the room; when anyone looked to him for an opinion he made no comment. The press had been given statements and the suits felt that, by the arrest of Art Mathews, they had been able at least to gain time. Even if they couldn't provide evidence that Mathews had murdered all the victims, they were satisfied that by his own admittance and subsequent suicide he had been guilty of at least three.

Andrew Fellows had come in and they had been in deep discussion with him for two hours. He did not disagree with their conclusions but raised doubts that Mathews was the killer. Not until they seemed to have grown tired of their own voices did Rooney ease his bulk from the chair. 'You mind if I put my two cents in?'

They had forgotten he was even in the room. The Chief looked pointedly at his watch. 'Is it about the Lorraine Page woman?'

Andrew Fellows frowned. 'Lorraine Page?'

'We're still looking for her but it shouldn't be long.'

Rooney squeezed between a row of chairs.

'Lorraine Page?' Fellows asked again, but no one answered him and she was forgotten as Rooney prodded the photograph of Didi, the last victim.

'What if our killer – and I'm excluding Mathews just for a moment – was looking for this particular woman or man – the transsexual? Looking for her because she and Mathews were blackmailing him.' There was a low murmur and Rooney held up his hand. 'Let me finish. Take a look at them. Tough, hard-faced women, all bleached blondes, all prostitutes, as was this victim.' Again he tapped Didi's picture. 'It's a possible motive because I think Hastings was also being blackmailed and possibly by Mathews . . .'

The men listened, giving each other sidelong looks. The Chief loosened his tie. Mathews had admitted at no time to blackmailing anyone. Rooney continued to repeat almost verbatim what Lorraine had said to him. He did not mention her part in piecing it together, or that she was the witness who had been attacked by the killer. Just before he gave the name of her suspect, he felt a hot flush spread through his body. The Thorburn family were powerful and all Rooney had was Lorraine's theory. They did not have enough evidence: her own admission that Janklow had been her attacker would, as she rightly surmised, be tough to prove. As she had said, it would be her word against his. And as yet no incriminating evidence linked him to the murders. Until he had more on Janklow, Rooney decided he would keep his identity to himself.

The room was silent. The Chief stared at Rooney – they all did – and Andrew Fellows's face wore a half smile. It was hard to determine whether it was through disbelief or because he was impressed.

Rooney decided he might as well go for the big prize. He nodded to Hastings's picture. 'He used a garage to park his car, the S and A company. I've not gone into this in any depth but a number of the company's employees were checked out against the description we had from the anonymous witness. The S and A garage is owned by a Brad Thorburn.' Fellows gasped at this but no one paid him any attention. Rooney continued, 'I'm not suggesting anything without further evidence. Obviously considering the family's connections, I have not, until tonight, even voiced my suspicions.'

'Just what are you implying?' Fellows asked, his face pink with agitation. Rooney looked at him then, and at the Chief who became aware that Fellows should not have been privy to this statement and suggested that he might wish to leave.

Fellows had not disclosed that he knew Brad Thorburn. He was unsure as to why not but, then, he hadn't been asked. He intended to drive straight home but changed his mind and headed for Thorburn's house.

Jake saw the patrol car even before he turned into the road. Lorraine was in the back seat.

'You want me to drive past the cops?' Jake asked.

'Yeah, but not for the reason you think. I'll go in but in my own time. There's somebody I want to talk to first. I misjudged Rooney. He must have told them about me.'

She ducked out of sight as Jake passed the police car, turning left at the top of the road before he stopped.

'Where we going?' Rosie asked.

'I need to talk to Andrew Fellows. I won't do anything crazy, believe me. I just want to run a few things past him.'

'I'll drive you,' said Rosie.

Lorraine hesitated before she agreed. Jake got out and Rosie moved into the driving seat. He watched them drawing away from the pavement but not until they were almost out of sight did he walk off.

The car backfired. Jake whipped round. It had sounded like a gun blast. It made him uneasy and he wished he'd stayed with the two women. He also wished he'd asked a lot more questions, but as he walked on he also realized that he had been part of Lorraine's cover-up story about the attack. He shook his head. He had known as soon as he saw the injury that it hadn't been caused by a fall, as she'd said. With all her lies, Lorraine had not only used Rosie but himself. The more he thought about it, the more angry he became, and now he started to wonder where Lorraine got all that money from. He remembered the way she clutched it when he'd stitched up her wound. She was one hell of a liar, he told himself. Maybe there was more to the cops hanging around than either he or Rosie knew.

Rooney had now told the agents about Craig Lyall, again using Lorraine's evidence. When the Chief got back, Rooney was in the hot seat. Berillo wanted to know why he had been withholding so much evidence, and neither discussed it with him nor provided the agents with the information on Mathews's blackmailing activities.

'I only pieced it together tonight. Like I said, it's just supposition. I've been up all night on this. I hadn't finished interviewing Mathews when the FBI took over. You tell *me* how such an important suspect with all this high-tech surveillance on his cell was able to slit his wrists. Don't lay that on me, I wasn't even in the station. It's down to the FBI.'

The agents took his gibes and accusations without expression. One of them, a blond, square-jawed man, was making copious notes as Rooney spoke.

'You're seriously saying that Brad Thorburn is a suspect?' demanded his chief. The atmosphere in the room was uneasy. Bean remained silent throughout: he was wondering why Rooney had never mentioned any of his findings to him.

'I never said Thorburn *was* a suspect. I believe it's his brother, Steven Janklow.'

The blond agent, tight-lipped with anger, asked if Janklow fitted the description of the killer given to Rooney's department after Hastings's body had been found. Rooney shifted uneasily. As he had never seen Janklow or interviewed him, he was hesitant.

'I've not interviewed him. All I know is he knew Hastings and —'

'And?' snapped the Chief. Rooney felt as if they were all against him, closing in on him. He pulled at his bulbous nose, half wishing he'd kept his big mouth shut. He took a flyer, lying through his teeth. 'I held back giving you this information until I'd checked in the files for a possible vice charge against Janklow in the past. So far I've not been able to trace it and it was just told to me by one of the workers at the garage. I didn't want to act on hearsay – well, not until I'd run it past you. I could be wrong on all counts.'

The Chief glanced at his watch and then said, 'You go through those vice records, Bill, immediately – but until you have more evidence we make no contact with the Thorburn family for two reasons. If our man is Janklow, we need hard facts to arrest him, and the Thorburn family is high society and powerful.' The Chief said the last sentence directly to the blond FBI man: 'In other words, back off the Thorburns until I say so.'

The agents departed, with a show of obvious irritation towards Rooney, and the Chief called him into his office. He turned on him in a fury, demanding to know what the fuck he'd been playing at.

'Just trying to do my job.'

'Come on, Bill, who are you kiddin'? You're just pissed off because the FBI have been brought in. If you'd even had half of what you blurted out tonight we could have held them off. What else are you holding back? You'd better come clean with me, Bill.' He stared hard at Rooney and then asked about Lorraine Page.

Rooney covered like an old trooper. 'She's my informant but I didn't know until tonight that she knew Mathews or that she was with him the night Holly was murdered.'

'I want her brought in because I want to talk to her. I want to know just what the hell Mathews was up to.'

'It's in his file. He's been in for blackmail and extortion, along with his porno rap.'

'Is that it?'

'That's it. Like I said, let me dig into Janklow's past a bit more and then I'll get straight back to you.'

The Chief agreed but told Rooney to call him, no matter what the time was, if he discovered anything else.

Rooney returned to his office where Bean was waiting. He couldn't stop smiling; he felt he'd shown the bastards. He kicked the door closed. 'You and me got work to do.'

Bean took off his jacket and hung it over the back of a chair. Rooney was rummaging through his desk drawers. 'What about Lorraine Page?' Bean asked. 'According to officers Hully and Maynard you were at her place. They said you were bringing her in.'

'I left when she didn't show – that all right with you?'

Bean's face was quizzical. 'You just done a hell of a lot of legwork since you left here last night, but you've not mentioned any of this to me – Janklow, the Thorburn family. If you'd seen those agents' faces, talk about jaws dropping open. I was impressed. They were really pissed. They were patting each other on the back ten minutes earlier about Art Mathews. They really upped the pressure on him, you know, he was crying his eyes out. She tip you off about him?'

Rooney raised his eyebrow in mock surprise. 'God no, that was supreme detective work on my part, Lieutenant.' Then he scowled. 'If Mathews said he killed them, I reckon he'd have said he'd shot his mother just to get those suits off him. He was scared – I reckon he was scared shitless about being done for blackmail again. He'd have done eighteen years this time and the little prick knew it. They just wanted to make an arrest, period. I reckon they were lucky he did kill himself because if I'd got my hands on him, I might have got a different result, like negative.'

Bean sighed. 'So why did he kill himself, then?'

'Because maybe he knew he was in very deep and we'd have dug up something. Christ almighty, I gave them his fucking file, he was serving time when two of the victims were done. I don't care what any of that FBI crowd want

328

to say about copy-cat killings, those victims were all done by the same man.'

Bean sucked in his breath. 'Or woman. That's what Fellows threw in tonight.'

'Bullshit.'

'No. He said that all the crap that's written about male or female strength is hyped up out of all proportion. If a woman wanted to kill, she could have done it. He even said that was why the victims took a blow to the back of the head first – incapacitated them.'

'Well, Fellows is looking up his own tight-assed backside. We got that witness, the one that gave us the description, right?' He almost disclosed who she was but stopped himself. Instead he leaned over the desk. 'She described her attacker as a man, right?'

Bean jangled the change in his pocket. 'Lorraine Page. Where does she figure in it all, then? What if they were doing it together? She was with Mathews the night Holly was murdered, he said so.'

'I know, I know . . .' He felt his stomach turn over. What if Bean was right? Could she be that much involved?

Bean sank into a chair. 'Well, you put the cat among the pigeons. It sounded like hot shit to me.' Rooney looked puzzled. 'It was nice to watch you in action, Captain.'

Rooney smiled. 'I was always one of the best. Now, why don't you go get some sandwiches and coffee?'

Bean picked up his jacket again. 'Gonna be a long night, is it?'

As the door closed behind him Rooney slumped in his chair. He wasn't one of the best – he doubted if he ever had been – but she was. It was *she* who was hot shit and she'd proved it. He just hoped to God she was right, that she hadn't done a runner. Did he want to crack this so badly he was going to let her risk her neck? He knew he still had the trump card that she was the witness. If he was forced into a corner he'd bring it out. He wondered how long it would be before they brought her in, then suddenly felt cold. What if Bean was right? What if she had been ducking and diving all along? What if she'd never been a witness but a killer, and the description was just to put them all off the scent? He picked up the phone and punched out her number. No answer. Where the hell was she? If she wasn't brought in within the hour, he'd go out looking for her personally. She wasn't the killer – that was dumb, that was *crazy* – but he felt a horrible nag at his gut. She was connected to Didi and Mathews; he'd told the FBI that she had been with Mathews the night Holly was murdered. He should have brought her in with him, he shouldn't have trusted her. She might even now be in some bar drinking herself into a stupor – she'd threatened as much . . .

Bean came in. He'd called for a takeout to be brought in rather than schlepp out for it himself.

'What else did Fellows say about it maybe being a woman?'

'None of the victims had been sexually abused, there'd been no trace of semen, not even on Holly. Victims all struck from behind, just their faces mangled.'

Rooney swallowed and tapped the edge of his desk. 'Is Lorraine Page being brought in?'

'Changing your theory, are you?'

Rooney sniffed and waved to Bean to get out, but he hovered at the door. 'She was an ex-cop, right? She's capable of taking care of herself, she's tough, I've heard you say it, and she's been out hooking. She's got a record. Maybe, just maybe, she's also got a lot of venom in her, a hatred of women that look like her.'

Rooney hit the desk hard. 'No. No way.'

He watched Bean walk away down the corridor. He couldn't have lost his touch to that extent. He shut his eyes and recalled Lorraine's face, the way her pale eyes bored into him, the scar making her face switch between vulnerable and street tough. He read through her file again: the arrests, the charges, the no-shows at court, the attacks on arresting officers, even that she had been held in a strait-jacket. Drunk and disorderly was recorded time and again. Drunk in charge of a vehicle, drunk when arrested for breaking into a liquor store – she had fought the arresting officer, bitten him, kicked him and punched him in the face. It had taken four of them to get her into the wagon. She'd been held in the cells for three days, charged with assault and spent two months in the women's jail. If he hadn't known her, he would have described her without hesitation as dangerous. Could she be capable of murder? His feet ached as he walked up and down, swearing alternately at Fellows – for throwing this 'woman killer' angle into the investigation – at Lorraine, and lastly at himself.

When Bean returned with the food, Rooney seemed distracted and had taken a bottle from one of the drawers. He took the top off his coffee, gulped a few mouthfuls and topped it up with bourbon. 'Check that vice charge, the Janklow thing, get on that first.' Bean didn't say he was already working on it, he just left Rooney alone. He'd seen these dark moods often and didn't want to be at the receiving end of one today.

Rooney closed Lorraine's file. She had sunk lower than he could ever have imagined and he felt a certain remorse. The question uppermost in his mind was, had she sunk so low then forced herself back up just to take revenge? Should he warn all officers that she might be dangerous? He knew if he gave that out, and she resisted arrest, she might be shot.

Rooney opened the lowest drawer in his desk, took out his gun and searched for his holster. He rarely, if ever, wore it, even though he knew he should. Now he strapped it on, checked the weapon, and slipped it into place. He shrugged back into his jacket and was just about to walk out when

Bean returned. 'We got no record in any Vice section regarding Steven Janklow. This is the second time I've checked, so now I've requested they go back in Records to the time of the first murder. There's nothing on him or the Thorburns. Nothing. Even if there had been a possible charge, we'd at least have a record or it would have been on file – that includes if charges were dropped for any reason, like string-pulling.'

Rooney passed Bean, reeking of bourbon. 'You got your peppermints handy?' he asked him, as if he knew what he was thinking.

'You going home?' Bean asked.

'Nope, I'll call in. I need some fresh air.'

'What about the extra cars out looking for Lorraine Page? They still haven't picked her up.'

'I'll bring her. Just hang out here until I find her.'

'Don't you want me to drive?'

Rooney turned on him. 'No, I fucking don't. Just stay put – I'll call in soon as I find her!'

He slammed the door so hard the blinds rattled.

Lorraine asked Rosie to wait and she walked up the drive to Andrew Fellows's home. She rang a couple of times before Dilly answered. She was wearing a nightgown with a shawl wrapped round her shoulders.

'I'm sorry, did I get you out of bed?'

'No, didn't feel like getting up today, I was just watching TV. Sit down, I'll get us some tea. He shouldn't be too long – he called in to say he was on his way home hours ago.'

Lorraine sat down within sight of Brad's portrait. Dilly came to sit on the sofa, curling her feet up beneath her. 'He went to meet the FBI agents at the station. He gets talking and then he forgets the time.'

'Dilly, tell me about Brad.'

She giggled. 'Oh, another conquest, is it? Well, just let me warn you, he's some hunk but don't get too interested. He's got a terrible reputation – screws them, sometimes marries them, but then he gets icy, ditches them. He's ditched more than I can count.'

The kettle boiled and she went to make the tea. Lorraine looked at the portrait again.

'He had it all, you see, given on a plate. Loaded and handsome, always a fatal combination.' Dilly's head appeared above the kitchen counter. 'He's so glamorous, motor racing – God, he looks so sexy in those white jumpsuits. Now he's writing thrillers, or whatever he calls them, but he'll never finish a book, I know him . . . Do you take sugar?'

'What about his family?' Lorraine asked.

'Oh, you *are* hooked – or are you seeing cash registers?'

'Just interested.'

'I bet. His family are mega-rich. I'll tell you something weird. His brother – he's got an older brother, did I tell you?'

'Go on . . .'

Dilly snuggled down and sipped her tea. She loved to gossip. 'Well I only met him once. They're like chalk and cheese. He's quite small whereas Brad is tall and well-built, dark. Steven's fairish, short-sighted, sort of prissy. I only saw him for a few minutes when I was up at their house. They have Christ knows how many homes – well, Brad does, he was left everything. They have different fathers – obvious, I suppose, they got different names, right? Janklow was her first husband, wealthy, I think, but it was Thorburn who had the big bucks. She was a great socialite, beautiful, pampered and I think she was in movies at one time, very early on. She's ancient.'

'And she's still alive?'

'Oh, yeah, in some expensive home. I've never met her but I think Andrew has. But he's useless, I ask him all these questions about his patients and he won't gossip but I love it.'

'She was a patient?'

'Oh no – well, I don't think so. I just knew he met her once and she sometimes stays with Brad. She has this bedroom, very Greta-Garbo-style, different from Brad's taste. His is all macho wood and the bare essentials.'

Lorraine was getting impatient.

'How long will Andrew be, do you think?'

Dilly shrugged. 'You asking me? All I know is he phoned to say he was on his way. Do you want another cup of tea?'

Brad offered Fellows a glass of wine, which he refused. They walked into the living room.

'What did you want to talk to me about?'

Fellows sat down, unsure how to begin. 'Is Steven home?'

Brad looked perplexed. 'He may be. He keeps to his part of the house. Why do you ask?'

Fellows fiddled with the fringe on the sofa. 'Just something I overheard tonight. I was at the cop shop – FBI agents, they've been brought in to oversee these murders. Have you read about them?'

Brad sipped his wine. 'Be hard not to. Are you working on them?'

Fellows tugged frantically at his ear. 'They brought up this guy Norman Hastings, one of the victims. Did we talk about him?'

Brad leaned back. 'I don't remember.'

'Well, I suggested they dig deep – may be they'd missed something. As it turned out, I was right.' He smiled. 'He was a cross-dresser, you know, a transvestite.'

'And?' Brad said softly. His voice was deep, attractive, and he sank down lower on the sofa.

Fellows looked away. 'I don't think I was supposed to

334

hear it, about this Hastings guy. Did you know he parked his car at your garage?'

Brad frowned. 'Somebody mentioned it to me but I have no idea who parks there half the time. It's supposed to be just for the employees.'

'Have you been questioned?'

'No, but the police have been talking to all the employees – in fact I was meaning to talk to you about it . . . because I think I might write something, and I know you sometimes assist the homicide squad. I just thought maybe you could help me.'

Fellows stood up. 'Maybe I'll have a glass of wine, after all.'

'Sure,' Brad said easily. He uncoiled his perfect body, picked up his glass and walked out towards the kitchen. Fellows followed. As he passed the stairs he looked upwards, instinctively, as if he knew someone was looking down at him, but there was no one in sight. 'Is Steven home?' Fellows asked again. Brad poured two glasses of Chablis and offered one to him. 'Just I thought I saw someone on the landing.'

'You asked that already, Andrew! You tired or something? You never did say why you came. Are you cancelling our squash game?'

'Oh, no, that's fine, it was—'

Brad walked ahead of him. 'Remember the last time we played? That woman was waiting to see you – Lorraine Page? Maybe I should have told you, she came here.' Brad was sprawled on the sofa again. 'She was looking for someone up the road.'

Fellows sipped his wine, wondering if he should tell his friend what he had come to say. He couldn't make up his mind.

Brad balanced his glass on the sofa arm, twisting the stem. 'Actually, she's rather attractive, has an odd way of looking at you, sort of sly but not—'

Fellows drained his glass and stood up. 'Stay away from her, she's bad news. She's not what she seems.'

'What's that supposed to mean? I thought she was a friend of yours. She was at your place for dinner, wasn't she?'

Fellows decided he'd tell Brad, whether it was ethical or not. 'She's a hooker and a police informer. She's also wanted in connection with these murders. But there's something else . . . The cops were discussing your garage and the fact that Hastings parked his car there.'

'They don't suspect anyone at the garage, do they?'

'They were discussing your brother. Apparently he knew Hastings. He was found dead in his own car so maybe someone at your place had access to it. Look, I'm just repeating what I overheard. Maybe you can tip Steven off, have a chat to him.'

Brad walked Fellows to the front door. 'He's not mentioned any of this to me but we're not exactly best of friends. But thanks, I'll have a word with him.'

Fellows stood on the porch. 'This is advice, Brad. I'd stay clear of Lorraine Page if she should make contact. The lady could be desirable but her past life isn't.'

Brad watched Fellows drive away. He would have liked his friend to explain himself, but then he saw Steven standing on the first-floor balcony. Brad banged the gate with his fist and walked back into the house. He ran up the stairs two and three at a time until he reached his brother's quarters. He tried the door, but it was locked. 'Steven, open the door – I know you're in there so open the fucking door. I want to talk to you.' He waited, hit the door again, but there was silence. 'Steven, open the door or I'll get the master keys. *Steven?*'

He pressed his ear to the door. He could hear water running. He fetched the spare keys. He returned to his brother's bedroom and slipped in the key. He walked inside, bare-foot, leaving the door wide open behind him.

Brad looked round the immaculate room. He could still hear the sound of the bathwater running as he crept across the room. He'd wait, Steven would have to come out at some time. The room was different from his own, but similar to his mother's – floral drapes at the window, a canopied bed with swathes of silk caught in a coronet and tied with large satin bows. The carpet was oyster pink, as were the silk-covered walls. The stereo equipment was built into banks of mirrors; the television section was mirror-fronted to match the rows of wardrobes. Steven's tapes and videos were neatly stacked and listed in alphabetical order, hundreds of CDs, old records and tapes. Brad caught his own reflection over and over again. There was no corner of the room in which you couldn't see yourself. It was all elegant, expensive, even tasteful, if you liked that kind of décor. Brad hated it.

He looked over the dressing table – more fitting for a woman than a man, with jars of creams and perfumes in neat symmetrical rows, silver-backed mirrors and hair-brushes, and rows of silver-framed photographs. Brad had only ever entered this room two or three times and now he looked around slowly, taking everything in. He opened one wardrobe door after another to reveal rows of linen jackets and a vast array of shirts, each one covered in plastic. The shoes were packed in boxes with colour coordinations marked. There were racks of ties, silk handkerchiefs, even straw hats, a few he recognized as having belonged to his father.

He could hear the bathwater draining away. He knocked, waited a moment, then knocked again. The softly playing classical music was turned off.

'Come on, Steven, I have to talk to you. It's important.' He punched the bathroom door. 'Okay, fucking stay in there. You can come to me, I'm not waiting any longer. But you'd better come and see me, you hear? That was Andrew Fellows, my friend from the college, the professor.

He's working with the police. He had something to tell me about you, about that Norman Hastings friend of yours. If you want to know what he told me, then . . . screw you, Steven!'

Brad waited another few moments, then spotted the briefcase, placed neatly at the side of the dressing table. He picked it up and tried to open it, but it was locked. He looked over the dressing table and found a thin paper-knife. He prised open the lock, removed a file of papers, and then replaced the briefcase. His brother had still not made a sound so he left.

Two minutes later the bathroom door opened and Janklow walked out, draped in a silk dressing gown, naked beneath it. He bolted the bedroom door, to ensure his privacy, then walked casually towards the dressing table and sat on the small frilled stool. He opened a bottle of lotion and began carefully to cream his hands. Every move was studied, each finger massaged, each perfectly manicured nail scrutinized. He used pointed cotton-wool sticks to wipe around the cuticles and then looked along his row of clear varnishes, choosing one and carefully painting each nail. His hands were steady; he was calm. He slipped off the robe and stood naked, surveying himself in the mirrors. His slim body was still pinkish from the bath, a pale, white-skinned body, but muscular. He never went in the sun, unlike Brad – he never did any of the things Brad did, not as a child or as a man.

He began to do his yoga exercises, studying every posture in his mirrors. His testicles were small, like marbles, and his penis flaccid. He knelt forwards, squeezing his thighs together, pushing his penis out of sight until he knelt upwards, seemingly devoid of any sex organ. His nipples were erect, pink, and he slowly massaged his breasts, breathing deeply. The only blemish on his hairless skin was the mark at the side of his neck. He had used oil of arnica, even make-up to disguise the toothmarks of the bitch who had bitten him. He had been desperate to find her again. She could hurt him much more than the bite had. He breathed deeply, not wanting to become agitated.

It was almost over, he was almost free. It had been a terrible long nightmare. He had even thought of suffocating his mother just so that she would never find out; he had done it all for her because he loved her with an all-consuming passion. But they were not like mother and son, they were one. That was why he couldn't kill her. He couldn't bear the thought of losing her, just as he could not tolerate her knowing about him.

Brad stood in his mother's room. He wasn't sure why he had come here, possibly because it reminded him of Steven's. He stood at her dressing table looking at the photographs and then slipped his finger into the small drawer in the centre. Everything here had a place and not one perfume bottle was out of line. He sniffed a cut-glass stopper and recognized the same smell from his brother's room. As he was about to replace the stopper, he accidentally knocked over the bottle, which tipped into the open drawer, perfume splashing over the leather jewel boxes. He swore, snatched a tissue from the white-embroidered box and dabbed at the leather, then took out the large, fan-styled box to make sure it was not stained. He clicked it open. The velvet-lined case that had once contained four fabulous ropes of perfectly matched pearls was empty. He closed it and then opened the other boxes. All were empty.

He whistled softly as he shut the drawers. He checked that the perfume bottle was once more in line with the others and walked out.

Just as Brad left his mother's room, he heard the front door close. 'Steven? *Steven?*'

He ran down the stairs just in time to see his brother drive out in the Mercedes.

Lorraine hadn't seen it coming. She was totally taken aback when Dilly Fellows, midway through talking about Brad Thorburn, burst into tears. She sobbed loudly, hands over her face. 'This is so stupid, but just talking about him hurts me so much because I love him. I don't know what to do about it sometimes. I can usually control it but sometimes it just bursts out of me.'

Lorraine stood up. 'Look, I'd better go. My friend's waiting outside.'

Dilly sniffed. 'You should have brought her in. I don't know what's happened to Andrew and I'm so sorry about this, I don't know what you must think of me. Andrew doesn't know. Oh, God, you won't tell him, will you?' Lorraine shook her head. 'He's got no idea. He knows I had a passion for Brad – well, it was obvious to begin with – but he doesn't know just how much I care. I think about him all the time, I make up excuses to call him. I'm like a teenager – but I like it. I like this feeling. It's like a pain, it's almost sexual it gets so intense, and then when he comes here with Andrew, I have an orgasm just looking at him. I do, I honestly do, and it's an incredible feeling. I put it back into my work when he's been around, I can paint for hours. Did he touch you?'

Lorraine felt more and more uneasy. Dilly was over-bright, over-excited and her voice was verging on hysterical. 'Why did you ask me all those questions about him? Did you fuck him?'

Lorraine picked up her purse. 'No, I didn't, and I have to go. Thank you for the tea.' She couldn't wait to get into the car.

*

'Jesus, you took your time, I was just about to come in and get you. A few minutes, you said,' Rosie growled. She was hungry and it was way past lunchtime.

Lorraine apologized. 'That woman is freaky. I really liked her at first – she seemed so warm and friendly, so bloody normal.'

They drove off. 'Where to next, home or what?' Rosie asked.

Lorraine hesitated. 'Look, we drive home, then I've got to go some place else. I'll take the car on alone because I don't want to keep you hanging around any longer.'

'Great, some fucking partner I am, I'm not in on anything. I don't know what you're talking about half the time.'

Lorraine jerked her thumb back at the house. 'That was the wife of the guy the cops brought in to help solve the case. He's a professor of psychology, working for Rooney. If you ask me, he should do some work on his wife. She just blurted out she was infatuated with Brad Thorburn, I couldn't believe it.'

Lorraine knew she would go and see him, as soon as she got rid of Rosie, and it was strange, she had a dull, low ache in the pit of her stomach. She wanted to see him but it wasn't just about the case. She wouldn't admit that to herself, or that she was feeling sexually aroused. She refused even to contemplate that.

Rosie was still pissed off about being dumped back home when Lorraine dropped her off a little way from the apartment. Just as she turned the corner past the grocery store, Rooney screeched to a halt alongside her.

'Where's Lorraine? This is important, Rosie, there's a warrant out for her arrest. If you know where she is you'll be doing her a favour because they got every available officer out looking for her and if she resists arrest, she could get hurt.' Rosie said nothing and Rooney got out of the car. 'Come on, sweetheart, where is she? If you care anything about her you'll tell me.'

Rosie looked down the road. 'She's gone off in the car.'

Rooney asked her for the registration number. Rosie was in a quandary but then she blurted it out. She'd said enough now and started off down the road.

'Where you going?'

'I got to go home, feed my cat.'

Rooney told her to stay in the apartment. If Lorraine came back she was to call him immediately. 'You sure you don't know where she is or where she was heading? When did you last see her?'

Rosie shouted that she'd told him all she knew and she hadn't seen Lorraine since early morning. She hurried to her apartment and went up the stairs. She looked down at Rooney as he parked opposite the house watching her. 'I don't know where she is!' she yelled as she let herself in and slammed the screen door behind her. She looked out of the window. Rooney was still there. She was about to call Jake when she heard Rooney's car move off. She decided to wait for half an hour or so. If Lorraine hadn't returned, if she hadn't heard anything, she'd call Jake and ask him what she should do.

Andrew Fellows let himself in and called his wife. She gave no answer. In the kitchen, he noticed the two cups and saucers left on the draining board. He found her in the bedroom, huddled beneath the duvet, the TV on. 'You had a visitor?' She looked at him, eyes red-rimmed. 'You okay?'

'I'm fine. It's a sad movie.'

'Who was here?'

Dilly sat up. 'Your friend Lorraine Page. She wanted to speak to you – waited ages.' She swallowed and her eyes filled with tears. 'She asked me questions about Brad and then she left. She had a friend waiting, she said.'

Fellows sat on the edge of the bed. 'Just tell me exactly what she said, what questions she asked.'

Dilly switched off the TV by remote control. She repeated everything Lorraine had said but deleted any reference to her own outburst. Fellows went into his den. He called the police station.

Bean listened as Fellows reported that Lorraine Page had been at his home and had talked to his wife. He was very agitated and angry. Bean said he would send someone over straight away.

'She's not here now, she's left.'

Bean called Rooney to let him know that Lorraine had been with Fellows's wife. Rooney took the address; he was on his way. He'd just left Lorraine's place, and had already put out the registration number of her vehicle. It would only be a matter of time before they brought her in.

Brad sifted through the file he had taken from Steven's room, bank statements and other private papers. He knew it had been going on for some considerable time – it was obvious from the receipts. Steven, meticulous as ever, had carefully recorded each sale of every item he had removed from his mother's jewel drawer. The four strands of pearls had been sold for five thousand dollars, although they were insured for three times that amount. The diamond rings, necklaces, the ruby and sapphire bracelets, the topaz ring, all had been listed but with a dash at the side of each item. Brad calculated that his brother had accrued over a hundred and fifty thousand dollars, yet he had not paid it into his own bank accounts – unless he had another one somewhere.

Brad was aware that on his mother's death she would leave the jewels to Steven. But that was no reason for him to have been selling them off without her permission – unless she knew of it. It was just after three. He decided against calling the nursing home: better to face Steven first when he came home.

He replaced the papers in the briefcase, then went back

343

into his mother's room. One of the wardrobe doors was slightly ajar and he opened it to close it properly. He looked at the rows of her wigs. He found them distasteful, as he found everything about her obsessive drive to retain her youth. The wardrobe was crammed with flimsy gowns and négligés, not fitting for a woman in her seventies, of an era when she had been in her prime. Brad was sweating from the overheated room and the cloying smell of her perfume. He felt slightly nauseous, also guilty. She had always hated anyone touching her things. She herself had never liked to be touched. How often as a child he had run to embrace her, but she had always held up her perfectly manicured hands as if she was scared to be held by her own child. It had been different with Steven. If anything, she had encouraged him because he was so much older than Brad. She pointedly preferred his company. Brad remembered his father in one of his rages shouting up the stairs, as she stood quivering in pale lime chiffon, that if she didn't want him, he would find other women who did. 'Other women?' She had leered down at his father, her perfect red lips drawn back in a snarling smile. 'No decent woman would come within a mile of you. Whores! You can only get a whore and that's because you pay her!'

'You'd know all about that, wouldn't you? Janklow picked you out of the chorus line. You were a ten-cent stripper – you think I don't know? Movie star? The closest you ever got to a real movie was paying at the ticket window.'

She would throw things, she would rant and rage at him whenever he referred to her first husband, or her chorus line days, and he would roar with laughter, enjoying her fury, her humiliation, encouraging Brad to listen, warning him never to marry someone else's used goods. She would become so hysterical that she would smash mirrors and crockery, and lock herself into her room for days on end. The only person who was ever able to calm her was Steven.

Back in his own room, Brad lay down, looking up at his mirrored ceiling. The mirror remained, a legacy from Tom Thorburn. Brad wondered if the other legacy was his predilection for young blondes. He had certainly married enough of them. But of late, like his father, he chose to go with whores rather than get involved in yet another relationship. It was rare for women to say no to him: on the polo field, at the racetrack, they were always available, like clutches of twittering starlings.

He was a man to whom few women said no. That was why he had liked Lorraine Page. She had said no but she had almost said yes. Just thinking about her gave him an erection. He was no longer pondering on his brother or what Andrew Fellows had hinted at. He was even able to put aside the Norman Hastings query, simply because he felt sure that the reason Steven had been so secretive was because of his systematic siphoning off of his mother's jewellery. He wished he had just come out and asked Andrew for Lorraine's phone number.

But even his relationship with Andrew was a mess because his wife was always wanting Brad to screw her, and she wasn't the first – a lot of his friends' wives wanted him. Some he had obliged but it always ended badly.

His erection dispersed as he looked over his life. He had wasted it, he knew that. Even his attempt at writing a novel was futile. He had millions at his disposal, his vast charitable donations taken care of by trustees, but there never seemed any point. He hated what he had become: a dilettante, worse, a clone of his father.

Lorraine headed up Beverly Glen. She passed Brad Thorburn's home, parking the car a few houses up, half hidden from the road. She then walked back, wishing Rosie was with her. The house looked peacefully silent, the faint sound of a lawn mower buzzing from somewhere in the grounds, and she pressed the intercom at the side of the gates. She rang again as the dog appeared. He barked and then stood looking at her through the gates. Brad answered. 'Who is it?'

'Lorraine Page.' She was fazed when he laughed. He didn't say anything else but the gates clicked open. He stepped out onto the porch and leaned against the door frame, a glass of wine in his hand. He was smiling, watching her as she walked slowly towards him. She was so tall and the sun made her hair seem more white than blonde. She wore high-heeled slingback shoes, a straight skirt with a slit to one side, revealing a fraction of her thigh. The jacket was ill-fitting, a little too large, and she had a white shirt beneath, open at the neck. She wore no jewellery and it didn't look as if she had on any make-up. She carried only a clutch purse, in her right hand. As she reached the first white stone step on the porch, she tilted her head; even from this distance, he could see the scar on her cheek.

'I was just thinking about you,' he said quietly. She wasn't expecting him to be so gentle, just as she didn't expect him to hold out his hand to her. It felt strong, gripping hers tightly. 'Do you know the police are looking for you?' he said, not taking his eyes from hers, trying to see what she wanted from him, but her fine hair hid her face.

'Yes, but I have to talk to you.'

He guided her towards the hallway, his hand now at her elbow, with a firm but not threatening hold. They walked into the drawing room. He remained at the door, finishing his wine, watching her.

'Is your brother home?'

'No.'

'Are there any servants here?'

'Just the housekeeper, she'll be leaving at four.' He ran his hand over his neck to the back of his hairline. The T-shirt moved aside and she could see part of his shoulder.

She was silent. She stared hard at him and his eyes slid away, as if embarrassed by her clear, direct gaze. She opened her purse and took out her cigarettes, flicked open the packet and placed one between her lips. 'Do you have a light?'

He came in and put down his empty glass. She thought he was going to pick up a table lighter but instead he came close, took the cigarette out of her mouth and tossed it aside. He then slipped his hand to the small of her back and pressed her to him. In her high heels she was almost as tall as he was. He kissed her and let his hand fall to her buttocks, pulling her even closer to him. He kissed her again and she responded, her tongue traced his mouth and she moved back just a fraction, taking his free hand to place on her heart. She was trembling. He scooped her up into his arms – she was so incredibly light – and carried her with ease out of the drawing room and up the stairs. One of her shoes fell off, then the other, as she rested against him. She was crying, her head buried in his shoulder. He had never known such sweetness, and by the time he laid her down on his bed, she was sobbing. He just held her, rocking her, soothing her, kissing her hair, kissing the tears that poured down her cheeks. He looked up and saw himself cradling her as if she was a child. He was scared of his own tenderness towards this woman, who both excited him sexually and aroused emotions he had not thought himself still capable of having. His arms tightened around her, until the weeping subsided and she lifted her lips to him. This time his kiss was not gentle but passionate, hard and crushing, and she responded.

Steven Janklow walked into the house. He looked into the spotless empty kitchen. The housekeeper had already left. He picked up his brother's empty wine-glass, took it into the kitchen, and put it carefully in the dishwasher. He lifted the lids of two covered dishes left out for dinner. He was hungry but he didn't know what he felt like eating; nothing tempted him.

He started up the stairs and stopped. He saw Lorraine's shoes, first one then the other. He held them in disgust, cheap shoes, and carried them up the stairs, turning towards his brother's quarters. He was just about to put them outside his door – he'd done it before, not just with shoes, but brassières, skirts and, more often than not, panties – when, as he drew closer, he could hear a high-pitched moan, like a mewing. It made him cringe. They all sounded alike, all his brother's whores – even his wives. Janklow had intended simply to leave the shoes but the door was ajar. He put out his hand to close it, averting his eyes in case he got so much as a glimpse of their writhing naked bodies. The woman moaned again, and even though he didn't want to look, he couldn't help himself.

Her face was tilted towards him, eyes closed, mouth half open. She was astride his brother, her body like a young boy's rather than a woman's – that, perhaps, was what had made him stare. As she moved, thrusting forwards, Janklow gasped, quickly covering his mouth with his hand. He didn't shut the door; he didn't dare make a sound as he backed away silently. Not until he was safely along the corridor did he turn and run. He clung to the toilet rim as he vomited, retching with terror, his whole body breaking out in an icy sweat. He couldn't be mistaken, it wasn't possible. There couldn't be two women with that face, that scar. It was *her* – the woman he had picked up, the woman who had bitten his neck until he bled like a pig.

He ran cold water over his face to try to calm himself, but his hands trembled violently. His mind screamed out questions. Why was she here? How could she have got to him here, traced him here? He tried to control his breathing, stop himself panting. Brad often dragged back whores and cheap bitches but he'd never have believed he would

348

have sunk this low, not with *that* woman – she was disgusting. He flopped on his bed, saying to himself it was just a coincidence, it was that and nothing more, just a terrible coincidence. He rolled over, clenching his fists, trying not to break down and weep with fear. It was then that he saw his briefcase, knew at a glance that it had been moved, and worse, that it had been opened.

A thought struck him. He got up and went to his mother's room where he checked her jewellery drawer. He knew that the boxes had been taken out – they were all in the wrong order. Someone had been in here and into his own room, checking him out. Was it Brad? Or was it that woman? He returned to his bedroom and bolted the door. He had to get rid of her. If she was a call-girl, if Brad had done his usual, brought her back to the house, he would just have to wait. They never stayed all night. When he saw her leave, he would follow. It was simple. He would kill her as he had almost done before, only this time he would make sure. He looked at his bedside clock, it was almost five. If she was like the others, she would probably be leaving after an hour or so to start work at night. Walking the streets as she had been doing when she had picked him up. He remembered how she had rested her hand on the car door, asked if he needed her help. There hadn't been a car in the drive, had she come by taxi? Or parked out in the street?

Janklow crept around the house. He found Lorraine's purse, opened it and searched through. She had little money, no cards or check books. All she had in her purse was a packet of cigarettes, a used lipstick, a comb, and, he smiled to himself, car keys.

He left the house and went down the driveway. He saw Bruno look up and wag his tail, and hoped he wouldn't start barking. He stood, frozen to the spot, until the dog lowered his head. The gardener was on the other side of the tennis courts, using some kind of spray, intent on his work. Janklow opened the gates and walked along the road, sure that no one had seen him. There was no one on the road and not even a car passed him.

He found Lorraine's car and checked the keys against the registration number. He was feeling better now, more in control, already working out in his mind how he would kill her, because she was going to die.

Rooney rang Andrew Fellows's doorbell, keeping his finger on the button. Fellows opened up and sighed when he saw who it was. 'I said everything on the phone to Lieutenant Bean. I didn't think it was necessary for anyone to come out, especially not now. She was here before lunch.'

Rooney smiled. 'Sorry about this. I just wanted to go over a few things, and I'd like to speak to Mrs Fellows.'

They went into the kitchen where Dilly was sitting. She looked upset, tear-stained. She repeated everything to Rooney, again without any mention of her disclosure to Lorraine about Brad Thorburn.

'Can I speak to you alone, Professor?' Rooney asked.

'Of course. Dilly, this won't take long.'

Fellows took Rooney into his den. He looked a little sheepish.

'You know the Thorburns?'

'Yes.'

'You didn't mention it this morning.'

'No one asked me if I did or didn't know them.'

'When you left the station, did you come straight back home?'

Fellows flushed a deep red. 'No, I did not. I – I went to the Thorburn house.'

Rooney stared hard, in disbelief as Fellows told him what he had said to Brad. He was obviously ashamed and knew he had behaved unethically. Rooney asked for Thorburn's address and phone number. He left shortly after, not reprimanding Fellows, not saying much at all.

Fellows found his wife in the bedroom. She was crying again. He stared at her for a moment and then walked out. In a fit of rage he dragged Brad's portrait off the wall, smashed it against the open fireplace until the canvas ripped apart and the frame snapped. He stamped on it, then lit the log fire and watched it blaze. He had never felt so angry in his life – angry and bitter, but above all foolish. He hated that most of all. He had just jeopardized his work with the police and doubted if he would ever be called upon again.

As the flames slowly destroyed the painting, his anger subsided. Now he felt nothing but humiliation. Brad Thorburn's nakedness had dominated his home and he had allowed it, joked about it, encouraged Brad to visit Dilly. What made it worse was that Brad had known of her instability, which made his affair with her even more of a betrayal. Fellows vowed never to speak to or see him again. He couldn't even stay in this room, even though the painting was no longer hanging on the wall. The vast space where the life-size portrait had hung added insult to injury. He picked up a cup of cold coffee and headed into the den. As he shut the door, he could hear his wife still crying but he had no intention of discussing Brad with her again. Fellows didn't care if he had screwed her once or twice, it was immaterial. The fact that he had fucked her at all was what mattered.

Fellows found little solace in his den. There were photographs of him and Brad together all over the walls, the two of them fishing, playing baseball, water-skiing in Miami, at squash tournaments, on tennis courts. Brad Thorburn and Andrew Fellows had known each other for many years, had always been competitive with each other as sportsmen. In the women stakes, Fellows had never moved in Brad's social sphere, had never wanted to, could never have been any competition there. No man could, not with Brad's looks and wealth.

Fellows sat at his desk. He drew the file on the murder

351

investigation closer and began to go over every detail once again. He had been so sure that Brad Thorburn could have no connection with the killings but what if he had been wrong? What if he had missed something? If he had, he was determined to find it. It made him feel better. He wanted to hurt Brad Thorburn – better still, destroy him.

Rooney reached his car and picked up the radio to tell Bean he was now on his way to the Thorburns'.

'You going to interview Janklow?' Bean asked.

'Nope, I think Lorraine Page is trying to though so get a squad car out there. It's Beverly Glen, you got the address? Okay, I'll see you.'

CHAPTER 17

THEY LAY naked side by side, the sheet loosely covering their bodies. She was face downwards, her eyes closed. Brad drew the sheet back and brushed his hand gently over her body. 'How did you get these marks?' He leaned up on his elbow, to trace the scar on her face. 'And this?'

She pulled away from him, and suddenly swished the entire sheet from the bed and wrapped it around herself. 'I'd better get dressed.'

He remained lying naked on the bed as she crossed the room. Trailing the sheet, she started to pick up her clothes. Skirt in one hand, she looked around. 'Where are my shoes?'

Brad got up and opened a wardrobe. He took out a white kaftan and dragged it on over his head. 'They must be downstairs. I'll get them.' He stood behind her and wrapped his arms round her, kissing the nape of her neck. Then he frowned and brushed the short hair at the nape of her neck upwards. 'Jesus Christ, how did you get this one?'

The scar, still pink and raised, zig-zagged across her hair line. She tried to move away but he gripped her tightly. 'Why don't you answer me? Who did this to you?'

She tried to release herself but he held her tighter. 'I need to get dressed.'

He let go of her shoulders. 'I'll be downstairs.'

'Don't go, not yet, we have to talk, the reason I came here.'

Brad sighed. 'You want to talk but if I ask you a question you refuse to answer. So you go ahead, you talk.' His face was tight with anger because he had thought she had come to see him, be with him. She continued to gather her clothes as he sat waiting.

'Look, if it makes it any easier I know you're a whore, you told me that yourself. Is it money you want?'

She moved so fast and it was so unexpected that he did nothing to defend himself. The slap was hard and it hurt. He rubbed his cheek and laughed.

'I didn't come here for what we just did.' She stepped back and her fists were clenched. He reached out his hand to her but she wouldn't take it. She began to pace up and down, the sheet trailing on the floor. She looked astonishingly beautiful. There was a mannish quality to her as she tightened the sheet round her body. 'The scars I got from times when I was on the streets. I used to get drunk, I don't know what I did, who I went with. I'm not proud of the hideous things or the cigarette burns, but I never felt them. I didn't care enough about myself to care.'

'And now?' he asked.

'Now I just want you to listen – don't interrupt me, just listen.'

'Fine.' He leaned back against the pillows. He was not disgusted by anything she had said – in some ways he didn't really believe it.

'The scar on my cheek was a bar-room fight over a bottle of vodka, that's about as much as I can remember, nothing dramatic, nothing romantic. I got it, I live with it, and I was, so I was told, lucky not to lose the sight of my eye. I was a hooker but who I was with and when I don't know. I don't have AIDS, or any venereal disease, just in case you're freaking out. I had myself checked. There's a lot of my life I don't remember. But I do know about this scar,

354

this one at the back of my head, because this is one of the reasons I'm here.'

She was very still, standing like a statue in front of him. She seemed to be watching him for a reaction, some kind of revulsion that would help her continue, but he gave none. Instead he patted the bed, indicating for her to lie beside him, but she shook her head.

'I used to be a police officer. I was a lieutenant with the LAPD Homicide Unit.'

He half smiled and she glared at him. He lifted his hands in an apologetic gesture. She continued: she was now acting as a paid street informer for Captain Rooney. He had hired her because she knew the girls on the streets and he needed information about the hammer killer. She looked directly at him as he sat up, no longer smiling, but staring at her. Without any emotion she told him about the night she had been attacked, half turning to reveal the scar again. She then told him how she had made an anonymous call to the police describing the man who had attacked her. As she gave Brad the description, she didn't take her eyes off him. If she had described his brother, he showed not the slightest sign of recognition. She explained how she had taken Hastings's wallet. She watched him all the time as she told him about Art Mathews, Didi and Nula. He listened in silence. He only became tense when she described the cufflinks, the S and A logo, the cufflinks worn by the man who had attacked her. Brad got off the bed and crossed to a pine dresser. He opened the drawer and took out a small leather case. He threw it onto the bed. 'Like those?'

Lorraine opened the box and took out the cufflinks. She looked at them and nodded. He stood with his hands on his hips and after a moment he asked her to go on. She told him how she had gone to his garage, checked out the workers, checked out the cars in the hangar and had discovered that Norman Hastings had parked his car there the day before he was murdered. That no one could recall what time he had removed it or if he took it away himself. Perhaps it had been taken by someone working at the company.

Brad returned to the bed. Seeing a muscle working at the side of his neck, she knew he was on edge. His eyes also betrayed him, but he never mentioned his brother, just indicated for her to continue. The more she talked, the more he realized that, just as she had said, Lorraine Page had not come to his home for any sexual or romantic reason, but for information. He had misjudged her, misjudged his own prowess, he didn't know this woman at all; he was becoming more and more wary of her.

Lorraine detected his anxiety but continued, keeping her eyes on him constantly. She noticed that it was almost five thirty on the bedside clock, and she started to hurry, telling Brad how she and her friend had photographed each of the workers and had eliminated them one by one. The reason she was outside his house was to continue the elimination process. 'You mean me?' he asked.

'Yes, we even took some photographs of your brother, but none were of much use, so I returned to the Hastings murder, to his wife, and to the man who had taken photographs of Hastings. His name is Craig Lyall.' She waited a beat but he didn't react so she continued.

'Norman Hastings was a transvestite.'

Brad's eyebrows lifted slightly. It was an open reaction without guilt.

'I think the killer was being blackmailed,' Lorraine went on, 'and probably for some considerable time. I think Hastings was too, but he was only able to pay small sums that wouldn't alert his wife and family. He was very protective towards them, terrified his private life would be disclosed. I believe the blackmailers were Art Mathews and Didi, one of the victims, transsexual. She made up the men for photographs taken by Lyall. She was then able to tip off Mathews and he, I think, instigated the blackmail.'

356

She had seen it, just a flicker in his eyes, on the word blackmail but he covered it well, nodding as if he wanted her to continue. She was combing her hair, watching him in the mirror. 'I wouldn't mind a cup of coffee,' she said, and smiled, then remembered the housekeeper would have left.

He stood up immediately. 'I'll make it.'

'And I still can't find my shoes.'

Brad opened the bedroom door. The shoes were neatly placed outside. He picked them up, held them by the straps and tossed them to her. Lorraine slipped her feet into them before she remembered they had fallen off as he carried her up the stairs. Who had placed them outside the door? The housekeeper? Or someone else? Down in the kitchen, Brad sweated. Had Steven come home? He couldn't recollect the alarm being triggered, and the security system worked on a timer device so would have automatically switched on. By now the gardener would also have left. He looked out of the window and couldn't see the Mercedes. He was sure he hadn't heard Steven return. Maybe he was still out. But if he was, who had put Lorraine's shoes outside the bedroom door?

Brad jumped when he heard her footsteps on the marble hall. She went into the drawing room and collected her purse and then he heard her walking towards the kitchen.

'Did you say the housekeeper left at four?' she asked nonchalantly, as he ground the coffee beans. She was trying to remember what time they had gone up to the bedroom. 'I wondered who left my shoes outside your door.'

'Probably Maria, she's obsessively tidy. Am I one of your suspects?' he asked, smiling.

'No, of course not.'

He sat on the stool next to her. 'Do you need me to call you a cab?'

She touched his face. 'No, I have a car. Now, can we

357

stop playing games?' She withdrew her hand. 'Tell me about Steven.'

'What about him? Oh, you wanted to see him. Well, he's out but if you leave me your number I can get him to call you tomorrow.'

'Don't protect him, Brad. You'd better be honest with me. That's what I meant about stopping playing games. I want to talk about him, I want to see him to eliminate him. It was your brother I came to see – see him face to face.'

Brad pointed at her. 'Why don't *you* stop? You eliminate him? *You*? There's a warrant out for your arrest, as we both know.' Brad smiled as he poured the coffee. 'You know, I've been fascinated by this monologue you've just delivered. The rogue cop, is that how you see yourself? Maybe the booze did something to your head, Lorraine. I know why you're here.'

She was off the stool, heading towards him. 'Who told *you* about the warrant out for me? – was it Rooney? Did he speak to your brother?' Brad put his cup down. She'd changed suddenly. He thought she was just scared but she said, steadily, 'You'd better tell me, Brad. This man has killed nine times. He knows I'm alive and he's looking for me. I'll be the next. Who was here and what did he tell you? Was it Captain Rooney?'

'No, it wasn't him, whoever he is.'

She pushed at him. 'Who was it? Did he speak to Steven? *For God's sake, stop playing around and tell me who was here.*'

Brad gripped her wrist. 'It doesn't matter. What matters to me is you have to stop this right now – whatever you've dug up on Steven, whatever filth you want to make up about him, about this family.'

She jerked free. 'What are you talking about?'

'How much do you fucking want? You're very clever at what you do, Lorraine. I've had it before, I just didn't think I could be so wrong about someone. So how much and what have you got on Steven? Is that why you took such pains to explain the blackmail by those two whatever-their-names-were?'

'You think I want to blackmail you?'

'Isn't that what you came here for? This family has always been an easy mark, so name your price.'

She snatched up her purse. 'Nothing you could pay, Brad Thorburn. You just think what you want, I didn't come here for any other reason than to—'

'What?' he interrupted. He was angry but controlled.

'I think your brother is a killer. You won't be able to protect him or buy him out of this. You know why? Because I'll prove it.'

Brad sneered, 'You expect me to believe a word you've told me? I've had threats from a lot better than you, sweetheart.'

'What about your brother? Has he had threats?'

'My brother is no concern of yours. Now get the hell out of my house! Now! Get out!' Lorraine turned on her heel. He could hear her walking across the marble hallway, the front door slamming behind her. He waited a moment before he called his lawyer, asking him to come to the house immediately.

She was almost at the gates when she saw a reflected blue light and knew a patrol car was near or heading close by. She pushed the gate closed and ran to the shrubbery. She only just made it out of sight as Rooney appeared.

The front doorbell rang and rang. Brad stared out of the window and could see a figure standing outside the gates. For a moment he thought Lorraine had returned. He went out onto the porch, and Rooney announced himself. Brad stood at the door as Rooney walked up the path and stopped on the bottom step. 'Is Steven Janklow home?'

Brad shook his head and introduced himself. Rooney showed his ID, badge and repeated his name as they entered the house, Brad ushering him ahead. As he closed the door, he saw a police patrol car draw up outside the gates.

Lorraine watched the interaction from the shrubbery. She felt safer now that Rooney was here. She wanted to get back inside the house and remembered the door at the rear opening onto the small corridor leading up to Brad's bedroom. She crossed her fingers that it would be open and that the alarms had not been switched on.

Rooney looked around the impressive drawing room. Brad offered a drink but he refused. 'Do you know where your brother is, Mr Thorburn?'

'No, I'm sorry, I don't. What is this about?'

'I think you know. Andrew Fellows called by earlier, didn't he? So let's cut the bullshit. Is Lorraine Page here?'

'She was but she left.'

'Do you know where she went?'

'No, I don't. I'm surprised you didn't see her, she was here about ten minutes ago.'

'Mr Thorburn, I won't keep you, I'd just like a recent picture of your brother, Steven Janklow.'

Rooney wandered over to a grand piano and looked at the silver-framed photographs. He picked one up and held it out. 'This him?'

Brad said no, it was his father. He suggested that the following morning, when he had had time to speak to his brother, he would ask him to let Rooney have a photograph.

'I'd like to take a look at one now,' Rooney said stubbornly.

'Is it really necessary?'

'Yes, sir. This is a murder investigation.'

Brad disappeared and Rooney stood with his feet planted apart. He was on dangerous ground, he knew, standing in the Thorburn household demanding a photograph without any warrant or back-up evidence except Lorraine's theory.

He waited, then crossed to the telephone and punched out Lorraine's number. Rosie answered.

'It's Rooney. Is she back yet?'

'No.'

'Call me as soon as she gets in.'

He put in another call to Bean. Still no sign of Lorraine. Suddenly, Rooney heard a car driving up the gravel path. He wondered if it was Janklow. His heart sank as he heard voices, Brad saying something about a police officer, a long, whispered conversation. Then Brad walked into the drawing room, with a small balding man wearing rimless glasses and carrying a briefcase.

'This is Alfred Kophch, Captain Rooney.'

Rooney shook the pallid little man's damp hand and remained standing. He didn't need to be told that the balding man was one of the most high-powered criminal lawyers in LA. Kophch sat down and opened his case. 'You want a photograph of my client Steven Janklow, is that correct? Do you have a warrant to be on the premises?'

Rooney huffed and said that at this stage of his inquiries he did not require a warrant. It was an informal visit and Brad Thorburn had invited him in.

'Why do you want a photograph of my client?'

Rooney went a deep red. 'Elimination purposes.'

'I would like to know why no one has contacted Mr Janklow before, and why you have made an informal house call at six thirty p.m.'

Rooney sat on the edge of the plush sofa. He was beginning to sweat, not with nerves but with contained agitation. This grilling made him feel as if he was the guilty party. He reached into his pocket and took out a dog-eared envelope with scrawled dates on the back.

'I would also like to ask – informally – Steven Janklow to tell me where he was on these dates. As he is not here, you can bring him with you in the morning, with a photograph.'

'Why do you need this photograph if Mr Janklow is prepared to come in to see you in person?'

'An attack took place in a multi-level garage. We believe the man that attacked the woman, our witness, is involved in the murders.'

Kophch sighed. 'So now you're saying that Mr Janklow is also a suspect for this attack?'

'Possibly.'

'And the name of the witness?'

Brad leaned forward. 'It's a prostitute called Lorraine Page. There's a warrant out for her arrest and she's involved in a blackmail case.'

'Is this correct?' snapped Kophch.

Rooney shuffled uneasily. 'I am not prepared to disclose the identity of the witness.'

Kophch gave Rooney a warning look. 'Blackmail? This is all getting out of hand, isn't it? I suggest that when you have charges you wish to relate to my client, you contact my office. Until then you should leave these premises immediately and I will forward a complaint to your superiors.'

Rooney stood up slowly. 'Fine. All I'm trying to do is track down a killer.'

Kophch faced Rooney. 'And I am protecting my client. As you must be aware, the Thorburns are an influential family and have in the past been subjected to various blackmail threats and—'

Rooney interrupted, taking a flyer, 'Then there was the vice charge against Mr Janklow that was dismissed. I am aware of certain activities in the past concerning this family, which is why I chose to make this an informal visit.' Suddenly, he was on a roll. He could see the hooded looks passing between the lawyer and Brad, and pushed it further. 'However, this is not just a homosexual cruising or pick-up, but a murder and one that has been the focus of huge media attention.'

Kophch was good. He didn't back off as Rooney had expected but came straight back at him. 'And in the late edition of the papers today there was an announcement that a man arrested for these murders had subsequently committed suicide. Are you now saying this man was not the perpetrator of these crimes?'

Rooney sniffed and pulled at his nose. 'Possibly not.'

His face tight with contained anger, Brad snapped, 'It appears that everything and everyone concerned in this investigation is only "possibly" attached. I suggest that my lawyer should contact your superior and discuss it with him. Now I'd like you to leave my house.'

Rooney was shown the door. The gates opened and he stepped out, hearing them clang shut behind him. As he crossed to his car, he looked down the road, walked a few yards and then squinted in the semi-darkness at the registration number of the parked vehicle. It was Lorraine's. Two uniformed officers were already peering inside. Rooney called his office again to check if Lorraine had been traced. When he heard that she had not, his heart sank. He walked back to the Thorburn house as the alarm floodlights went out. The house seemed ominously dark and quiet apart from the ground floor, where he suspected Thorburn and Kophch were still talking. The officers asked what he wanted done about Lorraine's car. 'Open it up and search it,' he snarled. In truth, he wasn't sure about his next move. He felt a dull panic. Where the hell was she?

Lorraine had found the hidden door open and, in darkness, had made her way back up the narrow staircase into Brad's bedroom. The sheet she had used was on the floor where it had dropped, the pillows on the bed where she and Brad had made love were still dented from his body.

Lorraine crept along the landing. She had seen Rooney enter, and the lawyer, though she didn't know who he was, but was glad of the diversion as she went silently towards the bedrooms, trying to determine which was Janklow's. Below she could hear Brad talking and the low tones of another male voice she wrongly presumed was Rooney's.

She tried two or three rooms before she entered what she thought must be Janklow's and quietly closed the door. She looked around, checked the bathroom and wardrobes, half hoping to find female clothes or wigs but there was nothing. She was disappointed. All she wanted was a photograph, something she could take with her, but while there were many of his mother, and of him and Brad as boys, there were none of Janklow as a man. She was about to leave the room when she saw the briefcase.

She picked it up and froze when the locks clicked open loudly but all she could hear was the low murmur from downstairs. She sifted through the papers as Brad had done, searching for a diary, anything that would give her an insight into Janklow. She found the receipts, all the recorded sales of jewellery, but replaced them and then studied Janklow's bank statements. Again, like Brad, she noted that none of the sums paid to him for the jewels had been put into his accounts. And there was the neat methodical list of jewellery items – maybe these were to be sold? She gave up and went out of the room.

Then she found the mother's bedroom. She went over to the dressing table and glanced at one silver-framed picture after another. Still none of Janklow as an adult. Lorraine picked up a photo of the glamorous Mrs Thorburn – so like the woman driving the Mercedes as photographed by Rosie. It looked posed, well lit and touched up. She turned the frame over, about to replace it, when she decided to see if the photographer was identified on the back of the picture.

As she opened the frame she almost dropped the glass but caught it in time. A second photograph had been placed inside. At first glance it looked like another photograph of Mrs Thorburn, but on closer inspection it obviously wasn't. The blonde wig was identical, even the diamond necklace, the way the gloved hand rested beneath the sitter's chin. But this sitter was not Mrs Thorburn. It was someone attempting to look like her, but no amount of airbrushing and touching up could disguise the fact that the sitter was a man.

Lorraine took the photograph and replaced the frame. She checked three more before she found another hidden photograph of the same man. She could not be sure it was Janklow, or even the man who had attacked her, only that it was some man impersonating Mrs Thorburn. She then heard an ominous creaking sound from above: footsteps pacing up and down.

Quickly, she peered at the back of the photograph and made out a pale imprint of the photographer's name and contact number. It was so blurred that she needed more light, but she suspected it would be either Art Mathews or Craig Lyall. As she eased open the door, she jumped back as she heard voices, louder now. She hurried to the landing to look down to the hall. Should she confront Brad and Rooney together? Or get out, drive herself to the station, and show them the photographs? She crept further along the landing; they were still talking. Then she heard the same pacing coming from above. Was it Janklow? She dithered a moment and then moved silently down one stair at a time. She was within yards of the drawing room and she could hear clearly now.

'How serious is this?' she heard Brad ask.

'I have no idea but I will tomorrow, I'll go there personally. It's best not to worry about it. Just leave it with me.'

Lorraine was at the foot of the stairs, her heart pounding. She could easily have walked in, admitted being there – but why couldn't she hear Rooney's voice? She turned suddenly, certain someone was watching her. She pressed against the wall, trying to look up the stairs.

'You don't think there's any possibility of there being any truth in all this, do you?' Brad sounded tired. The clipped tone of the other man replied that he doubted there was anything to be worried about, he was fully aware of Steven's sexual preference and he would make sure it was never disclosed. But he would like to talk to him at the first opportunity. Where was he? Brad had no idea, but knew that he had been home earlier.

Why couldn't she hear Rooney's voice? Was he there? She looked to the open kitchen doorway, then back to the drawing room, and stepped out of her shoes. She made it to the kitchen and then stopped. She looked again to the first landing, again sure she had seen someone.

'I'll show you out.' It was Brad, and they were walking towards the hall. She dodged into the kitchen, seconds before the two men emerged from the drawing room. Lorraine could see them through a narrow chink between the door and its frame but she still couldn't see Rooney. He must have already left.

'One thing's bothering me, Alfred. Do you know if Mother instructed Steven to sell off her jewellery?'

'I don't deal with Mrs Thorburn's private accounts, it's an entirely different department, but I'll get it checked out.'

'I'm sure there'll be a reasonable explanation. I know the jewellery will be left to Steven on Mother's death – it's just that I find it strange that neither Mother nor Steven has mentioned it to me.'

Lorraine was terrified to move: they were so close. She was hoping and praying that if the front door was going to open, she could get out through the back door as the security system would be off. She was about to head for what she presumed was the back door when something Brad said made her freeze.

'This last business, I thought there was no possible way it could get out. You told me there would never be any repercussions and yet that Rooney brought it up as if it was still on the police files.'

Kophch again said that he would look into it. Although he had made certain there was no documented evidence left on any police file, he could not guarantee the silence of any officer who had been involved.

'Then pay them off, if necessary, whatever the cost.'

Lorraine flattened her body against the wall inching towards the back door.

'You know, Brad, there's only so much I can do. I cannot in any way jeopardize myself. Do you have any reason to believe that Steven could be involved in this? Because if you do, you must be honest with me. For example, this witness, do you know any more about her?'

Lorraine heard Brad discussing her visit, that he was sure she had only been trying to get money out of him. He sounded angry, his voice rising. 'Well, I can have her taken care of if she contacts me again.'

He was interrupted. 'No, you listen to me. If this woman shows up, you do nothing. Nothing. As I said, I was able to take care of things last time but this is bigger – this is murder, and if the press get wind that either you or your brother have any involvement, you'll be hounded. Now do you understand? You do not do anything without first discussing it with me!'

Brad walked out onto the porch with his lawyer. They shook hands and Brad watched Kophch take out his car keys. Then he walked back to the house, his hand on the buzzer to open the gates.

Lorraine edged to the back door. She tried the handle: it was open. She said a silent prayer, only to find she was in the garage rather than the garden as she had expected. The kitchen door closed behind her, just as Brad closed the front door and switched on the alarm circuit.

She looked round the vast dark garage, which had room for at least six cars. At the side of the sliding doors was a row of numbered buttons to open them and above the buttons was an ominous unblinking red dot. She tried to go back the way she had come, but the door was now locked. She was trapped inside the garage.

Rooney was sitting in his car as the lawyer drove past. Kophch stared at him but did not stop. Lorraine's car remained parked along the road; the two officers had found nothing inside. Rooney sat, hoping to see her and becoming more and more worried as the minutes ticked by. He wondered if she was in the house. He even wondered if he should go back in and demand to search the place, but he had no warrant.

The two officers hovered, waiting for instruction. Rooney rubbed his chin; his stubble itched. He was dog tired. 'I think she's maybe up at the house. I want one of you to call, ask if you can look around the grounds. I doubt if he'll let you in but it's worth a try. If we get no luck, take her car back to the station.'

Lorraine looked about her. A Rolls-Royce Silver Shadow, plus Brad's sports car, two Harley Davidson motorcycles, a Porsche and, hidden from her sight at first, the Mercedes. She was sure it would be alarmed, like everything else in the house. She looked at the garage doors, could see wires threaded everywhere. It was like a fortress. No way would she be able to get out that way; she'd have to return to the house. Then she heard the ringing of a distant doorbell. The garage doors began to slide open. She ducked behind a car as they began to whir and grind, pulling back. She peered up and could see Brad standing right outside the garage with a uniformed police officer.

'Take a look around in here and then wherever else you like but not in the house.'

She could see Brad's bare feet beneath the cars, and the dark trouser legs of the police officer, his black rubber-soled shoes.

'I'll show you round the back way,' Brad said. He hadn't expected to see Steven's car there and it had freaked him. He was sure his brother wasn't in but he covered his initial reaction by quickly offering to show the officer the gardens.

Lorraine waited until they were out of sight before she dashed out of the garage towards the grass verge and ran flat out until she reached the open gates.

Rooney and the officer were standing by her car, Rooney leaning forward for his cigarette to be lit. She headed to his car. It was open and she threw herself inside, onto the back seat. Rooney inhaled and let the smoke drift out of his nostrils. He checked the time again; it was almost seven o'clock. His stomach grumbling for food, he plodded back to the gates as the second officer appeared, a young, fresh-faced boy, who worked out. His muscles rippled beneath his pristine cop shirt and badge and he edged his night stick aside from his leg.

'There's no one in the grounds, Captain, and Mr Thorburn wants to lock up for the night. What do you want me to do? This place is alarmed all over, he's standing with his hand on the buzzer, says we can't go into the house.'

Rooney waddled towards him. 'You didn't see anything?'

'Been round the back, summer-house, tennis courts, swimming pool, checked all over. She's not in the grounds.'

Rooney went back to his car but he couldn't just walk away. As the two officers stood in the road waiting to know what he wanted them to do, he reached in for his radio.

'Don't let them take me in, Bill,' Lorraine said quietly from the back seat. 'Please don't.'

Rooney turned back to the officers but they hadn't seen

her. 'One of you take her car into the holding bays, the other follow. I'll see you back at base.'

Rooney got into his car and watched the two men split up, one going for Lorraine's car, the other getting a set of pliers out of the patrol car. He started his engine and drew away, leaving them as they decided who should drive Lorraine's car. The young muscular cop laughed as they reached down to fix the wires to start the engine. He said it had been a long time since he'd been caught doin' this.

'You go first, Rambo, I'll follow.'

Rooney didn't even head up Mulholland but pulled over about a mile away. She'd have felt better if he'd slammed on the brakes and yelled at her, but instead he engaged the handbrake gently and switched off the engine, then slowly swivelled around to face her.

'What the fuck do you think you're doing?' He hit the seat with the flat of his hand.

She unfolded the photographs. 'These were behind pictures of Mrs Thorburn. Look at the back. Can you see who took them?'

Rooney snatched the pictures and reached into his glove compartment for a torch. He shone it onto the creased photograph.

'Can you make it out?'

'Can you?' He passed the torch across to her and she shone it on the faded photographer's stamp. 'Professional Photo Studio,' she said slowly, disappointed it had not said Art Mathews – yet it could have been his studio, or even Craig Lyall's.

'So you got photographs of a woman,' Rooney said flatly.

'They're not of a woman, Bill, it's a man dressed up. And it's not just any woman he's dressed up to look like, but Mrs Thorburn. I think it's Janklow.'

'Jesus Christ, now what you tellin' me? That he's a homo

or a transvestite, or what? Is he or isn't he the man who fucking attacked you, Lorraine?'

'I don't know.'

'You don't know. Well, that is fucking great.'

'I didn't see him, Bill – that's why I went there.'

'I told you to stay in the apartment. You promised me. You done nothing but jerk me off, Lorraine.'

She sighed, watching her car being driven past followed by the patrol car. They tooted and waved at Rooney. As Lorraine's car drove away, the patrol car slowed.

'Everything okay, Captain?' The officer stared at Lorraine in the back seat.

Rooney jerked his thumb at Lorraine. 'Yeah, it's all fine. I found her. Go on, I'll see you back there.'

They watched the patrol car move off and Rooney turned back to her. 'I got to take you in. You got no option, I got no option.'

'I went to an AA meeting, I was going to go straight back and wait for you but . . .'

He fished in his pocket for his cigarettes, lighting one from the butt and tossing it out of his window. 'But you didn't. I've been running all over Pasadena, all over LA looking for you. They got half the cops on duty out looking for you. What the hell have you been doing?'

'Getting laid,' she said flippantly.

'Very funny, Lorraine, you always liked a joke. Well, this time the laugh is on me. Why didn't you tell me you were with Art Mathews the night of Holly's murder, with him all night? You were his friggin' alibi.'

She sighed, leaning forward to rest her arms along the seat. 'I wasn't with him all night. I left quite late . . . Rosie'll remember, maybe after twelve.'

He passed her a cigarette without her asking for one. 'I'm out of matches.'

She delved into her purse. 'What time was Holly

371

murdered, or near as damn it?' He took the matches, struck one, then held the flame out to her. 'Thanks.' She exhaled, waiting for him to answer her question.

Rooney plucked at his eyebrows. There had been so many murders, he couldn't remember offhand what time they had verified that Holly had died.

Lorraine tapped his arm. 'About eleven, wasn't it? She was just starting work so it'd be around ten thirty or eleven. I was with him so he couldn't have done it.'

Rooney lowered his window. 'Doesn't matter to him, he's dead, but it matters to *you* because the FBI got your name from him. I can't not take you in.'

He started the engine.

'Where are we going?' she asked.

'Back to the fucking station, where do you think? I just told you. I'm handing you over, I want you out of my hair, out of my life. You and your theory will land me in a strait-jacket, never mind retiring me. You've been feeding me a line of bullshit from day one.'

'Bill, I swear to you I haven't.'

He looked at her in the driving mirror, his eyes watering from tiredness and smoke. 'Holly was murdered after twelve. Lorraine, I was just testing you.'

She punched his shoulder. He stopped the car. Suddenly he was really angry, his jowled face set rigid. 'What the fuck were you doing at Thorburn's house? And from what I gathered, you weren't there for any interview with his brother. Trying to make a few bucks for yourself – is that what you were up to? I wouldn't put anything past you. Well, now I'm through with you.'

'Was he in there?' she asked.

'You tell me. We won't get a foot in there without more evidence than that load of shit you got. I'm gonna get it in the neck about this.'

He crashed the gears as the car shot forward. They headed up Mulholland, the road becoming steeper. His car coughed, protesting, but they picked up speed as they moved downhill. Suddenly Rooney stamped on his brakes as they came to the traffic lights at a dangerous multiple crossing. The patrol car was there plus two more cars, and rammed between them, the entire driver's side smashed to smithereens, was Lorraine's car. The officer was still inside, his blood spattering the broken windshield and soaking his muscular dead body.

Rooney barked at Lorraine to stay out of sight. As he got out and crossed to the wreckage, she peered out of the window. An ambulance and medic truck arrived and they began to release the driver.

When Rooney came back, he didn't turn to speak to her but stared straight ahead. 'He's dead. He was just a kid.'

'Was it an accident?' she asked.

'What would you say? There's one, two, three other vehicles involved. He jumped the lights, this junction's known to be a death trap. He drove straight into it.' He faced her. 'This is *your* fault. It's due to you, you hear me?'

'Why?' she snapped back. 'I wasn't driving the god-damned car, was I?'

Rooney walked back to the scene of the crash. A few people were gathering around to gawp, more police, and now they had the dead man free. Lorraine saw Rooney and another officer prise open the car's buckled hood. As they peered inside with a torch, another man crawled beneath it. Rooney was there for almost fifteen minutes. When he got back he sat half in and half out of his car, his feet still on the roadside. 'Brake cable's smothered in grease, sliced almost in two, and the handbrake cable's cut. Did anyone have access to the car keys?'

'They were in my purse.'

'They still there?'

Lorraine fumbled and took them out.

'Did you leave it unattended while you were there?'

'Yeah. For quite a while when I was talking to Brad

Thorburn. We were in the bedroom. I left my purse downstairs.' She flushed.

He looked at her and shook his head. 'Christ, I thought you were joking before. Did you screw him?'

'I wanted information, Bill.'

'I bet you did.'

'Why don't we go back up there, Bill, just you and me? If Janklow's there, it's him you should be taking in, never mind me! If I'd been in my car, it would have been me who was dead.'

Rooney slammed the car door and started the engine. 'No way. Not until I've discussed this with the Chief. I'm sorry, but that's the way it's got to be.'

Lorraine had been hoping againt all hope that this would never happen but now there was no alternative. She would become a witness for the prosecution and all it entailed. Any idea she had had of starting up as a private investigator would be ruined: when the press got to hear about her part in the murder investigation she and her past would make the headlines. She stared out of the window as they drove towards the precinct. She wanted a drink, could feel it sweeping over her. She wanted a drink rather than face it all.

She hardly said a word as Rooney led her into the station. The duty sergeant noted down all her particulars, she was photographed, and her prints taken. Then she was led away to Rooney's office.

Rooney had called the Chief and was waiting for him. He had shaved and changed his shirt for what looked like an even more crumpled one from his locker. He was drinking coffee and talking to Bean when Lorraine was brought into the room. Rooney introduced Bean who shook her hand and drew out a chair. 'When we're ready, we'll take your statement. We'll also tape it and film you, okay?'

Lorraine asked if someone was preparing the movie

rights but no one laughed. Bean fetched her some water and cigarettes and, as he seemed so helpful, she asked him if she could call her friend Rosie to let her know she was okay.

Lorraine waited in Rooney's office for some time. She was told they'd be held up until the FBI agents arrived; neither Rooney nor the Chief could deny them access to her. When she was eventually taken into the large room where everyone was gathered, it was eleven thirty. She remained closeted there for a further four hours. In that time she gave a clear statement of everything that had happened since the day she had first been attacked in the car park. When asked why she had not come forward, she said it was because she had removed Norman Hastings's wallet. She didn't lie, she could see no point. She answered all their questions directly and truthfully. No one appeared impressed by her subsequent investigation or her attempts at piecing together the evidence she had accumulated.

'Why are you so keen on continuing this investigation, even placing yourself at risk?' one of the agents asked. She didn't like the look of this one: his square jaw, which worked overtime, his clean-cut face, his blond crew-cut and neat suit, like a comic-strip man.

She looked over at Rooney who nodded quickly. 'I needed the money, I was being paid to do it by Captain Rooney.'

Although they knew about her record since leaving the police force, they seemed loath to believe that that was the only reason she had taken such risks. Surely she had another motive?

'I suppose I did. I hoped that if I succeeded in assisting the department, then it would stand me in good stead for the future if I ever wanted to start up as a private investigator. But if I have to be a prosecution witness, then it'll destroy that chance. I know this case'll get a load of publicity and like me, well, they'll go for the jugular – that's a joke. The ex-cop ex-hooker'll make good copy, might even get a headline "Madame Dracula". I doubt I'll be able to live it down. I might be able to move away, but I've got contacts here and you need contacts in the investigation business, right?'

They made no answer but glanced at each other before they all left the room, leaving her with a stone-faced policewoman. They returned an hour later. It was almost dawn. But Lorraine detected another undercurrent.

The Chief gave a grimace – she supposed it was some kind of smile but because he was so tense his lips just curled over his top teeth. 'Mrs Page, would you be willing to continue assisting this inquiry?' Rooney wouldn't meet her eyes and the Chief continued, 'There could be certain risks involved.'

Lorraine looked at the Chief, then Rooney. 'You want to make a deal with me, don't you? Well, I guess it would depend—'

'On what?' the Chief asked.

'On what exactly you want me to do. If I work with you, you'll have a tough time bringing me into court as a prosecution witness, won't you? I'd put any money on it that anything connected to the Thorburns you'll have to tread on lightly. What is it you want me to do? Is Janklow going in a line-up?'

'The situation is this. If you pick Steven Janklow out of a line-up, it will be his word against yours. You are a chronic alcoholic, ex-prostitute, drug user—'

She snapped, 'I am also an ex-cop.'

The FBI agent retorted, 'We know that, and we'd be out of our minds to put that out. With your record, it would make you sound an even worse witness than a hooker.'

The comic-strip man leaned on the desk. 'I think we got Janklow to agree to come into the station. He'll be accompanied by his lawyer. What we don't want is a line-up at this stage. But you came face to face with him, you were attacked, so what I want from you is just a good look. We'll set him up in an interview room with a one-way viewing section so you can watch him at your leisure. Because you have to be one hundred per cent sure that the man you say attacked you was Steven Janklow.'

Rooney took over. 'You're the only witness we have but, that said, we'll need a lot more. If he did attack you, then he will be charged with assault. If you're sure it's him, we can even press charges, but you and I both know, because of who you are and his powerful back-up, he'll walk.'

'What about the couple that saw me in the garage?'

'At no time were they able to describe the man in the car with you, so they can't be brought on as witnesses – well, not yet.'

So far Lorraine couldn't see any risk, but then she intercepted the looks between the men. As Rooney moved closer, Here it comes, she thought.

'You know Brad Thorburn, you've had sexual intercourse with him. He inferred that you may have been attempting to blackmail him. We don't know yet if he has played any part in the murders but he *is* Janklow's brother, and you've told us he even has a pair of cufflinks, so—'

'You want me to blackmail Brad Thorburn?' she asked smiling.

'No, we want you – and only if you're sure that Steven Janklow is the man who attacked you—'

The comic-strip man was gradually taking over and Lorraine began to try to assess him and to fathom what they wanted her to do. He was steely, assured. She determined that he was trying to make her offer to assist them without them saying it for themselves; whatever it was must be either illegal or, as they had implied, risky. They were all watching her, waiting for her to take the bait . . .

'I think I get what you're after. If I do recognize him and I'm a hundred per cent sure that the man who attacked me was Steven Janklow, then you've still only got him on assault. You want to use me to do – what? Put pressure on him and see what it throws up, and at the same time find out if Brad Thorburn is also involved?'

They all straightened and she knew she had not only bitten their bait but was offering to reel herself in. She looked over at Rooney and smiled. 'I'll do it but there are certain conditions. If I can get Janklow to admit his part in the murders, maybe by confronting him at his home, if I can get him to admit it and I'm wired up, you won't need to call me as a prosecution witness. So there will be a guilty plea? That what you're after?'

They didn't say a word.

'I'll have a try, but I want your word you won't release my part in any of this to the press.'

'We can't guarantee that,' snapped the Chief.

'Then bring him in and charge him. Just do what you have to do.'

There was a low murmur and she looked to the only other woman present and asked if she could go to the bathroom. She took her time: she was tired out and her clothes were crumpled. She sat on the toilet, thinking about everything they had discussed. When she was led back into the room, only Rooney and his chief remained. Everyone else had gone.

The Chief motioned her to a chair. 'We cannot agree to any deal, Lorraine, you know that, but what we will do is not press charges against you for withholding evidence, and we will endeavour to keep your name out of the proceedings. Your identity will be kept secret, but only if you're able to ascertain that Janklow is the killer.'

She looked at Rooney and gave a half smile. 'Okay, I'll do it. Though it's a very one-sided deal to your advantage. Now, I'll need some new clothes and I need to get some rest. I also need a car so I'll want a clean licence – just so I don't get picked up.'

Rooney winked at her as a warning not to press too hard for anything more.

'When is Janklow coming in?' she asked the Chief.

'Not sure, but we don't want to make it seem too urgent, so you'll have time to change and rest up.'

'Can Bill be my back-up?' she asked, and smiled at Rooney who looked at the ceiling. 'He was always a good back-up man, one of the best.'

'No, I'm afraid not. Bill's been seen in your company and by the look of him if he doesn't get some sleep, he'll fall down. You'll have his lieutenant, Josh Bean. He's a good man, and he's waiting to drive you home right now.'

Lorraine was confident, almost arrogant, as she said, 'He gonna take me shopping? I want to look good.'

The Chief replied that they might not need the new clothes. First she had to view Janklow, then they'd see about the other things she'd asked for – just as they'd also have to set her up with a wire. She walked out of the room before the Chief had finished talking, saying over her shoulder, 'I guess you'll call me when you need me.'

'Can we trust her?' the Chief asked Rooney.

'Much as any woman and she hasn't had a drink for nine months. She wants to go straight.'

'It never was your theory, was it?' the Chief said quietly and Rooney grunted. He knew that by bringing her in it'd come out in the open.

'No. She ran rings around most officers and, so help me God, I'll never know why she blew it those years ago.'

'Just hope she doesn't blow it with us. If she puts a foot out of line, Bill, I'll haul her in so fast, I'll have her charged and put away for a long time. You should make sure she's aware of just how serious this is. We've got to get this case wrapped up. And if she fucks up, it's not just us, it'll be the FBI who'll make sure she never works again, not here or in any other state. Let her know that. Make sure she knows we can't have any mistakes – there's been too many as it is.'

CHAPTER 18

ROONEY HAD shaved, and was wearing a clean-looking shirt and a new suit. He'd had a good lunch before he drove into the station. He knew that Janklow was being brought in by his lawyer at four thirty because his chief, who seemed to be in a growing state of panic, had called him three times.

Bean was sweating as he hit a traffic jam. Lorraine sat beside him. If she was nervous she didn't show it but Josh grew increasingly agitated. He kept on tapping the dashboard clock, then checking his wrist-watch. It was almost four. His hair was damp at the nape of his neck and he leaned out of the window to look at the lines of traffic up ahead. He knew if she wasn't at the station by four fifteen he'd be hauled over the carpet. He wiped his face.

Lorraine tapped his shoulder. 'Get your light on or we'll never make it. Shut it off before we get to the precinct.'

Subtle it wasn't but in the end Bean switched on his siren and his blinking roof-light and began to edge his way down the centre of the road. Even less subtly, he yelled out of the window for other drivers to move over.

On arrival at the station, they were met by Rooney.

'Is he here yet?' she asked breathlessly.

Rooney shook his head as he and Bean hurried her along towards the viewing room. It was just an anteroom, with a table and two hard-backed chairs facing a square-curtained window that adjoined the main interview room. There were

380

microphones at ceiling level, the controls at the side of the room. Lorraine was ushered in. She noticed that, like Bean, Rooney was sweating. She knew a lot was riding for Rooney on her identification of Janklow.

'You just make notes and watch, look and listen. You'll be able to hear every word they say.'

'Come on, Bill, I know the set-up. Who's taking the interview?'

'Ed Bickerstaff, one of the suits. He's the blond crew-cut guy.'

It was four twenty-five, five minutes to go. Rooney left the room. Lorraine lit up and her hands were shaking. She picked up her pen and began to doodle on the notepad, then said to Bean, 'What if there's something I think Janklow should be asked?'

Bean hesitated. 'Give it to me and I'll see if I can go into the interview room but only if it's—'

'Important?' she said smiling.

'Yeah.'

'He's gonna know he's being viewed – any two-bit criminal knows by the window – so why all the secrecy?'

'Protection.'

'His?'

'Yours. You're a valuable witness, Mrs Page.'

Janklow and Kophch's arrival in a chauffeur-driven Cadillac sent whispers through almost every department. Even though secrecy had surrounded the request to bring in Janklow, rumour spread fast; any suspect being brought in for questioning about the hammer murders would have attracted interest, but a high-society man like one of the Thorburn family. . .

Rooney stood in the corridor as they filed past him. He was surprised at how confident Janklow appeared, not paying anyone any attention but staring ahead, his face partly hidden by dark glasses. As they passed, Rooney sniffed. He could smell expensive cologne like delicate flowers. He noticed the way Kophch stayed close to Janklow, his steely eyes taking in everyone and everything.

Bean replaced the intercom phone and looked at Lorraine. 'They're coming in now.' He drew back the curtain to expose the dark square window-pane and returned to his seat.

The microphones picked up the sounds of the room beyond. Bickerstaff was sitting to one side, hardly visible. The table was stacked with files and photographs. As the door opened, he rose to his feet. Lorraine leaned forward: she couldn't see Janklow as the men were introduced. Kophch turned and stared at the one-way glass, aware of what it was, but said nothing and drew out a chair for Janklow.

Lorraine watched closely as Janklow sat down facing her directly, his chair positioned towards the viewing window opposite Bickerstaff. Kophch sat on his left, and clicked open his briefcase. Janklow was wearing a fawn cashmere jacket and a white shirt with a tie, but Lorraine couldn't see his trousers. He had mouse-blond hair combed back from his face which was angular, more handsome than she had expected. His nose was thinnish, again not as she had remembered and she doubted immediately that this was the man by whom she had been attacked. She didn't recognize him. She sat back, her heart beating rapidly. She'd been wrong. She twisted her pen. 'Can they get him to take off his glasses?'

'They will, just relax.' Bean could see that she was tense: she was frowning, cocking her head first on one side then the other.

No one spoke in the adjoining room. It was eerie: the silence, the waiting.

'Would you please remove your glasses, Mr Janklow?' It was the quiet voice of Bickerstaff.

'If you require my client to look at any evidence, he will need to use his glasses. They are not decorative but prescription. I'm sorry but your request is denied.'

Bickerstaff opened his file. 'Take off your glasses, please, Mr Janklow. When it is required you may replace them.'

Janklow slowly removed them. Lorraine felt chilled for the first time. His eyes were pale blue, washed out, and he stared ahead as if straight at her. She caught her breath as he moistened his lips. His mouth had been tightly closed until this moment but when he licked round both lips his face took on a different quality, as if his lips had come to life, wide lips, wide, wet lips. She scribbled on her notepad. This was the man who had attacked her, she knew it. His lips had given him away.

'It's him,' she said softly, barely audible. Bean stared at her and then back to the window as the interview began in earnest.

Bickerstaff, quiet and authoritative, first explained that he would require from Mr Janklow his whereabouts on certain dates. He was aware that some were several years ago but he should answer to the best of his knowledge. When the date of the first murder was given, Janklow frowned. 'I have no idea.'

His lawyer jotted something in his leatherbound notebook. The second date and Janklow was unable to answer, the third and still nothing – he was even apologetic at his memory failure. Bickerstaff persisted. As the more recent dates came up, Janklow gave alibi times and places. He mentioned his brother and his mother. Both, his lawyer said, would verify his client's whereabouts.

Bickerstaff then laid out the victims' photographs in front of Janklow. He studied each one intently, in silence, before shaking his head. 'No, I don't know any of these people.'

Lorraine watched every gesture he made, his hands, long delicate fingers, and she made a note of the ring on his right-hand pinky finger. She was sure that this was the man who had attacked her, even though she didn't recognize his voice, or remember the ring. It was his face and hands that convinced her: he was left-handed.

Bickerstaff was unhurried, taking his time over each question, each photograph. He was saving Norman Hastings and Didi – or David Burrows – until last. When he presented Janklow with the picture of Hastings, Janklow said he knew him quite well. He described how Hastings had used his garage to park his car but denied any social interaction between them. When asked if he was aware of Hastings's transvestite tendencies he looked shocked, and when Bickerstaff asked if he knew Art Mathews he looked nonplussed. To his knowledge, he said, he had never heard the name. He was then asked if he knew Craig Lyall. This time he paused and touched his mouth, he started to shake his head and then changed his mind. 'Craig Lyall? Er, yes, I think I've been to his studio. He's a photographer. I took my mother there to be photographed, but he was not as professional as I'd hoped and the session was terminated. My mother is very particular, and this refers back to her days in the movies. She was a film star when she was in her twenties.'

Bickerstaff let him talk, quietly turning pages, before he interrupted. 'Were you being blackmailed, Mr Janklow?'

Janklow sat back in his chair. 'Blackmailed? Do you mean by Lyall?'

'By anyone,' Bickerstaff replied.

'Absolutely not.'

He now presented Janklow with the photograph of Didi. Again, Janklow spent a considerable time looking at it, shifting his glasses on and off. 'No, I've never met this woman.'

'It's a man.' Bickerstaff waited. 'She or he never made you up for a photograph?'

Lorraine saw Janklow's mouth snap shut. Then he licked

his lips again and gave a humourless laugh. 'No, I was never made up – I presume you mean in female attire – for any photograph.'

Bickerstaff didn't flicker but continued, head down, still nonchalant, as he asked if Janklow was homosexual.

'No, I am not,' Janklow snapped.

'Are you a transvestite?'

'No, I am not.'

'Have you ever in the past been charged with any homosexual crime?'

'No.'

Kophch reached out and touched Janklow's arm. He was becoming agitated and he constantly licked his lips. Lorraine chewed her pen, willing Bickerstaff to push for more, but he remained composed, even apologetic, looking at Kophch and saying that he was sorry if some of the questions were distasteful to his client but he must understand they had to be asked.

Kophch leaned towards Bickerstaff, his voice low. 'Mr Bickerstaff, please feel free to ask my client any question – that is what we are here for, to confirm my client's innocence – but please let me remind you, he is here of his own free will.'

'I am aware of that, Mr Kophch. The sooner we have completed all the questions, then the sooner your presence will no longer be necessary.'

Lorraine sighed. If anything, Bickerstaff seemed to be on Janklow's side. She had never witnessed anyone taking so long, pussy-footing around. His methodical approach was driving her crazy. She asked Bean when Bickerstaff was going to up the ante. He made no reply but stared at the glass partition.

Bickerstaff presented Holly's picture next and Janklow denied any knowledge of her. Then Bickerstaff gave him Didi's photograph again.

'I have already said I do not know this person.'

385

Bickerstaff pushed the photograph closer. 'This person sometimes calls herself Didi.'

'I don't know her – whoever it is. I don't know them.'

'You have also denied knowing or meeting Art Mathews.'

'I don't know him. You're repeating the same questions.'

Bickerstaff was beginning to step up the pressure, just a little. 'Now, Mr Janklow, can we return to the dates and the alibis you have given. It seems convenient that both your brother and your mother are always your only alibi. You have no other witness to—'

Janklow's voice rose as he interrupted. 'It happens to be the truth.'

'Mr Bickerstaff,' Kophch intervened, 'it is obvious that you are beginning to repeat yourself. If you have no further questions to ask my client, then perhaps we can close this interview.'

'I'm afraid not, Mr Kophch, because your client has so far been unable to present to me any alibi for a number of these cases.'

'But they took place some years ago. If we are given time we will attempt to present you with the whereabouts of my client on those specific dates.'

Kophch stood up but was ordered by Bickerstaff to remain seated. Lorraine clasped her hands tightly together. This was more like it.

'Mr Janklow, you've stated that you are not homosexual.'

'Yes.'

'You are not a transvestite.'

'No, I am not.'

'Is your brother?'

'No, that's ridiculous.'

'And you have never at any time in the past eight years been arrested on a homosexual-related incident.'

'No, I have not.'

'You have stated that on the night of Norman Hastings's death you were not in Santa Monica, you were not—'

'I was with my mother.'

'Is this your mother, Mr Janklow?'

Bickerstaff placed one of the photographs Lorraine had removed from the Thorburn house before him. Janklow looked at his lawyer, then looked back at the photographs. He was visibly shocked. 'Is this your mother, Mr Janklow?'

Kophch frowned and looked at the pictures. He seemed confused as Janklow sat tight-lipped with fury.

'Is this a photograph of your mother, Mr Janklow?'

'Yes.'

'Are you sure?'

'*Yes.*'

Bickerstaff removed a picture of Mrs Thorburn and placed it on the table. 'Do you notice any difference, Mr Janklow, between this photograph of Mrs Thorburn and the one I am now placing in front of you?'

The two photographs lay side by side, one of Mrs Thorburn, the other, everyone was certain, of Janklow himself.

He picked up the photographs and stared at them. 'Where did you get these?'

'Would your client please answer the question?'

Janklow was becoming agitated. Lorraine stood up. Bickerstaff should go for him now. *What was he waiting for? Why didn't he push Janklow now?* Kophch requested a few moments alone with his client. As they were led out, Lorraine slapped the table. 'I don't believe this – *I don't believe it!*'

The door opened; Bickerstaff walked in and asked quietly if she had anything to tell him.

'You bet I have! It's him and I would stand up in any court. In fact, if you want me to I'll walk in there and confront him.'

'No, you won't,' Bickerstaff said firmly, and left.

They waited over half an hour before Janklow and Kophch returned. Janklow was calm again. Kophch opened the interview this time.

'My client and I would like to know how you came by these photographs.'

Bickerstaff kept his head down as if studying his papers. 'I am afraid, Mr Kophch, I am unable to give that information to you. We feel we require to place your client under oath and that anything he subsequently says—'

'If you have any charges related to my client, I want to hear them. If any relate to these murders, then we will not, at this interview, discuss or refer—'

Bickerstaff snapped, 'You will not, Mr Kophch, tell me what I can or cannot do. I am more than aware of the law and I am now ready to charge your client with assault.'

'*What?*' Mr Kophch's studied calm cracked. He had been unprepared for an assault charge.

Bickerstaff continued, 'I wish formally to charge your client that he did, on the night of the seventeenth of April, assault a woman, whose identity I have every right at this stage of my inquiry not to disclose.'

'You never at any time told me my client was suspected of an assault,' Kophch interjected. 'You have brought my client and myself here on false pretences.'

Bickerstaff and Kophch argued for more than ten minutes. Lorraine was becoming impressed with Bickerstaff, who had remained in control. Kophch was one of the most high-powered lawyers and knew every legal loophole but Bickerstaff was one jump ahead. He had wanted, from the outset, to force Janklow to talk on oath but without Lorraine's verification of his identity he had not had sufficient evidence. Now he had, and at seven o'clock that evening Janklow was sworn in and read the charges of assault against him. As yet there was still not enough evidence to charge him with any of the murders. All were more than aware that when Kophch received Lorraine's statements and was allowed access to the evidence against Janklow, they would be in trouble. But they had enough to hold him for another twenty-four hours.

At nine o'clock that evening, with only an hour's break for a light supper, Janklow was brought back into the interview room. He and Kophch had spent the time alone in a cell.

Lorraine had sat in the incident room with Bickerstaff over sandwiches and coffee.

'I think you should put more pressure on his homosexual activities.'

'The blackmail's a strong murder motive and if he and Hastings ever discussed the blackmail—'

Lorraine leaned close, excited. 'Of *course* he was being blackmailed. What about all the missing jewellery belonging to Mrs Thorburn? We don't know if it was sold with her permission but it's a good area to get Janklow to talk about – even more so as Mrs Thorburn is his only alibi for the night I was attacked.' Bickerstaff wiped a crumb from his lips with his paper napkin. 'Is anyone talking to her?' Lorraine asked.

Bickerstaff was getting irritated, but he listened – he felt obliged to. 'Don't tell me what I should and shouldn't do, Lorraine, I'm quite capable of interrogating a suspect.' He finally asked her if she felt that Janklow was the killer.

'Yes, I do,' she stated. 'He has the motive, heavy blackmail and possibly over a long period of time.'

'But you don't have any proof of that, it's just supposition and we don't have a motive for each of these women.'

Lorraine looked at Bickerstaff, her head on one side. 'What about Kophch? He's not as tough as I expected – he seems to be taking a back seat. Couple of times he could have got Janklow off the hook but he let it ride. Why?'

Bickerstaff grinned. 'We got him. Here, read that. This retired cop has spilled the beans, and that softly spoken lawyer's in it up to his neck.' He pushed forward a neatly typed statement. 'Steven Janklow had been arrested for soliciting in a red-light district. He was given a warning, but three nights later was arrested again in the same area. This time they took him down to the station to book him. His lawyer subsequently bought off the vice charges against Janklow and paid the cop to pull his arrest sheet. Kophch would be struck off if it was known that the client he bought out subsequently went on to kill eight women. But don't let him fool you, he's a vicious little shark. His prowess is in court – you'd be surprised what he's like and what he can do. A lot of this is knocking him sideways – but don't think he's a pussy because he's got razor-sharp claws.'

The time was up. Janklow was being led back into the interview room. The session began again. Bickerstaff repeated almost every question he had asked earlier. Janklow answered virtually word for word. He denied any knowledge of the victims and confidently repeated the same alibis. It was only when he was asked about his sexuality that he became hesitant. He was quiet, subdued, when he admitted that he was homosexual but was now celibate; he had not had a relationship with any man for ten years. He was near tears when he admitted that he did, on occasion, use women's clothes, but only his mother's. He had never been outside his home dressed as a woman. The photographs Lorraine had found were taken a long time ago.

'Who took these photographs, Mr Janklow?'

Janklow became distressed. He sniffed, then took out a clean laundered handkerchief and blew his nose. 'Art Mathews, or one of his assistants.'

'Where, Mr Janklow?'

Again he sniffed, wiping his nose. 'Santa Monica.'

'Are you or were you being blackmailed by Mathews, Mr Janklow?'

'No, and I haven't seen that wretched man since that session.'

'Who did the hair and make-up for it?' Bickerstaff pressed, repeating the question.

Janklow wriggled in his seat. 'It might have been David.'

'David?'

'Oh, stop this! You know who I mean. That David Burrows – Didi.'

'So was David "Didi" Burrows blackmailing you, Mr Janklow?'

'*No.* Why do you keep asking me this? I've told you I'm not being blackmailed. Not by that Art, or Burrows or anybody. I haven't seen them since that session years ago.'

Bickerstaff doodled with his pencil. 'And you have not dressed as a woman for, as you said, many years?'

'*That is correct,*' he snapped loudly.

Janklow was now confronted by Rosie's photograph. He stared at it, pursed his lips. He seemed disgusted by it. '*That* isn't me.'

'Please look more closely, Mr Janklow. Is that person in the photograph you?'

'No, it is not. It's my mother.'

'Your mother?'

Janklow blew his nose again. His eyes watering, he wriggled and then whispered, 'It's me.' He had already lied – and under oath. Bickerstaff went after him again, demanding to know just how deeply entrenched he was in the world of transvestites and transsexuals, swinging his questioning round to prostitutes – whether Janklow had ever picked up transsexual prostitutes. 'No, I have not.'

'You sure about that, Steven? You never picked up other men like yourself, dressed like this . . .' He pushed the photo of Janklow forward again.

'I do not pick up any of the filth from the streets.'

'Tell me about David Burrows.'

391

'I don't know him.'

'Didi. Come on, Steven, you've admitted he made you up, fixed your hair for the photographs and now you're saying you didn't know him. You're lying.'

Janklow looked helplessly to Kophch who examined his nails, refusing to meet Janklow's eye.

Bickerstaff leaned back. 'Okay, Steven, you didn't know Didi, you didn't know Art Mathews. So tell me about the jewellery you've been selling off. It's a lot of money and it belongs to your mother.'

'You leave her out of this.' He was back on the defensive.

'But, Steven, if you've been selling it without her permission then we'll have to discuss it with her.'

'Leave her alone. She's not well.'

'I can't do that, Steven, because she's also your alibi for the night of the assault and the night of Norman Hastings's murder. We're going to have to bring her in, you must know that.'

Janklow slapped the table near to Kophch. 'Tell them they can't do that.'

'They can, Steven.'

Janklow put his head in his hands. When Bickerstaff asked him again about the jewellery, he began to sob. This was not what Bickerstaff wanted: if he became too distressed, by law Kophch could take a break. Bickerstaff switched the subject away from Mrs Thorburn.

Lorraine was furious. 'What the hell is he doing? He's got him sobbing his heart out. Why doesn't he push for more about the jewellery? I don't believe it.'

Rooney walked in and saw her angry face. 'Mrs Thorburn has just told us that she gave her son permission to sell all her jewellery and that he was, on the night he was supposed to have attacked you, with her . . . I got to tell Bickerstaff.'

'Shit.' Lorraine looked at him. 'But somebody must have got to her – like Brad.'

'According to the nursing staff she's had no visitors, just one phone call. Late last night. From Kophch. But as her legal advisor he has every right to call her, and I'm telling you, she's a tough old broad and she's got all her marbles – told me to get the hell out.'

Bickerstaff was back on the subject of Janklow's relationship with Norman Hastings.

'He was a fool, a stupid idiot.' Janklow was no longer tearful, and both Lorraine and Rooney listened intently. It was eerie watching him, his face twisted, his lips wetter and shinier. 'Stupid, boring, fat, bloated fool.' Kophch gave a warning touch to Janklow's arm. 'Get off me, don't *you* touch me, you're a useless waste of money. This is *your* fault, all your fault – you should never have brought me in here. I'd be better off on my own. I don't want you here any more.'

Bickerstaff ploughed on, asking Janklow why he didn't like Hastings, a man he had said he hardly knew. Janklow whipped round and pointed at Bickerstaff. Kophch attempted to calm him but he swiped him aside. 'You have nothing to keep me here! You've been fishing around for hours and I know you have not one shred of evidence against me.'

'What about a witness, Steven?'

'Lies. There was never any witness.' Janklow was pulling at his jacket and smirking now, rocking backwards and forwards in his chair.

'We have a witness, Steven, someone you attacked on the same day Norman Hastings was killed.'

Janklow laughed. 'Oh, yes? You think I don't know who she is? She'd never stand a chance coming up against me. She's an ex-cop, ex-drunkard with a string of vice charges against her. She killed a kid when she was on duty. I know who you're protecting! I know – and it's a joke.'

Kophch was white, his face so tight with anger because his client was blowing it. He should never have admitted what he knew about Lorraine. Kophch rose to his feet. 'I insist we take a break now.'

'Sit down,' Janklow leered. 'I'm beginning to enjoy myself. This is fascinating. Go on, ask me anything you want.'

Bickerstaff said evenly, 'Listen to me, I don't care if we scooped a witness off the streets. All that matters to me is that she's a witness, you tried to kill her, you used a claw hammer. You know the type because there must be a hundred of them at your garage. I am quite prepared to let you go, Mr Janklow, but I will need a blood test. You see, you made a big mistake with the assault. She attacked you as well, didn't she? She made you bleed, didn't she? And, Mr Janklow, we have a sample of blood taken from the vehicle, the same vehicle into which you stuffed Norman Hastings's body. We have what I think is your blood. And now would you open your shirt.'

Janklow had become still, his face drawn, his hands clenched in front of him.

'Open your shirt and remove your tie.'

Lorraine clutched Rooney as Janklow slowly loosened his tie, slipping it away from his neck, and undid his shirt, one button after the next. It was horribly sexual – he was flicking glances to each of the men in the room and then he pulled away his shirt, revealing his white neck.

Bickerstaff got up, hiding Janklow from Lorraine and Rooney as he peered at the man's neck. He stepped back. 'You've got a mark the right side of your neck. Where did you get it?'

Janklow shrugged his shoulders. 'I have a German shepherd dog. He bit me a few weeks ago, maybe a couple of months. You can ask my brother, he was there, he saw it.'

Bickerstaff returned to his seat. He asked the other officer to contact Brad Thorburn. Janklow did up his shirt.

'Did you ever use Norman Hastings's car, Mr Janklow?'

'Oh, I might have – yes, I did . . . well, not drive it. I sat in it once, and – oh, I remember it very well. I was sitting talking to Norman, and I had a dreadful nosebleed because I have a weak septum.'

'What date would that be?'

'I borrowed his handkerchief to stem the bloodflow. Brad saw it, because I looked dreadful, very white and shaking. So I have a witness to that as well.'

Janklow buttoned up his shirt and unbelted his trousers as he tucked in the shirt tails, giving hideous flirtatious glances round the room. 'I did not kill anyone, I did not attack anyone, I am an innocent man, and now I would like to go home as I'm tired.'

Bickerstaff would not let up. He asked again where exactly Janklow had had the nosebleed, and on what date. Janklow yawned and said in the front seat of Hastings's car – he'd been parking it for him in the garage.

'What date would that have been?'

'I have no idea, around the sixteenth, I suppose. That was why I didn't come into work the following day, the seventeenth, because I felt poorly. I spent the day with my mother instead.'

Bickerstaff began to collect his files. 'I think, Mr Janklow, you can leave. We will, of course, have to check all this information, make inquiries to verify your alibis, both with Mr Brad Thorburn and Mrs Thorburn. I would also like you to pass to us further details of your whereabouts on the other dates you were unable to recall where you were.'

'Yes, of course. I'll check back in my diaries, give the relevant information to Mr Kophch and, as they say in the movies, I'll get back to you.'

Lorraine looked at Rooney in disbelief. 'He's going to walk! They're going to let him walk out of here.'

'Looks like it,' Rooney said bluntly.

'But it's obviously him! You know it, they must know it.'

'We're not through with him yet.'

Lorraine kicked at her chair. 'What about me? Don't I count? I've said it was him, I *know* it was him – he did *this* to me!' She showed Rooney the scar at the back of her head and then slumped in her chair. 'Jesus Christ, I even feel like some of the women I used to take statements from, the whores beaten within an inch of their lives. They always used to say to me, "Nothing will happen, nobody cares about us, nobody cares if they beat us to a pulp, because we don't matter." Are all those dead women of no consequence? Because you know, Rooney, if he walks now he'll never be brought back in.'

As if to confirm what she was saying, the chairs were scraping back in the interview room, Kophch assisting Janklow to stand up. He was joking about his crumpled shirt.

Lorraine pushed past Rooney and made for the door. He grabbed her. 'No, don't do it, Lorraine, you don't go out there.'

She wrenched her arm free. 'He's *walking out*, Bill! I swear before God I'll make a citizen's arrest! I'm not going to let him get away with this—'

'He just did. Now sit down.'

When Janklow and Kophch had departed, the atmosphere in the incident room was of exhaustion and depression. Bickerstaff looked at Lorraine and lifted his hands in a gesture of defeat. Lorraine's hands were on her hips. 'Get me a wire – get me set up. I'll get him to incriminate himself. I swear before God I'll bring that piece of shit in.'

Bickerstaff was worn out, but he grinned at her. 'That's what I hoped you'd say. Go home and get some rest. We'll talk in the morning.'

Bean drove her home and, as he had been instructed, remained with her, sleeping outside in the patrol car. Bickerstaff had taken him aside and warned him to keep her under watch day and night. Janklow knew who she was, maybe even knew her address. The following morning he was to get her some decent clothes before he brought her back into the precinct. Now she was all they had and everything depended on her. He was not to let her out of his sight for a moment.

Lorraine, accompanied by Bean and Rosie, set off early for Rodeo Drive. She chose an elegant suit, with a tight, pencil-slim skirt with a thigh-length slit, and loose jacket with a soft creamy silk blouse beneath. She chose high-heeled shoes with matching clutch bag. Conscious that she was to be wired, she also bought a fitted, slightly padded, brassière and matching panties. A suspender belt and fine pale stockings completed the outfit. She had her hair streaked, cut and blown dry, a manicure and a facial. Rosie and Bean trailed from one place to the next, sitting in the salon as she was made up by an expert. The whole process took three hours so she did not arrive at the station until after twelve.

Rooney gaped at the bill and even more when he saw her. He flushed with embarrassment. She always had been one hell of a looker, but now she was stunning. He blew it, however, when he said, intending a compliment, 'Holy shit, they sure done a hell of a job on you.'

Rooney was not the only one taken aback by Lorraine's appearance. Bickerstaff's jaw dropped and the Chief, who had screamed bloody murder when he had seen the cost, also complimented her. Lorraine found it almost amusing the way they suddenly drew out chairs for her, jumped to light her cigarette. She loved the feel of the soft kid leather handbag, containing new lipstick, powder compact, silk handkerchief, calf-leather wallet, silver lighter and cigarette case.

She was to wear a small pick-up mike disguised as a decorative pin attached to a gold chain round her neck. It was in the shape of a heart and could record from a five-

397

mile radius. She was impressed by its sophistication: she had half expected the old box in a belt strapped to her waist as she had been used to in the past. Even if she was stripped naked, Rooney said half in jest, it would be hard to find. She had flicked him a look, wondering if they were all aware she had been to bed with Brad Thorburn. It seemed likely as she was warned that the only time she would lose contact with the radio surveillance truck would be if she took a shower.

Lorraine was then closeted with Bickerstaff and his team, Rooney standing glumly to one side as they discussed her approach to Janklow. They knew he was at home and they also knew that Brad Thorburn was with him but a telephone tap had revealed that Thorburn was intending to leave for France and had been arranging his flight. Janklow had returned to the house directly after leaving the precinct but had made no phone calls. Mrs Thorburn had been interviewed again and repeated the statement she had made. Brad Thorburn had also verified everything his brother had said. Two calls had been recorded from the tap on the Thorburn home, both from Alfred Kophch, requesting that Janklow visit him in his office at his earliest convenience. Kophch had also said that on no account should Janklow make outgoing calls, but speak to him only personally at his office.

As Bickerstaff and Lorraine discussed the new developments, a report came in that Mrs Thorburn had just called Brad and asked him to visit her. She had refused to speak to Steven.

'That's good,' Lorraine said. 'The only time I saw Janklow really upset was whenever you made any reference to her and if she's not talking to her nasty little pervert son, he might be even more on edge.'

'You're very confident, Lorraine. How can you be sure you'll get into the Thorburn house?'

'I'm sure.'

Bickerstaff was growing to like her. He patted her shoulder. 'Well, you take care – and I mean it. Use your back-up and scream the fuckin' place down when you feel any kind of threat.'

Bickerstaff looked up as Rooney returned, tapping his wrist-watch. It was really time for Lorraine to leave. She tried to make light of it – they were all so concerned – and asked if Andrew Fellows was still working for them. Rooney dismissed him out of hand: the last thing he had suggested was that the killer might be a woman. They had all joked that she had even been under suspicion, and Lorraine laughed out loud.

She was presented with a clean driving licence and a Mustang, also wired up to the main base, was ready in the yard. The only thing she did not have was a weapon.

Rooney walked her to the car. He opened the driving door, winking to warn her not to say anything because she was wired. Then he took his gun from his shoulder holster and stashed it in the glove compartment. 'We're all with you and we'll be on hand. You know what to do?'

Lorraine nodded. They had given her the code word 'Rosie'. If she mentioned it the back-up cops were to stand by; it meant she was heading into deeper trouble than she could handle. If 'Rosie' was coupled with 'Partner' they were to come in no matter what else she said. This was an old scam she and Lubrinski had worked, just the name of someone they could start to talk about, which would give no warning to the suspect that it was, in fact, a warning.

Lorraine shut the glove compartment. 'Thanks, Bill.'

Rooney pulled at his nose. 'Fuck off, and get a move on.' He'd always said that and it touched her but she slammed the door and started the engine. She didn't look back but headed for Beverly Glen. It would take an easy hour and a quarter. She knew Brad and Janklow were in, and that no further outgoing or incoming calls had been made. The housekeeper and gardener were there but Lorraine knew

399

they left about four. From then on, it would just be the brothers.

Moving way behind Lorraine was a dry-cleaning truck with two overalled police officers up front. In the back were Bickerstaff, Rooney and another FBI agent. Lorraine's car bleeped on the grid up ahead of them but they made no effort to sit on her tail. They didn't need to – they knew where she was heading and even if they were miles back they could still monitor the car, and her personal microphone.

Lorraine parked right outside the gates, clearly visible from the house, and rang the doorbell by the intercom. The dry cleaning truck parked a good distance down the tree-lined street.

'Who is it?'

Lorraine recognized Brad's voice. 'Let me come in – it's Lorraine.'

'Are you alone?'

'No, I got surveillance trucks and a couple of uniformed cops. What the hell do you think, Brad? Let me in.'

The gates opened and Brad came out onto the porch. He watched her as she walked up the gravel path, then frowned. 'What have you done to yourself?'

She did a slow turn, hands out, one holding her purse. 'I've spent all day at the beauty parlour. How do I look?'

'What do you want?' he asked abruptly.

'To talk.' He stared at her and she laughed. 'What are you so suspicious of? Here, you want to check my bag?' She tossed it to him and remained standing on the pathway.

He caught it in one hand but didn't open it. 'I don't think I've got anything to say to you.'

She moved closer. 'You let me in, though. How about a coffee?'

He looked back to the hallway and then down at her as she remained on the lower step. 'I'm going away – this isn't a good idea.'

'Why don't you just hear me out – hear why I've come? I have a reason.'

'I gathered,' he said, as he turned and walked into the house. She followed him, eyes flicking upwards to the bedroom above. Was he there? Was he watching her? She saw nothing; no curtain moved aside; it was very still.

In the kitchen, Brad took her things out of her bag, laid them all out.

'Satisfied?'

He went to the fridge and took out a bottle of chilled wine, held it up and then slammed the fridge door. He poured himself a glass as she perched on a stool and began to put everything back into her purse. He switched on the coffee percolator and leaned against the sink.

'Don't you ever wear shoes?' she asked, smiling.

'What's this, a rerun of last night?'

'I know they took your brother in for questioning.'

'They also released him.'

'So I gather.'

He sipped his wine, leaning against the sink.

'Where are you going?'

'France.'

'For how long?'

'I don't know. What do you want?'

She opened the cigarette case, held it up as if for his permission, and he fetched a cup for her coffee. She still found attractive every move he made, even just pouring coffee. He had such a great body, but his ease was what made him so sexy. When he moved close to give her the coffee he smelt of soap. 'You just showered?'

'Yeah, I had a game of tennis. I was going to play squash with Andrew but he refused to speak to me.'

'Why?'

He smiled. 'Maybe his wife has told him about her fantasy, that she and I were a hot number, but it's all in her head.'

'Is it made up, or did you fuck her?'

He passed her an ashtray. 'You like to talk dirty? What does it mean to you if I screwed her or not?'

'It was just a question. I like her – he's okay too.'

Brad picked up his glass, tilted it towards her, and drank the contents. 'What do you want?'

'Money.'

He ran his glass under the sink. 'So what's your hourly rate, then?'

She chortled. 'Oh, this isn't *hourly*! This is going to cost you and Steven a lot, lot more.'

'*Steven?*'

Lorraine blew on the hot black coffee, looking at him over the rim of the cup. 'Let's not waste any more time playing games. I want money, Brad. Your brother may have walked but you take a good look at me. Now put me in court in front of a jury. You think they're gonna say, "Oh, she's just a hooker, oh, she's just a fucked-up piece of shit, an ex-cop who killed a kid." You take a good look at me, Brad, because I reckon I look good. I look good enough to sway a jury, make them doubt all that shit about me, make them look at me, see the scar on the back of my head. They'll listen real good when I say it with tears, and I can conjure up tears, Brad, I'll have them running down my cheeks when I tell them what he did to me.'

He couldn't deal with her at all. It was as if she'd become two, even three people. This hard, sophisticated woman was not the same woman who had wept in his arms.

He looked so confused that she felt suddenly guilty, wanting to comfort him. It was stupid. She lit a cigarette, blowing the smoke out high above her head. 'I'll have your brother charged with assault and then they'll think again about the murders, same blow as the one to the back of my head. He wanted to kill me – he *tried* to kill me – and you may say in court that he was bitten by your dog, big Mr Brad Thorburn, but wait till I tell them, weeping, holding my head in my hands, that when he struck me with the hammer I fought for my life. I bit him in the neck and I hung on until my teeth broke his skin, until he screamed like a stuck pig. . . It was Steven who attacked me, Brad. Why don't we stop all the bullshit and get down to just how much you'll pay me to keep my mouth shut?'

He looked at her with open hostility. She revolted him.

'Okay, I'll give you more. I had a tooth missing. They get a match on those marks on his neck, they'll be able to verify it was my teeth – not your dog's, but mine.'

He wouldn't look at her.

'You don't like hearing me talk this way? Well, why don't you get Steven down here? Why don't the three of us discuss just how much it'll take to buy me off, maybe to send *me* to France and forget I was ever attacked.'

'You'd do that?'

'Sure. You wanted to know why I was here, well, now you do.' Brad was so obviously out of his depth she felt almost sorry for him, sorry to have to be so hard, but she had no option. In some ways she wanted him to throw her out, wanted him to be straight and honest because she liked him so much.

'How much?' he said gruffly, not even looking at her.

She inhaled and let the smoke drift out slowly, then rested her chin on her hand. 'A million. You can afford it. But I want it in cash, used notes.'

He made a sound that was half laugh, half sob. 'A million.'

'And I guarantee that I'll disappear, any charges will be dropped. Suddenly he didn't look like your brother, suddenly I guess I was just mistaken. He'd never even have to go to court.'

'I doubt if he will, anyway,' Brad snapped.

'You want a bet? Because if they don't press charges, then I will take out a private prosecution. I'll have every feminist group backing me up. You wouldn't believe the stink I could create. You and your precious brother and your beloved mother would be hounded by the press. You won't buy out of that but you can buy me out now. Go talk to Steven. Is he in?'

Brad made it to the doorway, his fists clenched. He wanted to grab her by her hair and throw her out bodily. He had never felt such loathing for another human being – let alone a woman.

'Oh, I can see I got you real angry. Well, it's up to you, I think I'm being fair and square. What's a million to you, rich boy?' He moved so fast, one moment in the doorway the next at her side. He slapped her face hard. She held her cheek. 'That make you feel better, rich boy? It's just gone up another ten grand. Touch me again and, so help me God, I'll walk out of here and start screaming my fucking head off. Now go talk to your sick pervert of a brother – better still bring his ass down here. Let's hear what he has to say.'

He walked out. She was shaking all over – he had really hurt her. She rubbed her aching jaw and checked her face in her compact mirror. Her cheek was inflamed but otherwise she looked better than she had in years. She snapped the compact shut, moved to the hall and looked up. Brad was nowhere in sight. She went into the empty drawing room.

'He's gone upstairs, I'm now in the drawing room.' She said it softly, tilting her head down to the tiny gold heart.

Lorraine heard footsteps and leaned against the piano, as if she was looking over the framed photographs.

'He's agreed, a million, but he can't get it for at least a couple of months.'

Lorraine propped both elbows on the piano. 'No deal, I can't wait that long. I want it today. Why don't you pay me? You got the dough, haven't you?'

'This has nothing to do with me. I wouldn't pay you a cent.'

'No, but you'd stand up in court and tell a jury that your dog bit him on the neck, your mother would say on oath that her son was with her all day and all night on the night he nearly killed me. You're sick, you know that? Well, fuck you and fuck your brother. I'm getting out of here, I can make enough selling my story to the press.'

Brad stood across the door. 'He doesn't have that amount of cash and nor do I. Everything's tied up in property, trust funds. I can't get that amount of money released in a day, it would be impossible.'

'I don't believe you and I wanna talk to your brother. You're a pain in the butt. *Steven!*'

She heard footsteps; he was coming down the stairs.

Steven Janklow walked into view and stood in the hallway.

'Hi, you remember me, don't you, Steve? You said you needed to be sucked off in a public place, twenty dollars. We drove to the garage in the shopping mall. Sure you remember. Look at him, Brad, he remembers me. Maybe it's my scar.'

Janklow's face twisted in rage. 'I don't know you. Throw her out of here, Brad.'

Lorraine remained where she was. She felt safe with Brad between her and Janklow. 'Fine, Brad, you throw me out, but first fill him in, tell him what the deal is. If you don't have the cash, then I'll take a couple of items belonging to your mother. Art Mathews said he was getting good prices for the stuff in Europe.'

Janklow looked as if he would attack her but Brad gripped him. 'Just calm down, Steven. Have you ever seen her before?'

They moved out of sight further into the hall. Lorraine had to hold on to the piano top, her legs were shaking so much. She could hear Janklow insisting that he did not know her, that she was lying. She hurtled out and confronted both men. 'I'm lying, am I? Right, you'll see, and I'll see you in court.'

She strode into the kitchen and picked up her bag. She was about to walk past them to the front door, when she heard Brad's low voice, 'Give that to me! Give it.'

She turned round just in time to see Janklow with the gun but he hadn't even got it to waist level before Brad had taken it from him. Then he sank onto the bottom stair. Brad slipped the weapon into his pocket. He spoke to Lorraine.

'You'll get your money as soon as I can arrange it.'

'Well, what about the jewellery? Don't you have any left? Art seemed to think you had more'n the Queen of England.'

Janklow's head was in his hands, but he said, 'He was a thieving piece of shit.'

Lorraine sniggered. 'Yeah, he was that all right but you got no worries about him talking.' She was on firmer ground, testing how much she could say. 'They had him arrested for the murders, didn't you know? Apparently he even admitted to a couple, then he got scared and killed himself – cut his wrists on his glasses.'

Janklow looked at her with his pale, expressionless eyes. Lorraine held his gaze. 'You shouldn't have hurt Didi, though. She was a friend of mine. I know she was into the blackmail with Art, but he forced her to do it.'

Janklow looked up at his brother. 'There's nothing left, Brad. I've got no money – I can't pay her.'

'What about your mother? She's sitting on a load, isn't she? How would you think she'd feel if I paid her a visit? It's all the same to me. Look, I don't want to walk away empty-handed. If Art and Didi cleaned you out, then why not—'

'You don't go anywhere near my mother.' Janklow's temper surfaced.

'Then I'll just walk out of here. But I warned your

brother – you ask him – I'm not gonna let you off. I'll sell my story to the papers and then she'll wish she could get up and run because they won't leave her alone. They'll dig up every inch of dirt on her, on this family—'

Janklow shoved Brad away and dived at Lorraine, but again Brad caught him before he laid a finger on her. He pushed him up against the wall. 'Tell me the truth, Steven. Was it you who attacked her?'

He screamed and tried to wriggle out of Brad's grasp, but Brad thumped him in the stomach so hard he buckled over. Then he yanked his brother up against the wall by his hair. 'You'd better tell me, Steven, because if what she says is true, then we've got to pay her off.'

She pressed her back against the wall. 'He attacked me and he murdered the others. He did it, Brad! Ask him. *Go on, ask him!*'

'*Yes! Yes! Yes!*' screamed Janklow.

Brad released his hold but was still too close for his brother, who was gasping for breath, to try anything on her. Brad looked at Lorraine, then at Janklow. 'Okay, we'll pay. I'll pay you whatever you want.'

Janklow pulled at Brad's arm. 'You fool, you pay her and she'll be back like that other bitch. They'll never leave you alone. You let her walk out of here and she'll be on your back like a leech. She's a leech, a blood-sucker.'

'What you gonna do, Steven? Kill me like the others?'

Lorraine spat it out and Janklow tried again to reach her. Again Brad dragged him back, shoving him against the wall. He was frothing at the mouth with impotent fury, but Brad was too strong for him to escape. 'They deserved it! And even if he's stupid enough to pay you off, I'll find you, wherever you are, no matter how long it takes.'

She pointed at Janklow and then back at Brad. 'You did hear that, didn't you? You're gettin' off real light. He's killed eight women and all I'm doing is asking for a million dollars. I could push for a lot more.'

Brad looked first at her then Janklow as the implication sank in. His face was drained. He hauled his brother slowly to his feet, and stared into his twisted face. Janklow was near to weeping. 'Is this true, Steven?' Brad shook him so hard his head cracked against the wall. '*Is it true?*' He gripped his brother's face in his hands. '*Is it true?*'

Deflated, Janklow lifted his hands up like a child to his mother. He was half pleading with Brad to hold him. He started crying, his wet lips hung open as he blubbered and began slowly to slide down the wall. 'I'm taking him upstairs to his room. You stay down here.'

Lorraine watched as Brad half carried his brother upstairs. There was no fight or anger left in him: he was crying more loudly – she could hear him – he sounded like a little boy. 'Brad,' she said flatly. Half-way up the stairs, he stopped. 'You'd better stay with him. Will you put the gun down that you took from him?'

They both looked towards her, as different as Dilly Fellows had said, like chalk and cheese. Brad took the gun out of his pocket and for a split second she thought he was going to fire it straight into her head, but she said calmly, matter-of-fact, 'I'm wired up, Brad. Every word we've said has been recorded. Just put down the gun.'

He let it drop and half carried, half lifted Janklow into his room. As the door closed she went to the intercom in the hallway and said they should come in and that he was in the top right-hand front bedroom. She pressed open the gates and went to wait on the porch. The truck was now pulling up outside. Rooney was first out and gave her the thumbs-up. Next out was Bickerstaff. Lorraine had turned away to look over the beautiful gardens, the flowers, the swimming pool, the tennis courts. It was so perfect, so incongruously peaceful. The sound of squad cars arriving cut through the silence. Lorraine joined Rooney. She removed the wire from her neck and asked if she could go home. She was told by Bickerstaff that she must return to the station.

Brad Thorburn was led out between two uniformed police officers followed by Steven Janklow handcuffed between another two. Janklow began to sob out a wretched, sickening confession inside the vehicle, and two hours after he was arrested, admitted to six murders, but seemed vague about Holly and Didi, and one of the as yet unidentified victims. The other two remained unidentified because Janklow didn't know their names but agreed when shown the photographs that he had killed them. He said one was called Ellen and the other something like Susanna but he hadn't known their surnames.

Lorraine did not get home until late that night. Rosie was waiting expectantly to hear all that had happened. She gave her friend a bear hug and was disappointed when Lorraine didn't want to go out for a celebration dinner.

'But it's all over, isn't it?'

Lorraine sighed, exhausted. 'Yes, I guess it is, but I don't feel like celebrating.'

The next few days were long and drawn out. She was asked to be on call should they require her at the station. Something nagged at her but she couldn't pin it down. In the end she put it down to the possibility that she still might be used as a prosecution witness.

The good news came at the beginning of the following week. Janklow would plead guilty – which meant Lorraine would not have to take the stand – to five counts of murder.

A month after his brother's arrest, Brad Thorburn left Los Angeles to escape media attention, but remained in touch with his brother via their lawyer. Lorraine followed the progress of the case through Rooney, or by dropping into the station. Money was tight, and Rosie kept up her daily check of want ads, but their financial situation put paid to the prospect of starting up their own agency.

Rooney was the one to tell Lorraine that her theory had been wrong although so had everyone else's. Further interviews with Steven Janklow elicited that he had been blackmailed by Art Mathews for much longer than they had thought – almost nine years – but he had only met Art once. Didi had made the calls and collected the money and the jewellery. Janklow had always liked Didi, he said, because she fixed his wigs and make-up. The other women had been murdered because they were like his father's whores, dirty hookers he had brought home to flaunt in front of Janklow's beloved mother. There was no blackmail link to the dead women, only Didi. Norman Hastings had been killed because, as he was being blackmailed himself, he felt that he and Janklow could help each other out – even go to the police to press charges. Janklow had not wanted anyone to know about his private life; he was disgusted that a fat middle-aged man like Norman Hastings could ever think that they were alike, so he killed him. When pressed for further details on the murder of Angela 'Holly' Hollow and David 'Didi' Burrows he said that he couldn't remember and he supposed he must have killed them.

Janklow also admitted attacking Lorraine, again saying that she was just like his father's whores and he had been right to attack her as she was now his brother's whore. His obsessive love for his mother had so twisted him that half the time he believed that he was her, and when he eventually admitted everything he had done, did not hold it against her that she had not come to see him.

To his surprise Rooney was called in to see his chief and given a big bonus; a whip-round from all the officers had paid for a gold travel clock and leather case. He hated the thought of retirement but his part in tracking down Janklow had made good press coverage, and he grudgingly thanked Lorraine but then said that if the truth be known she should thank him.

Lorraine's part in Janklow's arrest was not leaked to the press. The only thing she got out of it was the few bucks from Rooney, the clean driving licence and the new clothes. She had to hand back Rooney's gun because he had to return it with his badge. She and Rosie were flat broke.

'The bastards! Don't you get a reward?'

Lorraine laughed. 'No! But I got my self respect, Rosie.'

'Well, it ain't gonna pay the rent, sweet face, so now what do you do?'

She was looking good, she knew it; she'd been back on form and she knew that too. Working again had filled in her days, her nights, and yet somehow she wanted or expected more. She studied her reflection in the bathroom mirror: so much for respect. If they really thought she was something, how come they didn't offer her a job? How come, at the end, she was still broke, and worse, back to square one? She gripped the washbasin and bowed her head.

'Tea's ready,' Rosie yelled out.

Lorraine looked up at herself; it wasn't over, she hadn' beaten it. 'Jesus Christ, I want a drink.'

Rosie cut a thick slice of banana bread and poured tea for each of them. 'Home-made that – got it at the deli near the corner.' Lorraine choked suddenly. 'What's the matter? Don't you like it?'

Rosie watched as she grabbed the file from the Janklow case and began to thumb through it. Half an hour later she looked up. 'I got to go out. If you want something to do can you find out who we contact to rent that place Art Mathews had as a gallery, and how much? I'm gonna see if I can raise some dough, then we'll open up Page Investigation Services. I'll be back or I'll call in, okay?'

Rosie followed her onto the steps outside the apartment. 'Where are you going?'

411

Lorraine ran down the stairs, turning at the bottom. She waved and called back something about the banana bread, then she formed her right hand into the shape of a gun, and pretended to fire it. Rosie went back inside and glanced at the papers wondering what Lorraine had been so excited about. The file was open at Didi's autopsy report. Rosie grimaced in distaste and went back to her bread. It didn't taste so good. The pathologist's findings stated that David Burrows's last meal had been banana bread.

CHAPTER 19

E D BICKERSTAFF had been in a heavy meeting all morning discussing Janklow's mental deterioration. His family, via their lawyers, were insisting he be declared insane and therefore incapable of standing trial.

Bickerstaff had spent many hours with Janklow since his arrest, during which he talked compulsively, almost with pride, about what he had done. He showed no guilt or remorse, but the reverse; he gloated in detailing how the women had died. He was still sketchy when it came to Didi and Holly, but was adamant that he had killed them. He was constantly smiling, always polite and cheerful, and continued to talk freely when he was alone in his cell.

The last meeting Bickerstaff had with Janklow had been two days ago. His head was bruised and swollen and he was wearing a white gown with ties at the back as he had just been for a brain scan. He sat on the bed dangling his feet, and midway through the interview he started to sing some long-forgotten song. He could only remember the chorus, and repeated the same words over and over. 'If you say you love me, do you care? If you say you love me, do you care?'

When Bickerstaff was told that Lorraine Page was asking for him, he agreed to see her. He hadn't liked the way she'd

413

been hanging around the station so he intended making this meeting short and sweet. She was ushered into his office – Rooney's old patch. He got up as she entered and shook hands.

'Is he insane, then?' she asked without any preamble.

'Well, they're certainly trying to prove it.'

'What do you think?' she asked.

'Well, he may be putting up one hell of a performance – who's to tell? I don't know.'

Bickerstaff rested his chin in his hands. 'That was one hell of a performance you gave at his place. Class act – but then old Rooney said you were good. What he never said was just how good. You mind if I ask you something personal?'

'Go ahead.'

'That shooting incident – one with the kid – how come you fired six times when you could have brought him down with one shot?'

She hadn't expected him to bring up the shooting and it caught her off guard. 'I'd had a few drinks. I didn't see the boy, just his jacket. It had this yellow stripe down the back . . . I had a partner I was fond of. He was in a shoot-out. The man that killed him had a black sweater with a yellow stripe and I didn't see the boy – it wasn't him I was firing at but somebody else.'

He stood up and, just like Rooney used to do, flicked at the blind. 'You could be useful to me, maybe, sometime in the future. You got any plans?'

Lorraine reminded him about the investigation agency. She caught him looking at his watch and knew he wanted her to leave, but she hadn't come for praise or even a tentative offer of future work. Not that she believed him about that. 'I need money. I'm broke.'

He frowned. She lit a cigarette and kept it between her lips as she spoke. 'I don't think Janklow murdered David Burrows or Holly.'

414

Bickerstaff leaned on the back of his chair. 'He's admitted both.'

'Way it sounds, he's admitting to any stiff we had in or around LA since nineteen sixty-five.' He laughed and she took the cigarette out of her mouth. 'How much if I get you proof that it was Art Mathews? You wouldn't look so dumb about his suicide. As it stands now, Janklow said he killed them which makes Art Mathews look as if he was put under so much pressure he killed himself—'

'You want me to hire you?'

'You can call it what you like. I just need cash to get cards printed, a word processor, pay a bit of rent.'

'You withholding further evidence, Mrs Page?'

'No, and maybe I'm wrong but I think Art Mathews killed both Holly and Didi. And if he didn't, I'd like to find out who did. And, if you don't have Janklow on the stand, maybe you'll have somebody else, because I'm sure Art didn't do the murders alone.'

'You gonna give me a name?'

'I don't have one yet, but I'm workin' on it. Come on, I know there's a kitty for informers – you can call me that if you like. It's not as if the FBI are broke, and it might be useful to you, Mr Bickerstaff.'

He smarted at her audacity. 'How much?'

She stubbed out her cigarette. 'Ten grand, in cash, in an envelope.'

He sucked in his breath and stuffed his hands in his pockets. 'Make it five and you've got a deal – if you get the proof that Art Mathews did the murders.'

She tossed the hair out of her eyes. 'You just got a deal, Mr Bickerstaff. I'll be in touch.'

Lorraine headed off in search of Curtis. She found him in a bar with a blonde Holly-lookalike on his arm. When he saw her he whistled and she pivoted for him like a model.

'I want to talk to you, Curtis, some place private.' She swore she was on the level and they headed into a back room. They were only there for about ten minutes before they returned to the bar.

'You want a drink, Lorraine?'

'I'm not drinking today, but thanks for the offer.' She banged out of the bar into the brilliant afternoon sunshine. She hadn't thought he'd bite but he *had* cared for Holly and what was a couple of grand? His girls were making that in a night for him.

She hailed a taxi and went home, where Rosie was waiting. Half an hour later they left together with an overnight bag. They hired not a wreck but a decent car. They had a long drive ahead of them, maybe six or seven hours: they were heading for San Francisco.

Rosie did most of the driving while Lorraine map-read. They only stopped for gasoline but it was after midnight when they arrived in San Francisco and booked into a cheap motel on the outskirts. Rosie was hungry so went out for a takeout hamburger and french fries, bringing one back for Lorraine, who was deeply asleep so Rosie ate it herself. She couldn't sleep, and tossed and turned, her bed creaking ominously, but Lorraine slept on. Rosie propped herself up on her elbow and looked over to her friend. In the blue light from the forecourt that broke through the motel's thin curtains, she studied Lorraine's sleeping face. The transformation from when they had first met was astonishing. She was a different woman in every way – less aggressive, more content within herself, more confident, more womanly.

Lorraine woke early. Rosie was dead to the world so she slipped into the bathroom and took a shower. As she soaped herself she thought about Brad Thorburn. She heard the way she had spoken to him, saw him so hurt, so bewildered. They would probably never meet again and he would never know just how much he had meant to her, what he had done for her. He had made her feel loved, wanted, had made some dead part of her revive. Brad Thorburn had woken her as a woman.

After breakfast, Lorraine took a street map of San Francisco, marked their destination with a cross and passed it over to Rosie. 'You're the driver. That's where we got to get to.'

'Who we seeing?'

·Lorraine hesitated. In all fairness Rosie should know why they had come here. 'I *think* that Janklow didn't kill Holly or Didi. Nula lied to me. She said that she and Didi were working together the night Holly was killed but Holly's pimp said Nula was on her own. I think it's got something to do with Art. Also, I think Nula lied about where Didi was the night she was murdered. It's Nula we're going to see. Curtis gave me the address but I don't want to scare her off. I just want her to tell me a few things.'

'Are you gonna get paid for this?'

'Five thousand dollars from Ed Bickerstaff, and Curtis said he'd give me two grand if I got Holly's killer, so we'll have enough to open the agency.'

Lorraine called Nula's number. A sleepy voice answered and she hung up. She recognized Nula's voice.

She and Rosie left the motel, bought a morning paper and Rosie headed into the city. They were hemmed in by traffic and the streets were a confusing mass of one-way systems but they finally turned into Delaware Road.

'Slow right down, real slow,' Lorraine said. 'Let's check the numbers, it's apartment building 182. There it is!'

Rosie pulled up outside a dilapidated four-storey building.

Lorraine gazed up at it, checked the fire escape and then opened the car door. 'I'll be about half an hour. Sit tight.' Rosie picked up the newspaper and prepared herself for the wait. Lorraine checked the names on the apartments and then made her way up an old stone staircase littered with garbage to the third floor. She rapped hard on the door of apartment 23 and waited.

'Who is it?'

'Surprise, Nula, open up, it's me.'

The eye-hole slid back, and bolts and chain locks were removed. Nula opened the door. 'Jesus Christ, how did you find me?'

'Curtis said you were here. As I was passing, I thought I'd call in.' Nula opened the door wider and Lorraine stepped inside. Nula was wearing a tatty kimono and she was barefoot. 'It's only nine o'clock, for chrissakes.'

Lorraine apologized and followed her into the bed-sitting room. It was a mess, crammed with dresses and bags, cases half unpacked and old food cartons. 'I just moved in, bit of a come-down but then I'm not gonna be here permanently. It used to belong to a friend and they're on tour in a big show so I've got it for a few months. Sit down.' Nula folded her arms and looked over Lorraine. She pursed her lips. 'Looking very chic, dear, come into money? That's a very expensive suit.' She sat at her dressing table, fiddled with her hair and checked her face. 'I look like a piece of shit but I was working nearly all night. Girl's got to do what she has to do to earn a living but Christ, this is a shit-hole. The pay isn't half as good as in LA.'

Lorraine told Nula about Janklow, how he had admitted all the murders, including Didi and Holly. Nula closed her eyes. 'Thank God. I've been praying they get the bastard and I know about Art. I cried my heart out but he took his life so I guess that's what he wanted. Those bastards pushed him, the shits, and he was innocent. But why are you here?'

'Work. I'm with an investigation agency.'

Nula shrieked with laughter, then pointed at Lorraine. 'You were a cop, weren't you? Well, I hope you've not

418

come to arrest me.' She brushed her hair, looking at Lorraine in the mirror. She was getting uneasy, Lorraine could sense it.

'What *do* you want?' Nula asked.

'Well, I'm trying to piece a few things together. You said on the night Holly died Didi was with you, that you both saw her cross the road but Curtis said Didi wasn't there, you were alone.' She paused.

Nula motioned for her to continue.

'Nula, I think Art killed Holly *and* Didi but I got to have evidence to prove it. Whatever you tell me won't be used against you – I'll keep your name out of it and it won't hurt Art because he's dead. It'll really help me. It's Mrs Thorburn's jewellery I'm interested in or what pieces you've got left.'

Nula blinked rapidly and swivelled round. 'I don't know what you're talking about.'

Lorraine got up and walked towards Nula. 'The last meal Didi ate was home-made banana bread. She was at home, wasn't she? Not, as you said, out working. Curtis said she didn't show that night because her foot was still hurting. You said she'd been out all day with a regular, but that wasn't true, was it? Now, did Art come round?'

Nula began to paint her nails. 'Bullshit, dear. She went out, and then I was told she'd been murdered. You even called the apartment.'

'The ring on Didi's finger, the one you said she couldn't take off, was Mrs Thorburn's, wasn't it? Well, I'd never seen her wearing it before so she must have been able to get it off. So I think it's something to do with that ring. Is that why Art killed her? Because of the ring?'

Nula painted the last nail of her right hand and began on the left with studied concentration. Lorraine moved closer. 'Didi and Art were blackmailing Steven Janklow. Art was cleaning up, wasn't he? He used Didi to make contact and to pick up the jewels. Where did she pick them up from? Janklow's garage? Was that where they did the exchange?'

Nula continued to paint her nails. 'Listen, dear, why don't you go and do your Perry Mason someplace else? Didi was my closest friend, we adored each other and we both loved little Holly – neither of us would hurt her. Whatever she was doing with Art – she never let on about it to me.'

'Maybe not, but Art might have got angry with her. Maybe it was Art that picked Holly up?'

Nula wafted her nails about to dry them. 'To be honest, dear, I don't know what you're getting at. You've had a wasted journey.'

'Come on, Nula, I know you have to be in on it. Janklow listed a lot of Mrs Thorburn's jewellery but he didn't sell it. Did he give it to Art?'

'I don't know,' Nula snapped.

Lorraine shrugged. 'Fine, I'll go, but I won't keep quiet. You must know something because you had to be in on it.' She tried a different tactic. 'Look, I don't like to do this but I'm broke. Maybe I'll keep quiet if you give me a cut. I want money to keep my mouth shut, Nula. I lied about the agency crap – who's ever gonna employ me?

Nula began to shake a bottle of foundation cream furiously and started to make up her face. 'Obviously I have so much money that I get some perverse kick out of living in this shit-hole and getting twenty dollars a blow-job if I'm lucky. I don't have any dough, all right?'

Lorraine walked slowly to the door. 'Well, if you won't help me, Nula, I'll go to the cops – see if they'll dole me out a few dollars for the information.'

Nula smirked and then said loudly, 'Craig, why don't you come in and say hello to Perry Mason, dear?'

Lorraine pressed her back against the door as Craig Lyall walked in from the bathroom. Nula started to collect her clothes, relaxed and seemingly no longer interested in

420

Lorraine. She held up a dress, checking herself in the mirror, while Lyall moved closer to Lorraine.

Nula giggled. 'Sit down, sweetheart. We're going to have a little party, just the three of us. Well, *you* are. Open the bottle, Craig dear, she won't be able to resist.' She minced out into the bathroom.

Lorraine's heart thudded. How long had she been in the apartment? Ten, fifteen minutes? Would Rosie do anything? Did she even know which was Nula's apartment?

Lyall produced a bottle of vodka.

'Don't do this, Craig. I just wanted a cut of the jewellery, nothing more, and Janklow's already admitted the murders. I won't go to the cops, I promise, it was just a threat. I didn't mean it – all I wanted was some dough.'

Nula shrieked from the bathroom, 'What do you think we are? What are you so scared about? All we're going to do is have a little party.'

She reappeared, wearing a black silk underskirt and stockings. She held out a pair of shoes. 'If you think your shoes are nice, look at these, three hundred dollars, hand-made.' She slipped on first one then the other.

Lyall opened a bottle of vodka and poured a tumblerful. 'Have a drink, Lorraine dear. *Go on, drink it!*'

She swiped Lyall's hand away. The glass smashed against the wall.

'Hold her down and pour it down her throat.' Nula had opened a suitcase full of new clothes. She selected a smart navy dress with a white collar. Lyall gripped Lorraine's wrist and dragged her towards the bed. She struggled and Nula smacked her hard across the face. 'Listen, you'd better do what we want or we'll mark your other cheek. Is that what you want, Miss Goody-Two-Shoes? I knew you were a cunt the moment you ripped us off at the gallery. You blackmailed Art. Now *drink*.'

Lorraine was trying to locate the fire escape. Did the apartment face the street? How long had she told Rosie she would be? She'd fouled up so badly. Had she really felt so sure she'd be able to face out Nula, get the information she needed and return to Bickerstaff? She'd been so off the wall, she'd lost her touch – she almost needed a drink she was so angry with herself.

'Drink,' Lyall said, but she still hadn't taken the glass.

Nula moved to his side. 'Pour it down her throat! What are you waiting for? Few glasses and she'll be begging for more. Go on, do it.'

Lorraine looked up into his scared face. 'Don't do this to me, Craig. I promise I won't tell anybody you've got the jewellery—'

He gripped her cheeks and forced the glass to her lips. Nula grabbed her hair and held her head back, screaming at Lyall to get on with it.

Rosie had read the entire newspaper. She tossed it aside and checked her watch. She looked at the front entrance, drumming her fingers on the steering wheel. Then she got out of the car, trying to remember the name of the person Lorraine was seeing. She looked down the row of names by the intercom but most were scratched out or blank. She pushed open the main door, walked into the corridor, which stank of urine, and climbed the stairs to the first floor. Half-way up she stopped when a door opened and two kids ran out. She had to flatten herself against the stairwell as they charged past her. A woman came to the door and Rosie hurried towards her. 'Have you seen a tall blonde woman?' The door slammed in her face.

She continued up to the second floor, where a male voice demanded to know what she wanted. She turned to face an elderly black man wearing overalls and carrying a broom. 'You live here? What you doin' here?' Rosie explained she was looking for someone. 'What apartment?' he demanded.

'I dunno. She came in about half an hour ago to visit a friend – Nula. You know anyone called Nula?'

He shook his head and shoved the brush at her feet. 'Get out, go on, get out. This is private property.'

She got to the car in time to see the kids who had pushed past her breaking one of its rear-view mirrors and the window on the driver's side had been smashed. Rosie kicked at the glass in fury as the kids ran off shrieking. She carefully removed the glass from the seat. Where the hell was Lorraine? As she straightened up she saw a man walking out of the building with two suitcases. He was in one hell of a hurry and she was about to shout to him when he turned into a yard. Rosie followed, reaching the entrance as the man was throwing suitcases into the trunk of a car. Just as she was about to cross towards him, a woman shouted and he looked up to the fire escape.

Nula was leaning over the railings. 'Get another bottle, and hurry up.'

Lyall got into his car and started the engine. Rosie stared hard at Nula, sure it was the right woman. She wasn't sure what to do. If Lorraine was with her, maybe they were just talking and she'd go nuts if Rosie suddenly barged in. On the other hand, if Lorraine was in trouble and Rosie did nothing she'd be just as mad. 'Think like a detective, Rosie, come on,' she muttered. 'What would Mrs Super Sleuth Lorraine Page do?'

Standing on an old crate, she managed to drag the pull-ladder of the fire escape loose and started to climb upwards. One or two rungs snapped off as she put her weight on them so she almost fell back to the ground. Half-way up she wondered what the hell she was doing but by then she was almost at the first landing.

She grabbed the railings and ducked under the barrier to stand on the first escape. She was scared that if someone saw her they might push her off, so she picked up a garbage bag and tried to look like a resident dumping it. She passed one window after another, peering in, looking for Lorraine. The apartments were run down and squalid, and she saw no one until the fourth window revealed a couple eating. She dodged back the way she had come and headed up towards the second floor. Suddenly, the bag split and refuse clattered down the fire escape. She froze. The landing window opened below. 'What the fuck's goin' on up there?' The window banged shut again and Rosie held on grimly, heart pounding. She nearly fell off again when another of the rusted steps gave way and felt her arm wrench almost out of its socket as she hung on. It was only her anger with Lorraine that kept her climbing.

It took Lyall just a few minutes to get to the corner store, buy two more bottles of vodka and return to the apartment block. He parked right behind Rosie's car, ran up the stairs two at a time to the third floor, and banged on the door for Nula to let him in.

Lorraine was on the bed, her feet tied together with a pair of Nula's tights and her hands bound in front of her. The empty bottle was on the bed beside her. Nula was dressed and everything was packed ready to leave. Lyall locked the door and chucked the bottles onto the bed beside Lorraine. He was sweating with nerves. 'There's a car smashed up outside, a rental from LA – that hers?'

'Why don't you ask her yourself?' Nula snapped.

Lyall picked up the cases. 'I'm not hanging around, Nula, I'm getting out now with or without you. If that bitch could find us so can the cops. She's probably workin' for them.'

Nula was unscrewing the cap of a fresh bottle, glaring at him. 'You'll do just what I tell you and so will she.' Nula pushed the bottle between Lorraine's lips, tilting it. The vodka dribbled down her chin covering her chest. 'Drink it, Lorraine! *Swallow it!*'

The vodka hit the back of Lorraine's throat. She had to swallow but she turned her head away. Nula slapped her face hard and pinched her nose so that when she forced the bottle between Lorraine's lips she had to swallow. The liquor made her body feel as if it was on fire and the room began to blur. 'That's a good girl, come on, let's see you finish the bottle.'

Lyall was frightened. 'Christ, you'll kill her.'

Nula laughed. 'What the fuck do you think I'm trying to do? Get those bags down to the car.' He opened the door and suddenly Nula sprang off the bed and ran towards him. '*No*! I don't want you pissing your pants and driving off. We'll go together. Open the other bottle.'

'I'm not doing it!'

Nula punched him and pushed him up against the wall. 'We got to do this, we've no choice. She knows enough to get them sniffing round us and if they pick me up I swear before God you'll go down with me.'

Nula sat astride Lorraine pouring the vodka down her throat. Lorraine heaved as if to vomit and Nula withdrew the bottle and again slapped her hard across the face. Her eyes closed and her body went limp, and Nula poured the rest into her slack mouth. The liquid dribbled down her face, into her hair, saturating her.

Nula got off the bed, Lorraine was motionless. 'Let's go,' Lyall pressed. 'We'll miss the plane, Nula! *Come on!*'

Rosie, meanwhile, was on the third floor, edging along the fire escape, peering into one window after another, as Nula and Lyall got into their car and drove off. Her legs were shaking, her hands cut from the rusted rails as she inched towards the landing window. She'd break the glass if need be – she was not going to go any higher or climb down. Now she didn't even care if she was arrested for breaking and entering. She got to her knees and began to crawl the last few yards. It was then she saw Lorraine.

She banged on the window. Lorraine half turned her head but then went back to untying her legs. She kept flopping over and she was giggling. Rosie banged on the window again but Lorraine seemed oblivious. Rosie attempted to open the window but it held firm. She pressed her face closer as Lorraine tried to stand, lurching into the wall, then into the dressing table. She rolled around laughing and then she saw the bottle of vodka that had fallen off the bed.

Rosie kicked at the window. The glass cracked but only after she had used both feet was there a hole big enough for her to undo the lock.

Lorraine paid her no attention. She was trying unsuccessfully to drink from the bottle. Rosie heaved her bulk through the window. The glass cut her leg and she was gasping for breath from the effort. She reached Lorraine as she lifted up the bottle to drink and grabbed it. Lorraine screamed and tried to hold onto it but Rosie wouldn't give way. She tore the bottle from her, ran with it into the bathroom and poured the contents down the sink.

She became aware of an ominous silence from the other room and dropped the bottle. Lorraine had passed out. She looked green, her breathing rasping, rattling. Rosie was terrified that she was choking and dragged her to the bathroom, hung her over the bath, then ran water over her, pushing at her lungs. Lorraine heaved and coughed, then vomited. Rosie forced her under the cold water tap. She was like a pitiful rag doll, unable to fend Rosie off, unable to do anything as she retched.

Rosie got her to her feet and forced her to walk up and down. Her head lolled on her chest; she couldn't speak; her eyes were unfocused and she didn't seem to know who Rosie was. She mumbled incoherently and then slithered to the floor. 'Lemme sleep.'

Rosie dragged her up again, walking her up and down.

She was crying – she was so afraid. She didn't know if she should call an ambulance and she kept asking Lorraine her name but she couldn't reply, just kept saying that she wanted to sleep. It wasn't until she had been violently sick again that Rosie helped her to the bed. She stripped off Lorraine's clothes and drew back the sheets, rolling her naked body further onto the bed.

'Lorraine? It's Rosie.'

Lorraine's eyes drooped and she gave a weak smile. Rosie went into the filthy kitchen, where she brewed some coffee. She went back to the bed and shook Lorraine, who moaned and flapped at Rosie to leave her alone. But Rosie persisted, made her sit up and tried to get her to drink the coffee. After half an hour, Rosie could tell she was coming round. She asked where she was and Rosie said they were in San Francisco but it didn't seem to sink in. She closed her eyes again but Rosie still wouldn't let her sleep: she pressed ice cubes wrapped in a pillow slip to Lorraine's head. 'Rosie, I have to sleep. Leave me alone.'

Finally, Rosie lost patience. '*Right*. I'm going to leave you. You disgust me – just as you got everything going for you. Why did you do it?'

Lorraine threw aside the sheet. 'I got to have a drink, Rosie, I'm going crazy, my head aches. Just get me a drink.' She held her head in her hands. 'I got to make a call – got to call Bickerstaff. Is there a phone here?'

'The state you're in you can't call anyone.'

Lorraine squinted up at her. 'They forced it down me.' She tried to stand but the room spun and she had to sit down again. 'Nula, you got to get her arrested, she's with that photographer Craig Lyall. I got to call Bickerstaff.'

Rosie didn't know whether to believe her or not. She stood with her feet planted like a solid oak. 'Well, you can't do nothin' about that now. They've gone.'

'Shit.' Lorraine picked up the ice pack and rested it against her head. 'You saw them leave?'

427

'Yeah.'

Rosie poured more coffee and a glass of water. 'Start drinking this and as much water as you can take – go on, take it.'

Lorraine did as she was told but when she attempted to move off the bed she felt faint. 'Rosie, start looking in the garbage. See if they left anything that might tell us where they're heading.'

Rosie found nothing in the kitchen but in the bedroom she spotted a small trash can by the dressing table filled with cotton-wool balls and tissues smeared with make-up. She tipped them out onto an old newspaper and poked around. She found nothing and wrapped up the mess in the newspaper – then opened it again. There were marks around the air-flight ads. 'There's this. What do you think?'

Lorraine forced herself to look at the paper: two airlines had been underlined and there were crosses against them. 'Call these airlines, see if any flights are leaving this afternoon with a Mr Lyall on board.'

'They won't tell me. They never tell you what passengers are boarding – that's a law, isn't it?'

Lorraine craved a drink – her whole body screamed for one – but she gulped the water. 'Say it's an emergency, something to do with kids . . . Anything, just find out which airline they're with.' Lorraine hung on to the bed-head as she stood up. She inched her way into the bathroom where she saw the vodka bottle and reached out for it. A single drop remained in the bottom and she drank it before she retched again, clinging to the wash-basin. She saw herself in the mirror: her face was pale green, her eyes red-rimmed and her lips swollen.

Rosie barged in. 'Two seats booked by Mr Lyall for the four-fifteen flight to Las Vegas. Now what?'

Lorraine's eyes were closed. 'Did they go off in a cab?'

'No, a car. So, now what do I do?'

She told Rosie to call Ed Bickerstaff. 'This is what you say to him. Tell him you're my partner – Jesus, just tell him anything – that it's to do with the murders of David Burrows and Holly, you got that?'

Rosie reached for the phone as Lorraine crashed to the floor.

Ed Bickerstaff hung up. He wondered if he could trust the information. He would have been happier if it had been Lorraine herself who had called – she have never made any mention of a partner. He decided there was nothing to lose so he put in the call to send agents to Las Vegas to arrest Craig Lyall and his companion. He then arranged for a search warrant to look over Lyall's studio. As he was leaving his office, he received the phone call he had been half expecting: Steven Janklow's plea would stand as guilty on seven counts of murder, but his mental state had been scrutinized and eight doctors and four psychiatrists had declared him criminally insane and medically unfit to stand trial. He would be held in a secure mental institution for life, with no hope of release. Mrs Thorburn had still not made any contact with him. Brad Thorburn continued to monitor his brother's welfare via the family lawyers but no more than that.

The subsequent arrest of Lyall and Nula would be welcome as a show of the FBI's thoroughness but Bickerstaff was wondering if he had made a mistake. He called Rooney to double-check on Lorraine but he was away, and although he'd already ordered that Nula and Lyall be brought in he still had to run it by the Chief. Bickerstaff embroidered the facts a little, pointing out that Lyall's arrest might further clarify Janklow's guilt. It might also confirm that Art Mathews had instigated the murders of Angela Hollow and David Burrows. It sounded so good to him that he felt more confident.

'Who's the informant, Ed? And how come you haven't discussed this with anyone else from my department?'

Bickerstaff flushed. 'It's Lorraine Page.'

The Chief gave a fish-eyed stare.

'Lorraine Page? You'd better hope to Christ that it pans out as well as the Janklow tapes she did.' He hesitated. 'Has she got something else on Janklow?'

'I'll get back to you as soon as I hear anything.'

The Chief glared. 'So you'll be staying on?'

Bickerstaff seemed fazed. 'Of course. This is tied in with the original investigation.'

'You sure it's not tied in with you trying to whitewash your fuck-up with Art Mathews?'

Bickerstaff stood square-jawed in front of the desk. He'd have liked to punch a hole right through it but he retained his composure. 'I'm just trying to do my job. Nothing has been whitewashed and I'm not making any excuses for the Art Mathews fuck-up but I would like to check any new evidence that may come to light.'

'How much did Page hit you for?'

Bickerstaff smiled but it was without humour. 'She doesn't get a cent.' He closed the door behind him silently. He had not added that Lorraine's payout depended on her providing Bickerstaff with evidence that proved Mathews's part in the hammer murders. If she could, it would help cover the FBI's public humiliation at having erroneously named Mathews as the sole killer. If she did bring in the goods, five thousand dollars was not much to pay for the FBI coming out smelling like roses.

As Bickerstaff was about to enter his office, he was handed a fax informing him that Lyall and Nula had been arrested in Las Vegas. Lyall insisted they were there to get married and they had said they had nothing to do with Steven Janklow. Bickerstaff requested they be brought in for questioning in connection with a 'homicide investigation' and a possible 'accessory to murder' charge.

He grew impatient as he received no reply to his calls to Lorraine's apartment. Nula and Lyall were on their way to Pasadena from Las Vegas and he hadn't the slightest idea what he was going to question them about. What had they overlooked in previous interviews? Or was it possible that Lorraine Page had, yet again, withheld vital evidence? If she had she was now in dangerous waters and Bickerstaff would make sure she drowned.

Rosie and Lorraine hardly spoke throughout the long drive home. It took all Lorraine's will-power not to beg Rosie to buy a bottle. The need to drink was stronger than her headache and sickness. She felt despairing and, worse, inadequate. It was the end of the agency, the partnership – she was back at square one again and it hurt. But nothing was stronger than the urge to drink. She had not beaten it. She felt it had beaten her.

The phone was ringing as they opened the front door. It was Bickerstaff. Rosie asked him to call back, and hung up before he could remonstrate. She then called Jake who said he'd be right over. When he arrived Rosie had cooked some spaghetti and laid the table. Jake put his arm round her shoulder. 'How you doing?'

'Fucked! I had a future and a job yesterday but today, well, I dunno. You got to talk to her – this guy Bickerstaff keeps calling.'

Jake nodded and went into the bedroom. Lorraine was awake, sitting on the edge of the bed. She had on a bathrobe and looked pale, sickly. She gave that look of hers, tilting her head, that slight squint. 'It's no good, Jake, I'm not going to make it. I blew it so badly. I got over-confident, arrogant. You know, I thought I was so damned clever, and if it wasn't for Rosie I'd probably be dead.'

He squeezed her hand. 'It'll always be a part of your life. You can never have one drink. Even if you think you're strong enough to deal with it you won't be because it's an illness, Lorraine.'

Lorraine was crying. 'All I want is a drink, Jake.'

He stood up. 'Lemme tell you something. I want one, Rosie wants one, we all want one, you're no different. We all feel like you do so get your ass off that bed and come in and eat.'

He walked out and she got up slowly. When she joined them at the table, he drew out a chair.

'Thanks for helping me out this afternoon, Rosie.'

'Think nothing of it, partner, but next time you tell me to wait outside, I want to know how many minutes, who you're going to see and why.'

Lorraine doubted if there would be another time. The phone rang. Rosie answered and handed it to Lorraine. 'You better talk to him, it's Bickerstaff.'

'Hi, Ed. We just got back. It was a long drive . . . Yeah, yeah, no problem. I'll be there . . . sure, thanks.' She hung up. 'They want me at the station. They're sending a squad car. I can't think straight – I can't even see straight. They're going to take one look at me and they're gonna know. I'm still plastered.'

Jake took off his jacket and rolled up his sleeves.

'Let's get that shower running.'

Lorraine looked at them dead-eyed. 'Oh, God, not again . . .'

CHAPTER 20

NULA HAD been separated from Lyall on the way to Pasadena but the flight to Las Vegas had been long enough for them to get their story straight. Lorraine had not arrived at the station when their lawyer angrily confronted Bickerstaff, insinuating that he was wrongfully holding them on the word of a known drunkard, a woman who had arrived at his clients' apartment in San Francisco attempting to blackmail them. He doubted if Bickerstaff would be able to make any sense of what Mrs Page had levelled against his clients as she had been so drunk when they had last seen her that they had left her in the apartment. Time was against Bickerstaff because without strong evidence implicating them he could not hold Lyall and Nula longer than twenty-four hours. He was in a hot-seat of his own making and could ask for no help from the local police. This had been an FBI arrest and Bickerstaff was on his own.

Jake and Rosie were still plying Lorraine with water and coffee. She had no hangover now but her confidence had gone. She was afraid to confront Bickerstaff, and Rosie knew it.

The doorbell rang, and Lorraine jumped. Bickerstaff stood on the step, his shirt sticking to him, his tie loosened.

'I was just on my way,' Lorraine said lamely.

'Let's move it. We've got them for twenty-four hours and time's running out. You'd better have a fucking good

433

reason for setting this scene up. I got my boss and their lawyer at me and I got the entire department wondering what the hell is goin' on and they aren't the only ones.'

Lorraine followed him down the stairs. She stepped into the back of the patrol car, he slammed the door, and got into the front.

'They both said you were drunk.'

'They poured a bottle of vodka down my throat, so I guess I was.'

'You okay now?'

'Just a bit shaky.'

'You should have told me who you were going after, and more important why. You wanna fill me in before we get there?'

Lorraine took a deep breath. 'I wasn't sure, I knew Nula was possibly involved. What I didn't know was that Lyall was too.'

Ed started the engine. 'I've given them both a tough grilling and they stuck to their story. They were in Vegas to get married, or were gonna try for some kind of ceremony – they got preachers there that'd marry them. They also maintain they don't know nothin' about Holly's or David Burrows's murder and they know that Janklow's admitted to killing them. They also said you were drunk when you visited them and that they told you if you needed them they'd fly back after they got hitched.'

There was silence for a moment. Then Bickerstaff asked bluntly, 'How do you want to work this?'

Lorraine was desperate for a drink. She didn't dare take out a cigarette as her hands were shaking so much. 'Maybe talk to Lyall first, break him. I don't think he killed anybody. He's dominated by Nula, maybe even scared of her, so go for him first.'

Bickerstaff was uneasy. His brain ticked like the small hand on his watch as he tried to assimilate what she had just said.

434

'It's something to do with Mrs Thorburn's jewellery,' she added. 'I need to look at the lists Janklow made out and I want to see the morgue shot of Didi – David Burrows.'

Lorraine followed Bickerstaff through the corridors, stopping off at his office. He asked for Lyall to be brought up from the cells and taken to a small interview room with a one-way glass. Lyall was nervous and asked repeatedly for his lawyer. He sat with his hands splayed out on the small bare table, his face set, his mouth a rigid line. Watched by Lorraine and Bickerstaff, he stared around the small windowless room and then looked directly at the one-way glass.

'You want to go in?' Bickerstaff asked.

Lorraine could feel the tension disappearing. 'Just let him sweat a few more minutes. I'll need a glass of water, some kind of official-looking file, good photographs of the dead women, lot of documents, pens, notepad – and keep his lawyer out for as long as you can.'

Bickerstaff glanced at his watch, constantly monitoring the time as it ticked away. Lorraine was calmly checking down Janklow's list of jewellery. She felt positive. She looked through the glass partition at Lyall, watching his every move, the way he clenched and unclenched his hands, ran a finger round the inside of his collar and cleared his throat. They could hear him crossing and uncrossing his legs, his shoes scuffing the floor.

Ten minutes later Bickerstaff handed Lorraine the articles she had requested. She patted her pockets to make sure she had the cigarettes and lighter; she was no longer shaking but was feeling a buzz inside her. She was almost ready.

'Get someone to take water and glasses in, but not to say a word, even if he asks a question.'

She watched an officer enter the room. They heard Lyall asking how long he was to be kept waiting but the officer didn't even look at him. Lorraine nodded to Bickerstaff. 'I'm ready.'

As she left the room, he murmured, 'Good luck,' but she didn't turn back.

When Lorraine walked in, Lyall covered his surprise fast, turning away as she sat in the chair opposite. She paid him no attention but opened the dummy file and her notebook, carefully laid out her pens, cigarettes and lighter. Then she reached over to the jug and poured herself a glass of water.

Lyall cleared his throat again and tapped his foot. Bickerstaff waited.

Lorraine slowly got out the photographs of Holly and placed them in front of Lyall. 'Please look at the photographs, Craig.'

He turned away.

'She was only seventeen and she was beautiful, wasn't she? Take a look at her pretty face.'

He glanced at the ten-by-six photograph. Then Lorraine pointed to the morgue shots, which showed the injuries that virtually obliterated her face, broken nose, eye-sockets filled with blood and the gaping mouth with the front teeth smashed.

'Someone hammered her face, broke her skull, her nose, even her teeth. What kind of person do you think would do this? What kind of *madness* did this?'

Lyall wouldn't look at the photographs but kept his eyes on the wall.

'I keep on telling them that you couldn't have done it but they won't believe me, you know why? Because—'

'I didn't do that. I'm innocent.' His voice was high-pitched, bordering on hysterical.

'I know you are – of course you are – all you were involved in was blackmail. I know that but—'

'Janklow did it, he admitted it – so why don't you piss off and leave me alone? I want my lawyer here.' He sounded less hesitant now, his voice lower.

436

'Your lawyer will be here, Craig, but he's just finalizing Nula's release. She's going, so I hope you've made arrangements for your share of any money you had, because she . . .'

Bickerstaff covered his face. She was really pushing it.

'I don't believe you,' Lyall said sullenly.

'Believe what? That she's being released?' Lorraine flicked through the dummy documents. 'This is her statement. You can read it, if you like, but you won't be released, Craig, because Nula has stated that you were involved in murdering this girl and David Burrows.'

Lyall sneered, 'I know you're lying.'

Lorraine pushed forward Didi's photographs, the before and after shots. 'Am I? That's naïve of you, Craig. You know Nula killed Didi, even though she insists that you did it – that you drove her to the apartment, sat and drank tea, even offered her the banana bread. Didi lived on that banana bread of hers, didn't she? Anyway, according to Nula, the three of you started to argue because Didi had kept a ring, one of Mrs Thorburn's pieces. You'd all agreed to get rid of everything because the items could be traced, but Didi kept a ring. This one. Look at this picture, Craig – that is the ring, isn't it? On the third finger of her right hand.'

Bickerstaff had no idea what Lorraine was talking about. What ring? Was it in the files? He turned to his back-up. 'Get me the files down here, will you? And fast.' He turned his attention back to the interview room.

Lyall's fists were clenched so tight the knuckles stood out white. Lorraine placed in front of him the full-length mortuary shot of Didi in which she was wearing the ring.

'Just nod if it is the ring, Craig. You don't have to say anything. I'm only trying to help you, you must know that. I'm not even pressing charges about your part in trying to kill me.'

'What are you?' he snapped.

437

'I'm a private investigator, not even attached to the station or the FBI, but because I was there in San Francisco they're allowing me to talk to you. You both tried to kill me and you almost succeeded but what you didn't know was that I was wired, so everything you said in that apartment has been recorded. That's why you were both arrested in Las Vegas.'

He still didn't believe a word.

'Nula knew that she had to frame somebody to get herself released and that was you, Craig, because as soon as she saw me with the FBI agents she knew the game was up. She's been talking since they brought her in. Look at these statements. Don't you think it's strange your lawyer isn't here?'

Bickerstaff could feel sweat running down his back. He was relieved no one else was privy to what Lorraine was saying as all hell would have broken loose.

'I never killed anybody,' Lyall snapped, but his hands were shaking now.

Lorraine sipped her water. 'I know that, Craig, but let me read you a section of Nula's statement . . .'

Lyall was sweating even more than Bickerstaff, who couldn't believe Lorraine's audacity – the way she was lying.

She sifted through the dummy documents, and continued to talk quietly and calmly. She drew a page forward and started to read.

'"It started as an argument between the three of us. Didi wouldn't give the ring back, she said she couldn't get it off her finger so then Craig said he would cut it off and she started to get hysterical."'

'That's not true,' he interjected. Lorraine held up her hand as if to tell him to be patient, then carried on reading in the same steady voice.

'"Craig became more and more angry because Didi could get us all into trouble. We'd been selling Mrs Thorburn's jewellery for years, bits and pieces. Art would find the buyer

438

and we would just collect, but because of the killings it was dangerous for Didi to walk around showing off this big ring. It was a topaz with a row of diamonds around it and it was worth a lot of money."'

Lorraine was making it up as she went along. All she had pieced together was that according to Janklow's lists and description the ring belonged to Mrs Thorburn and it was possibly the ring Didi was wearing. She looked at Lyall. 'I presume when she says Art she is referring to Art Mathews, is that correct?'

'Why are you asking me these questions?'

'I used to be a cop, now I'm freelance, insurance claims, that kind of thing. Before they charge you I want to get my facts straight and until your lawyer is available they can't talk to you. There's nothing illegal about it – there's nobody else here.'

He was really sweating now. 'You mean it's true? They're releasing Nula?'

She nodded, tapped the dummy file. 'She's given her statement and all I want to do is get onto her for my clients and before she skips the country. I don't care who did what to whom just so long as I hold onto my job.'

Lyall tried to fathom how she was sitting in front of him. He knew she'd been dead drunk. How in hell had she got herself together?

Bickerstaff shook his head. Lorraine was giving to him, piece by piece, a section of the jigsaw puzzle, the stolen jewellery, the blackmail scam, but Lyall had not as yet implicated himself in any way.

Lorraine asked, 'You took the photographs of Janklow, didn't you?'

Lyall sighed. 'Art did. Well, some of them, years ago when he had a studio in Santa Monica. Janklow had this thing about looking like his mother, you know, all dragged up. At first Art didn't know who he was – he'd used some false name, they all do – and then he saw him at some society dinner with his mother, years ago, and started milking him. That's all I know. I swear before God, I honestly had nothing to do with it. I didn't even know it was going on . . .' He trailed off. 'I don't know what to do,' he said suddenly, helplessly.

'Maybe tell me the truth. Then I'll tell you what I think, as a friend, you should do, and in return, you tell me about the whereabouts of the stolen jewellery. I'm not interested in the murders. If you did them with Nula that's your business.'

'I didn't,' he said flatly. 'I'm so confused, I don't know who I can trust and I don't believe a word you're telling me.'

Lorraine snapped the file closed. 'If that's the way you feel I'll walk. All I wanted to do was get my insurance claims sorted out. There's more than three million dollars' worth of gems missing. Mrs Thorburn's son Brad asked me to look into it. They've let me talk to you because they aren't quite ready to charge you.' Bickerstaff's mouth was bone dry. She was fishing in dangerous waters again: actually *naming* people – that could get him into real trouble.

'They can't charge me with anything,' Lyall said shrilly.

Lorraine slapped her hand hard on the table and Lyall jumped. 'Don't be so fucking stupid. Nula's named you as Holly and Didi's killer. You're crazy if you think they're not going to lock you up for a very long time. Art Mathews is dead so she's only got you to blame. Now, if you're saying you didn't have any part in those murders then you'd better have a good alibi because she's given them evidence to prove you killed them both. Because you were in Didi's apartment, weren't you? If you didn't kill her then Nula did, right?'

He sniffed. 'I didn't touch her.'

'So who did?'

'She did, of course. Nula.'

440

Lorraine felt as if she had been punched. She'd expected him to say Mathews, not Nula.

'You saw her?'

Lyall put his head in his hands. 'Yes, she said she pushed Didi and she fell and hit her head against the coffee table. We couldn't find any pulse and she began to panic. Well, she had reason to.'

'Because of Mrs Thorburn's jewellery?'

'*Yes*. And then I panicked, it was just all confused and terrible. We couldn't get it off her finger, the ring . . . we couldn't get it off.'

He broke down and started to sob.

'So who decided to make it look as if it was one of the hammer murders?'

'She did. She said no one would believe it if they just found her, especially not after Holly.'

He sobbed, muttered to himself that it wasn't him, he hadn't done anything.

Lorraine touched his hand. 'Craig, what do you mean "after Holly"? What about Holly?'

Lyall flapped his hands wildly. 'Oh, Christ, this is terrible, it isn't right, I know it.'

'Come on, Craig, get it off your chest, tell me.'

He steadied himself. 'Holly had somehow found out about the blackmail – God knows how but she had. She'd been picked up by some john, taken back to his place and–'

'Do you know who it was?'

Lyall chewed his lip. 'I think it was – you said his name before – Brad Thorburn.'

Lorraine couldn't believe what she was hearing. '*Brad Thorburn*? You mean he's involved in all this?'

'Yes, in as much as he picked up Holly and took her back to his house. I dunno what happened but she somehow knew what we were all doing – maybe she saw Janklow there – but she started pushing Nula and Didi for money.

They got on to Art – they were really worried – and next thing I read she was murdered. I don't know which one of them did it but they got away with it because they made it look like this serial killer had done it. I think Art was involved. I swear before God I don't know. I was caught up in it all because I'd taken photographs of that Norman Hastings and he was a friend of Janklow's but I didn't know that. It was just, well, I knew *they* were doing it and it seemed so easy.'

Lorraine was trying to take on board what he was saying and then it clicked. 'Were you blackmailing Norman Hastings?'

'Yes, but then he went to Janklow and asked him what he should do about it. I suppose the two of them discussed it together. I've told you all I know. I had nothing to do with any of the murders. All I did was a bit of blackmail.'

Bickerstaff checked his watch, told one of his aides to bring in Brad Thorburn. He said he didn't give a shit if he was still in France. He was feeling elated and couldn't wait to get his own hands on Lyall. And he couldn't wait to lay it all before the Chief for the sheer pleasure of seeing his face.

Lorraine continued to question Lyall as he sobbed out his part in the blackmail racket. She made only a few notes, knowing that Bickerstaff would go over everything. She didn't even feel self-congratulatory. She couldn't stop Brad Thorburn's face drifting into her mind and she only half listened as Lyall talked, freely now as if relieved it was all out in the open.

Lyall had used Didi to make up the men who came to him for secret photographic sessions. They had met through Mathews when they worked together in Santa Monica. When they met again in Los Angeles they continued their old tricks and Mathews let Didi and Nula use his apartment for photo sessions. He moved out, leaving them there. Didi continued to pass on potential blackmail victims. Janklow was paying first Art, then all three to keep silent. None had any indication that he was also a killer. He had always paid up without argument, regaining one negative after another, until he began to get edgy, saying he had no more money, no more jewellery.

Lyall asked for water, sipped it and then traced the rim of the glass with his finger. 'Hastings didn't have much cash but he paid up, fifty bucks here and there. But when Art found out he went crazy.' The rim of the glass squeaked as he ran his finger round and round.

'Did you kill Norman Hastings, Craig?'

'No, I didn't, and I had nothing to do with any of those others.'

Lorraine leaned forward. 'What about Didi?'

Lyall closed his eyes and sighed. 'I saw her – she was already dead, she was at their apartment. Nula called me. She was lying on the floor. I never touched her. I think they had something to do with that girl Holly, but I don't know what – they knew something, I'm sure of it.'

'What about Mathews? Was he involved in Holly's murder? That's what you're suggesting, isn't it? That Nula and Didi had something to do with Holly's death?'

His voice was quiet, almost a whisper. 'Yes, but I don't know if Art was involved.' He started to cry, biting his bottom lip to stop the tears. 'I swear all I'm guilty of is helping Nula to—' He broke down, and Lorraine waited until he had composed himself. 'I helped move her body, carry it to the stolen car.'

'When you carried Didi, did she have these injuries?'

Lorraine brought out the photograph of Didi's hideously beaten face again and he straightened up.

'No. When I last saw her her head was covered in a black plastic bag, I never saw her face, and after she was put in the car, I went home.'

When he had finished Lyall seemed more relaxed. He had stopped crying and seemed resigned. As Lorraine gathered her notes and files together, he gave her a weak smile. 'I loved her, you know, really loved Nula. We were going to be married in Vegas – that's why I helped her. It wasn't anything but that, I didn't do anything.'

Lorraine walked across to the door. 'They'll want a statement from you, Craig, and I think you'd be wise to tell them everything you know, just as you've told me. Don't let her get away with it.'

Bickerstaff didn't congratulate Lorraine. He almost grabbed her notes from her while directing his men to begin the detailed requestioning of Craig Lyall. Lorraine sat in his office, drained, as the atmosphere around grew charged with excitement. She felt ill, her head thudded, but all she could think of was Brad Thorburn. Had she been wrong? Could he be implicated in the murders? Had she always known more than he had indicated?

'What about Thorburn?' she asked Bickerstaff quietly.

'We're having him brought back from France.' He hesitated and leaned over her. 'How involved do you reckon the smooth bastard is?'

'I don't know.'

'You mean there's something you *don't* know about this business?'

'I didn't think he was involved.'

Bickerstaff tapped her shoulder. 'We'll find out soon enough.'

Now it was Nula's turn. Bickerstaff was moving like a man on speed, talking non-stop, firing instructions right, left and centre. Lorraine remained sitting in his office until they were ready for her, thinking about Brad Thorburn.

Nula was brought up from the cells. She screamed for her lawyer and wanted to see Lyall. She was aggressive and abusive, and had to be half dragged into an interview room, kicking and spitting. Only when she saw Lorraine did she quieten down. As the door closed behind her, Lorraine entered the adjoining room, looking through the one-way glass as Nula knocked over the jug of water.

She refused to say one word without her lawyer present. He was, in fact, sitting beside Lyall, now under oath to tell the truth. He made a formal statement detailing his part in the blackmail of Norman Hastings and describing how Nula had killed Didi. He could give no details about Holly's murder as he had not been involved.

Bickerstaff waited until Lyall's statement was ready before interviewing Nula. By law she had to be allowed time to talk to the lawyer and he would be present throughout. Bickerstaff formally requested that Lorraine not only be present but a party to the interrogation. The entire station was buzzing with the new developments. There was no animosity, just strong professional back-up: anything Bickerstaff wanted he got.

They were ready to interrogate Nula, the last piece in the jigsaw. She now knew how serious the charges were, and that there was no hope of her being released from custody. She had become calmer, having been kept waiting for hours. She was sitting at the table, and had redone her make-up and hair. She looked almost perfect, every hair in place, her lips a deep dark vermilion with a sheen of gloss but small flecks of the lipstick stained her front teeth.

Bickerstaff, two uniformed officers and a stenographer entered the room, followed by Lorraine. Nula turned slowly to face her and then laughed. 'I underestimated you,' she said, completely relaxed, and apparently unconcerned by the formidable line-up. If anything, she seemed almost to be enjoying the attention. Her lawyer waited until everyone had been seated and the tape recorder switched on; the stenographer's hands were poised.

Nula was facing two separate charges: blackmail and extortion, and first degree murder. She stated that her birth name was Nigel Simmons. Her lawyer now turned to

445

Bickerstaff. 'My client categorically denies any part in the charges levelled at her and she has the right to remain silent. She has been made aware of certain statements by Craig Lyall, implicating her in these said crimes, and again denies playing any part in the said crimes but will, if required, be prepared to stand trial for the prosecution and to implicate Craig Lyall as being solely responsible for the crimes.'

There was a short pause before Bickerstaff began by asking Nula directly if she had been involved in the blackmail of Steven Janklow.

No comment.

Had she struck David Burrows (Didi) during an argument and then with the assistance of Craig Lyall, carried his body to a stolen car and deposited it?

No comment.

Bickerstaff asked detailed questions for almost half an hour. Each one was answered with, 'No comment.'

Throughout, Nula sat checking her nails, fixing her skirt, straightening her frilled blouse. She sometimes looked at Lorraine, raising an eyebrow, and then, as if bored by the proceedings, yawned, crossing and recrossing her legs. When the photographs of Didi were displayed, she averted her face and stared at the wall. When she was asked again to look at the photographs, she sighed and glanced down, then looked at her lawyer.

Holly's pictures were laid in front of her. This time her lawyer asked her to look at the photographs as requested. She picked one up, glared around the room, and then let it drop back on the table, drumming her nails on it.

'No comment.'

'Are you saying you do not recognize her? Or that you do not know her?' Bickerstaff asked impatiently.

'My client refuses to answer that question in case it may implicate her request to act as a prosecution witness.'

Bickerstaff turned towards Lorraine. He gave a brief nod

and they requested a break in the interview to enable them to confer. Both left the room.

Bickerstaff shoved his hands into his pockets. 'This could go on for days. You want to have a try, see if we can hurry it up in there?'

'Okay. Is it legal for the same lawyer to represent both parties?'

'Lyall has already given his statement. It'll be up to him to hire someone else. I would, if I was him, but that's not my main concern right now.'

They went back into the interview room and the tape was turned on again. Lorraine pulled her chair up close. Nula giggled and leaned across the table. 'Your turn now, is it?'

Lorraine ignored her remark. 'She was just seventeen, Nula. Why did you have to kill her? What harm had she ever done you?'

Nula conferred with her lawyer and then sat back.

'My client wants to know why Mrs Page is present at this interview. She is aware that she is not attached to the FBI or the police homicide division. She is also aware that Mrs Page is a chronic alcoholic. I would also like to lodge my own formal complaint as to such a woman being present.'

Bickerstaff leaned back in his chair. 'No comment.'

'Is she some kind of witness?' the lawyer asked tersely.

Nula smirked. 'They couldn't get her on a stand in any court of law, she'd be laughed off. She's a drunkard, she's a whore and she's even been paid for working with Art Mathews. She more than likely instigated the blackmail – she was certainly paid enough to keep quiet. Ask her! Has anyone asked her how much Art Mathews paid her? I never touched Holly, nor did I hurt my best friend. She's making it all up, probably with that pervert Lyall. I can even smell the booze on her – it's coming out of her pores. Look at the way her hands are shaking.'

447

Lorraine refused to be goaded. She turned to Bickerstaff and got a steely glint stare. She leaned back and imitated Nula's smiling face. 'I'm as sober as she is and she's lying. I was never paid a cent by Art Mathews.'

'You lying cunt,' Nula spat out.

'Takes one to know one,' Lorraine snapped back. 'But then you don't have one. Is that your problem? Is that why you had to kill little Holly? Because she was young, beautiful, everything you wanted to be but—'

Nula stood up, pushing away the restraining hand of her lawyer. 'She was about as innocent as my ass!'

'Taking your clients away, was she?' Lorraine shot out and Nula swiped at her across the table.

Lorraine was on her feet. 'That's it, Nula, come on, show what you're really like. Show just what a mean bitch you are – and you *are* mean. The way you hammered poor Didi's face after all she'd done for you.'

No one in the room acknowledged what was going on. They sat stony-faced as Nula and Lorraine shouted at each other. At one point, an officer half rose but Bickerstaff glared. He wanted this row to continue.

Nula snarled, 'It was *me* that did everything for *her*. Don't you know anything?' She pointed a red-tipped talon at Lorraine. 'She doesn't know what she's talking about.'

'Without Didi you were nothing. She had to tout you around—you couldn't even pick up a john without her.'

'Fuck you, that's bullshit.' Nula's hands were on her hips. Her lawyer tried to make her sit down but she stepped away.

'She told me, said you were a useless piece of garbage.'

Nula swiped at her again.

'And then when you found out she'd kept a ring, you just snapped, didn't you?'

Nula looked at them all smugly. 'I know what you're trying to do. Well, I'm not saying another word.'

She sat down and smoothed her skirt as Lorraine walked

to the side of the room and propped herself against the wall. 'Nobody's asking you to, Nula, because we know. We know that you tried to get the ring off her finger – even threatened to cut it off – but she wouldn't part with it. She told you to piss off so you punched her, like the man you really are. All this paint and wig, all the glam clothes, you're just a heavy-handed man underneath it all, aren't you, Mr Simmons? But Didi, she was really beautiful, wasn't she?'

Nula elbowed her lawyer. 'Tell her to shut the fuck up. This isn't legal. I want to leave.'

Bickerstaff calmly looked at the lawyer. 'Tell her she won't be leaving here for a long time.'

Nula stood up again and lunged forward. 'You're all jerks, all of you, you've got nothing on me, nothin' but what that wimp Lyall has told you and he's full of shit.'

'Then why don't you tell us what really happened?' Bickerstaff asked.

'No fucking way, you asshole, I'm not sayin' another word. I know my rights, I don't have to tell you anything because I know all you've got is his word against mine. That's *all* you've got and until we make a deal and make me a prosecution witness, I'm not talking.'

Lorraine was still standing by the wall, arms folded. 'Tell us about Holly. Why did you kill Holly?'

Nula shouted, 'I never touched her, I never touched Didi, I never did anything and I know you got nothing on me, nothing. Janklow killed them, just like he killed all the others – it's in the papers. It's Janklow – I've got nothin' to do with anything.'

'But he didn't kill Holly and he didn't kill Didi.'

'*Yes, he did.*' Nula was red in the face with fury. 'He was a sicko, everybody knows it, he's nuts, can't even stand trial. Don't you follow what's going on with your so-called investigations? I know what you did. You put poor Art in prison and you killed him. You gave a big press conference, "We got the killer" and you were wrong. How come nobody is standing trial for that? He was innocent. I'm innocent.'

Getting no reaction from anyone she turned back to Lorraine, pointing at her. 'I'll scream it all out to the papers about you, Mrs Page, about what's going on in this room. Janklow has admitted to killing Holly and Didi, Janklow is a sicko, a pervert and—'

'So are you,' Lorraine said softly.

'*Get her out of this room or I'll—*'

'You'll what, Nula? Kill me like Holly?'

'This isn't right, she shouldn't be allowed to do this to me, she's saying things to get me going. Well, I'm not gonna say another word. If you got the evidence then arrest me, charge me. Go on, let's hear you do it.'

Bickerstaff checked his watch. It was almost nine thirty. He suggested they take a break and continue the interview the following morning.

'Does that mean I can go?' Nula asked.

'You will be held in custody pending further inquiries.'

'But you haven't charged me,' she said. 'Can they do this?' she asked the lawyer.

'Yes.'

'Bastards,' she muttered.

'You'll meet plenty of them, Nigel,' Lorraine said quietly. 'How many will be in her cell with her? Three or four?' she asked Bickerstaff. He made no answer.

'I want to be put in the women's section,' Nula demanded.

'That won't be possible,' Bickerstaff said flatly and turned to the lawyer. 'Please explain to your client that as she is listed as male on her birth certificate she cannot be placed in a female wing.'

For the first time, Nula seemed frightened. She clung to her lawyer. 'But I'm a woman. They can't do this to me.' He whispered to her and she looked at Bickerstaff, then Lorraine, lunging at her, knocking over the table. 'You

450

bitch! *You did this to me!* You know what'll happen to me in with those animals.'

Lorraine ducked and sidestepped Nula as an officer grabbed her. 'Then talk, Nula. At least they can segregate you. Tell us the truth about Holly.'

'Shut up, you schmuck.'

'Tell the truth, Nula. It was an accident, wasn't it? You never meant to kill Didi, did you? She was your best friend – I know that, I've seen you two together.' Lorraine saw the change sweep over Nula in her body language; she lost all the fight.

'Yes, she was,' Nula said softly, and then averted her face. Her eyes filled with tears. 'Best friend I ever had.'

The room fell silent as if everyone knew it was coming. Nula looked up at the ceiling, her eyes brimming with tears, and Lorraine moved silently back to her own seat. Nula blew her nose on a tissue and then began plucking at it. 'Oh, all right, there's no point, is there? You'll find out, I suppose. She fell and hit her head on the side of the glass coffee table. Craig started to panic because we couldn't find her pulse. We thought she was dead and what with—'

'The blackmail? You were worried about that, were you?' Lorraine asked softly.

'It was all getting out of hand, right? We suspected Janklow was doing these killings because he was a real crazy fucker. He always paid up like it was a joke, like he got off on it. He never argued or nothing but paid up once a month regular as clockwork. But Art began to get greedy, kept on pushing him for more and what was so sick, we were blackmailing him because of all his drag pictures but he still wanted more of them. We all kinda knew he was going to crack someday. That was maybe why Art kept asking him for more money, more jewellery, like he knew he was gonna break.'

'But why did you think it was him murdering these women?'

451

Nula was tired; she supported herself on her elbow. 'Art put it all together, don't ask me how. He always was an intuitive shit but instead of backing off, he asked for more. We were against it but he wouldn't listen to us. I mean, we were doing okay, we had dough and then he opened that gallery. There was no need to be so greedy, we even had the other business, the photo sessions. We'd all never had it so good—'

'How did you collect the money?'

'We'd just go to his garage, one or other of us, pretend we were looking for cars. Art used to drive an old Bentley. He'd bought it from S and A, so he was able to go in and out of Janklow's place. We'd not go in dragged up, anything like that. We were pretty cool, changed into straight gear.'

'How did Hastings fit into it?' Lorraine asked.

'Well, Art and Didi saw him at the garage. Didi recognized Hastings, because she'd been doing his wigs and make-up at Craig's studio. Well, this panicked Art for a while, then he discovered that Craig's at it, like he's picked up our tricks and he's only doing Norman Hastings himself. Craig's such an oaf, he couldn't even pick a guy with dough. Art was furious – it could've all come out – and what got him worried was that Janklow and Hastings knew each other, and could put two and two together, cause trouble.'

'But Janklow must have known who you were?' Lorraine said.

Nula shrugged. 'Maybe, but if he did he never contacted the cops. Like I said, he seemed to get off on it, like it was punishment. Anyway, we thought we should just back off – besides Art had plenty more, not with as much dough as Janklow, but he did all right . . .'

'So did Hastings talk to Janklow about the blackmail?'

Nula sighed. 'I dunno, but when he was found dead, we freaked. Then fucking Janklow appeared and said he needed Art to cover for him, like say he was someplace when he wasn't. He'd done something.'

Lorraine asked if Nula remembered the date. She thought for a moment and then said it was the fifteenth, she wasn't too sure. But it was the same date Lorraine had been attacked. Nula cried for a few moments and then sniffed, wiping her check with her hand. 'He said he'd pay well for Art to cover for him. He couldn't get cash so he handed over a box of jewellery, said it was all he had left.'

'Did you sell it?'

Nula blew her nose. 'In the past when we'd got a few things we'd used Curtis to fence it for us. We didn't say where we got it and he wasn't going to ask.' Nula sighed. Everyone hung on her every word. 'Curtis gave one of the pieces we were selling off – a ring – to Holly and she used to wear it, showed it to everyone. He'd said it was like an engagement ring. It was the big topaz, with diamonds round it. Anyway, she gets picked up by a john who takes her back to his place and he says where did she get the ring as his mother had one like it but—'

'Who was it?'

'Janklow's brother. Anyway, Holly puts two and two together and comes up with sixteen. She asks us about the stuff we fenced to Curtis and then tells us about this john, Brad Thorburn. We tell Art and he's going fucking ape-shit because he knows it's bloody Janklow's brother, and that Curtis, if he smells a good racket, would want in on it, and Curtis would cause trouble.'

Lorraine lit two cigarettes and passed one to Nula. She puffed for a while and then bowed her head. 'We had to do something about the ring – we could have all been implicated, know what I mean? She showed it off to everyone – not that Curtis would have ever married her. He's got a wife and kids anyway.' She sucked at the cigarette. 'We knew we had to get rid of Holly. We figured she hadn't said anything to Curtis – he never came on to us. Art was working the night we decided to do it at the gallery. After we left, we went back to the apartment and Didi got into

453

men's gear. We nabbed a car and parked it not far away from the apartment. Didi left, then I left. I went on my patch, waited for Holly to arrive.'

She sobbed and was given a clean tissue. She took the cigarette from the ashtray and smoked. 'Holly, well, she was always jumping into johns' cars. We knew if she saw a decent car she'd duck and dive to it. Didi drew up across the road and sort of waved towards Holly and, sure enough, she shot across the road so fast I had a tough time following her. Course, soon as she got into the car she knew something was up but by that time I'd gone over, got the back door open and got in; then Didi drove off. We wanted just to get the bloody ring off her, warn her, but she was like a wildcat. We didn't even drive far – we couldn't, she was screaming and shouting so much. I think Didi hit her first, then me, but we never meant . . . We didn't mean to hurt her. She was suddenly just like a rag doll, it was awful, so we stuffed her into the trunk. Didi was supposed to dump it, leave her in it and get back to work, meet up with me. I went back on the streets, to sort of give us an alibi, you know, saying Didi had got a john and I was to talk to Curtis.'

'So where did Art come into all this?'

Nula stubbed out the cigarette. 'That stupid bitch Didi, she didn't turn up. We'd agreed to meet in the Bar Q but she never showed because she went back to the gallery. She was hysterical because as she was driving around, Holly must have come round. She started banging on the trunk, screaming again.' Nula rested her head in her hands. 'Art was mad as hell that she'd gone to the gallery with Holly in the car and Didi's face was scratched and bruised. Holly was a tough kid – she'd put up a fight. If she hadn't we'd never have hurt her.'

'So what happened at the gallery?'

Nula licked her lips. 'I'm not sure but Art said he'd check on Holly, and he went out. Then he came back in and got a hammer. Didi knew what he was gonna do and tried to stop him and it fell on her foot. Anyway, Art did it and came back and told Didi to dump the car. He gave her the ring – he'd taken it off Holly.'

'So Didi got back in the car, knowing Holly was dead in the trunk. Then what?'

'All the stupid cow had to do was dump it and piss off, but she gets into a terrible state. Her foot all swelled up, and she drove home in it because she said she couldn't have walked and she was scared of anyone seeing her. *I* had to dump it. I gave it a good clean in case there were any prints. It wasn't so bad because there was no blood or anything. In fact it wasn't until I got out and was walking past it that I saw this bit of cloth sticking out and then freaked. I just ran like hell back home.'

Lorraine sounded friendly and understanding. 'It must have been realy hard for you.'

'It was, but then it was un-fucking-believable. Didi started wearing the ring. And she wouldn't part with it, it was like some kind of obsession, as if she wanted to be caught. She was always crying and she couldn't sleep. Nothin' I said made any difference. She wouldn't listen to me and that's why we had this row. I was trying to get it off her but she went hysterical, saying it was hers.'

'So you had to get the ring away from Didi, is that right?'

'Course I did but she wouldn't give it up and so we had this argument. She pushed me, then I pushed her and she fell. I thought she was dead, but when . . . It was like Holly happening all over again.'

Nula started to cry, her shoulders shaking, and Lorraine reached across the table for her hand. 'It's okay, everything's going to be okay. After she'd fallen what happened?'

Nula's lipstick smeared, her mascara running down her face. 'I called Art and he came over. He said we should make it look like this serial killer had murdered her, like we'd done with Holly. But he said as he'd fixed it with Holly, I should do Didi, that he was having nothing to do with it and then he left—'

'And?' Lorraine asked.

'I hit her with the hammer and it must have been just like Holly because she moaned. She was still alive, just like Holly. I could hear her voice, telling me about Holly, and I just kept on hitting and hitting her until she was quiet.' Nula accepted another cigarette, inhaled deeply and then sipped some water. 'After I'd done it, I didn't know what to do next. I couldn't lift her by myself so I called Craig. All he did was help me get her to the car.' She fell silent. No one spoke. She smoked the cigarette down to the cork, then looked at it.

Lorraine took the stub from her and tossed it into the ashtray. She stood up.

'Where are you going?' Nula asked.

'They can charge you now.'

Nula watched fearfully as Lorraine walked to the door. She didn't even look back; she just walked out.

It was after midnight. Ed Bickerstaff was jubilant. Lyall's and Nula's statements were signed and they had been taken to their cells. He passed a small white envelope to Lorraine. 'Five thousand dollars in used notes. You did good. I didn't think she'd crack.'

'I won't be needed at the trial, will I?'

'Not unless she changes her plea but I don't think she will.'

'What about Brad Thorburn?'

'I reckon the only thing he was guilty of was screwing a prostitute but we'll need him for questioning. He's on his way back from France.'

Bickerstaff guided her to the door, then paused. 'If I ever need you again . . .'

Lorraine smiled. 'I'll send you my card. I can set up an office now.'

'Just one more thing, if you don't mind me asking. You seemed pretty friendly in there with Nula.'

'Just doing my job. She's scum – she almost killed me.'

'You don't want to press charges, though, do you?'

She gave him a wry look. 'No.'

Rosie was sitting on the sofa watching TV when Lorraine got home. Lorraine looked at her and grinned. 'You're a good friend, Rosie.'

'Bed's all made up. I'll kip on the sofa.'

Lorraine winked. 'Thanks.'

Just as she walked into the bedroom, the phone rang. 'If that's for me, I'm not back yet.' She switched on the shower and couldn't hear properly what Rosie was calling through the door. She had to switch it off.

'That was Brad Thorburn. He said he'd ring again tomorrow morning.'

Lorraine stripped off and stepped beneath the cool water, tilting her face up to the jet spray. She was unnerved by his call and she hadn't expected to hear from him again.

'Is he back in LA?' she shouted.

Rosie appeared in the doorway again. 'On his way, be here in the morning. He said he was at the airport in Paris. Did you want to speak to him?'

Lorraine wrapped the towel around herself and frowned. Brad had picked up Holly, taken her back to that house, had probably screwed her in the same bed as he'd fucked her in, little seventeen-year-old Holly. Brad Thorburn would probably always pick up the wrong kind. As much as she wanted to see him, she thought he was probably calling her to find out if she knew why the police wanted to talk to him.

'If he calls again, I'm out. He's no good – well, not for me.'

'Okay, whatever you say. You want a cup of tea?'

'Sounds good.'

Lorraine lay down on the bed. Tomorrow she would open up the agency, get cards made, get a word processor. By the time Rosie came in with the tea she was deeply asleep. Rosie didn't wake her but gently wrapped the bedcover over her. Lorraine didn't stir.

The last item on her list had been blurred, only half considered, but it was the first thing she thought of in the morning.

Rosie looked up sleepily from the couch when Lorraine walked in. 'What did you say?'

'Let's go to a meeting this morning.'

Brad Thorburn stared around the empty house with all its furnishings draped in dust sheets. He walked out, slamming the front door. He drove to the police station and was introduced to Ed Bickerstaff. The interview was formal and he gave a detailed statement of the night he had picked up a young blonde hooker. He couldn't recall her name; she was just one of so many. Bickerstaff questioned him as to what time of night, how long she had stayed and then asked if on the night in question he had noticed anything unusual about her. Brad shrugged, he couldn't remember clearly.

'How about an item of jewellery?'

Brad thought, and then it dawned on him. 'She was wearing a large ring. I only remember because it was similar to one my mother used to wear, but she took it off and slipped it into her purse and I never gave it much thought.'

'Was this it?' Bickerstaff held out the ring taken from Didi's finger.

Brad stared at it. 'Yes, well, it was similar.'

'Could this be your mother's ring?'

458

'Possibly. It *is* similar but whether it's hers or not I couldn't say. She had a large collection of jewels – she was a collector. Some of them were worth thousands, others cheap replicas. She was always terrified of being mugged. I'm sorry not to be of more help.'

Bickerstaff didn't bother to explain how important the ring had been in so many people's lives – or deaths.

Brad left and returned to his car. He drove to the real-estate agents, signed over the documents for the contents of the house to be sold along with the property, and then went to Beverly Glen. The sale notices already hung outside. Brad collected the items he wanted to take with him and put little red stickers on the rest so the storage men would be able to ascertain which articles were to be removed. He walked from room to room in the shrouded house. There was little he needed or wanted, it was mostly his personal belongings from his own quarters. He did, however, stick red dots on all the silver-framed family photographs. He found it difficult to look at the faces of his brother and mother but went about his work as fast as possible. Steven's room was more difficult than he had anticipated, with his precious collections of shells and snuff-boxes, the banks of photographs of their mother. He closed the door, refusing to allow himself to think about Steven. Not until he was in his own room did he relax as he checked his books and record collections, his sports equipment. There was so little with which he had any emotional ties – everything could easily be replaced. All he knew was that he would never come back to this house and its memories.

Brad arrived at his mother's nursing home in the late afternoon. He had called Lorraine's number four times but received no reply. He decided he would try once more before he left. He didn't know why he wanted to see her; he was not infatuated or in love with her, but he couldn't shake off the memory of how gentle he had felt towards her, how good it had been to hold her in his arms.

Mrs Thorburn was seated by the windows overlooking the elegant gardens. The nursing home was ludicrously expensive, with two or three nursing staff to every resident. She was reading *Vogue*, the arthritic hands with their perfectly manicured nails gliding over the pages, pausing to tap a particular photograph and then ripping off a yellow sticker from a pad and carefully applying it to a page. She still bought lavish clothes – sometimes an entire collection – which were delivered to the home.

Brad watched her for a few more minutes. Everything about her was immaculate: her wig, false eyelashes and pale powdered skin drawn tightly over the high cheekbones. The many face-lifts had given her a surreal look so she could, at a distance, be taken for a thirty-year-old woman; only at close-up did one see the stretched, taut, ageing skin. He called her name softly as he approached and bent to kiss her cheek. As always she averted her face.

'Watch out for my hair, darling.'

He drew up a chair, sitting to one side. She shut the magazine and held it out as if to an unseen butler. Brad took it and pushed it into the side of her wheelchair.

'How are you?'

'Dreadful. How do you expect me to be?'

Her perfect lips, dark crimson, with smears across her over-large, over-white false teeth, grimaced in a sneering smile. 'I hear you're selling the house? I always hated it. Will we get a good price?'

'I should think so.'

'Where are you going to live?'

'South of France.'

'Always loved Cannes but it's not what it used to be. Your father took me there often in the early days but we had problems with the staff, probably because he was fucking them.'

Brad smiled at the way she dropped in the word 'fucking' as if to shock, but he was used to it. She could swear better

460

than any man he'd ever met and he felt something akin to fondness for her, which surprised him. She suddenly pointed one frail, red-nailed finger to the gardens. 'They're putting in a new border and a fountain. I just hope it's not some awful cherub pissing. I hate those little penises spurting water. I'm always surprised how many people choose them, very distasteful, nasty things, penises – uncircumcised ones in particular. I made sure you were circumcised – much more attractive, especially if you're being sucked off.' She gave a shrill laugh, and placed her hands over her lips like a naughty schoolgirl, her diamonds glinting in the sunlight.

'Do you remember that big topaz ring? It had diamonds all round it, very large, set in platinum,' he said quietly, surprised at even bringing the subject up.

'Hard to forget. Your father would always give me something extravagant when he was screwing somebody else. The more expensive it was the higher the chance of it being a close friend. The topaz was good quality and they were rose diamonds, excellent carat. Why do you ask?'

'No reason.'

'Ah, my darling, there's always a reason. I suppose it was one of the items Steven stole or sold or whatever they wish to call it. Well, it was a beautiful ring but too ostentatious for my taste.' She turned to face Brad, her eyes even at eighty still china blue.

'Why did he have so many other women? My father. It's always struck me as odd. You must have loved each other at one time?'

'Love never came into it, sweetheart.' He wanted to hold her clawlike hand but she was turning to one of the other wealthy inmates, waving like royalty. 'That was why he hated me so much and tried to hurt me in every way possible. He hated me because I could not find him attractive. I married him for his money. I told him but I don't think he believed me.'

461

'Is that true?'

She turned back to face him, her blue eyes like ice chips. 'What do you think?'

'I don't know and I have to go.' He stood up. She waved again across the elegant room and murmured that it was tea-time. 'Will you write to Steven?' he asked.

'He's dead to me. I can't bring myself to write or make any contact. He does not exist. I've already changed my will. You'll get everything.'

He touched her shoulder. 'I'll write, and then, as soon as I'm settled, you'll come visit me.'

'That would be very pleasant, dear.' Both knew the other was lying; there would be no visits. There was no antagonism or reprimand in her bright eyes. She held out her hand and he kissed it gently. How often had he smelt that sweet floral perfume? How many times had he as a child wanted this woman to hold him and kiss him? He felt it even now: he wanted some sign that she cared for him. But she gave none, dismissing him by withdrawing her hand.

He walked away across the polished wood floor, then turned back, half hoping she would still be watching him. But she was already flicking through the pages of *Vogue* again, positioning a yellow sticker on a long cream evening gown worn by a doe-eyed model.

She hadn't worn an evening gown for more than thirty years but she hadn't wept for much longer. Tears ruined her make-up, made her false eyelashes unstick. It had taken many long years of practice not to weep. She could recall the last time she had cried herself to exhaustion. It had been when she had found her husband in bed with her closest friend. The two of them naked, moaning with orgasmic pleasure. She had never had an orgasm in her entire life; she was frigid; she was, as her husband had called her, the 'Ice Maiden'. Only little Steven had broken through to her heart. Only Steven had known how to love her, seemed to know intuitively the fear she had of allowing herself to be loved. He had known how to kiss her without pawing or fumbling. Only Steven knew how delicate she was – and now even he had betrayed her. He had been as brutal as every man she had ever encountered. Sitting trapped in her wheelchair, she remembered his slim, delicate body, his sweet, tender kisses, his perfect circumcised penis that she had loved to kiss awake and then to rub his semen over her skin, because it was better than any expensive creams. They had discussed its therapeutic powers endlessly, lying together in her overheated bedroom. She had never believed that what they were doing was wrong – it was only natural. She bore no blame for what he had subsequently done: that was nothing to do with her. The women were whores, just like the bitches her husband had brought home. They had meant nothing to her, and she refused to feel any remorse for the women her beloved son had killed. She started to sing softly to herself, snatches of a song she'd sung in a chorus someplace a long time ago.

'If I say I love you, do you mind,
If I shower you with kisses, if I tell you, honey . . . this is . . .'

but she could no longer recall all the lyrics.

Steven Janklow was being led from his neatly made bed in the white-walled room. He liked night time. Every night on the way to the bathroom with his warder, he passed a window. He always stopped in his tracks when he saw his reflection in his white cotton institution gown. 'Oh, hello, darling,' he whispered, before he was led into the bathroom. He never spoke to anyone else, only to the image in the dark window-pane, but he was always smiling. He seemed happy and contented. Often singing the same few lines from some half-remembered song.

'If I say I love you, do you mind,
If I shower you with kisses . . .'

Brad Thorburn returned to France. He made one last attempt to contact Lorraine but received no reply. 'If I say I love you, do you mind . . .'

Rosie and Lorraine had worked hard all week. They had bought some cheap office furniture, a bookcase and filing cabinets. They had arranged for the phone to be connected and delivery of a word processor. Lorraine dropped by the gym to see Hector and explained that she was taking over the office next door. The close proximity of the gym would make it very convenient for workouts.

They did not hire a sign painter as no good agency wants their work broadcast. They were to keep a low profile and advertise in newspapers and magazines. Lorraine would require a licence and a permit to carry a weapon but she felt she should give Bickerstaff a few weeks before she asked a favour. She'd left the number and the address in case he wanted to talk to her but he hadn't called.

She and Rosie were surveying their handiwork when there was a rap on the door. Lorraine turned. 'I thought you were doing Europe.'

Rooney took off his hat. 'The wife still is. I was called back for the Craig Lyall business.'

She tilted her head on one side and he gave an odd, rueful smile.

'Okay, I'm lying. I called Josh to see what was happening and, well, in case they needed me I thought I should come back.'

'Do they?' she asked, wanting to give him a hug but deciding against it. Rooney was not the kind of man you hugged often.

'Got the bum's rush. They're all very pleased with

themselves and now there's no nasty smears about the Art Mathews suicide, which makes the FBI happier.'

He edged further into the new office and looked around. 'You won't get a licence, you know,' he said flatly.

She shrugged. A lot of agencies were working without one.

'Won't get the good clients. You won't even get a weapon licence.'

'I'll take it day by day, Bill.'

He sniffed and looked around, twisting his hat. 'You got my home number?' he asked. He had something on his mind but was too embarrassed to come out with it so he merely shrugged his shoulders. 'I might go and have a curry. I don't suppose you're in the mood for a vindaloo?'

'Not right now, but thanks for the offer.' She let him plod all the way to the door before she called his name. 'Bill . . .'

He turned, plonking his hat on. 'Yep?'

She walked slowly towards him, arms folded. 'I know you're retired and looking forward to sitting back and enjoying a life of leisure, but I was just wondering . . .'

He couldn't hide it: his face lit up as he looked at her expectantly.

'Well, as you said, I couldn't get an investigator's licence or a weapon permit. I've only got my driving licence thanks to you. What would you say to helping me out – not full time, I wouldn't ask that of you, maybe just a couple days a week?'

She let him do a lot of frowning and head scratching but then he smiled. 'I'll make the licence application today. I've got a lot of contacts – we could make a go of it.'

She put out her hand and he shook it and then he pulled her towards him. The big man that nobody dared hug clasped her tightly, his voice was hoarse with emotion. 'Always said you were one of the best. I'm proud you pulled yourself back up. I'm proud of you, Lorraine.'

Rosie watched him walk off before she snapped, 'I thought I was your partner!'

'You are. We need him, Rosie, he's got his retirement bonus, he's got contacts. It's all to do with contacts and he'll be a good front man.' She put her arm around her fat friend's shoulders. 'I'm feeling good, Rosie, positive. How about you?'

Rosie was as tickled as old Rooney had been. Lorraine had this ability to draw you to her, make you want to please her – kill her at times too – but more than that, you felt if she was happy then you were part of that happiness.

'I'm feeling good, partner. I know we'll make a go of it, I just know it.'

Rosie and Lorraine went on to an AA meeting. They both went regularly twice a week. Jake was waiting for them to join him. He was the greeter at the door as they took their places in front of the small informal platform. This meeting was important because Lorraine was going to share her story. Rosie glowed with pride. She herself was not ready yet to stand up and be counted, as Jake called it, but she was closer than she'd ever been before and she felt she owed it to her friend Lorraine. Rosie had a future. It wouldn't all be plain sailing, she knew that – she was no fool – but at least she was in a far better position than she had ever dreamed possible. She was thankful that she'd taken that crazy chance on the strange skinny woman minus a front tooth because they'd both come through. To see Lorraine sitting up there, elegant, strong and vital, made the long, hard journey they'd travelled together worth every minute.

Jake took out a big square handkerchief. He couldn't stop himself: Lorraine was making him cry, not because of what she was saying but because, like Rosie, he was so proud of her, and it was hard for him to believe that the wretched creature Rosie had brought back from the institution was now facing the demon head on. She had fought it, and almost been beaten, but now he was sure she was on her way to recovery. You could almost feel her energy, her optimism.

'My name is Lorraine and I'm alcoholic. Eight years ago, I was a police lieutenant. I was also a drunk. I committed a terrible injustice. I mistakenly took a young boy's life because I was drunk. There is no excuse. Nothing will ever take away the guilt I felt, still feel, will always feel.' Lorraine continued the story of her life, how she had lost her children and her husband, how she had sunk into prostitution, how she had fallen downwards to every kind of depravity simply to earn enough money to drink herself into oblivion. She talked about meeting Rosie, about her introduction to Jake, how she came to be there, and lastly that she had opened up a private investigation agency and was hoping she would make a success of it. She then thanked everyone for listening to her story.

'I don't want oblivion any more, I want my life, I want to live my life and I want to live it sober. I will always be indebted to AA and to my friends. At last I feel more at peace with myself and with God.'

Lynda La Plante
The Governor   £5.99

Scarcely a day passes without an incident at one of Britain's most notorious top security prisons. But what happens when the tension boils over and there's a woman in charge?

Helen Hewitt is the boss. The first woman Governor of a top security men's prison – home to some of the country's hardest criminals. And case-hardened male officers who'll pounce at the first sign of weakness.

Helen Hewitt is tough. She has to survive. But she is also a woman. She can play the hard games too. But sometimes with a different set of rules . . .

The Governor. The exclusive novelization of the hit TV series from Lynda La Plante. Hard-hitting, exciting, true-to-life drama from the phenomenally successful author of *Prime Suspect* and *Widows*.

Lynda La Plante
Entwined   £6.99

In the newly liberated streets of modern Berlin two women, a pampered, beautiful Baroness, losing control of her mind, and a fearless wild animal trainer, facing the greatest challenge of her career, are drawn together by a series of tragic and extraordinary coincidences.

When a man is found brutally murdered, their lives become entangled by an investigation that uncovers a web of darkness and opens up secrets that have long been condemned to silence . . .

Who were they, all those years ago? What nightmare did they share? And what is the truth about the undying nature of their love?

Lynda La Plante
The Legacy £6.99

was a curse . . .

For Hugh – the hard-drinking, two-fisted lion of the Welsh valleys. For his loyal daughter Evelyne – who lost her heart and her father's trust to the charm of a travelling gypsy. And for handsome prizefighter Freedom – saved from the gallows to do battle for the heavyweight championship of the world . . .

From the poverty of the Welsh pit valleys to the glories of the prize ring, from the dangers of Prohibition America to the terrors of Britain at war, Lynda La Plante begins the bestselling saga of their lives and their fortunes . . . and the curse that made their name . . .

'A torrid tale of love, intrigue and passion . . . packed with glamour, big business and big, big money'   *Daily Express*